A NORTON CRITICAL EDITION

E. M. Forster
HOWARDS END

"ONLY CONNECT . . ."

AUTHORITATIVE TEXT
TEXTUAL APPENDIX
BACKGROUNDS AND CONTEXTS
CRITICISM

Edited by

PAUL B. ARMSTRONG

BROWN UNIVERSITY

W • W • NORTON & COMPANY • *New York* • *London*

Copyright (c) 1998 by W. W. Norton & Company, Inc.

The text of this book is composed in Electra
with the display set in Bernhard Modern
Composition by Publishing Synthesis Ltd., New York
Manufacturing by The Maple-Vail Book Manufacturing Group
Cover illustration: Forster at age six on a pony with his mother in front of Rooksnest.

Library of Congress Cataloging-in-Publication Data

Forster, E. M. (Edward Morgan), 1879–1970.
Howards End : authoritative text, textual appendix, backgrounds and contexts,
criticism / E. M. Forster ; edited by Paul B. Armstrong.
p.   cm.—(A Norton critical edition)
"Only connect . . . "
Includes bibliographical references.

ISBN 0-393-97011-6 (pbk.)

1. Forster, E. M. (Edward Morgan), 1879–1970. Howards End.   2. Inheritance and
succession—England—Fiction.   3. Man-woman relationships—England—Fiction.
4. Social conflict—England—Fiction.   5. Young women—England—Fiction.
6. Sisters—England—Fiction.   I. Armstrong, Paul B., 1949–   .   II. Title.
PR6011.058H6 1997
823'.912—dc21   97-9678

W. W. Norton & Company, Inc., 500 Fifth Avenue, New York, N.Y. 10110
www.wwnorton.com

W. W. Norton & Company Ltd., Castle House, 75/76 Wells Street,
London W1T 3QT

4 5 6 7 8 9 0

The Editor

PAUL B. ARMSTRONG is Dean of the College at Brown University. He has been Dean of the College of Arts and Sciences and Professor of English at the State University of New York at Stony Brook and has also taught at the University of Oregon, the University of Copenhagen, the Free University of Berlin, the Georgia Institute of Technology, and the University of Virginia. He is the author of *Conflicting Readings: Variety and Validity in Interpretation, The Challenge of Bewilderment: Understanding and Representation in James, Conrad, and Ford,* and *The Phenomenology of Henry James.*

Contents

Preface   ix

The Text of *Howards End*

Howards End   5

TEXTUAL APPENDIX   245

Textual Variants   245

Selections from the Manuscripts   250

Backgrounds and Contexts

THE AUTHOR AND THE NOVEL   269

E. M. Forster • Journal Entries   269

- Working Notes   275
- Selected Letters   276

To Goldsworthy Lowes Dickinson (12 May 1907)   276

To Edward Arnold (13 Jan. 1909; 12 Feb. 1909;
23 March 1909; 19 April 1909; 22 March 1910;
6 April 1910; 9 Aug. 1910; 14 Sept. 1910)   277

To Edward Garnett (10 Nov. 1910; 12 Nov. 1910)   280

To Goldsworthy Lowes Dickinson (21 Nov. 1910)   281

To Arthur Christopher Benson (13 Dec. 1910)   281

To Edward Arnold (23 Feb. 1911)   282

To E. J. Dent (7 May 1911)   282

To Edward Arnold (3 June 1911)   282

To Florence Barger (8 Nov. 1916)   283

- Recollection of Rooksnest   283
- Map of Rooksnest   285
- Boyhood Recollection of Rooksnest   286
- Interview   291
- From His *Commonplace Book*   294

- People 294
- Not Listening to Music 303

THE AUTHOR ON POLITICS

E. M. Forster • *From* Notes on the English Character 306
- What I Believe 310
- Tolerance 318
- The Challenge of Our Time 321

INTERPRETATIONS OF FORSTER'S LIBERALISM

Lionel Trilling • [The Liberal Imagination and *Howards End*] 326

Frederick Crews • [Forster and the Liberal Tradition] 331

Wilfred Stone • E. M. Forster's Subversive Individualism 340

Michael Levenson • Liberalism and Symbolism in *Howards End* 353

Daniel Born • Private Gardens, Public Swamps: *Howards End* and the Revaluation of Liberal Guilt 365

Criticism

CONTEMPORARY RESPONSES 381

Unsigned Review • From the *Times Literary Supplement* 381

R. A. Scott-James • From the *Daily News* 382

Edward Garnett • Villadom 383

Unsigned Review • From the *Westminster Gazette* 385

Unsigned Review • From the *Athenaeum* 386

A. C. Benson • Letter to E. M. Forster (9 Dec. 1910) 387

Katherine Mansfield • Journal Entry (May 1917) 388

Frieda Lawrence • Letter to E. M. Forster (5 Feb. 1915) 388

D. H. Lawrence • Letter to Bertrand Russell (12 Feb. 1915) 389
- Letter to E. M. Forster (20 Sept. 1922) 391

Virginia Woolf • The Novels of E. M. Forster 391

CONTENTS

ESSAYS IN CRITICISM

Wilfred Stone • *Howards End*: Red-Bloods and
Mollycoddles · 396

Barbara Rosecrance • [The Ambivalent Narrator of
Howards End] · 408

Perry Meisel • *Howards End*: Private Worlds and
Public Languages · 416

Kenneth Graham • [The Indirect Style of *Howards End*] · 425

Elizabeth Langland • Gesturing toward an Open Space:
Gender, Form, and Language in E. M. Forster's
Howards End · 438

Fredric Jameson • [Modernism, Imperialism, and
Howards End] · 451

REVIEWS OF THE MERCHANT-IVORY FILM

Vincent Canby • [A Triumphant Adaptation] · 459

John Simon • Demolition Jobs · 461

Terrence Rafferty • Yes, But · 463

Anne Billson • Our Kind of People · 467

E. M. Forster: A Chronology · 469

Selected Bibliography · 471

Preface

When *Howards End* was first published in England in November 1910, it was an immediate critical and popular success. A proud but somewhat insecure and private person, E. M. Forster was both pleased and embarrassed by the attention he received. The novel has been in print ever since. Although critics may disagree about whether *Howards End* or Forster's later novel *A Passage to India* is the better work, the two together have established his position as one of the great English writers of the twentieth century. *Howards End* has recently received renewed attention thanks to the popular film adaptation by Ismail Merchant and James Ivory. Interest in the novel has also increased because of recent critical concern with the social bases and implications of modernism. Almost from the beginning, critics recognized that a central value of *Howards End* is the analysis it offers of the condition of England of its time. The recent revival of interest in the question of liberalism has also caused readers to return to *Howards End*, a novel whose reception and reputation have been intimately linked to debates about this controversial term. This Norton Critical Edition of the novel attempts to provide a rich and various set of materials that suggest how *Howards End* has been interpreted, criticized, and debated from many different perspectives, artistic and formal as well as social and political, in ways that have kept the novel alive even though—or, rather, precisely because—readers have not always known what to make of this seemingly straightforward but elusive, often ambiguous work.

The text of this edition of *Howards End* is based on the first English edition published by Edward Arnold. The publishing history of the novel has been vexed. Even the most authoritative scholarly edition, the 1973 Abinger edition, is not entirely reliable, as the "Textual Variants" section explains. I have followed more conservative editorial practices than the Abinger editor did, who relied on a later edition for his copy text and often corrected it by making inferences about Forster's intentions that may or may not be justified. The problems in establishing the text go back in part to Forster himself, who was a notoriously sloppy proofreader, but they also reflect a complicated publishing history in which some egregious misprints went unnoticed for long periods ("goblin footfall" was rendered "goblin football" in a number of editions, for example, and from 1924 to 1951 the crucial epigraph "Only connect . . ." vanished from the English editions). I have corrected obvious errors, as the list of variants shows, but I have refrained from trying to construct an ideal text based on hunches and guesses. With only very minor changes, the text offered here is the text Forster saw through publication when it first appeared.

Forster's comments about *Howards End* in his diaries and letters are typically brief, but they are often extremely revealing. This Norton Critical Edition includes extended excerpts from Forster's journals that have not been previously published, as well as many letters to his publisher that are also not readily available. Forster's early notebook entry of 26 June 1908 gives the germ of the novel and shows that "the spiritual cleavage" between the Schlegel and Wilcox families was firmly in his mind from the outset. But his working notes show that he was still playing with various ideas for ending the novel far into the process of composition. An extensive selection of Forster's manuscript revisions reveals that many crucial elements of the novel were only discovered in the process of composition and that many of its memorable phrases were arrived at only through laborious trial and error.

Other materials in the "Backgrounds and Contexts" section place the novel in relation to Forster's personal experiences, give suggestions about his artistic methods, and provide his own evaluation of his achievement. Two different recollections of his boyhood home, Rooksnest, on which the house Howards End is based, are accompanied by his own pen-and-ink sketch of its grounds as a child. His comments in his essay "People" from *Aspects of the Novel*, where he introduces his influential distinction between "flat" and "round" characters, offer important explanations of why character matters to him in fiction. The amusing reflections in "Not Listening to Music" provide insights into how to understand not only the many musical references in *Howards End* but also his use of leitmotivs in this very musical novel.

Forster's reputation has been closely tied to his status as a representative of what Lionel Trilling famously called the "liberal imagination." Understanding Forster's liberalism is crucial for making sense of the social and political implications of *Howards End*. Forster's essays on politics are entertaining, provocative, and often moving, and they provide an invaluable context for understanding the social purposes of his fiction. Forster's liberalism lays primary stress on personal relations even when questions of public policy are at stake. Hence his well-known statement in "What I Believe": "If I had to choose between betraying my country and betraying my friend, I hope I should have the guts to betray my country." The role of private obligations is, of course, a central theme in *Howards End*. There and elsewhere Forster understands the condition of England and the state of society through the lens of personal relations. His description of the English character faults his countrymen for having an "undeveloped heart," a criticism that resonates with his portrayal of the Wilcoxes. His essays illustrate how, throughout his career, he grappled with the contradiction and the tension between the personal and the political.

Liberalism is a notoriously slippery term. In "The Challenge of Our Time," Forster aligns himself with "the fag-end of Victorian liberalism," but this ironically deprecatory self-description is vague and misleading. Where Trilling lauds the refusal of Forster's "liberal imagination" to simplify contradictory issues, later critics have found the novel problematic either because it proposes unsatisfactory resolutions or because it refuses to answer the questions it raises. These critics have disagreed, though, over whether these problems are a result of flaws in the novel's construction, a symptom of social dilemmas Forster's work reflects and cannot overcome, or a consequence of weaknesses in the liberal position that neither Forster nor Trilling recognizes. The essays in the section "Interpretations of Forster's Liberalism" provide backgrounds and evaluations that should make clearer what is involved in these disputes.

Frederick Crews usefully places Forster's political affiliations and social values within the liberal tradition, from John Stuart Mill's classic denunciation of the dehumanizing doctrines of utilitarianism to the ethics of personal relations advocated by Forster's contemporaries G. E. Moore and Goldsworthy Lowes Dickinson. Trilling's classic advocacy of Forster's "liberal imagination" was meant to oppose the ideological rigidities of 1940s America with an ironic appreciation of the ambiguities and indeterminacies of social life. Crews is joined by Wilfred Stone in countering this praise with appreciative but critical interpretations of Forster's position that see its weaknesses as well as its strengths as evidence of the unresolved problems that shadow the enduring values of the liberal tradition. Michael Levenson argues that Forster responds to the failure of liberal social reforms by replacing politics with symbolic imagination to encourage readers to see correspondences and imagine ways of overcoming divergences. Daniel Born uses Forster's rigorous self-scrutiny to criticize the less conflicted liberalism of the present-day philosopher Richard Rorty, suggesting that *Howards End*, although a text very much of the philosophical and political climate of its time, still has much to say to the intellectual debates of ours.

The first reviews of the novel were almost exclusively laudatory and praised *Howards End* as evidence that Forster had entered the first rank of English novelists. Isolated voices of dissent questioned the plausibility of Helen Schlegel conceiving a child with Leonard Bast or Margaret marrying Henry Wilcox. Others complained that the intellectual and symbolic design of the novel forced distortions in plot and character. These are criticisms echoed by later readers (Katherine Mansfield quipped that Leonard Bast could not have fathered Helen's child, but perhaps his umbrella did). These readers include Forster's powerful contemporaries D. H. Lawrence and Virginia Woolf, whose reactions to his work reveal much about themselves.

The novel's epigraph, "Only connect . . .", may seem like a simple and straightforward admonition. It is not at all certain, however, whether this advice should be read literally or ironically because the syntheses offered by the text are often problematic and typically leave the poles they would join still far apart: the "prose" and the "passion," artistic imagination and pragmatic business sense, personal relations and social responsibility, individual culture and public involvement, modern urbanization and rural tradition, to name but a few of the dualities that define this novel's thematic domain. As the selections from the criticism suggest, later readers have disagreed in interesting ways about whether the novel is deliberately ambiguous or seriously flawed because of the many oppositions it seems to want to unify but ultimately leaves unresolved.

Where Trilling lauds the novel's "moral realism" and complexity because it refuses to synthesize intractable contradictions, later critics have found the text evasive, confusing, or duplicitous. For example, Stone acuses Forster of presenting "a moral failure as a triumph" in the novel's seeming endorsement of the Schlegel sisters' "spiritual-esthetic withdrawal." Barbara Rosecrance traces the novel's contradictions to the peculiar ambivalences of the narrator, who is both an omniscient authority and an idiosyncratic, eccentric personality, and the *Howards End* she describes is considerably more complex and unstable than the authoritative narrative of the realist tradition it is often taken to be. Kenneth Graham similarly regards indirection and ambiguity as characteristic of the novel's style. Elizabeth Langland finds in these ambivalences evidence of Forster's "fear of the feminine in himself," a fear that sometimes results in "a misogynistic homosexuality" but that *Howards End* at its best moments overcomes by subverting conventional notions of the feminine and "gestur[ing]" toward an alternative to binary thinking" about gender. Perry Meisel sees these duplicities and subversions as criticisms of the modernist desire for wholeness, a longing Forster shares even as he demonstrates its impossibility through an irony that affirms the irreducible doubleness of language. The Marxist critic Fredric Jameson also sees *Howards End* as evidence of the modernist dilemma, but unlike Meisel, he claims Forster shares in the self-deceptions of his time. The variety of opinion outlined above itself resists synthesis, but it suggests the way Forster has been able to transform his own inability to resolve the dilemmas of his time into a provocation to later readers to wrestle with the contradictions that troubled and intrigued him.

The novel's enduring appeal also owes much to the interest of its characters, however one evaluates them, as well as to the verbal wit and entertainment of the writing and to the transport into another world its portrait of a receding time and place offers. The popular Merchant-Ivory film captures something of Forster's cleverness with language in its dialogue, even if the interesting and ambiguous narrator cannot survive the translation into another medium. Precisely by what it necessarily omits from the novel, however, the film also helps to show how much interest there is in what remains—most basically, the characters, the story, and the evocation of place. Here too, like the novel, *Howards End* the film has been controversial in interesting ways. As the selection of reviews in this edition shows, not all critics felt the film adaptation was successful. Their conflicting points of view raise questions about the relations between written narrative and film—about whether translation from one medium to the other is ever possible—and about whether the film's portrayal of England at the turn of the century is escapist or historically authentic. Those disagreements in turn call on us to reconsider the novel's manner of narration, the purposes of its representation of English manners, and its treatment of its characters. It is often unclear whether the film critics' evaluations and disagreements are about the film or the text it renders, a double possibility of which many of them are not aware.

It is a pleasure to thank the many people who helped me as I assembled this edition. I am grateful to the several librarians who gave me invaluable assistance. Jacqueline Cox, the modern archivist at the King's College library in Cambridge, was gracious, attentive, and efficient in responding to my requests before, during, and after the time I spent working on the Forster materials under her care. Scott Duvall, chair of Special Collections and Manuscripts at the Brigham Young University Library, generously provided me with a copy of the English first edition of the novel. I received assistance as well from the staff at the New York Public Library, the British Library, the Harry Ransom Humanities Research Center at the University of Texas, and the Knight Library at the University of Oregon. I would also like to thank Jeremy Hawthorn, Christopher Wheeler, Mary Lago, Steven Arkin, and Richard Stein for answering various queries. The incomparable Keith Carabine was an always reliable source of knowledge about things British. My friend and colleague Marianne Nicols gave much good advice about the intricacies of Latin. I also could not have done without Libby Tolson's efficient and resourceful help. As always, but more with each passing year, I am grateful to Timmy and Maggie for the joy they bring to my life. My gratitude to Beverly Haviland is more recent but no less happy and profound.

The Text of
HOWARDS END

HOWARDS END

BY

E. M. FORSTER

"Only connect . . ."

Chapter I

One may as well begin with Helen's letters to her sister.

> "Howards End,
> "Tuesday.

"Dearest Meg,

"It isn't going to be what we expected. It is old and little, and altogether delightful—red brick. We can scarcely pack in as it is, and the dear knows what will happen when Paul (younger son) arrives to-morrow. From hall you go right or left into dining-room or drawing-room. Hall itself is practically a room. You open another door in it, and there are the stairs going up in a sort of tunnel to the first-floor. Three bedrooms in a row there, and three attics in a row above. That isn't all the house really, but it's all that one notices—nine windows as you look up from the front garden.

"Then there's a very big wych-elm[1]—to the left as you look up—leaning a little over the house, and standing on the boundary between the garden and meadow. I quite love that tree already. Also ordinary elms, oaks—no nastier than ordinary oaks—pear-trees, apple-trees, and a vine. No silver birches, though. However, I must get on to my host and hostess. I only wanted to show that it isn't the least what we expected. Why did we settle that their house would be all gables and wiggles, and their garden all gamboge-coloured[2] paths? I believe simply because we associate them with expensive hotels—Mrs. Wilcox trailing in beautiful dresses down long corridors, Mr. Wilcox bullying porters, etc. We females are that unjust.

"I shall be back Saturday; will let you know train later. They are as angry as I am that you did not come too; really Tibby is too tiresome, he starts a new mortal disease every month. How could he have got hay fever in London? and even if he could, it seems hard that you should give up a visit to hear a schoolboy sneeze. Tell him that Charles Wilcox (the son who is here) has hay fever too, but he's brave, and gets quite cross when we inquire after it. Men like the Wilcoxes would do Tibby a power of good. But you won't agree, and I'd better change the subject.

"This long letter is because I'm writing before breakfast. Oh, the beautiful vine leaves! The house is covered with a vine. I looked out earlier, and Mrs. Wilcox was already in the garden. She evidently loves it. No wonder she sometimes looks tired. She was watching the large red poppies come out. Then she walked off the lawn to the meadow, whose corner to the right I can just see. Trail, trail, went her long dress over the

---

1. A tree of this kind, with broader leaves and more spreading branches than the common elm, was a prominent feature of the garden at Rooksnest, Forster's boyhood home.
2. Yellow.

5

sopping grass, and she came back with her hands full of the hay that was cut yesterday—I suppose for rabbits or something, as she kept on smelling it. The air here is delicious. Later on I heard the noise of cro-quet balls, and looked out again, and it was Charles Wilcox practising; they are keen on all games. Presently he started sneezing and had to stop. Then I hear more clicketing, and it is Mr. Wilcox practising, and then, 'a-tissue, a-tissue': he has to stop too. Then Evie comes out, and does some calisthenic exercises on a machine that is tacked on to a greengage-tree—they put everything to use—and then she says 'a-tissue,' and in she goes. And finally Mrs. Wilcox reappears, trail, trail, still smelling hay and looking at the flowers. I inflict all this on you because once you said that life is sometimes life and sometimes only a drama, and one must learn to distinguish tother from which,[3] and up to now I have always put that down as 'Meg's clever nonsense.' But this morning, it really does seem not life but a play, and it did amuse me enormously to watch the W's. Now Mrs. Wilcox has come in.

"I am going to wear [omission]. Last night Mrs. Wilcox wore an [omission], and Evie [omission]. So it isn't exactly a go-as-you-please place, and if you shut your eyes it still seems the wiggly hotel that we expected. Not if you open them. The dog-roses are too sweet. There is a great hedge of them over the lawn—magnificently tall, so that they fall down in garlands, and nice and thin at the bottom, so that you can see ducks through it and a cow. These belong to the farm, which is the only house near us. There goes the breakfast gong. Much love. Modified love to Tibby. Love to Aunt Juley; how good of her to come and keep you com-pany, but what a bore. Burn this. Will write again Thursday.

"Helen."

                                                      "Howards End,
                                                            "Friday.

    "Dearest Meg,

        "I am having a glorious time. I like them all. Mrs. Wilcox, if qui-eter than in Germany, is sweeter than ever, and I never saw anything like her steady unselfishness, and the best of it is that the others do not take advantage of her. They are the very happiest, jolliest family that you can imagine. I do really feel that we are making friends. The fun of it is that they think me a noodle, and say so—at least, Mr. Wilcox does—and when that happens, and one doesn't mind, it's a pretty sure test, isn't it? He says the most horrid things about women's suffrage[4] so nicely, and when I said I believed in equality he just folded his arms and gave me such a setting down as I've never had. Meg, shall we ever learn to talk

3. One from the other.
4. The campaign of women for the right to vote

less? I never felt so ashamed of myself in my life. I couldn't point to a time when men had been equal, nor even to a time when the wish to be equal had made them happier in other ways. I couldn't say a word. I had just picked up the notion that equality is good from some book—probably from poetry, or you. Anyhow, it's been knocked into pieces, and, like all people who are really strong, Mr. Wilcox did it without hurting me. On the other hand, I laugh at them for catching hay fever. We live like fighting-cocks, and Charles takes us out every day in the motor—a tomb with trees in it, a hermit's house, a wonderful road that was made by the Kings of Mercia[5]—tennis—a cricket match—bridge—and at night we squeeze up in this lovely house. The whole clan's here now—it's like a rabbit warren. Evie is a dear. They want me to stop over Sunday—I suppose it won't matter if I do. Marvellous weather and the views marvellous—views westward to the high ground. Thank you for your letter. Burn this.

> "Your affectionate
> "Helen."

> "Howards End,
>   "Sunday.

"Dearest dearest Meg,—I do not know what you will say: Paul and I are in love—the younger son who only came here Wednesday."

Chapter II

Margaret glanced at her sister's note and pushed it over the breakfast-table to her aunt. There was a moment's hush, and then the flood-gates opened.

"I can tell you nothing, Aunt Juley. I know no more than you do. We met—we only met the father and mother abroad last spring. I know so little that I didn't even know their son's name. It's all so——" She waved her hand and laughed a little.

"In that case it is far too sudden."

"Who knows, Aunt Juley, who knows?"

"But, Margaret dear, I mean, we mustn't be unpractical now that we've come to facts. It is too sudden, surely."

"Who knows!"

"But Margaret dear——"

"I'll go for her other letters," said Margaret. "No, I won't, I'll finish my breakfast. In fact, I haven't them. We met the Wilcoxes on an awful expedition that we made from Heidelberg to Speyer. Helen and I had got it into our heads that there was a grand old cathedral at Speyer—the Archbishop of Speyer was one of the seven electors—you know—

5. An Old English kingdom in south central Britain.

'Speyer, Maintz, and Köln.'[1] Those three sees once commanded the Rhine Valley and got it the name of Priest Street."

"I still feel quite uneasy about this business, Margaret."

"The train crossed by a bridge of boats, and at first sight it looked quite fine. But oh, in five minutes we had seen the whole thing. The cathedral had been ruined, absolutely ruined, by restoration; not an inch left of the original structure. We wasted a whole day, and came across the Wilcoxes as we were eating our sandwiches in the public gardens. They too, poor things, had been taken in—they were actually stopping at Speyer—and they rather liked Helen insisting that they must fly with us to Heidelberg. As a matter of fact, they did come on next day. We all took some drives together. They knew us well enough to ask Helen to come and see them—at least, I was asked too, but Tibby's illness prevented me, so last Monday she went alone. That's all. You know as much as I do now. It's a young man out the unknown. She was to have come back Saturday, but put off till Monday, perhaps on account of—I don't know."

She broke off, and listened to the sounds of a London morning. Their house was in Wickham Place, and fairly quiet, for a lofty promontory of buildings separated it from the main thoroughfare. One had the sense of a backwater, or rather of an estuary, whose waters flowed in from the invisible sea, and ebbed into a profound silence while the waves without were still beating. Though the promontory consisted of flats—expensive, with cavernous entrance halls, full of concierges and palms—it fulfilled its purpose, and gained for the older houses opposite a certain measure of peace. These, too, would be swept away in time, and another promontory would arise upon their site, as humanity piled itself higher and higher on the precious soil of London.

Mrs. Munt had her own method of interpreting her nieces. She decided that Margaret was a little hysterical, and was trying to gain time by a torrent of talk. Feeling very diplomatic, she lamented the fate of Speyer, and declared that never, never should she be so misguided as to visit it, and added of her own accord that the principles of restoration were ill understood in Germany. "The Germans," she said, "are too thorough, and this is all very well sometimes, but at other times it does not do."

"Exactly," said Margaret; "Germans are too thorough." And her eyes began to shine.

"Of course I regard you Schlegels as English," said Mrs. Munt hastily—"English to the backbone."

Margaret leaned forward and stroked her hand.

"And that reminds me—Helen's letter——"

"Oh yes, Aunt Juley, I am thinking all right about Helen's letter. I

1. The seven electors chose the Holy Roman Emperor.

know—I must go down and see her. I am thinking about her all right. I am meaning to go down."

"But go with some plan," said Mrs. Munt, admitting into her kindly voice a note of exasperation. "Margaret, if I may interfere, don't be taken by surprise. What do you think of the Wilcoxes? Are they our sort? Are they likely people? Could they appreciate Helen, who is to my mind a very special sort of person? Do they care about Literature and Art? That is most important when you come to think of it. Literature and Art. Most important. How old would the son be? She says 'younger son.' Would he be in a position to marry? Is he likely to make Helen happy? Did you gather——"

"I gathered nothing."

They began to talk at once.

"Then in that case——"

"In that case I can make no plans, don't you see."

"On the contrary——"

"I hate plans. I hate lines of action. Helen isn't a baby."

"Then in that case, my dear, why go down?"

Margaret was silent. If her aunt could not see why she must go down, she was not going to tell her. She was not going to say "I love my dear sister; I must be near her at this crisis of her life." The affections are more reticent than the passions, and their expression more subtle. If she herself should ever fall in love with a man, she, like Helen, would proclaim it from the house-tops, but as she only loved a sister she used the voiceless language of sympathy.

"I consider you odd girls," continued Mrs. Munt, "and very wonderful girls, and in many ways far older than your years. But—you won't be offended?—frankly, I feel you are not up to this business. It requires an older person. Dear, I have nothing to call me back to Swanage." She spread out her plump arms. "I am all at your disposal. Let me go down to this house whose name I forget instead of you."

"Aunt Juley"—she jumped up and kissed her—"I must, must go to Howards End myself. You don't exactly understand, though I can never thank you properly for offering."

"I do understand," retorted Mrs. Munt, with immense confidence. "I go down in no spirit of interference, but to make inquiries. Inquiries are necessary. Now, I am going to be rude. You would say the wrong thing; to a certainty you would. In your anxiety for Helen's happiness you would offend the whole of these Wilcoxes by asking one of your impetuous questions—not that one minds offending them."

"I shall ask no questions. I have it in Helen's writing that she and a man are in love. There is no question to ask as long as she keeps to that. All the rest isn't worth a straw. A long engagement if you like, but inquiries, questions, plans, lines of action—no, Aunt Juley, no."

Away she hurried, not beautiful, not supremely brilliant, but filled

with something that took the place of both qualities—something best
described as a profound vivacity, a continual and sincere response to all
that she encountered in her path through life.

"If Helen had written the same to me about a shop-assistant or a penniless clerk——"

"Dear Margaret, do come into the library and shut the door. Your
good maids are dusting the banisters."

"—or if she had wanted to marry the man who calls for Carter
Paterson,[2] I should have said the same." Then, with one of those turns
that convinced her aunt that she was not mad really, and convinced
observers of another type that she was not a barren theorist, she added:
"Though in the case of Carter Paterson I should want it to be a very long
engagement indeed, I must say."

"I should think so," said Mrs. Munt; "and, indeed, I can scarcely follow you. Now, just imagine if you said anything of that sort to the
Wilcoxes. I understand it, but most good people would think you mad.
Imagine how disconcerting for Helen! What is wanted is a person who
will go slowly, slowly in this business, and see how things are and where
they are likely to lead to."

Margaret was down on this.

"But you implied just now that the engagement must be broken off."

"I think probably it must; but slowly."

"Can you break an engagement off slowly?" Her eyes lit up. "What's
an engagement made of, do you suppose? I think it's made of some hard
stuff, that may snap, but can't break. It is different to the other ties of life.
They stretch or bend. They admit of degree. They're different."

"Exactly so. But won't you let me just run down to Howards House,
and save you all the discomfort? I will really not interfere, but I do so
thoroughly understand the kind of thing you Schlegels want that one
quiet look round will be enough for me."

Margaret again thanked her, again kissed her, and then ran upstairs to
see her brother.

He was not so well.

The hay fever had worried him a good deal all night. His head ached,
his eyes were wet, his mucous membrane, he informed her, in a most
unsatisfactory condition. The only thing that made life worth living was
the thought of Walter Savage Landor,[3] from whose "Imaginary Conversations" she had promised to read at frequent intervals during the day.

It was rather difficult. Something must be done about Helen. She
must be assured that it is not a criminal offence to love at first sight. A
telegram to this effect would be cold and cryptic, a personal visit seemed

---

2. A shipping or transport firm.
3. An English poet and essayist (1775–1864) who wrote a voluminous book of fictional dialogues
   between famous ancient and modern figures.

each moment more impossible. Now the doctor arrived, and said that Tibby was quite bad. Might it really be best to accept Aunt Juley's kind offer, and to send her down to Howards End with a note?

Certainly Margaret was impulsive. She did swing rapidly from one decision to another. Running downstairs into the library, she cried: "Yes, I have changed my mind; I do wish that you would go."

There was a train from King's Cross[4] at eleven. At half-past ten Tibby, with rare self-effacement, fell asleep, and Margaret was able to drive her aunt to the station.

"You will remember, Aunt Juley, not to be drawn into discussing the engagement. Give my letter to Helen, and say whatever you feel yourself, but do keep clear of the relatives. We have scarcely got their names straight yet, and, besides, that sort of thing is so uncivilized and wrong."

"So uncivilized?" queried Mrs. Munt, fearing that she was losing the point of some brilliant remark.

"Oh, I used an affected word. I only meant would you please only talk the thing over with Helen."

"Only with Helen."

"Because——" But it was no moment to expound the personal nature of love. Even Margaret shrank from it, and contented herself with stroking her good aunt's hand, and with meditating, half sensibly and half poetically, on the journey that was about to begin from King's Cross.

Like many others who have lived long in a great capital, she had strong feelings about the various railway termini. They are our gates to the glorious and the unknown. Through them we pass out into adventure and sunshine, to them, alas! we return. In Paddington all Cornwall is latent and the remoter west; down the inclines of Liverpool Street lie fenlands and the illimitable Broads; Scotland is through the pylons of Euston; Wessex behind the poised chaos of Waterloo. Italians realize this, as is natural; those of them who are so unfortunate as to serve as waiters in Berlin call the Anhalt Bahnhof the Stazione d'Italia, because by it they must return to their homes. And he is a chilly Londoner who does not endow his stations with some personality, and extend to them, however shyly, the emotions of fear and love.

To Margaret—I hope that it will not set the reader against her—the station of King's Cross had always suggested Infinity. Its very situation—withdrawn a little behind the facile splendours of St. Pancras[5]—implied a comment on the materialism of life. Those two great arches, colourless, indifferent, shouldering between them an unlovely clock, were fit portals for some eternal adventure, whose issue might be prosperous, but would certainly not be expressed in the ordinary language of prosperity. If you think this ridiculous, remember that it is not Margaret who is

---

4. A station from which trains leave London for points north.
5. A station near King's Cross.

telling you about it; and let me hasten to add that they were in plenty of
time for the train; that Mrs. Munt, though she took a second-class ticket, was put by the guard into a first (only two seconds on the train, one
smoking and the other babies—one cannot be expected to travel with
babies); and that Margaret, on her return to Wickham Place, was confronted with the following telegram:

"All over. Wish I had never written. Tell no one.—Helen."

But Aunt Juley was gone—gone irrevocably, and no power on earth
could stop her.

Chapter III

Most complacently did Mrs. Munt rehearse her mission. Her nieces
were independent young women, and it was not often that she was able
to help them. Emily's daughters had never been quite like other girls.
They had been left motherless when Tibby was born, when Helen was
five and Margaret herself but thirteen. It was before the passing of the
Deceased Wife's Sister Bill,[1] so Mrs. Munt could without impropriety
offer to go and keep house at Wickham Place. But her brother-in-law,
who was peculiar and a German, had referred the question to Margaret,
who with the crudity of youth had answered, 'No, they could manage
much better alone.' Five years later Mr. Schlegel had died too, and Mrs.
Munt had repeated her offer. Margaret, crude no longer, had been grateful and extremely nice, but the substance of her answer had been the
same. "I must not interfere a third time," thought Mrs. Munt. However,
of course she did. She learnt, to her horror, that Margaret, now of age,
was taking her money out of the old safe investments and putting it into
Foreign Things, which always smash. Silence would have been criminal. Her own fortune was invested in Home Rails,[2] and most ardently did
she beg her niece to imitate her. "Then we should be together, dear."
Margaret, out of politeness, invested a few hundreds in the Nottingham
and Derby Railway, and though the Foreign Things did admirably and
the Nottingham and Derby declined with the steady dignity of which
only Home Rails are capable, Mrs. Munt never ceased to rejoice, and to
say, "I did manage that, at all events. When the smash comes poor
Margaret will have a nest-egg to fall back upon." This year Helen came
of age, and exactly the same thing happened in Helen's case; she also
would shift her money out of Consols, but she, too, almost without
being pressed, consecrated a fraction of it to the Nottingham and Derby
Railway. So far so good, but in social matters their aunt had accomplished nothing. Sooner or later the girls would enter on the process
known as throwing themselves away, and if they had delayed hitherto, it

1. Until 1907 it was illegal in England for a widower to marry his sister-in-law.
2. English railroad companies.

was only that they might throw themselves more vehemently in the future. They saw too many people at Wickham Place—unshaven musicians, an actress even, German cousins (one knows what foreigners are), acquaintances picked up at Continental hotels (one knows what they are too). It was interesting, and down at Swanage no one appreciated culture more than Mrs. Munt; but it was dangerous, and disaster was bound to come. How right she was, and how lucky to be on the spot when the disaster came!

The train sped northward, under innumerable tunnels. It was only an hour's journey, but Mrs. Munt had to raise and lower the window again and again. She passed through the South Welwyn Tunnel, saw light for a moment, and entered the North Welwyn Tunnel, of tragic fame.[3] She traversed the immense viaduct, whose arches span untroubled meadows and the dreamy flow of Tewin Water. She skirted the parks of politicians. At times the Great North Road accompanied her, more suggestive of infinity than any railway, awakening, after a nap of a hundred years, to such life as is conferred by the stench of motor-cars, and to such culture as is implied by the advertisements of antibilious pills.[4] To history, to tragedy, to the past, to the future, Mrs. Munt remained equally indifferent; hers but to concentrate on the end of her journey, and to rescue poor Helen from this dreadful mess.

The station for Howards End was at Hilton, one of the large villages that are strung so frequently along the North Road, and that owe their size to the traffic of coaching and pre-coaching days. Being near London, it had not shared in the rural decay, and its long High Street had budded out right and left into residential estates. For about a mile a series of tiled and slated houses passed before Mrs. Munt's inattentive eyes, a series broken at one point by six Danish tumuli[5] that stood shoulder to shoulder along the highroad, tombs of soldiers. Beyond these tumuli habitations thickened, and the train came to a standstill in a tangle that was almost a town.

The station, like the scenery, like Helen's letters, struck an indeterminate note. Into which country will it lead, England or Suburbia? It was new, it had island platforms and a subway, and the superficial comfort exacted by business men. But it held hints of local life, personal intercourse, as even Mrs. Munt was to discover.

"I want a house," she confided to the ticket boy. "Its name is Howards Lodge. Do you know where it is?"

"Mr. Wilcox!" the boy called.

A young man in front of them turned round.

"She's wanting Howards End."

There was nothing for it but to go forward, though Mrs. Munt was too

3. Site of a three-train crash in 1866.
4. Medicine for indigestion and peevishness caused by excessive secretions from the liver.
5. Viking burial mounds, later referred to as the "Six Hills."

much agitated even to stare at the stranger. But remembering that there were two brothers, she had the sense to say to him, "Excuse me asking, but are you the younger Mr. Wilcox or the elder?"

"The younger. Can I do anything for you?"

"Oh, well"—she controlled herself with difficulty. "Really. Are you? I——" She moved away from the ticket boy and lowered her voice. "I am Miss Schlegel's aunt. I ought to introduce myself, oughtn't I? My name is Mrs. Munt."

She was conscious that he raised his cap and said quite coolly, "Oh, rather; Miss Schlegel is stopping with us. Did you want to see her?"

"Possibly——"

"I'll call you a cab. No; wait a mo." He thought. "Our motor's here. I'll run you up in it."

"That is very kind——"

"Not at all, if you'll just wait till they bring out a parcel from the office. This way."

"My niece is not with you by any chance?"

"No; I came over with my father. He has gone on south in your train. You'll see Miss Schlegel at lunch. You're coming up to lunch, I hope?"

"I should like to come *up*," said Mrs. Munt, not committing herself to nourishment until she had studied Helen's lover a little more. He seemed a gentleman, but had so rattled her round that her powers of observation were numbed. She glanced at him stealthily. To a feminine eye there was nothing amiss in the sharp depressions at the corners of his mouth, nor in the rather box-like construction of his forehead. He was dark, clean-shaven, and seemed accustomed to command.

"In front or behind? Which do you prefer? It may be windy in front."

"In front if I may; then we can talk."

"But excuse me one moment—I can't think what they're doing with that parcel." He strode into the booking-office, and called with a new voice: "Hi! hi, you there! Are you going to keep me waiting all day? Parcel for Wilcox, Howards End. Just look sharp!" Emerging, he said in quieter tones: "This station's abominably organized; if I had my way, the whole lot of 'em should get the sack. May I help you in?"

"This is very good of you," said Mrs. Munt, as she settled herself into a luxurious cavern of red leather, and suffered her person to be padded with rugs and shawls. She was more civil than she had intended, but really this young man was very kind. Moreover, she was a little afraid of him: his self-possession was extraordinary. "Very good indeed," she repeated, adding: "It is just what I should have wished."

"Very good of you to say so," he replied, with a slight look of surprise, which, like most slight looks, escaped Mrs. Munt's attention. "I was just tooling my father over to catch the down train."

"You see, we heard from Helen this morning."

Young Wilcox was pouring in petrol, starting his engine, and performing other actions with which this story has no concern. The great car began to rock, and the form of Mrs. Munt, trying to explain things, sprang agreeably up and down among the red cushions. "The mater will be very glad to see you," he mumbled. "Hi! I say. Parcel. Parcel for Howards End. Bring it out. Hi!"

A bearded porter emerged with the parcel in one hand and an entry book in the other. With the gathering whir of the motor these ejaculations mingled: "Sign, must I? Why the —— should I sign after all this bother? Not even got a pencil on you? Remember next time I report you to the station-master. My time's of value, though yours mayn't be. Here"—here being a tip.

"Extremely sorry, Mrs. Munt."

"Not at all, Mr. Wilcox."

"And do you object to going through the village? It is rather a longer spin, but I have one or two commissions."

"I should love going through the village. Naturally I am very anxious to talk things over with you."

As she said this she felt ashamed, for she was disobeying Margaret's instructions. Only disobeying them in the letter, surely. Margaret had only warned her against discussing the incident with outsiders. Surely it was not 'uncivilized or wrong' to discuss it with the young man himself, since chance had thrown them together.

A reticent fellow, he made no reply. Mounting by her side, he put on gloves and spectacles, and off they drove, the bearded porter—life is a mysterious business—looking after them with admiration.

The wind was in their faces down the station road, blowing the dust into Mrs. Munt's eyes. But as soon as they turned into the Great North Road she opened fire. "You can well imagine," she said, "that the news was a great shock to us."

"What news?"

"Mr. Wilcox," she said frankly, "Margaret has told me everything—everything. I have seen Helen's letter."

He could not look her in the face, as his eyes were fixed on his work; he was travelling as quickly as he dared down the High Street. But he inclined his head in her direction, and said, "I beg your pardon; I didn't catch."

"About Helen. Helen, of course. Helen is a very exceptional person—I am sure you will let me say this, feeling towards her as you do—indeed, all the Schlegels are exceptional. I come in no spirit of interference, but it was a great shock."

They drew up opposite a draper's. Without replying, he turned round in his seat, and contemplated the cloud of dust that they had raised in their passage through the village. It was settling again, but not all into the road from which he had taken it. Some of it had percolated through the open windows, some had whitened the roses and gooseberries of the wayside gardens, while a certain proportion had entered the lungs of the villagers. "I wonder when they'll learn wisdom and tar the roads," was his comment. Then a man ran out of the draper's with a roll of oilcloth, and off they went again.

"Margaret could not come herself, on account of poor Tibby, so I am here to represent her and to have a good talk."

"I'm sorry to be so dense," said the young man, again drawing up outside a shop. "But I still haven't quite understood."

"Helen, Mr. Wilcox—my niece and you."

He pushed up his goggles and gazed at her, absolutely bewildered. Horror smote her to the heart, for even she began to suspect that they were at cross-purposes, and that she had commenced her mission by some hideous blunder.

"Miss Schlegel and myself?" he asked, compressing his lips.

"I trust there has been no misunderstanding," quavered Mrs. Munt. "Her letter certainly read that way."

"What way?"

"That you and she——" She paused, then drooped her eyelids.

"I think I catch your meaning," he said stickily. "What an extraordinary mistake!"

"Then you didn't the least——" she stammered, getting blood-red in the face, and wishing she had never been born.

"Scarcely, as I am already engaged to another lady." There was a moment's silence, and then he caught his breath and exploded with, "Oh, good God! Don't tell me it's some silliness of Paul's."

"But you are Paul."

"I'm not."

"Then why did you say so at the station?"

"I said nothing of the sort."

"I beg your pardon, you did."

"I beg your pardon, I did not. My name is Charles."

"Younger" may mean son as opposed to father, or second brother as opposed to first. There is much to be said for either view, and later on they said it. But they had other questions before them now.

"Do you mean to tell me that Paul——"

But she did not like his voice. He sounded as if he was talking to a porter, and, certain that he had deceived her at the station, she too grew angry.

"Do you mean to tell me that Paul and your niece——"

Mrs. Munt—such is human nature—determined that she would champion the lovers. She was not going to be bullied by a severe young man. "Yes, they care for one another very much indeed," she said. "I dare say they will tell you about it by-and-by. We heard this morning."

And Charles clenched his fist and cried, "The idiot, the idiot, the little fool!"

Mrs. Munt tried to divest herself of her rugs. "If that is your attitude, Mr. Wilcox, I prefer to walk."

"I beg you will do no such thing. I take you up this moment to the house. Let me tell you the thing's impossible, and must be stopped."

Mrs. Munt did not often lose her temper, and when she did it was only to protect those whom she loved. On this occasion she blazed out. "I quite agree, sir. The thing is impossible, and I will come up and stop it. My niece is a very exceptional person, and I am not inclined to sit still while she throws herself away on those who will not appreciate her."

Charles worked his jaws.

"Considering she has only known your brother since Wednesday, and only met your father and mother at a stray hotel——"

"Could you possibly lower your voice? The shopman will overhear."

"Esprit de classe"[6]—if one may coin the phrase—was strong in Mrs. Munt. She sat quivering while a member of the lower orders deposited a metal funnel, a saucepan, and a garden squirt[7] beside the roll of oil-cloth.

"Right behind?"

"Yes, sir." And the lower orders vanished in a cloud of dust.

"I warn you: Paul hasn't a penny; it's useless."

"No need to warn us, Mr. Wilcox, I assure you. The warning is all the other way. My niece has been very foolish, and I shall give her a good scolding and take her back to London with me."

"He has to make his way out in Nigeria. He couldn't think of marrying for years, and when he does it must be a woman who can stand the climate, and is in other ways—— Why hasn't he told us? Of course he's ashamed. He knows he's been a fool. And so he has—a damned fool."

She grew furious.

"Whereas Miss Schlegel has lost no time in publishing the news."

"If I were a man, Mr. Wilcox, for that last remark I'd box your ears. You're not fit to clean my niece's boots, to sit in the same room with her, and you dare—you actually dare—— I decline to argue with such a person."

"All I know is, she's spread the thing and he hasn't, and my father's away and I——"

"And all that I know is——"

"Might I finish my sentence, please?"

"No."

Charles clenched his teeth and sent the motor swerving all over the lane.

6. Class solidarity.
7. A portable syringe for watering the garden.

She screamed.

So they played the game of Capping Families, a round of which is always played when love would unite two members of our race. But they played it with unusual vigour, stating in so many words that Schlegels were better than Wilcoxes, Wilcoxes better than Schlegels. They flung decency aside. The man was young, the woman deeply stirred; in both a vein of coarseness was latent. Their quarrel was no more surprising than are most quarrels—inevitable at the time, incredible afterwards. But it was more than usually futile. A few minutes, and they were enlightened. The motor drew up at Howards End, and Helen, looking very pale, ran out to meet her aunt.

"Aunt Juley, I have just had a telegram from Margaret; I—I meant to stop your coming. It isn't—it's over."

The climax was too much for Mrs. Munt. She burst into tears.

"Aunt Juley dear, don't. Don't let them know I've been so silly. It wasn't anything. Do bear up for my sake."

"Paul," cried Charles Wilcox,.pulling his gloves off.

"Don't let them know. They are never to know."

"Oh, my darling Helen——"

"Paul! Paul!"

A very young man came out of the house.

"Paul, is there any truth in this?"

"I didn't—I don't——"

"Yes or no, man; plain question, plain answer. Did or didn't Miss Schlegel——"

"Charles dear," said a voice from the garden. "Charles, dear Charles, one doesn't ask plain questions. There aren't such things."

They were all silent. It was Mrs. Wilcox.

She approached just as Helen's letter had described her, trailing noiselessly over the lawn, and there was actually a wisp of hay in her hands. She seemed to belong not to the young people and their motor, but to the house, and to the tree that overshadowed it. One knew that she worshipped the past, and that the instinctive wisdom the past can alone bestow had descended upon her—that wisdom to which we give the clumsy name of aristocracy. High born she might not be. But assuredly she cared about her ancestors, and let them help her. When she saw Charles angry, Paul frightened, and Mrs. Munt in tears, she heard her ancestors say, "Separate those human beings who will hurt each other most. The rest can wait." So she did not ask questions. Still less did she pretend that nothing had happened, as a competent society hostess would have done. She said, "Miss Schlegel, would you take your aunt up to your room or to my room, whichever you think best. Paul, do find Evie, and tell her lunch for six, but I'm not sure whether we shall all be downstairs for it." And when they had obeyed her, she turned to her elder son, who still stood in the throbbing, stinking car, and smiled at him with tenderness, and without saying a word, turned away from him towards her flowers.

"Mother," he called, "are you aware that Paul has been playing the fool again?"

"It is all right, dear. They have broken off the engagement."

"Engagement——!"

"They do not love any longer, if you prefer it put that way," said Mrs. Wilcox, stooping down to smell a rose.

Chapter IV

Helen and her aunt returned to Wickham Place in a state of collapse, and for a little time Margaret had three invalids on her hands. Mrs. Munt soon recovered. She possessed to a remarkable degree the power of distorting the past, and before many days were over she had forgotten the part played by her own imprudence in the catastrophe. Even at the crisis she had cried, "Thank goodness, poor Margaret is saved this!" which during the journey to London evolved into, "It had to be gone through by someone," which in its turn ripened into the permanent form of "The one time I really did help Emily's girls was over the Wilcox business." But Helen was a more serious patient. New ideas had burst upon her like a thunder clap, and by them and by their reverberations she had been stunned.

The truth was that she had fallen in love, not with an individual, but with a family.

Before Paul arrived she had, as it were, been tuned up into his key. The energy of the Wilcoxes had fascinated her, had created new images of beauty in her responsive mind. To be all day with them in the open air, to sleep at night under their roof, had seemed the supreme joy of life, and had led to that abandonment of personality that is a possible prelude to love. She had liked giving in to Mr. Wilcox, or Evie, or Charles; she had liked being told that her notions of life were sheltered or academic; that Equality was nonsense, Votes for Women nonsense, Socialism nonsense, Art and Literature, except when conducive to strengthening the character, nonsense. One by one the Schlegel fetiches had been overthrown, and, though professing to defend them, she had rejoiced. When Mr. Wilcox said that one sound man of business did more good to the world than a dozen of your social reformers, she had swallowed the curious assertion without a gasp, and had leant back luxuriously among the cushions of his motor-car. When Charles said, "Why be so polite to servants? they don't understand it," she had not given the Schlegel retort of, "If they don't understand it, I do." No; she had vowed to be less polite to servants in the future. "I am swathed in cant," she thought, "and it is good for me to be stripped of it." And all that she thought or did or breathed was a quiet preparation for Paul. Paul was inevitable. Charles was taken up with another girl, Mr. Wilcox was so old, Evie so young, Mrs. Wilcox so different. Round the absent brother she began to throw the halo of Romance, to irradiate him with all the splendour of those happy days, to feel that in him she should draw nearest to the robust ideal. He and she were about the same age, Evie said. Most people thought Paul handsomer than his brother. He was certainly a better shot, though not so good at golf. And when Paul appeared, flushed with the triumph of getting through an examination, and ready to flirt with any pretty girl, Helen met him halfway, or more than halfway, and turned towards him on the Sunday evening.

He had been talking of his approaching exile in Nigeria, and he should have continued to talk of it, and allowed their guest to recover. But the heave of her bosom flattered him. Passion was possible, and he became passionate. Deep down in him something whispered, "This girl would let you kiss her; you might not have such a chance again."

That was "how it happened," or, rather, how Helen described it to her sister, using words even more unsympathetic than my own. But the poetry of that kiss, the wonder of it, the magic that there was in life for hours after it—who can describe that? It is so easy for an Englishman to sneer at these chance collisions of human beings. To the insular cynic and the insular moralist they offer an equal opportunity. It is so easy to talk of "passing emotion," and to forget how vivid the emotion was ere it passed. Our impulse to sneer, to forget, is at root a good one. We recognize that emotion is not enough, and that men and women are personalities capable of sustained relations, not mere opportunities for an electrical discharge. Yet we rate the impulse too highly. We do not admit that by collisions of this trivial sort the doors of heaven may be shaken open. To Helen, at all events, her life was to bring nothing more intense than the embrace of this boy who played no part in it. He had drawn her out of the house, where there was danger of surprise and light; he had led her by a path he knew, until they stood under the column of the vast wych-elm. A man in the darkness, he had whispered "I love you" when she was desiring love. In time his slender personality faded, the scene that he had evoked endured. In all the variable years that followed she never saw the like of it again.

"I understand," said Margaret—"at least, I understand as much as ever is understood of these things. Tell me now what happened on the Monday morning."

"It was over at once."

"How, Helen?"

"I was still happy while I dressed, but as I came downstairs I got nervous, and when I went into the dining-room I knew it was no good. There was Evie—I can't explain—managing the tea-urn, and Mr. Wilcox reading the 'Times.'"

"Was Paul there?"

"Yes; and Charles was talking to him about Stocks and Shares, and he looked frightened."

By slight indications the sisters could convey much to each other. Margaret saw horror latent in the scene, and Helen's next remark did not surprise her.

"Somehow, when that kind of man looks frightened it is too awful. It is all right for us to be frightened, or for men of another sort—father, for instance; but for men like that! When I saw all the others so placid, and Paul mad with terror in case I said the wrong thing, I felt for a moment that the whole Wilcox family was a fraud, just a wall of newspapers and motor-cars and golf-clubs, and that if it fell I should find nothing behind it but panic and emptiness."

"I don't think that. The Wilcoxes struck me as being genuine people, particularly the wife."

"No, I don't really think that. But Paul was so broad-shouldered; all kinds of extraordinary things made it worse, and I knew that it would never do—never. I said to him after breakfast, when the others were practising strokes, 'We rather lost our heads,' and he looked better at once, though frightfully ashamed. He began a speech about having no money to marry on, but it hurt him to make it, and I stopped him. Then he said, 'I must beg your pardon over this, Miss Schlegel; I can't think what came over me last night.' And I said, 'Nor what over me; never mind.' And then we parted—at least, until I remembered that I had written straight off to tell you the night before, and that frightened him again. I asked him to send a telegram for me, for he knew you would be coming or something; and he tried to get hold of the motor, but Charles and Mr. Wilcox wanted it to go to the station; and Charles offered to send the telegram for me, and then I had to say that the telegram was of no consequence, for Paul said Charles might read it, and though I wrote it out several times, he always said people would suspect something. He took it himself at last, pretending that he must walk down to get cartridges, and, what with one thing and the other, it was not handed in at the Post Office until too late. It was the most terrible morning. Paul disliked me more and more, and Evie talked cricket averages till I nearly screamed. I cannot think how I stood her all the other days. At last Charles and his father started for the station, and then came your telegram warning me that Aunt Juley was coming by that train, and Paul—oh, rather horrible—said that I had muddled it. But Mrs. Wilcox knew."

"Knew what?"

"Everything; though we neither of us told her a word, and had known all along, I think."

"Oh, she must have overheard you."

"I suppose so, but it seemed wonderful. When Charles and Aunt Juley drove up, calling each other names, Mrs. Wilcox stepped in from the garden and made everything less terrible. Ugh! but it has been a disgusting business. To think that——" She sighed.

"To think that because you and a young man meet for a moment, there must be all these telegrams and anger," supplied Margaret.

Helen nodded.

"I've often thought about it, Helen. It's one of the most interesting things in the world. The truth is that there is a great outer life that you and I have never touched—a life in which telegrams and anger count. Personal relations, that we think supreme, are not supreme there. There love means marriage settlements, death, death duties. So far I'm clear. But here my difficulty. This outer life, though obviously horrid, often seems the real one—there's grit in it. It does breed character. Do personal relations lead to sloppiness in the end?"

"Oh, Meg, that's what I felt, only not so clearly, when the Wilcoxes were so competent, and seemed to have their hands on all the ropes."

"Don't you feel it now?"

"I remember Paul at breakfast," said Helen quietly. "I shall never forget him. He had nothing to fall back upon. I know that personal relations are the real life, for ever and ever."

"Amen!"

So the Wilcox episode fell into the background, leaving behind it memories of sweetness and horror that mingled, and the sisters pursued the life that Helen had commended. They talked to each other and to other people, they filled the tall thin house at Wickham Place with those whom they liked or could befriend. They even attended public meetings. In their own fashion they cared deeply about politics, though not as politicians would have us care; they desired that public life should mirror whatever is good in the life within. Temperance, tolerance, and sexual equality were intelligible cries to them; whereas they did not follow our Forward Policy in Thibet[1] with the keen attention that it merits, and would at times dismiss the whole British Empire with a puzzled, if reverent, sigh. Not out of them are the shows of history erected: the world would be a grey, bloodless place were it entirely composed of Miss Schlegels. But the world being what it is, perhaps they shine out in it like stars.

A word on their origin. They were not "English to the backbone," as their aunt had piously asserted. But, on the other hand, they were not "Germans of the dreadful sort." Their father had belonged to a type that was more prominent in Germany fifty years ago than now. He was not the aggressive German, so dear to the English journalist, nor the domestic German, so dear to the English wit. If one classed him at all it would be as the countryman of Hegel and Kant, as the idealist, inclined to be

1. Britain's use of force to open up Tibet for trade.

dreamy, whose Imperialism was the Imperialism of the air. Not that his
life had been inactive. He had fought like blazes against Denmark,
Austria, France.[2] But he had fought without visualizing the results of victory. A hint of the truth broke on him after Sedan, when he saw the dyed
moustaches of Napoleon going grey; another when he entered Paris,
and saw the smashed windows of the Tuileries.[3] Peace came — it was all
very immense, one had turned into an Empire — but he knew that some
quality had vanished for which not all Alsace-Lorraine could compensate him. Germany a commercial Power, Germany a naval Power,
Germany with colonies here and a Forward Policy there, and legitimate
aspirations in the other place, might appeal to others, and be fitly served
by them; for his own part, he abstained from the fruits of victory, and nat-
uralized himself in England. The more earnest members of his family
never forgave him, and knew that his children, though scarcely English
of the dreadful sort, would never be German to the backbone. He had
obtained work in one of our provincial Universities, and there married
Poor Emily (or Die Engländerin,[4] as the case may be), and as she had
money, they proceeded to London, and came to know a good many people. But his gaze was always fixed beyond the sea. It was his hope that
the clouds of materialism obscuring the Fatherland would part in time,
and the mild intellectual light re-emerge. "Do you imply that we
Germans are stupid, Uncle Ernst?" exclaimed a haughty and magnificent nephew. Uncle Ernst replied, "To my mind. You use the intellect,
but you no longer care about it. That I call stupidity." As the haughty
nephew did not follow, he continued, "You only care about the things
that you can use, and therefore arrange them in the following order:
Money, supremely useful; intellect, rather useful; imagination, of no use
at all. No" — for the other had protested — "your Pan-Germanism[5] is no
more imaginative than is our Imperialism over here. It is the vice of a
vulgar mind to be thrilled by bigness, to think that a thousand square
miles are a thousand times more wonderful than one square mile, and
that a million square miles are almost the same as heaven. That is not
imagination. No, it kills it. When their poets over here try to celebrate
bigness they are dead at once, and naturally. Your poets too are dying,
your philosophers, your musicians, to whom Europe has listened for two
hundred years. Gone. Gone with the little courts that nurtured them —

2. Mr. Schlegel fought in each of the three wars launched by Otto von Bismarck (1815–98) to
   expand Prussia and establish the German Empire, first by annexing Schleswig-Holstein from
   Denmark (1864), then by defeating Austria (1866), previously its ally in the war against
   Denmark, and finally by taking the disputed Alsace-Lorraine from France in the Franco-
   Prussian War (1870–71).
3. Emperor Napoleon III (1808–73), nephew of the great Napoleon Bonaparte, was defeated by
   Prussia at the Battle of Sedan in northeastern France (1 September 1870) and deposed (4
   September 1870) after a bloodless revolution in Paris. The Tuileries was his palace.
4. The English woman.
5. Bismarck's nationalist aim of unifying all German-speaking peoples in one country.

gone with Esterhaz and Weimar.[6] What? What's that? Your Universities? Oh yes, you have learned men, who collect more facts than do the learned men of England. They collect facts, and facts, and empires of facts. But which of them will rekindle the light within?"

To all this Margaret listened, sitting on the haughty nephew's knee.

It was a unique education for the little girls. The haughty nephew would be at Wickham Place one day, bringing with him an even haughtier wife, both convinced that Germany was appointed by God to govern the world. Aunt Juley would come the next day, convinced that Great Britain had been appointed to the same post by the same authority. Were both these loud-voiced parties right? On one occasion they had met, and Margaret, with clasped hands had implored them to argue the subject out in her presence. Whereat they blushed, and began to talk about the weather. "Papa," she cried—she was a most offensive child—"why will they not discuss this most clear question?" Her father, surveying the parties grimly, replied that he did not know. Putting her head on one side, Margaret then remarked, "To me one of two things is very clear; either God does not know his own mind about England and Germany, or else these do not know the mind of God." A hateful little girl, but at thirteen she had grasped a dilemma that most people travel through life without perceiving. Her brain darted up and down; it grew pliant and strong. Her conclusion was, that any human being lies nearer to the unseen than any organization, and from this she never varied.

Helen advanced along the same lines, though with a more irresponsible tread. In character she resembled her sister, but she was pretty, and so apt to have a more amusing time. People gathered round her more readily, especially when they were new acquaintances, and she did enjoy a little homage very much. When their father died and they ruled alone at Wickham Place, she often absorbed the whole of the company, while Margaret—both were tremendous talkers—fell flat. Neither sister bothered about this. Helen never apologized afterwards, Margaret did not feel the slightest rancour. But looks have their influence upon character. The sisters were alike as little girls, but at the time of the Wilcox episode their methods were beginning to diverge; the younger was rather apt to entice people, and, in enticing them, to be herself enticed; the elder went straight ahead, and accepted an occasional failure as part of the game.

Little need be premised about Tibby. He was now an intelligent man of sixteen, but dyspeptic and difficile.[7]

6. The princely Esterhazy family in Hungary were lavish patrons of art and music in the seventeenth and eighteenth centuries. Weimar was the cultural center of eighteenth-century Germany and home to Bach, Goethe, and Schiller.
7. Irritable and hard to please.

Chapter V

It will be generally admitted that Beethoven's Fifth Symphony[1] is the most sublime noise that has ever penetrated into the ear of man. All sorts and conditions are satisfied by it. Whether you are like Mrs. Munt, and tap surreptitiously when the tunes come—of course, not so as to disturb the others—or like Helen, who can see heroes and shipwrecks in the music's flood; or like Margaret, who can only see the music; or like Tibby, who is profoundly versed in counterpoint, and holds the full score open on his knee; or like their cousin, Fräulein Mosebach, who remembers all the time that Beethoven is "echt Deutsch";[2] or like Fräulein Mosebach's young man, who can remember nothing but Fräulein Mosebach: in any case, the passion of your life becomes more vivid, and you are bound to admit that such a noise is cheap at two shillings. It is cheap, even if you hear it in the Queen's Hall, dreariest music-room in London, though not as dreary as the Free Trade Hall, Manchester; and even if you sit on the extreme left of that hall, so that the brass bumps at you before the rest of the orchestra arrives, it is still cheap.

"Who is Margaret talking to?" said Mrs. Munt, at the conclusion of the first movement. She was again in London on a visit to Wickham Place.

Helen looked down the long line of their party, and said that she did not know.

"Would it be some young man or other whom she takes an interest in?"

"I expect so," Helen replied. Music enwrapped her, and she could not enter into the distinction that divides young men whom one takes an interest in from young men whom one knows.

"You girls are so wonderful in always having—— Oh dear! one mustn't talk."

For the Andante[3] had begun—very beautiful, but bearing a family likeness to all the other beautiful Andantes that Beethoven had written, and, to Helen's mind, rather disconnecting the heroes and shipwrecks of the first movement from the heroes and goblins of the third. She heard the tune through once, and then her attention wandered, and she gazed at the audience, or the organ, or the architecture. Much did she censure the attenuated Cupids who encircle the ceiling of the Queen's Hall, inclining each to each with vapid gesture, and clad in sallow pantaloons,

---

1. The Symphony No. 5 in C Minor (1808) by Ludwig van Beethoven (1770–1827). It opens with perhaps the most memorable phrase in symphonic history (three quickly repeated notes followed by a longer lower one) of which Beethoven said: "So knocks fate at the door."
2. Genuinely German.
3. The slow movement. The four movements of the Fifth Symphony are allegro con brio (fast with spirit), andante con moto (moderate with motion), scherzo allegro (fast and sprightly), finale allegro.

on which the October sunlight struck. "How awful to marry a man like those Cupids!" thought Helen. Here Beethoven started decorating his tune, so she heard him through once more, and then she smiled at her cousin Frieda. But Frieda, listening to Classical Music, could not respond. Herr Liesecke, too, looked as if wild horses could not make him inattentive; there were lines across his forehead, his lips were part-ed, his pince-nez[4] at right angles to his nose, and he had laid a thick, white hand on either knee. And next to her was Aunt Juley, so British, and wanting to tap. How interesting that row of people was! What diverse influences had gone to the making! Here Beethoven, after hum-ming and hawing with great sweetness, said "Heigho," and the Andante came to an end. Applause, and a round of "wunderschöning" and "pracht" volleying[5] from the German contingent. Margaret started talk-ing to her new young man; Helen said to her aunt: "Now comes the wonderful movement: first of all the goblins, and then a trio of elephants dancing;" and Tibby implored the company generally to look out for the transitional passage on the drum.

"On the what, dear?"

"On the *drum*, Aunt Juley."

"No; look out for the part where you think you have done with the goblins and they come back," breathed Helen, as the music started with a goblin walking quietly over the universe, from end to end. Others fol-lowed him. They were not aggressive creatures; it was that that made them so terrible to Helen. They merely observed in passing that there was no such thing as splendour or heroism in the world. After the inter-lude of elephants dancing, they returned and made the observation for the second time. Helen could not contradict them, for, once at all events, she had felt the same, and had seen the reliable walls of youth collapse. Panic and emptiness! Panic and emptiness! The goblins were right.

Her brother raised his finger: it was the transitional passage on the drum.

For, as if things were going too far, Beethoven took hold of the gob-lins and made them do what he wanted. He appeared in person. He gave them a little push, and they began to walk in a major key instead of in a minor, and then—he blew with his mouth and they were scattered! Gusts of splendour, gods and demi-gods contending with vast swords, colour and fragrance broadcast on the field of battle, magnificent victo-ry, magnificent death! Oh, it all burst before the girl, and she even stretched out her gloved hands as if it was tangible. Any fate was titanic; any contest desirable; conqueror and conquered would alike be applauded by the angels of the utmost stars.

4. Eyeglasses held on by pinching the nose.
5. "Wonderful-ing" and "splendid-ing."

And the goblins—they had not really been there at all? They were only the phantoms of cowardice and unbelief? One healthy human impulse would dispel them? Men like the Wilcoxes, or President Roosevelt,[6] would say yes. Beethoven knew better. The goblins really had been there. They might return—and they did. It was as if the splendour of life might boil over and waste to steam and froth. In its dissolution one heard the terrible, ominous note, and a goblin, with increased malignity, walked quietly over the universe from end to end. Panic and emptiness! Panic and emptiness! Even the flaming ramparts of the world might fall.

Beethoven chose to make all right in the end. He built the ramparts up. He blew with his mouth for the second time, and again the goblins were scattered. He brought back the gusts of splendour, the heroism, the youth, the magnificence of life and of death, and, amid vast roarings of a superhuman joy, he led his Fifth Symphony to its conclusion. But the goblins were there. They could return. He had said so bravely, and that is why one can trust Beethoven when he says other things.

Helen pushed her way out during the applause. She desired to be alone. The music had summed up to her all that had happened or could happen in her career. She read it as a tangible statement, which could never be superseded. The notes meant this and that to her, and they could have no other meaning, and life could have no other meaning. She pushed right out of the building, and walked slowly down the outside staircase, breathing the autumnal air, and then she strolled home.

"Margaret," called Mrs. Munt, "is Helen all right?"

"Oh yes."

"She is always going away in the middle of a programme," said Tibby.

"The music has evidently moved her deeply," said Fräulein Mosebach.

"Excuse me," said Margaret's young man, who had for some time been preparing a sentence, "but that lady has, quite inadvertently, taken my umbrella."

"Oh, good gracious me!—I am so sorry. Tibby, run after Helen."

"I shall miss the Four Serious Songs[7] if I do."

"Tibby love, you must go."

"It isn't of any consequence," said the young man, in truth a little uneasy about his umbrella.

"But of course it is. Tibby! Tibby!"

Tibby rose to his feet, and wilfully caught his person on the backs of the chairs. By the time he had tipped up the seat and had found his hat, and had deposited his full score in safety, it was "too late" to go after

---

6. Theodore Roosevelt (1858–1919), twenty-sixth president of the United States (1901–9), known for his robustness, activism, and militaristic nationalism.
7. By the German romantic composer Johannes Brahms (1833–97).

Helen. The Four Serious Songs had begun, and one could not move during their performance.

"My sister is so careless," whispered Margaret.

"Not at all," replied the young man; but his voice was dead and cold.

"If you would give me your address——"

"Oh, not at all, not at all;" and he wrapped his greatcoat over his knees.

Then the Four Serious Songs rang shallow in Margaret's ears. Brahms, for all his grumbling and grizzling, had never guessed what it felt like to be suspected of stealing an umbrella. For this fool of a young man thought that she and Helen and Tibby had been playing the confidence trick on him, and that if he gave his address they would break into his rooms some midnight or other and steal his walking-stick too. Most ladies would have laughed, but Margaret really minded, for it gave her a glimpse into squalor. To trust people is a luxury in which only the wealthy can indulge; the poor cannot afford it. As soon as Brahms had grunted himself out, she gave him her card and said, "That is where we live; if you preferred, you could call for the umbrella after the concert, but I didn't like to trouble you when it has all been our fault."

His face brightened a little when he saw that Wickham Place was W.[8] It was sad to see him corroded with suspicion, and yet not daring to be impolite, in case these well-dressed people were honest after all. She took it as a good sign that he said to her, "It's a fine programme this afternoon, is it not?" for this was the remark with which he had originally opened, before the umbrella intervened.

"The Beethoven's fine," said Margaret, who was not a female of the encouraging type. "I don't like the Brahms, though, nor the Mendelssohn that came first—and ugh! I don't like this Elgar[9] that's coming."

"What, what?" called Herr Liesecke, overhearing. "The 'Pomp and Circumstance' will not be fine?"

"Oh, Margaret, you tiresome girl!" cried her aunt. "Here have I been persuading Herr Liesecke to stop for 'Pomp and Circumstance,' and you are undoing all my work. I am so anxious for him to hear what we are doing in music. Oh, you mustn't run down our English composers, Margaret."

"For my part, I have heard the composition at Stettin," said Fräulein Mosebach. "On two occasions. It is dramatic, a little."

"Frieda, you despise English music. You know you do. And English art. And English literature, except Shakespeare, and he's a German.[1] Very well, Frieda, you may go."

8. Postal code for the well-to-do West End of London.
9. Felix Mendelssohn (1809–47), German composer; Sir Edward William Elgar (1857–1934), English composer best known for his five *Pomp and Circumstance* marches (1901–30), the first of which is the patriotic *Land of Hope and Glory*.
1. German writers like Goethe and Schiller felt a special affinity to Shakespeare because of the depth and complexity of his tragic vision.

The lovers laughed and glanced at each other. Moved by a common impulse, they rose to their feet and fled from "Pomp and Circumstance."

"We have this call to pay in Finsbury Circus, it is true," said Herr Liesecke, as he edged past her and reached the gangway just as the music started.

"Margaret——" loudly whispered by Aunt Juley. "Margaret, Margaret! Fräulein Mosebach has left her beautiful little bag behind her on the seat."

Sure enough, there was Frieda's reticule,[2] containing her address book, her pocket dictionary, her map of London, and her money.

"Oh, what a bother—what a family we are! Fr—frieda!"

"Hush!" said all those who thought the music fine.

"But it's the number they want in Finsbury Circus——"

"Might I—couldn't I——" said the suspicious young man, and got very red.

"Oh, I would be so grateful."

He took the bag—money clinking inside it—and slipped up the gangway with it. He was just in time to catch them at the swing-door, and he received a pretty smile from the German girl and a fine bow from her cavalier. He returned to his seat upsides with the world. The trust that they had reposed in him was trivial, but he felt that it cancelled his mistrust for them, and that probably he would not be "had" over his umbrella. This young man had been "had" in the past—badly, perhaps overwhelmingly—and now most of his energies went in defending himself against the unknown. But this afternoon—perhaps on account of music—he perceived that one must slack off occasionally, or what is the good of being alive? Wickham Place, W., though a risk, was as safe as most things, and he would risk it.

So when the concert was over and Margaret said, "We live quite near; I am going there now. Could you walk round with me, and we'll find your umbrella?" he said, "Thank you," peaceably, and followed her out of the Queen's Hall. She wished that he was not so anxious to hand a lady downstairs, or to carry a lady's programme for her—his class was near enough her own for its manners to vex her. But she found him interesting on the whole—everyone interested the Schlegels on the whole at that time—and while her lips talked culture, her heart was planning to invite him to tea.

"How tired one gets after music!" she began.

"Do you find the atmosphere of Queen's Hall oppressive?"

"Yes, horribly."

"But surely the atmosphere of Covent Garden[3] is even more oppressive."

2. Small purse.
3. Site in London of the Royal Opera.

"Do you go there much?"

"When my work permits, I attend the gallery for the Royal Opera."

Helen would have exclaimed, "So do I. I love the gallery," and thus have endeared herself to the young man. Helen could do these things. But Margaret had an almost morbid horror of "drawing people out," of "making things go." She had been to the gallery at Covent Garden, but she did not "attend" it, preferring the more expensive seats; still less did she love it. So she made no reply.

"This year I have been three times—to 'Faust,' 'Tosca,' and——" Was it 'Tannhouser' or 'Tannhoyser'?[4] Better not risk the word.

Margaret disliked "Tosca" and "Faust." And so, for one reason and another, they walked on in silence, chaperoned by the voice of Mrs. Munt, who was getting into difficulties with her nephew.

"I do in a *way* remember the passage, Tibby, but when every instrument is so beautiful, it is difficult to pick out one thing rather than another. I am sure that you and Helen take me to the very nicest concerts. Not a dull note from beginning to end. I only wish that our German friends would have stayed till it finished."

"But surely you haven't forgotten the drum steadily beating on the low C, Aunt Juley?" came Tibby's voice. "No one could. It's unmistakable."

"A specially loud part?" hazarded Mrs. Munt. "Of course I do not go in for being musical," she added, the shot failing. "I only care for music—a very different thing. But still I will say this for myself—I do know when I like a thing and when I don't. Some people are the same about pictures. They can go into a picture gallery—Miss Conder can—and say straight off what they feel, all round the wall. I never could do that. But music is so different to pictures, to my mind. When it comes to music I am as safe as houses, and I assure you, Tibby, I am by no means pleased by everything. There was a thing—something about a faun in French[5]—which Helen went into ecstasies over, but I thought it most tinkling and superficial, and said so, and I held to my opinion too."

"Do you agree?" asked Margaret. "Do you think music is so different to pictures?"

"I—I should have thought so, kind of," he said.

"So should I. Now, my sister declares they're just the same. We have great arguments over it. She says I'm dense; I say she's sloppy." Getting under way, she cried: "Now, doesn't it seem absurd to you? What *is* the good of the Arts if they're interchangeable? What *is* the good of the ear if it tells you the same as the eye? Helen's one aim is to translate tunes into the language of painting, and pictures into the language of music. It's very ingenious, and she says several pretty things in the process, but what's gained, I'd like to know? Oh, it's all rubbish, radically false. If

---

4. *Tannhäuser* is an opera by the German romantic composer Richard Wagner (1813–83).
5. Impressionistic tone poem *Prelude to the Afternoon of a Faun* (1894) by the French composer Claude Debussy (1862–1918).

Monet's[6] really Debussy, and Debussy's really Monet, neither gentleman is worth his salt—that's my opinion."

Evidently these sisters quarrelled.

"Now, this very symphony that we've just been having—she won't let it alone. She labels it with meanings from start to finish; turns it into literature. I wonder if the day will ever return when music will be treated as music. Yet I don't know. There's my brother—behind us. He treats music as music, and oh, my goodness! He makes me angrier than anyone, simply furious. With him I daren't even argue."

An unhappy family, if talented.

"But, of course, the real villain is Wagner. He has done more than any man in the nineteenth century towards the muddling of the arts. I do feel that music is in a very serious state just now, though extraordinarily interesting. Every now and then in history there do come these terrible geniuses, like Wagner, who stir up all the wells of thought at once. For a moment it's splendid. Such a splash as never was. But afterwards—such a lot of mud; and the wells—as it were, they communicate with each other too easily now, and not one of them will run quite clear. That's what Wagner's done."

Her speeches fluttered away from the young man like birds. If only he could talk like this, he would have caught the world. Oh, to acquire culture! Oh, to pronounce foreign names correctly! Oh, to be well informed, discoursing at ease on every subject that a lady started! But it would take one years. With an hour at lunch and a few shattered hours in the evening, how was it possible to catch up with leisured women, who had been reading steadily from childhood? His brain might be full of names, he might have even heard of Monet and Debussy; the trouble was that he could not string them together into a sentence, he could not make them "tell," he could not quite forget about his stolen umbrella. Yes, the umbrella was the real trouble. Behind Monet and Debussy the umbrella persisted, with the steady beat of a drum. "I suppose my umbrella will be all right," he was thinking. "I don't really mind about it. I will think about music instead. I suppose my umbrella will be all right." Earlier in the afternoon he had worried about seats. Ought he to have paid as much as two shillings? Earlier still he had wondered, "Shall I try to do without a programme?" There had always been something to worry him ever since he could remember, always something that distracted him in the pursuit of beauty. For he did pursue beauty, and, therefore, Margaret's speeches did flutter away from him like birds.

Margaret talked ahead, occasionally saying, "Don't you think so? don't you feel the same?" And once she stopped, and said, "Oh, do interrupt me!" which terrified him. She did not attract him, though she filled him with awe. Her figure was meagre, her face seemed all teeth and

6. Claude Monet (1840–1926), French impressionist painter.

eyes, her references to her sister and her brother were uncharitable. For all her cleverness and culture, she was probably one of those soulless, atheistical women who have been so shown up by Miss Corelli.[7] It was surprising (and alarming) that she should suddenly say, "I do hope that you'll come in and have some tea."

"I do hope that you'll come in and have some tea. We should be so glad. I have dragged you so far out of your way."

They had arrived at Wickham Place. The sun had set, and the back-water, in deep shadow, was filling with a gentle haze. To the right the fantastic sky-line of the flats towered black against the hues of evening; to the left the older houses raised a square-cut, irregular parapet against the grey. Margaret fumbled for her latchkey. Of course she had forgotten it. So, grasping her umbrella by its ferrule, she leant over the area and tapped at the dining-room window.

"Helen! Let us in!"

"All right," said a voice.

"You've been taking this gentleman's umbrella."

"Taken a what?" said Helen, opening the door. "Oh, what's that? Do come in! How do you do?"

"Helen, you must not be so ramshackly. You took this gentleman's umbrella away from Queen's Hall, and he has had the trouble of coming round for it."

"Oh, I am so sorry!" cried Helen, all her hair flying. She had pulled off her hat as soon as she returned, and had flung herself into the big dining-room chair. "I do nothing but steal umbrellas. I am so very sorry! Do come in and choose one. Is yours a hooky or a nobbly? Mine's a nobbly—at least, I *think* it is."

The light was turned on, and they began to search the hall, Helen, who had abruptly parted with the Fifth Symphony, commenting with shrill little cries.

"Don't you talk, Meg! You stole an old gentleman's silk top-hat. Yes, she did, Aunt Juley. It is a positive fact. She thought it was a muff. Oh, heavens! I've knocked the In and Out card down. Where's Frieda? Tibby, why don't you ever— No, I can't remember what I was going to say. That wasn't it, but do tell the maids to hurry tea up. What about this umbrella?" She opened it. "No, it's all gone along the seams. It's an appalling umbrella. It must be mine."

But it was not.

He took it from her, murmured a few words of thanks, and then fled, with the lilting step of the clerk.

"But if you will stop——" cried Margaret. "Now, Helen, how stupid you've been!"

7. On her deathbed, the heroine of Marie Corelli's novel *The Sorrows of Satan* (1895) repents her denial of God's existence.

"Whatever have I done?"

"Don't you see that you've frightened him away? I meant him to stop to tea. You oughtn't to talk about stealing or holes in an umbrella. I saw his nice eyes getting so miserable. No, it's not a bit of good now." For Helen had darted out into the street, shouting, "Oh, do stop!"

"I dare say it is all for the best," opined Mrs. Munt. "We know nothing about the young man, Margaret, and your drawing-room is full of very tempting little things."

But Helen cried: "Aunt Juley, how can you! You make me more and more ashamed. I'd rather he *had* been a thief and taken all the apostle spoons[8] than that I—— Well, I must shut the front-door, I suppose. One more failure for Helen."

"Yes, I think the apostle spoons could have gone as rent," said Margaret. Seeing that her aunt did not understand, she added: "You remember 'rent'? It was one of father's words—Rent to the ideal, to his own faith in human nature. You remember how he would trust strangers, and if they fooled him he would say, 'It's better to be fooled than to be suspicious'—that the confidence trick is the work of man, but the want-of-confidence-trick is the work of the devil."

"I remember something of the sort now," said Mrs. Munt, rather tartly, for she longed to add, "It was lucky that your father married a wife with money." But this was unkind, and she contented herself with, "Why, he might have stolen the little Ricketts[9] picture as well."

"Better that he had," said Helen stoutly.

"No, I agree with Aunt Juley," said Margaret. "I'd rather mistrust people than lose my little Ricketts. There are limits."

Their brother, finding the incident commonplace, had stolen upstairs to see whether there were scones for tea. He warmed the teapot—almost too deftly—rejected the Orange Pekoe that the parlour-maid had provided, poured in five spoonfuls of a superior blend, filled up with really boiling water, and now called to the ladies to be quick or they would lose the aroma.

"All right, Auntie Tibby," called Helen, while Margaret, thoughtful again, said: "In a way, I wish we had a real boy in the house—the kind of boy who cares for men. It would make entertaining so much easier."

"So do I," said her sister. "Tibby only cares for cultured females singing Brahms." And when they joined him she said rather sharply: "Why didn't you make that young man welcome, Tibby? You must do the host a little, you know. You ought to have taken his hat and coaxed him into stopping, instead of letting him be swamped by screaming women."

Tibby sighed, and drew a long strand of hair over his forehead.

---

8. Rare silver antique spoons depicting Christ's apostles.
9. Charles Ricketts (1866–1931), British illustrator.

"Oh, it's no good looking superior. I mean what I say."

"Leave Tibby alone!" said Margaret, who could not bear her brother to be scolded.

"Here's the house a regular hen-coop!" grumbled Helen.

"Oh, my dear!" protested Mrs. Munt. "How can you say such dreadful things! The number of men you get here has always astonished me. If there is any danger it's the other way round."

"Yes, but it's the wrong sort of men, Helen means."

"No, I don't," corrected Helen. "We get the right sort of man, but the wrong side of him, and I say that's Tibby's fault. There ought to be a something about the house—an—I don't know what."

"A touch of the W.'s, perhaps?"

Helen put out her tongue.

"Who are the W.'s?" asked Tibby.

"The W.'s are things I and Meg and Aunt Juley know about and you don't, so there!"

"I suppose that ours is a female house," said Margaret, "and one must just accept it. No, Aunt Juley, I don't mean that this house is full of women. I am trying to say something much more clever. I mean that it was irrevocably feminine, even in father's time. Now I'm sure you understand! Well, I'll give you another example. It'll shock you, but I don't care. Suppose Queen Victoria gave a dinner-party, and that the guests had been Leighton, Millais, Swinburne, Rossetti, Meredith, Fitzgerald, etc.[1] Do you suppose that the atmosphere of that dinner would have been artistic? Heavens, no! The very chairs on which they sat would have seen to that. So with our house—it must be feminine, and all we can do is to see that it isn't effeminate. Just as another house that I can mention, but won't, sounded irrevocably masculine, and all its inmates can do is to see that it isn't brutal."

"That house being the W.'s house, I presume," said Tibby.

"You're not going to be told about the W.'s, my child," Helen cried, "so don't you think it. And on the other hand, I don't the least mind if you find out, so don't you think you've done anything clever, in either case. Give me a cigarette."

"You do what you can for the house," said Margaret. "The drawing-room reeks of smoke."

"If you smoked too, the house might suddenly turn masculine. Atmosphere is probably a question of touch and go. Even at Queen Victoria's dinner-party—if something had been just a little different— perhaps if she'd worn a clinging Liberty tea-gown instead of a magenta satin——"

"With an Indian shawl over her shoulders——"

---

1. Artists and poets with whom the conventional Queen Victoria would presumably have had little in common.

"Fastened at the bosom with a Cairngorm-pin——"

Bursts of disloyal laughter—you must remember that they are half German—greeted these suggestions, and Margaret said pensively, "How inconceivable it would be if the Royal Family cared about Art." And the conversation drifted away and away, and Helen's cigarette turned to a spot in the darkness, and the great flats opposite were sown with lighted windows, which vanished and were relit again, and vanished incessantly. Beyond them the thoroughfare roared gently—a tide that could never be quiet, while in the east, invisible behind the smokes of Wapping,[2] the moon was rising.

"That reminds me, Margaret. We might have taken that young man into the dining-room, at all events. Only the majolica plate[3]—and that is so firmly set in the wall. I am really distressed that he had no tea."

For that little incident had impressed the three women more than might be supposed. It remained as a goblin footfall, as a hint that all is not for the best in the best of all possible worlds,[4] and that beneath these superstructures of wealth and art there wanders an ill-fed boy, who has recovered his umbrella indeed, but who has left no address behind him, and no name.

Chapter VI

We are not concerned with the very poor. They are unthinkable, and only to be approached by the statistician or the poet. This story deals with gentlefolk, or with those who are obliged to pretend that they are gentlefolk.

The boy, Leonard Bast, stood at the extreme verge of gentility. He was not in the abyss, but he could see it, and at times people whom he knew had dropped in, and counted no more. He knew that he was poor, and would admit it: he would have died sooner than confess any inferiority to the rich. This may be splendid of him. But he was inferior to most rich people, there is not the least doubt of it. He was not as courteous as the average rich man, nor as intelligent, nor as healthy, nor as lovable. His mind and his body had been alike underfed, because he was poor, and because he was modern they were always craving better food. Had he lived some centuries ago, in the brightly coloured civilizations of the past, he would have had a definite status, his rank and his income would have corresponded. But in his day the angel of Democracy had arisen, enshadowing the classes with leathern wings, and proclaiming, "All men are equal—all men, that is to say, who possess umbrellas," and so he was

2. Smokestacks from the area of docks and warehouses east of London on the Thames River.
3. Valuable hand-painted earthenware.
4. "Goblin footfall": the footstep of a ghost; "all is not for the best . . .": Pangloss, a comic figure in Voltaire's tale *Candide*, declares repeatedly (and ridiculously) that "All is for the best in the best of all possible worlds."

obliged to assert gentility, lest he slipped into the abyss where nothing counts, and the statements of Democracy are inaudible.

As he walked away from Wickham Place, his first care was to prove that he was as good as the Miss Schlegels. Obscurely wounded in his pride, he tried to wound them in return. They were probably not ladies. Would real ladies have asked him to tea? They were certainly ill-natured and cold. At each step his feeling of superiority increased. Would a real lady have talked about stealing an umbrella? Perhaps they were thieves after all, and if he had gone into the house they would have clapped a chloroformed handkerchief over his face. He walked on complacently as far as the Houses of Parliament. There an empty stomach asserted itself, and told him that he was a fool.

"Evening, Mr. Bast."

"Evening, Mr. Dealtry."

"Nice evening."

"Evening."

Mr. Dealtry, a fellow clerk, passed on, and Leonard stood wondering whether he would take the tram as far as a penny would take him, or whether he would walk. He decided to walk—it is no good giving in, and he had spent money enough at Queen's Hall—and he walked over Westminster Bridge, in front of St. Thomas's Hospital, and through the immense tunnel that passes under the South-Western main line at Vauxhall. In the tunnel he paused and listened to the roar of the trains. A sharp pain darted through his head, and he was conscious of the exact form of his eye sockets. He pushed on for another mile, and did not slacken speed until he stood at the entrance of a road called Camelia Road, which was at present his home.

Here he stopped again, and glanced suspiciously to right and left, like a rabbit that is going to bolt into its hole. A block of flats, constructed with extreme cheapness, towered on either hand. Farther down the road two more blocks were being built, and beyond these an old house was being demolished to accommodate another pair. It was the kind of scene that may be observed all over London, whatever the locality—bricks and mortar rising and falling with the restlessness of the water in a fountain, as the city receives more and more men upon her soil. Camelia Road would soon stand out like a fortress, and command, for a little, an exten-sive view. Only for a little. Plans were out for the erection of flats in Magnolia Road also. And again a few years, and all the flats in either road might be pulled down, and new buildings, of a vastness at present unimaginable, might arise where they had fallen.

"Evening, Mr. Bast."

"Evening, Mr. Cunningham."

"Very serious thing this decline of the birth-rate in Manchester."

"I beg your pardon?"

"Very serious thing this decline of the birth-rate in Manchester," repeated Mr. Cunningham, tapping the Sunday paper, in which the calamity in question had just been announced to him.

"Ah, yes," said Leonard, who was not going to let on that he had not bought a Sunday paper.

"If this kind of thing goes on the population of England will be stationary in 1960."

"You don't say so."

"I call it a very serious thing, eh?"

"Good-evening, Mr. Cunningham."

"Good-evening, Mr. Bast."

Then Leonard entered Block B of the flats, and turned, not upstairs, but down, into what is known to house agents as a semi-basement, and to other men as a cellar. He opened the door, and cried "Hullo!" with the pseudo-geniality of the Cockney. There was no reply. "Hullo!" he repeated. The sitting-room was empty, though the electric light had been left burning. A look of relief came over his face, and he flung himself into the armchair.

The sitting-room contained, besides the armchair, two other chairs, a piano, a three-legged table, and a cosy corner. Of the walls, one was occupied by the window, the other by a draped mantelshelf bristling with Cupids. Opposite the window was the door, and beside the door a bookcase, while over the piano there extended one of the masterpieces of Maud Goodman.[1] It was an amorous and not unpleasant little hole when the curtains were drawn, and the lights turned on, and the gas-stove unlit. But it struck that shallow makeshift note that is so often heard in the modern dwelling-place. It had been too easily gained, and could be relinquished too easily.

As Leonard was kicking off his boots he jarred the three-legged table, and a photograph frame, honourably poised upon it, slid sideways, fell off into the fireplace, and smashed. He swore in a colourless sort of way, and picked the photograph up. It represented a young lady called Jacky, and had been taken at the time when young ladies called Jacky were often photographed with their mouths open. Teeth of dazzling whiteness extended along either of Jacky's jaws, and positively weighed her head sideways, so large were they and so numerous. Take my word for it, that smile was simply stunning, and it is only you and I who will be fastidious, and complain that true joy begins in the eyes, and that the eyes of Jacky did not accord with her smile, but were anxious and hungry.

Leonard tried to pull out the fragments of glass, and cut his fingers and swore again. A drop of blood fell on the frame, another followed, spilling over on to the exposed photograph. He swore more vigorously, and dashed into the kitchen, where he bathed his hands. The kitchen was the same size as the sitting-room: through it was a bedroom. This

1. Popular illustrator of questionable taste.

completed his home. He was renting the flat furnished: of all the objects that encumbered it none were his own except the photograph frame, the Cupids, and the books.

"Damn, damn, damnation!" he murmured, together with such other words as he had learnt from older men. Then he raised his hand to his forehead and said, "Oh, damn it all——" which meant something different. He pulled himself together. He drank a little tea, black and silent, that still survived upon an upper shelf. He swallowed some dusty crumbs of a cake. Then he went back to the sitting-room, settled himself anew, and began to read a volume of Ruskin.[2]

'Seven miles to the north of Venice——'

How perfectly the famous chapter opens! How supreme its command of admonition and of poetry! The rich man is speaking to us from his gondola.

'Seven miles to the north of Venice the banks of sand which nearer the city rise little above low-water mark attain by degrees a higher level, and knit themselves at last into fields of salt morass, raised here and there into shapeless mounds, and intercepted by narrow creeks of sea.'

Leonard was trying to form his style on Ruskin: he understood him to be the greatest master of English Prose. He read forward steadily, occasionally making a few notes.

'Let us consider a little each of these characters in succession, and first (for of the shafts enough has been said already), what is very peculiar to this church—its luminousness.'

Was there anything to be learnt from this fine sentence? Could he adapt it to the needs of daily life? Could he introduce it, with modifications, when he next wrote a letter to his brother, the lay-reader? For example—

'Let us consider a little each of these characters in succession, and first (for of the absence of ventilation enough has been said already), what is very peculiar to this flat—its obscurity.'

Something told him that the modifications would not do; and that something, had he known it, was the spirit of English Prose. 'My flat is dark as well as stuffy.' Those were the words for him.

And the voice in the gondola rolled on, piping melodiously of Effort and Self-Sacrifice, full of high purpose, full of beauty, full even of sympathy and the love of men, yet somehow eluding all that was actual and insistent in Leonard's life. For it was the voice of one who had never been dirty or hungry, and had not guessed successfully what dirt and hunger are.

Leonard listened to it with reverence. He felt that he was being done good to, and that if he kept on with Ruskin, and the Queen's Hall Concerts, and some pictures by Watts,[3] he would one day push his head out of the grey waters and see the universe. He believed in sudden con-

2. John Ruskin (1819–1900), English critic, author of *The Stones of Venice* (1851–53).
3. George Frederic Watts (1817–1904), English painter and sculptor.

version, a belief which may be right, but which is peculiarly attractive to a half-baked mind. It is the basis of much popular religion: in the domain of business it dominates the Stock Exchange, and becomes that "bit of luck" by which all successes and failures are explained. "If only I had a bit of luck, the whole thing would come straight. . . . He's got a most magnificent place down at Streatham and a 20 h.-p. Fiat, but then, mind you, he's had luck. . . . I'm sorry the wife's so late, but she never has any luck over catching trains." Leonard was superior to these people; he did believe in effort and in a steady preparation for the change that he desired. But of a heritage that may expand gradually, he had no conception: he hoped to come to Culture suddenly, much as the Revivalist hopes to come to Jesus. Those Miss Schlegels had come to it; they had done the trick; their hands were upon the ropes,[4] once and for all. And meanwhile, his flat was dark, as well as stuffy.

Presently there was a noise on the staircase. He shut up Margaret's card in the pages of Ruskin, and opened the door. A woman entered, of whom it is simplest to say that she was not respectable. Her appearance was awesome. She seemed all strings and bell-pulls—ribbons, chains, bead necklaces that clinked and caught—and a boa of azure feathers hung round her neck, with the ends uneven. Her throat was bare, wound with a double row of pearls, her arms were bare to the elbows, and might again be detected at the shoulder, through cheap lace. Her hat, which was flowery, resembled those punnets, covered with flannel, which we sowed with mustard and cress[5] in our childhood, and which germinated here yes, and there no. She wore it on the back of her head. As for her hair, or rather hairs, they are too complicated to describe, but one system went down her back, lying in a thick pad there, while another, created for a lighter destiny, rippled around her forehead. The face—the face does not signify. It was the face of the photograph, but older, and the teeth were not so numerous as the photographer had suggested, and certainly not so white. Yes, Jacky was past her prime, whatever that prime may have been. She was descending quicker than most women into the colourless years, and the look in her eyes confessed it.

"What ho!" said Leonard, greeting the apparition with much spirit, and helping it off with its boa.

Jacky, in husky tones, replied, "What ho!"

"Been out?" he asked. The question sounds superfluous, but it cannot have been really, for the lady answered, "No," adding, "Oh, I am so tired."

"You tired?"

"Eh?"

"I'm tired," said he, hanging the boa up.

"Oh, Len, I am so tired."

---

4. Had the necessary competence or understanding (as in "knew the ropes").
5. Punnets: small flat baskets; mustard and cress: related leafy, lettuce-like plants.

"I've been to that classical concert I told you about," said Leonard.

"What's that?"

"I came back as soon as it was over."

"Anyone been round to our place?" asked Jacky.

"Not that I've seen. I met Mr. Cunningham outside, and we passed a few remarks."

"What, not Mr. Cunningham?"

"Yes."

"Oh, you mean Mr. Cunningham."

"Yes. Mr. Cunningham."

"I've been out to tea at a lady friend's."

Her secret being at last given to the world, and the name of the lady-friend being even adumbrated, Jacky made no further experiments in the difficult and tiring art of conversation. She never had been a great talker. Even in her photographic days she had relied upon her smile and her figure to attract, and now that she was—

> "On the shelf,
> On the shelf,
> Boys, boys, I'm on the shelf,"

she was not likely to find her tongue. Occasional bursts of song (of which the above is an example) still issued from her lips, but the spoken word was rare.

She sat down on Leonard's knee, and began to fondle him. She was now a massive woman of thirty-three, and her weight hurt him, but he could not very well say anything. Then she said, "Is that a book you're reading?" and he said, "That's a book," and drew it from her unreluctant grasp. Margaret's card fell out of it. It fell face downwards, and he murmured, "Bookmarker."

"Len——"

"What is it?" he asked, a little wearily, for she only had one topic of conversation when she sat upon his knee.

"You do love me?"

"Jacky, you know that I do. How can you ask such questions!"

"But you do love me, Len, don't you?"

"Of course I do."

A pause. The other remark was still due.

"Len——"

"Well? What is it?"

"Len, you will make it all right?"

"I can't have you ask me that again," said the boy, flaring up into a sudden passion. "I've promised to marry you when I'm of age, and that's enough. My word's my word. I've promised to marry you as soon as ever I'm twenty-one, and I can't keep on being worried. I've worries enough. It isn't likely I'd throw you over, let alone my word, when I've spent all this money. Besides, I'm an Englishman, and I never go back on my word. Jacky, do be reasonable. Of course I'll marry you. Only do stop badgering me."

"When's your birthday, Len?"

"I've told you again and again, the eleventh of November next. Now get off my knee a bit; someone must get supper, I suppose."

Jacky went through to the bedroom, and began to see to her hat. This meant blowing at it with short sharp puffs. Leonard tidied up the sitting-room, and began to prepare their evening meal. He put a penny into the slot of the gas-meter, and soon the flat was reeking with metallic fumes. Somehow he could not recover his temper, and all the time he was cooking he continued to complain bitterly.

"It really is too bad when a fellow isn't trusted. It makes one feel so wild, when I've pretended to the people here that you're my wife—all right, all right, you *shall* be my wife—and I've bought you the ring to wear, and I've taken this flat furnished, and it's far more than I can afford, and yet you aren't content, and I've also not told the truth when I've written home." He lowered his voice. "He'd stop it." In a tone of horror, that was a little luxurious, he repeated: "My brother 'd stop it. I'm going against the whole world, Jacky.

"That's what I am, Jacky. I don't take any heed of what anyone says. I just go straight forward, I do. That's always been my way. I'm not one of your weak knock-kneed chaps. If a woman's in trouble, I don't leave her in the lurch. That's not my street. No, thank you.

"I'll tell you another thing too. I care a good deal about improving myself by means of Literature and Art, and so getting a wider outlook. For instance, when you came in I was reading Ruskin's 'Stones of Venice.' I don't say this to boast, but just to show you the kind of man I am. I can tell you, I enjoyed that classical concert this afternoon."

To all his moods Jacky remained equally indifferent. When supper was ready—and not before—she emerged from the bedroom, saying: "But you do love me, don't you?"

They began with a soup square, which Leonard had just dissolved in some hot water. It was followed by the tongue—a freckled cylinder of meat, with a little jelly at the top, and a great deal of yellow fat at the bottom—ending with another square dissolved in water (jelly : pineapple), which Leonard had prepared earlier in the day. Jacky ate contentedly enough, occasionally looking at her man with those anxious eyes, to which nothing else in her appearance corresponded, and which yet seemed to mirror her soul. And Leonard managed to convince his stomach that it was having a nourishing meal.

After supper they smoked cigarettes and exchanged a few statements. She observed that her 'likeness' had been broken. He found occasion to remark, for the second time, that he had come straight back home after the concert at Queen's Hall. Presently she sat upon his knee. The inhabıtants of Camelia Road tramped to and fro outside the window, just on a level with their heads, and the family in the flat on the ground-floor began to sing, "Hark, my soul, it is the Lord."

"That tune fairly gives me the hump,"[6] said Leonard.

Jacky followed this, and said that, for her part, she thought it a lovely tune.

"No; I'll play you something lovely. Get up, dear, for a minute."

He went to the piano and jingled out a little Grieg.[7] He played badly and vulgarly, but the performance was not without its effect, for Jacky said she thought she'd be going to bed. As she receded, a new set of interests possessed the boy, and he began to think of what had been said about music by that odd Miss Schlegel—the one that twisted her face about so when she spoke. Then the thoughts grew sad and envious. There was the girl named Helen, who had pinched his umbrella, and the German girl who had smiled at him pleasantly, and Herr someone, and Aunt someone, and the brother—all, all with their hands on the ropes. They had all passed up that narrow, rich staircase at Wickham Place, to some ample room, whither he could never follow them, not if he read for ten hours a day. Oh, it was no good, this continual aspiration. Some are born cultured; the rest had better go in for whatever comes easy. To see life steadily and to see it whole[8] was not for the likes of him.

From the darkness beyond the kitchen a voice called, "Len?"

"You in bed?" he asked, his forehead twitching.

"M'm."

"All right."

Presently she called him again.

"I must clean my boots ready for the morning," he answered.

Presently she called him again.

"I rather want to get this chapter done."

"What?"

He closed his ears against her.

"What's that?"

"All right, Jacky, nothing; I'm reading a book."

"What?"

"What?" he answered, catching her degraded deafness.

Presently she called him again.

Ruskin had visited Torcello by this time, and was ordering his gondoliers to take him to Murano. It occurred to him, as he glided over the whispering lagoons, that the power of Nature could not be shortened by the folly, nor her beauty altogether saddened by the misery, of such as Leonard.

6. Annoys or vexes (slang).
7. Edvard Grieg (1843–1907), Norwegian composer, known for his songs, author of *Peer Gynt* (1876).
8. From "To a Friend," a poem by the English critic Matthew Arnold (1822–88).

Chapter VII

"Oh, Margaret," cried her aunt next morning, "such a most unfortunate thing has happened. I could not get you alone."

The most unfortunate thing was not very serious. One of the flats in the ornate block opposite had been taken furnished by the Wilcox family, "coming up, no doubt, in the hope of getting into London society." That Mrs. Munt should be the first to discover the misfortune was not remarkable, for she was so interested in the flats, that she watched their every mutation with unwearying care. In theory she despised them—they took away that old-world look—they cut off the sun—flats house a flashy type of person. But if the truth had been known, she found her visits to Wickham Place twice as amusing since Wickham Mansions had arisen, and would in a couple of days learn more about them than her nieces in a couple of months, or her nephew in a couple of years. She would stroll across and make friends with the porters, and inquire what the rents were, exclaiming for example: "What! a hundred and twenty for a basement? You'll never get it!" And they would answer: "One can but try, madam." The passenger lifts, the provision lifts, the arrangement for coals (a great temptation for a dishonest porter), were all familiar matters to her, and perhaps a relief from the politico-economical-æsthetic atmosphere that reigned at the Schlegels'.

Margaret received the information calmly, and did not agree that it would throw a cloud over poor Helen's life.

"Oh, but Helen isn't a girl with no interests," she explained. "She has plenty of other things and other people to think about. She made a false start with the Wilcoxes, and she'll be as willing as we are to have nothing more to do with them."

"For a clever girl, dear, how very oddly you do talk. Helen'll *have* to have something more to do with them, now that they're all opposite. She may meet that Paul in the street. She cannot very well not bow."

"Of course she must bow. But look here; let's do the flowers. I was going to say, the will to be interested in him has died, and what else matters? I look on that disastrous episode (over which you were so kind) as the killing of a nerve in Helen. It's dead, and she'll never be troubled with it again. The only things that matter are the things that interest one. Bowing, even calling and leaving cards, even a dinner-party—we can do all those things to the Wilcoxes, if they find it agreeable; but the other thing, the one important thing—never again. Don't you see?"

Mrs. Munt did not see, and indeed Margaret was making a most questionable statement—that any emotion, any interest once vividly aroused, can wholly die.

"I also have the honour to inform you that the Wilcoxes are bored with us. I didn't tell you at the time—it might have made you angry, and you had enough to worry you—but I wrote a letter to Mrs. W., and apologized for the trouble that Helen had given them. She didn't answer it."

"How very rude!"

"I wonder. Or was it sensible?"

"No, Margaret, most rude."

"In either case one can class it as reassuring."

Mrs. Munt sighed. She was going back to Swanage on the morrow, just as her nieces were wanting her most. Other regrets crowded upon her: for instance, how magnificently she would have cut Charles if she had met him face to face. She had already seen him, giving an order to the porter—and very common he looked in a tall hat. But unfortunately his back was turned to her, and though she had cut his back, she could not regard this as a telling snub.

"But you will be careful, won't you?" she exhorted.

"Oh, certainly. Fiendishly careful."

"And Helen must be careful, too."

"Careful over what?" cried Helen, at that moment coming into the room with her cousin.

"Nothing," said Margaret, seized with a momentary awkwardness.

"Careful over what, Aunt Juley?"

Mrs. Munt assumed a cryptic air. "It is only that a certain family, whom we know by name but do not mention, as you said yourself last night after the concert, have taken the flat opposite from the Mathesons—where the plants are in the balcony."

Helen began some laughing reply, and then disconcerted them all by blushing. Mrs. Munt was so disconcerted that she exclaimed, "What, Helen, you don't mind them coming, do you?" and deepened the blush to crimson.

"Of course I don't mind," said Helen a little crossly. "It is that you and Meg are both so absurdly grave about it, when there's nothing to be grave about at all."

"I'm not grave," protested Margaret, a little cross in her turn.

"Well, you look grave; doesn't she, Frieda?"

"I don't feel grave, that's all I can say; you're going quite on the wrong tack."

"No, she does not feel grave," echoed Mrs. Munt. "I can bear witness to that. She disagrees——"

"Hark!" interrupted Fräulein Mosebach. "I hear Bruno entering the hall."

For Herr Liesecke was due at Wickham Place to call for the two younger girls. He was not entering the hall—in fact, he did not enter it for quite five minutes. But Frieda detected a delicate situation, and said that she and Helen had much better wait for Bruno down below, and leave Margaret and Mrs. Munt to finish arranging the flowers. Helen acquiesced. But, as if to prove that the situation was not delicate really, she stopped in the doorway and said:

"Did you say the Mathesons' flat, Aunt Juley? How wonderful you are! I never knew that the woman who laced too tightly's name was Matheson."

"Come, Helen," said her cousin.

"Go, Helen," said her aunt; and continued to Margaret almost in the same breath: "Helen cannot deceive me. She does mind."

"Oh, hush!" breathed Margaret. "Frieda'll hear you, and she can be so tiresome."

"She minds," persisted Mrs. Munt, moving thoughtfully about the room, and pulling the dead chrysanthemums out of the vases. "I knew she'd mind—and I'm sure a girl ought to! Such an experience! Such awful coarse-grained people! I know more about them than you do, which you forget, and if Charles had taken you that motor drive—well, you'd have reached the house a perfect wreck. Oh, Margaret, you don't know what you are in for. They're all bottled up against the drawing-room window. There's Mrs. Wilcox—I've seen her. There's Paul. There's Evie, who is a minx. There's Charles—I saw him to start with. And who would an elderly man with a moustache and a copper-coloured face be?"

"Mr. Wilcox, possibly."

"I knew it. And there's Mr. Wilcox."

"It's a shame to call his face copper colour," complained Margaret. "He has a remarkably good complexion for a man of his age."

Mrs. Munt, triumphant elsewhere, could afford to concede Mr. Wilcox his complexion. She passed on from it to the plan of campaign that her nieces should pursue in the future. Margaret tried to stop her.

"Helen did not take the news quite as I expected, but the Wilcox nerve is dead in her really, so there's no need for plans."

"It's as well to be prepared."

"No—it's as well not to be prepared."

"Why?"

"Because——"

Her thought drew being from the obscure borderland. She could not explain in so many words, but she felt that those who prepare for all the emergencies of life beforehand may equip themselves at the expense of joy. It is necessary to prepare for an examination, or a dinner-party, or a possible fall in the price of stock: those who attempt human relations must adopt another method, or fail. "Because I'd sooner risk it," was her lame conclusion.

"But imagine the evenings," exclaimed her aunt, pointing to the Mansions with the spout of the watering-can. "Turn the electric light on here or there, and it's almost the same room. One evening they may forget to draw their blinds down, and you'll see them; and the next, you yours, and they'll see you. Impossible to sit out on the balconies. Impossible to water the plants, or even speak. Imagine going out of the front-door, and they come out opposite at the same moment. And yet you tell me that plans are unnecessary, and you'd rather risk it."

"I hope to risk things all my life."

"Oh, Margaret, most dangerous."

"But after all," she continued with a smile, "there's never any great risk as long as you have money."

"Oh, shame! What a shocking speech!"

"Money pads the edges of things," said Miss Schlegel. "God help those who have none."

"But this is something quite new!" said Mrs. Munt, who collected new ideas as a squirrel collects nuts, and was especially attracted by those that are portable.

"New for me; sensible people have acknowledged it for years. You and I and the Wilcoxes stand upon money as upon islands. It is so firm beneath our feet that we forget its very existence. It's only when we see someone near us tottering that we realize all that an independent income means. Last night, when we were talking up here round the fire, I began to think that the very soul of the world is economic, and that the lowest abyss is not the absence of love, but the absence of coin."

"I call that rather cynical."

"So do I. But Helen and I, we ought to remember, when we are tempted to criticize others, that we are standing on these islands, and that most of the others are down below the surface of the sea. The poor cannot always reach those whom they want to love, and they can hardly ever escape from those whom they love no longer. We rich can. Imagine the tragedy last June, if Helen and Paul Wilcox had been poor people, and couldn't invoke railways and motor-cars to part them."

"That's more like Socialism," said Mrs. Munt suspiciously.

"Call it what you like. I call it going through life with one's hand spread open on the table. I'm tired of these rich people who pretend to be poor, and think it shows a nice mind to ignore the piles of money that keep their feet above the waves. I stand each year upon six hundred pounds,[1] and Helen upon the same, and Tibby will stand upon eight, and as fast as our pounds crumble away into the sea they are renewed — from the sea, yes, from the sea. And all our thoughts are the thoughts of six-hundred-pounders, and all our speeches; and because we don't want to steal umbrellas ourselves, we forget that below the sea people do want

1. Forster's biographer Nicola Beauman suggests that one should multiply by 45 to approximate the current value of monetary sums at the turn of the century, so that Helen's annual income of £600 would equal £27,000 ($43,200) and Tibby's £800 would be worth £36,000 ($57,600). However, because costs have changed so greatly (the wages of servants, for example), these comparisons should be taken with a grain of salt.

to steal them, and do steal them sometimes, and that what's a joke up here is down there reality——"

"There they go—there goes Fräulein Mosebach. Really, for a German she does dress charmingly. Oh——!"

"What is it?"

"Helen was looking up at the Wilcoxes' flat."

"Why shouldn't she?"

"I beg your pardon, I interrupted you. What was it you were saying about reality?"

"I had worked round to myself, as usual," answered Margaret in tones that were suddenly preoccupied.

"Do tell me this, at all events. Are you for the rich or for the poor?"

"Too difficult. Ask me another. Am I for poverty or for riches? For riches. Hurrah for riches!"

"For riches!" echoed Mrs. Munt, having, as it were, at last secured her nut.

"Yes. For riches. Money for ever!"

"So am I, and so, I am afraid, are most of my acquaintances at Swanage, but I am surprised that you agree with us."

"Thank you so much, Aunt Juley. While I have talked theories, you have done the flowers."

"Not at all, dear. I wish you would let me help you in more important things."

"Well, would you be very kind? Would you come round with me to the registry office?[2] There's a housemaid who won't say yes but doesn't say no."

On their way thither they too looked up at the Wilcoxes' flat. Evie was in the balcony, "staring most rudely," according to Mrs. Munt. Oh yes, it was a nuisance, there was no doubt of it. Helen was proof against a passing encounter, but—— Margaret began to lose confidence. Might it reawake the dying nerve if the family were living close against her eyes? And Frieda Mosebach was stopping with them for another fortnight, and Frieda was sharp, abominably sharp, and quite capable of remarking, "You love one of the young gentlemen opposite, yes?" The remark would be untrue, but of the kind which, if stated often enough, may become true; just as the remark, 'England and Germany are bound to fight,' renders war a little more likely each time that it is made, and is therefore made the more readily by the gutter press of either nation.[3] Have the private emotions also their gutter press? Margaret thought so, and feared that good Aunt Juley and Frieda were typical specimens of it. They might, by continual chatter, lead Helen into a repetition of the

2. Employment office for domestic help.
3. During the years preceding World War I, the mass-circulation newspapers in both England and Germany published much nationalistic, patriotic rhetoric demonizing the other country. The war broke out in 1914, four years after the publication of *Howards End*.

desires of June. Into a repetition—they could not do more; they could not lead her into lasting love. They were—she saw it clearly—Journalism; her father, with all his defects and wrong-headedness, had been Literature, and had he lived, he would have persuaded his daughter rightly.

The registry office was holding its morning reception. A string of carriages filled the street. Miss Schlegel waited her turn, and finally had to be content with an insidious "temporary," being rejected by genuine housemaids on the ground of her numerous stairs. Her failure depressed her, and though she forgot the failure, the depression remained. On her way home she again glanced up at the Wilcoxes' flat, and took the rather matronly step of speaking about the matter to Helen.

"Helen, you must tell me whether this thing worries you."

"If what?" said Helen, who was washing her hands for lunch.

"The W.'s coming."

"No, of course not."

"Really?"

"Really." Then she admitted that she was a little worried on Mrs. Wilcox's account; she implied that Mrs. Wilcox might reach backward into deep feelings, and be pained by things that never touched the other members of that clan. "I shan't mind if Paul points at our house and says, 'There lives the girl who tried to catch me.' But she might."

"If even that worries you, we could arrange something. There's no reason we should be near people who displease us or whom we displease, thanks to our money. We might even go away for a little."

"Well, I am going away. Frieda's just asked me to Stettin, and I shan't be back till after the New Year. Will that do? Or must I fly the country altogether? Really, Meg, what has come over you to make such a fuss?"

"Oh, I'm getting an old maid, I suppose. I thought I minded nothing, but really I—I should be bored if you fell in love with the same man twice and"—she cleared her throat—"you did go red, you know, when Aunt Juley attacked you this morning. I shouldn't have referred to it otherwise."

But Helen's laugh rang true, as she raised a soapy hand to heaven and swore that never, nowhere and nohow, would she again fall in love with any of the Wilcox family, down to its remotest collaterals.

Chapter VIII

The friendship between Margaret and Mrs. Wilcox, which was to develop so quickly and with such strange results, may perhaps have had its beginnings at Speyer, in the spring. Perhaps the elder lady, as she gazed at the vulgar, ruddy cathedral, and listened to the talk of Helen and her husband, may have detected in the other and less charming of the sisters a deeper sympathy, a sounder judgment. She was capable of detecting such things. Perhaps it was she who had desired the Miss Schlegels to be invited to Howards End, and Margaret whose presence she had particularly desired. All this is speculation: Mrs. Wilcox has left few clear indications behind her. It is certain that she came to call at Wickham Place a fortnight later, the very day that Helen was going with her cousin to Stettin.

"Helen!" cried Fräulein Mosebach in awestruck tones (she was now in her cousin's confidence)—"his mother has forgiven you!" And then, remembering that in England the new-comer ought not to call before she is called upon, she changed her tone from awe to disapproval, and opined that Mrs. Wilcox was "keine Dame."[1]

"Bother the whole family!" snapped Margaret. "Helen, stop giggling and pirouetting, and go and finish your packing. Why can't the woman leave us alone?"

"I don't know what I shall do with Meg," Helen retorted, collapsing upon the stairs. "She's got Wilcox and Box[2] upon the brain. Meg, Meg, I don't love the young genterman; I don't love the young genterman, Meg, Meg. Can a body speak plainer?"

"Most certainly her love has died," asserted Fräulein Mosebach.

"Most certainly it has, Frieda, but that will not prevent me from being bored with the Wilcoxes if I return the call."

Then Helen simulated tears, and Fräulein Mosebach, who thought her extremely amusing, did the same. "Oh, boo hoo! boo hoo hoo! Meg's going to return the call, and I can't. 'Cos why? 'Cos I'm going to German-eye."

"If you are going to Germany, go and pack; if you aren't, go and call on the Wilcoxes instead of me."

"But, Meg, Meg, I don't love the young genterman; I don't love the young—O lud, who's that coming down the stairs? I vow 'tis my brother. O crimini!"

A male—even such a male as Tibby—was enough to stop the foolery. The barrier of sex, though decreasing among the civilized, is still high, and higher on the side of women. Helen could tell her sister all, and her cousin much about Paul; she told her brother nothing. It was not prudishness, for she now spoke of "the Wilcox ideal" with laughter, and even with a growing brutality. Nor was it precaution, for Tibby seldom repeated any news that did not concern himself. It was rather the feeling that she betrayed a secret into the camp of men, and that, however trivial it was on this side of the barrier, it would become important on that. So she stopped, or rather began to fool on other subjects, until her long-suffering relatives drove her upstairs. Fräulein Mosebach followed her, but

1. No lady.
2. A reference to the nineteenth-century musical comedy *Cox and Box*, according to Forster's editor Oliver Stallybrass. Helen imitates music hall diction in the subsequent dialogue.

lingered to say heavily over the banisters to Margaret, "It is all right—she does not love the young man—he has not been worthy of her."

"Yes, I know; thanks very much."

"I thought I did right to tell you."

"Ever so many thanks."

"What's that?" asked Tibby. No one told him, and he proceeded into the dining-room, to eat Elvas plums.

That evening Margaret took decisive action. The house was very quiet, and the fog—we are in November now—pressed against the windows like an excluded ghost. Frieda and Helen and all their luggages had gone. Tibby, who was not feeling well, lay stretched on a sofa by the fire. Margaret sat by him, thinking. Her mind darted from impulse to impulse, and finally marshalled them all in review. The practical person, who knows what he wants at once, and generally knows nothing else, will accuse her of indecision. But this was the way her mind worked. And when she did act, no one could accuse her of indecision then. She hit out as lustily as if she had not considered the matter at all. The letter that she wrote Mrs. Wilcox glowed with the native hue of resolution. The pale cast of thought[3] was with her a breath rather than a tarnish, a breath that leaves the colours all the more vivid when it has been wiped away.

"Dear Mrs. Wilcox,

"I have to write something discourteous. It would be better if we did not meet. Both my sister and my aunt have given displeasure to your family, and, in my sister's case, the grounds for displeasure might recur. As far as I know, she no longer occupies her thoughts with your son. But it would not be fair, either to her or to you, if they met, and it is therefore right that our acquaintance, which began so pleasantly, should end.

"I fear that you will not agree with this; indeed, I know that you will not, since you have been good enough to call on us. It is only an instinct on my part, and no doubt the instinct is wrong. My sister would, undoubtedly, say that it is wrong. I write without her knowledge, and I hope that you will not associate her with my discourtesy.

"Believe me,
"Yours truly,
"M. J. Schlegel."

Margaret sent this letter round by the post. Next morning she received the following reply by hand:

"Dear Miss Schlegel,

"You should not have written me such a letter. I called to tell you that Paul has gone abroad.

"Ruth Wilcox."

---

3. "Thus the native hue of resolution / Is sicklied o'er with the pale cast of thought," from *Hamlet*, 3.1.84–85.

Margaret's cheeks burnt. She could not finish her breakfast. She was on fire with shame. Helen had told her that the youth was leaving England, but other things had seemed more important, and she had forgotten. All her absurd anxieties fell to the ground, and in their place arose the certainty that she had been rude to Mrs. Wilcox. Rudeness affected Margaret like a bitter taste in the mouth. It poisoned life. At times it is necessary, but woe to those who employ it without due need. She flung on a hat and shawl, just like a poor woman, and plunged into the fog, which still continued. Her lips were compressed, the letter remained in her hand, and in this state she crossed the street, entered the marble vestibule of the flats, eluded the concierges, and ran up the stairs till she reached the second-floor.

She sent in her name, and to her surprise was shown straight into Mrs. Wilcox's bedroom.

"Oh, Mrs. Wilcox, I have made the baddest blunder. I am more, more ashamed and sorry than I can say."

Mrs. Wilcox bowed gravely. She was offended, and did not pretend to the contrary. She was sitting up in bed, writing letters on an invalid table that spanned her knees. A breakfast tray was on another table beside her. The light of the fire, the light from the window, and the light of a candle-lamp, which threw a quivering halo round her hands, combined to create a strange atmosphere of dissolution.

"I knew he was going to India in November, but I forgot."

"He sailed on the 17th for Nigeria, in Africa."

"I knew—I know. I have been too absurd all through. I am very much ashamed."

Mrs. Wilcox did not answer.

"I am more sorry than I can say, and I hope that you will forgive me."

"It doesn't matter, Miss Schlegel. It is good of you to have come round so promptly."

"It does matter," cried Margaret. "I have been rude to you; and my sister is not even at home, so there was not even that excuse."

"Indeed?"

"She has just gone to Germany."

"She gone as well," murmured the other. "Yes, certainly, it is quite safe—safe, absolutely, now."

"You've been worrying too!" exclaimed Margaret, getting more and more excited, and taking a chair without invitation. "How perfectly extraordinary! I can see that you have. You felt as I do; Helen mustn't meet him again."

"I did think it best."

"Now why?"

"That's a most difficult question," said Mrs. Wilcox, smiling, and a little losing her expression of annoyance. "I think you put it best in your letter—it was an instinct, which may be wrong."

"It wasn't that your son still——"

"Oh no; he often—my Paul is very young, you see."

"Then what was it?"

She repeated: "An instinct which may be wrong."

"In other words, they belong to types that can fall in love, but couldn't live together. That's dreadfully probable. I'm afraid that in nine cases out of ten Nature pulls one way and human nature another."

"These are indeed 'other words,'" said Mrs. Wilcox. "I had nothing so coherent in my head. I was merely alarmed when I knew that my boy cared for your sister."

"Ah, I have always been wanting to ask you. How *did* you know? Helen was so surprised when our aunt drove up, and you stepped forward and arranged things. Did Paul tell you?"

"There is nothing to be gained by discussing that," said Mrs. Wilcox after a moment's pause.

"Mrs. Wilcox, were you very angry with us last June? I wrote you a letter and you didn't answer it."

"I was certainly against taking Mrs. Matheson's flat. I knew it was opposite your house."

"But it's all right now?"

"I think so."

"You only think? You aren't sure? I do love these little muddles tidied up?"

"Oh yes, I'm sure," said Mrs. Wilcox, moving with uneasiness beneath the clothes. "I always sound uncertain over things. It is my way of speaking."

"That's all right, and I'm sure too."

Here the maid came in to remove the breakfast-tray. They were interrupted, and when they resumed conversation it was on more normal lines.

"I must say good-bye now—you will be getting up."

"No—please stop a little longer—I am taking a day in bed. Now and then I do."

"I thought of you as one of the early risers."

"At Howards End—yes; there is nothing to get up for in London."

"Nothing to get up for?" cried the scandalized Margaret. "When there are all the autumn exhibitions, and Ysaye[4] playing in the afternoon! Not to mention people."

"The truth is, I am a little tired. First came the wedding, and then Paul went off, and, instead of resting yesterday, I paid a round of calls."

"A wedding?"

"Yes; Charles, my elder son, is married."

4. Eugène-Auguste Ysaye (1858–1931), Belgian violinist.

"Indeed!"

"We took the flat chiefly on that account, and also that Paul could get his African outfit. The flat belongs to a cousin of my husband's, and she most kindly offered it to us. So before the day came we were able to make the acquaintance of Dolly's people, which we had not yet done."

Margaret asked who Dolly's people were.

"Fussell. The father is in the Indian army—retired; the brother is in the army. The mother is dead."

So perhaps these were the "chinless sunburnt men" whom Helen had espied one afternoon through the window. Margaret felt mildly interested in the fortunes of the Wilcox family. She had acquired the habit on Helen's account, and it still clung to her. She asked for more information about Miss Dolly Fussell that was, and was given it in even, unemotional tones. Mrs. Wilcox's voice, though sweet and compelling, had little range of expression. It suggested that pictures, concerts, and people are all of small and equal value. Only once had it quickened— when speaking of Howards End.

"Charles and Albert Fussell have known one another some time. They belong to the same club, and are both devoted to golf. Dolly plays golf too, though I believe not so well, and they first met in a mixed four-some. We all like her, and are very much pleased. They were married on the 11th, a few days before Paul sailed. Charles was very anxious to have his brother as best man, so he made a great point of having it on the 11th. The Fussells would have preferred it after Christmas, but they were very nice about it. There is Dolly's photograph—in that double frame."

"Are you quite certain that I'm not interrupting, Mrs. Wilcox?"

"Yes, quite."

"Then I will stay. I'm enjoying this."

Dolly's photograph was now examined. It was signed "For dear Mims," which Mrs. Wilcox interpreted as "the name she and Charles had settled that she should call me." Dolly looked silly, and had one of those triangular faces that so often prove attractive to a robust man. She was very pretty. From her Margaret passed to Charles, whose features prevailed opposite. She speculated on the forces that had drawn the two together till God parted them. She found time to hope that they would be happy.

"They have gone to Naples for their honeymoon."

"Lucky people!"

"I can hardly imagine Charles in Italy."

"Doesn't he care for travelling?"

"He likes travel, but he does see through foreigners so. What he enjoys most is a motor tour in England, and I think that would have carried the day if the weather had not been so abominable. His father gave him a car of his own for a wedding present, which for the present is being stored at Howards End."

"I suppose you have a garage there?"

"Yes. My husband built a little one only last month, to the west of the house, not far from the wych-elm, in what used to be the paddock for the pony."

The last words had an indescribable ring about them.

"Where's the pony gone?" asked Margaret after a pause.

"The pony? Oh, dead, ever so long ago."

"The wych-elm I remember. Helen spoke of it as a very splendid tree."

"It is the finest wych-elm in Hertfordshire. Did your sister tell you about the teeth?"

"No."

"Oh, it might interest you. There are pigs' teeth stuck into the trunk, about four feet from the ground. The country people put them in long ago, and they think that if they chew a piece of the bark, it will cure the toothache. The teeth are almost grown over now, and no one comes to the tree."

"I should. I love folklore and all festering superstitions."

"Do you think that the tree really did cure toothache, if one believed in it?"

"Of course it did. It would cure anything—once."

"Certainly I remember cases—you see I lived at Howards End long, long before Mr. Wilcox knew it. I was born there."

The conversation again shifted. At the time it seemed little more than aimless chatter. She was interested when her hostess explained that Howards End was her own property. She was bored when too minute an account was given of the Fussell family, of the anxieties of Charles concerning Naples, of the movements of Mr. Wilcox and Evie, who were motoring in Yorkshire. Margaret could not bear being bored. She grew inattentive, played with the photograph frame, dropped it, smashed Dolly's glass, apologized, was pardoned, cut her finger thereon, was pitied, and finally said she must be going—there was all the housekeeping to do, and she had to interview Tibby's riding-master.

Then the curious note was struck again.

"Good-bye, Miss Schlegel, good-bye. Thank you for coming. You have cheered me up."

"I'm so glad!"

"I—I wonder whether you ever think about yourself?"

"I think of nothing else," said Margaret, blushing, but letting her hand remain in that of the invalid.

"I wonder. I wondered at Heidelberg."

"*I'm* sure!"

"I almost think——"

"Yes?" asked Margaret, for there was a long pause—a pause that was somehow akin to the flicker of the fire, the quiver of the reading-lamp upon their hands, the white blur from the window; a pause of shifting and eternal shadows.

"I almost think you forget you're a girl."

Margaret was startled and a little annoyed. "I'm twenty-nine," she remarked. "That's not so wildly girlish."

Mrs. Wilcox smiled.

"What makes you say that? Do you mean that I have been gauche and rude?"

A shake of the head. "I only meant that I am fifty-one, and that to me, both of you—— Read it all in some book or other; I cannot put things clearly."

"Oh, I've got it—inexperience. I'm no better than Helen, you mean, and yet I presume to advise her."

"Yes. You have got it. Inexperience is the word."

"Inexperience," repeated Margaret, in serious yet buoyant tones. "Of course, I have everything to learn—absolutely everything—just as much as Helen. Life's very difficult and full of surprises. At all events, I've got as far as that. To be humble and kind, to go straight ahead, to love people rather than pity them, to remember the submerged—well, one can't do all these things at once, worse luck, because they're so contradictory. It's then that proportion comes in—to live by proportion. Don't *begin* with proportion. Only prigs do that. Let proportion come in as a last resource, when the better things have failed, and a deadlock—— Gracious me, I've started preaching!"

"Indeed, you put the difficulties of life splendidly," said Mrs. Wilcox, withdrawing her hand into the deeper shadows. "It is just what I should have liked to say about them myself."

Chapter IX

Mrs. Wilcox cannot be accused of giving Margaret much information about life. And Margaret, on the other hand, has made a fair show of modesty, and has pretended to an inexperience that she certainly did not feel. She had kept house for over ten years; she had entertained, almost with distinction; she had brought up a charming sister, and was bringing up a brother. Surely, if experience is attainable, she had attained it.

Yet the little luncheon-party that she gave in Mrs. Wilcox's honour was not a success. The new friend did not blend with the "one or two delightful people" who had been asked to meet her, and the atmosphere was one of polite bewilderment. Her tastes were simple, her knowledge of culture slight, and she was not interested in the New English Art Club,[1]

---

1. Founded in 1886, a rival to the more conservative Royal Academy.

nor in the dividing-line between Journalism and Literature, which was started as a conversational hare. The delightful people darted after it with cries of joy, Margaret leading them, and not till the meal was half over did they realize that the principal guest had taken no part in the chase. There was no common topic. Mrs. Wilcox, whose life had been spent in the service of husband and sons, had little to say to strangers who had never shared it, and whose age was half her own. Clever talk alarmed her, and withered her delicate imaginings; it was the social counterpart of a motor-car, all jerks, and she was a wisp of hay, a flower. Twice she deplored the weather, twice criticized the train service on the Great Northern Railway. They vigorously assented, and rushed on, and when she inquired whether there was any news of Helen, her hostess was too much occupied in placing Rothenstein[2] to answer. The question was repeated: "I hope that your sister is safe in Germany by now." Margaret checked herself and said "Yes, thank you; I heard on Tuesday." But the demon of vociferation was in her, and the next moment she was off again.

"Only on Tuesday, for they live right away at Stettin.[3] Did you ever know anyone living at Stettin?"

"Never," said Mrs. Wilcox gravely, while her neighbour, a young man low down in the Education Office, began to discuss what people who lived at Stettin ought to look like. Was there such a thing as Stettininty? Margaret swept on.

"People at Stettin drop things into boats out of overhanging warehouses. At least, our cousins do, but aren't particularly rich. The town isn't interesting, except for a clock that rolls its eyes, and the view of the Oder, which truly is something special. Oh, Mrs. Wilcox, you would love the Oder! The river, or rather rivers—there seem to be dozens of them—are intense blue, and the plain they run through an intensest green."

"Indeed! That sounds like a most beautiful view, Miss Schlegel."

"So I say, but Helen, who will muddle things, says no, it's like music. The course of the Oder is to be like music. It's obliged to remind her of a symphonic poem. The part by the landing-stage is in B minor, if I remember rightly, but lower down things get extremely mixed. There is a slodgy theme in several keys at once, meaning mud-banks, and another for the navigable canal, and the exit into the Baltic is in C sharp major, pianissimo."[4]

"What do the overhanging warehouses make of that?" asked the man, laughing.

"They make a great deal of it," replied Margaret, unexpectedly rush-

2. William Rothenstein (1872–1945), English painter.
3. A seaport in eastern Germany (now northwest Poland), where the river Oder empties into the Baltic Sea.
4. Very soft.

ing off on a new track. "I think it's affectation to compare the Oder to music, and so do you, but the overhanging warehouses of Stettin take beauty seriously, which we don't, and the average Englishman doesn't, and despises all who do. Now don't say 'Germans have no taste,' or I shall scream. They haven't. But—but—such a tremendous but!—they take poetry seriously. They do take poetry seriously."

"Is anything gained by that?"

"Yes, yes. The German is always on the lookout for beauty. He may miss it through stupidity, or misinterpret it, but he is always asking beauty to enter his life, and I believe that in the end it will come. At Heidelberg I met a fat veterinary surgeon whose voice broke with sobs as he repeated some mawkish poetry. So easy for me to laugh—I, who never repeat poetry, good or bad, and cannot remember one fragment of verse to thrill myself with. My blood boils—well, I'm half German, so put it down to patriotism—when I listen to the tasteful contempt of the average islander for things Teutonic, whether they're Böcklin[5] or my veterinary surgeon. 'Oh, Böcklin,' they say; 'he strains after beauty, he peoples Nature with gods too consciously.' Of course Böcklin strains, because he wants something—beauty and all the other intangible gifts that are floating about the world. So his landscapes don't come off, and Leader's[6] do."

"I am not sure that I agree. Do you?" said he, turning to Mrs. Wilcox.

She replied: "I think Miss Schlegel puts everything splendidly"; and a chill fell on the conversation.

"Oh, Mrs. Wilcox, say something nicer than that. It's such a snub to be told you put things splendidly."

"I do not mean it as a snub. Your last speech interested me so much. Generally people do not seem quite to like Germany. I have long wanted to hear what is said on the other side."

"The other side? Then you do disagree. Oh, good! Give us your side."

"I have no side. But my husband"—her voice softened, the chill increased—"has very little faith in the Continent, and our children have all taken after him."

"On what grounds? Do they feel that the Continent is in bad form?"

Mrs. Wilcox had no idea; she paid little attention to grounds. She was not intellectual, nor even alert, and it was odd that, all the same, she should give the idea of greatness. Margaret, zigzagging with her friends over Thought and Art, was conscious of a personality that transcended their own and dwarfed their activities. There was no bitterness in Mrs. Wilcox; there was not even criticism; she was lovable, and no ungracious or uncharitable word had passed her lips. Yet she and daily life were out of focus: one or the other must show blurred. And at lunch she seemed more

---

5. Arnold Böcklin (1827–1901), Swiss painter allied to German classicism.
6. Benjamin Williams Leader (1831–1923), popular English landscape painter.

out of focus than usual, and nearer the line that divides daily life from a life that may be of greater importance.

"You will admit, though, that the Continent—it seems silly to speak of 'the Continent,' but really it is all more like itself than any part of it is like England. England is unique. Do have another jelly first. I was going to say that the Continent, for good or for evil, is interested in ideas. Its Literature and Art have what one might call the kink of the unseen about them, and this persists even through decadence and affectation. There is more liberty of action in England, but for liberty of thought go to bureaucratic Prussia.[7] People will there discuss with humility vital questions that we here think ourselves too good to touch with tongs."

"I do not want to go to Prussia," said Mrs. Wilcox—"not even to see that interesting view that you were describing. And for discussing with humility I am too old. We never discuss anything at Howards End."

"Then you ought to!" said Margaret. "Discussion keeps a house alive. It cannot stand by bricks and mortar alone."

"It cannot stand without them," said Mrs. Wilcox, unexpectedly catching on to the thought, and rousing, for the first and last time, a faint hope in the breasts of the delightful people. "It cannot stand without them, and I sometimes think——But I cannot expect your generation to agree, for even my daughter disagrees with me here."

"Never mind us or her. Do say!"

"I sometimes think that it is wiser to leave action and discussion to men."

There was a little silence.

"One admits that the arguments against the suffrage *are* extraordinarily strong," said a girl opposite, leaning forward and crumbling her bread.

"Are they? I never follow any arguments. I am only too thankful not to have a vote myself."

"We didn't mean the vote, though, did we?" supplied Margaret. "Aren't we differing on something much wider, Mrs. Wilcox? Whether women are to remain what they have been since the dawn of history; or whether, since men have moved forward so far, they too may move forward a little now. I say they may. I would even admit a biological change."

"I don't know, I don't know."

"I must be getting back to my overhanging warehouse," said the man. "They've turned disgracefully strict."

Mrs. Wilcox also rose.

"Oh, but come upstairs for a little. Miss Quested plays. Do you like

7. A kingdom in the eastern part of Germany, which was Bismarck's base in building the modern German state.

MacDowell?[8] Do you mind him only having two noises? If you must really go, I'll see you out. Won't you even have coffee?"

They left the dining-room, closing the door behind them, and as Mrs. Wilcox buttoned up her jacket, she said: "What an interesting life you all lead in London!"

"No, we don't," said Margaret, with a sudden revulsion. "We lead the lives of gibbering monkeys. Mrs. Wilcox—really—— We have something quiet and stable at the bottom. We really have. All my friends have. Don't pretend you enjoyed lunch, for you loathed it, but forgive me by coming again, alone, or by asking me to you."

"I am used to young people," said Mrs. Wilcox, and with each word she spoke the outlines of known things grew dim. "I hear a great deal of chatter at home, for we, like you, entertain a great deal. With us it is more sport and politics, but—I enjoyed my lunch very much, Miss Schlegel, dear, and am not pretending, and only wish I could have joined in more. For one thing, I'm not particularly well just to-day. For another, you younger people move so quickly that it dazes me. Charles is the same, Dolly the same. But we are all in the same boat, old and young. I never forget that."

They were silent for a moment. Then, with a newborn emotion, they shook hands. The conversation ceased suddenly when Margaret re-entered the dining-room: her friends had been talking over her new friend, and had dismissed her as uninteresting.

Chapter X

Several days passed.

Was Mrs. Wilcox one of the unsatisfactory people—there are many of them—who dangle intimacy and then withdraw it? They evoke our interests and affections, and keep the life of the spirit dawdling round them. Then they withdraw. When physical passion is involved, there is a definite name for such behaviour—flirting—and if carried far enough it is punishable by law. But no law—not public opinion even—punishes those who coquette with friendship, though the dull ache that they inflict, the sense of misdirected effort and exhaustion, may be as intolerable. Was she one of these?

Margaret feared so at first, for, with a Londoner's impatience, she wanted everything to be settled up immediately. She mistrusted the periods of quiet that are essential to true growth. Desiring to book Mrs. Wilcox as a friend, she pressed on the ceremony, pencil, as it were, in hand, pressing the more because the rest of the family were away, and the opportunity seemed favourable. But the elder woman would not be hurried. She refused to fit in with the Wickham Place set, or to reopen

8. Edward MacDowell (1860–1908), American composer.

discussion of Helen and Paul, whom Margaret would have utilized as a short-cut. She took her time, or perhaps let time take her, and when the crisis did come all was ready.

The crisis opened with a message: would Miss Schlegel come shopping? Christmas was nearing, and Mrs. Wilcox felt behindhand with the presents. She had taken some more days in bed, and must make up for lost time. Margaret accepted, and at eleven o'clock one cheerless morning they started out in a brougham.[1]

"First of all," began Margaret, "we must make a list and tick off the people's names. My aunt always does, and this fog may thicken up any moment. Have you any ideas?"

"I thought we would go to Harrod's or the Haymarket Stores,"[2] said Mrs. Wilcox rather hopelessly. "Everything is sure to be there. I am not a good shopper. The din is so confusing, and your aunt is quite right—one ought to make a list. Take my note-book, then, and write your own name at the top of the page."

"Oh, hooray!" said Margaret, writing it. "How very kind of you to start with me!" But she did not want to receive anything expensive. Their acquaintance was singular rather than intimate, and she divined that the Wilcox clan would resent any expenditure on outsiders; the more compact families do. She did not want to be thought a second Helen, who would snatch presents since she could not snatch young men, nor to be exposed, like a second Aunt Juley, to the insults of Charles. A certain austerity of demeanour was best, and she added: "I don't really want a Yuletide gift, though. In fact, I'd rather not."

"Why?"

"Because I've odd ideas about Christmas. Because I have all that money can buy. I want more people, but no more things."

"I should like to give you something worth your acquaintance, Miss Schlegel, in memory of your kindness to me during my lonely fortnight. It has so happened that I have been left alone, and you have stopped me from brooding. I am too apt to brood."

"If that is so," said Margaret, "if I have happened to be of use to you, which I didn't know, you cannot pay me back with anything tangible."

"I suppose not, but one would like to. Perhaps I shall think of something as we go about."

Her name remained at the head of the list, but nothing was written opposite it. They drove from shop to shop. The air was white, and when they alighted it tasted like cold pennies. At times they passed through a clot of grey. Mrs. Wilcox's vitality was low that morning, and it was Margaret who decided on a horse for this little girl, a golliwog[3] for that, for the rector's wife a copper warming-tray. "We always give the servants

1. A horse-drawn carriage with the driver outside in front.
2. Popular department stores.
3. A grotesque black doll.

money." "Yes, do you, yes, much easier," replied Margaret, but felt the grotesque impact of the unseen upon the seen, and saw issuing from a forgotten manger at Bethlehem this torrent of coins and toys. Vulgarity reigned. Public-houses, besides their usual exhortation against temperance reform, invited men to "Join our Christmas goose club"—one bottle of gin, etc., or two, according to subscription. A poster of a woman in tights heralded the Christmas pantomime, and little red devils, who had come in again that year, were prevalent upon the Christmas-cards. Margaret was no morbid idealist. She did not wish this spate of business and self-advertisement checked. It was only the occasion of it that struck her with amazement annually. How many of these vacillating shoppers and tired shop-assistants realized that it was a divine event that drew them together? She realized it, though standing outside in the matter. She was not a Christian in the accepted sense; she did not believe that God had ever worked among us as a young artisan. These people, or most of them, believed it, and if pressed, would affirm it in words. But the visible signs of their belief were Regent Street or Drury Lane, a little mud displaced, a little money spent, a little food cooked, eaten, and forgotten. Inadequate. But in public who shall express the unseen adequately? It is private life that holds out the mirror to infinity; personal intercourse, and that alone, that ever hints at a personality beyond our daily vision.

"No, I do like Christmas on the whole," she announced. "In its clumsy way, it does approach Peace and Goodwill. But oh, it is clumsier every year."

"Is it? I am only used to country Christmases."

"We are usually in London, and play the game with vigour—carols at the Abbey, clumsy midday meal, clumsy dinner for the maids, followed by Christmas-tree and dancing of poor children, with songs from Helen. The drawing-room does very well for that. We put the tree in the powder-closet, and draw a curtain when the candles are lighted, and with the looking-glass behind it looks quite pretty. I wish we might have a powder-closet in our next house. Of course, the tree has to be very small, and the presents don't hang on it. No; the presents reside in a sort of rocky landscape made of crumpled brown paper."

"You spoke of your 'next house,' Miss Schlegel. Then are you leaving Wickham Place?"

"Yes, in two or three years, when the lease expires. We must."

"Have you been there long?"

"All our lives."

"You will be very sorry to leave it."

"I suppose so. We scarcely realize it yet. My father——" She broke off, for they had reached the stationery department of the Haymarket Stores, and Mrs. Wilcox wanted to order some private greeting cards.

"If possible, something distinctive," she sighed. At the counter she found a friend, bent on the same errand, and conversed with her insipidly, wasting much time. "My husband and our daughter are motoring." "Bertha too? Oh, fancy, what a coincidence!" Margaret, though not practical, could shine in such company as this. While they talked, she went through a volume of specimen cards, and submitted one for Mrs. Wilcox's inspection. Mrs. Wilcox was delighted—so original, words so sweet; she would order a hundred like that, and could never be sufficiently grateful. Then, just as the assistant was booking the order, she said: "Do you know, I'll wait. On second thoughts, I'll wait. There's plenty of time still, isn't there, and I shall be able to get Evie's opinion."

They returned to the carriage by devious paths; when they were in, she said, "But couldn't you get it renewed?"

"I beg your pardon?" asked Margaret.

"The lease, I mean."

"Oh, the lease! Have you been thinking of that all the time? How very kind of you!"

"Surely something could be done."

"No; values have risen too enormously. They mean to pull down Wickham Place, and build flats like yours."

"But how horrible!"

"Landlords are horrible."

Then she said vehemently: "It is monstrous, Miss Schlegel; it isn't right. I had no idea that this was hanging over you. I do pity you from the bottom of my heart. To be parted from your house, your father's house—it oughtn't to be allowed. It is worse than dying. I would rather die than——Oh, poor girls! Can what they call civilization be right, if people mayn't die in the room where they were born? My dear, I am so sorry——"

Margaret did not know what to say. Mrs. Wilcox had been overtired by the shopping, and was inclined to hysteria.

"Howards End was nearly pulled down once. It would have killed me."

"Howards End must be a very different house to ours. We are fond of ours, but there is nothing distinctive about it. As you saw, it is an ordinary London house. We shall easily find another."

"So you think."

"Again my lack of experience, I suppose!" said Margaret, easing away from the subject. "I can't say anything when you take up that line, Mrs. Wilcox. I wish I could see myself as you see me—foreshortened into a backfisch.[4] Quite the ingénue. Very charming—wonderfully well read for my age, but incapable——"

Mrs. Wilcox would not be deterred. "Come down with me to Howards End now," she said, more vehemently than ever. "I want you to

4. Adolescent (German).

see it. You have never seen it. I want to hear what you say about it, for you do put things so wonderfully."

Margaret glanced at the pitiless air and then at the tired face of her companion. "Later on I should love it," she continued, "but it's hardly the weather for such an expedition, and we ought to start when we're fresh. Isn't the house shut up, too?"

She received no answer. Mrs. Wilcox appeared to be annoyed.

"Might I come some other day?"

Mrs. Wilcox bent forward and tapped the glass. "Back to Wickham Place, please!" was her order to the coachman. Margaret had been snubbed.

"A thousand thanks, Miss Schlegel, for all your help."

"Not at all."

"It is such a comfort to get the presents off my mind—the Christmas-cards especially. I do admire your choice."

It was her turn to receive no answer. In her turn Margaret became annoyed.

"My husband and Evie will be back the day after to-morrow. That is why I dragged you out shopping to-day. I stayed in town chiefly to shop, but got through nothing, and now he writes that they must cut their tour short, the weather is so bad, and the police-traps have been so bad—nearly as bad as in Surrey. Ours is such a careful chauffeur, and my husband feels it particularly hard that they should be treated like road-hogs."

"Why?"

"Well, naturally he—he isn't a road-hog."

"He was exceeding the speed-limit, I conclude. He must expect to suffer with the lower animals."

Mrs. Wilcox was silenced. In growing discomfort they drove homewards. The city seemed Satanic, the narrower streets oppressing like the galleries of a mine. No harm was done by the fog to trade, for it lay high, and the lighted windows of the shops were thronged with customers. It was rather a darkening of the spirit which fell back upon itself, to find a more grievous darkness within. Margaret nearly spoke a dozen times, but something throttled her. She felt petty and awkward, and her meditations on Christmas grew more cynical. Peace? It may bring other gifts, but is there a single Londoner to whom Christmas is peaceful? The craving for excitement and for elaboration has ruined that blessing. Goodwill? Had she seen any example of it in the hordes of purchasers? Or in herself? She had failed to respond to this invitation merely because it was a little queer and imaginative—she, whose birthright it was to nourish imagination! Better to have accepted, to have tired themselves a little by the journey, than coldly to reply, "Might I come some other day?" Her cynicism left her. There would be no other day. This shadowy woman would never ask her again.

They parted at the Mansions. Mrs. Wilcox went in after due civilities, and Margaret watched the tall, lonely figure sweep up the hall to the lift. As the glass doors closed on it she had the sense of an imprisonment. The beautiful head disappeared first, still buried in the muff; the long trailing skirt followed. A woman of undefinable rarity was going up heavenward, like a specimen in a bottle. And into what a heaven—a vault as of hell, sooty black, from which soots descended!

At lunch her brother, seeing her inclined for silence, insisted on talking. Tibby was not ill-natured, but from babyhood something drove him to do the unwelcome and the unexpected. Now he gave her a long account of the day-school that he sometimes patronized. The account was interesting, and she had often pressed him for it before, but she could not attend now, for her mind was focussed on the invisible. She discerned that Mrs. Wilcox, though a loving wife and mother, had only one passion in life—her house—and that the moment was solemn when she invited a friend to share this passion with her. To answer "another day" was to answer as a fool. "Another day" will do for brick and mortar, but not for the Holy of Holies into which Howards End had been transfigured. Her own curiosity was slight. She had heard more than enough about it in the summer. The nine windows, the vine, and the wych-elm had no pleasant connections for her, and she would have preferred to spend the afternoon at a concert. But imagination triumphed. While her brother held forth she determined to go, at whatever cost, and to compel Mrs. Wilcox to go, too. When lunch was over she stepped over to the flats.

Mrs. Wilcox had just gone away for the night.

Margaret said that it was of no consequence, hurried downstairs, and took a hansom to King's Cross. She was convinced that the escapade was important, though it would have puzzled her to say why. There was question of imprisonment and escape, and though she did not know the time of the train, she strained her eyes for St. Pancras' clock.

Then the clock of King's Cross swung into sight, a second moon in that infernal sky, and her cab drew up at the station. There was a train for Hilton in five minutes. She took a ticket, asking in her agitation for a single. As she did so, a grave and happy voice saluted her and thanked her.

"I will come if I still may," said Margaret, laughing nervously.

"You are coming to sleep, dear, too. It is in the morning that my house is most beautiful. You are coming to stop. I cannot show you my meadow properly except at sunrise. These fogs"—she pointed at the station roof—"never spread far. I dare say they are sitting in the sun in Hertfordshire, and you will never repent joining them."

"I shall never repent joining you."

"It is the same."

They began the walk up the long platform. Far at its end stood the train, breasting the darkness without. They never reached it. Before imagination could triumph, there were cries of "Mother! mother!" and a heavy-browed girl darted out of the cloak-room and seized Mrs. Wilcox by the arm.

"Evie!" she gasped—"Evie, my pet——"

The girl called, "Father! I say! look who's here."

"Evie, dearest girl, why aren't you in Yorkshire?"

"No—motor smash—changed plans—father's coming."

"Why, Ruth!" cried Mr. Wilcox, joining them. "What in the name of all that's wonderful are you doing here, Ruth?"

Mrs. Wilcox had recovered herself.

"Oh, Henry dear!—here's a lovely surprise—but let me introduce—but I think you know Miss Schlegel."

"Oh yes," he replied, not greatly interested. "But how's yourself, Ruth?"

"Fit as a fiddle," she answered gaily.

"So are we, and so was our car, which ran A1 as far as Ripon, but there a wretched horse and cart which a fool of a driver——"

"Miss Schlegel, our little outing must be for another day."

"I was saying that this fool of a driver, as the policeman himself admits——"

"Another day, Mrs. Wilcox. Of course."

"—But as we've insured against third party risks, it won't so much matter——"

"—Cart and car being practically at right angles——"

The voices of the happy family rose high. Margaret was left alone. No one wanted her. Mrs. Wilcox walked out of King's Cross between her husband and her daughter, listening to both of them.

Chapter XI

The funeral was over. The carriages had rolled away through the soft mud, and only the poor remained. They approached to the newly-dug shaft and looked their last at the coffin, now almost hidden beneath the spadefuls of clay. It was their moment. Most of them were women from the dead woman's district, to whom black garments had been served out by Mr. Wilcox's orders. Pure curiosity had brought others. They thrilled with the excitement of a death, and of a rapid death, and stood in groups or moved between the graves, like drops of ink. The son of one of them, a wood-cutter, was perched high above their heads, pollarding[1] one of the churchyard elms. From where he sat he could see the village of Hilton, strung upon the North Road, with its accreting suburbs; the sunset beyond, scarlet and orange, winking at him beneath brows of grey; the church; the plantations; and behind him an unspoilt country of

1. Cutting a tree back almost to the trunk to produce a dense growth of branches.

fields and farms. But he, too, was rolling the event luxuriously in his mouth. He tried to tell his mother down below all that he had felt when he saw the coffin approaching: how he could not leave his work, and yet did not like to go on with it; how he had almost slipped out of the tree, he was so upset; the rooks had cawed, and no wonder—it was as if rooks knew too. His mother claimed the prophetic power herself—she had seen a strange look about Mrs. Wilcox for some time. London had done the mischief, said others. She had been a kind lady; her grandmother had been kind, too—a plainer person, but very kind. Ah, the old sort was dying out! Mr. Wilcox, he was a kind gentleman. They advanced to the topic again and again, dully, but with exaltation. The funeral of a rich person was to them what the funeral of Alcestis or Ophelia[2] is to the edu-cated. It was Art; though remote from life, it enhanced life's values, and they witnessed it avidly.

The grave-diggers, who had kept up an undercurrent of disapproval— they disliked Charles; it was not a moment to speak of such things, but they did not like Charles Wilcox—the grave-diggers finished their work and piled up the wreaths and crosses above it. The sun set over Hilton: the grey brows of the evening flushed a little, and were cleft with one scarlet frown. Chattering sadly to each other, the mourners passed through the lych-gate[3] and traversed the chestnut avenues that led down to the village. The young wood-cutter stayed a little longer, poised above the silence and swaying rhythmically. At last the bough fell beneath his saw. With a grunt, he descended, his thoughts dwelling no longer on death, but on love, for he was mating. He stopped as he passed the new grave; a sheaf of tawny chrysanthemums had caught his eye. "They did-n't ought to have coloured flowers at buryings," he reflected. Trudging on a few steps, he stopped again, looked furtively at the dusk, turned back, wrenched a chrysanthemum from the sheaf, and hid it in his pock-et.

After him came silence absolute. The cottage that abutted on the churchyard was empty, and no other house stood near. Hour after hour the scene of the interment remained without an eye to witness it. Clouds drifted over it from the west; or the church may have been a ship, high-prowed, steering with all its company towards infinity. Towards morning the air grew colder, the sky clearer, the surface of the earth hard and sparkling above the prostrate dead. The wood-cutter, returning after a night of joy, reflected: "They lilies, they chrysants; it's a pity I didn't take them all."

Up at Howards End they were attempting breakfast. Charles and Evie sat in the dining-room, with Mrs. Charles. Their father, who could not bear to see a face, breakfasted upstairs. He suffered acutely. Pain came

2. Women from classical mythology and Shakespeare's *Hamlet* who take their own lives.
3. The roofed gate to a churchyard.

over him in spasms, as if it was physical, and even while he was about to eat, his eyes would fill with tears, and he would lay down the morsel untasted.

He remembered his wife's even goodness during thirty years. Not anything in detail—not courtship or early raptures—but just the unvarying virtue, that seemed to him a woman's noblest quality. So many women are capricious, breaking into odd flaws of passion or frivolity. Not so his wife. Year after year, summer and winter, as bride and mother, she had been the same, he had always trusted her. Her tenderness! Her innocence! The wonderful innocence that was hers by the gift of God. Ruth knew no more of worldly wickedness and wisdom than did the flowers in her garden, or the grass in her field. Her idea of business—"Henry, why do people who have enough money try to get more money?" Her idea of politics—"I am sure that if the mothers of various nations could meet, there would be no more wars." Her idea of religion—ah, this had been a cloud, but a cloud that passed. She came of Quaker stock, and he and his family, formerly Dissenters,[4] were now members of the Church of England. The rector's sermons had at first repelled her, and she had expressed a desire for "a more inward light,"[5] adding, "not so much for myself as for baby" (Charles). Inward light must have been granted, for he heard no complaints in later years. They brought up their three children without dispute. They had never disputed.

She lay under the earth now. She had gone, and as if to make her going the more bitter, had gone with a touch of mystery that was all unlike her. "Why didn't you tell me you knew of it?" he had moaned, and her faint voice had answered: "I didn't want to, Henry—I might have been wrong—and everyone hates illnesses." He had been told of the horror by a strange doctor, whom she had consulted during his absence from town. Was this altogether just? Without fully explaining, she had died. It was a fault on her part, and—tears rushed into his eyes—what a little fault! It was the only time she had deceived him in those thirty years.

He rose to his feet and looked out of the window, for Evie had come in with the letters, and he could meet no one's eye. Ah yes—she had been a good woman—she had been steady. He chose the word deliberately. To him steadiness included all praise.

He himself, gazing at the wintry garden, is in appearance a steady man. His face was not as square as his son's, and, indeed, the chin, though firm enough in outline, retreated a little, and the lips, ambiguous, were curtained by a moustache. But there was no external hint of weakness. The eyes, if capable of kindness and good-fellowship, if ruddy for the moment with tears, were the eyes of one who could not be driven. The forehead, too, was like Charles's. High and straight, brown and

4. English Protestants who refuse to conform to the established Church.
5. Members of the Religious Society of Friends, or Quakers, believe that everyone's "inner light" can establish communion with God and that the assistance of priests is unnecessary.

polished, merging abruptly into temples and skull, it had the effect of a bastion that protected his head from the world. At times it had the effect of a blank wall. He had dwelt behind it, intact and happy, for fifty years.

"The post's come, father," said Evie awkwardly.

"Thanks. Put it down."

"Has the breakfast been all right?"

"Yes, thanks."

The girl glanced at him and at it with constraint. She did not know what to do.

"Charles says do you want the 'Times'?"

"No, I'll read it later."

"Ring if you want anything, father, won't you?"

"I've all I want."

Having sorted the letters from the circulars, she went back to the dining-room.

"Father's eaten nothing," she announced, sitting down with wrinkled brows behind the tea-urn.

Charles did not answer, but after a moment he ran quickly upstairs, opened the door, and said: "Look here, father, you must eat, you know;" and having paused for a reply that did not come, stole down again. "He's going to read his letters first, I think," he said evasively; "I dare say he will go on with his breakfast afterwards." Then he took up the 'Times,' and for some time there was no sound except the clink of cup against saucer and of knife on plate.

Poor Mrs. Charles sat between her silent companions, terrified at the course of events, and a little bored. She was a rubbishy little creature, and she knew it. A telegram had dragged her from Naples to the death-bed of a woman whom she had scarcely known. A word from her husband had plunged her into mourning. She desired to mourn inwardly as well, but she wished that Mrs. Wilcox, since fated to die, could have died before the marriage, for then less would have been expected of her. Crumbling her toast, and too nervous to ask for the butter, she remained almost motionless, thankful only for this, that her father-in-law was having his breakfast upstairs.

At last Charles spoke. "They had no business to be pollarding those elms yesterday," he said to his sister.

"No indeed."

"I must make a note of that," he continued. "I am surprised that the rector allowed it."

"Perhaps it may not be the rector's affair."

"Whose else could it be?"

"The lord of the manor."

"Impossible."

"Butter, Dolly?"

"Thank you, Evie dear. Charles——"

"Yes, dear?"

"I didn't know one could pollard elms. I thought one only pollarded willows."

"Oh no, one can pollard elms."

"Then why oughtn't the elms in the churchyard to be pollarded?" Charles frowned a little, and turned again to his sister.

"Another point. I must speak to Chalkeley."

"Yes, rather; you must complain to Chalkeley."

"It's no good him saying he is not responsible for those men. He is responsible."

"Yes, rather."

Brother and sister were not callous. They spoke thus, partly because they desired to keep Chalkeley up to the mark—a healthy desire in its way—partly because they avoided the personal note in life. All Wilcoxes did. It did not seem to them of supreme importance. Or it may be as Helen supposed: they realized its importance, but were afraid of it. Panic and emptiness, could one glance behind. They were not callous, and they left the breakfast-table with aching hearts. Their mother never had come in to breakfast. It was in the other rooms, and especially in the garden, that they felt her loss most. As Charles went out to the garage, he was reminded at every step of the woman who had loved him and whom he could never replace. What battles he had fought against her gentle conservatism! How she had disliked improvements, yet how loyally she had accepted them when made! He and his father—what trouble they had had to get this very garage! With what difficulty had they persuaded her to yield them the paddock for it— the paddock that she loved more dearly than the garden itself! The vine—she had got her way about the vine. It still encumbered the south wall with its unproductive branches. And so with Evie, as she stood talking to the cook. Though she could take up her mother's work inside the house, just as the man could take it up without, she felt that something unique had fallen out of her life. Their grief, though less poignant than their father's, grew from deeper roots, for a wife may be replaced; a mother never.

Charles would go back to the office. There was little to do at Howards End. The contents of his mother's will had been long known to them. There were no legacies, no annuities, none of the posthumous bustle with which some of the dead prolong their activities. Trusting her husband, she had left him everything without reserve. She was quite a poor woman—the house had been all her dowry, and the house would come to Charles in time. Her watercolours Mr. Wilcox intended to reserve for Paul, while Evie would take the jewellery and lace. How easily she slipped out of life! Charles thought the habit laudable, though he did not intend to adopt it himself, whereas Margaret would have seen in it an almost culpable indifference to earthly fame. Cynicism—not the superficial cynicism that snarls and sneers, but the cynicism that can go with courtesy and tenderness—that was the note of Mrs. Wilcox's will. She wanted not to vex people. That accomplished, the earth might freeze over her for ever.

No, there was nothing for Charles to wait for. He could not go on with his honeymoon, so he would go up to London and work—he felt too miserable hanging about. He and Dolly would have the furnished flat while his father rested quietly in the country with Evie. He could also keep an eye on his own little house, which was being painted and decorated for him in one of the Surrey suburbs, and in which he hoped to instal himself soon after Christmas. Yes, he would go up after lunch in his new motor, and the town servants, who had come down for the funeral, would go up by train.

He found his father's chauffeur in the garage, said "Morning" without looking at the man's face, and, bending over the car, continued: "Hullo! my new car's been driven!"

"Has it, sir?"

"Yes," said Charles, getting rather red; "and whoever's driven it hasn't cleaned it properly, for there's mud on the axle. Take it off."

The man went for the cloths without a word. He was a chauffeur as ugly as sin—not that this did him disservice with Charles, who thought charm in a man rather rot, and had soon got rid of the little Italian beast with whom they had started.

"Charles——" His bride was tripping after him over the hoar-frost, a dainty black column, her little face and elaborate mourning hat forming the capital thereof.

"One minute, I'm busy. Well, Crane, who's been driving it, do you suppose?"

"Don't know, I'm sure, sir. No one's driven it since I've been back, but, of course, there's the fortnight I've been away with the other car in Yorkshire."

The mud came off easily.

"Charles, your father's down. Something's happened. He wants you in the house at once. Oh, Charles!"

"Wait, dear, wait a minute. Who had the key of the garage while you were away, Crane?"

"The gardener, sir."

"Do you mean to tell me that old Penny can drive a motor?"

"No, sir; no one's had the motor out, sir."

"Then how do you account for the mud on the axle?"

"I can't, of course, say for the time I've been in Yorkshire. No more mud now, sir."

Charles was vexed. The man was treating him as a fool, and if his heart had not been so heavy he would have reported him to his father. But it was not a morning for complaints. Ordering the motor to be round after lunch, he joined his wife, who had all the while been pouring out some incoherent story about a letter and a Miss Schlegel.

"Now, Dolly, I can attend to you. Miss Schlegel? What does she want?"

When people wrote a letter Charles always asked what they wanted. Want was to him the only cause of action. And the question in this case was correct, for his wife replied, "She wants Howards End."

"Howards End? Now, Crane, just don't forget to put on the Stepney wheel."[6]

"No, sir."

"Now, mind you don't forget, for I —— Come, little woman." When they were out of the chauffeur's sight he put his arm round her waist and pressed her against him. All his affection and half his attention—it was what he granted her throughout their happy married life.

"But you haven't listened, Charles——"

"What's wrong?"

"I keep on telling you—Howards End. Miss Schlegel's got it."

"Got what?" said Charles, unclasping her. "What the dickens are you talking about?"

"Now, Charles, you promised not to say those naughty——"

"Look here, I'm in no mood for foolery. It's no morning for it either."

"I tell you—I keep on telling you—Miss Schlegel—she's got it—your mother's left it to her—and you've all got to move out!"

"*Howards End?*"

"*Howards End!*" she screamed, mimicking him, and as she did so Evie came dashing out of the shubbery.

"Dolly, go back at once! My father's much annoyed with you. Charles"—she hit herself wildly—"come in at once to father. He's had a letter that's too awful."

Charles began to run, but checked himself, and stepped heavily across the gravel path. There the house was—the nine windows, the unprolific vine. He exclaimed, "Schlegels again!" and as if to complete chaos, Dolly said, "Oh no, the matron of the nursing home has written instead of her."

"Come in, all three of you!" cried his father, no longer inert. "Dolly, why have you disobeyed me?"

"Oh, Mr. Wilcox——"

"I told you not to go out to the garage. I've heard you all shouting in the garden. I won't have it. Come in."

He stood in the porch, transformed, letters in his hand.

"Into the dining-room, every one of you. We can't discuss private matters in the middle of all the servants. Here, Charles, here; read these. See what you make."

6. Spare tire.

Charles took two letters, and read them as he followed the procession. The first was a covering note from the matron. Mrs. Wilcox had desired her, when the funeral should be over, to forward the enclosed. The enclosed—it was from his mother herself. She had written: "To my husband: I should like Miss Schlegel (Margaret) to have Howards End."

"I suppose we're going to have a talk about this?" he remarked, ominously calm.

"Certainly. I was coming out to you when Dolly——"

"Well, let's sit down."

"Come, Evie, don't waste time, sit down."

In silence they drew up to the breakfast-table. The events of yesterday—indeed, of this morning—suddenly receded into a past so remote that they seemed scarcely to have lived in it. Heavy breathings were heard. They were calming themselves. Charles, to steady them further, read the enclosure out loud: "A note in my mother's handwriting, in an envelope addressed to my father, sealed. Inside: 'I should like Miss Schlegel (Margaret) to have Howards End.' No date, no signature. Forwarded through the matron of that nursing home. Now, the question is——"

Dolly interrupted him. "But I say that note isn't legal. Houses ought to be done by a lawyer, Charles, surely."

Her husband worked his jaw severely. Little lumps appeared in front of either ear—a symptom that she had not yet learnt to respect, and she asked whether she might see the note. Charles looked at his father for permission, who said abstractedly, "Give it her." She seized it, and at once exclaimed: "Why, it's only in pencil! I said so. Pencil never counts."

"We know that it is not legally binding, Dolly," said Mr. Wilcox, speaking from out of his fortress. "We are aware of that. Legally, I should be justified in tearing it up and throwing it into the fire. Of course, my dear, we consider you as one of the family, but it will be better if you do not interfere with what you do not understand."

Charles, vexed both with his father and his wife, then repeated: "The question is——" He had cleared a space of the breakfast-table from plates and knives, so that he could draw patterns on the tablecloth. "The question is whether Miss Schlegel, during the fortnight we were all away, whether she unduly——" He stopped.

"I don't think that," said his father, whose nature was nobler than his son's.

"Don't think what?"

"That she would have—that it is a case of undue influence. No, to my mind the question is the—the invalid's condition at the time she wrote."

"My dear father, consult an expert if you like, but I don't admit it is my mother's writing."

"Why, you just said it was!" cried Dolly.

"Never mind if I did," he blazed out; "and hold your tongue."

The poor little wife coloured at this, and, drawing her handkerchief from her pocket, shed a few tears. No one noticed her. Evie was scowling like an angry boy. The two men were gradually assuming the manner of the committee-room. They were both at their best when serving on committees. They did not make the mistake of handling human affairs in the bulk, but disposed of them item by item, sharply. Caligraphy was the item before them now, and on it they turned their well-trained brains. Charles, after a little demur, accepted the writing as genuine, and they passed on to the next point. It is the best—perhaps the only—way of dodging emotion. They were the average human article, and had they considered the note as a whole it would have driven them miserable or mad. Considered item by item, the emotional content was minimized, and all went forward smoothly. The clock ticked, the coals blazed higher, and contended with the white radiance that poured in through the windows. Unnoticed, the sun occupied his sky, and the shadows of the tree stems, extraordinarily solid, fell like trenches of purple across the frosted lawn. It was a glorious winter morning. Evie's fox terrier, who had passed for white, was only a dirty grey dog now, so intense was the purity that surrounded him. He was discredited, but the blackbirds that he was chasing glowed with Arabian darkness, for all the conventional colouring of life had been altered. Inside, the clock struck ten with a rich and confident note. Other clocks confirmed it, and the discussion moved towards its close.

To follow it is unnecessary. It is rather a moment when the commentator should step forward. Ought the Wilcoxes to have offered their home to Margaret? I think not. The appeal was too flimsy. It was not legal; it had been written in illness, and under the spell of a sudden friendship; it was contrary to the dead woman's intentions in the past, contrary to her very nature, so far as that nature was understood by them. To them Howards End was a house: they could not know that to her it had been a spirit, for which she sought a spiritual heir. And—pushing one step farther in these mists—may they not have decided even better than they supposed? Is it credible that the possessions of the spirit can be bequeathed at all? Has the soul offspring? A wych-elm tree, a vine, a wisp of hay with dew on it—can passion for such things be transmitted where there is no bond of blood? No; the Wilcoxes are not to be blamed. The problem is too terrific, and they could not even perceive a problem. No; it is natural and fitting that after due debate they should tear the note up and throw it on to their dining-room fire. The practical moralist may acquit them absolutely. He who strives to look deeper may acquit them—almost. For one hard fact remains. They did neglect a personal appeal. The woman who had died did say to them, "Do this," and they answered, "We will not."

The incident made a most painful impression on them. Grief mounted into the brain and worked there disquietingly. Yesterday they had

lamented: "She was a dear mother, a true wife: in our absence she
neglected her health and died." To-day they thought: "She was not as
true, as dear, as we supposed." The desire for a more inward light had
found expression at last, the unseen had impacted on the seen, and all
that they could say was "Treachery." Mrs. Wilcox had been treacherous
to the family, to the laws of property, to her own written word. How did
she expect Howards End to be conveyed to Miss Schlegel? Was her husband, to whom it legally belonged, to make it over to her as a free gift?
Was the said Miss Schlegel to have a life interest in it, or to own it
absolutely? Was there to be no compensation for the garage and other
improvements that they had made under the assumption that all would
be theirs some day? Treacherous! treacherous and absurd! When we
think the dead both treacherous and absurd, we have gone far towards
reconciling ourselves to their departure. That note, scribbled in pencil,
sent through the matron, was unbusinesslike as well as cruel, and de-
creased at once the value of the woman who had written it.

"Ah, well!" said Mr. Wilcox, rising from the table. "I shouldn't have
thought it possible."

"Mother couldn't have meant it," said Evie, still frowning.

"No, my girl, of course not."

"Mother believed so in ancestors too—it isn't like her to leave anything to an outsider, who'd never appreciate."

"The whole thing is unlike her," he announced. "If Miss Schlegel had
been poor, if she had wanted a house, I could understand it a little. But
she has a house of her own. Why should she want another? She wouldn't
have any use for Howards End."

"That time may prove," murmured Charles.

"How?" asked his sister.

"Presumably she knows—mother will have told her. She got twice or
three times into the nursing home. Presumably she is awaiting developments."

"What a horrid woman!" And Dolly, who had recovered, cried, "Why,
she may be coming down to turn us out now!"

Charles put her right. "I wish she would," he said ominously. "I could
then deal with her."

"So could I," echoed his father, who was feeling rather in the cold.
Charles had been kind in undertaking the funeral arrangements and in
telling him to eat his breakfast, but the boy as he grew up was a little dic-
tatorial, and assumed the post of chairman too readily. "I could deal with
her, if she comes, but she won't come. You're all a bit hard on Miss
Schlegel."

"That Paul business was pretty scandalous, though."

"I want no more of the Paul business, Charles, as I said at the time,
and besides, it is quite apart from this business. Margaret Schlegel has
been officious and tiresome during this terrible week, and we have all

suffered under her, but upon my soul she's honest. She's *not* in collusion with the matron. I'm absolutely certain of it. Nor was she with the doctor, I'm equally certain of that. She did not hide anything from us, for up to that very afternoon she was as ignorant as we are. She, like ourselves, was a dupe——" He stopped for a moment. "You see, Charles, in her terrible pain your poor mother put us all in false positions. Paul would not have left England, you would not have gone to Italy, nor Evie and I into Yorkshire, if only we had known. Well, Miss Schlegel's position has been equally false. Take all in all, she has not come out of it badly."

Evie said: "But those chrysanthemums——"

"Or coming down to the funeral at all——" echoed Dolly.

"Why shouldn't she come down? She had the right to, and she stood far back among the Hilton women. The flowers—certainly we should not have sent such flowers, but they may have seemed the right thing to her, Evie, and for all you know they may be the custom in Germany."

"Oh, I forget she isn't really English," cried Evie. "That would explain a lot."

"She's a cosmopolitan," said Charles, looking at his watch. "I admit I'm rather down on cosmopolitans. My fault, doubtless. I cannot stand them, and a German cosmopolitan is the limit. I think that's about all, isn't it? I want to run down and see Chalkeley. A bicycle will do. And, by the way, I wish you'd speak to Crane some time. I'm certain he's had my new car out."

"Has he done it any harm?"

"No."

"In that case I shall let it pass. It's not worth while having a row."

Charles and his father sometimes disagreed. But they always parted with an increased regard for one another, and each desired no doughtier[7] comrade when it was necessary to voyage for a little past the emotions. So the sailors of Ulysses voyaged past the Sirens, having first stopped one another's ears with wool.[8]

Chapter XII

Charles need not have been anxious. Miss Schlegel had never heard of his mother's strange request. She was to hear of it in after years, when she had built up her life differently, and it was to fit into position as the headstone of the corner. Her mind was bent on other questions now, and by her also it would have been rejected as the fantasy of an invalid.

She was parting from these Wilcoxes for the second time. Paul and his mother, ripple and great wave, had flowed into her life and ebbed out of

7. More loyal, more courageous.
8. The hero of Homer's *Odyssey* had his crew plug their ears and tie him to a mast so that he could hear the seductive singing of these mythological women who drove sailors to their death.

it for ever. The ripple had left no traces behind: the wave had strewn at her feet fragments torn from the unknown. A curious seeker, she stood for a while at the verge of the sea that tells so little, but tells a little, and watched the outgoing of this last tremendous tide. Her friend had vanished in agony, but not, she believed, in degradation. Her withdrawal had hinted at other things besides disease and pain. Some leave our life with tears, others with an insane frigidity; Mrs. Wilcox had taken the middle course, which only rarer natures can pursue. She had kept proportion. She had told a little of her grim secret to her friends, but not too much; she had shut up her heart—almost, but not entirely. It is thus, if there is any rule, that we ought to die—neither as victim nor as fanatic, but as the seafarer who can greet with an equal eye the deep that he is entering, and the shore that he must leave.

The last word—whatever it would be—had certainly not been said in Hilton churchyard. She had not died there. A funeral is not death, any more than baptism is birth or marriage union. All three are the clumsy devices, coming now too late, now too early, by which Society would register the quick motions of man. In Margaret's eyes Mrs. Wilcox had escaped registration. She had gone out of life vividly, her own way, and no dust was so truly dust as the contents of that heavy coffin, lowered with ceremonial until it rested on the dust of the earth, no flowers so utterly wasted as the chrysanthemums that the frost must have withered before morning. Margaret had once said she "loved superstition." It was not true. Few women had tried more earnestly to pierce the accretions in which body and soul are enwrapped. The death of Mrs. Wilcox had helped her in her work. She saw a little more clearly than hitherto what a human being is, and to what he may aspire. Truer relationships gleamed. Perhaps the last word would be hope—hope even on this side of the grave.

Meanwhile, she could take an interest in the survivors. In spite of her Christmas duties, in spite of her brother, the Wilcoxes continued to play a considerable part in her thoughts. She had seen so much of them in the final week. They were not "her sort," they were often suspicious and stupid, and deficient where she excelled; but collision with them stimulated her, and she felt an interest that verged into liking, even for Charles. She desired to protect them, and often felt that they could protect her, excelling where she was deficient. Once past the rocks of emotion, they knew so well what to do, whom to send for; their hands were on all the ropes, they had grit as well as grittiness, and she valued grit enormously. They led a life that she could not attain to—the outer life of "telegrams and anger," which had detonated when Helen and Paul had touched in June, and had detonated again the other week. To Margaret this life was to remain a real force. She could not despise it, as Helen and Tibby affected to do. It fostered such virtues as neatness, decision, and obedience, virtues of the second rank, no doubt, but they have formed our civilization. They form character, too; Margaret could not doubt it: they keep the soul from becoming sloppy. How dare Schlegels despise Wilcoxes, when it takes all sorts to make a world?

"Don't brood too much," she wrote to Helen, "on the superiority of the unseen to the seen. It's true, but to brood on it is medieval. Our business is not to contrast the two, but to reconcile them."

Helen replied that she had no intention of brooding on such a dull subject. What did her sister take her for? The weather was magnificent. She and the Mosebachs had gone tobogganing on the only hill that Pomerania[1] boasted. It was fun, but overcrowded, for the rest of Pomerania had gone there too. Helen loved the country, and her letter glowed with physical exercise and poetry. She spoke of the scenery, quiet, yet august; of the snow-clad fields, with their scampering herds of deer; of the river and its quaint entrance into the Baltic Sea; of the Oderberge,[2] only three hundred feet high, from which one slid all too quickly back into the Pomeranian plains, and yet these Oderberge were real mountains, with pine-forests, streams, and views complete. "It isn't size that counts so much as the way things are arranged." In another paragraph she referred to Mrs. Wilcox sympathetically, but the news had not bitten into her. She had not realized the accessories of death, which are in a sense more memorable than death itself. The atmosphere of precautions and recriminations, and in the midst a human body growing more vivid because it was in pain; the end of that body in Hilton churchyard; the survival of something that suggested hope, vivid in its turn against life's workaday cheerfulness; — all these were lost to Helen, who only felt that a pleasant lady could now be pleasant no longer. She returned to Wickham Place full of her own affairs — she had had another proposal — and Margaret, after a moment's hesitation, was content that this should be so.

The proposal had not been a serious matter. It was the work of Fräulein Mosebach, who had conceived the large and patriotic notion of winning back her cousins to the Fatherland by matrimony. England had played Paul Wilcox, and lost; Germany played Herr Förstmeister[3] someone — Helen could not remember his name. Herr Förstmeister lived in a wood, and, standing on the summit of the Oderberge, he had pointed out his house to Helen, or rather, had pointed out the wedge of pines in which it lay. She had exclaimed, "Oh, how lovely! That's the place for me!" and in the evening Frieda appeared in her bedroom. "I have a message, dear Helen," etc., and so she had, but had been very nice when Helen laughed; quite understood — a forest too solitary and damp — quite agreed, but Herr Förstmeister believed he had assurance to the contrary. Germany had lost, but with good-humour; holding the manhood of the world, she felt bound to win. "And there will even be someone for Tibby," concluded

1. Northern seacoast province of eastern Germany.
2. Mountains near the Oder River.
3. Chief forester.

Helen. "There now, Tibby, think of that; Frieda is saving up a little girl for you, in pig-tails and white worsted stockings, but the feet of the stockings are pink, as if the little girl had trodden in strawberries. I've talked too much. My head aches. Now you talk."

Tibby consented to talk. He too was full of his own affairs, for he had just been up to try for a scholarship at Oxford. The men were down,[4] and the candidates had been housed in various colleges, and had dined in hall. Tibby was sensitive to beauty, the experience was new, and he gave a description of his visit that was almost glowing. The august and mellow University, soaked with the richness of the western counties that it has served for a thousand years, appealed at once to the boy's taste: it was the kind of thing he could understand, and he understood it all the better because it was empty. Oxford is—Oxford: not a mere receptacle for youth, like Cambridge. Perhaps it wants its inmates to love it rather than to love one another: such at all events was to be its effect on Tibby. His sisters sent him there that he might make friends, for they knew that his education had been cranky, and had severed him from other boys and men. He made no friends. His Oxford remained Oxford empty, and he took into life with him, not the memory of a radiance, but the memory of a colour scheme.

It pleased Margaret to hear her brother and sister talking. They did not get on overwell as a rule. For a few moments she listened to them, feeling elderly and benign. Then something occurred to her, and she interrupted:

"Helen, I told you about poor Mrs. Wilcox; that sad business?"

"Yes."

"I have had a correspondence with her son. He was winding up the estate, and wrote to ask me whether his mother had wanted me to have anything. I thought it good of him, considering I knew her for so little. I said that she had once spoken of giving me a Christmas present, but we both forgot about it afterwards."

"I hope Charles took the hint."

"Yes—that is to say, her husband wrote later on, and thanked me for being a little kind to her, and actually gave me her silver vinaigrette. Don't you think that is extraordinarily generous? It has made me like him very much. He hopes that this will not be the end of our acquaintance, but that you and I will go and stop with Evie some time in the future. I like Mr. Wilcox. He is taking up his work—rubber—it is a big business. I gather he is launching out rather. Charles is in it, too. Charles is married—a pretty little creature, but she doesn't seem wise. They took on the flat, but now they have gone off to a house of their own."

Helen, after a decent pause, continued her account of Stettin. How quickly a situation changes! In June she had been in a crisis; even in

4. The regular students were on vacation.

November she could blush and be unnatural; now it was January, and the whole affair lay forgotten. Looking back on the past six months, Margaret realized the chaotic nature of our daily life, and its difference from the orderly sequence that has been fabricated by historians. Actual life is full of false clues and sign-posts that lead nowhere. With infinite effort we nerve ourselves for a crisis that never comes. The most successful career must show a waste of strength that might have removed mountains, and the most unsuccessful is not that of the man who is taken unprepared, but of him who has prepared and is never taken. On a tragedy of that kind our national morality is duly silent. It assumes that preparation against danger is in itself a good, and that men, like nations, are the better for staggering through life fully armed. The tragedy of preparedness has scarcely been handled, save by the Greeks. Life is indeed dangerous, but not in the way morality would have us believe. It is indeed unmanageable, but the essence of it is not a battle. It is unmanageable because it is a romance, and its essence is romantic beauty.

Margaret hoped that for the future she would be less cautious, not more cautious, than she had been in the past.

Chapter XIII

Over two years passed, and the Schlegel household continued to lead its life of cultured, but not ignoble, ease, still swimming gracefully on the grey tides of London. Concerts and plays swept past them, money had been spent and renewed, reputations won and lost, and the city herself, emblematic of their lives, rose and fell in a continual flux, while her shallows washed more widely against the hills of Surrey and over the fields of Hertfordshire. This famous building had arisen, that was doomed. To-day Whitehall had been transformed: it would be the turn of Regent Street to-morrow. And month by month the roads smelt more strongly of petrol, and were more difficult to cross, and human beings heard each other speak with greater difficulty, breathed less of the air, and saw less of the sky. Nature withdrew: the leaves were falling by midsummer; the sun shone through dirt with an admired obscurity.

To speak against London is no longer fashionable. The Earth as an artistic cult has had its day, and the literature of the near future will probably ignore the country and seek inspiration from the town. One can understand the reaction. Of Pan[1] and the elemental forces, the public has heard a little too much—they seem Victorian, while London is Georgian[2]—and those who care for the earth with sincerity may wait long ere the pendulum swings back to her again. Certainly London fascinates. One visualizes it as a tract of quivering grey, intelligent without

1. The Greek god of forests and pastures, half man and half goat.
2. Queen Victoria ruled from 1837 to 1901, King George V (her grandson) from 1910 to 1936. In 1910 things Victorian would have seemed old-fashioned, things Georgian—modern.

purpose, and excitable without love; as a spirit that has altered before it can be chronicled; as a heart that certainly beats, but with no pulsation of humanity. It lies beyond everything: Nature, with all her cruelty, comes nearer to us than do these crowds of men. A friend explains himself: the earth is explicable—from her we came, and we must return to her. But who can explain Westminster Bridge Road or Liverpool Street in the morning—the city inhaling—or the same thoroughfares in the evening—the city exhaling her exhausted air? We reach in desperation beyond the fog, beyond the very stars, the voids of the universe are ransacked to justify the monster, and stamped with a human face. London is religion's opportunity—not the decorous religion of theologians, but anthropomorphic, crude. Yes, the continuous flow would be tolerable if a man of our own sort—not anyone pompous or tearful—were caring for us up in the sky.

The Londoner seldom understands his city until it sweeps him, too, away from his moorings, and Margaret's eyes were not opened until the lease of Wickham Place expired. She had always known that it must expire, but the knowledge only became vivid about nine months before the event. Then the house was suddenly ringed with pathos. It had seen so much happiness. Why had it to be swept away? In the streets of the city she noted for the first time the architecture of hurry, and heard the language of hurry on the mouths of its inhabitants—clipped words, formless sentences, potted expressions of approval or disgust. Month by month things were stepping livelier, but to what goal? The population still rose, but what was the quality of the men born? The particular millionaire who owned the freehold of Wickham Place, and desired to erect Babylonian[3] flats upon it—what right had he to stir so large a portion of the quivering jelly? He was not a fool—she had heard him expose Socialism—but true insight began just where his intelligence ended, and one gathered that this was the case with most millionaires. What right had such men—— But Margaret checked herself. That way lies madness. Thank goodness she, too, had some money, and could purchase a new home.

Tibby, now in his second year at Oxford, was down for the Easter vacation, and Margaret took the opportunity of having a serious talk with him. Did he at all know where he wanted to live? Tibby didn't know that he did know. Did he at all know what he wanted to do? He was equally uncertain, but when pressed remarked that he should prefer to be quite free of any profession. Margaret was not shocked, but went on sewing for a few minutes before she replied:

"I was thinking of Mr. Vyse. He never strikes me as particularly happy."

"Ye-es," said Tibby, and then held his mouth open in a curious quiver,

3. Decadent, sinful.

as if he, too, had thought of Mr. Vyse, had seen round, through, over, and beyond Mr. Vyse, had weighed Mr. Vyse, grouped him, and finally dismissed him as having no possible bearing on the subject under discussion. That bleat of Tibby's infuriated Helen. But Helen was now down in the dining-room preparing a speech about political economy. At times her voice could be heard declaiming through the floor.

"But Mr. Vyse is rather a wretched, weedy man, don't you think? Then there's Guy. That was a pitiful business. Besides"—shifting to the general—"everyone is the better for some regular work."

Groans.

"I shall stick to it," she continued, smiling. "I am not saying it to educate you; it is what I really think. I believe that in the last century men have developed the desire for work, and they must not starve it. It's a new desire. It goes with a great deal that's bad, but in itself it's good, and I hope that for women, too, 'not to work' will soon become as shocking as 'not to be married' was a hundred years ago."

"I have no experience of this profound desire to which you allude," enunciated Tibby.

"Then we'll leave the subject till you do. I'm not going to rattle you round. Take your time. Only do think over the lives of the men you like most, and see how they've arranged them."

"I like Guy and Mr. Vyse most," said Tibby faintly, and leant so far back in his chair that he extended in a horizontal line from knees to throat.

"And don't think I'm not serious because I don't use the traditional arguments—making money, a sphere awaiting you, and so on—all of which are, for various reasons, cant." She sewed on. "I'm only your sister. I haven't any authority over you, and I don't want to have any. Just to put before you what I think the truth. You see"—she shook off the pince-nez to which she had recently taken—"in a few years we shall be the same age practically, and I shall want you to help me. Men are so much nicer than women."

"Labouring under such a delusion, why do you not marry?"

"I sometimes jolly well think I would if I got the chance."

"Has no body arst you?"

"Only ninnies."

"Do people ask Helen?"

"Plentifully."

"Tell me about them."

"No."

"Tell me about your ninnies, then."

"They were men who had nothing better to do," said his sister, feeling that she was entitled to score this point. "So take warning: you must work, or else you must pretend to work, which is what I do. Work, work, work if you'd save your soul and your body. It is honestly a necessity, dear boy. Look at the Wilcoxes, look at Mr. Pembroke. With all their defects of temper and understanding, such men give me more pleasure than many who are better equipped, and I think it is because they have worked regularly and honestly."

"Spare me the Wilcoxes," he moaned.

"I shall not. They are the right sort."

"Oh, goodness me, Meg!" he protested, suddenly sitting up, alert and angry. Tibby, for all his defects, had a genuine personality.

"Well, they're as near the right sort as you can imagine."

"No, no—oh, no!"

"I was thinking of the younger son, whom I once classed as a ninny, but who came back so ill from Nigeria. He's gone out there again, Evie Wilcox tells me—out to his duty."

'Duty' always elicited a groan.

"He doesn't want the money, it is work he wants, though it is beastly work—dull country, dishonest natives, an eternal fidget over fresh water and food. A nation who can produce men of that sort may well be proud. No wonder England has become an Empire."

"*Empire!*"

"I can't bother over results," said Margaret, a little sadly. "They are too difficult for me. I can only look at the men. An Empire bores me, so far, but I can appreciate the heroism that builds it up. London bores me, but what thousands of splendid people are labouring to make London——"

"What it is," he sneered.

"What it is, worse luck. I want activity without civilization. How paradoxical! Yet I expect that is what we shall find in heaven."

"And I," said Tibby, "want civilization without activity, which, I expect, is what we shall find in the other place."

"You needn't go as far as the other place, Tibbikins, if you want that. You can find it at Oxford."

"Stupid——"

"If I'm stupid, get me back to the house-hunting. I'll even live in Oxford if you like—North Oxford. I'll live anywhere except Bournemouth, Torquay, and Cheltenham. Oh yes, or Ilfracombe and Swanage and Tunbridge Wells and Surbiton and Bedford. There on no account."

"London, then."

"I agree, but Helen rather wants to get away from London. However, there's no reason we shouldn't have a house in the country and also a flat in town, provided we all stick together and contribute. Though of course—— Oh, how one does maunder on, and to think, to think of the people who are really poor. How do they live? Not to move about the world would kill me."

As she spoke, the door was flung open, and Helen burst in in a state of extreme excitement.

"Oh, my dears, what do you think? You'll never guess. A woman's been here asking me for her husband. Her *what*?" (Helen was fond of supplying her own surprise.) "Yes, for her husband, and it really is so."

"Not anything to do with Bracknell?" cried Margaret, who had lately taken on an unemployed of that name to clean the knives and boots.

"I offered Bracknell, and he was rejected. So was Tibby. (Cheer up, Tibby!) It's no one we know. I said, 'Hunt, my good woman; have a good look round, hunt under the tables, poke up the chimney, shake out the antimacassars. Husband? husband?' Oh, and she so magnificently dressed and tinkling like a chandelier."

"Now, Helen, what did happen really?"

"What I say. I was, as it were, orating my speech. Annie opens the door like a fool, and shows a female straight in on me, with my mouth open. Then we began—very civilly. 'I want my husband, what I have reason to believe is here.' No—how unjust one is. She said 'whom,' not 'what.' She got it perfectly. So I said, 'Name, please?' and she said, 'Lan, Miss,' and there we were."

"Lan?"

"Lan or Len. We were not nice about our vowels. Lanoline."

"But what an extraordinary——"

"I said, 'My good Mrs. Lanoline, we have some grave misunderstanding here. Beautiful as I am, my modesty is even more remarkable than my beauty, and never, never has Mr. Lanoline rested his eyes on mine.'"

"I hope you were pleased," said Tibby.

"Of course," Helen squeaked. "A perfectly delightful experience. Oh, Mrs. Lanoline's a dear—she asked for a husband as if he was an umbrella. She mislaid him Saturday afternoon—and for a long time suffered no inconvenience. But all night, and all this morning her apprehensions grew. Breakfast didn't seem the same—no, no more did lunch, and so she strolled up to 2, Wickham Place as being the most likely place for the missing article."

"But how on earth——"

"Don't begin how on earthing. 'I know what I know,' she kept repeating, not uncivilly, but with extreme gloom. In vain I asked her what she did know. Some knew what others knew, and others didn't, and if they didn't, then others again had better be careful. Oh dear, she was incompetent! She had a face like a silkworm, and the dining-room reeks of orris-root.[4] We chatted pleasantly a little about husbands, and I wondered where hers was too, and advised her to go to the police. She thanked me. We agreed that Mr. Lanoline's a notty, notty man, and hasn't no business to go on the lardy-da. But I think she suspected me up to the last. Bags I writing to Aunt Juley about this. Now, Meg, remember—bags I."[5]

4. Perfume.
5. Slang for laying claim to something: "I get to tell this to Aunt Juley."

"Bag it by all means," murmured Margaret, putting down her work. "I'm not sure that this is so funny, Helen. It means some horrible volcano smoking somewhere, doesn't it?"

"I don't think so—she doesn't really mind. The admirable creature isn't capable of tragedy."

"Her husband may be, though," said Margaret, moving to the window.

"Oh no, not likely. No one capable of tragedy could have married Mrs. Lanoline."

"Was she pretty?"

"Her figure may have been good once."

The flats, their only outlook, hung like an ornate curtain between Margaret and the welter of London. Her thoughts turned sadly to house-hunting. Wickham Place had been so safe. She feared, fantastically, that her own little flock might be moving into turmoil and squalor, into nearer contact with such episodes as these.

"Tibby and I have again been wondering where we'll live next September," she said at last.

"Tibby had better first wonder what he'll do," retorted Helen; and that topic was resumed, but with acrimony. Then tea came, and after tea Helen went on preparing her speech, and Margaret prepared one, too, for they were going out to a discussion society on the morrow. But her thoughts were poisoned. Mrs. Lanoline had risen out of the abyss, like a faint smell, a goblin footfall, telling of a life where love and hatred had both decayed.

Chapter XIV

The mystery, like so many mysteries, was explained. Next day, just as they were dressed to go out to dinner, a Mr. Bast called. He was a clerk in the employment of the Porphyrion[1] Fire Insurance Company. Thus much from his card. He had come "about the lady yesterday." Thus much from Annie, who had shown him into the dining-room.

"Cheers, children!" cried Helen. "It's Mr. Lanoline."

Even Tibby was interested. The three hurried downstairs, to find, not the gay dog they expected, but a young man, colourless, toneless, who had already the mournful eyes above a drooping moustache that are so common in London, and that haunt some streets of the city like accusing presences. One guessed him as the third generation, grandson to the shepherd or ploughboy whom civilization had sucked into the town; as one of the thousands who have lost the life of the body and failed to reach the life of the spirit. Hints of robustness survived in him, more

---

1. In Greek mythology, Porphyrion is a figure of upheaval, a giant who attempts to ravish Hera, the queen of the heavens (divinity of fertility and childbirth), and is slain by her brother-husband Zeus.

than a hint of primitive good looks, and Margaret, noting the spine that might have been straight, and the chest that might have broadened, wondered whether it paid to give up the glory of the animal for a tail coat and a couple of ideas. Culture had worked in her own case, but during the last few weeks she had doubted whether it humanized the majority, so wide and so widening is the gulf that stretches between the natural and the philosophic man, so many the good chaps who are wrecked in trying to cross it. She knew this type very well—the vague aspirations, the mental dishonesty, the familiarity with the outsides of books. She knew the very tones in which he would address her. She was only unprepared for an example of her own visiting-card.

"You wouldn't remember giving me this, Miss Schlegel?" said he, uneasily familiar.

"No; I can't say I do."

"Well, that was how it happened, you see."

"Where did we meet, Mr. Bast? For the minute I don't remember."

"It was a concert at the Queen's Hall. I think you will recollect," he added pretentiously, "when I tell you that it included a performance of the Fifth Symphony of Beethoven."

"We hear the Fifth practically every time it's done, so I'm not sure— do you remember, Helen?"

"Was it the time the sandy cat walked round the balustrade?"

He thought not.

"Then I don't remember. That's the only Beethoven I ever remember specially."

"And you, if I may say so, took away my umbrella, inadvertently of course."

"Likely enough," Helen laughed, "for I steal umbrellas even oftener than I hear Beethoven. Did you get it back?"

"Yes, thank you, Miss Schlegel."

"The mistake arose out of my card, did it?" interposed Margaret.

"Yes, the mistake arose—it was a mistake."

"The lady who called here yesterday thought that you were calling too, and that she could find you?" she continued, pushing him forward, for, though he had promised an explanation, he seemed unable to give one.

"That's so, calling too—a mistake."

"Then why——?" began Helen, but Margaret laid a hand on her arm.

"I said to my wife," he continued more rapidly—"I said to Mrs. Bast, 'I have to pay a call on some friends,' and Mrs. Bast said to me, 'Do go.' While I was gone, however, she wanted me on important business, and thought I had come here, owing to the card, and so came after me, and I beg to tender my apologies, and hers as well, for any inconvenience we may have inadvertently caused you."

"No inconvenience," said Helen; "but I still don't understand."

An air of evasion characterized Mr. Bast. He explained again, but was obviously lying, and Helen didn't see why he should get off. She had the cruelty of youth. Neglecting her sister's pressure, she said, "I still don't understand. When did you say you paid this call?"

"Call? What call?" said he, staring as if her question had been a foolish one, a favourite device of those in mid-stream.

"This afternoon call."

"In the afternoon, of course!" he replied, and looked at Tibby to see how the repartee went. But Tibby, himself a repartee, was unsympathetic, and said, "Saturday afternoon or Sunday afternoon?"

"S—Saturday."

"Really!" said Helen; "and you were still calling on Sunday, when your wife came here. A long visit."

"I don't call that fair," said Mr. Bast, going scarlet and handsome. There was fight in his eyes. "I know what you mean, and it isn't so."

"Oh, don't let us mind," said Margaret, distressed again by odours from the abyss.

"It was something else," he asserted, his elaborate manner breaking down. "I was somewhere else to what you think, so there!"

"It was good of you to come and explain," she said. "The rest is naturally no concern of ours."

"Yes, but I want—I wanted—have you ever read 'The Ordeal of Richard Feverel'?"[2]

Margaret nodded.

"It's a beautiful book. I wanted to get back to the Earth, don't you see, like Richard does in the end. Or have you ever read Stevenson's 'Prince Otto'?"[3]

Helen and Tibby groaned gently.

"That's another beautiful book. You get back to the Earth in that. I wanted——" He mouthed affectedly. Then through the mists of his culture came a hard fact, hard as a pebble. "I walked all the Saturday night," said Leonard. "I walked." A thrill of approval ran through the sisters. But culture closed in again. He asked whether they had ever read E. V. Lucas's "Open Road."[4]

Said Helen, "No doubt it's another beautiful book, but I'd rather hear about your road."

"Oh, I walked."

"How far?"

"I don't know, nor for how long. It got too dark to see my watch."

"Were you walking alone, may I ask?"

"Yes," he said, straightening himself; "but we'd been talking it over

2. Novel by George Meredith (1828–1909) in which the hero spends a night walking through a forest.
3. Novel by Robert Louis Stevenson (1850–94) with many idealized celebrations of nature.
4. Edward Verrell Lucas (1868–1938), author of several travel books.

at the office. There's been a lot of talk at the office lately about these things. The fellows there said one steers by the Pole Star, and I looked it up in the celestial atlas, but once out of doors everything gets so mixed——"

"Don't talk to me about the Pole Star," interrupted Helen, who was becoming interested. "I know its little ways. It goes round and round, and you go round after it."

"Well, I lost it entirely. First of all the street lamps, then the trees, and towards morning it got cloudy."

Tibby, who preferred his comedy undiluted, slipped from the room. He knew that this fellow would never attain to poetry, and did not want to hear him trying. Margaret and Helen remained. Their brother influenced them more than they knew: in his absence they were stirred to enthusiasm more easily.

"Where did you start from?" cried Margaret. "Do tell us more."

"I took the Underground to Wimbledon. As I came out of the office I said to myself, 'I must have a walk once in a way. If I don't take this walk now, I shall never take it.' I had a bit of dinner at Wimbledon, and then——"

"But not good country there, is it?"

"It was gas-lamps for hours. Still, I had all the night, and being out was the great thing. I did get into woods, too, presently."

"Yes, go on," said Helen.

"You've no idea how difficult uneven ground is when it's dark."

"Did you actually go off the roads?"

"Oh yes. I always meant to go off the roads, but the worst of it is that it's more difficult to find one's way."

"Mr. Bast, you're a born adventurer," laughed Margaret. "No professional athlete would have attempted what you've done. It's a wonder your walk didn't end in a broken neck. Whatever did your wife say?"

"Professional athletes never move without lanterns and compasses," said Helen. "Besides, they can't walk. It tires them. Go on."

"I felt like R. L. S. You probably remember how in 'Virginibus——' "[5]

"Yes, but the wood. This 'ere wood. How did you get out of it?"

"I managed one wood, and found a road the other side which went a good bit uphill. I rather fancy it was those North Downs, for the road went off into grass, and I got into another wood. That was awful, with gorse bushes. I did wish I'd never come, but suddenly it got light—just while I seemed going under one tree. Then I found a road down to a station, and took the first train I could back to London."

"But was the dawn wonderful?" asked Helen.

With unforgettable sincerity he replied, "No." The word flew again like a pebble from the sling. Down toppled all that had seemed ignoble

5. Stevenson's *Virginibus Puerisque* (1881) includes the essay "Walking Tours."

or literary in his talk, down toppled tiresome R. L. S. and the "love of the earth" and his silk top-hat. In the presence of these women Leonard had arrived, and he spoke with a flow, an exultation, that he had seldom known.

"The dawn was only grey, it was nothing to mention——"

"Just a grey evening turned upside down. I know."

"—and I was too tired to lift up my head to look at it, and so cold too. I'm glad I did it, and yet at the time it bored me more than I can say. And besides—you can believe me or not as you choose—I was very hungry. That dinner at Wimbledon—I meant it to last me all night like other dinners. I never thought that walking would make such a difference. Why, when you're walking you want, as it were, a breakfast and luncheon and tea during the night as well, and I'd nothing but a packet of Woodbines.[6] Lord, I did feel bad! Looking back, it wasn't what you may call enjoyment. It was more a case of sticking to it. I did stick. I—I was determined. Oh, hang it all! what's the good—I mean, the good of living in a room for ever? There one goes on day after day, same old game, same up and down to town, until you forget there is any other game. You ought to see once in a way what's going on outside, if it's only nothing particular after all."

"I should just think you ought," said Helen, sitting on the edge of the table.

The sound of a lady's voice recalled him from sincerity, and he said: "Curious it should all come about from reading something of Richard Jefferies."[7]

"Excuse me, Mr. Bast, but you're wrong there. It didn't. It came from something far greater."

But she could not stop him. Borrow was imminent after Jefferies— Borrow, Thoreau, and sorrow.[8] R. L. S. brought up the rear, and the outburst ended in a swamp of books. No disrespect to these great names. The fault is ours, not theirs. They mean us to use them for sign-posts, and are not to blame if, in our weakness, we mistake the sign-post for the destination. And Leonard had reached the destination. He had visited the county of Surrey when darkness covered its amenities, and its cosy villas had re-entered ancient night. Every twelve hours this miracle happens, but he had troubled to go and see for himself. Within his cramped little mind dwelt something that was greater than Jefferies' books—the spirit that led Jefferies to write them; and his dawn, though revealing nothing but monotones, was part of the eternal sunrise that shows George Borrow Stonehenge.

6. Cigarettes.
7. Richard Jefferies (1848–87), naturalist and author of books about the English countryside.
8. George Henry Borrow (1803–81), English author and traveler, wrote extensively about his wanderings. Henry David Thoreau (1817–62), American writer and naturalist, celebrated the solitary life in harmony with nature.

"Then you don't think I was foolish?" he asked, becoming again the naïve and sweet-tempered boy for whom Nature had intended him.

"Heavens, no!" replied Margaret.

"Heaven help us if we do!" replied Helen.

"I'm very glad you say that. Now, my wife would never understand— not if I explained for days."

"No, it wasn't foolish!" cried Helen, her eyes aflame. "You've pushed back the boundaries; I think it splendid of you."

"You've not been content to dream as we have——"

"Though we have walked, too——"

"I must show you a picture upstairs——"

Here the door-bell rang. The hansom had come to take them to their evening party.

"Oh, bother, not to say dash—I had forgotten we were dining out; but do, do, come round again and have a talk."

"Yes, you must—do," echoed Margaret.

Leonard, with extreme sentiment, replied: "No, I shall not. It's better like this."

"Why better?" asked Margaret.

"No, it is better not to risk a second interview. I shall always look back on this talk with you as one of the finest things in my life. Really. I mean this. We can never repeat. It has done me real good, and there we had better leave it."

"That's rather a sad view of life, surely."

"Things so often get spoiled."

"I know," flashed Helen, "but people don't."

He could not understand this. He continued in a vein which min-gled true imagination and false. What he said wasn't wrong, but it wasn't right, and a false note jarred. One little twist, they felt, and the instrument might be in tune. One little strain, and it might be silent for ever. He thanked the ladies very much, but he would not call again. There was a moment's awkwardness, and then Helen said: "Go, then; perhaps you know best; but never forget you're better than Jefferies." And he went. Their hansom caught him up at the corner, passed with a waving of hands, and vanished with its accomplished load into the evening.

London was beginning to illuminate herself against the night. Electric lights sizzled and jagged in the main thoroughfares, gas-lamps in the side streets glimmered a canary gold or green. The sky was a crimson battlefield of spring, but London was not afraid. Her smoke mitigated the splendour, and the clouds down Oxford Street were a delicately painted ceiling, which adorned while it did not distract. She has never known the clear-cut armies of the purer air. Leonard hurried through her tinted wonders, very much part of the picture. His was a grey life, and to brighten it he had ruled off a few corners for Romance.

The Miss Schlegels—or, to speak more accurately, his interview with
them—were to fill such a corner, nor was it by any means the first time
that he had talked intimately to strangers. The habit was analogous to
a debauch, an outlet, though the worst of outlets, for instincts that
would not be denied. Terrifying him, it would beat down his suspicions
and prudence until he was confiding secrets to people whom he had
scarcely seen. It brought him many fears and some pleasant memories.
Perhaps the keenest happiness he had ever known was during a railway journey to Cambridge, where a decent-mannered undergraduate
had spoken to him. They had got into conversation, and gradually
Leonard flung reticence aside, told some of his domestic troubles, and
hinted at the rest. The undergraduate, supposing they could start a
friendship, asked him to "coffee after hall," which he accepted, but
afterwards grew shy, and took care not to stir from the commercial
hotel where he lodged. He did not want Romance to collide with the
Porphyrion, still less with Jacky, and people with fuller, happier lives
are slow to understand this. To the Schlegels, as to the undergraduate, he was an interesting creature, of whom they wanted to see more.
But they to him were denizens of Romance, who must keep to the corner he had assigned them, pictures that must not walk out of their
frames.

His behaviour over Margaret's visiting-card had been typical. His had
scarcely been a tragic marriage. Where there is no money and no inclination to violence tragedy cannot be generated. He could not leave his
wife, and he did not want to hit her. Petulance and squalor was
enough. Here "that card" had come in. Leonard, though furtive, was
untidy, and left it lying about. Jacky found it, and then began, "What's
that card, eh?" "Yes, don't you wish you knew what that card was?"
"Len, who's Miss Schlegel?" etc. Months passed, and the card, now as
a joke, now as a grievance, was handed about, getting dirtier and dirtier. It followed them when they moved from Camelia Road to Tulse
Hill. It was submitted to third parties. A few inches of pasteboard, it
became the battlefield on which the souls of Leonard and his wife contended. Why did he not say, "A lady took my umbrella, another gave
me this that I might call for my umbrella"? Because Jacky would have
disbelieved him? Partly, but chiefly because he was sentimental. No
affection gathered round the card, but it symbolized the life of culture,
that Jacky should never spoil. At night he would say to himself, "Well,
at all events, she doesn't know about that card. Yah! done her there!"

Poor Jacky! she was not a bad sort, and had a great deal to bear. She
drew her own conclusion—she was only capable of drawing one conclusion—and in the fulness of time she acted upon it. All the Friday
Leonard had refused to speak to her, and had spent the evening observing the stars. On the Saturday he went up, as usual, to town, but he
came not back Saturday night, nor Sunday morning, nor Sunday after-

noon. The inconvenience grew intolerable, and though she was now of a retiring habit, and shy of women, she went up to Wickham Place. Leonard returned in her absence. The card, the fatal card, was gone from the pages of Ruskin, and he guessed what had happened.

"Well?" he had exclaimed, greeting her with peals of laughter. "I know where you've been, but you don't know where I've been."

Jacky sighed, said, "Len, I do think you might explain," and resumed domesticity.

Explanations were difficult at this stage, and Leonard was too silly— or it is tempting to write, too sound a chap to attempt them. His reticence was not entirely the shoddy article that a business life promotes, the reticence that pretends that nothing is something, and hides behind the 'Daily Telegraph.' The adventurer, also, is reticent, and it is an adventure for a clerk to walk for a few hours in darkness. You may laugh at him, you who have slept nights out on the veldt,[9] with your rifle beside you and all the atmosphere of adventure pat. And you also may laugh who think adventures silly. But do not be surprised if Leonard is shy whenever he meets you, and if the Schlegels rather than Jacky hear about the dawn.

That the Schlegels had not thought him foolish became a permanent joy. He was at his best when he thought of them. It buoyed him as he journeyed home beneath fading heavens. Somehow the barriers of wealth had fallen, and there had been—he could not phrase it—a general assertion of the wonder of the world. "My conviction," says the mystic, "gains infinitely the moment another soul will believe in it,"[1] and they had agreed that there was something beyond life's daily grey. He took off his top-hat and smoothed it thoughtfully. He had hitherto supposed the unknown to be books, literature, clever conversation, culture. One raised oneself by study, and got upsides with the world. But in that quick interchange a new light dawned. Was that "something" walking in the dark among the suburban hills?

He discovered that he was going bareheaded down Regent Street. London came back with a rush. Few were about at this hour, but all whom he passed looked at him with a hostility that was the more impressive because it was unconscious. He put his hat on. It was too big; his head disappeared like a pudding into a basin, the ears bending outwards at the touch of the curly brim. He wore it a little backwards, and its effect was greatly to elongate the face and to bring out the distance between the eyes and the moustache. Thus equipped, he escaped criticism. No one felt uneasy as he titupped along the pavements, the heart of a man ticking fast in his chest.

9. Plains of South Africa.
1. A line from the German romantic poet Novalis (1772–1801), which Joseph Conrad uses as the epigraph to *Lord Jim* (1900).

Chapter XV

The sisters went out to dinner full of their adventure, and when they were both full of the same subject, there were few dinner-parties that could stand up against them. This particular one, which was all ladies, had more kick in it than most, but succumbed after a struggle. Helen at one part of the table, Margaret at the other, would talk of Mr. Bast and of no one else, and somewhere about the entrée their monologues collided, fell ruining, and became common property. Nor was this all. The dinner-party was really an informal discussion club; there was a paper after it, read amid coffee-cups and laughter in the drawing-room, but dealing more or less thoughtfully with some topic of general interest. After the paper came a debate, and in this debate Mr. Bast also figured, appearing now as a bright spot in civilization, now as a dark spot, according to the temperament of the speaker. The subject of the paper had been, "How ought I to dispose of my money?" the reader professing to be a millionaire on the point of death, inclined to bequeath her fortune for the foundation of local art galleries, but open to conviction from other sources. The various parts had been assigned beforehand, and some of the speeches were amusing. The hostess assumed the ungrateful rôle of 'the millionaire's eldest son,' and implored her expiring parent not to dislocate Society by allowing such vast sums to pass out of the family. Money was the fruit of self-denial, and the second generation had a right to profit by the self-denial of the first. What right had 'Mr. Bast' to profit? The National Gallery[1] was good enough for the likes of him. After property had had its say—a saying that is necessarily ungracious—the various philanthropists stepped forward. Something must be done for 'Mr. Bast': his conditions must be improved without impairing his independence; he must have a free library, or free tennis-courts; his rent must be paid in such a way that he did not know it was being paid; it must be made worth his while to join the Territorials;[2] he must be forcibly parted from his uninspiring wife, the money going to her as compensation; he must be assigned a Twin Star, some member of the leisured classes who would watch over him ceaselessly (groans from Helen); he must be given food but no clothes, clothes but no food, a third-return ticket to Venice, without either food or clothes when he arrived there. In short, he might be given anything and everything so long as it was not the money itself.

And here Margaret interrupted.

"Order, order, Miss Schlegel!" said the reader of the paper. "You are here, I understand, to advise me in the interests of the Society for the Preservation of Places of Historic Interest or Natural Beauty. I cannot

---

1. Public art museum in London.
2. Local militia, part of the British Territorial Army.

have you speaking out of your rôle. It makes my poor head go round, and I think you forget that I am very ill."

"Your head won't go round if only you'll listen to my argument," said Margaret. "Why not give him the money itself? You're supposed to have about thirty thousand a year."

"Have I? I thought I had a million."

"Wasn't a million your capital? Dear me! we ought to have settled that. Still, it doesn't matter. Whatever you've got, I order you to give as many poor men as you can three hundred a year each."

"But that would be pauperizing them," said an earnest girl, who liked the Schlegels, but thought them a little unspiritual at times.

"Not if you gave them so much. A big windfall would not pauperize a man. It is these little driblets, distributed among too many, that do the harm. Money's educational. It's far more educational than the things it buys." There was a protest. "In a sense," added Margaret, but the protest continued. "Well, isn't the most civilized thing going, the man who has learnt to wear his income properly?"

"Exactly what your Mr. Basts won't do."

"Give them a chance. Give them money. Don't dole them out poetry-books and railway-tickets like babies. Give them the wherewithal to buy these things. When your Socialism comes it may be different, and we may think in terms of commodities instead of cash. Till it comes give people cash, for it is the warp of civilization, whatever the woof may be. The imagination ought to play upon money and realize it vividly, for it's the—the second most important thing in the world. It is so slurred over and hushed up, there is so little clear thinking—oh, political economy, of course, but so few of us think clearly about our own private incomes, and admit that independent thoughts are in nine cases out of ten the result of independent means. Money: give Mr. Bast money, and don't bother about his ideals. He'll pick up those for himself."

She leant back while the more earnest members of the club began to misconstrue her. The female mind, though cruelly practical in daily life, cannot bear to hear ideals belittled in conversation, and Miss Schlegel was asked however she could say such dreadful things, and what it would profit Mr. Bast if he gained the whole world and lost his own soul. She answered, "Nothing, but he would not gain his soul until he had gained a little of the world." Then they said, "No, they did not believe it," and she admitted that an overworked clerk may save his soul in the superterrestrial sense, where the effort will be taken for the deed, but she denied that he will ever explore the spiritual resources of this world, will ever know the rarer joys of the body, or attain to clear and passionate intercourse with his fellows. Others had attacked the fabric of Society—Property, Interest, etc.; she only fixed her eyes on a few human beings, to see how, under present conditions, they could be made happier. Doing good to humanity was useless: the many-coloured efforts thereto spreading over the vast area like films and resulting in a universal grey. To do good to one, or, as in this case, to a few, was the utmost she dare hope for.

Between the idealists, and the political economists, Margaret had a bad time. Disagreeing elsewhere, they agreed in disowning her, and in keeping the administration of the millionaire's money in their own hands. The earnest girl brought forward a scheme of "personal supervision and mutual help," the effect of which was to alter poor people until they became exactly like people who were not so poor. The hostess pertinently remarked that she, as eldest son, might surely rank among the millionaire's legatees. Margaret weakly admitted the claim, and another claim was at once set up by Helen, who declared that she had been the millionaire's housemaid for over forty years, overfed and underpaid; was nothing to be done for her, so corpulent and poor? The millionaire then read out her last will and testament, in which she left the whole of her fortune to the Chancellor of the Exchequer.[3] Then she died. The serious parts of the discussion had been of higher merit than the playful—in a men's debate is the reverse more general?—but the meeting broke up hilariously enough, and a dozen happy ladies dispersed to their homes.

Helen and Margaret walked the earnest girl as far as Battersea Bridge Station, arguing copiously all the way. When she had gone they were conscious of an alleviation, and of the great beauty of the evening. They turned back towards Oakley Street. The lamps and the plane-trees, following the line of the embankment, struck a note of dignity that is rare in English cities. The seats, almost deserted, were here and there occupied by gentlefolk in evening dress, who had strolled out from the houses behind to enjoy fresh air and the whisper of the rising tide. There is something continental about Chelsea Embankment. It is an open space used rightly, a blessing more frequent in Germany than here. As Margaret and Helen sat down, the city behind them seemed to be a vast theatre, an opera-house in which some endless trilogy was performing, and they themselves a pair of satisfied subscribers, who did not mind losing a little of the second act.

"Cold?"

"No."

"Tired?"

"Doesn't matter."

The earnest girl's train rumbled away over the bridge.

"I say, Helen——"

"Well?"

"Are we really going to follow up Mr. Bast?"

"I don't know."

"I think we won't."

3. Comparable to the secretary of the treasury in the United States.

"As you like."

"It's no good, I think, unless you really mean to know people. The discussion brought that home to me. We got on well enough with him in a spirit of excitement, but think of rational intercourse. We mustn't play at friendship. No, it's no good."

"There's Mrs. Lanoline, too," Helen yawned. "So dull."

"Just so, and possibly worse than dull."

"I should like to know how he got hold of your card."

"But he said—something about a concert and an umbrella——"

"Then did the card see the wife——"

"Helen, come to bed."

"No, just a little longer, it is so beautiful. Tell me; oh yes; did you say money is the warp of the world?"

"Yes."

"Then what's the woof?"

"Very much what one chooses," said Margaret. "It's something that isn't money—one can't say more."

"Walking at night?"

"Probably."

"For Tibby, Oxford?"

"It seems so."

"For you?"

"Now that we have to leave Wickham Place, I begin to think it's that. For Mrs. Wilcox it was certainly Howards End."

One's own name will carry immense distances. Mr. Wilcox, who was sitting with friends many seats away, heard his, rose to his feet, and strolled along towards the speakers.

"It is sad to suppose that places may ever be more important than people," continued Margaret.

"Why, Meg? They're so much nicer generally. I'd rather think of that forester's house in Pomerania than of the fat Herr Förstmeister who lived in it."

"I believe we shall come to care about people less and less, Helen. The more people one knows the easier it becomes to replace them. It's one of the curses of London. I quite expect to end my life caring most for a place."

Here Mr. Wilcox reached them. It was several weeks since they had met.

"How do you do?" he cried. "I thought I recognized your voices. Whatever are you both doing down here?"

His tones were protective. He implied that one ought not to sit out on Chelsea Embankment without a male escort. Helen resented this, but Margaret accepted it as part of the good man's equipment.

"What an age it is since I've seen you, Mr. Wilcox. I met Evie in the Tube, though, lately. I hope you have good news of your son."

"Paul?" said Mr. Wilcox, extinguishing his cigarette, and sitting down between them. "Oh, Paul's all right. We had a line from Madeira.[4] He'll be at work again by now."

"Ugh——" said Helen, shuddering from complex causes.

"I beg your pardon?"

"Isn't the climate of Nigeria too horrible?"

"Someone's got to go," he said simply. "England will never keep her trade overseas unless she is prepared to make sacrifices. Unless we get firm in West Africa, Ger——[5] untold complications may follow. Now tell me all your news."

"Oh, we've had a splendid evening," cried Helen, who always woke up at the advent of a visitor. "We belong to a kind of club that reads papers, Margaret and I—all women, but there is a discussion after. This evening it was on how one ought to leave one's money—whether to one's family, or to the poor, and if so how—oh, most interesting."

The man of business smiled. Since his wife's death he had almost doubled his income. He was an important figure at last, a reassuring name on company prospectuses, and life had treated him very well. The world seemed in his grasp as he listened to the River Thames, which still flowed inland from the sea. So wonderful to the girls, it held no mysteries for him. He had helped to shorten its long tidal trough by taking shares in the lock at Teddington, and if he and other capitalists thought good, some day it could be shortened again. With a good dinner inside him and an amiable but academic woman on either flank, he felt that his hands were on all the ropes of life, and that what he did not know could not be worth knowing.

"Sounds a most original entertainment!" he exclaimed, and laughed in his pleasant way. "I wish Evie would go to that sort of thing. But she hasn't the time. She's taken to breed Aberdeen terriers—jolly little dogs."

"I expect we'd better be doing the same, really."

"We pretend we're improving ourselves, you see," said Helen a little sharply, for the Wilcox glamour is not of the kind that returns, and she had bitter memories of the days when a speech such as he had just made would have impressed her favourably. "We suppose it a good thing to waste an evening once a fortnight over a debate, but, as my sister says, it may be better to breed dogs."

"Not at all. I don't agree with your sister. There's nothing like a debate to teach one quickness. I often wish I had gone in for them when I was a youngster. It would have helped me no end."

"Quickness——?"

4. Portuguese island off the northwest coast of Africa.
5. Togoland and Cameroon, German colonies on either side of Nigeria, were among the African territories where Britain and Germany contested one another's imperial claims before World War I.

"Yes. Quickness in argument. Time after time I've missed scoring a point because the other man has had the gift of the gab and I haven't. Oh, I believe in these discussions."

The patronizing tone, thought Margaret, came well enough from a man who was old enough to be their father. She had always maintained that Mr. Wilcox had a charm. In times of sorrow or emotion his inadequacy had pained her, but it was pleasant to listen to him now, and to watch his thick brown moustache and high forehead confronting the stars. But Helen was nettled. The aim of *their* debates she implied was Truth.

"Oh yes, it doesn't much matter what subject you take," said he.

Margaret laughed and said, "But this is going to be far better than the debate itself." Helen recovered herself and laughed too. "No, I won't go on," she declared. "I'll just put our special case to Mr. Wilcox."

"About Mr. Bast? Yes, do. He'll be more lenient to a special case."

"But, Mr. Wilcox, do first light another cigarette. It's this. We've just come across a young fellow, who's evidently very poor, and who seems interest——"

"What's his profession?"

"Clerk."

"What in?"

"Do you remember, Margaret?"

"Porphyrion Fire Insurance Company."

"Oh yes; the nice people who gave Aunt Juley a new hearth-rug. He seems interesting, in some ways very, and one wishes one could help him. He is married to a wife whom he doesn't seem to care for much. He likes books, and what one may roughly call adventure, and if he had a chance—— But he is so poor. He lives a life where all the money is apt to go on nonsense and clothes. One is so afraid that circumstances will be too strong for him and that he will sink. Well, he got mixed up in our debate. He wasn't the subject of it, but it seemed to bear on his point. Suppose a millionaire died, and desired to leave money to help such a man. How should he be helped? Should he be given three hundred pounds a year direct, which was Margaret's plan? Most of them thought this would pauperize him. Should he and those like him be given free libraries? I said 'No!' He doesn't want more books to read, but to read books rightly. My suggestion was he should be given something every year towards a summer holiday, but then there is his wife, and they said she would have to go too. Nothing seemed quite right! Now what do you think? Imagine that you were a millionaire, and wanted to help the poor. What would you do?"

Mr. Wilcox, whose fortune was not so very far below the standard indicated, laughed exuberantly. "My dear Miss Schlegel, I will not rush in where your sex has been unable to tread. I will not add another plan to the numerous excellent ones that have been already suggested. My only contribution is this: let your young friend clear out of the Porphyrion Fire Insurance Company with all possible speed."

"Why?" said Margaret.

He lowered his voice. "This is between friends. It'll be in the Receiver's hands before Christmas. It'll smash," he added, thinking that she had not understood.

"Dear me, Helen, listen to that. And he'll have to get another place!"

"*Will* have? Let him leave the ship before it sinks. Let him get one now."

"Rather than wait, to make sure?"

"Decidedly."

"Why's that?"

Again the Olympian laugh, and the lowered voice. "Naturally the man who's in a situation when he applies stands a better chance, is in a stronger position, than the man who isn't. It looks as if he's worth something. I know by myself—(this is letting you into the State secrets)—it affects an employer greatly. Human nature, I'm afraid."

"I hadn't thought of that," murmured Margaret, while Helen said, "Our human nature appears to be the other way round. We employ people because they're unemployed. The boot man, for instance."

"And how does he clean the boots?"

"Not well," confessed Margaret.

"There you are!"

"Then do you really advise us to tell this youth——?"

"I advise nothing," he interrupted, glancing up and down the Embankment, in case his indiscretion had been overheard. "I oughtn't to have spoken—but I happen to know, being more or less behind the scenes. The Porphyrion's a bad, bad concern—— Now, don't say I said so. It's outside the Tariff Ring."[6]

"Certainly I won't say. In fact, I don't know what that means."

"I thought an insurance company never smashed," was Helen's contribution. "Don't the others always run in and save them?"

"You're thinking of reinsurance," said Mr. Wilcox mildly. "It is exactly there that the Porphyrion is weak. It has tried to undercut, has been badly hit by a long series of small fires, and it hasn't been able to reinsure. I'm afraid that public companies don't save one another for love."

"'Human nature,' I suppose," quoted Helen, and he laughed and agreed that it was. When Margaret said that she supposed that clerks, like everyone else, found it extremely difficult to get situations in these days, he replied, "Yes, extremely," and rose to rejoin his friends. He knew by his own office—seldom a vacant post, and hundreds of applicants for it; at present no vacant post.

"And how's Howards End looking?" said Margaret, wishing to change

6. An alliance of insurance companies.

the subject before they parted. Mr. Wilcox was a little apt to think one wanted to get something out of him.

"It's let."

"Really. And you wandering homeless in long-haired Chelsea? How strange are the ways of Fate!"

"No; it's let unfurnished. We've moved."

"Why, I thought of you both as anchored there for ever. Evie never told me."

"I dare say when you met Evie the thing wasn't settled. We only moved a week ago. Paul has rather a feeling for the old place, and we held on for him to have his holiday there; but, really, it is impossibly small. Endless drawbacks. I forget whether you've been up to it?"

"As far as the house, never."

"Well, Howards End is one of those converted farms. They don't really do, spend what you will on them. We messed away with a garage all among the wych-elm roots, and last year we enclosed a bit of the meadow and attempted a rockery. Evie got rather keen on Alpine plants. But it didn't do—no, it didn't do. You remember, or your sister will remember, the farm with those abominable guinea-fowls, and the hedge that the old woman never would cut properly, so that it all went thin at the bottom. And, inside the house, the beams—and the staircase through a door—picturesque enough, but not a place to live in." He glanced over the parapet cheerfully. "Full tide. And the position wasn't right either. The neighbourhood's getting suburban. Either be in London or out of it, I say; so we've taken a house in Ducie Street, close to Sloane Street, and a place right down in Shropshire—Oniton Grange. Ever heard of Oniton? Do come and see us—right away from everywhere, up towards Wales."

"What a change!" said Margaret. But the change was in her own voice, which had become most sad. "I can't imagine Howards End or Hilton without you."

"Hilton isn't without us," he replied. "Charles is there still."

"Still?" said Margaret, who had not kept up with the Charleses. "But I thought he was still at Epsom. They were furnishing that Christmas—one Christmas. How everything alters! I used to admire Mrs. Charles from our windows very often. Wasn't it Epsom?"

"Yes, but they moved eighteen months ago. Charles, the good chap"—his voice dropped—"thought I should be lonely. I didn't want him to move, but he would, and took a house at the other end of Hilton, down by the Six Hills. He had a motor, too. There they all are, a very jolly party—he and she and the two grandchildren."

"I manage other people's affairs so much better than they manage them themselves," said Margaret as they shook hands. "When you moved out of Howards End, I should have moved Mr. Charles Wilcox into it. I should have kept so remarkable a place in the family."

"So it is," he replied. "I haven't sold it, and don't mean to."

"No; but none of you are there."

"Oh, we've got a splendid tenant—Hamar Bryce, an invalid. If Charles ever wanted it—but he won't. Dolly is so dependent on modern conveniences. No, we have all decided against Howards End. We like it in a way, but now we feel that it is neither one thing nor the other. One must have one thing or the other."

"And some people are lucky enough to have both. You're doing yourself proud, Mr. Wilcox. My congratulations."

"And mine," said Helen.

"Do remind Evie to come and see us—two, Wickham Place. We shan't be there very long, either."

"You, too, on the move?"

"Next September," Margaret sighed.

"Everyone moving! Good-bye."

The tide had begun to ebb. Margaret leant over the parapet and watched it sadly. Mr. Wilcox had forgotten his wife, Helen her lover; she herself was probably forgetting. Everyone moving. Is it worth while attempting the past when there is this continual flux even in the hearts of men?

Helen roused her by saying: "What a prosperous vulgarian Mr. Wilcox has grown! I have very little use for him in these days. However, he did tell us about the Porphyrion. Let us write to Mr. Bast as soon as ever we get home, and tell him to clear out of it at once."

"Do; yes, that's worth doing. Let us."

"Let's ask him to tea."

Chapter XVI

Leonard accepted the invitation to tea next Saturday. But he was right; the visit proved a conspicuous failure.

"Sugar?" said Margaret.

"Cake?" said Helen. "The big cake or the little deadlies? I'm afraid you thought my letter rather odd, but we'll explain—we aren't odd, really—nor affected, really. We're over-expressive: that's all."

As a lady's lap-dog Leonard did not excel. He was not an Italian, still less a Frenchman, in whose blood there runs the very spirit of persiflage and of gracious repartee. His wit was the Cockney's; it opened no doors into imagination, and Helen was drawn up short by "The more a lady has to say, the better," administered waggishly.

"Oh yes," she said.

"Ladies brighten——"

"Yes, I know. The darlings are regular sunbeams. Let me give you a plate."

"How do you like your work?" interposed Margaret.

He, too, was drawn up short. He would not have these women prying into his work. They were Romance, and so was the room to which he had at last penetrated, with the queer sketches of people bathing upon its walls, and so were the very tea-cups, with their delicate borders of wild strawberries. But he would not let Romance interfere with his life. There is the devil to pay then.

"Oh, well enough," he answered.

"Your company is the Porphyrion, isn't it?"

"Yes, that's so"—becoming rather offended. "It's funny how things get round."

"Why funny?" asked Helen, who did not follow the workings of his mind. "It was written as large as life on your card, and considering we wrote to you there, and that you replied on the stamped paper——"

"Would you call the Porphyrion one of the big Insurance Companies?" pursued Margaret.

"It depends what you call big."

"I mean by big, a solid, well-established concern, that offers a reason-ably good career to its employés."

"I couldn't say—some would tell you one thing and others another," said the employé uneasily. "For my own part"—he shook his head—"I only believe half I hear. Not that even; it's safer. Those clever ones come to the worse grief, I've often noticed. Ah, you can't be too careful."

He drank, and wiped his moustache, which was going to be one of those moustaches that always droop into tea-cups—more bother than they're worth, surely, and not fashionable either.

"I quite agree, and that's why I was curious to know: is it a solid, well-established concern?"

Leonard had no idea. He understood his own corner of the machine, but nothing beyond it. He desired to confess neither knowledge nor ignorance, and under these circumstances, another motion of the head seemed safest. To him, as to the British public, the Porphyrion was the Porphyrion of the advertisement—a giant, in the classical style, but draped sufficiently, who held in one hand a burning torch, and pointed with the other to St. Paul's and Windsor Castle.[1] A large sum of money was inscribed below, and you drew your own conclusions. This giant caused Leonard to do arithmetic and write letters, to explain the regula-tions to new clients, and re-explain them to old ones. A giant was of an impulsive morality—one knew that much. He would pay for Mrs. Munt's hearth-rug with ostentatious haste, a large claim he would repu-diate quietly, and fight court by court. But his true fighting weight, his antecedents, his amours with other members of the commercial Pantheon[2]—all these were as uncertain to ordinary mortals as were the

1. St. Paul's Cathedral, largest and finest church in London; Windsor Castle, residence of the royal family.
2. Temple of the gods.

escapades of Zeus. While the gods are powerful, we learn little about them. It is only in the days of their decadence that a strong light beats into heaven.

"We were told the Porphyrion's no go," blurted Helen. "We wanted to tell you; that's why we wrote."

"A friend of ours did think that it is insufficiently reinsured," said Margaret.

Now Leonard had his clue. He must praise the Porphyrion. "You can tell your friend," he said, "that he's quite wrong."

"Oh, good!"

The young man coloured a little. In his circle to be wrong was fatal. The Miss Schlegels did not mind being wrong. They were genuinely glad that they had been misinformed. To them nothing was fatal but evil.

"Wrong, so to speak," he added.

"How 'so to speak'?"

"I mean I wouldn't say he's right altogether."

But this was a blunder. "Then he is right partly," said the elder woman, quick as lightning.

Leonard replied that everyone was right partly, if it came to that.

"Mr. Bast, I don't understand business, and I dare say my questions are stupid, but can you tell me what makes a concern 'right' or 'wrong'?"

Leonard sat back with a sigh.

"Our friend, who is also a business man, was so positive. He said before Christmas——"

"And advised you to clear out of it," concluded Helen. "But I don't see why he should know better than you do."

Leonard rubbed his hands. He was tempted to say that he knew nothing about the thing at all. But a commercial training was too strong for him. Nor could he say it was a bad thing, for this would be giving it away; nor yet that it was good, for this would be giving it away equally. He attempted to suggest that it was something between the two, with vast possibilities in either direction, but broke down under the gaze of four sincere eyes. As yet he scarcely distinguished between the two sisters. One was more beautiful and more lively, but "the Miss Schlegels" still remained a composite Indian god, whose waving arms and contradictory speeches were the product of a single mind.[3]

"One can but see," he remarked, adding, "as Ibsen says, 'things happen.'"[4] He was itching to talk about books and make the most of his romantic hour. Minute after minute slipped away, while the ladies, with imperfect skill, discussed the subject of reinsurance or praised their anonymous friend. Leonard grew annoyed—perhaps rightly. He made

---

3. The numerous gods and goddesses of Hinduism are considered various forms of the single supreme being.
4. This quote is most likely sheer invention, perhaps signaling Leonard's desperation.

vague remarks about not being one of those who minded their affairs being talked over by others, but they did not take the hint. Men might have shown more tact. Women, however tactful elsewhere, are heavy-handed here. They cannot see why we should shroud our incomes and our prospects in a veil. "How much exactly have you, and how much do you expect to have next June?" And these were women with a theory, who held that reticence about money matters is absurd, and that life would be truer if each would state the exact size of the golden island upon which he stands, the exact stretch of warp over which he throws the woof that is not money. How can we do justice to the pattern otherwise?

And the precious minutes slipped away, and Jacky and squalor came nearer. At last he could bear it no longer, and broke in, reciting the names of books feverishly. There was a moment of piercing joy when Margaret said, "So *you* like Carlyle,"[5] and then the door opened, and "Mr. Wilcox, Miss Wilcox" entered, preceded by two prancing puppies.

"Oh, the dears! Oh, Evie, how too impossibly sweet!" screamed Helen, falling on her hands and knees.

"We brought the little fellows round," said Mr. Wilcox.

"I bred 'em myself."

"Oh, really! Mr. Bast, come and play with puppies."

"I've got to be going now," said Leonard sourly.

"But play with puppies a little first."

"This is Ahab, that's Jezebel," said Evie, who was one of those who name animals after the less successful characters of Old Testament history.[6]

"I've got to be going."

Helen was too much occupied with puppies to notice him.

"Mr. Wilcox, Mr. Ba—— Must you be really? Good-bye!"

"Come again," said Helen from the floor.

Then Leonard's gorge rose. Why should he come again? What was the good of it? He said roundly: "No, I shan't; I knew it would be a failure."

Most people would have let him go. "A little mistake. We tried knowing another class—impossible." But the Schlegels had never played with life. They had attempted friendship, and they would take the consequences. Helen retorted, "I call that a very rude remark. What do you want to turn on me like that for?" and suddenly the drawing-room re-echoed to a vulgar row.

"You ask me why I turn on you?"

"Yes."

"What do you want to have me here for?"

---

5. Thomas Carlyle (1795–1881), English philosopher and social critic, notorious for his difficult style.
6. See 1 Kings 16.28 and 22.40.

"To help you, you silly boy!" cried Helen. "And don't shout."

"*I* don't want your patronage. *I* don't want your tea. I was quite happy. What do you want to unsettle me for?" He turned to Mr. Wilcox. "I put it to this gentleman. I ask you, sir, am I to have my brain picked?"

Mr. Wilcox turned to Margaret with the air of humorous strength that he could so well command. "Are we intruding, Miss Schlegel? Can we be of any use, or shall we go?"

But Margaret ignored him.

"I'm connected with a leading insurance company, sir. I receive what I take to be an invitation from these—ladies" (he drawled the word). "I come, and it's to have my brain picked. I ask you, is it fair?"

"Highly unfair," said Mr. Wilcox, drawing a gasp from Evie, who knew that her father was becoming dangerous.

"There, you hear that? Most unfair, the gentleman says. There! Not content with"—pointing at Margaret—"you can't deny it." His voice rose: he was falling into the rhythm of a scene with Jacky. "But as soon as I'm useful it's a very different thing. 'Oh yes, send for him. Cross-question him. Pick his brains.' Oh yes. Now, take me on the whole, I'm a quiet fellow: I'm law-abiding, I don't wish any unpleasantness; but I—I——"

"You," said Margaret—"you—you——"

Laughter from Evie, as at a repartee.

"You are the man who tried to walk by the Pole star."

More laughter.

"You saw the sunrise."

Laughter.

"You tried to get away from the fogs that are stifling us all—away past books and houses to the truth. You were looking for a real home."

"I fail to see the connection," said Leonard, hot with stupid anger.

"So do I." There was a pause. "You were that last Sunday—you are this to-day. Mr. Bast! I and my sister have talked you over. We wanted to help you; we also supposed you might help us. We did not have you here out of charity—which bores us—but because we hoped there would be a connection between last Sunday and other days. What is the good of your stars and trees, your sunrise and the wind, if they do not enter into our daily lives? They have never entered into mine, but into yours, we thought—— Haven't we all to struggle against life's daily greyness, against pettiness, against mechanical cheerfulness, against suspicion? I struggle by remembering my friends; others I have known by remembering some place—some beloved place or tree—we thought you one of these."

"Of course, if there's been any misunderstanding," mumbled Leonard, "all I can do is to go. But I beg to state——" He paused. Ahab and Jezebel danced at his boots and made him look ridiculous. "You were picking my brain for official information—I can prove it—I——" He blew his nose and left them.

"Can I help you now?" said Mr. Wilcox, turning to Margaret. "May I have one quiet word with him in the hall?"

"Helen, go after him—do anything—*anything*—to make the noodle understand."

Helen hesitated.

"But really——" said their visitor. "Ought she to?"

At once she went.

He resumed. "I would have chimed in, but I felt that you could polish him off for yourselves—I didn't interfere. You were splendid, Miss Schlegel—absolutely splendid. You can take my word for it, but there are very few women who could have managed him."

"Oh yes," said Margaret distractedly.

"Bowling him over with those long sentences was what fetched me," cried Evie.

"Yes, indeed," chuckled her father; "all that part about 'mechanical cheerfulness'—oh, fine!"

"I'm very sorry," said Margaret, collecting herself. "He's a nice creature really. I cannot think what set him off. It has been most unpleasant for you."

"Oh, *I* didn't mind." Then he changed his mood. He asked if he might speak as an old friend, and, permission given, said: "Oughtn't you really to be more careful?"

Margaret laughed, though her thoughts still strayed after Helen. "Do you realize that it's all your fault?" she said. "You're responsible."

"I?"

"This is the young man whom we were to warn against the Porphyrion. We warn him, and—look!"

Mr. Wilcox was annoyed. "I hardly consider that a fair deduction," he said.

"Obviously unfair," said Margaret. "I was only thinking how tangled things are. It's our fault mostly—neither yours nor his."

"Not his?"

"No."

"Miss Schlegel, you are too kind."

"Yes, indeed," nodded Evie, a little contemptuously.

"You behave much too well to people, and then they impose on you. I know the world and that type of man, and as soon as I entered the room, I saw you had not been treating him properly. You must keep that type at a distance. Otherwise they forget themselves. Sad, but true. They aren't our sort, and one must face the fact."

"Ye-es."

"Do admit that we should never have had the outburst if he was a gentleman."

"I admit it willingly," said Margaret, who was pacing up and down the room. "A gentleman would have kept his suspicions to himself."

Mr. Wilcox watched her with a vague uneasiness.

"What did he suspect you of?"

"Of wanting to make money out of him."

"Intolerable brute! But how were you to benefit?"

"Exactly. How indeed! Just horrible, corroding suspicion. One touch of thought or of goodwill would have brushed it away. Just the senseless fear that does make men intolerable brutes."

"I come back to my original point. You ought to be more careful, Miss Schlegel. Your servants ought to have orders not to let such people in."

She turned to him frankly. "Let me explain exactly why we like this man, and want to see him again."

"That's your clever way of talking. I shall never believe you like him."

"I do. Firstly, because he cares for physical adventure, just as you do. Yes, you go motoring and shooting; he would like to go camping out. Secondly, he cares for something special *in* adventure. It is quickest to call that special something poetry——"

"Oh, he's one of that writer sort."

"No—oh no! I mean he may be, but it would be loathsome stuff. His brain is filled with the husks of books, culture—horrible; we want him to wash out his brain and go to the real thing. We want to show him how he may get upsides with life. As I said, either friends or the country, some"—she hesitated—"either some very dear person or some very dear place seems necessary to relieve life's daily grey, and to show that it is grey. If possible, one should have both."

Some of her words ran past Mr. Wilcox. He let them run past. Others he caught and criticized with admirable lucidity.

"Your mistake is this, and it is a very common mistake. This young bounder has a life of his own. What right have you to conclude it is an unsuccessful life, or, as you call it, 'grey'?"

"Because——"

"One minute. You know nothing about him. He probably has his own joys and interests—wife, children, snug little home. That's where we practical fellows"—he smiled—"are more tolerant than you intellectuals. We live and let live, and assume that things are jogging on fairly well elsewhere, and that the ordinary plain man may be trusted to look after his own affairs. I quite grant—I look at the faces of the clerks in my own office, and observe them to be dull, but I don't know what's going on beneath. So, by the way, with London. I have heard you rail against London, Miss Schlegel, and it seems a funny thing to say but I was very angry with you. What do you know about London? You only see civilization from the outside. I don't say in your case, but in too many cases that attitude leads to morbidity, discontent, and Socialism."

She admitted the strength of his position, though it undermined imagination. As he spoke, some outposts of poetry and perhaps of sympathy fell ruining, and she retreated to what she called her "second line"—to the special facts of the case.

"His wife is an old bore," she said simply. "He never came home last Saturday night because he wanted to be alone, and she thought he was with us."

"With *you?*"

"Yes." Evie tittered. "He hasn't got the cosy home that you assumed. He needs outside interests."

"Naughty young man!" cried the girl.

"Naughty?" said Margaret, who hated naughtiness more than sin. "When you're married, Miss Wilcox, won't you want outside interests?"

"He has apparently got them," put in Mr. Wilcox slyly.

"Yes, indeed, father."

"He was tramping in Surrey, if you mean that," said Margaret, pacing away rather crossly.

"Oh, I dare say!"

"Miss Wilcox, he was!"

"M-m-m-m!" from Mr. Wilcox, who thought the episode amusing, if risqué. With most ladies he would not have discussed it, but he was trading on Margaret's reputation as an emancipated woman.

"He said so, and about such a thing he wouldn't lie."

They both began to laugh.

"That's where I differ from you. Men lie about their positions and prospects, but not about a thing of that sort."

He shook his head. "Miss Schlegel, excuse me, but I know the type."

"I said before—he isn't a type. He cares about adventures rightly. He's certain that our smug existence isn't all. He's vulgar and hysterical and bookish, but don't think that sums him up. There's manhood in him as well. Yes, that's what I'm trying to say. He's a real man."

As she spoke their eyes met, and it was as if Mr. Wilcox's defences fell. She saw back to the real man in him. Unwittingly she had touched his emotions. A woman and two men—they had formed the magic triangle of sex, and the male was thrilled to jealousy, in case the female was attracted by another male. Love, say the ascetics, reveals our shameful kinship with the beasts. Be it so: one can bear that; jealousy is the real shame. It is jealousy, not love, that connects us with the farmyard intolerably, and calls up visions of two angry cocks and a complacent hen. Margaret crushed complacency down because she was civilized. Mr. Wilcox, uncivilized, continued to feel anger long after he had rebuilt his defences, and was again presenting a bastion to the world.

"Miss Schlegel, you're a pair of dear creatures, but you really *must* be careful in this uncharitable world. What does your brother say?"

"I forget."

"Surely he has some opinion?"

"He laughs, if I remember correctly."

"He's very clever, isn't he?" said Evie, who had met and detested Tibby at Oxford.

"Yes, pretty well—but I wonder what Helen's doing."

"She is very young to undertake this sort of thing," said Mr. Wilcox.

Margaret went out into the landing. She heard no sound, and Mr. Bast's topper was missing from the hall.

"Helen!" she called.

"Yes!" replied a voice from the library.

"You in there?"

"Yes—he's gone some time."

Margaret went to her. "Why, you're all alone," she said.

"Yes—it's all right, Meg. Poor, poor creature——"

"Come back to the Wilcoxes and tell me later—Mr. W. much concerned, and slightly titillated."

"Oh, I've no patience with him. I hate him. Poor dear Mr. Bast! he wanted to talk literature, and we would talk business. Such a muddle of a man, and yet so worth pulling through. I like him extraordinarily."

"Well done," said Margaret, kissing her, "but come into the drawing-room now, and don't talk about him to the Wilcoxes. Make light of the whole thing."

Helen came and behaved with a cheerfulness that reassured their visitor—this hen at all events was fancy-free.

"He's gone with my blessing," she cried, "and now for puppies."

As they drove away, Mr. Wilcox said to his daughter:

"I am really concerned at the way those girls go on. They are as clever as you make 'em, but unpractical—God bless me! One of these days they'll go too far. Girls like that oughtn't to live alone in London. Until they marry, they ought to have someone to look after them. We must look in more often—we're better than no one. You like them, don't you, Evie?"

Evie replied: "Helen's right enough, but I can't stand the toothy one. And I shouldn't have called either of them girls."

Evie had grown up handsome. Dark-eyed, with the glow of youth under sunburn, built firmly and firm-lipped, she was the best the Wilcoxes could do in the way of feminine beauty. For the present, puppies and her father were the only things she loved, but the net of matrimony was being prepared for her, and a few days later she was attracted to a Mr. Percy Cahill, an uncle of Mrs. Charles', and he was attracted to her.

Chapter XVII

The Age of Property holds bitter moments even for a proprietor. When a move is imminent, furniture becomes ridiculous, and Margaret now lay awake at nights wondering where, where on earth they and all their belongings would be deposited in September next. Chairs, tables, pictures, books, that had rumbled down to them through the generations, must rumble forward again like a slide of rubbish to which she longed to give the final push, and send toppling into the sea. But there were all their father's books—they never read them, but they were their father's, and must be kept. There was the marble-topped cheffonier—their mother had set store by it, they could not remember why. Round every knob and cushion in the house sentiment gathered, a sentiment that was at times personal, but more often a faint piety to the dead, a prolongation of rites that might have ended at the grave.

It was absurd, if you came to think of it; Helen and Tibby came to think of it: Margaret was too busy with the house-agents. The feudal ownership of land did bring dignity, whereas the modern ownership of movables is reducing us again to a nomadic horde. We are reverting to the civilization of luggage, and historians of the future will note how the middle classes accreted possessions without taking root in the earth, and may find in this the secret of their imaginative poverty. The Schlegels were certainly the poorer for the loss of Wickham Place. It had helped to balance their lives, and almost to counsel them. Nor is their ground-landlord spiritually the richer. He has built flats on its site, his motor-cars grow swifter, his exposures of Socialism more trenchant. But he has split the precious distillation of the years, and no chemistry of his can give it back to society again.

Margaret grew depressed; she was anxious to settle on a house before they left town to pay their annual visit to Mrs. Munt. She enjoyed this visit, and wanted to have her mind at ease for it. Swanage, though dull, was stable, and this year she longed more than usual for its fresh air and for the magnificent downs that guard it on the north. But London thwarted her; in its atmosphere she could not concentrate. London only stimulates, it cannot sustain; and Margaret, hurrying over its surface for a house without knowing what sort of a house she wanted, was paying for many a thrilling sensation in the past. She could not even break loose from culture, and her time was wasted by concerts which it would be a sin to miss, and invitations which it would never do to refuse. At last she grew desperate; she resolved that she would go nowhere and be at home to no one until she found a house, and broke the resolution in half an hour.

Once she had humorously lamented that she had never been to Simpson's restaurant in the Strand. Now a note arrived from Miss Wilcox, asking her to lunch there. Mr. Cahill was coming, and the three would have such a jolly chat, and perhaps end up at the Hippodrome.[1] Margaret had no strong regard for Evie, and no desire to meet her fiancé, and she was surprised that Helen, who had been far funnier about Simpson's, had not been asked instead. But the invitation touched her by its intimate tone. She must know Evie Wilcox better than she supposed, and declaring that she "simply must," she accepted.

But when she saw Evie at the entrance of the restaurant, staring

1. Vaudeville theater.

fiercely at nothing after the fashion of athletic women, her heart failed her anew. Miss Wilcox had changed perceptibly since her engagement. Her voice was gruffer, her manner more downright, and she was inclined to patronize the more foolish virgin. Margaret was silly enough to be pained at this. Depressed at her isolation, she saw not only houses and furniture, but the vessel of life itself slipping past her, with people like Evie and Mr. Cahill on board.

There are moments when virtue and wisdom fail us, and one of them came to her at Simpson's in the Strand. As she trod the staircase, narrow, but carpeted thickly, as she entered the eating-room, where saddles of mutton were being trundled up to expectant clergymen, she had a strong, if erroneous, conviction of her own futility, and wished she had never come out of her backwater, where nothing happened except art and literature, and where no one ever got married or succeeded in remaining engaged. Then came a little surprise. 'Father might be of the party—yes, father was.' With a smile of pleasure she moved forward to greet him, and her feeling of loneliness vanished.

"I thought I'd get round if I could," said he. "Evie told me of her little plan, so I just slipped in and secured a table. Always secure a table first. Evie, don't pretend you want to sit by your old father, because you don't. Miss Schlegel, come in my side, out of pity. My goodness, but you look tired! Been worrying round after your young clerks?"

"No, after houses," said Margaret, edging past him into the box. "I'm hungry, not tired; I want to eat heaps."

"That's good. What'll you have?"

"Fish pie," said she, with a glance at the menu.

"Fish pie! Fancy coming for fish pie to Simpson's. It's not a bit the thing to go for here."

"Go for something for me, then," said Margaret, pulling off her gloves. Her spirits were rising, and his reference to Leonard Bast had warmed her curiously.

"Saddle of mutton," said he after profound reflection; "and cider to drink. That's the type of thing. I like this place, for a joke, once in a way. It is so thoroughly Old English. Don't you agree?"

"Yes," said Margaret, who didn't. The order was given, the joint rolled up, and the carver, under Mr. Wilcox's direction, cut the meat where it was succulent, and piled their plates high. Mr. Cahill insisted on sirloin, but admitted that he had made a mistake later on. He and Evie soon fell into a conversation of the 'No, I didn't; yes, you did' type—conversation which, though fascinating to those who are engaged in it, neither desires nor deserves the attention of others.

"It's a golden rule to tip the carver. Tip everywhere's my motto."

"Perhaps it does make life more human."

"Then the fellows know one again. Especially in the East, if you tip, they remember you from year's end to year's end."

"Have you been in the East?"

"Oh, Greece and the Levant.[2] I used to go out for sport and business to Cyprus; some military society of a sort there. A few piastres,[3] properly distributed, help to keep one's memory green. But you, of course, think this shockingly cynical. How's your discussion society getting on? Any new Utopias lately?"

"No, I'm house-hunting, Mr. Wilcox, as I've already told you once. Do you know of any houses?"

"Afraid I don't."

"Well, what's the point of being practical if you can't find two distressed females a house? We merely want a small house with large rooms, and plenty of them."

"Evie, I like that! Miss Schlegel expects me to turn house agent for her!"

"What's that, father?"

"I want a new home in September, and someone must find it. I can't."

"Percy, do you know of anything?"

"I can't say I do," said Mr. Cahill.

"How like you! You're never any good."

"Never any good. Just listen to her! Never any good. Oh, come!"

"Well, you aren't. Miss Schlegel, is he?"

The torrent of their love, having splashed these drops at Margaret, swept away on its habitual course. She sympathized with it now, for a little comfort had restored her geniality. Speech and silence pleased her equally, and while Mr. Wilcox made some preliminary inquiries about cheese, her eyes surveyed the restaurant, and admired its well-calculated tributes to the solidity of our past. Though no more Old English than the works of Kipling,[4] it had selected its reminiscences so adroitly that her criticism was lulled, and the guests whom it was nourishing for imperial purposes bore the outer semblance of Parson Adams or Tom Jones.[5] Scraps of their talk jarred oddly on the ear. "Right you are! I'll cable out to Uganda this evening," came from the table behind. "Their Emperor wants war; well, let him have it," was the opinion of a clergyman. She smiled at such incongruities. "Next time," she said to Mr. Wilcox, "you shall come to lunch with me at Mr. Eustace Miles's."

"With pleasure."

"No, you'd hate it," she said, pushing her glass towards him for some more cider. "It's all proteids and body buildings, and people come up to you and beg your pardon, but you have such a beautiful aura."[6]

2. The area on the eastern Mediterranean including Lebanon, Syria, and Israel.
3. Coins.
4 Rudyard Kipling (1865–1936), patriotic author who celebrated British heroism and romanticized imperialism.
5. Characters in novels by Henry Fielding (1707–54).
6. Margaret is teasing Henry with the language of vegetarianism and astrology.

"A what?"

"Never heard of an aura? Oh, happy, happy man! I scrub at mine for hours. Nor of an astral plane?"

He had heard of astral planes, and censured them.

"Just so. Luckily it was Helen's aura, not mine, and she had to chaperone it and do the politenesses. I just sat with my handkerchief in my mouth till the man went."

"Funny experiences seem to come to you two girls. No one's ever asked me about my—what d'ye call it? Perhaps I've not got one."

"You're bound to have one, but it may be such a terrible colour that no one dares mention it."

"Tell me, though, Miss Schlegel, do you really believe in the supernatural and all that?"

"Too difficult a question."

"Why's that? Gruyère or Stilton?"[7]

"Gruyère, please."

"Better have Stilton."

"Stilton. Because, though I don't believe in auras, and think Theosophy's[8] only a halfway-house——"

"—Yet there may be something in it all the same," he concluded, with a frown.

"Not even that. It may be halfway in the wrong direction. I can't explain. I don't believe in all these fads, and yet I don't like saying that I don't believe in them."

He seemed unsatisfied, and said: "So you wouldn't give me your word that you *don't* hold with astral bodies and all the rest of it?"

"I could," said Margaret, surprised that the point was of any importance to him. "Indeed, I will. When I talked about scrubbing my aura, I was only trying to be funny. But why do you want this settled?"

"I don't know."

"Now, Mr. Wilcox, you do know."

"Yes, I am," "No, you're not," burst from the lovers opposite. Margaret was silent for a moment, and then changed the subject.

"How's your house?"

"Much the same as when you honoured it last week."

"I don't mean Ducie Street. Howards End, of course."

"Why 'of course'?"

"Can't you turn out your tenant and let it to us? We're nearly demented."

"Let me think. I wish I could help you. But I thought you wanted to be in town. One bit of advice: fix your district, then fix your price, and then don't budge. That's how I got both Ducie Street and Oniton. I said

---

7. French and English cheeses.
8. A mystical philosophy popularized in the late nineteenth century by the Theosophical Society.

to myself, 'I mean to be exactly here,' and I was, and Oniton's a place in a thousand."

"But I do budge. Gentlemen seem to mesmerize houses—cow them with an eye, and up they come, trembling. Ladies can't. It's the houses that are mesmerizing me. I've no control over the saucy things. Houses are alive. No?"

"I'm out of my depth," he said, and added: "Didn't you talk rather like that to your office boy?"

"Did I?—I mean I did, more or less. I talk the same way to everyone— or try to."

"Yes, I know. And how much do you suppose that he understood of it?"

"That's his lookout. I don't believe in suiting my conversation to my company. One can doubtless hit upon some medium of exchange that seems to do well enough, but it's no more like the real thing than money is like food. There's no nourishment in it. You pass it to the lower classes, and they pass it back to you, and this you call 'social intercourse' or 'mutual endeavour,' when it's mutual priggishness if it's anything. Our friends at Chelsea don't see this. They say one ought to be at all costs intelligible, and sacrifice——"

"Lower classes," interrupted Mr. Wilcox, as it were thrusting his hand into her speech. "Well, you do admit that there are rich and poor. That's something."

Margaret could not reply. Was he incredibly stupid, or did he understand her better than she understood herself?

"You do admit that, if wealth was divided up equally, in a few years there would be rich and poor again just the same. The hard-working man would come to the top, the wastrel sink to the bottom."

"Everyone admits that."

"Your Socialists don't."

"My Socialists do. Yours mayn't; but I strongly suspect yours of being not Socialists, but ninepins, which you have constructed for your own amusement. I can't imagine any living creature who would bowl over quite so easily."

He would have resented this had she not been a woman. But women may say anything—it was one of his holiest beliefs—and he only retorted, with a gay smile: "I don't care. You've made two damaging admissions, and I'm heartily with you in both."

In time they finished lunch, and Margaret, who had excused herself from the Hippodrome, took her leave. Evie had scarcely addressed her, and she suspected that the entertainment had been planned by the father. He and she were advancing out of their respective families towards a more intimate acquaintance. It had begun long ago. She had been his wife's friend, and, as such, he had given her that silver vinaigrette as a memento. It was pretty of him to have given that vinaigrette, and he had always preferred her to Helen—unlike most men. But the advance had been astonishing lately. They had done more in a week than in two years, and were really beginning to know each other.

She did not forget his promise to sample Eustace Miles, and asked him as soon as she could secure Tibby as his chaperon. He came, and partook of body-building dishes with humility.

Next morning the Schlegels left for Swanage. They had not succeeded in finding a new home.

Chapter XVIII

As they were seated at Aunt Juley's breakfast-table at The Bays, parrying her excessive hospitality and enjoying the view of the bay, a letter came for Margaret and threw her into perturbation. It was from Mr. Wilcox. It announced an "important change" in his plans. Owing to Evie's marriage, he had decided to give up his house in Ducie Street, and was willing to let it on a yearly tenancy. It was a businesslike letter, and stated frankly what he would do for them and what he would not do. Also the rent. If they approved, Margaret was to come up *at once*—the words were underlined, as is necessary when dealing with women—and to go over the house with him. If they disapproved, a wire would oblige, as he should put it into the hands of an agent.

The letter perturbed, because she was not sure what it meant. If he liked her, if he had manoeuvred to get her to Simpson's, might this be a manoeuvre to get her to London, and result in an offer of marriage? She put it to herself as indelicately as possible, in the hope that her brain would cry, "Rubbish, you're a self-conscious fool!" But her brain only tingled a little and was silent, and for a time she sat gazing at the mincing waves, and wondering whether the news would seem strange to the others.

As soon as she began speaking, the sound of her own voice reassured her. There could be nothing in it. The replies also were typical, and in the burr of conversation her fears vanished.

"You needn't go though——" began her hostess.

"I needn't, but hadn't I better? It's really getting rather serious. We let chance after chance slip, and the end of it is we shall be bundled out bag and baggage into the street. We don't know what we *want*, that's the mischief with us——"

"No, we have no real ties," said Helen, helping herself to toast.

"Shan't I go up to town to-day, take the house if it's the least possible, and then come down by the afternoon train to-morrow, and start enjoying myself. I shall be no fun to myself or to others until this business is off my mind."

"But you won't do anything rash, Margaret?"

"There's nothing rash to do."

"Who *are* the Wilcoxes?" said Tibby, a question that sounds silly, but was really extremely subtle, as his aunt found to her cost when she tried to answer it. "I don't *manage* the Wilcoxes; I don't see where they come *in*."

"No more do I," agreed Helen. "It's funny that we just don't lose sight of them. Out of all our hotel acquaintances, Mr. Wilcox is the only one who has stuck. It is now over three years, and we have drifted away from far more interesting people in that time."

"Interesting people don't get one houses."

"Meg, if you start in your honest-English vein, I shall throw the treacle[1] at you."

"It's a better vein than the cosmopolitan," said Margaret, getting up. "Now, children, which is it to be? You know the Ducie Street house. Shall I say yes or shall I say no? Tibby love—which? I'm specially anxious to pin you both."

"It all depends what meaning you attach to the word 'possi——' "

"It depends on nothing of the sort. Say 'yes.' "

"Say 'no.' "

Then Margaret spoke rather seriously. "I think," she said, "that our race is degenerating. We cannot settle even this little thing; what will it be like when we have to settle a big one?"

"It will be as easy as eating," returned Helen.

"I was thinking of father. How could he settle to leave Germany as he did, when he had fought for it as a young man, and all his feelings and friends were Prussian? How could he break loose with Patriotism and begin aiming at something else? It would have killed me. When he was nearly forty he could change countries and ideals—and we, at our age, can't change houses. It's humiliating."

"Your father may have been able to change countries," said Mrs. Munt with asperity, "and that may or may not be a good thing. But he could change houses no better than you can, in fact, much worse. Never shall I forget what poor Emily suffered in the move from Manchester."

"I knew it," cried Helen. "I told you so. It is the little things one bungles at. The big, real ones are nothing when they come."

"Bungle, my dear! You are too little to recollect—in fact, you weren't there. But the furniture was actually in the vans and on the move before the lease for Wickham Place was signed, and Emily took train with baby—who was Margaret then—and the smaller luggage for London, without so much as knowing where her new home would be. Getting away from that house may be hard, but it is nothing to the misery that we all went through getting you into it."

Helen, with her mouth full, cried:

"And that's the man who beat the Austrians, and the Danes, and the

1. Molasses.

French, and who beat the Germans that were inside himself. And we're like him."

"Speak for yourself," said Tibby. "Remember that I am cosmopolitan, please."

"Helen may be right."

"Of course she's right," said Helen.

Helen might be right, but she did not go up to London. Margaret did that. An interrupted holiday is the worst of the minor worries, and one may be pardoned for feeling morbid when a business letter snatches one away from the sea and friends. She could not believe that her father had ever felt the same. Her eyes had been troubling her lately, so that she could not read in the train, and it bored her to look at the landscape, which she had seen but yesterday. At Southampton she "waved" to Frieda: Frieda was on her way down to join them at Swanage, and Mrs. Munt had calculated that their trains would cross. But Frieda was looking the other way, and Margaret travelled on to town feeling solitary and old-maidish. How like an old maid to fancy that Mr. Wilcox was courting her! She had once visited a spinster—poor, silly, and unattractive—whose mania it was that every man who approached her fell in love. How Margaret's heart had bled for the deluded thing! How she had lectured, reasoned, and in despair acquiesced! "I may have been deceived by the curate, my dear, but the young fellow who brings the midday post really is fond of me, and has, as a matter of fact——" It had always seemed to her the most hideous corner of old age, yet she might be driven into it herself by the mere pressure of virginity.

Mr. Wilcox met her at Waterloo himself. She felt certain that he was not the same as usual; for one thing, he took offence at everything she said.

"This is awfully kind of you," she began, "but I'm afraid it's not going to do. The house has not been built that suits the Schlegel family."

"What! Have you come up determined not to deal?"

"Not exactly."

"Not exactly? In that case let's be starting."

She lingered to admire the motor, which was new, and a fairer creature than the vermilion giant that had borne Aunt Juley to her doom three years before.

"Presumably it's very beautiful," she said. "How do you like it, Crane?"

"Come, let's be starting," repeated her host. "How on earth did you know that my chauffeur was called Crane?"

"Why, I know Crane: I've been for a drive with Evie once. I know that you've got a parlourmaid called Milton. I know all sorts of things."

"Evie!" he echoed in injured tones. "You won't see her. She's gone out with Cahill. It's no fun, I can tell you, being left so much alone. I've got my work all day—indeed, a great deal too much of it—but when I come home in the evening, I tell you, I can't stand the house."

"In my absurd way, I'm lonely too," Margaret replied. "It's heart-break-ing to leave one's old home. I scarcely remember anything before Wickham Place, and Helen and Tibby were born there. Helen says——"

"You, too, feel lonely?"

"Horribly. Hullo, Parliament's back!"

Mr. Wilcox glanced at Parliament contemptuously. The more impor-tant ropes of life lay elsewhere. "Yes, they are talking again," said he. "But you were going to say——"

"Only some rubbish about furniture. Helen says it alone endures while men and houses perish, and that in the end the world will be a desert of chairs and sofas—just imagine it!—rolling through infinity with no one to sit upon them."

"Your sister always likes her little joke."

"She says 'Yes,' my brother says 'No,' to Ducie Street. It's no fun help-ing us, Mr. Wilcox, I assure you."

"You are not as unpractical as you pretend. I shall never believe it."

Margaret laughed. But she was—quite as unpractical. She could not concentrate on details. Parliament, the Thames, the irresponsive chauf-feur, would flash into the field of house-hunting, and all demand some comment or response. It is impossible to see modern life steadily and see it whole, and she had chosen to see it whole. Mr. Wilcox saw steadily. He never bothered over the mysterious or the private. The Thames might run inland from the sea, the chauffeur might conceal all passion and philosophy beneath his unhealthy skin. They knew their own busi-ness, and he knew his.

Yet she liked being with him. He was not a rebuke, but a stimulus, and banished morbidity. Some twenty years her senior, he preserved a gift that she supposed herself to have already lost—not youth's creative power, but its self-confidence and optimism. He was so sure that it was a very pleasant world. His complexion was robust, his hair had receded but not thinned, the thick moustache and the eyes that Helen had compared to brandy-balls had an agreeable menace in them, whether they were turned towards the slums or towards the stars. Some day—in the millennium—there may be no need for his type. At present, homage is due to it from those who think themselves superior, and who possibly are.

"At all events you responded to my telegram promptly," he remarked.

"Oh, even I know a good thing when I see it."

"I'm glad you don't despise the goods of this world."

"Heavens, no! Only idiots and prigs do that."

"I am glad, very glad," he repeated, suddenly softening and turning to her, as if the remark had pleased him. "There is so much cant talked in would-be intellectual circles. I am glad you don't share it. Self-denial is all very well as a means of strengthening the character. But I can't stand those people who run down comforts. They have usually some axe to grind. Can you?"

"Comforts are of two kinds," said Margaret, who was keeping herself in hand—"those we can share with others, like fire, weather, or music; and those we can't—food, for instance. It depends."

"I mean reasonable comforts, of course. I shouldn't like to think that you——" He bent nearer; the sentence died unfinished. Margaret's head turned very stupid, and the inside of it seemed to revolve like the beacon in a lighthouse. He did not kiss her, for the hour was half-past twelve, and the car was passing by the stables of Buckingham Palace. But the atmosphere was so charged with emotion that people only seemed to exist on her account, and she was surprised that Crane did not realize this, and turn round. Idiot though she might be, surely Mr. Wilcox was more—how should one put it?—more psychological than usual. Always a good judge of character for business purposes, he seemed this afternoon to enlarge his field, and to note qualities outside neatness, obedience, and decision.

"I want to go over the whole house," she announced when they arrived. "As soon as I get back to Swanage, which will be to-morrow afternoon, I'll talk it over once more with Helen and Tibby, and wire you 'yes' or 'no.'"

"Right. The dining-room." And they began their survey.

The dining-room was big, but over-furnished. Chelsea would have moaned aloud. Mr. Wilcox had eschewed those decorative schemes that wince, and relent, and refrain, and achieve beauty by sacrificing comfort and pluck. After so much self-colour and self-denial, Margaret viewed with relief the sumptuous dado, the frieze, the gilded wall-paper, amid whose foliage parrots sang. It would never do with her own furniture, but those heavy chairs, that immense sideboard loaded with presentation plate, stood up against its pressure like men. The room suggested men, and Margaret, keen to derive the modern capitalist from the warriors and hunters of the past, saw it as an ancient guest-hall, where the lord sat at meat among his thanes. Even the Bible—the Dutch Bible that Charles had brought back from the Boer War[2]—fell into position. Such a room admitted loot.

"Now the entrance-hall."

The entrance-hall was paved.

"Here we fellows smoke."

We fellows smoked in chairs of maroon leather. It was as if a motor-car had spawned. "Oh, jolly!" said Margaret, sinking into one of them.

"You do like it?" he said, fixing his eyes on her upturned face, and surely betraying an almost intimate note. "It's all rubbish not making oneself comfortable. Isn't it?"

"Ye-es. Semi-rubbish. Are those Cruikshanks?"

"Gillrays.[3] Shall we go on upstairs?"

2. War between Britain and the Dutch settlers of South Africa (1899–1902).
3. James Gillray (1756–1815) and George Cruikshank (1792–1878), popular English caricaturists.

"Does all this furniture come from Howards End?"

"The Howards End furniture has all gone to Oniton."

"Does—— However, I'm concerned with the house, not the furniture. How big is this smoking-room?"

"Thirty by fifteen. No, wait a minute. Fifteen and a half."

"Ah, well. Mr. Wilcox, aren't you ever amused at the solemnity with which we middle classes approach the subject of houses?"

They proceeded to the drawing-room. Chelsea managed better here. It was sallow and ineffective. One could visualize the ladies withdrawing to it, while their lords discussed life's realities below, to the accompaniment of cigars. Had Mrs. Wilcox's drawing-room looked thus at Howards End? Just as this thought entered Margaret's brain, Mr. Wilcox did ask her to be his wife, and the knowledge that she had been right so overcame her that she nearly fainted.

But the proposal was not to rank among the world's great love scenes.

"Miss Schlegel"—his voice was firm—"I have had you up on false pretences. I want to speak about a much more serious matter than a house."

Margaret almost answered: "I know——"

"Could you be induced to share my—is it probable——"

"Oh, Mr. Wilcox!" she interrupted, holding the piano and averting her eyes. "I see, I see. I will write to you afterwards if I may."

He began to stammer. "Miss Schlegel—Margaret—you don't understand."

"Oh yes! Indeed, yes!" said Margaret.

"I am asking you to be my wife."

So deep already was her sympathy, that when he said, "I am asking you to be my wife," she made herself give a little start. She must show surprise if he expected it. An immense joy came over her. It was indescribable. It had nothing to do with humanity, and most resembled the all-pervading happiness of fine weather. Fine weather is due to the sun, but Margaret could think of no central radiance here. She stood in his drawing-room happy, and longing to give happiness. On leaving him she realized that the central radiance had been love.

"You aren't offended, Miss Schlegel?"

"How could I be offended?"

There was a moment's pause. He was anxious to get rid of her, and she knew it. She had too much intuition to look at him as he struggled for possessions that money cannot buy. He desired comradeship and affection, but he feared them, and she, who had taught herself only to desire, and could have clothed the struggle with beauty, held back, and hesitated with him.

"Good-bye," she continued. "You will have a letter from me—I am going back to Swanage to-morrow."

"Thank you."

"Good-bye, and it's you I thank."

"I may order the motor round, mayn't I?"

"That would be most kind."

"I wish I had written instead. Ought I to have written?"

"Not at all."

"There's just one question——"

She shook her head. He looked a little bewildered, and they parted.

They parted without shaking hands: she had kept the interview, for his sake, in tints of the quietest grey. Yet she thrilled with happiness ere she reached her own house. Others had loved her in the past, if one may apply to their brief desires so grave a word, but those others had been "ninnies"—young men who had nothing to do, old men who could find nobody better. And she had often "loved," too, but only so far as the facts of sex demanded: mere yearnings for the masculine, to be dismissed for what they were worth, with a smile. Never before had her personality been touched. She was not young or very rich, and it amazed her that a man of any standing should take her seriously. As she sat trying to do accounts in her empty house, amidst beautiful pictures and noble books, waves of emotion broke, as if a tide of passion was flowing through the night air. She shook her head, tried to concentrate her attention, and failed. In vain did she repeat: "But I've been through this sort of thing before." She had never been through it; the big machinery, as opposed to the little, had been set in motion, and the idea that Mr. Wilcox loved, obsessed her before she came to love him in return.

She would come to no decision yet. "Oh, sir, this is so sudden"—that prudish phrase exactly expressed her when her time came. Premonitions are not preparation. She must examine more closely her own nature and his; she must talk it over judicially with Helen. It had been a strange love-scene—the central radiance unacknowledged from first to last. She, in his place, would have said "Ich liebe dich,"[4] but perhaps it was not his habit to open the heart. He might have done it if she had pressed him—as a matter of duty, perhaps; England expects every man to open his heart once; but the effort would have jarred him, and never, if she could avoid it, should he lose those defences that he had chosen to raise against the world. He must never be bothered with emotional talk, or with a display of sympathy. He was an elderly man now, and it would be futile and impudent to correct him.

Mrs. Wilcox strayed in and out, ever a welcome ghost; surveying the scene, thought Margaret, without one hint of bitterness.

Chapter XIX

If one wanted to show a foreigner England, perhaps the wisest course would be to take him to the final section of the Purbeck Hills, and stand

4. I love you (German).

him on their summit, a few miles to the east of Corfe. Then system after system of our island would roll together under his feet. Beneath him is the valley of the Frome, and all the wild lands that come tossing down from Dorchester, black and gold, to mirror their gorse in the expanses of Poole.[1] The valley of the Stour is beyond, unaccountable stream, dirty at Blandford, pure at Wimborne—the Stour, sliding out of fat fields, to marry the Avon beneath the tower of Christchurch.[2] The valley of the Avon—invisible, but far to the north the trained eye may see Clearbury Ring that guards it, and the imagination may leap beyond that on to Salisbury Plain itself, and beyond the Plain to all the glorious downs of Central England.[3] Nor is Suburbia absent. Bournemouth's[4] ignoble coast cowers to the right, heralding the pine-trees that mean, for all their beauty, red houses, and the Stock Exchange, and extend to the gates of London itself. So tremendous is the City's trail! But the cliffs of Freshwater it shall never touch, and the island will guard the Island's purity till the end of time. Seen from the west, the Wight[5] is beautiful beyond all laws of beauty. It is as if a fragment of England floated forward to greet the foreigner—chalk of our chalk, turf of our turf, epitome of what will follow. And behind the fragment lie Southampton, hostess to the nations, and Portsmouth, a latent fire,[6] and all around it, with double and treble collision of tides, swirls the sea. How many villages appear in this view! How many castles! How many churches, vanished or triumphant! How many ships, railways, and roads! What incredible variety of men working beneath that lucent sky to what final end! The reason fails, like a wave on the Swanage beach; the imagination swells, spreads, and deepens, until it becomes geographic and encircles England.

So Frieda Mosebach, now Frau Architect Liesecke, and mother to her husband's baby, was brought up to these heights to be impressed, and, after a prolonged gaze, she said that the hills were more swelling here than in Pomerania, which was true, but did not seem to Mrs. Munt apposite. Poole Harbour was dry, which led her to praise the absence of muddy foreshore at Friedrich Wilhelms Bad, Rügen,[7] where beech-trees hang over the tideless Baltic, and cows may contemplate the brine. Rather unhealthy Mrs. Munt thought this would be, water being safer when it moved about.

---

1. Purbeck Hills: chalk hills on the English Channel just northeast of Swanage; Corfe: a village about five miles northwest of Swanage. Both are in Dorset (county seat—Dorchester), a region in southwest England with a harbor at Poole and fertile valleys of the Blackmore, Stour, and Frome rivers.
2. The Stour flows south through Blandford Forum and Wimbourne Minster to merge with the River Avon before emptying into Poole Bay in the English Channel at Christchurch.
3. Clearbury Ring: a hill south of Salisbury encircled by an earth rampart; downs: undulating grassy uplands.
4. Town on Poole Bay in the pine-wooded valley of the Bourne.
5. Island in the English Channel to the east of Dorset.
6. Southampton, England's main harbor for passenger ships, and Portsmouth, a fortified naval base, both lie on the southern coast across from the Isle of Wight.
7. Large island off the coast of eastern Germany.

"And your English lakes—Vindermere, Grasmere[8]—are they, then, unhealthy?"

"No, Frau Liesecke; but that is because they are fresh water, and different. Salt water ought to have tides, and go up and down a great deal, or else it smells. Look, for instance, at an aquarium."

"An aquarium! Oh, *Meesis* Munt, you mean to tell me that fresh aquariums stink less than salt? Why, then Victor, my brother-in-law, collected many tadpoles——"

"You are not to say 'stink,' " interrupted Helen; "at least, you may say it, but you must pretend you are being funny while you say it."

"Then 'smell.' And the mud of your Pool down there—does it not smell, or may I say 'stink, ha, ha'?"

"There always has been mud in Poole Harbour," said Mrs. Munt, with a slight frown. "The rivers bring it down, and a most valuable oyster-fishery depends upon it."

"Yes, that is so," conceded Frieda; and another international incident was closed.

" 'Bournemouth is,' " resumed their hostess, quoting a local rhyme to which she was much attached—" 'Bournemouth is, Poole was, and Swanage is to be the most important town of all and biggest of the three.' Now, Frau Liesecke, I have shown you Bournemouth, and I have shown you Poole, so let us walk backward a little, and look down again at Swanage."

"Aunt Juley, wouldn't that be Meg's train?"

A tiny puff of smoke had been circling the harbour, and now was bearing southwards towards them over the black and the gold.

"Oh, dearest Margaret, I do hope she won't be overtired."

"Oh, I do wonder—I do wonder whether she's taken the house."

"I hope she hasn't been hasty."

"So do I—oh, *so* do I."

"Will it be as beautiful as Wickham Place?" Frieda asked.

"I should think it would. Trust Mr. Wilcox for doing himself proud. All those Ducie Street houses are beautiful in their modern way, and I can't think why he doesn't keep on with it. But it's really for Evie that he went there, and now that Evie's going to be married——"

"Ah!"

"You've never seen Miss Wilcox, Frieda. How absurdly matrimonial you are!"

"But sister to that Paul?"

"Yes."

"And to that Charles," said Mrs. Munt with feeling. "Oh, Helen, Helen, what a time that was!"

8. Lakes in the Lake District in northwestern England.

Helen laughed. "Meg and I haven't got such tender hearts. If there's a chance of a cheap house, we go for it."

"Now look, Frau Liesecke, at my niece's train. You see, it is coming towards us—coming, coming; and, when it gets to Corfe, it will actually go *through* the downs, on which we are standing, so that, if we walk over, as I suggested, and look down on Swanage, we shall see it coming on the other side. Shall we?"

Frieda assented, and in a few minutes they had crossed the ridge and exchanged the greater view for the lesser. Rather a dull valley lay below, backed by the slope of the coastward downs. They were looking across the Isle of Purbeck and on to Swanage, soon to be the most important town of all, and ugliest of the three. Margaret's train reappeared as promised, and was greeted with approval by her aunt. It came to a standstill in the middle distance, and there it had been planned that Tibby should meet her, and drive her, and a tea-basket, up to join them.

"You see," continued Helen to her cousin, "the Wilcoxes collect houses as your Victor collects tadpoles. They have, one, Ducie Street; two, Howards End, where my great rumpus was; three, a country seat in Shropshire; four, Charles has a house in Hilton; and five, another near Epsom; and six, Evie will have a house when she marries, and probably a pied-à-terre in the country—which makes seven. Oh yes, and Paul a hut in Africa makes eight. I wish we could get Howards End. That was something like a dear little house! Didn't you think so, Aunt Juley?"

"I had too much to do, dear, to look at it," said Mrs. Munt, with a gracious dignity. "I had everything to settle and explain, and Charles Wilcox to keep in his place besides. It isn't likely I should remember much. I just remember having lunch in your bedroom."

"Yes, so do I. But, oh dear, dear, how dreadful it all seems! And in the autumn there began that anti-Pauline movement—you, and Frieda, and Meg, and Mrs. Wilcox, all obsessed with the idea that I might yet marry Paul."

"You yet may," said Frieda despondently.

Helen shook her head. "The Great Wilcox Peril will never return. If I'm certain of anything it's of that."

"One is certain of nothing but the truth of one's own emotions."

The remark fell damply on the conversation. But Helen slipped her arm round her cousin, somehow liking her the better for making it. It was not an original remark, nor had Frieda appropriated it passionately, for she had a patriotic rather than a philosophic mind. Yet it betrayed that interest in the universal which the average Teuton possesses and the average Englishman does not. It was, however illogically, the good, the beautiful, the true, as opposed to the respectable, the pretty, the adequate. It was a landscape of Böcklin's beside a landscape of Leader's,[9]

---

9. Benjamin Williams Leader (1831–1923), popular English landscape painter and member of the Royal Academy.

strident and ill-considered, but quivering into supernatural life. It sharpened idealism, stirred the soul. It may have been a bad preparation for what followed.

"Look!" cried Aunt Juley, hurrying away from generalities over the narrow summit of the down. "Stand where I stand, and you will see the pony-cart coming. I see the pony-cart coming."

They stood and saw the pony-cart coming. Margaret and Tibby were presently seen coming in it. Leaving the outskirts of Swanage, it drove for a little through the budding lanes, and then began the ascent.

"Have you got the house?" they shouted, long before she could possibly hear.

Helen ran down to meet her. The highroad passed over a saddle, and a track went thence at right angles along the ridge of the down.

"Have you got the house?"

Margaret shook her head.

"Oh, what a nuisance! So we're as we were?"

"Not exactly."

She got out, looking tired.

"Some mystery," said Tibby. "We are to be enlightened presently."

Margaret came close up to her and whispered that she had had a proposal of marriage from Mr. Wilcox.

Helen was amused. She opened the gate on to the downs so that her brother might lead the pony through. "It's just like a widower," she remarked. "They've cheek enough for anything, and invariably select one of their first wife's friends."

Margaret's face flashed despair.

"That type——" She broke off with a cry. "Meg, not anything wrong with you?"

"Wait one minute," said Margaret, whispering always.

"But you've never conceivably—you've never——" She pulled herself together. "Tibby, hurry up through; I can't hold this gate indefinitely. Aunt Juley! I say, Aunt Juley, make the tea, will you, and Frieda; we've got to talk houses, and 'll come on afterwards." And then, turning her face to her sister's, she burst into tears.

Margaret was stupefied. She heard herself saying, "Oh, really——" She felt herself touched with a hand that trembled.

"Don't," sobbed Helen, "don't, don't, Meg, don't!" She seemed incapable of saying any other word. Margaret, trembling herself, led her forward up the road, till they strayed through another gate on to the down.

"Don't, don't do such a thing! I tell you not to—don't! I know—don't!"

"What do you know?"

"Panic and emptiness," sobbed Helen. "Don't!"

Then Margaret thought, "Helen is a little selfish. I have never behaved like this when there has seemed a chance of her marrying." She said: "But we would still see each other very often, and you——"

"It's not a thing like that," sobbed Helen. And she broke right away and wandered distractedly upwards, stretching her hands towards the view and crying.

"What's happened to you?" called Margaret, following through the wind that gathers at sundown on the northern slopes of hills. "But it's stupid!" And suddenly stupidity seized her, and the immense landscape was blurred. But Helen turned back.

"Meg——"

"I don't know what's happened to either of us," said Margaret, wiping her eyes. "We must both have gone mad." Then Helen wiped hers, and they even laughed a little.

"Look here, sit down."

"All right; I'll sit down if you'll sit down."

"There. (One kiss.) Now, whatever, whatever is the matter?"

"I do mean what I said. Don't; it wouldn't do."

"Oh, Helen, stop saying 'don't'! It's ignorant. It's as if your head wasn't out of the slime. 'Don't' is probably what Mrs. Bast says all the day to Mr. Bast."

Helen was silent.

"Well?"

"Tell me about it first, and meanwhile perhaps I'll have got my head out of the slime."

"That's better. Well, where shall I begin? When I arrived at Waterloo—no, I'll go back before that, because I'm anxious you should know everything from the first. The 'first' was about ten days ago. It was the day Mr. Bast came to tea and lost his temper. I was defending him, and Mr. Wilcox became jealous about me, however slightly. I thought it was the involuntary thing, which men can't help any more than we can. You know—at least, I know in my own case—when a man has said to me, 'So-and-so's a pretty girl,' I am seized with a momentary sourness against So-and-so, and long to tweak her ear. It's a tiresome feeling, but not an important one, and one easily manages it. But it wasn't only this in Mr. Wilcox's case, I gather now."

"Then you love him?"

Margaret considered. "It is wonderful knowing that a real man cares for you," she said. "The mere fact of that grows more tremendous. Remember, I've known and liked him steadily for nearly three years."

"But loved him?"

Margaret peered into her past. It is pleasant to analyze feelings while they are still only feelings, and unembodied in the social fabric. With her arm round Helen, and her eyes shifting over the view, as if this county or that could reveal the secret of her own heart, she meditated honestly, and said, "No."

"But you will?"

"Yes," said Margaret, "of that I'm pretty sure. Indeed, I began the moment he spoke to me."

"And have settled to marry him?"

"I had, but am wanting a long talk about it now. What *is* it against him, Helen? You must try and say."

Helen, in her turn, looked outwards. "It is ever since Paul," she said finally.

"But what has Mr. Wilcox to do with Paul?"

"But he was there, they were all there that morning when I came down to breakfast, and saw that Paul was frightened—the man who loved me frightened and all his paraphernalia fallen, so that I knew it was impossible, because personal relations are the important thing for ever and ever, and not this outer life of telegrams and anger."

She poured the sentence forth in one breath, but her sister understood it, because it touched on thoughts that were familiar between them.

"That's foolish. In the first place, I disagree about the outer life. Well, we've often argued that. The real point is that there is the widest gulf between my love-making and yours. Yours was romance; mine will be prose. I'm not running it down—a very good kind of prose, but well considered, well thought out. For instance, I know all Mr. Wilcox's faults. He's afraid of emotion. He cares too much about success, too little about the past. His sympathy lacks poetry, and so isn't sympathy really. I'd even say"—she looked at the shining lagoons—"that, spiritually, he's not as honest as I am. Doesn't that satisfy you?"

"No, it doesn't," said Helen. "It makes me feel worse and worse. You must be mad."

Margaret made a movement of irritation.

"I don't intend him, or any man or any woman, to be all my life—good heavens, no! There are heaps of things in me that he doesn't, and shall never, understand."

Thus she spoke before the wedding ceremony and the physical union, before the astonishing glass shade had fallen that interposes between married couples and the world. She was to keep her independence more than do most women as yet. Marriage was to alter her fortunes rather than her character, and she was not far wrong in boasting that she understood her future husband. Yet he did alter her character—a little. There was an unforeseen surprise, a cessation of the winds and odours of life, a social pressure that would have her think conjugally.

"So with him," she continued. "There are heaps of things in him—more especially things that he does—that will always be hidden from me. He has all those public qualities which you so despise and enable all this——" She waved her hand at the landscape, which confirmed anything. "If Wilcoxes hadn't worked and died in England for thousands of years, you and I couldn't sit here without having our throats cut.

There would be no trains, no ships to carry us literary people about in, no fields even. Just savagery. No—perhaps not even that. Without their spirit life might never have moved out of protoplasm. More and more do I refuse to draw my income and sneer at those who guarantee it. There are times when it seems to me——"

"And to me, and to all women. So one kissed Paul."

"That's brutal," said Margaret. "Mine is an absolutely different case. I've thought things out."

"It makes no difference thinking things out. They come to the same."

"Rubbish!"

There was a long silence, during which the tide returned into Poole Harbour. "One would lose something," murmured Helen, apparently to herself. The water crept over the mud-flats towards the gorse and the blackened heather. Branksea Island lost its immense foreshores, and became a sombre episode of trees. Frome was forced inward towards Dorchester, Stour against Wimborne, Avon towards Salisbury, and over the immense displacement the sun presided, leading it to triumph ere he sank to rest. England was alive, throbbing through all her estuaries, crying for joy through the mouths of all her gulls, and the north wind, with contrary motion, blew stronger against her rising seas. What did it mean? For what end are her fair complexities, her changes of soil, her sinuous coast? Does she belong to those who have moulded her and made her feared by other lands, or to those who have added nothing to her power, but have somehow seen her, seen the whole island at once, lying as a jewel in a silver sea, sailing as a ship of souls, with all the brave world's fleet accompanying her towards eternity?

Chapter XX

Margaret had often wondered at the disturbance that takes place in the world's waters, when Love, who seems so tiny a pebble, slips in. Whom does Love concern beyond the beloved and the lover? Yet his impact deluges a hundred shores. No doubt the disturbance is really the spirit of the generations, welcoming the new generation, and chafing against the ultimate Fate, who holds all the seas in the palm of her hand. But Love cannot understand this. He cannot comprehend another's infinity; he is conscious only of his own—flying sunbeam, falling rose, pebble that asks for one quiet plunge below the fretting interplay of space and time. He knows that he will survive at the end of things, and be gathered by Fate as a jewel from the slime, and be handed with admiration round the assembly of the gods. "Men did produce this," they will say, and, saying, they will give men immortality. But meanwhile—what agitations meanwhile! The foundations of Property and Propriety are laid bare, twin rocks; Family Pride flounders to the surface, puffing and blowing, and refusing to be comforted; Theology, vaguely ascetic, gets up a nasty ground swell. Then the lawyers are aroused—cold brood—and creep out of their holes. They do what they can; they tidy up Property and Propriety, reassure Theology and Family Pride. Half-guineas are poured on the troubled waters, the lawyers creep back, and, if all has gone well, Love joins one man and woman together in Matrimony.

Margaret had expected the disturbance, and was not irritated by it. For a sensitive woman she had steady nerves, and could bear with the incongruous and the grotesque; and, besides, there was nothing excessive about her love-affair. Good-humour was the dominant note of her relations with Mr. Wilcox, or, as I must now call him, Henry. Henry did not encourage romance, and she was no girl to fidget for it. An acquaintance had become a lover, might become a husband, but would retain all that she had noted in the acquaintance; and love must confirm an old relation rather than reveal a new one.

In this spirit she promised to marry him.

He was in Swanage on the morrow, bearing the engagement-ring. They greeted one another with a hearty cordiality that impressed Aunt Juley. Henry dined at The Bays, but had engaged a bedroom in the principal hotel: he was one of those men who know the principal hotel by instinct. After dinner he asked Margaret if she wouldn't care for a turn on the Parade.[1] She accepted, and could not repress a little tremor; it would be her first real love scene. But as she put on her hat she burst out laughing. Love was so unlike the article served up in books: the joy, though genuine, was different; the mystery an unexpected mystery. For one thing, Mr. Wilcox still seemed a stranger.

For a time they talked about the ring; then she said:

"Do you remember the Embankment at Chelsea? It can't be ten days ago."

"Yes," he said, laughing. "And you and your sister were head and ears deep in some Quixotic scheme. Ah well!"

"I little thought then, certainly. Did you?"

"I don't know about that; I shouldn't like to say."

"Why, was it earlier?" she cried. "Did you think of me this way earlier! How extraordinarily interesting, Henry! Tell me."

But Henry had no intention of telling. Perhaps he could not have told, for his mental states became obscure as soon as he had passed through them. He misliked the very word "interesting," connoting it with wasted energy and even with morbidity. Hard facts were enough for him.

"I didn't think of it," she pursued. "No; when you spoke to me in the drawing-room, that was practically the first. It was all so different from what it's supposed to be. On the stage, or in books, a proposal is—how shall I put it?—a full-blown affair, a kind of bouquet; it loses its literal meaning. But in life a proposal really is a proposal——"

1. Promenade.

"By the way——"

"—a suggestion, a seed," she concluded; and the thought flew away into darkness.

"I was thinking, if you didn't mind, that we ought to spend this evening in a business talk; there will be so much to settle."

"I think so too. Tell me, in the first place, how did you get on with Tibby?"

"With your brother?"

"Yes, during cigarettes."

"Oh, very well."

"I am so glad," she answered, a little surprised. "What did you talk about? Me, presumably."

"About Greece too."

"Greece was a very good card, Henry. Tibby's only a boy still, and one has to pick and choose subjects a little. Well done."

"I was telling him I have shares in a currant-farm near Calamata."

"What a delightful thing to have shares in! Can't we go there for our honeymoon?"

"What to do?"

"To eat the currants. And isn't there marvelous scenery?"

"Moderately, but it's not the kind of place one could possibly go to with a lady."

"Why not?"

"No hotels."

"Some ladies do without hotels. Are you aware that Helen and I have walked alone over the Apennines,[2] with our luggage on our backs?"

"I wasn't aware, and, if I can manage it, you will never do such a thing again."

She said more gravely: "You haven't found time for a talk with Helen yet, I suppose?"

"No."

"Do, before you go. I am so anxious you two should be friends."

"Your sister and I have always hit it off," he said negligently. "But we're drifting away from our business. Let me begin at the beginning. You know that Evie is going to marry Percy Cahill."

"Dolly's uncle."

"Exactly. The girl's madly in love with him. A very good sort of fellow, but he demands—and rightly—a suitable provision with her. And in the second place, you will naturally understand, there is Charles. Before leaving town, I wrote Charles a very careful letter. You see, he has an increasing family and increasing expenses, and the I. and W. A.[3] is nothing particular just now, though capable of development."

2. Mountain range in Italy.
3. The Imperial and West African Rubber Company, the Wilcox family firm (see chapter XXIII).

"Poor fellow!" murmured Margaret, looking out to sea, and not under-standing.

"Charles being the elder son, some day Charles will have Howards End; but I am anxious, in my own happiness, not to be unjust to others."

"Of course not," she began, and then gave a little cry. "You mean money. How stupid I am! Of course not!"

Oddly enough, he winced a little at the word. "Yes. Money, since you put it so frankly. I am determined to be just to all—just to you, just to them. I am determined that my children shall have no case against me."

"Be generous to them," she said sharply. "Bother justice!"

"I am determined—and have already written to Charles to that effect——"

"But how much have you got?"

"What?"

"How much have you a year? I've six hundred."

"My income?"

"Yes. We must begin with how much you have, before we can settle how much you can give Charles. Justice, and even generosity, depend on that."

"I must say you're a downright young woman," he observed, patting her arm and laughing a little. "What a question to spring on a fellow!"

"Don't you know your income? Or don't you want to tell it me?"

"I——"

"That's all right"—now she patted him—"don't tell me. I don't want to know. I can do the sum just as well by proportion. Divide your income into ten parts. How many parts would you give to Evie, how many to Charles, how many to Paul?"

"The fact is, my dear, I hadn't any intention of bothering you with details. I only wanted to let you know that—well, that something must be done for the others, and you've understood me perfectly, so let's pass on to the next point."

"Yes, we've settled that," said Margaret, undisturbed by his strategic blunderings. "Go ahead; give away all you can, bearing in mind. I've a clear six hundred. What a mercy it is to have all this money about one."

"We've none too much, I assure you; you're marrying a poor man."

"Helen wouldn't agree with me here," she continued. "Helen daren't slang the rich, being rich herself, but she would like to. There's an odd notion, that I haven't yet got hold of, running about at the back of her brain, that poverty is somehow 'real.' She dislikes all organization, and probably confuses wealth with the technique of wealth. Sovereigns[4] in a stocking wouldn't bother her; cheques do. Helen is too relentless. One can't deal in her high-handed manner with the world."

4. Gold coins worth one British pound.

"There's this other point, and then I must go back to my hotel and write some letters. What's to be done now about the house in Ducie Street?"

"Keep it on—at least, it depends. When do you want to marry me?"

She raised her voice, as too often, and some youths, who were also taking the evening air, overheard her. "Getting a bit hot, eh?" said one. Mr. Wilcox turned on them, and said sharply, "I say!" There was silence. "Take care I don't report you to the police." They moved away quietly enough, but were only biding their time, and the rest of the conversation was punctuated by peals of ungovernable laughter.

Lowering his voice and infusing a hint of reproof into it, he said: "Evie will probably be married in September. We could scarcely think of anything before then."

"The earlier the nicer, Henry. Females are not supposed to say such things, but the earlier the nicer."

"How about September for us too?" he asked, rather dryly.

"Right. Shall we go into Ducie Street ourselves in September? Or shall we try to bounce Helen and Tibby into it? That's rather an idea. They are so unbusinesslike, we could make them do anything by judicious management. Look here—yes. We'll do that. And we ourselves could live at Howards End or Shropshire."

He blew out his cheeks. "Heavens! how you women do fly round! My head's in a whirl. Point by point, Margaret. Howards End's impossible. I let it to Hamar Bryce on a three years' agreement last March. Don't you remember? Oniton. Well, that is much, much too far away to rely on entirely. You will be able to be down there entertaining a certain amount, but we must have a house within easy reach of Town. Only Ducie Street has huge drawbacks. There's a mews[5] behind."

Margaret could not help laughing. It was the first she had heard of the mews behind Ducie Street. When she was a possible tenant it had suppressed itself, not consciously, but automatically. The breezy Wilcox manner, though genuine, lacked the clearness of vision that is imperative for truth. When Henry lived in Ducie Street he remembered the mews; when he tried to let he forgot it; and if anyone had remarked that the mews must be either there or not, he would have felt annoyed, and afterwards have found some opportunity of stigmatizing the speaker as academic. So does my grocer stigmatize me when I complain of the quality of his sultanas,[6] and he answers in one breath that they are the best sultanas, and how can I expect the best sultanas at that price? It is a flaw inherent in the business mind, and Margaret may do well to be tender to it, considering all that the business mind has done for England.

5. A courtyard with stables or a garage.
6. Raisins.

"Yes, in summer especially, the mews is a serious nuisance. The smoking-room, too, is an abominable little den. The house opposite has been taken by operatic people. Ducie Street's going down, it's my private opinion."

"How sad! It's only a few years since they built those pretty houses."

"Shows things are moving. Good for trade."

"I hate this continual flux of London. It is an epitome of us at our worst—eternal formlessness; all the qualities, good, bad, and indifferent, streaming away—streaming, streaming for ever. That's why I dread it so. I mistrust rivers, even in scenery. Now, the sea——"

"High tide, yes."

"Hoy toid"—from the promenading youths.

"And these are the men to whom we give the vote," observed Mr. Wilcox, omitting to add that they were also the men to whom he gave work as clerks—work that scarcely encouraged them to grow into other men. "However, they have their own lives and interests. Let's get on."

He turned as he spoke, and prepared to see her back to The Bays. The business was over. His hotel was in the opposite direction, and if he accompanied her his letters would be late for the post. She implored him not to come, but he was obdurate.

"A nice beginning, if your aunt saw you slip in alone!"

"But I always do go about alone. Considering I've walked over the Apennines, it's common sense. You will make me so angry. I don't the least take it as a compliment."

He laughed, and lit a cigar. "It isn't meant as a compliment, my dear. I just won't have you going about in the dark. Such people about too! It's dangerous."

"Can't I look after myself? I do wish——"

"Come along, Margaret; no wheedling."

A younger woman might have resented his masterly ways, but Margaret had too firm a grip of life to make a fuss. She was, in her own way, as masterly. If he was a fortress she was a mountain peak, whom all might tread, but whom the snows made nightly virginal. Disdaining the heroic outfit, excitable in her methods, garrulous, episodical, shrill, she misled her lover much as she had misled her aunt. He mistook her fertility for weakness. He supposed her "as clever as they make 'em," but no more, not realizing that she was penetrating to the depths of his soul, and approving of what she found there.

And if insight were sufficient, if the inner life were the whole of life, their happiness had been assured.

They walked ahead briskly. The parade and the road after it were well lighted, but it was darker in Aunt Juley's garden. As they were going up by the side-paths, through some rhododendrons, Mr. Wilcox, who was in front, said "Margaret" rather huskily, turned, dropped his cigar, and took her in his arms.

She was startled, and nearly screamed, but recovered herself at once, and kissed with genuine love the lips that were pressed against her own. It was their first kiss, and when it was over he saw her safely to the door and rang the bell for her, but disappeared into the night before the maid answered it. On looking back, the incident displeased her. It was so isolated. Nothing in their previous conversation had heralded it, and, worse still, no tenderness had ensued. If a man cannot lead up to passion he can at all events lead down from it, and she had hoped, after her complaisance, for some interchange of gentle words. But he had hurried away as if ashamed, and for an instant she was reminded of Helen and Paul.

Chapter XXI

Charles had just been scolding his Dolly. She deserved the scolding, and had bent before it, but her head, though bloody, was unsubdued, and her chirrupings began to mingle with his retreating thunder.

"You've woken the baby. I knew you would. (Rum-ti-foo, Rackety-tackety-Tompkin!) I'm not responsible for what Uncle Percy does, nor for anybody else or anything, so there!"

"Who asked him while I was away? Who asked my sister down to meet him? Who sent them out in the motor day after day?"

"Charles, that reminds me of some poem."

"Does it indeed? We shall all be dancing to a very different music presently. Miss Schlegel has fairly got us on toast."

"I could simply scratch that woman's eyes out, and to say it's my fault is most unfair."

"It's your fault, and five minutes ago you admitted it."

"I didn't."

"You did."

"Tootle, tootle, playing on the pootle!" exclaimed Dolly, suddenly devoting herself to the child.

"It's all very well to turn the conversation, but father would never have dreamt of marrying as long as Evie was there to make him comfortable. But you must needs start match-making. Besides, Cahill's too old."

"Of course, if you're going to be rude to Uncle Percy——"

"Miss Schlegel always meant to get hold of Howards End, and, thanks to you, she's got it."

"I call the way you twist things round and make them hang together most unfair. You couldn't have been nastier if you'd caught me flirting. Could he, diddums?"

"We're in a bad hole, and must make the best of it. I shall answer the pater's letter civilly. He's evidently anxious to do the decent thing. But I do not intend to forget these Schlegels in a hurry. As long as they're on their best behaviour—Dolly, are you listening?—we'll behave, too. But if I find them giving themselves airs, or monopolizing my father, or at all

ill-treating him, or worrying him with their artistic beastliness, I intend
to put my foot down, yes, firmly. Taking my mother's place! Heaven
knows what poor old Paul will say when the news reaches him."

The interlude closes. It has taken place in Charles's garden at Hilton.
He and Dolly are sitting in deck-chairs, and their motor is regarding
them placidly from its garage across the lawn. A short-frocked edition of
Charles also regards them placidly; a perambulator edition is squeaking;
a third edition is expected shortly. Nature is turning out Wilcoxes in this
peaceful abode, so that they may inherit the earth.

Chapter XXII

Margaret greeted her lord with peculiar tenderness on the morrow.
Mature as he was, she might yet be able to help him to the building of
the rainbow bridge that should connect the prose in us with the passion.
Without it we are meaningless fragments, half monks, half beasts,
unconnected arches that have never joined into a man. With it love is
born, and alights on the highest curve, glowing against the grey, sober
against the fire. Happy the man who sees from either aspect the glory of
these outspread wings. The roads of his soul lie clear, and he and his
friends shall find easy-going.

It was hard-going in the roads of Mr. Wilcox's soul. From boyhood he
had neglected them. "I am not a fellow who bothers about my own
inside." Outwardly he was cheerful, reliable, and brave; but within, all
had reverted to chaos, ruled, so far as it was ruled at all, by an incomplete asceticism. Whether as boy, husband, or widower, he had always
the sneaking belief that bodily passion is bad, a belief that is desirable
only when held passionately. Religion had confirmed him. The words
that were read aloud on Sunday to him and to other respectable men
were the words that had once kindled the souls of St. Catharine and St.
Francis[1] into a white-hot hatred of the carnal. He could not be as the
saints and love the Infinite with a seraphic ardour, but he could be a little ashamed of loving a wife. 'Amabat, amare timebat.'[2] And it was here
that Margaret hoped to help him.

It did not seem so difficult. She need trouble him with no gift of her
own. She would only point out the salvation that was latent in his own
soul, and in the soul of every man. Only connect! That was the whole of
her sermon. Only connect the prose and the passion, and both will be
exalted, and human love will be seen at its height. Live in fragments no
longer. Only connect, and the beast and the monk, robbed of the isolation that is life to either, will die.

Nor was the message difficult to give. It need not take the form of a

---

1. Catharine of Alexandria (ca. 310 A.D.), virgin Christian martyr; Francis of Assisi (1182?–1226),
   Christian saint converted from a worldly life to a devout existence of self-denial.
2. "He loved, he was afraid to love." (Latin)

good "talking." By quiet indications the bridge would be built and span their lives with beauty.

But she failed. For there was one quality in Henry for which she was never prepared, however much she reminded herself of it: his obtuseness. He simply did not notice things, and there was no more to be said. He never noticed that Helen and Frieda were hostile, or that Tibby was not interested in currant plantations; he never noticed the lights and shades that exist in the greyest conversation, the finger-posts, the milestones, the collisions, the illimitable views. Once—on another occasion—she scolded him about it. He was puzzled, but replied with a laugh: "My motto is Concentrate. I've no intention of frittering away my strength on that sort of thing." "It isn't frittering away the strength," she protested. "It's enlarging the space in which you may be strong." He answered: "You're a clever little woman, but my motto's Concentrate." And this morning he concentrated with a vengeance.

They met in the rhododendrons of yesterday. In the daylight the bushes were inconsiderable and the path was bright in the morning sun. She was with Helen, who had been ominously quiet since the affair was settled. "Here we all are!" she cried, and took him by one hand, retaining her sister's in the other.

"Here we are. Good-morning, Helen."

Helen replied, "Good-morning, Mr. Wilcox."

"Henry, she has had such a nice letter from the queer, cross boy. Do you remember him? He had a sad moustache, but the back of his head was young."

"I have had a letter too. Not a nice one—I want to talk it over with you:" for Leonard Bast was nothing to him now that she had given him her word; the triangle of sex was broken for ever.

"Thanks to your hint, he's clearing out of the Porphyrion."

"Not a bad business that Porphyrion," he said absently, as he took his own letter out of his pocket.

"Not a *bad*——" she exclaimed, dropping his hand. "Surely, on Chelsea Embankment——"

"Here's our hostess. Good-morning, Mrs. Munt. Fine rhododendrons. Good-morning, Frau Liesecke; we manage to grow flowers in England, don't we?"

"Not a *bad* business?"

"No. My letter's about Howards End. Bryce has been ordered abroad, and wants to sublet it. I am far from sure that I shall give him permission. There was no clause in the agreement. In my opinion, subletting is a mistake. If he can find me another tenant, whom I consider suitable, I may cancel the agreement. Morning, Schlegel. Don't you think that's better than subletting?"

Helen had dropped her hand now, and he had steered her past the whole party to the seaward side of the house. Beneath them was the bourgeois little bay, which must have yearned all through the centuries for just such a watering-place as Swanage to be built on its margin. The waves were colourless, and the Bournemouth steamer, drawn up against the pier and hooting wildly for excursionists, gave a further touch of insipidity.

"When there is a sublet I find that damage——"

"Do excuse me, but about the Porphyrion. I don't feel easy—might I just bother you, Henry?"

Her manner was so serious that he stopped, and asked her a little sharply what she wanted.

"You said on Chelsea Embankment, surely, that it was a bad concern, so we advised this clerk to clear out. He writes this morning that he's taken our advice, and now you say it's not a bad concern."

"A clerk who clears out of any concern, good or bad, without securing a berth somewhere else first, is a fool, and I've no pity for him."

"He has not done that. He's going into a bank in Camden Town, he says. The salary's much lower, but he hopes to manage—a branch of Dempster's Bank. Is that all right?"

"Dempster! My goodness me, yes."

"More right than the Porphyrion?"

"Yes, yes, yes; safe as houses—safer."

"Very many thanks. I'm sorry—if you sublet——?"

"If he sublets, I shan't have the same control. In theory there should be no more damage done at Howards End; in practice there will be. Things may be done for which no money can compensate. For instance, I shouldn't want that fine wych-elm spoilt. It hangs—— Margaret, we must go and see the old place some time. It's pretty in its way. We'll motor down and have lunch with Charles."

"I should enjoy that," said Margaret bravely.

"What about next Wednesday?"

"Wednesday? No, I couldn't well do that. Aunt Juley expects us to stop here another week at least."

"But you can give that up now."

"Er—no," said Margaret, after a moment's thought.

"Oh, that'll be all right. I'll speak to her."

"This visit is a high solemnity. My aunt counts on it year after year. She turns the house upside down for us; she invites our special friends— she scarcely knows Frieda, and we can't leave her on her hands. I missed one day, and she would be so hurt if I didn't stay the full ten."

"But I'll say a word to her. Don't you bother."

"Henry, I won't go. Don't bully me."

"You want to see the house, though?"

"Very much—I've heard so much about it, one way or the other. Aren't there pigs' teeth in the wych-elm?"

"*Pigs' teeth?*"

"And you chew the bark for toothache."

"What a rum notion! Of course not!"

"Perhaps I have confused it with some other tree. There are still a great number of sacred trees in England, it seems."

But he left her to intercept Mrs. Munt, whose voice could be heard in the distance: to be intercepted himself by Helen.

"Oh, Mr. Wilcox, about the Porphyrion——" she began, and went scarlet all over her face.

"It's all right," called Margaret, catching them up. "Dempster's Bank's better."

"But I think you told us the Porphyrion was bad, and would smash before Christmas."

"Did I? It was still outside the Tariff Ring, and had to take rotten policies. Lately it came in—safe as houses now."

"In other words, Mr. Bast need never have left it."

"No, the fellow needn't."

"—and needn't have started life elsewhere at a greatly reduced salary."

"He only says 'reduced,'" corrected Margaret, seeing trouble ahead.

"With a man so poor, every reduction must be great. I consider it a deplorable misfortune."

Mr. Wilcox, intent on his business with Mrs. Munt, was going steadily on, but the last remark made him say: "What? What's that? Do you mean that I'm responsible?"

"You're ridiculous, Helen."

"You seem to think——" He looked at his watch. "Let me explain the point to you. It is like this. You seem to assume, when a business concern is conducting a delicate negotiation, it ought to keep the public informed stage by stage. The Porphyrion, according to you, was bound to say, 'I am trying all I can to get into the Tariff Ring. I am not sure that I shall succeed, but it is the only thing that will save me from insolvency, and I am trying.' My dear Helen——"

"Is that your point? A man who had little money has less—that's mine."

"I am grieved for your clerk. But it is all in the day's work. It's part of the battle of life."

"A man who had little money," she repeated, "has less, owing to us. Under these circumstances I do not consider 'the battle of life' a happy expression."

"Oh come, come!" he protested pleasantly. "You're not to blame. No one's to blame."

"Is no one to blame for anything?"

"I wouldn't say that, but you're taking it far too seriously. Who is this fellow?"

"We have told you about the fellow twice already," said Helen. "You have even met the fellow. He is very poor and his wife is an extravagant imbecile. He is capable of better things. We—we, the upper classes—thought we would help him from the height of our superior knowledge—and here's the result!"

He raised his finger. "Now, a word of advice."

"I require no more advice."

"A word of advice. Don't take up that sentimental attitude over the poor. See that she doesn't, Margaret. The poor are poor, and one's sorry for them, but there it is. As civilization moves forward, the shoe is bound to pinch in places, and it's absurd to pretend that anyone is responsible personally. Neither you, nor I, nor my informant, nor the man who informed him, nor the directors of the Porphyrion, are to blame for this clerk's loss of salary. It's just the shoe pinching—no one can help it; and it might easily have been worse."

Helen quivered with indignation.

"By all means subscribe to charities—subscribe to them largely—but don't get carried away by absurd schemes of Social Reform. I see a good deal behind the scenes, and you can take it from me that there is no Social Question—except for a few journalists who try to get a living out of the phrase. There are just rich and poor, as there always have been and always will be. Point me out a time when men have been equal——"

"I didn't say——"

"Point me out a time when desire for equality has made them happier. No, no. You can't. There always have been rich and poor. I'm no fatalist. Heaven forbid! But our civilization is moulded by great impersonal forces" (his voice grew complacent; it always did when he eliminated the personal), "and there always will be rich and poor. You can't deny it" (and now it was a respectful voice)—"and you can't deny that, in spite of all, the tendency of civilization has on the whole been upward."

"Owing to God, I suppose," flashed Helen.

He stared at her.

"You grab the dollars. God does the rest."

It was no good instructing the girl if she was going to talk about God in that neurotic modern way. Fraternal to the last, he left her for the quieter company of Mrs. Munt. He thought, "She rather reminds me of Dolly."

Helen looked out at the sea.

"Don't ever discuss political economy with Henry," advised her sister. "It'll only end in a cry."

"But he must be one of those men who have reconciled science with religion," said Helen slowly. "I don't like those men. They are scientific themselves, and talk of the survival of the fittest, and cut down the salaries of their clerks, and stunt the independence of all who may menace their comfort, but yet they believe that somehow good—it is always that sloppy 'somehow'—will be the outcome, and that in some mystical way the Mr. Basts of the future will benefit because the Mr. Basts of to-day are in pain."

"He is such a man in theory. But oh, Helen, in theory!"

"But oh, Meg, what a theory!"

"Why should you put things so bitterly, dearie?"

"Because I'm an old maid," said Helen, biting her lip. "I can't think why I go on like this myself." She shook off her sister's hand and went into the house. Margaret, distressed at the day's beginning, followed the Bournemouth steamer with her eyes. She saw that Helen's nerves were exasperated by the unlucky Bast business beyond the bounds of polite-ness. There might at any minute be a real explosion, which even Henry would notice. Henry must be removed.

"Margaret!" her aunt called. "Magsy! It isn't true, surely, what Mr. Wilcox says, that you want to go away early next week?"

"Not 'want,'" was Margaret's prompt reply; "but there is so much to be settled, and I do want to see the Charleses'."

"But going away without taking the Weymouth trip, or even the Lulworth?" said Mrs. Munt, coming nearer. "Without going once more up Nine Barrows Down?"

"I'm afraid so."

Mr. Wilcox rejoined her with, "Good! I did the breaking of the ice."

A wave of tenderness came over her. She put a hand on either shoul-der, and looked deeply into the black, bright eyes. What was behind their competent stare? She knew, but was not disquieted.

Chapter XXIII

Margaret had no intention of letting things slide, and the evening before she left Swanage she gave her sister a thorough scolding. She censured her, not for disapproving of the engagement, but for throwing over her disapproval a veil of mystery. Helen was equally frank. "Yes," she said, with the air of one looking inwards, "there is a mystery. I can't help it. It's not my fault. It's the way life has been made." Helen in those days was over-interested in the subconscious self. She exaggerated the Punch and Judy aspect of life, and spoke of mankind as puppets, whom an invis-ible showman twitches into love and war. Margaret pointed out that if she dwelt on this she, too, would eliminate the personal. Helen was silent for a minute, and then burst into a queer speech, which cleared the air. "Go on and marry him. I think you're splendid; and if anyone can pull it off, you will." Margaret denied that there was anything to "pull off," but she continued: "Yes, there is, and I wasn't up to it with Paul. I can only do what's easy. I can only entice and be enticed. I can't, and won't, attempt difficult relations. If I marry, it will either be a man who's strong enough to boss me or whom I'm strong enough to boss. So

I shan't ever marry, for there aren't such men. And Heaven help anyone whom I do marry, for I shall certainly run away from him before you can say 'Jack Robinson.' There! Because I'm uneducated. But you, you're different; you're a heroine."

"Oh, Helen! Am I? Will it be as dreadful for poor Henry as all that?"

"You mean to keep proportion, and that's heroic, it's Greek, and I don't see why it shouldn't succeed with you. Go on and fight with him and help him. Don't ask me for help, or even for sympathy. Henceforward I'm going my own way. I mean to be thorough, because thoroughness is easy. I mean to dislike your husband, and to tell him so. I mean to make no concessions to Tibby. If Tibby wants to live with me, he must lump me. I mean to love you more than ever. Yes, I do. You and I have built up something real, because it is purely spiritual. There's no veil of mystery over us. Unreality and mystery begin as soon as one touches the body. The popular view is, as usual, exactly the wrong one. Our bothers are over tangible things—money, husbands, house-hunting. But Heaven will work of itself."

Margaret was grateful for this expression of affection, and answered, "Perhaps." All vistas close in the unseen—no one doubts it—but Helen closed them rather too quickly for her taste. At every turn of speech one was confronted with reality and the absolute. Perhaps Margaret grew too old for metaphysics, perhaps Henry was weaning her from them, but she felt that there was something a little unbalanced in the mind that so readily shreds the visible. The business man who assumes that this life is everything, and the mystic who asserts that it is nothing, fail, on this side and on that, to hit the truth. "Yes, I see, dear; it's about halfway between," Aunt Juley had hazarded in earlier years. No; truth, being alive, was not halfway between anything. It was only to be found by continuous excursions into either realm, and though proportion is the final secret, to espouse it at the outset is to insure sterility.

Helen, agreeing here, disagreeing there, would have talked till midnight, but Margaret, with her packing to do, focussed the conversation on Henry. She might abuse Henry behind his back, but please would she always be civil to him in company? "I definitely dislike him, but I'll do what I can," promised Helen. "Do what you can with my friends in return."

This conversation made Margaret easier. Their inner life was so safe that they could bargain over externals in a way that would have been incredible to Aunt Juley, and impossible for Tibby or Charles. There are moments when the inner life actually "pays," when years of self-scrutiny, conducted for no ulterior motive, are suddenly of practical use. Such moments are still rare in the West; that they come at all promises a fairer future. Margaret, though unable to understand her sister, was assured against estrangement, and returned to London with a more peaceful mind.

The following morning, at eleven o'clock, she presented herself at the offices of the Imperial and West African Rubber Company. She was glad to go there, for Henry had implied his business rather than described it, and the formlessness and vagueness that one associates with Africa itself had hitherto brooded over the main sources of his wealth. Not that a visit to the office cleared things up. There was just the ordinary surface scum of ledgers and polished counters and brass bars that began and stopped for no possible reason, of electric-light globes blossoming in triplets, of little rabbit-hutches faced with glass or wire, of little rabbits. And even when she penetrated to the inner depths, she found only the ordinary table and Turkey carpet, and though the map over the fireplace did depict a helping of West Africa, it was a very ordinary map. Another map hung opposite, on which the whole continent appeared, looking like a whale marked out for a blubber, and by its side was a door, shut, but Henry's voice came through it, dictating a "strong" letter. She might have been at the Porphyrion, or Dempster's Bank, or her own wine-merchant's. Everything seems just alike in these days. But perhaps she was seeing the Imperial side of the company rather than its West African, and Imperialism always had been one of her difficulties.

"One minute!" called Mr. Wilcox on receiving her name. He touched a bell, the effect of which was to produce Charles.

Charles had written his father an adequate letter—more adequate than Evie's, through which a girlish indignation throbbed. And he greeted his future stepmother with propriety.

"I hope that my wife—how do you do?—will give you a decent lunch," was his opening. "I left instructions, but we live in a rough-and-ready way. She expects you back to tea, too, after you have had a look at Howards End. I wonder what you'll think of the place. I wouldn't touch it with tongs myself. Do sit down! It's a measly little place."

"I shall enjoy seeing it," said Margaret, feeling, for the first time, shy.

"You'll see it at its worst, for Bryce decamped abroad last Monday without even arranging for a charwoman to clear up after him. I never saw such a disgraceful mess. It's unbelievable. He wasn't in the house a month."

"I've more than a little bone to pick with Bryce," called Henry from the inner chamber.

"Why did he go so suddenly?"

"Invalid type; couldn't sleep."

"Poor fellow!"

"Poor fiddlesticks!" said Mr. Wilcox, joining them. "He had the impudence to put up notice-boards without as much as saying with your leave or by your leave. Charles flung them down."

"Yes, I flung them down," said Charles modestly.

"I've sent a telegram after him, and a pretty sharp one, too. He, and he in person, is responsible for the upkeep of that house for the next three years."

"The keys are at the farm; we wouldn't have the keys."

"Quite right."

"Dolly would have taken them, but I was in, fortunately."

"What's Mr. Bryce like?" asked Margaret.

But nobody cared. Mr. Bryce was the tenant, who had no right to sublet; to have defined him further was a waste of time. On his misdeeds they descanted profusely, until the girl who had been typing the strong letter came out with it. Mr. Wilcox added his signature. "Now we'll be off," said he.

A motor-drive, a form of felicity detested by Margaret, awaited her. Charles saw them in, civil to the last, and in a moment the offices of the Imperial and West African Rubber Company faded away. But it was not an impressive drive. Perhaps the weather was to blame, being grey and banked high with weary clouds. Perhaps Hertfordshire is scarcely intended for motorists. Did not a gentleman once motor so quickly through Westmoreland that he missed it? and if Westmoreland can be missed, it will fare ill with a county whose delicate structure particularly needs the attentive eye. Hertfordshire is England at its quietest, with little emphasis of river and hill; it is England meditative. If Drayton[1] were with us again to write a new edition of his incomparable poem, he would sing the nymphs of Hertfordshire as indeterminate of feature, with hair obfuscated by the London smoke. Their eyes would be sad, and averted from their fate towards the Northern flats, their leader not Isis or Sabrina, but the slowly flowing Lea.[2] No glory of raiment would be theirs, no urgency of dance; but they would be real nymphs.

The chauffeur could not travel as quickly as he had hoped, for the Great North Road was full of Easter traffic. But he went quite quick enough for Margaret, a poor-spirited creature, who had chickens and children on the brain.

"They're all right," said Mr. Wilcox. "They'll learn—like the swallows and the telegraph-wires."

"Yes, but, while they're learning——"

"The motor's come to stay," he answered. "One must get about. There's a pretty church—oh, you aren't sharp enough. Well, look out, if the road worries you—right outward at the scenery."

She looked at the scenery. It heaved and merged like porridge. Presently it congealed. They had arrived.

---

1. Michael Drayton (1563–1631), author of the long poem "Poly-Olbion, or a Chorographicall Description of all the Tracts, Rivers, Mountaines, Forests, & other Parts . . . of Great Britaine" (1613).
2. Isis, Egyptian goddess of fertility; Sabrina, in British legend, the nymph of the river Severn who saves distressed maidens. The river Lea flows south from Hertfordshire to London.

Charles's house on the left; on the right the swelling forms of the Six Hills. Their appearance in such a neighbourhood surprised her. They interrupted the stream of residences that was thickening up towards Hilton. Beyond them she saw meadows and a wood, and beneath them she settled that soldiers of the best kind lay buried. She hated war and liked soldiers—it was one of her amiable inconsistencies.

But here was Dolly, dressed up to the nines, standing at the door to greet them, and here were the first drops of the rain. They ran in gaily, and after a long wait in the drawing-room, sat down to the rough-and-ready lunch, every dish in which concealed or exuded cream. Mr. Bryce was the chief topic of conversation. Dolly described his visit with the key, while her father-in-law gave satisfaction by chaffing her and contradicting all she said. It was evidently the custom to laugh at Dolly. He chaffed Margaret, too, and Margaret, roused from a grave meditation, was pleased, and chaffed him back. Dolly seemed surprised, and eyed her curiously. After lunch the two children came down. Margaret disliked babies, but hit it off better with the two-year-old, and sent Dolly into fits of laughter by talking sense to him. "Kiss them now, and come away," said Mr. Wilcox. She came, but refused to kiss them: it was such hard luck on the little things, she said, and though Dolly proffered Chorly-worly and Porgly-woggles in turn, she was obdurate.

By this time it was raining steadily. The car came round with the hood up, and again she lost all sense of space. In a few minutes they stopped, and Crane opened the door of the car.

"What's happened?" asked Margaret.

"What do you suppose?" said Henry.

A little porch was close up against her face.

"Are we there already?"

"We are."

"Well, I never! In years ago it seemed so far away."

Smiling, but somehow disillusioned, she jumped out, and her impetus carried her to the front-door. She was about to open it, when Henry said: "That's no good; it's locked. Who's got the key?"

As he had himself forgotten to call for the key at the farm, no one replied. He also wanted to know who had left the front gate open, since a cow had strayed in from the road, and was spoiling the croquet lawn. Then he said rather crossly: "Margaret, you wait in the dry. I'll go down for the key. It isn't a hundred yards."

"Mayn't I come too?"

"No; I shall be back before I'm gone."

Then the car turned away, and it was as if a curtain had risen. For the second time that day she saw the appearance of the earth.

There were the greengage-trees that Helen had once described, there the tennis lawn, there the hedge that would be glorious with dog-roses in June, but the vision now was of black and palest green. Down by the dell-hole[3] more vivid colours were awakening, and Lent lilies stood sentinel on its margin, or advanced in battalions over the grass. Tulips were a tray of jewels. She could not see the wych-elm tree, but a branch of the celebrated vine, studded with velvet knobs, had covered the porch. She was struck by the fertility of the soil; she had seldom been in a garden where the flowers looked so well, and even the weeds she was idly plucking out of the porch were intensely green. Why had poor Mr. Bryce fled from all this beauty? For she had already decided that the place was beautiful.

"Naughty cow! Go away!" cried Margaret to the cow, but without indignation.

Harder came the rain, pouring out of a windless sky, and spattering up from the notice-boards of the house-agents, which lay in a row on the lawn where Charles had hurled them. She must have interviewed Charles in another world—where one did have interviews. How Helen would revel in such a notion! Charles dead, all people dead, nothing alive but houses and gardens. The obvious dead, the intangible alive, and—no connection at all between them! Margaret smiled. Would that her own fancies were as clear-cut! Would that she could deal as high-handedly with the world! Smiling and sighing, she laid her hand upon the door. It opened. The house was not locked up at all.

She hesitated. Ought she to wait for Henry? He felt strongly about property, and might prefer to show her over himself. On the other hand, he had told her to keep in the dry, and the porch was beginning to drip. So she went in, and the draught from inside slammed the door behind.

Desolation greeted her. Dirty finger-prints were on the hall-windows, flue[4] and rubbish on its unwashed boards. The civilization of luggage had been here for a month, and then decamped. Dining-room and drawing-room—right and left—were guessed only by their wall-papers. They were just rooms where one could shelter from the rain. Across the ceiling of each ran a great beam. The dining-room and hall revealed theirs openly, but the drawing-room's was match-boarded[5]—because the facts of life must be concealed from ladies? Drawing-room, dining-room, and hall—how petty the names sounded! Here were simply three rooms where children could play and friends shelter from the rain. Yes, and they were beautiful.

Then she opened one of the doors opposite—there were two—and exchanged wall-papers for whitewash. It was the servants' part, though she scarcely realized that: just rooms again, where friends might shelter. The garden at the back was full of flowering cherries and plums. Farther on were hints of the meadow and a black cliff of pines. Yes, the meadow was beautiful.

---

3. A deep natural hollow or pit.
4. Dust, fluff.
5. Covered over with wooden paneling.

Penned in by the desolate weather, she recaptured the sense of space which the motor had tried to rob from her. She remembered again that ten square miles are not ten times as wonderful as one square mile, that a thousand square miles are not practically the same as heaven. The phantom of bigness, which London encourages, was laid for ever when she paced from the hall at Howards End to its kitchen and heard the rains run this way and that where the watershed of the roof divided them.

Now Helen came to her mind, scrutinizing half Wessex from the ridge of the Purbeck Downs, and saying: "You will have to lose something." She was not so sure. For instance, she would double her kingdom by opening the door that concealed the stairs.

Now she thought of the map of Africa; of empires; of her father; of the two supreme nations, streams of whose life warmed her blood, but, mingling, had cooled her brain. She paced back into the hall, and as she did so the house reverberated.

"Is that you, Henry?" she called.

There was no answer, but the house reverberated again.

"Henry, have you got in?"

But it was the heart of the house beating, faintly at first, then loudly, martially. It dominated the rain.

It is the starved imagination, not the well-nourished, that is afraid. Margaret flung open the door to the stairs. A noise as of drums seemed to deafen her. A woman, an old woman, was descending, with figure erect, with face impassive, with lips that parted and said dryly:

"Oh! Well, I took you for Ruth Wilcox."

Margaret stammered: "I—— Mrs. Wilcox—I?"

"In fancy, of course—in fancy. You had her way of walking. Good-day." And the old woman passed out into the rain.

Chapter XXIV

"It gave her quite a turn," said Mr. Wilcox, when retailing the incident to Dolly at tea-time. "None of you girls have any nerves, really. Of course, a word from me put it all right, but silly old Miss Avery—she frightened you, didn't she, Margaret? There you stood clutching a bunch of weeds. She might have said something, instead of coming down the stairs with that alarming bonnet on. I passed her as I came in. Enough to make the car shy. I believe Miss Avery goes in for being a character; some old maids do." He lit a cigarette. "It is their last resource. Heaven knows what she was doing in the place; but that's Bryce's business, not mine."

"I wasn't as foolish as you suggest," said Margaret. "She only startled me, for the house had been silent so long."

"Did you take her for a spook?" asked Dolly, for whom "spooks" and "going to church" summarized the unseen.

"Not exactly."

"She really did frighten you," said Henry, who was far from discouraging timidity in females. "Poor Margaret! And very naturally. Uneducated classes are so stupid."

"Is Miss Avery uneducated classes?" Margaret asked, and found herself looking at the decoration scheme of Dolly's drawing-room.

"She's just one of the crew at the farm. People like that always assume things. She assumed you'd know who she was. She left all the Howards End keys in the front lobby, and assumed that you'd seen them as you came in, that you'd lock up the house when you'd done, and would bring them on down to her. And there was her niece hunting for them down at the farm. Lack of education makes people very casual. Hilton was full of women like Miss Avery once."

"I shouldn't have disliked it, perhaps."

"Or Miss Avery giving me a wedding present," said Dolly.

Which was illogical but interesting. Through Dolly, Margaret was destined to learn a good deal.

"But Charles said I must try not to mind, because she had known his grandmother."

"As usual, you've got the story wrong, my good Dorothea."

"I meant great-grandmother—the one who left Mrs. Wilcox the house. Weren't both of them and Miss Avery friends when Howards End, too, was a farm?"

Her father-in-law blew out a shaft of smoke. His attitude to his dead wife was curious. He would allude to her, and hear her discussed, but never mentioned her by name. Nor was he interested in the dim, bucolic past. Dolly was—for the following reason.

"Then hadn't Mrs. Wilcox a brother—or was it an uncle? Anyhow, he popped the question, and Miss Avery, she said 'No.' Just imagine, if she'd said 'Yes,' she would have been Charles's aunt. (Oh, I say, that's rather good! 'Charlie's Aunt'! I must chaff him about that this evening.) And the man went out and was killed. Yes, I'm certain I've got it right now. Tom Howard—he was the last of them."

"I believe so," said Mr. Wilcox negligently.

"I say! Howards End—Howards Ended!" cried Dolly. "I'm rather on the spot this evening, eh?"

"I wish you'd ask whether Crane's ended."

"Oh, Mr. Wilcox, how *can* you?"

"Because, if he has had enough tea, we ought to go.—Dolly's a good little woman," he continued, "but a little of her goes a long way. I couldn't live near her if you paid me."

Margaret smiled. Though presenting a firm front to outsiders, no Wilcox could live near, or near the possessions of, any other Wilcox. They had the colonial spirit, and were always making for some spot where the white man might carry his burden unobserved. Of course,

Howards End was impossible, so long as the younger couple were established in Hilton. His objections to the house were plain as daylight now.

Crane had had enough tea, and was sent to the garage, where their car had been trickling muddy water over Charles's. The downpour had surely penetrated the Six Hills by now, bringing news of our restless civilization. "Curious mounds," said Henry, "but in with you now; another time." He had to be up in London by seven—if possible, by six-thirty. Once more she lost the sense of space; once more trees, houses, people, animals, hills, merged and heaved into one dirtiness, and she was at Wickham Place.

Her evening was pleasant. The sense of flux which had haunted her all the year disappeared for a time. She forgot the luggage and the motor-cars, and the hurrying men who know so much and connect so little. She recaptured the sense of space, which is the basis of all earthly beauty, and, starting from Howards End, she attempted to realize England. She failed—visions do not come when we try, though they may come through trying. But an unexpected love of the island awoke in her, connecting on this side with the joys of the flesh, on that with the inconceivable. Helen and her father had known this love, poor Leonard Bast was groping after it, but it had been hidden from Margaret till this afternoon. It had certainly come through the house and old Miss Avery. Through them: the notion of "through" persisted; her mind trembled towards a conclusion which only the unwise have put into words. Then, veering back into warmth, it dwelt on ruddy bricks, flowering plum-trees, and all the tangible joys of spring.

Henry, after allaying her agitation, had taken her over his property, and had explained to her the use and dimensions of the various rooms. He had sketched the history of the little estate. "It is so unlucky," ran the monologue, "that money wasn't put into it about fifty years ago. Then it had four—five—times the land—thirty acres at least. One could have made something out of it then—a small park, or at all events shrubberies, and rebuilt the house farther away from the road. What's the good of taking it in hand now? Nothing but the meadow left, and even that was heavily mortgaged when I first had to do with things—yes, and the house too. Oh, it was no joke." She saw two women as he spoke, one old, the other young, watching their inheritance melt away. She saw them greet him as a deliverer. "Mismanagement did it—besides, the days for small farms are over. It doesn't pay—except with intensive cultivation. Small holdings, back to the land—ah! philanthropic bunkum. Take it as a rule that nothing pays on a small scale. Most of the land you see (they were standing at an upper window, the only one which faced west) belongs to the people at the Park—they made their pile over copper—good chaps. Avery's Farm, Sishe's—what they call the Common, where you see that ruined oak—one after the other fell in, and so did this, as near as is no matter." But Henry had saved it, without fine feelings or deep insight; but he had saved it, and she loved him for the deed. "When I had more control I did what I could: sold off the two and a half animals, and the mangy pony, and the superannuated tools; pulled down the outhouses; drained; thinned out I don't know how many guelder-roses and elder-trees; and inside the house I turned the old kitchen into a hall, and made a kitchen behind where the dairy was. Garage and so on came later. But one could still tell it's been an old farm. And yet it isn't the place that would fetch one of your artistic crew." No, it wasn't; and if he did not quite understand it, the artistic crew would still less: it was English, and the wych-elm that she saw from the window was an English tree. No report had prepared her for its peculiar glory. It was nei-ther warrior, nor lover, nor god; in none of these rôles do the English excel. It was a comrade, bending over the house, strength and adventure in its roots, but in its utmost fingers tenderness, and the girth, that a dozen men could not have spanned, became in the end evanescent, till pale bud clusters seemed to float in the air. It was a comrade. House and tree transcended any similes of sex. Margaret thought of them now, and was to think of them through many a windy night and London day, but to compare either to man, to woman, always dwarfed the vision. Yet they kept within limits of the human. Their message was not of eternity, but of hope on this side of the grave. As she stood in the one, gazing at the other, truer relationship had gleamed.

Another touch, and the account of her day is finished. They entered the garden for a minute, and to Mr. Wilcox's surprise she was right. Teeth, pigs' teeth, could be seen in the bark of the wych-elm tree—just the white tips of them showing. "Extraordinary!" he cried. "Who told you?"

"I heard of it one winter in London," was her answer, for she, too, avoided mentioning Mrs. Wilcox by name.

Chapter XXV

Evie heard of her father's engagement when she was in for a tennis tour-nament, and her play went simply to pot. That she should marry and leave him had seemed natural enough; that he, left alone, should do the same was deceitful; and now Charles and Dolly said that it was all her fault. "But I never dreamt of such a thing," she grumbled. "Dad took me to call now and then, and made me ask her to Simpson's. Well, I'm alto-gether off dad." It was also an insult to their mother's memory; there they were agreed, and Evie had the idea of returning Mrs. Wilcox's lace and jewellery "as a protest." Against what it would protest she was not clear; but being only eighteen, the idea of renunciation appealed to her, the more as she did not care for jewellery or lace. Dolly then suggested that she and Uncle Percy should pretend to break off their engagement, and then perhaps Mr. Wilcox would quarrel with Miss Schlegel, and break off his; or Paul might be cabled for. But at this point Charles told them not to talk nonsense. So Evie settled to marry as soon as possible; it was no good hanging about with these Schlegels eyeing her. The date of her wedding was consequently put forward from September to August, and in the intoxication of presents she recovered much of her good-humour.

Margaret found that she was expected to figure at this function, and to figure largely; it would be such an opportunity, said Henry, for her to get to know his set. Sir James Bidder would be there, and all the Cahills and the Fussells, and his sister-in-law, Mrs. Warrington Wilcox, had fortunately got back from her tour round the world. Henry she loved, but his set promised to be another matter. He had not the knack of surrounding himself with nice people—indeed, for a man of ability and virtue his choice had been singularly unfortunate; he had no guiding principle beyond a certain preference for mediocrity; he was content to settle one of the greatest things in life haphazard, and so, while his investments went right, his friends generally went wrong. She would be told, "Oh, So-and-so's a good sort—a thundering good sort," and find, on meeting him, that he was a brute or a bore. If Henry had shown real affection, she would have understood, for affection explains everything. But he seemed without sentiment. The "thundering good sort" might at any moment become "a fellow for whom I never did have much use, and have less now," and be shaken off cheerily into oblivion. Margaret had done the same as a schoolgirl. Now she never forgot anyone for whom she had once cared; she connected, though the connection might be bitter, and she hoped that some day Henry would do the same.

Evie was not to be married from Ducie Street. She had a fancy for something rural, and, besides, no one would be in London then, so she left her boxes for a few weeks at Oniton Grange, and her banns were duly published[1] in the parish church, and for a couple of days the little town, dreaming between the ruddy hills, was roused by the clang of our civilization, and drew up by the roadside to let the motors pass. Oniton had been a discovery of Mr. Wilcox's—a discovery of which he was not altogether proud. It was up towards the Welsh border, and so difficult of access that he had concluded it must be something special. A ruined castle stood in the grounds. But having got there, what was one to do? The shooting was bad, the fishing indifferent, and women-folk reported the scenery as nothing much. The place turned out to be in the wrong part of Shropshire, damn it, and though he never damned his own property aloud, he was only waiting to get it off his hands, and then to let fly. Evie's marriage was its last appearance in public. As soon as a tenant was found, it became a house for which he never had had much use, and had less now, and, like Howards End, faded into Limbo.

But on Margaret Oniton was destined to make a lasting impression. She regarded it as her future home, and was anxious to start straight with

---

1. Her marriage was announced.

the clergy, etc., and, if possible, to see something of the local life. It was a market-town[2]—as tiny a one as England possesses—and had for ages served that lonely valley, and guarded our marches against the Kelt.[3] In spite of the occasion, in spite of the numbing hilarity that greeted her as soon as she got into the reserved saloon at Paddington, her senses were awake and watching, and though Oniton was to prove one of her innumerable false starts, she never forgot it, nor the things that happened there.

The London party only numbered eight—the Fussells, father and son, two Anglo-Indian[4] ladies named Mrs. Plynlimmon and Lady Edser, Mrs. Warrington Wilcox and her daughter, and, lastly, the little girl, very smart and quiet, who figures at so many weddings, and who kept a watchful eye on Margaret, the bride-elect. Dolly was absent—a domestic event detained her at Hilton; Paul had cabled a humorous message; Charles was to meet them with a trio of motors at Shrewsbury. Helen had refused her invitation; Tibby had never answered his. The management was excellent, as was to be expected with anything that Henry undertook; one was conscious of his sensible and generous brain in the background. They were his guests as soon as they reached the train; a special label for their luggage; a courier; a special lunch; they had only to look pleasant and, where possible, pretty. Margaret thought with dismay of her own nuptials—presumably under the management of Tibby. "Mr. Theobald Schlegel and Miss Helen Schlegel request the pleasure of Mrs. Plynlimmon's company on the occasion of the marriage of their sister Margaret." The formula was incredible, but it must soon be printed and sent, and though Wickham Place need not compete with Oniton, it must feed its guests properly, and provide them with sufficient chairs. Her wedding would either be ramshackly or bourgeois—she hoped the latter. Such an affair as the present, staged with a deftness that was almost beautiful, lay beyond her powers and those of her friends.

The low rich purr of a Great Western express is not the worst background for conversation, and the journey passed pleasantly enough. Nothing could have exceeded the kindness of the two men. They raised windows for some ladies, and lowered them for others, they rang the bell for the servant, they identified the colleges as the train slipped past Oxford, they caught books or bag-purses in the act of tumbling on to the floor. Yet there was nothing finicking about their politeness: it had the Public School touch, and, though sedulous, was virile. More battles than Waterloo have been won on our playing-fields,[5] and Margaret

2. A town with the privilege of holding a public market.
3. The Welsh. Wales became a principality of England in 1282 when Edward I defeated Llewelyn the Last; the Welsh actively resisted English rule sporadically for centuries.
4. English residents of colonial India.
5. After defeating Napoleon, the Duke of Wellington is reported to have said: "The battle of Waterloo was won on the playing fields of Eton," one of the ancient boarding schools that train the English ruling class.

bowed to a charm of which she did not wholly approve, and said nothing when the Oxford colleges were identified wrongly. "Male and
female created He them";[6] the journey to Shrewsbury confirmed this
questionable statement, and the long glass saloon, that moved so easily
and felt so comfortable, became a forcing-house[7] for the idea of sex.

At Shrewsbury came fresh air. Margaret was all for sight-seeing, and
while the others were finishing their tea at the Raven, she annexed a
motor and hurried over the astonishing city.[8] Her chauffeur was not the
faithful Crane, but an Italian, who dearly loved making her late.
Charles, watch in hand, though with a level brow, was standing in front
of the hotel when they returned. It was perfectly all right, he told her;
she was by no means the last. And then he dived into the coffee-room,
and she heard him say, "For God's sake, hurry the women up; we shall
never be off," and Albert Fussell reply, "Not I; I've done my share," and
Colonel Fussell opine that the ladies were getting themselves up to kill.
Presently Myra (Mrs. Warrington's daughter) appeared, and as she was
his cousin, Charles blew her up a little: she had been changing her
smart travelling hat for a smart motor hat. Then Mrs. Warrington herself, leading the quiet child; the two Anglo-Indian ladies were always last.
Maids, courier, heavy luggage, had already gone on by a branch-line to
a station nearer Oniton, but there were five hat-boxes and four dressing-
bags to be packed, and five dust-cloaks to be put on, and to be put off at
the last moment, because Charles declared them not necessary. The
men presided over everything with unfailing good-humour. By half-past
five the party was ready, and went out of Shrewsbury by the Welsh
Bridge.

Shropshire had not the reticence of Hertfordshire. Though robbed of
half its magic by swift movement, it still conveyed the sense of hills.
They were nearing the buttresses that force the Severn eastward and
make it an English stream, and the sun, sinking over the Sentinels of
Wales, was straight in their eyes. Having picked up another guest, they
turned southward, avoiding the greater mountains, but conscious of an
occasional summit, rounded and mild, whose colouring differed in quality from that of the lower earth, and whose contours altered more slowly. Quiet mysteries were in progress behind those tossing horizons: the
West, as ever, was retreating with some secret which may not be worth
the discovery, but which no practical man will ever discover.

They spoke of Tariff Reform.[9]

Mrs. Warrington was just back from the Colonies. Like many other
critics of Empire, her mouth had been stopped with food, and she could

6. Genesis 1.27.
7. Greenhouse for accelerating the growth of plants and flowers.
8. Perhaps Shrewsbury is "astonishing" because, a modern commercial town, it nevertheless has
   many historic buildings and ancient churches.
9. A proposal for increasing the duties on imports from territories outside the British Empire.

only exclaim at the hospitality with which she had been received, and warn the Mother Country against trifling with young Titans. "They threaten to cut the painter,"[1] she cried, "and where shall we be then? Miss Schlegel, you'll undertake to keep Henry sound about Tariff Reform? It is our last hope."

Margaret playfully confessed herself on the other side, and they began to quote from their respective hand-books while the motor carried them deep into the hills. Curious these were rather than impressive, for their outlines lacked beauty, and the pink fields on their summits suggested the handkerchiefs of a giant spread out to dry. An occasional outcrop of rock, an occasional wood, an occasional "forest," treeless and brown, all hinted at wildness to follow, but the main colour was an agricultural green. The air grew cooler; they had surmounted the last gradient, and Oniton lay below them with its church, its radiating houses, its castle, its river-girt peninsula. Close to the castle was a grey mansion, unintellectual but kindly, stretching with its grounds across the peninsula's neck— the sort of mansion that was built all over England in the beginning of the last century, while architecture was still an expression of the national character. That was the Grange, remarked Albert, over his shoulder, and then he jammed the break on, and the motor slowed down and stopped. "I'm sorry," said he, turning round. "Do you mind getting out— by the door on the right. Steady on."

"What's happened?" asked Mrs. Warrington.

Then the car behind them drew up, and the voice of Charles was heard saying: "Get out the women at once." There was a concourse of males, and Margaret and her companions were hustled out and received into the second car. What had happened? As it started off again, the door of a cottage opened, and a girl screamed wildly at them.

"What is it?" the ladies cried.

Charles drove them a hundred yards without speaking. Then he said: "It's all right. Your car just touched a dog."

"But stop!" cried Margaret, horrified.

"It didn't hurt him."

"Didn't really hurt him?" asked Myra.

"No."

"Do *please* stop!" said Margaret, leaning forward. She was standing up in the car, the other occupants holding her knees to steady her. "I want to go back, please."

Charles took no notice.

"We've left Mr. Fussell behind," said another; "and Angelo, and Crane."

"Yes, but no woman."

1. The rope towing a boat.

"I expect a little of"—Mrs. Warrington scratched her palm—"will be more to the point than one of us!"

"The insurance company see to that," remarked Charles, "and Albert will do the talking."

"I want to go back, though, I say!" repeated Margaret, getting angry.

Charles took no notice. The motor, loaded with refugees, continued to travel very slowly down the hill. "The men are there," chorused the others. "Men will see to it."

"The men *can't* see to it. Oh, this is ridiculous! Charles, I ask you to stop."

"Stopping's no good," drawled Charles.

"Isn't it?" said Margaret, and jumped straight out of the car.

She fell on her knees, cut her gloves, shook her hat over her ear. Cries of alarm followed her. "You've hurt yourself," exclaimed Charles, jumping after her.

"Of course I've hurt myself!" she retorted.

"May I ask what——"

"There's nothing to ask," said Margaret.

"Your hand's bleeding."

"I know."

"I'm in for a frightful row from the pater."

"You should have thought of that sooner, Charles."

Charles had never been in such a position before. It was a woman in revolt who was hobbling away from him, and the sight was too strange to leave any room for anger. He recovered himself when the others caught them up: their sort he understood. He commanded them to go back.

Albert Fussell was seen walking towards them.

"It's all right!" he called. "It wasn't a dog, it was a cat."

"There!" exclaimed Charles triumphantly. "It's only a rotten cat."

"Got room in your car for a little un? I cut as soon as I saw it wasn't a dog; the chauffeurs are tackling the girl." But Margaret walked forward steadily. Why should the chauffeurs tackle the girl? Ladies sheltering behind men, men sheltering behind servants—the whole system's wrong, and she must challenge it.

"Miss Schlegel! 'Pon my word, you've hurt your hand."

"I'm just going to see," said Margaret. "Don't you wait, Mr. Fussell."

The second motor came round the corner. "It is all right, madam," said Crane in his turn. He had taken to call her madam.

"What's all right? The cat?"

"Yes, madam. The girl will receive compensation for it."

"She was a very ruda girla," said Angelo from the third motor thoughtfully.

"Wouldn't you have been rude?"

The Italian spread out his hands, implying that he had not thought of rudeness, but would produce it if it pleased her. The situation became absurd. The gentlemen were again buzzing round Miss Schlegel with offers of assistance, and Lady Edser began to bind up her hand. She yielded, apologizing slightly, and was led back to the car, and soon the landscape resumed its motion, the lonely cottage disappeared, the castle swelled on its cushion of turf, and they had arrived. No doubt she had disgraced herself. But she felt their whole journey from London had been unreal. They had no part with the earth and its emotions. They were dust, and a stink, and cosmopolitan chatter, and the girl whose cat had been killed had lived more deeply than they.

"Oh, Henry," she exclaimed, "I have been so naughty," for she had decided to take up this line. "We ran over a cat. Charles told me not to jump out, but I would, and look!" She held out her bandaged hand. "Your poor Meg went such a flop."

Mr. Wilcox looked bewildered. In evening dress, he was standing to welcome his guests in the hall.

"Thinking it was a dog," added Mrs. Warrington.

"Ah, a dog's a companion!" said Colonel Fussell. "A dog'll remember you."

"Have you hurt yourself, Margaret?"

"Not to speak about; and it's my left hand."

"Well, hurry up and change."

She obeyed, as did the others. Mr. Wilcox then turned to his son.

"Now, Charles, what's happened?"

Charles was absolutely honest. He described what he believed to have happened. Albert had flattened out a cat, and Miss Schlegel had lost her nerve, as any woman might. She had been got safely into the other car, but when it was in motion had leapt out again, in spite of all that they could say. After walking a little on the road, she had calmed down and had said that she was sorry. His father accepted this explanation, and neither knew that Margaret had artfully prepared the way for it. It fitted in too well with their view of feminine nature. In the smoking-room, after dinner, the Colonel put forward the view that Miss Schlegel had jumped it out of devilry. Well he remembered as a young man, in the harbour of Gibraltar once, how a girl—a handsome girl, too—had jumped overboard for a bet. He could see her now, and all the lads overboard after her. But Charles and Mr. Wilcox agreed it was much more probably nerves in Miss Schlegel's case. Charles was depressed. That woman had a tongue. She would bring worse disgrace on his father before she had done with them. He strolled out on to the castle mound to think the matter over. The evening was exquisite. On three sides of him a little river whispered, full of messages from the west; above his head the ruins made patterns against the sky. He carefully reviewed their dealings with this family, until he fitted Helen, and Margaret, and Aunt Juley into an orderly conspiracy. Paternity had made him suspicious. He had two children to look after, and more coming, and day by day they seemed less likely to grow up rich men. "It is all very well," he reflected, "the pater saying that he will be just to all, but one can't be just indefinitely. Money isn't elastic. What's to happen if Evie has a family? And, come to that, so may the pater. There'll not be enough to go round, for there's none coming in, either through Dolly or Percy. It's damnable!" He looked enviously at the Grange, whose windows poured light and laughter. First and last, this wedding would cost a pretty penny. Two ladies were strolling up and down the garden terrace, and as the syllables "Imperialism" were wafted to his ears, he guessed that one of them was his aunt. She might have helped him, if she too had not had a family to provide for. "Everyone for himself," he repeated—a maxim which had cheered him in the past, but which rang grimly enough among the ruins of Oniton. He lacked his father's ability in business, and so had an ever higher regard for money; unless he could inherit plenty, he feared to leave his children poor.

As he sat thinking, one of the ladies left the terrace and walked into the meadow; he recognized her as Margaret by the white bandage that gleamed on her arm, and put out his cigar, lest the gleam should betray him. She climbed up the mound in zigzags, and at times stooped down, as if she was stroking the turf. It sounds absolutely incredible, but for a moment Charles thought that she was in love with him, and had come out to tempt him. Charles believed in temptresses, who are indeed the strong man's necessary complement, and having no sense of humour, he could not purge himself of the thought by a smile. Margaret, who was engaged to his father, and his sister's wedding-guest, kept on her way without noticing him, and he admitted that he had wronged her on this point. But what was she doing? Why was she stumbling about amongst the rubble and catching her dress in brambles and burrs? As she edged round the keep, she must have got to leeward and smelt his cigar-smoke, for she exclaimed, "Hullo! Who's that?"

Charles made no answer.

"Saxon or Kelt?"[2] she continued, laughing in the darkness. "But it doesn't matter. Whichever you are, you will have to listen to me. I love this place. I love Shropshire. I hate London. I am glad that this will be my home. Ah, dear"—she was now moving back towards the house— "what a comfort to have arrived!"

"That woman means mischief," thought Charles, and compressed his lips. In a few minutes he followed her indoors, as the ground was getting damp. Mists were rising from the river, and presently it became invisible, though it whispered more loudly. There had been a heavy downpour in the Welsh hills.

---

2. "English or Welsh?" In a joking allusion to their long history of conflict, Margaret pretends to be a guard challenging a stranger.

Chapter XXVI

Next morning a fine mist covered the peninsula. The weather promised well, and the outline of the castle mound grew clearer each moment that Margaret watched it. Presently she saw the keep,[1] and the sun painted the rubble gold, and charged the white sky with blue. The shadow of the house gathered itself together, and fell over the garden. A cat looked up at her window and mewed. Lastly the river appeared, still holding the mists between its banks and its overhanging alders, and only visible as far as a hill, which cut off its upper reaches.

Margaret was fascinated by Oniton. She had said that she loved it, but it was rather its romantic tension that held her. The rounded Druids[2] of whom she had caught glimpses in her drive, the rivers hurrying down from them to England, the carelessly modelled masses of the lower hills, thrilled her with poetry. The house was insignificant, but the prospect from it would be an eternal joy, and she thought of all the friends she would have to stop in it, and of the conversion of Henry himself to a rural life. Society, too, promised favourably. The rector of the parish had dined with them last night, and she found that he was a friend of her father's, and so knew what to find in her. She liked him. He would introduce her to the town. While, on her other side, Sir James Bidder sat, repeating that she only had to give the word, and he would whip up the county families for twenty miles round. Whether Sir James, who was Garden Seeds,[3] had promised what he could perform, she doubted, but so long as Henry mistook them for the county families when they did call, she was content.

Charles and Albert Fussell now crossed the lawn. They were going for a morning dip, and a servant followed them with their bathing dresses. She had meant to take a stroll herself before breakfast, but saw that the day was still sacred to men, and amused herself by watching their contretemps.[4] In the first place the key of the bathing-shed could not be found. Charles stood by the riverside with folded hands, tragical, while the servant shouted, and was misunderstood by another servant in the garden. Then came a difficulty about a spring-board, and soon three people were running backwards and forwards over the meadow, with orders and counter orders and recriminations and apologies. If Margaret wanted to jump from a motor-car, she jumped; if Tibby thought paddling would benefit his ankles, he paddled; if a clerk desired adventure, he took a walk in the dark. But these athletes seemed paralyzed. They could not bathe without their appliances, though the morning sun was calling and the last mists were rising from the dimpling stream. Had they

1. The strongest, most secure part of a medieval castle.
2. Figuratively, Welsh hills; literally, members of an ancient Celtic priesthood.
3. An amateur gardener, not a prominent farmer from the region's long-established families.
4. Mix-ups.

found the life of the body after all? Could not the men whom they despised as milksops[5] beat them, even on their own ground?

She thought of the bathing arrangements as they should be in her day—no worrying of servants, no appliances, beyond good sense. Her reflections were disturbed by the quiet child, who had come out to speak to the cat, but was now watching her watch the men. She called, "Good-morning, dear," a little sharply. Her voice spread consternation. Charles looked round, and though completely attired in indigo blue, vanished into the shed, and was seen no more.

"Miss Wilcox is up——" the child whispered, and then became unintelligible.

"What's that?"

It sounded like, "——cut-yoke—sack-back——"[6]

"I can't hear."

"—On the bed—tissue-paper——"

Gathering that the wedding-dress was on view, and that a visit would be seemly, she went to Evie's room. All was hilarity here. Evie, in a petticoat, was dancing with one of the Anglo-Indian ladies, while the other was adoring yards of white satin. They screamed, they laughed, they sang, and the dog barked.

Margaret screamed a little too, but without conviction. She could not feel that a wedding was so funny. Perhaps something was missing in her equipment.

Evie gasped: "Dolly is a rotter not to be here! Oh, we would rag just then!" Then Margaret went down to breakfast.

Henry was already installed; he ate slowly and spoke little, and was, in Margaret's eyes, the only member of their party who dodged emotion successfully. She could not suppose him indifferent either to the loss of his daughter or to the presence of his future wife. Yet he dwelt intact, only issuing orders occasionally—orders that promoted the comfort of his guests. He inquired after her hand; he set her to pour out the coffee and Mrs. Warrington to pour out the tea. When Evie came down there was a moment's awkwardness, and both ladies rose to vacate their places. "Burton," called Henry, "serve tea and coffee from the sideboard!" It wasn't genuine tact, but it was tact, of a sort—the sort that is as useful as the genuine, and saves even more situations at Board meetings. Henry treated a marriage like a funeral, item by item, never raising his eyes to the whole, and "Death, where is thy sting? Love, where is thy victory?"[7] one would exclaim at the close.

After breakfast she claimed a few words with him. It was always best to approach him formally. She asked for the interview, because he was

5. Unmanly men.
6. Sewing terms.
7. A variation on 1 Corinthians 15.55, a common funerary text: "O death, where is thy sting? O grave, where is thy victory?"

going on to shoot grouse to-morrow, and she was returning to Helen in town.

"Certainly, dear," said he. "Of course, I have the time. What do you want?"

"Nothing."

"I was afraid something had gone wrong."

"No; I have nothing to say, but you may talk."

Glancing at his watch, he talked of the nasty curve at the lych-gate. She heard him with interest. Her surface could always respond to his without contempt, though all her deeper being might be yearning to help him. She had abandoned any plan of action. Love is the best, and the more she let herself love him, the more chance was there that he would set his soul in order. Such a moment as this, when they sat under fair weather by the walls of their future home, was so sweet to her that its sweetness would surely pierce to him. Each lift of his eyes, each parting of the thatched lip from the clean-shaven, must prelude the tenderness that kills the Monk and the Beast at a single blow. Disappointed a hundred times, she still hoped. She loved him with too clear a vision to fear his cloudiness. Whether he droned trivialities, as to-day, or sprang kisses on her in the twilight, she could pardon him, she could respond.

"If there is this nasty curve," she suggested, "couldn't we walk to the church? Not, of course, you and Evie; but the rest of us might very well go on first, and that would mean fewer carriages."

"One can't have ladies walking through the Market Square. The Fussells wouldn't like it; they were awfully particular at Charles's wedding. My—she—one of our party was anxious to walk, and certainly the church was just round the corner, and I shouldn't have minded; but the Colonel made a great point of it."

"You men shouldn't be so chivalrous," said Margaret thoughtfully.

"Why not?"

She knew why not, but said that she did not know. He then announced that, unless she had anything special to say, he must visit the wine-cellar, and they went off together in search of Burton. Though clumsy and a little inconvenient, Oniton was a genuine country-house. They clattered down flagged passages, looking into room after room, and scaring unknown maids from the performance of obscure duties. The wedding-breakfast must be in readiness when they came back from church, and tea would be served in the garden. The sight of so many agitated and serious people made Margaret smile, but she reflected that they were paid to be serious, and enjoyed being agitated. Here were the lower wheels of the machine that was tossing Evie up into nuptial glory. A little boy blocked their way with pig-pails. His mind could not grasp their greatness, and he said: "By your leave; let me pass, please." Henry asked him where Burton was. But the servants were so new that they did not know one another's names. In the still-room sat the band, who had stipulated for champagne as part of their fee, and who were already drinking beer. Scents of Araby[8] came from the kitchen, mingled with cries. Margaret knew what had happened there, for it happened at Wickham Place. One of the wedding dishes had boiled over, and the cook was throwing cedar-shavings to hide the smell. At last they came upon the butler. Henry gave him the keys, and handed Margaret down the cellar-stairs. Two doors were unlocked. She, who kept all her wine at the bottom of the linen-cupboard, was astonished at the sight. "We shall never get through it!" she cried, and the two men were suddenly drawn into brotherhood, and exchanged smiles. She felt as if she had again jumped out of the car while it was moving.

Certainly Oniton would take some digesting. It would be no small business to remain herself, and yet to assimilate such an establishment. She must remain herself, for his sake as well as her own, since a shadowy wife degrades the husband whom she accompanies; and she must assimilate for reasons of common honesty, since she had no right to marry a man and make him uncomfortable. Her only ally was the power of Home. The loss of Wickham Place had taught her more than its possession. Howards End had repeated the lesson. She was determined to create new sanctities among these hills.

After visiting the wine-cellar, she dressed, and then came the wedding, which seemed a small affair when compared with the preparations for it. Everything went like one o'clock.[9] Mr. Cahill materialized out of space, and was waiting for his bride at the church door. No one dropped the ring or mispronounced the responses, or trod on Evie's train, or cried. In a few minutes the clergymen performed their duty, the register was signed, and they were back in their carriages, negotiating the dangerous curve by the lych-gate. Margaret was convinced that they had not been married at all, and that the Norman church had been intent all the time on other business.

There were more documents to sign at the house, and the breakfast to eat, and then a few more people dropped in for the garden party. There had been a great many refusals, and after all it was not a very big affair — not as big as Margaret's would be. She noted the dishes and the strips of red carpet, that outwardly she might give Henry what was proper. But inwardly she hoped for something better than this blend of Sunday church and fox-hunting. If only someone had been upset! But this wedding had gone off so particularly well—"quite like a Durbar"[1] in the opinion of Lady Edser, and she thoroughly agreed with her.

So the wasted day lumbered forward, the bride and bridegroom drove off, yelling with laughter, and for the second time the sun retreated

8. Smells of exotic spices.
9. Without a hitch.
1. Court held by an Indian prince to receive pledges of loyalty from his subjects, or where native princes declare allegiance to the British monarchy.

towards the hills of Wales. Henry, who was more tired than he owned, came up to her in the castle meadow, and, in tones of unusual softness, said that he was pleased. Everything had gone off so well. She felt that he was praising her, too, and blushed; certainly she had done all she could with his intractable friends, and had made a special point of kowtowing to the men. They were breaking camp this evening: only the Warringtons and quiet child would stay the night, and the others were already moving towards the house to finish their packing. "I think it did go off well," she agreed. "Since I had to jump out of the motor, I'm thankful I lighted on my left hand. I am so very glad about it, Henry dear; I only hope that the guests at ours may be half as comfortable. You must all remember that we have no practical person among us, except my aunt, and she is not used to entertainments on a large scale."

"I know," he said gravely. "Under the circumstances, it would be better to put everything into the hands of Harrod's or Whiteley's,[2] or even to go to some hotel."

"You desire a hotel?"

"Yes, because—well, I mustn't interfere with you. No doubt you want to be married from your old home."

"My old home's falling into pieces, Henry. I only want my new. Isn't it a perfect evening——"

"The Alexandrina isn't bad——"

"The Alexandrina," she echoed, more occupied with the threads of smoke that were issuing from their chimneys, and ruling the sunlit slopes with parallels of grey.

"It's off Curzon Street."

"Is it? Let's be married from off Curzon Street."

Then she turned westward, to gaze at the swirling gold. Just where the river rounded the hill the sun caught it. Fairyland must lie above the bend, and its precious liquid was pouring towards them past Charles's bathing-shed. She gazed so long that her eyes were dazzled, and when they moved back to the house, she could not recognize the faces of people who were coming out of it. A parlour-maid was preceding them.

"Who are those people?" she asked.

"They're callers!" exclaimed Henry. "It's too late for callers."

"Perhaps they're town people who want to see the wedding presents."

"I'm not at home yet to townees."

"Well, hide among the ruins, and if I can stop them, I will."

He thanked her.

Margaret went forward, smiling socially. She supposed that these were unpunctual guests, who would have to be content with vicarious civility, since Evie and Charles were gone, Henry tired, and the others in their rooms. She assumed the airs of a hostess; not for long. For one of

2. Caterers.

the group was Helen—Helen in her oldest clothes, and dominated by that tense, wounding excitement that had made her a terror in their nursery days.

"What is it?" she called. "Oh, what's wrong? Is Tibby ill?"

Helen spoke to her two companions, who fell back. Then she bore forward furiously.

"They're starving!" she shouted. "I found them starving!"

"Who? Why have you come?"

"The Basts."

"Oh, Helen!" moaned Margaret. "Whatever have you done now?"

"He has lost his place. He has been turned out of his bank. Yes, he's done for. We upper classes have ruined him, and I suppose you'll tell me it's the battle of life. Starving. His wife is ill. Starving. She fainted in the train."

"Helen, are you mad?"

"Perhaps. Yes. If you like, I'm mad. But I've brought them. I'll stand injustice no longer. I'll show up the wretchedness that lies under this luxury, this talk of impersonal forces, this cant about God doing what we're too slack to do ourselves."

"Have you actually brought two starving people from London to Shropshire, Helen?"

Helen was checked. She had not thought of this, and her hysteria abated. "There was a restaurant car on the train," she said.

"Don't be absurd. They aren't starving, and you know it. Now, begin from the beginning. I won't have such theatrical nonsense. How dare you! Yes, how dare you!" she repeated, as anger filled her, "bursting in to Evie's wedding in this heartless way. My goodness! but you've a perverted notion of philanthropy. Look"—she indicated the house—"servants, people out of the windows. They think it's some vulgar scandal, and I must explain, 'Oh no, it's only my sister screaming, and only two hangers-on of ours, whom she has brought here for no conceivable reason.'"

"Kindly take back the word 'hangers-on,'" said Helen, ominously calm.

"Very well," conceded Margaret, who for all her wrath was determined to avoid a real quarrel. "I, too, am sorry about them, but it beats me why you've brought them here, or why you're here yourself."

"It's our last chance of seeing Mr. Wilcox."

Margaret moved towards the house at this. She was determined not to worry Henry.

"He's going to Scotland. I know he is. I insist on seeing him."

"Yes, to-morrow."

"I knew it was our last chance."

"How do you do, Mr. Bast?" said Margaret, trying to control her voice. "This is an odd business. What view do you take of it?"

"There is Mrs. Bast, too," prompted Helen.

Jacky also shook hands. She, like her husband, was shy, and, further-more, ill, and, furthermore, so bestially stupid that she could not grasp what was happening. She only knew that the lady had swept down like a whirlwind last night, had paid the rent, redeemed the furniture,[3] pro-vided them with a dinner and a breakfast, and ordered them to meet her at Paddington next morning. Leonard had feebly protested, and when the morning came, had suggested that they shouldn't go. But she, half mesmerized, had obeyed. The lady had told them to, and they must, and their bed-sitting-room had accordingly changed into Paddington, and Paddington into a railway carriage, that shook, and grew hot, and grew cold, and vanished entirely, and reappeared amid torrents of expensive scent. "You have fainted," said the lady in an awe-struck voice. "Perhaps the air will do you good." And perhaps it had, for here she was, feeling rather better among a lot of flowers.

"I'm sure I don't want to intrude," began Leonard, in answer to Margaret's question. "But you have been so kind to me in the past in warning me about the Porphyrion that I wondered—why, I wondered whether——"

"Whether we could get him back into the Porphyrion again," supplied Helen. "Meg, this has been a cheerful business. A bright evening's work that was on Chelsea Embankment."

Margaret shook her head and returned to Mr. Bast.

"I don't understand. You left the Porphyrion because we suggested it was a bad concern, didn't you?"

"That's right."

"And went into a bank instead?"

"I told you all that," said Helen; "and they reduced their staff after he had been in a month, and now he's penniless, and I consider that we and our informant are directly to blame."

"I hate all this," Leonard muttered.

"I hope you do, Mr. Bast. But it's no good mincing matters. You have done yourself no good by coming here. If you intend to confront Mr. Wilcox, and to call him to account for a chance remark, you will make a very great mistake."

"I brought them. I did it all," cried Helen.

"I can only advise you to go at once. My sister has put you in a false position, and it is kindest to tell you so. It's too late to get to town, but you'll find a comfortable hotel in Oniton, where Mrs. Bast can rest, and I hope you'll be my guests there."

"That isn't what I want, Miss Schlegel," said Leonard. "You're very kind, and no doubt it's a false position, but you make me miserable. I seem no good at all."

---

3. Repaid a loan for which the furniture was security.

"It's work he wants," interpreted Helen. "Can't you see?"

Then he said: "Jacky, let's go. We're more bother than we're worth. We're costing these ladies pounds and pounds already to get work for us, and they never will. There's nothing we're good enough to do."

"We would like to find you work," said Margaret rather conventionally. "We want to—I, like my sister. You're only down in your luck. Go to the hotel, have a good night's rest, and some day you shall pay me back the bill, if you prefer it."

But Leonard was near the abyss, and at such moments men see clearly. "You don't know what you're talking about," he said. "I shall never get work now. If rich people fail at one profession, they can try another. Not I. I had my groove, and I've got out of it. I could do one particular branch of insurance in one particular office well enough to command a salary, but that's all. Poetry's nothing, Miss Schlegel. One's thoughts about this and that are nothing. Your money, too, is nothing, if you'll understand me. I mean if a man over twenty once loses his own particular job, it's all over with him. I have seen it happen to others. Their friends give them money for a little, but in the end they fall over the edge. It's no good. It's the whole world pulling. There always will be rich and poor."

He ceased. "Won't you have something to eat?" said Margaret. "I don't know what to do. It isn't my house, and though Mr. Wilcox would have been glad to see you at any other time—as I say, I don't know what to do, but I undertake to do what I can for you. Helen, offer them something. Do try a sandwich, Mrs. Bast."

They moved to a long table behind which a servant was still standing. Iced cakes, sandwiches innumerable, coffee, claret-cup, champagne, remained almost intact: their overfed guests could do no more. Leonard refused. Jacky thought she could manage a little. Margaret left them whispering together, and had a few more words with Helen.

She said: "Helen, I like Mr. Bast. I agree that he's worth helping. I agree that we are directly responsible."

"No, indirectly. Via Mr. Wilcox."

"Let me tell you once for all that if you take up that attitude, I'll do nothing. No doubt you're right logically, and are entitled to say a great many scathing things about Henry. Only, I won't have it. So choose."

Helen looked at the sunset.

"If you promise to take them quietly to the George, I will speak to Henry about them—in my own way, mind; there is to be none of this absurd screaming about justice. I have no use for justice. If it was only a question of money, we could do it ourselves. But he wants work, and that we can't give him, but possibly Henry can."

"It's his duty to," grumbled Helen.

"Nor am I concerned with duty. I'm concerned with the characters of various people whom we know, and how, things being as they are, things may be made a little better. Mr. Wilcox hates being asked favours: all business men do. But I am going to ask him, at the risk of a rebuff, because I want to make things a little better."

"Very well. I promise. You take it very calmly."

"Take them off to the George, then, and I'll try. Poor creatures! but they look tired." As they parted, she added: "I haven't nearly done with you, though, Helen. You have been most self-indulgent. I can't get over it. You have less restraint rather than more as you grow older. Think it over and alter yourself, or we shan't have happy lives."

She rejoined Henry. Fortunately he had been sitting down: these physical matters were important. "Was it townees?" he asked, greeting her with a pleasant smile.

"You'll never believe me," said Margaret, sitting down beside him. "It's all right now, but it was my sister."

"Helen here?" he cried, preparing to rise. "But she refused the invitation. I thought she despised weddings."

"Don't get up. She has not come to the wedding. I've bundled her off to the George."

Inherently hospitable, he protested.

"No; she has two of her protégés with her, and must keep with them."

"Let 'em all come."

"My dear Henry, did you see them?"

"I did catch sight of a brown bunch of a woman, certainly."

"The brown bunch was Helen, but did you catch sight of a sea-green and salmon bunch?"

"What! are they out beanfeasting?"[4]

"No; business. They wanted to see me, and later on I want to talk to you about them."

She was ashamed of her own diplomacy. In dealing with a Wilcox, how tempting it was to lapse from comradeship, and to give him the kind of woman that he desired! Henry took the hint at once, and said: "Why later on? Tell me now. No time like the present."

"Shall I?"

"If it isn't a long story."

"Oh, not five minutes; but there's a sting at the end of it, for I want you to find the man some work in your office."

"What are his qualifications?"

"I don't know. He's a clerk."

"How old?"

"Twenty-five, perhaps."

"What's his name?"

"Bast," said Margaret, and was about to remind him that they had met at Wickham Place, but stopped herself. It had not been a successful meeting.

4. Partying.

"Where was he before?"

"Dempster's Bank."

"Why did he leave?" he asked, still remembering nothing.

"They reduced their staff."

"All right; I'll see him."

It was the reward of her tact and devotion through the day. Now she understood why some women prefer influence to rights. Mrs. Plynlimmon, when condemning suffragettes, had said: "The woman who can't influence her husband to vote the way she wants ought to be ashamed of herself." Margaret had winced, but she was influencing Henry now, and though pleased at her little victory, she knew that she had won it by the methods of the harem.

"I should be glad if you took him," she said, "but I don't know whether he's qualified."

"I'll do what I can. But, Margaret, this mustn't be taken as a precedent."

"No, of course—of course——"

"I can't fit in your protégés every day. Business would suffer."

"I can promise you he's the last. He—he's rather a special case."

"Protégés always are."

She let it stand at that. He rose with a little extra touch of complacency, and held out his hand to help her up. How wide the gulf between Henry as he was and Henry as Helen thought he ought to be! And she herself—hovering as usual between the two, now accepting men as they are, now yearning with her sister for Truth. Love and Truth—their warfare seems eternal. Perhaps the whole visible world rests on it, and if they were one, life itself, like the spirits when Prospero[5] was reconciled to his brother, might vanish into air, into thin air.

"Your protégé has made us late," said he. "The Fussells will just be starting."

On the whole she sided with men as they are. Henry would save the Basts as he had saved Howards End, while Helen and her friends were discussing the ethics of salvation. His was a slap-dash method, but the world has been built slap-dash, and the beauty of mountain and river and sunset may be but the varnish with which the unskilled artificer hides his joins. Oniton, like herself, was imperfect. Its apple-trees were stunted, its castle ruinous. It, too, had suffered in the border warfare between the Anglo-Saxon and the Kelt, between things as they are and as they ought to be. Once more the west was retreating, once again the orderly stars were dotting the eastern sky. There is certainly no rest for us on the earth. But there is happiness, and as Margaret descended the mound on her lover's arm, she felt that she was having her share.

5. Sorcerer from Shakespeare's *The Tempest*, who renounces his magical powers after winning back his dukedom from his usurping brother.

To her annoyance, Mrs. Bast was still in the garden; the husband and Helen had left her there to finish her meal while they went to engage rooms. Margaret found this woman repellent. She had felt, when shaking her hand, an overpowering shame. She remembered the motive of her call at Wickham Place, and smelt again odours from the abyss— odours the more disturbing because they were involuntary. For there was no malice in Jacky. There she sat, a piece of cake in one hand, an empty champagne glass in the other, doing no harm to anybody.

"She's overtired," Margaret whispered.

"She's something else," said Henry. "This won't do. I can't have her in my garden in this state."

"Is she——" Margaret hesitated to add "drunk." Now that she was going to marry him, he had grown particular. He discountenanced risqué conversations now.

Henry went up to the woman. She raised her face, which gleamed in the twilight like a puff-ball.

"Madam, you will be more comfortable at the hotel," he said sharply.

Jacky replied: "If it isn't Hen!"

"Ne crois pas que le mari lui ressemble," apologized Margaret. "Il est tout à fait différent."[6]

"Henry!" she repeated, quite distinctly.

Mr. Wilcox was much annoyed. "I can't congratulate you on your protégés," he remarked.

"Hen, don't go. You do love me, dear, don't you?"

"Bless us, what a person!" sighed Margaret, gathering up her skirts.

Jacky pointed with her cake. "You're a nice boy, you are." She yawned. "There now, I love you."

"Henry, I am awfully sorry."

"And pray why?" he asked, and looked at her so sternly that she feared he was ill. He seemed more scandalized than the facts demanded.

"To have brought this down on you."

"Pray don't apologize."

The voice continued.

"Why does she call you 'Hen'?" said Margaret innocently. "Has she ever seen you before?"

"Seen Hen before!" said Jacky. "Who hasn't seen Hen? He's serving you like me, my dear. These boys! You wait—— Still we love 'em."

"Are you now satisfied?" Henry asked.

Margaret began to grow frightened. "I don't know what it is all about," she said. "Let's come in."

But he thought she was acting. He thought he was trapped. He saw his whole life crumbling. "Don't you indeed?" he said bitingly. "I do. Allow me to congratulate you on the success of your plan."

6. "Don't think the husband resembles her. He is completely different." (French)

"This is Helen's plan, not mine."

"I now understand your interest in the Basts. Very well thought out. I am amused at your caution, Margaret. You are quite right—it was necessary. I am a man, and have lived a man's past. I have the honour to release you from your engagement."

Still she could not understand. She knew of life's seamy side as a theory; she could not grasp it as a fact. More words from Jacky were necessary—words unequivocal, undenied.

"So that——" burst from her, and she went indoors. She stopped herself from saying more.

"So what?" asked Colonel Fussell, who was getting ready to start in the hall.

"We were saying—Henry and I were just having the fiercest argument, my point being——" Seizing his fur coat from a footman, she offered to help him on. He protested, and there was a playful little scene.

"No, let me do that," said Henry, following.

"Thanks so much! You see—he has forgiven me!"

The Colonel said gallantly: "I don't expect there's much to forgive."

He got into the car. The ladies followed him after an interval. Maids, courier, and heavier luggage had been sent on earlier by the branchline. Still chattering, still thanking their host and patronizing their future hostess, the guests were borne away.

Then Margaret continued: "So that woman has been your mistress?"

"You put it with your usual delicacy," he replied.

"When, please?"

"Why?"

"When, please?"

"Ten years ago."

She left him without a word. For it was not her tragedy: it was Mrs. Wilcox's.

Chapter XXVII

Helen began to wonder why she had spent a matter of eight pounds in making some people ill and others angry. Now that the wave of excitement was ebbing, and had left her, Mr. Bast, and Mrs. Bast stranded for the night in a Shropshire hotel, she asked herself what forces had made the wave flow. At all events, no harm was done. Margaret would play the game properly now, and though Helen disapproved of her sister's methods, she knew that the Basts would benefit by them in the long-run.

"Mr. Wilcox is so illogical," she explained to Leonard, who had put his wife to bed, and was sitting with her in the empty coffee-room. "If we told him it was his duty to take you on, he might refuse to do it. The fact is, he isn't properly educated. I don't want to set you against him, but you'll find him a trial."

"I can never thank you sufficiently, Miss Schlegel," was all that Leonard felt equal to.

"I believe in personal responsibility. Don't you? And in personal everything. I hate—I suppose I oughtn't to say that—but the Wilcoxes are on the wrong tack surely. Or perhaps it isn't their fault. Perhaps the little thing that says 'I' is missing out of the middle of their heads, and then it's a waste of time to blame them. There's a nightmare of a theory that says a special race is being born which will rule the rest of us in the future just because it lacks the little thing that says 'I.' Had you heard that?"

"I get no time for reading."

"Had you thought it, then? That there are two kinds of people—our kind, who live straight from the middle of their heads, and the other kind who can't, because their heads have no middle? They can't say 'I.' They *aren't* in fact, and so they're supermen. Pierpont Morgan[1] has never said 'I' in his life."

Leonard roused himself. If his benefactress wanted intellectual conversation, she must have it. She was more important than his ruined past. "I never got on to Nietzsche,"[2] he said. "But I always understood that those supermen were rather what you may call egoists."

"Oh no, that's wrong," replied Helen. "No superman ever said 'I want,' because 'I want' must lead to the question, 'Who am I?' and so to Pity and to Justice. He only says 'want.' 'Want Europe,' if he's Napoleon; 'want wives,' if he's Bluebeard; 'want Botticelli,'[3] if he's Pierpont Morgan. Never the 'I'; and if you could pierce through him, you'd find panic and emptiness in the middle."

Leonard was silent for a moment. Then he said: "May I take it, Miss Schlegel, that you and I are both the sort that say 'I'?"

"Of course."

"And your sister too?"

"Of course," repeated Helen, a little sharply. She was annoyed with Margaret, but did not want her discussed. "All presentable people say 'I.'"

"But Mr. Wilcox—he is not perhaps——"

"I don't know that it's any good discussing Mr. Wilcox either."

"Quite so, quite so," he agreed. Helen asked herself why she had snubbed him. Once or twice during the day she had encouraged him to criticize, and then had pulled him up short. Was she afraid of him presuming? If so, it was disgusting of her.

But he was thinking the snub quite natural. Everything she did was natural, and incapable of causing offence. While the Miss Schlegels were together he had felt them scarcely human—a sort of admonitory

---

1. J. Pierpont Morgan (1837–1913), fabulously wealthy American banker and financier.
2. Friedrich Nietzsche (1844–1900), German philosopher whose "superman" exceeded the limits of ordinary morality.
3. Bluebeard, a fairytale character who marries and kills one wife after another; Botticelli (1445–1510), Italian Renaissance painter.

whirligig. But a Miss Schlegel alone was different. She was in Helen's case unmarried, in Margaret's about to be married, in neither case an echo of her sister. A light had fallen at last into this rich upper world, and he saw that it was full of men and women, some of whom were more friendly to him than others. Helen had become "his" Miss Schlegel, who scolded him and corresponded with him, and had swept down yesterday with grateful vehemence. Margaret, though not unkind, was severe and remote. He would not presume to help her, for instance. He had never liked her, and began to think that his original impression was true, and that her sister did not like her either. Helen was certainly lonely. She, who gave away so much, was receiving too little. Leonard was pleased to think that he could spare her vexation by holding his tongue and concealing what he knew about Mr. Wilcox. Jacky had announced her discovery when he fetched her from the lawn. After the first shock, he did not mind for himself. By now he had no illusions about his wife, and this was only one new stain on the face of a love that had never been pure. To keep perfection perfect, that should be his ideal, if the future gave him time to have ideals. Helen, and Margaret for Helen's sake, must not know.

Helen disconcerted him by turning the conversation to his wife. "Mrs. Bast—does she ever say 'I'?" she asked, half mischievously, and then, "Is she very tired?"

"It's better she stops in her room," said Leonard.

"Shall I sit up with her?"

"No, thank you; she does not need company."

"Mr. Bast, what kind of woman is your wife?"

Leonard blushed up to his eyes.

"You ought to know my ways by now. Does that question offend you?"

"No, oh no, Miss Schlegel, no."

"Because I love honesty. Don't pretend your marriage has been a happy one. You and she can have nothing in common."

He did not deny it, but said shyly: "I suppose that's pretty obvious; but Jacky never meant to do anybody any harm. When things went wrong, or I heard things, I used to think it was her fault, but, looking back, it's more mine. I needn't have married her, but as I have I must stick to her and keep her."

"How long have you been married?"

"Nearly three years."

"What did your people say?"

"They will not have anything to do with us. They had a sort of family council when they heard I was married, and cut us off altogether."

Helen began to pace up and down the room. "My good boy, what a mess!" she said gently. "Who are your people?"

He could answer this. His parents, who were dead, had been in trade; his sisters had married commercial travellers; his brother was a lay-reader.

"And your grandparents?"

Leonard told her a secret that he had held shameful up to now. "They were just nothing at all," he said—"agricultural labourers and that sort."

"So! From which part?"

"Lincolnshire mostly, but my mother's father—he, oddly enough, came from these parts round here."

"From this very Shropshire. Yes, that is odd. My mother's people were Lancashire. But why do your brother and your sisters object to Mrs. Bast?"

"Oh, I don't know."

"Excuse me, you do know. I am not a baby. I can bear anything you tell me, and the more you tell the more I shall be able to help. Have they heard anything against her?"

He was silent.

"I think I have guessed now," said Helen very gravely.

"I don't think so, Miss Schlegel; I hope not."

"We must be honest, even over these things. I have guessed. I am frightfully, dreadfully sorry, but it does not make the least difference to me. I shall feel just the same to both of you. I blame, not your wife for these things, but men."

Leonard left it at that—so long as she did not guess the man. She stood at the window and slowly pulled up the blinds. The hotel looked over a dark square. The mists had begun. When she turned back to him her eyes were shining.

"Don't you worry," he pleaded. "I can't bear that. We shall be all right if I get work. If I could only get work—something regular to do. Then it wouldn't be so bad again. I don't trouble after books as I used. I can imagine that with regular work we should settle down again. It stops one thinking."

"Settle down to what?"

"Oh, just settle down."

"And that's to be life!" said Helen, with a catch in her throat. "How can you, with all the beautiful things to see and do—with music—with walking at night——"

"Walking is well enough when a man's in work," he answered. "Oh, I did talk a lot of nonsense once, but there's nothing like a bailiff[4] in the house to drive it out of you. When I saw him fingering my Ruskins and Stevensons, I seemed to see life straight real, and it isn't a pretty sight. My books are back again, thanks to you, but they'll never be the same to me again, and I shan't ever again think night in the woods is wonderful."

"Why not?" asked Helen, throwing up the window.

"Because I see one must have money."

"Well, you're wrong."

4. An officer of the court.

"I wish I was wrong, but—the clergyman—he has money of his own, or else he's paid; the poet or the musician—just the same; the tramp—he's no different. The tramp goes to the workhouse in the end, and is paid for with other people's money. Miss Schlegel, the real thing's money, and all the rest is a dream."

"You're still wrong. <u>You've forgotten Death.</u>"

Leonard could not understand.

"If we lived for ever, what you say would be true. But we have to die, we have to leave life presently. Injustice and greed would be the real thing if we lived for ever. As it is, we must hold to other things, because Death is coming. I love Death—not morbidly, but because He explains. He shows me the emptiness of Money. Death and Money are the eternal foes. Not Death and Life. Never mind what lies behind Death, Mr. Bast, but be sure that the poet and the musician and the tramp will be happier in it than the man who has never learnt to say, 'I am I.' "

"I wonder."

"We are all in a mist—I know, but I can help you this far—men like the Wilcoxes are deeper in the mist than any. Sane, sound Englishmen! building up empires, levelling all the world into what they call common sense. But mention Death to them and they're offended, because Death's really Imperial, and He cries out against them for ever."

"I am as afraid of Death as anyone."

"But not of the idea of Death."

"But what is the difference?"

"Infinite difference," said Helen, more gravely than before.

Leonard looked at her wondering, and had the sense of great things sweeping out of the shrouded night. But he could not receive them, because his heart was still full of little things. As the lost umbrella had spoilt the concert at Queen's Hall, so the lost situation was obscuring the diviner harmonies now. Death, Life and Materialism were fine words, but would Mr. Wilcox take him on as a clerk? Talk as one would, Mr. Wilcox was king of this world, the superman, with his own morality, whose head remained in the clouds.

"I must be stupid," he said apologetically.

While to Helen the paradox became clearer and clearer. 'Death destroys a man: the idea of Death saves him.' Behind the coffins and the skeletons that stay the vulgar mind lies something so immense that all that is great in us responds to it. Men of the world may recoil from the charnel-house[5] that they will one day enter, but Love knows better. Death is his foe, but his peer, and in their age-long struggle the thews[6] of Love have been strengthened, and his vision cleared, until there is no one who can stand against him.

5. A place where the bodies of the dead are deposited.
6. Muscles.

"So never give in," continued the girl, and restated again and again the vague yet convincing plea that the Invisible lodges against the Visible. Her excitement grew as she tried to cut the rope that fastened Leonard to the earth. Woven of bitter experience, it resisted her. Presently the waitress entered and gave her a letter from Margaret. Another note, addressed to Leonard, was inside. They read them, listening to the murmurings of the river.

Chapter XXVIII

For many hours Margaret did nothing; then she controlled herself, and wrote some letters. She was too bruised to speak to Henry; she could pity him, and even determine to marry him, but as yet all lay too deep in her heart for speech. On the surface the sense of his degradation was too strong. She could not command voice or look, and the gentle words that she forced out through her pen seemed to proceed from some other person.

"My dearest boy," she began, "this is not to part us. It is everything or nothing, and I mean it to be nothing. It happened long before we ever met, and even if it had happened since, I should be writing the same, I hope. I do understand."

But she crossed out "I do understand"; it struck a false note. Henry could not bear to be understood. She also crossed out, "It is everything or nothing." Henry would resent so strong a grasp of the situation. She must not comment; comment is unfeminine.

"I think that'll about do," she thought.

Then the sense of his degradation choked her. Was he worth all this bother? To have yielded to a woman of that sort was everything, yes, it was, and she could not be his wife. She tried to translate his temptation into her own language, and her brain reeled. Men must be different, even to want to yield to such a temptation. Her belief in comradeship was stifled, and she saw life as from that glass saloon on the Great Western, which sheltered male and female alike from the fresh air. Are the sexes really races, each with its own code of morality, and their mutual love a mere device of Nature to keep things going? Strip human intercourse of the proprieties, and is it reduced to this? Her judgment told her no. She knew that out of Nature's device we have built a magic that will win us immortality. Far more mysterious than the call of sex to sex is the tenderness that we throw into that call; far wider is the gulf between us and the farmyard than between the farmyard and the garbage that nourishes it. We are evolving, in ways that Science cannot measure, to ends that Theology dares not contemplate. "Men did produce one jewel," the gods will say, and, saying, will give us immortality. Margaret knew all this, but for the moment she could not feel it, and transformed the marriage of Evie and Mr. Cahill into a carnival of fools, and her own marriage—too miserable to think of that, she tore up the letter, and then wrote another:

Dear Mr. Bast,

"I have spoken to Mr. Wilcox about you, as I promised, and am sorry to say that he has no vacancy for you.

"Yours truly,
"M. J. Schlegel."

She enclosed this in a note to Helen, over which she took less trouble than she might have done; but her head was aching, and she could not stop to pick her words:

"Dear Helen,

"Give him this. The Basts are no good. Henry found the woman drunk on the lawn. I am having a room got ready for you here, and will you please come round at once on getting this? The Basts are not at all the type we should trouble about. I may go round to them myself in the morning, and do anything that is fair.

"M."

In writing this, Margaret felt that she was being practical. Something might be arranged for the Basts later on, but they must be silenced for the moment. She hoped to avoid a conversation between the woman and Helen. She rang the bell for a servant, but no one answered it; Mr. Wilcox and the Warringtons were gone to bed, and the kitchen was abandoned to Saturnalia.[1] Consequently she went over to the George herself. She did not enter the hotel, for discussion would have been perilous, and, saying that the letter was important, she gave it to the waitress. As she recrossed the square she saw Helen and Mr. Bast looking out of the window of the coffee-room, and feared she was already too late. Her task was not yet over; she ought to tell Henry what she had done.

This came easily, for she saw him in the hall. The night wind had been rattling the pictures against the wall, and the noise had disturbed him.

"Who's there?" he called, quite the householder.

Margaret walked in and past him.

"I have asked Helen to sleep," she said. "She is best here; so don't lock the front-door."

"I thought someone had got in," said Henry.

"At the same time I told the man that we could do nothing for him. I don't know about later, but now the Basts must clearly go."

"Did you say that your sister is sleeping here, after all?"

"Probably."

"Is she to be shown up to your room?"

---

1. Revelry, partying.

"I have naturally nothing to say to her; I am going to bed. Will you tell the servants about Helen? Could someone go to carry her bag?"

He tapped a little gong, which had been bought to summon the servants.

"You must make more noise than that if you want them to hear."

Henry opened a door, and down the corridor came shouts of laughter. "Far too much screaming there," he said, and strode towards it. Margaret went upstairs, uncertain whether to be glad that they had met, or sorry. They had behaved as if nothing had happened, and her deepest instincts told her that this was wrong. For his own sake, some explanation was due.

And yet—what could an explanation tell her? A date, a place, a few details, which she could imagine all too clearly. Now that the first shock was over, she saw that there was every reason to premise a Mrs. Bast. Henry's inner life had long lain open to her—his intellectual confusion, his obtuseness to personal influence, his strong but furtive passions. Should she refuse him because his outer life corresponded? Perhaps. Perhaps, if the dishonour had been done to her, but it was done long before her day. She struggled against the feeling. She told herself that Mrs. Wilcox's wrong was her own. But she was not a barren theorist. As she undressed, her anger, her regard for the dead, her desire for a scene, all grew weak. Henry must have it as he liked, for she loved him, and some day she would use her love to make him a better man.

Pity was at the bottom of her actions all through this crisis. Pity, if one may generalize, is at the bottom of woman. When men like us, it is for our better qualities, and however tender their liking, we dare not be unworthy of it, or they will quietly let us go. But unworthiness stimulates woman. It brings out her deeper nature, for good or for evil.

Here was the core of the question. Henry must be forgiven, and made better by love; nothing else mattered. Mrs. Wilcox, that unquiet yet kindly ghost, must be left to her own wrong. To her everything was in proportion now, and she, too, would pity the man who was blundering up and down their lives. Had Mrs. Wilcox known of his trespass? An interesting question, but Margaret fell asleep, tethered by affection, and lulled by the murmurs of the river that descended all the night from Wales. She felt herself at one with her future home, colouring it and coloured by it, and awoke to see, for the second time, Oniton Castle conquering the morning mists.

Chapter XXIX

"Henry dear——" was her greeting.

He had finished his breakfast, and was beginning the 'Times.' His sister-in-law was packing. She knelt by him and took the paper from him, feeling that it was unusually heavy and thick. Then, putting her face where it had been, she looked up in his eyes.

"Henry dear, look at me. No, I won't have you shirking. Look at me. There. That's all."

"You're referring to last evening," he said huskily. "I have released you from your engagement. I could find excuses, but I won't. No, I won't. A thousand times no. I'm a bad lot, and must be left at that."

Expelled from his old fortress, Mr. Wilcox was building a new one. He could no longer appear respectable to her, so he defended himself instead in a lurid past. It was not true repentance.

"Leave it where you will, boy. It's not going to trouble us: I know what I'm talking about, and it will make no difference."

"No difference?" he inquired. "No difference, when you find that I am not the fellow you thought?" He was annoyed with Miss Schlegel here. He would have preferred her to be prostrated by the blow, or even to rage. Against the tide of his sin flowed the feeling that she was not altogether womanly. Her eyes gazed too straight; they had read books that are suitable for men only. And though he had dreaded a scene, and though she had determined against one, there was a scene, all the same. It was somehow imperative.

"I am unworthy of you," he began. "Had I been worthy, I should not have released you from your engagement. I know what I am talking about. I can't bear to talk of such things. We had better leave it."

She kissed his hand. He jerked it from her, and, rising to his feet, went on: "You, with your sheltered life, and refined pursuits, and friends, and books, you and your sister, and women like you—I say, how can you guess the temptations that lie round a man?"

"It is difficult for us," said Margaret; "but if we are worth marrying, we do guess."

"Cut off from decent society and family ties, what do you suppose happens to thousands of young fellows overseas? Isolated. No one near. I know by bitter experience, and yet you say it makes 'no difference.'"

"Not to me."

He laughed bitterly. Margaret went to the sideboard and helped herself to one of the breakfast dishes. Being the last down, she turned out the spirit-lamp that kept them warm. She was tender, but grave. She knew that Henry was not so much confessing his soul as pointing out the gulf between the male soul and the female, and she did not desire to hear him on this point.

"Did Helen come?" she asked.

He shook his head.

"But that won't do at all, at all! We don't want her gossiping with Mrs. Bast."

"Good God! no!" he exclaimed, suddenly natural. Then he caught himself up. "Let them gossip. My game's up, though I thank you for your unselfishness—little as my thanks are worth."

"Didn't she send me a message or anything?"

"I heard of none."

"Would you ring the bell, please?"

"What to do?"

"Why, to inquire."

He swaggered up to it tragically, and sounded a peal. Margaret poured herself out some coffee. The butler came, and said that Miss Schlegel had slept at the George, so far as he had heard. Should he go round to the George?

"I'll go, thank you," said Margaret, and dismissed him.

"It is no good," said Henry. "Those things leak out; you cannot stop a story once it has started. I have known cases of other men—I despised them once, I thought that *I'm* different, *I* shall never be tempted. Oh, Margaret——" He came and sat down near her, improvising emotion. She could not bear to listen to him. "We fellows all come to grief once in our time. Will you believe that? There are moments when the strongest man—— 'Let him who standeth, take heed lest he fall.' That's true, isn't it? If you knew all, you would excuse me. I was far from good influences—far even from England. I was very, very lonely, and longed for a woman's voice. That's enough. I have told you too much already for you to forgive me now."

"Yes, that's enough, dear."

"I have"—he lowered his voice—"I have been through hell."

Gravely she considered this claim. Had he? Had he suffered tortures of remorse, or had it been, "There! that's over. Now for respectable life again"? The latter, if she read him rightly. A man who has been through hell does not boast of his virility. He is humble and hides it, if, indeed, it still exists. Only in legend does the sinner come forth penitent, but terrible, to conquer pure woman by his resistless power. Henry was anxious to be terrible, but had not got it in him. He was a good average Englishman, who had slipped. The really culpable point—his faithlessness to Mrs. Wilcox—never seemed to strike him. She longed to mention Mrs. Wilcox.

And bit by bit the story was told her. It was a very simple story. Ten years ago was the time, a garrison town in Cyprus the place. Now and then he asked her whether she could possibly forgive him, and she answered, "I have already forgiven you, Henry." She chose her words carefully, and so saved him from panic. She played the girl, until he could rebuild his fortress and hide his soul from the world. When the butler came to clear away, Henry was in a very different mood—asked the fellow what he was in such a hurry for, complained of the noise last night in the servants' hall. Margaret looked intently at the butler. He, as a handsome young man, was faintly attractive to her as a woman—an attraction so faint as scarcely to be perceptible, yet the skies would have fallen if she had mentioned it to Henry.

On her return from the George the building operations were complete, and the old Henry fronted her, competent, cynical, and kind. He had made a clean breast, had been forgiven, and the great thing now was to forget his failure, and to send it the way of other unsuccessful investments. Jacky rejoined Howards End and Ducie Street, and the vermilion motor-car, and the Argentine Hard Dollars,[1] and all the things and people for whom he had never had much use, and had less now. Their memory hampered him. He could scarcely attend to Margaret, who brought back disquieting news from the George. Helen and her clients had gone.

"Well, let them go—the man and his wife, I mean, for the more we see of your sister the better."

"But they have gone separately—Helen very early, the Basts just before I arrived. They have left no message. They have answered neither of my notes. I don't like to think what it all means."

"What did you say in the notes?"

"I told you last night."

"Oh—ah—yes! Dear, would you like one turn in the garden?"

Margaret took his arm. The beautiful weather soothed her. But the wheels of Evie's wedding were still at work, tossing the guests outwards as deftly as they had drawn them in, and she could not be with him long. It had been arranged that they should motor to Shrewsbury, whence he would go north, and she back to London with the Warringtons. For a fraction of time she was happy. Then her brain recommenced.

"I am afraid there has been gossiping of some kind at the George. Helen would not have left unless she had heard something. I mismanaged that. It is wretched. I ought to have parted her from that woman at once."

"Margaret!" he exclaimed, loosing her arm impressively.

"Yes—yes, Henry?"

"I am far from a saint—in fact, the reverse—but you have taken me, for better or worse. Bygones must be bygones. You have promised to forgive me. Margaret, a promise is a promise. Never mention that woman again."

"Except for some practical reason—never."

"Practical! You practical!"

"Yes, I'm practical," she murmured, stooping over the mowing-machine and playing with the grass which trickled through her fingers like sand.

He had silenced her, but her fears made him uneasy. Not for the first time, he was threatened with blackmail. He was rich and supposed to be moral; the Basts knew that he was not, and might find it profitable to hint as much.

"At all events, you mustn't worry," he said. "This is a man's business." He thought intently. "On no account mention it to anybody."

Margaret flushed at advice so elementary, but he was really paving the way for a lie. If necessary he would deny that he had ever known Mrs.

1. An investment opportunity that turned sour.

Bast, and prosecute her for libel. Perhaps he never had known her. Here was Margaret, who behaved as if he had not. There the house. Round them were half a dozen gardeners, clearing up after his daughter's wedding. All was so solid and spruce, that the past flew up out of sight like a spring-blind,[2] leaving only the last five minutes unrolled.

Glancing at these, he saw that the car would be round during the next five, and plunged into action. Gongs were tapped, orders issued, Margaret was sent to dress, and the housemaid to sweep up the long trickle of grass that she had left across the hall. As is Man to the Universe, so was the mind of Mr. Wilcox to the minds of some men—a concentrated light upon a tiny spot, a little Ten Minutes moving self-contained through its appointed years. No Pagan he, who lives for the Now, and may be wiser than all philosophers. He lived for the five minutes that have past, and the five to come; he had the business mind.

How did he stand now, as his motor slipped out of Oniton and breasted the great round hills? Margaret had heard a certain rumour, but was all right. She had forgiven him, God bless her, and he felt the manlier for it. Charles and Evie had not heard it, and never must hear. No more must Paul. Over his children he felt great tenderness, which he did not try to track to a cause: Mrs. Wilcox was too far back in his life. He did not connect her with the sudden aching love that he felt for Evie. Poor little Evie! he trusted that Cahill would make her a decent husband.

And Margaret? How did she stand?

She had several minor worries. Clearly her sister had heard something. She dreaded meeting her in town. And she was anxious about Leonard, for whom they certainly were responsible. Nor ought Mrs. Bast to starve. But the main situation had not altered. She still loved Henry. His actions, not his disposition, had disappointed her, and she could bear that. And she loved her future home. Standing up in the car, just where she had leapt from it two days before, she gazed back with deep emotion upon Oniton. Besides the Grange and the Castle keep, she could now pick out the church and the black-and-white gables of the George. There was the bridge, and the river nibbling its green peninsula. She could even see the bathing-shed, but while she was looking for Charles's new springboard, the forehead of the hill rose up and hid the whole scene.

She never saw it again. Day and night the river flows down into England, day after day the sun retreats into the Welsh mountains, and the tower chimes, "See the Conquering Hero." But the Wilcoxes have no part in the place, nor in any place. It is not their names that recur in the parish register. It is not their ghosts that sigh among the alders at evening. They have swept into the valley and swept out of it, leaving a little dust and a little money behind.

---

2. A window-shade that rolls up, powered by a spring.

Chapter XXX

Tibby was now approaching his last year at Oxford. He had moved out of college, and was contemplating the Universe, or such portions of it as concerned him, from his comfortable lodgings in Long Wall. He was not concerned with much. When a young man is untroubled by passions and sincerely indifferent to public opinion, his outlook is necessarily limited. Tibby neither wished to strengthen the position of the rich nor to improve that of the poor, and so was well content to watch the elms nodding behind the mildly embattled parapets of Magdalen.[1] There are worse lives. Though selfish, he was never cruel; though affected in manner, he never posed. Like Margaret, he disdained the heroic equipment, and it was only after many visits that men discovered Schlegel to possess a character and a brain. He had done well in Mods,[2] much to the surprise of those who attended lectures and took proper exercise, and was now glancing disdainfully at Chinese in case he should some day consent to qualify as a Student Interpreter. To him thus employed Helen entered. A telegram had preceded her.

He noticed, in a distant way, that his sister had altered. As a rule he found her too pronounced, and had never come across this look of appeal, pathetic yet dignified—the look of a sailor who has lost everything at sea.

"I have come from Oniton," she began. "There has been a great deal of trouble there."

"Who's for lunch?" said Tibby, picking up the claret, which was warming in the hearth. Helen sat down submissively at the table. "Why such an early start?" he asked.

"Sunrise or something—when I could get away."

"So I surmise. Why?"

"I don't know what's to be done, Tibby. I am very much upset at a piece of news that concerns Meg, and do not want to face her, and I am not going back to Wickham Place. I stopped here to tell you this."

The landlady came in with the cutlets. Tibby put a marker in the leaves of his Chinese Grammar and helped them. Oxford—the Oxford of the vacation—dreamed and rustled outside, and indoors the little fire was coated with grey where the sunshine touched it. Helen continued her odd story.

"Give Meg my love and say that I want to be alone. I mean to go to Munich or else Bonn."

"Such a message is easily given," said her brother.

"As regards Wickham Place and my share of the furniture, you and she are to do exactly as you like. My own feeling is that everything may

---

1. A medieval college at Oxford University known for its beautiful tower.
2. The first public examination for a bachelor's degree at Oxford, conducted by officials called "moderators."

just as well be sold. What does one want with dusty economic books, which have made the world no better, or with mother's hideous chef-foniers?[3] I have also another commission for you. I want you to deliver a letter." She got up. "I haven't written it yet. Why shouldn't I post it, though?" She sat down again. "My head is rather wretched. I hope that none of your friends are likely to come in."

Tibby locked the door. His friends often found it in this condition. Then he asked whether anything had gone wrong at Evie's wedding.

"Not there," said Helen, and burst into tears.

He had known her hysterical—it was one of her aspects with which he had no concern—and yet these tears touched him as something unusual. They were nearer the things that did concern him, such as music. He laid down his knife and looked at her curiously. Then, as she continued to sob, he went on with his lunch.

The time came for the second course, and she was still crying. Apple Charlotte was to follow, which spoils by waiting. "Do you mind Mrs. Martlett coming in?" he asked, "or shall I take it from her at the door?"

"Could I bathe my eyes, Tibby?"

He took her to his bedroom, and introduced the pudding in her absence. Having helped himself, he put it down to warm in the hearth. His hand stretched towards the Grammar, and soon he was turning over the pages, raising his eyebrows scornfully, perhaps at human nature, perhaps at Chinese. To him thus employed Helen returned. She had pulled herself together, but the grave appeal had not vanished from her eyes.

"Now for the explanation," she said. "Why didn't I begin with it? I have found out something about Mr. Wilcox. He has behaved very wrongly indeed, and ruined two people's lives. It all came on me very suddenly last night; I am very much upset, and I do not know what to do. Mrs. Bast——"

"Oh, those people!"

Helen seemed silenced.

"Shall I lock the door again?"

"No thanks, Tibbikins. You're being very good to me. I want to tell you the story before I go abroad. You must do exactly what you like—treat it as part of the furniture. Meg cannot have heard it yet, I think. But I cannot face her and tell her that the man she is going to marry has miscon-ducted himself. I don't even know whether she ought to be told. Knowing as she does that I dislike him, she will suspect me, and think that I want to ruin her match. I simply don't know what to make of such a thing. I trust your judgment. What would you do?"

"I gather he has had a mistress," said Tibby.

Helen flushed with shame and anger. "And ruined two people's lives. And goes about saying that personal actions count for nothing, and there

3. Chest of drawers, bureau.

always will be rich and poor. He met her when he was trying to get rich out in Cyprus—I don't wish to make him worse than he is, and no doubt she was ready enough to meet him. But there it is. They met. He goes his way and she goes hers. What do you suppose is the end of such women?"

He conceded that it was a bad business.

"They end in two ways: Either they sink till the lunatic asylums and the workhouses are full of them, and cause Mr. Wilcox to write letters to the papers complaining of our national degeneracy, or else they entrap a boy into marriage before it is too late. She—I can't blame her."

"But this isn't all," she continued after a long pause, during which the landlady served them with coffee. "I come now to the business that took us to Oniton. We went all three. Acting on Mr. Wilcox's advice, the man throws up a secure situation and takes an insecure one, from which he is dismissed. There are certain excuses, but in the main Mr. Wilcox is to blame, as Meg herself admitted. It is only common justice that he should employ the man himself. But he meets the woman, and, like the cur that he is, he refuses, and tries to get rid of them. He makes Meg write. Two notes came from her late that evening—one for me, one for Leonard, dismissing him with barely a reason. I couldn't understand. Then it comes out that Mrs. Bast had spoken to Mr. Wilcox on the lawn while we left her to get rooms, and was still speaking about him when Leonard came back to her. This Leonard knew all along. He thought it natural he should be ruined twice. Natural! Could you have contained yourself?"

"It is certainly a very bad business," said Tibby.

His reply seemed to calm his sister. "I was afraid that I saw it out of proportion. But you are right outside it, and you must know. In a day or two—or perhaps a week—take whatever steps you think fit. I leave it in your hands."

She concluded her charge.

"The facts as they touch Meg are all before you," she added; and Tibby sighed and felt it rather hard that, because of his open mind, he should be empanelled to serve as a juror. He had never been interested in human beings, for which one must blame him, but he had had rather too much of them at Wickham Place. Just as some people cease to attend when books are mentioned, so Tibby's attention wandered when "personal relations" came under discussion. Ought Margaret to know what Helen knew the Basts to know? Similar questions had vexed him from infancy, and at Oxford he had learned to say that the importance of human beings has been vastly overrated by specialists. The epigram, with its faint whiff of the eighties, meant nothing. But he might have let it off now if his sister had not been ceaselessly beautiful.

"You see, Helen—have a cigarette—I don't see what I'm to do."

"Then there's nothing to be done. I dare say you are right. Let them marry. There remains the question of compensation."

"Do you want me to adjudicate that too? Had you not better consult an expert?"

"This part is in confidence," said Helen. "It has nothing to do with Meg, and do not mention it to her. The compensation—I do not see who is to pay it if I don't, and I have already decided on the minimum sum. As soon as possible I am placing it to your account, and when I am in Germany you will pay it over for me. I shall never forget your kindness, Tibbikins, if you do this."

"What is the sum?"

"Five thousand."[4]

"Good God alive!" said Tibby, and went crimson.

"Now, what is the good of driblets? To go through life having done one thing—to have raised one person from the abyss: not these puny gifts of shillings and blankets—making the grey more grey. No doubt people will think me extraordinary."

"I don't care a damn what people think!" cried he, heated to unusual manliness of diction. "But it's half what you have."

"Not nearly half." She spread out her hands over her soiled skirt. "I have far too much, and we settled at Chelsea last spring that three hundred a year is necessary to set a man on his feet. What I give will bring in a hundred and fifty between two. It isn't enough."

He could not recover. He was not angry or even shocked, and he saw that Helen would still have plenty to live on. But it amazed him to think what haycocks people can make of their lives. His delicate intonations would not work, and he could only blurt out that the five thousand pounds would mean a great deal of bother for him personally.

"I didn't expect you to understand me."

"I? I understand nobody."

"But you'll do it?"

"Apparently."

"I leave you two commissions, then. The first concerns Mr. Wilcox, and you are to use your discretion. The second concerns the money, and is to be mentioned to no one, and carried out literally. You will send a hundred pounds on account tomorrow."

He walked with her to the station, passing through those streets whose serried beauty never bewildered him and never fatigued. The lovely creature raised domes and spires into the cloudless blue, and only the ganglion of vulgarity round Carfax[5] showed how evanescent was the phantom, how faint its claim to represent England. Helen, rehearsing her commission, noticed nothing: the Basts were in her brain, and she retold the crisis in a meditative way, which might have made other men curious. She was seeing whether it would hold. He asked her once why

---

4. A gift worth roughly £225,000 ($360,000) in current terms.

5. Market square in Oxford, where the principal streets meet; hence a figure of trade or commerce in contrast to the spiritual values (as Tibby perceives them) of Oxford University.

she had taken the Basts right into the heart of Evie's wedding. She stopped like a frightened animal and said, "Does that seem to you so odd?" Her eyes, the hand laid on the mouth, quite haunted him, until they were absorbed into the figure of St. Mary the Virgin, before whom he paused for a moment on the walk home.

It is convenient to follow him in the discharge of his duties. Margaret summoned him the next day. She was terrified at Helen's flight, and he had to say that she had called in at Oxford. Then she said: "Did she seem worried at any rumour about Henry?" He answered, "Yes." "I knew it was that!" she exclaimed. "I'll write to her." Tibby was relieved.

He then sent the cheque to the address that Helen gave him, and stated that later on he was instructed to forward five thousand pounds. An answer came back, very civil and quiet in tone—such an answer as Tibby himself would have given. The cheque was returned, the legacy refused, the writer being in no need of money. Tibby forwarded this to Helen, adding in the fulness of his heart that Leonard Bast seemed somewhat a monumental person after all. Helen's reply was frantic. He was to take no notice. He was to go down at once and say that she commanded acceptance. He went. A scurf of books and china ornaments awaited him. The Basts had just been evicted for not paying their rent, and had wandered no one knew whither. Helen had begun bungling with her money by this time, and had even sold out her shares in the Nottingham and Derby Railway. For some weeks she did nothing. Then she reinvested, and, owing to the good advice of her stockbrokers, became rather richer than she had been before.

Chapter XXXI

Houses have their own ways of dying, falling as variously as the generations of men, some with a tragic roar, some quietly, but to an after-life in the city of ghosts, while from others—and thus was the death of Wickham Place—the spirit slips before the body perishes. It had decayed in the spring, disintegrating the girls more than they knew, and causing either to accost unfamiliar regions. By September it was a corpse, void of emotion, and scarcely hallowed by the memories of thirty years of happiness. Through its round-topped doorway passed furniture, and pictures, and books, until the last room was gutted and the last van had rumbled away. It stood for a week or two longer, open-eyed, as if astonished at its own emptiness. Then it fell. Navvies[1] came, and split it back into the grey. With their muscles and their beery good temper, they were not the worst of undertakers for a house which had always been human, and had not mistaken culture for an end.

The furniture, with a few exceptions, went down into Hertfordshire,

1. Manual laborers.

Mr. Wilcox having most kindly offered Howards End as a warehouse. Mr. Bryce had died abroad—an unsatisfactory affair—and as there seemed little guarantee that the rent would be paid regularly, he cancelled the agreement, and resumed possession himself. Until he relet the house, the Schlegels were welcome to stack their furniture in the garage and lower rooms. Margaret demurred, but Tibby accepted the offer gladly; it saved him from coming to any decision about the future. The plate and the more valuable pictures found a safer home in London, but the bulk of the things went country-ways, and were entrusted to the guardianship of Miss Avery.

Shortly before the move, our hero and heroine were married. They have weathered the storm, and may reasonably expect peace. To have no illusions and yet to love—what stronger surety can a woman find? She had seen her husband's past as well as his heart. She knew her own heart with a thoroughness that commonplace people believe impossible. The heart of Mrs. Wilcox was alone hidden, and perhaps it is superstitious to speculate on the feelings of the dead. They were married quietly—really quietly, for as the day approached she refused to go through another Oniton. Her brother gave her away, her aunt, who was out of health, presided over a few colourless refreshments. The Wilcoxes were represented by Charles, who witnessed the marriage settlement, and by Mr. Cahill. Paul did send a cablegram. In a few minutes, and without the aid of music, the clergyman made them man and wife, and soon the glass shade had fallen that cuts off married couples from the world. She, a monogamist, regretted the cessation of some of life's innocent odours; he, whose instincts were polygamous, felt morally braced by the change, and less liable to the temptations that had assailed him in the past.

They spent their honeymoon near Innsbruck. Henry knew of a reliable hotel there, and Margaret hoped for a meeting with her sister. In this she was disappointed. As they came south, Helen retreated over the Brenner, and wrote an unsatisfactory postcard from the shores of the Lake of Garda,[2] saying that her plans were uncertain and had better be ignored. Evidently she disliked meeting Henry. Two months are surely enough to accustom an outsider to a situation which a wife has accepted in two days, and Margaret had again to regret her sister's lack of self-control. In a long letter she pointed out the need of charity in sexual matters: so little is known about them; it is hard enough for those who are personally touched to judge; then how futile must be the verdict of Society. "I don't say there is no standard, for that would destroy morality; only that there can be no standard until our impulses are classified and better understood." Helen thanked her for her kind letter—rather a curious reply. She moved south again, and spoke of wintering in Naples.

---

2. The Brenner Pass traverses the Alps between Austria and Italy. The Lake of Garda lies in northern Italy.

Mr. Wilcox was not sorry that the meeting failed. Helen left him time to grow skin over his wound. There were still moments when it pained him. Had he only known that Margaret was awaiting him—Margaret, so lively and intelligent, and yet so submissive—he would have kept himself worthier of her. Incapable of grouping the past, he confused the episode of Jacky with another episode that had taken place in the days of his bachelorhood. The two made one crop of wild oats, for which he was heartily sorry, and he could not see that those oats are of a darker stock which are rooted in another's dishonour. Unchastity and infidelity were as confused to him as to the Middle Ages, his only moral teacher. Ruth (poor old Ruth!) did not enter into his calculations at all, for poor old Ruth had never found him out.

His affection for his present wife grew steadily. Her cleverness gave him no trouble, and, indeed, he liked to see her reading poetry or something about social questions; it distinguished her from the wives of other men. He had only to call, and she clapped the book up and was ready to do what he wished. Then they would argue so jollily, and once or twice she had him in quite a tight corner, but as soon as he grew really serious, she gave in. Man is for war, woman for the recreation of the warrior, but he does not dislike it if she makes a show of fight. She cannot win in a real battle, having no muscles, only nerves. Nerves make her jump out of a moving motor-car, or refuse to be married fashionably. The warrior may well allow her to triumph on such occasions; they move not the imperishable plinth[3] of things that touch his peace.

Margaret had a bad attack of these nerves during the honeymoon. He told her—casually, as was his habit—that Oniton Grange was let. She showed her annoyance, and asked rather crossly why she had not been consulted.

"I didn't want to bother you," he replied. "Besides, I have only heard for certain this morning."

"Where are we to live?" said Margaret, trying to laugh. "I loved the place extraordinarily. Don't you believe in having a permanent home, Henry?"

He assured her that she misunderstood him. It is home life that distinguishes us from the foreigner. But he did not believe in a damp home.

"This is news. I never heard till this minute that Oniton was damp."

"My dear girl!"—he flung out his hand—"have you eyes? have you a skin? How could it be anything but damp in such a situation? In the first place, the Grange is on clay, and built where the castle moat must have been; then there's that detestable little river, steaming all night like a kettle. Feel the cellar walls; look up under the eaves. Ask Sir James or anyone. Those Shropshire valleys are notorious. The only possible place for

3. The base of a column.

a house in Shropshire is on a hill; but, for my part, I think the country is too far from London, and the scenery nothing special."

Margaret could not resist saying, "Why did you go there, then?"

"I—because——" He drew his head back and grew rather angry. "Why have we come to the Tyrol, if it comes to that? One might go on asking such questions indefinitely."

One might; but he was only gaining time for a plausible answer. Out it came, and he believed it as soon as it was spoken.

"The truth is, I took Oniton on account of Evie. Don't let this go any further."

"Certainly not."

"I shouldn't like her to know that she nearly let me in for a very bad bargain. No sooner did I sign the agreement than she got engaged. Poor little girl! She was so keen on it all, and wouldn't even wait to make proper inquiries about the shooting. Afraid it would get snapped up— just like all of your sex. Well, no harm's done. She has had her country wedding, and I've got rid of my house to some fellows who are starting a preparatory school."

"Where shall we live, then, Henry? I should enjoy living somewhere."

"I have not yet decided. What about Norfolk?"

Margaret was silent. Marriage had not saved her from the sense of flux. London was but a foretaste of this nomadic civilization which is altering human nature so profoundly, and throws upon personal relations a stress greater than they have ever borne before. Under cosmopolitanism, if it comes, we shall receive no help from the earth. Trees and meadows and mountains will only be a spectacle, and the binding force that they once exercised on character must be entrusted to Love alone. May Love be equal to the task!

"It is now what?" continued Henry. "Nearly October. Let us camp for the winter at Ducie Street, and look out for something in the spring."

"If possible, something permanent. I can't be as young as I was, for these alterations don't suit me."

"But, my dear, which would you rather have—alterations or rheumatism?"

"I see your point," said Margaret, getting up. "If Oniton is really damp, it is impossible, and must be inhabited by little boys. Only, in the spring, let us look before we leap. I will take warning by Evie, and not hurry you. Remember that you have a free hand this time. These endless moves must be bad for the furniture, and are certainly expensive."

"What a practical little woman it is! What's it been reading? Theo— theo—how much?"

"Theosophy."

So Ducie Street was her first fate—a pleasant enough fate. The house, being only a little larger than Wickham Place, trained her for the immense establishment that was promised in the spring. They were frequently away, but at home life ran fairly regularly. In the morning Henry went to the business, and his sandwich—a relic this of some prehistoric craving—was always cut by her own hand. He did not rely upon the sandwich for lunch, but liked to have it by him in case he grew hungry at eleven. When he had gone, there was the house to look after, and the servants to humanize, and several kettles of Helen's to keep on the boil. Her conscience pricked her a little about the Basts; she was not sorry to have lost sight of them. No doubt Leonard was worth helping, but being Henry's wife, she preferred to help someone else. As for theatres and discussion societies, they attracted her less and less. She began to "miss" new movements, and to spend her spare time re-reading or thinking, rather to the concern of her Chelsea friends. They attributed the change to her marriage, and perhaps some deep instinct did warn her not to travel further from her husband than was inevitable. Yet the main cause lay deeper still; she had outgrown stimulants, and was passing from words to things. It was doubtless a pity not to keep up with Wedekind or John,[4] but some closing of the gates is inevitable after thirty, if the mind itself is to become a creative power.

Chapter XXXII

She was looking at plans one day in the following spring—they had finally decided to go down into Sussex and build—when Mrs. Charles Wilcox was announced.

"Have you heard the news?" Dolly cried, as soon as she entered the room. "Charles is so ang—I mean he is sure you know about it, or, rather, that you don't know."

"Why, Dolly!" said Margaret, placidly kissing her. "Here's a surprise! How are the boys and the baby?"

Boys and the baby were well, and in describing a great row that there had been at the Hilton Tennis Club, Dolly forgot her news. The wrong people had tried to get in. The rector, as representing the older inhabitants, had said—Charles had said—the tax-collector had said—Charles had regretted not saying—and she closed the description with, "But lucky you, with four courts of your own at Midhurst."

"It will be very jolly," replied Margaret.

"Are those the plans? Does it matter me seeing them?"

"Of course not."

"Charles has never seen the plans."

"They have only just arrived. Here is the ground floor—no, that's rather difficult. Try the elevation. We are to have a good many gables and a picturesque sky-line."

4. Frank Wedekind (1864–1918), German experimental dramatist who frankly explored sexual themes; Augustus John (1878–1961), British portrait painter known for his vigorous but unflattering representations.

"What makes it smell so funny?" said Dolly, after a moment's inspection. She was incapable of understanding plans or maps.

"I suppose the paper."

"And *which* way up is it?"

"Just the ordinary way up. That's the sky-line, and the part that smells strongest is the sky."

"Well, ask me another. Margaret—oh—what was I going to say? How's Helen?"

"Quite well."

"Is she never coming back to England? Everyone thinks it's awfully odd she doesn't."

"So it is," said Margaret, trying to conceal her vexation. She was getting rather sore on this point. "Helen is odd, awfully. She has now been away eight months."

"But hasn't she any address?"

"A poste restante[1] somewhere in Bavaria is her address. Do write her a line. I will look it up for you."

"No, don't bother. That's eight months she has been away, surely?"

"Exactly. She left just after Evie's wedding. It would be eight months."

"Just when baby was born, then?"

"Just so."

Dolly sighed, and stared enviously round the drawing-room. She was beginning to lose her brightness and good looks. The Charles' were not well off, for Mr. Wilcox, having brought up his children with expensive tastes, believed in letting them shift for themselves. After all, he had not treated them generously. Yet another baby was expected, she told Margaret, and they would have to give up the motor. Margaret sympathized, but in a formal fashion, and Dolly little imagined that the stepmother was urging Mr. Wilcox to make them a more liberal allowance. She sighed again, and at last the particular grievance was remembered. "Oh yes," she cried, "that is it: Miss Avery has been unpacking your packing-cases."

"Why has she done that? How unnecessary!"

"Ask another. I suppose you ordered her to."

"I gave no such orders. Perhaps she was airing the things. She did undertake to light an occasional fire."

"It was far more than an air," said Dolly solemnly. "The floor sounds covered with books. Charles sent me to know what is to be done, for he feels certain you don't know."

"Books!" cried Margaret, moved by the holy word. "Dolly, are you serious? Has she been touching our books?"

"Hasn't she, though! What used to be the hall's full of them. Charles thought for certain you knew of it."

---

1. A direction to hold a letter at a post office until called for by the addressee.

"I am very much obliged to you, Dolly. What can have come over Miss Avery? I must go down about it at once. Some of the books are my brother's, and are quite valuable. She had no right to open any of the cases."

"I say she's dotty. She was the one that never got married, you know. Oh, I say, perhaps she thinks your books are wedding-presents to herself. Old maids are taken that way sometimes. Miss Avery hates us all like poison ever since her frightful dust-up with Evie."

"I hadn't heard of that," said Margaret. A visit from Dolly had its compensations.

"Didn't you know she gave Evie a present last August, and Evie returned it, and then—oh, goloshes! You never read such a letter as Miss Avery wrote."

"But it was wrong of Evie to return it. It wasn't like her to do such a heartless thing."

"But the present was so expensive."

"Why does that make any difference, Dolly?"

"Still, when it costs over five pounds—I didn't see it, but it was a lovely enamel pendant from a Bond Street shop. You can't very well accept that kind of thing from a farm woman. Now, can you?"

"You accepted a present from Miss Avery when you were married."

"Oh, mine was old earthenware stuff—not worth a halfpenny. Evie's was quite different. You'd have to ask anyone to the wedding who gave you a pendant like that. Uncle Percy and Albert and father and Charles all said it was quite impossible, and when four men agree, what is a girl to do? Evie didn't want to upset the old thing, so thought a sort of joking letter best, and returned the pendant straight to the shop to save Miss Avery trouble."

"But Miss Avery said——"

Dolly's eyes grew round. "It was a perfectly awful letter. Charles said it was the letter of a madman. In the end she had the pendant back again from the shop and threw it into the duck-pond."

"Did she give any reasons?"

"We think she meant to be invited to Oniton, and so climb into society."

"She's rather old for that," said Margaret pensively. "May not she have given the present to Evie in remembrance of her mother?"

"That's a notion. Give everyone their due, eh? Well, I suppose I ought to be toddling. Come along Mr. Muff—you want a new coat, but I don't know who'll give it you, I'm sure;" and addressing her apparel with mournful humour, Dolly moved from the room.

Margaret followed her to ask whether Henry knew about Miss Avery's rudeness.

"Oh yes."

"I wonder, then, why he let me ask her to look after the house."

"But she's only a farm woman," said Dolly, and her explanation proved correct. Henry only censured the lower classes when it suited him. He bore with Miss Avery as with Crane—because he could get good value out of them. "I have patience with a man who knows his job," he would say, really having patience with the job, and not the man. Paradoxical as it may sound, he had something of the artist about him; he would pass over an insult to his daughter sooner than lose a good charwoman for his wife.

Margaret judged it better to settle the little trouble herself. Parties were evidently ruffled. With Henry's permission, she wrote a pleasant note to Miss Avery, asking her to leave the cases untouched. Then, at the first convenient opportunity, she went down herself, intending to repack her belongings and store them properly in the local warehouse: the plan had been amateurish and a failure. Tibby promised to accompany her, but at the last moment begged to be excused. So, for the second time in her life, she entered the house alone.

Chapter XXXIII

The day of her visit was exquisite, and the last of unclouded happiness that she was to have for many months. Her anxiety about Helen's extraordinary absence was still dormant, and as for a possible brush with Miss Avery—that only gave zest to the expedition. She had also eluded Dolly's invitation to luncheon. Walking straight up from the station, she crossed the village green and entered the long chestnut avenue that connects it with the church. The church itself stood in the village once. But it there attracted so many worshippers that the devil, in a pet, snatched it from its foundations, and poised it on an inconvenient knoll, three-quarters of a mile away. If this story is true, the chestnut avenue must have been planted by the angels. No more tempting approach could be imagined for the lukewarm Christian, and if he still finds the walk too long, the devil is defeated all the same, Science having built Holy Trinity, a Chapel of Ease, near the Charles', and roofed it with tin.

Up the avenue Margaret strolled slowly, stopping to watch the sky that gleamed through the upper branches of the chestnuts, or to finger the little horseshoes on the lower branches. Why has not England a great mythology? Our folklore has never advanced beyond daintiness, and the greater melodies about our country-side have all issued through the pipes of Greece. Deep and true as the native imagination can be, it seems to have failed here. It has stopped with the witches and the fairies. It cannot vivify one fraction of a summer field, or give names to half a dozen stars. England still waits for the supreme moment of her literature—for the great poet who shall voice her, or, better still, for the thousand little poets whose voices shall pass into our common talk.

At the church the scenery changed. The chestnut avenue opened into a road, smooth but narrow, which led into the untouched country. She followed it for over a mile. Its little hesitations pleased her. Having no urgent destiny, it strolled downhill or up as it wished, taking no trouble about the gradients, nor about the view, which nevertheless expanded. The great estates that throttle the south of Hertfordshire were less obtrusive here, and the appearance of the land was neither aristocratic nor suburban. To define it was difficult, but Margaret knew what it was not: it was not snobbish. Though its contours were slight, there was a touch of freedom in their sweep to which Surrey will never attain, and the distant brow of the Chilterns towered like a mountain. "Left to itself," was Margaret's opinion, "this county would vote Liberal." The comradeship, not passionate, that is our highest gift as a nation, was promised by it, as by the low brick farm where she called for the key.

But the inside of the farm was disappointing. A most finished young person received her. "Yes, Mrs. Wilcox; no, Mrs. Wilcox; oh yes, Mrs. Wilcox, auntie received your letter quite duly. Auntie has gone up to your little place at the present moment. Shall I send the servant to direct you?" Followed by: "Of course, auntie does not generally look after your place; she only does it to oblige a neighbour as something exceptional. It gives her something to do. She spends quite a lot of her time there. My husband says to me sometimes, 'Where's auntie?' I say, 'Need you ask? She's at Howards End.' Yes, Mrs. Wilcox. Mrs. Wilcox, could I prevail upon you to accept a piece of cake? Not if I cut it for you?"

Margaret refused the cake, but unfortunately this acquired her gentility in the eyes of Miss Avery's niece.

"I cannot let you go on alone. Now don't. You really mustn't. I will direct you myself if it comes to that. I must get my hat. Now"—roguishly—"Mrs. Wilcox, don't you move while I'm gone."

Stunned, Margaret did not move from the best parlour, over which the touch of art nouveau[1] had fallen. But the other rooms looked in keeping, though they conveyed the peculiar sadness of a rural interior. Here had lived an elder race, to which we look back with disquietude. The country which we visit at week-ends was really a home to it, and the graver sides of life, the deaths, the partings, the yearnings for love, have their deepest expression in the heart of the fields. All was not sadness. The sun was shining without. The thrush sang his two syllables on the budding guelder-rose. Some children were playing uproariously in heaps of golden straw. It was the presence of sadness at all that surprised Margaret, and ended by giving her a feeling of completeness. In these English farms, if anywhere, one might see life steadily and see it whole, group in one vision its transitoriness and its eternal youth, connect—connect without bitterness until all men are brothers. But her thoughts

---

1. A style of art, architecture, and furnishings in the late nineteenth and early twentieth centuries characterized by curved naturalistic forms and elaborate decoration.

were interrupted by the return of Miss Avery's niece, and were so tran-
quillizing that she suffered the interruption gladly.

It was quicker to go out by the back door, and, after due explanations,
they went out by it. The niece was now mortified by innumerable chickens, who rushed up to her feet for food, and by a shameless and maternal
sow. She did not know what animals were coming to. But her gentility
withered at the touch of the sweet air. The wind was rising, scattering
the straw and ruffling the tails of the ducks as they floated in families
over Evie's pendant. One of those delicious gales of spring, in which
leaves still in bud seem to rustle, swept over the land and then fell silent.
"Georgie," sang the thrush. "Cuckoo," came furtively from the cliff of
pine-trees. "Georgie, pretty Georgie," and the other birds joined in with
nonsense. The hedge was a half-painted picture which would be finished in a few days. Celandines grew on its banks, lords and ladies and
primroses in the defended hollows; the wild rose-bushes, still bearing
their withered hips, showed also the promise of blossom. Spring had
come, clad in no classical garb, yet fairer than all springs; fairer even
than she who walks through the myrtles of Tuscany with the graces
before her and the zephyr behind.[2]

The two women walked up the lane full of outward civility. But
Margaret was thinking how difficult it was to be earnest about furniture
on such a day, and the niece was thinking about hats. Thus engaged,
they reached Howards End. Petulant cries of "Auntie!" severed the air.
There was no reply, and the front door was locked.

"Are you sure that Miss Avery is up here?" asked Margaret.

"Oh yes, Mrs. Wilcox, quite sure. She is here daily."

Margaret tried to look in through the dining-room window, but the
curtain inside was drawn tightly. So with the drawing-room and the hall.
The appearance of these curtains was familiar, yet she did not remember
them being there on her other visit: her impression was that Mr. Bryce
had taken everything away. They tried the back. Here again they received
no answer, and could see nothing; the kitchen-window was fitted with a
blind, while the pantry and scullery had pieces of wood propped up
against them, which looked ominously like the lids of packing-cases.
Margaret thought of her books, and she lifted up her voice also. At the
first cry she succeeded.

"Well, well!" replied someone inside the house. "If it isn't Mrs.
Wilcox come at last!"

"Have you got the key, auntie?"

"Madge, go away," said Miss Avery, still invisible.

"Auntie, it's Mrs. Wilcox——"

Margaret supported her. "Your niece and I have come together——"

2. In Botticelli's painting *Primavera* (the first green of spring), Venus walks through the woods surrounded by various figures.

"Madge, go away. This is no moment for your hat."

The poor woman went red. "Auntie gets more eccentric lately," she said nervously.

"Miss Avery!" called Margaret. "I have come about the furniture. Could you kindly let me in?"

"Yes, Mrs. Wilcox," said the voice, "of course." But after that came silence. They called again without response. They walked round the house disconsolately.

"I hope Miss Avery is not ill," hazarded Margaret.

"Well, if you'll excuse me," said Madge, "perhaps I ought to be leaving you now. The servants need seeing to at the farm. Auntie is so odd at times." Gathering up her elegancies, she retired defeated, and, as if her departure had loosed a spring, the front door opened at once.

Miss Avery said, "Well, come right in, Mrs. Wilcox!" quite pleasantly and calmly.

"Thank you so much," began Margaret, but broke off at the sight of an umbrella-stand. It was her own.

"Come right into the hall first," said Miss Avery. She drew the curtain, and Margaret uttered a cry of despair. For an appalling thing had happened. The hall was fitted up with the contents of the library from Wickham Place. The carpet had been laid, the big work-table drawn up near the window; the bookcases filled the wall opposite the fireplace, and her father's sword—this is what bewildered her particularly—had been drawn from its scabbard and hung naked amongst the sober volumes. Miss Avery must have worked for days.

"I'm afraid this isn't what we meant," she began. "Mr. Wilcox and I never intended the cases to be touched. For instance, these books are my brother's. We are storing them for him and for my sister, who is abroad. When you kindly undertook to look after things, we never expected you to do so much."

"The house has been empty long enough," said the old woman.

Margaret refused to argue. "I dare say we didn't explain," she said civilly. "It has been a mistake, and very likely our mistake."

"Mrs. Wilcox, it has been mistake upon mistake for fifty years. The house is Mrs. Wilcox's, and she would not desire it to stand empty any longer."

To help the poor decaying brain, Margaret said:

"Yes, Mrs. Wilcox's house, the mother of Mr. Charles."

"Mistake upon mistake," said Miss Avery. "Mistake upon mistake."

"Well, I don't know," said Margaret, sitting down in one of her own chairs. "I really don't know what's to be done." She could not help laughing.

The other said: "Yes, it should be a merry house enough."

"I don't know—I dare say. Well, thank you very much, Miss Avery. Yes, that's all right. Delightful."

"There is still the parlour." She went through the door opposite and drew a curtain. Light flooded the drawing-room and the drawing-room furniture from Wickham Place. "And the dining-room." More curtains were drawn, more windows were flung open to the spring. "Then through here——" Miss Avery continued passing and repassing through the hall. Her voice was lost, but Margaret heard her pulling up the kitchen blind. "I've not finished here yet," she announced, returning. "There's still a deal to do. The farm lads will carry your great wardrobes upstairs, for there is no need to go into expense at Hilton."

"It is all a mistake," repeated Margaret, feeling that she must put her foot down. "A misunderstanding. Mr. Wilcox and I are not going to live at Howards End."

"Oh, indeed. On account of his hay fever?"

"We have settled to build a new home for ourselves in Sussex, and part of this furniture—my part—will go down there presently." She looked at Miss Avery intently, trying to understand the kink in her brain. Here was no maundering old woman. Her wrinkles were shrewd and humorous. She looked capable of scathing wit and also of high but unostentatious nobility.

"You think that you won't come back to live here, Mrs. Wilcox, but you will."

"That remains to be seen," said Margaret, smiling. "We have no intention of doing so for the present. We happen to need a much larger house. Circumstances oblige us to give big parties. Of course, some day—one never knows, does one?"

Miss Avery retorted: "Some day! Tcha! tcha! Don't talk about some day. You are living here now."

"Am I?"

"You are living here, and have been for the last ten minutes, if you ask me."

It was a senseless remark, but with a queer feeling of disloyalty Margaret rose from her chair. She felt that Henry had been obscurely censured. They went into the dining-room, where the sunlight poured in upon her mother's cheffonier, and upstairs, where many an old god peeped from a new niche. The furniture fitted extraordinarily well. In the central room—over the hall, the room that Helen had slept in four years ago—Miss Avery had placed Tibby's old bassinette.

"The nursery," she said.

Margaret turned away without speaking.

At last everything was seen. The kitchen and lobby were still stacked with furniture and straw, but, as far as she could make out, nothing had been broken or scratched. A pathetic display of ingenuity! Then they took a friendly stroll in the garden. It had gone wild since her last visit. The gravel sweep was weedy, and grass had sprung up at the very jaws of the garage. And Evie's rockery was only bumps. Perhaps Evie was responsible for Miss Avery's oddness. But Margaret suspected that the cause lay deeper, and that the girl's silly letter had but loosed the irritation of years.

"It's a beautiful meadow," she remarked. It was one of those open-air drawing-rooms that have been formed, hundreds of years ago, out of the smaller fields. So the boundary hedge zigzagged down the hill at right angles, and at the bottom there was a little green annex—a sort of powder-closet for the cows.

"Yes, the maidy's[3] well enough," said Miss Avery, "for those, that is, who don't suffer from sneezing." And she cackled maliciously. "I've seen Charlie Wilcox go out to my lads in hay time—oh, they ought to do this—they mustn't do that—he'd learn them to be lads. And just then the tickling took him. He has it from his father, with other things. There's not one Wilcox that can stand up against a field in June—I laughed fit to burst while he was courting Ruth."

"My brother gets hay fever too," said Margaret.

"This house lies too much on the land for them. Naturally, they were glad enough to slip in at first. But Wilcoxes are better than nothing, as I see you've found."

Margaret laughed.

"They keep a place going, don't they? Yes, it is just that."

"They keep England going, it is my opinion."

But Miss Avery upset her by replying: "Ay, they breed like rabbits. Well, well, it's a funny world. But He who made it knows what He wants in it, I suppose. If Mrs. Charles is expecting her fourth, it isn't for us to repine."

"They breed and they also work," said Margaret, conscious of some invitation to disloyalty, which was echoed by the very breeze and by the songs of the birds. "It certainly is a funny world, but so long as men like my husband and his sons govern it, I think it'll never be a bad one—never really bad."

"No, better'n nothing," said Miss Avery, and turned to the wych-elm.

On their way back to the farm she spoke of her old friend much more clearly than before. In the house Margaret had wondered whether she quite distinguished the first wife from the second. Now she said: "I never saw much of Ruth after her grandmother died, but we stayed civil. It was a very civil family. Old Mrs. Howard never spoke against anybody, nor let anyone be turned away without food. Then it was never 'Trespassers will be prosecuted' in their land, but would people please not come in? Mrs. Howard was never created to run a farm."

"Had they no men to help them?" Margaret asked.

Miss Avery replied: "Things went on until there were no men."

"Until Mr. Wilcox came along," corrected Margaret, anxious that her husband should receive his dues.

3. Dialect for *meadow*.

"I suppose so; but Ruth should have married a—no disrespect to you to say this, for I take it you were intended to get Wilcox any way, whether she got him first or no."

"Whom should she have married?"

"A soldier!" exclaimed the old woman. "Some real soldier."

Margaret was silent. It was a criticism of Henry's character far more trenchant than any of her own. She felt dissatisfied.

"But that's all over," she went on. "A better time is coming now, though you've kept me long enough waiting. In a couple of weeks I'll see your lights shining through the hedge of an evening. Have you ordered in coals?"

"We are not coming," said Margaret firmly. She respected Miss Avery too much to humour her. "No. Not coming. Never coming. It has all been a mistake. The furniture must be repacked at once, and I am very sorry, but I am making other arrangements, and must ask you to give me the keys."

"Certainly, Mrs. Wilcox," said Miss Avery, and resigned her duties with a smile.

Relieved at this conclusion, and having sent her compliments to Madge, Margaret walked back to the station. She had intended to go to the furniture warehouse and give directions for removal, but the muddle had turned out more extensive than she expected, so she decided to consult Henry. It was as well that she did this. He was strongly against employing the local man whom he had previously recommended, and advised her to store in London after all.

But before this could be done an unexpected trouble fell upon her.

Chapter XXXIV

It was not unexpected entirely. Aunt Juley's health had been bad all the winter. She had had a long series of colds and coughs, and had been too busy to get rid of them. She had scarcely promised her niece "to really take my tiresome chest in hand," when she caught a chill and developed acute pneumonia. Margaret and Tibby went down to Swanage. Helen was telegraphed for, and the spring party that after all gathered in that hospitable house had all the pathos of fair memories. On a perfect day, when the sky seemed blue porcelain, and the waves of the discreet little bay beat gentlest of tattoes upon the sand, Margaret hurried up through the rhododendrons, confronted again by the senselessness of Death. One death may explain itself, but it throws no light upon another: the groping inquiry must begin anew. Preachers or scientists may generalize, but we know that no generality is possible about those whom we love; not one heaven awaits them, not even one oblivion. Aunt Juley, incapable of tragedy, slipped out of life with odd little laughs and apologies for having stopped in it so long. She was very weak; she could not rise to the occasion, or realize the great mystery which all agree must await her; it only seemed to her that she was quite done up—more done up than ever before; that she saw and heard and felt less every moment; and that, unless something changed, she would soon feel nothing. Her spare strength she devoted to plans: could not Margaret take some steamer expeditions? were mackerel cooked as Tibby liked them? She worried herself about Helen's absence, and also that she should be the cause of Helen's return. The nurses seemed to think such interests quite natural, and perhaps hers was an average approach to the Great Gate. But Margaret saw Death stripped of any false romance; whatever the idea of Death may contain, the process can be trivial and hideous.

"Important—Margaret dear, take the Lulworth when Helen comes."

"Helen won't be able to stop, Aunt Juley. She has telegraphed that she can only get away just to see you. She must go back to Germany as soon as you are well."

"How very odd of Helen! Mr. Wilcox——"

"Yes, dear?"

"Can he spare you?"

Henry wished her to come, and had been very kind. Yet again Margaret said so.

Mrs. Munt did not die. Quite outside her will, a more dignified power took hold of her and checked her on the downward slope. She returned, without emotion, as fidgety as ever. On the fourth day she was out of danger.

"Margaret—important," it went on: "I should like you to have some companion to take walks with. Do try Miss Conder."

"I have been a little walk with Miss Conder."

"But she is not really interesting. If only you had Helen."

"I have Tibby, Aunt Juley."

"No, but he has to do his Chinese. Some real companion is what you need. Really, Helen is odd."

"Helen is odd, very," agreed Margaret.

"Not content with going abroad, why does she want to go back there at once?"

"No doubt she will change her mind when she sees us. She has not the least balance."

That was the stock criticism about Helen, but Margaret's voice trembled as she made it. By now she was deeply pained at her sister's behaviour. It may be unbalanced to fly out of England, but to stop away eight months argues that the heart is awry as well as the head. A sick-bed could recall Helen, but she was deaf to more human calls; after a glimpse at her aunt, she would retire into her nebulous life behind some poste restante. She scarcely existed; her letters had become dull and infrequent; she had no wants and no curiosity. And it was all put down to poor Henry's account! Henry, long pardoned by his wife, was still too infamous to be greeted by his sister-in-law. It was morbid, and, to her alarm, Margaret fancied that she could trace the growth of morbidity back in Helen's life for nearly four years. The flight from Oniton; the unbalanced patronage of the Basts; the explosion of grief up on the Downs—all connected with Paul, an insignificant boy whose lips had kissed hers for a fraction of time. Margaret and Mrs. Wilcox had feared that they might kiss again. Foolishly: the real danger was reaction. Reaction against the Wilcoxes had eaten into her life until she was scarcely sane. At twenty-five she had an idée fixe. What hope was there for her as an old woman?

The more Margaret thought about it the more alarmed she became. For many months she had put the subject away, but it was too big to be slighted now. There was almost a taint of madness. Were all Helen's actions to be governed by a tiny mishap, such as may happen to any young man or woman? Can human nature be constructed on lines so insignificant? The blundering little encounter at Howards End was vital. It propagated itself where graver intercourse lay barren; it was stronger than sisterly intimacy, stronger than reason or books. In one of her moods Helen had confessed that she still "enjoyed" it in a certain sense. Paul had faded, but the magic of his caress endured. And where there is enjoyment of the past there may also be reaction—propagation at both ends.

Well, it is odd and sad that our minds should be such seed-beds, and we without power to choose the seed. But man is an odd, sad creature as yet, intent on pilfering the earth, and heedless of the growths within himself. He cannot be bored about psychology. He leaves it to the specialist, which is as if he should leave his dinner to be eaten by a steam-engine. He cannot be bothered to digest his own soul. Margaret and Helen have been more patient, and it is suggested that Margaret has succeeded—so far as success is yet possible. She does understand herself, she has some rudimentary control over her own growth. Whether Helen has succeeded one cannot say.

The day that Mrs. Munt rallied Helen's letter arrived. She had posted it at Munich, and would be in London herself on the morrow. It was a disquieting letter, though the opening was affectionate and sane.

"Dearest Meg,

"Give Helen's love to Aunt Juley. Tell her that I love, and have loved, her ever since I can remember. I shall be in London Thursday.

"My address will be care of the bankers. I have not yet settled on a hotel, so write or wire to me there and give me detailed news. If Aunt Juley is much better, or if, for a terrible reason, it would be no good my coming down to Swanage, you must not think it odd if I do not come. I have all sorts of plans in my head. I am living abroad at present, and want to get back as quickly as possible. Will you please tell me where our furniture is. I should like to take out one or two books; the rest are for you.

"Forgive me, dearest Meg. This must read like rather a tiresome let-ter, but all letters are from your loving

"Helen."

It was a tiresome letter, for it tempted Margaret to tell a lie. If she wrote that Aunt Juley was still in danger her sister would come. Unhealthiness is contagious. We cannot be in contact with those who are in a morbid state without ourselves deteriorating. To "act for the best" might do Helen good, but would do herself harm, and, at the risk of disaster, she kept her colours flying a little longer. She replied that their aunt was much better, and awaited developments.

Tibby approved of her reply. Mellowing rapidly, he was a pleasanter companion than before. Oxford had done much for him. He had lost his peevishness, and could hide his indifference to people and his interest in food. But he had not grown more human. The years between eigh-teen and twenty-two, so magical for most, were leading him gently from boyhood to middle age. He had never known young-manliness, that quality which warms the heart till death, and gives Mr. Wilcox an imper-ishable charm. He was frigid, through no fault of his own, and without cruelty. He thought Helen wrong and Margaret right, but this family trouble was for him what a scene behind footlights is for most people. He had only one suggestion to make, and that was characteristic.

"Why don't you tell Mr. Wilcox?"

"About Helen?"

"Perhaps he has come across that sort of thing."

"He would do all he could, but——"

"Oh, you know best. But he is practical."

It was the student's belief in experts. Margaret demurred for one or two reasons. Presently Helen's answer came. She sent a telegram requesting the address of the furniture, as she would now return at once. Margaret replied, "Certainly not; meet me at the bankers at four." She and Tibby went up to London. Helen was not at the bankers, and they were refused her address. Helen had passed into chaos.

Margaret put her arm round her brother. He was all that she had left, and never had he seemed more unsubstantial.

"Tibby love, what next?"

He replied: "It is extraordinary."

"Dear, your judgment's often clearer than mine. Have you any notion what's at the back?"

"None, unless it's something mental."

"Oh—that!" said Margaret. "Quite impossible." But the suggestion had been uttered, and in a few minutes she took it up herself. Nothing else explained. And London agreed with Tibby. The mask fell off the city, and she saw it for what it really is—a caricature of infinity. The familiar barriers, the streets along which she moved, the houses between which she had made her little journeys for so many years, became negligible suddenly. Helen seemed one with the grimy trees and the traffic and the slowly-flowing slabs of mud. She had accomplished a hideous act of renunciation and returned to the One. Margaret's own faith held firm. She knew the human soul will be merged, if it be merged at all, with the stars and the sea. Yet she felt that her sister had been going amiss for many years. It was symbolic the catastrophe should come now, on a London afternoon, while rain fell slowly.

Henry was the only hope. Henry was definite. He might know of some paths in the chaos that were hidden from them, and she determined to take Tibby's advice and lay the whole matter in his hands. They must call at his office. He could not well make it worse. She went for a few moments into St. Paul's, whose dome stands out of the welter so bravely, as if preaching the gospel of form. But within, St. Paul's is as its surroundings—echoes and whispers, inaudible songs, invisible mosaics, wet footmarks crossing and recrossing the floor. Si monumentum requiris, circumspice:[1] it points us back to London. There was no hope of Helen here.

Henry was unsatisfactory at first. That she had expected. He was overjoyed to see her back from Swanage, and slow to admit the growth of a new trouble. When they told him of their search, he only chaffed Tibby and the Schlegels generally, and declared that it was "just like Helen" to lead her relatives a dance.

"That is what we all say," replied Margaret. "But why should it be just like Helen? Why should she be allowed to be so queer, and to grow queerer?"

"Don't ask me. I'm a plain man of business. I live and let live. My advice to you both is, don't worry. Margaret, you've got black marks again under your eyes. You know that's strictly forbidden. First your aunt—then your sister. No, we aren't going to have it. Are we, Theobald?" He rang the bell. "I'll give you some tea, and then you go straight to Ducie Street. I can't have my girl looking as old as her husband."

"All the same, you have not quite seen our point," said Tibby.

Mr. Wilcox, who was in good spirits, retorted, "I don't suppose I ever shall." He leant back, laughing at the gifted but ridiculous family, while the fire flickered over the map of Africa. Margaret motioned to her brother to go on. Rather diffident, he obeyed her.

"Margaret's point is this," he said. "Our sister may be mad."

Charles, who was working in the inner room, looked round.

"Come in, Charles," said Margaret kindly. "Could you help us at all? We are again in trouble."

1. In St. Paul's cathedral, the tomb of Sir Christopher Wren (1632–1723), the famous architect who designed St. Paul's and many other important London buildings, has this inscription in Latin: "If you want to see his monument, look around."

"I'm afraid I cannot. What are the facts? We are all mad more or less, you know, in these days."

"The facts are as follows," replied Tibby, who had at times a pedantic lucidity. "The facts are that she has been in England for three days and will not see us. She has forbidden the bankers to give us her address. She refuses to answer questions. Margaret finds her letters colourless. There are other facts, but these are the most striking."

"She has never behaved like this before, then?" asked Henry.

"Of course not!" said his wife, with a frown.

"Well, my dear, how am I to know?"

A senseless spasm of annoyance came over her. "You know quite well that Helen never sins against affection," she said. "You must have noticed that much in her, surely."

"Oh yes; she and I have always hit it off together."

"No, Henry—can't you see?—I don't mean that."

She recovered herself, but not before Charles had observed her. Stupid and attentive, he was watching the scene.

"I was meaning that when she was eccentric in the past, one could trace it back to the heart in the long-run. She behaved oddly because she cared for someone, or wanted to help them. There's no possible excuse for her now. She is grieving us deeply, and that is why I am sure that she is not well. 'Mad' is too terrible a word, but she is not well. I shall never believe it. I shouldn't discuss my sister with you if I thought she was well—trouble you about her, I mean."

Henry began to grow serious. Ill-health was to him something perfectly definite. Generally well himself, he could not realize that we sink to it by slow gradations. The sick had no rights; they were outside the pale; one could lie to them remorselessly. When his first wife was seized, he had promised to take her down into Hertfordshire, but meanwhile arranged with a nursing-home instead. Helen, too, was ill. And the plan that he sketched out for her capture, clever and well-meaning as it was, drew its ethics from the wolf-pack.

"You want to get hold of her?" he said. "That's the problem, isn't it? She has got to see a doctor."

"For all I know she has seen one already."

"Yes, yes; don't interrupt." He rose to his feet and thought intently. The genial, tentative host disappeared, and they saw instead the man who had carved money out of Greece and Africa, and bought forests from the natives for a few bottles of gin. "I've got it," he said at last. "It's perfectly easy. Leave it to me. We'll send her down to Howards End."

"How will you do that?"

"After her books. Tell her that she must unpack them herself. Then you can meet her there."

"But, Henry, that's just what she won't let me do. It's part of her— whatever it is—never to see me."

"Of course you won't tell her you're going. When she is there, looking at the cases, you'll just stroll in. If nothing is wrong with her, so much the better. But there'll be the motor round the corner, and we can run her up to a specialist in no time."

Margaret shook her head. "It's quite impossible."

"Why?"

"It doesn't seem impossible to me," said Tibby; "it is surely a very tippy plan."

"It is impossible, because——" She looked at her husband sadly. "It's not the particular language that Helen and I talk, if you see my meaning. It would do splendidly for other people, whom I don't blame."

"But Helen doesn't talk," said Tibby. "That's our whole difficulty. She won't talk your particular language, and on that account you think she's ill."

"No, Henry; it's sweet of you, but I couldn't."

"I see," he said; "you have scruples."

"I suppose so."

"And sooner than go against them you would have your sister suffer. You could have got her down to Swanage by a word, but you had scruples. And scruples are all very well. I am as scrupulous as any man alive, I hope; but when it is a case like this, when there is a question of madness——"

"I deny it's madness."

"You said just now——"

"It's madness when I say it, but not when you say it."

Henry shrugged his shoulders. "Margaret! Margaret!" he groaned. "No education can teach a woman logic. Now, my dear, my time is valuable. Do you want me to help you or not?"

"Not in that way."

"Answer my question. Plain question, plain answer. Do——"

Charles surprised them by interrupting. "Pater, we may as well keep Howards End out of it," he said.

"Why, Charles?"

Charles could give no reason; but Margaret felt as if, over tremendous distance, a salutation had passed between them.

"The whole house is at sixes and sevens," he said crossly. "We don't want any more mess."

"Who's 'we'?" asked his father. "My boy, pray, who's 'we'?"

"I am sure I beg your pardon," said Charles. "I appear always to be intruding."

By now Margaret wished she had never mentioned her trouble to her husband. Retreat was impossible. He was determined to push the matter to a satisfactory conclusion, and Helen faded as he talked. Her fair, flying hair and eager eyes counted for nothing, for she was ill, without rights, and any of her friends might hunt her. Sick at heart, Margaret joined in the chase. She wrote her sister a lying letter, at her husband's dictation;

she said the furniture was all at Howards End, but could be seen on Monday next at 3 p.m., when a charwoman would be in attendance. It was a cold letter, and the more plausible for that. Helen would think she was offended. And on Monday next she and Henry were to lunch with Dolly, and then ambush themselves in the garden.

After they had gone, Mr. Wilcox said to his son: "I can't have this sort of behaviour, my boy. Margaret's too sweet-natured to mind, but I mind for her."

Charles made no answer.

"Is anything wrong with you, Charles, this afternoon?"

"No, pater; but you may be taking on a bigger business than you reckon."

"How?"

"Don't ask me."

Chapter XXXV

One speaks of the moods of spring, but the days that are her true children have only one mood: they are all full of the rising and dropping of winds, and the whistling of birds. New flowers may come out, the green embroidery of the hedges increase, but the same heaven broods overhead, soft, thick, and blue, the same figures, seen and unseen, are wandering by coppice and meadow. The morning that Margaret had spent with Miss Avery, and the afternoon she set out to entrap Helen, were the scales of a single balance. Time might never have moved, rain never have fallen, and man alone, with his schemes and ailments, was troubling Nature until he saw her through a veil of tears.

She protested no more. Whether Henry was right or wrong, he was most kind, and she knew of no other standard by which to judge him. She must trust him absolutely. As soon as he had taken up a business, his obtuseness vanished. He profited by the slightest indications, and the capture of Helen promised to be staged as deftly as the marriage of Evie.

They went down in the morning as arranged, and he discovered that their victim was actually in Hilton. On his arrival he called at all the livery-stables in the village, and had a few minutes' serious conversation with the proprietors. What he said, Margaret did not know—perhaps not the truth; but news arrived after lunch that a lady had come by the London train, and had taken a fly to Howards End.

"She was bound to drive," said Henry. "There will be her books."

"I cannot make it out," said Margaret for the hundredth time.

"Finish your coffee, dear. We must be off."

"Yes, Margaret, you know you must take plenty," said Dolly.

Margaret tried, but suddenly lifted her hand to her eyes. Dolly stole glances at her father-in-law which he did not answer. In the silence the motor came round to the door.

"You're not fit for it," he said anxiously. "Let me go alone. I know exactly what to do."

"Oh yes, I am fit," said Margaret, uncovering her face. "Only most frightfully worried. I cannot feel that Helen is really alive. Her letters and telegrams seem to have come from someone else. Her voice isn't in them. I don't believe your driver really saw her at the station. I wish I'd never mentioned it. I know that Charles is vexed. Yes, he is——" She seized Dolly's hand and kissed it. "There, Dolly will forgive me. There. Now we'll be off."

Henry had been looking at her closely. He did not like this break-down.

"Don't you want to tidy yourself?" he asked.

"Have I time?"

"Yes, plenty."

She went to the lavatory by the front door, and as soon as the bolt slipped, Mr. Wilcox said quietly:

"Dolly, I'm going without her."

Dolly's eyes lit up with vulgar excitement. She followed him on tip-toe out to the car.

"Tell her I thought it best."

"Yes, Mr. Wilcox, I see."

"Say anything you like. All right."

The car started well, and with ordinary luck would have got away. But Porgly-woggles, who was playing in the garden, chose this moment to sit down in the middle of the path. Crane, in trying to pass him, ran one wheel over a bed of wallflowers. Dolly screamed. Margaret, hearing the noise, rushed out hatless, and was in time to jump on the footboard. She said not a single word: he was only treating her as she had treated Helen, and her rage at his dishonesty only helped to indicate what Helen would feel against them. She thought, "I deserve it: I am punished for lowering my colours."[1] And she accepted his apologies with a calmness that aston-ished him.

"I still consider you are not fit for it," he kept saying.

"Perhaps I was not at lunch. But the whole thing is spread clearly before me now."

"I was meaning to act for the best."

"Just lend me your scarf, will you. This wind takes one's hair so."

"Certainly, dear girl. Are you all right now?"

"Look! My hands have stopped trembling."

"And have quite forgiven me? Then listen. Her cab should already have arrived at Howards End. (We're a little late, but no matter.) Our first move will be to send it down to wait at the farm, as, if possible, one doesn't want a scene before servants. A certain gentleman"—he pointed

---

1. Surrendering her values (in heraldry, "colours" signify one's allegiances).

at Crane's back—"won't drive in, but will wait a little short of the front gate, behind the laurels. Have you still the keys of the house?"

"Yes."

"Well, they aren't wanted. Do you remember how the house stands?"

"Yes."

"If we don't find her in the porch, we can stroll round into the garden. Our object——"

Here they stopped to pick up the doctor.

"I was just saying to my wife, Mansbridge, that our main object is not to frighten Miss Schlegel. The house, as you know, is my property, so it should seem quite natural for us to be there. The trouble is evidently nervous—wouldn't you say so, Margaret?"

The doctor, a very young man, began to ask questions about Helen. Was she normal? Was there anything congenital or hereditary? Had anything occurred that was likely to alienate her from her family?

"Nothing," answered Margaret, wondering what would have happened if she had added: "Though she did resent my husband's immorality."

"She always was highly strung," pursued Henry, leaning back in the car as it shot past the church. "A tendency to spiritualism and those things, though nothing serious. Musical, literary, artistic, but I should say normal—a very charming girl."

Margaret's anger and terror increased every moment. How dare these men label her sister! What horrors lay ahead! What impertinences that shelter under the name of science! The pack was turning on Helen, to deny her human rights, and it seemed to Margaret that all Schlegels were threatened with her. "Were they normal?" What a question to ask! And it is always those who know nothing about human nature, who are bored by psychology and shocked by physiology, who ask it. However piteous her sister's state, she knew that she must be on her side. They would be made together if the world chose to consider them so.

It was now five minutes past three. The car slowed down by the farm, in the yard of which Miss Avery was standing. Henry asked her whether a cab had gone past. She nodded, and the next moment they caught sight of it, at the end of the lane. The car ran silently like a beast of prey. So unsuspicious was Helen that she was sitting in the porch, with her back to the road. She had come. Only her head and shoulders were visible. She sat framed in the vine, and one of her hands played with the buds. The wind ruffled her hair, the sun glorified it; she was as she had always been.

Margaret was seated next to the door. Before her husband could prevent her, she slipped out. She ran to the garden gate, which was shut, passed through it, and deliberately pushed it in his face. The noise alarmed Helen. Margaret saw her rise with an unfamiliar movement, and, rushing into the porch, learnt the simple explanation of all their fears—her sister was with child.

"Is the truant all right?" called Henry.

She had time to whisper: "Oh, my darling——" The keys of the house were in her hand. She unlocked Howards End and thrust Helen into it. "Yes, all right," she said, and stood with her back to the door.

Chapter XXXVI

"Margaret, you look upset!" said Henry.

Mansbridge had followed. Crane was at the gate, and the flyman had stood up on the box.[1] Margaret shook her head at them; she could not speak any more. She remained clutching the keys, as if all their future depended on them. Henry was asking more questions. She shook her head again. His words had no sense. She heard him wonder why she had let Helen in. "You might have given me a knock with the gate," was another of his remarks. Presently she heard herself speaking. She, or someone for her, said "Go away." Henry came nearer. He repeated, "Margaret, you look upset again. My dear, give me the keys. What are you doing with Helen?"

"Oh, dearest, do go away, and I will manage it all."

"Manage what?"

He stretched out his hand for the keys. She might have obeyed if it had not been for the doctor.

"Stop that at least," she said piteously; the doctor had turned back, and was questioning the driver of Helen's cab. A new feeling came over her; she was fighting for women against men. She did not care about rights, but if men came into Howards End, it should be over her body.

"Come, this is an odd beginning," said her husband.

The doctor came forward now, and whispered two words to Mr. Wilcox—the scandal was out. Sincerely horrified, Henry stood gazing at the earth.

"I cannot help it," said Margaret. "Do wait. It's not my fault. Please all four of you to go away now."

Now the flyman was whispering to Crane.

"We are relying on you to help us, Mrs. Wilcox," said the young doctor. "Could you go in and persuade your sister to come out?"

"On what grounds?" said Margaret, suddenly looking him straight in the eyes.

Thinking it professional to prevaricate, he murmured something about a nervous breakdown.

"I beg your pardon, but it is nothing of the sort. You are not qualified to attend my sister, Mr. Mansbridge. If we require your services, we will let you know."

"I can diagnose the case more bluntly if you wish," he retorted.

1. Helen's carriage-driver rose from his seat.

"You could, but you have not. You are, therefore, not qualified to attend my sister."

"Come, come, Margaret!" said Henry, never raising his eyes. "This is a terrible business, an appalling business. It's doctor's orders. Open the door."

"Forgive me, but I will not."

"I don't agree."

Margaret was silent.

"This business is as broad as it's long," contributed the doctor. "We had better all work together. You need us, Mrs. Wilcox, and we need you."

"Quite so," said Henry.

"I do not need you in the least," said Margaret.

The two men looked at each other anxiously.

"No more does my sister, who is still many weeks from her confinement."

"Margaret, Margaret!"

"Well, Henry, send your doctor away. What possible use is he now?"

Mr. Wilcox ran his eye over the house. He had a vague feeling that he must stand firm and support the doctor. He himself might need support, for there was trouble ahead.

"It all turns on affection now," said Margaret. "Affection. Don't you see?" Resuming her usual methods, she wrote the word on the house with her finger. "Surely you see. I like Helen very much, you not so much. Mr. Mansbridge doesn't know her. That's all. And affection, when reciprocated, gives rights. Put that down in your note-book, Mr. Mansbridge. It's a useful formula."

Henry told her to be calm.

"You don't know what you want yourselves," said Margaret, folding her arms. "For one sensible remark I will let you in. But you cannot make it. You would trouble my sister for no reason. I will not permit it. I'll stand here all the day sooner."

"Mansbridge," said Henry in a low voice, "perhaps not now."

The pack was breaking up. At a sign from his master, Crane also went back into the car.

"Now, Henry, you," she said gently. None of her bitterness had been directed at him. "Go away now, dear. I shall want your advice later, no doubt. Forgive me if I have been cross. But, seriously, you must go."

He was too stupid to leave her. Now it was Mr. Mansbridge who called in a low voice to him.

"I shall soon find you down at Dolly's," she called, as the gate at last clanged between them. The fly moved out of the way, the motor backed, turned a little, backed again, and turned in the narrow road. A string of farm carts came up in the middle; but she waited through all, for there was no hurry. When all was over and the car had started, she opened the door. "Oh, my darling!" she said. "My darling, forgive me." Helen was standing in the hall.

Chapter XXXVII

Margaret bolted the door on the inside. Then she would have kissed her sister, but Helen, in a dignified voice, that came strangely from her, said:

"Convenient! You did not tell me that the books were unpacked. I have found nearly everything that I want."

"I told you nothing that was true."

"It has been a great surprise, certainly. Has Aunt Juley been ill?"

"Helen, you wouldn't think I'd invent that?"

"I suppose not," said Helen, turning away, and crying a very little. "But one loses faith in everything after this."

"We thought it was illness, but even then—— I haven't behaved worthily."

Helen selected another book.

"I ought not to have consulted anyone. What would our father have thought of me?"

She did not think of questioning her sister, nor of rebuking her. Both might be necessary in the future, but she had first to purge a greater crime than any that Helen could have committed—that want of confidence that is the work of the devil.

"Yes, I am annoyed," replied Helen. "My wishes should have been respected. I would have gone through this meeting if it was necessary, but after Aunt Juley recovered, it was not necessary. Planning my life, as I now have to do——"

"Come away from those books," called Margaret. "Helen, do talk to me."

"I was just saying that I have stopped living haphazard. One can't go through a great deal of——" she missed out the noun—"without planning one's actions in advance. I am going to have a child in June, and in the first place conversations, discussions, excitement, are not good for me. I will go through them if necessary, but only then. In the second place I have no right to trouble people. I cannot fit in with England as I know it. I have done something that the English never pardon. It would not be right for them to pardon it. So I must live where I am not known."

"But why didn't you tell me, dearest?"

"Yes," replied Helen judicially. "I might have, but decided to wait."

"I believe you would never have told me."

"Oh yes, I should. We have taken a flat in Munich."

Margaret glanced out of the window.

"By 'we' I mean myself and Monica. But for her, I am and have been and always wish to be alone."

"I have not heard of Monica."

"You wouldn't have. She's an Italian—by birth at least. She makes her living by journalism. I met her originally on Garda. Monica is much the best person to see me through."

"You are very fond of her, then."

"She has been extraordinarily sensible with me."

Margaret guessed at Monica's type—'Italiano Inglesiato'[1] they had named it: the crude feminist of the South, whom one respects but avoids. And Helen had turned to it in her need!

"You must not think that we shall never meet," said Helen, with a measured kindness. "I shall always have a room for you when you can be spared, and the longer you can be with me the better. But you haven't understood yet, Meg, and of course it is very difficult for you. This is a shock to you. It isn't to me, who have been thinking over our futures for many months, and they won't be changed by a slight contretemps, such as this. I cannot live in England."

"Helen, you've not forgiven me for my treachery. You *couldn't* talk like this to me if you had."

"Oh, Meg dear, why do we talk at all?" She dropped a book and sighed wearily. Then, recovering herself, she said: "Tell me, how is it that all the books are down here?"

"Series of mistakes."

"And a great deal of the furniture has been unpacked."

"All."

"Who lives here, then?"

"No one."

"I suppose you are letting it, though."

"The house is dead," said Margaret, with a frown. "Why worry on about it?"

"But I am interested. You talk as if I had lost all my interest in life. I am still Helen, I hope. Now this hasn't the feel of a dead house. The hall seems more alive even than in the old days, when it held the Wilcoxes' own things."

"Interested, are you? Very well, I must tell you, I suppose. My husband lent it on condition we—but by a mistake all our things were unpacked, and Miss Avery, instead of——" She stopped. "Look here, I can't go on like this. I warn you I won't. Helen, why should you be so miserably unkind to me, simply because you hate Henry?"

"I don't hate him now," said Helen. "I have stopped being a school-girl, and, Meg, once again, I'm not being unkind. But as for fitting in with your English life—no, put it out of your head at once. Imagine a visit from me at Ducie Street! It's unthinkable."

Margaret could not contradict her. It was appalling to see her quietly moving forward with her plans, not bitter or excitable, neither asserting innocence nor confessing guilt, merely desiring freedom and the company of those who would not blame her. She had been through—how much? Margaret did not know. But it was enough to part her from old habits as well as old friends.

1. Anglicized Italian (Italian).

"Tell me about yourself," said Helen, who had chosen her books, and was lingering over the furniture.

"There's nothing to tell."

"But your marriage has been happy, Meg?"

"Yes, but I don't feel inclined to talk."

"You feel as I do."

"Not that, but I can't."

"No more can I. It is a nuisance, but no good trying."

Something had come between them. Perhaps it was Society, which henceforward would exclude Helen. Perhaps it was a third life, already potent as a spirit. They could find no meeting-place. Both suffered acutely, and were not comforted by the knowledge that affection survived.

"Look here, Meg, is the coast clear?"

"You mean that you want to go away from me?"

"I suppose so—dear old lady! it isn't any use. I knew we should have nothing to say. Give my love to Aunt Juley and Tibby, and take more yourself than I can say. Promise to come and see me in Munich later."

"Certainly, dearest."

"For that is all we can do."

It seemed so. Most ghastly of all was Helen's common sense: Monica had been extraordinarily good for her.

"I am glad to have seen you and the things." She looked at the bookcase lovingly, as if she was saying farewell to the past.

Margaret unbolted the door. She remarked: "The car has gone, and here's your cab."

She led the way to it, glancing at the leaves and the sky. The spring had never seemed more beautiful. The driver, who was leaning on the gate, called out, "Please, lady, a message," and handed her Henry's visiting-card through the bars.

"How did this come?" she asked.

Crane had returned with it almost at once.

She read the card with annoyance. It was covered with instructions in domestic French. When she and her sister had talked she was to come back for the night to Dolly's. "Il faut dormir sur ce sujet."[2] While Helen was to be found "une confortable chambre à l'hotel."[3] The final sentence displeased her greatly until she remembered that the Charles' had only one spare room, and so could not invite a third guest.

"Henry would have done what he could," she interpreted.

Helen had not followed her into the garden. The door once open, she lost her inclination to fly. She remained in the hall, going from bookcase to table. She grew more like the old Helen, irresponsible and charming.

2. "It is necessary to sleep on the subject." (French)
3. "A comfortable room at the hotel." (French)

"This *is* Mr. Wilcox's house?" she inquired.

"Surely you remember Howards End?"

"Remember? I who remember everything! But it looks to be ours now."

"Miss Avery was extraordinary," said Margaret, her own spirits lightening a little. Again she was invaded by a slight feeling of disloyalty. But it brought her relief, and she yielded to it. "She loved Mrs. Wilcox, and would rather furnish her house with our things than think of it empty. In consequence here are all the library books."

"Not all the books. She hasn't unpacked the Art Books, in which she may show her sense. And we never used to have the sword here."

"The sword looks well, though."

"Magnificent."

"Yes, doesn't it?"

"Where's the piano, Meg?"

"I warehoused that in London. Why?"

"Nothing."

"Curious, too, that the carpet fits."

"The carpet's a mistake," announced Helen. "I know that we had it in London, but this floor ought to be bare. It is far too beautiful."

"You still have a mania for under-furnishing. Would you care to come into the dining-room before you start? There's no carpet there."

They went in, and each minute their talk became more natural.

"Oh, *what* a place for mother's cheffonier!" cried Helen.

"Look at the chairs, though."

"Oh, look at them! Wickham Place faced north, didn't it?"

"North-west."

"Anyhow, it is thirty years since any of those chairs have felt the sun. Feel. Their dear little backs are quite warm."

"But why has Miss Avery made them set to partners? I shall just——"

"Over here, Meg. Put it so that anyone sitting will see the lawn."

Margaret moved a chair. Helen sat down in it.

"Ye-es. The window's too high."

"Try a drawing-room chair."

"No, I don't like the drawing-room so much. The beam has been match-boarded. It would have been so beautiful otherwise."

"Helen, what a memory you have for some things! You're perfectly right. It's a room that men have spoilt through trying to make it nice for women. Men don't know what we want——"

"And never will."

"I don't agree. In two thousand years they'll know."

"But the chairs show up wonderfully. Look where Tibby spilt the soup."

"Coffee. It was coffee surely."

Helen shook her head. "Impossible. Tibby was far too young to be given coffee at that time."

"Was father alive?"

"Yes."

"Then you're right and it must have been soup. I was thinking of much later—that unsuccessful visit of Aunt Juley's, when she didn't realize that Tibby had grown up. It was coffee then, for he threw it down on purpose. There was some rhyme, 'Tea, coffee—coffee, tea,' that she said to him every morning at breakfast. Wait a minute—how did it go?"

"I know—no, I don't. What a detestable boy Tibby was!"

"But the rhyme was simply awful. No decent person could have put up with it."

"Ah, that greengage tree," cried Helen, as if the garden was also part of their childhood. "Why do I connect it with dumb-bells? And there come the chickens. The grass wants cutting. I love yellowhammers——"

Margaret interrupted her. "I have got it," she announced.

> "'Tea, tea, coffee, tea,
>   Or chocolaritee.'

"That every morning for three weeks. No wonder Tibby was wild."

"Tibby is moderately a dear now," said Helen.

"There! I knew you'd say that in the end. Of course he's a dear."

A bell rang.

"Listen! what's that?"

Helen said, "Perhaps the Wilcoxes are beginning the siege."

"What nonsense—listen!"

And the triviality faded from their faces, though it left something behind—the knowledge that they never could be parted because their love was rooted in common things. Explanations and appeals had failed; they had tried for a common meeting-ground, and had only made each other unhappy. And all the time their salvation was lying round them—the past sanctifying the present; the present, with wild heart-throb, declaring that there would after all be a future, with laughter and the voices of children. Helen, still smiling, came up to her sister. She said, "It is always Meg." They looked into each other's eyes. The inner life had paid.

Solemnly the clapper[4] tolled. No one was in the front. Margaret went to the kitchen, and struggled between packing-cases to the window. Their visitor was only a little boy with a tin can. And triviality returned.

"Little boy, what do you want?"

"Please, I am the milk."

"Did Miss Avery send you?" said Margaret, rather sharply.

"Yes, please."

"Then take it back and say we require no milk." While she called to Helen, "No, it's not the siege, but possibly an attempt to provision us against one."

---

4. A bell's tongue.

"But I like milk," cried Helen. "Why send it away?"

"Do you? Oh, very well. But we've nothing to put it in, and he wants the can."

"Please, I'm to call in the morning for the can," said the boy.

"The house will be locked up then."

"In the morning would I bring eggs, too?"

"Are you the boy whom I saw playing in the stacks last week?"

The child hung his head.

"Well, run away and do it again."

"Nice little boy," whispered Helen. "I say, what's your name? Mine's Helen."

"Tom."

That was Helen all over. The Wilcoxes, too, would ask a child its name, but they never told their names in return.

"Tom, this one here is Margaret. And at home we've another called Tibby."

"Mine are lop-eareds," replied Tom, supposing Tibby to be a rabbit.

"You're a very good and rather a clever little boy. Mind you come again. —Isn't he charming?"

"Undoubtedly," said Margaret. "He is probably the son of Madge, and Madge is dreadful. But this place has wonderful powers."

"What do you mean?"

"I don't know."

"Because I probably agree with you."

"It kills what is dreadful and makes what is beautiful live."

"I do agree," said Helen, as she sipped the milk. "But you said that the house was dead not half an hour ago."

"Meaning that I was dead. I felt it."

"Yes, the house has a surer life than we, even if it was empty, and, as it is, I can't get over that for thirty years the sun has never shone full on our furniture. After all, Wickham Place was a grave. Meg, I've a startling idea."

"What is it?"

"Drink some milk to steady you."

Margaret obeyed.

"No, I won't tell you yet," said Helen, "because you may laugh or be angry. Let's go upstairs first and give the rooms an airing."

They opened window after window, till the inside, too, was rustling to the spring. Curtains blew, picture-frames tapped cheerfully. Helen uttered cries of excitement as she found this bed obviously in its right place, that in its wrong one. She was angry with Miss Avery for not having moved the wardrobes up. "Then one would see really." She admired the view. She was the Helen who had written the memorable letters four years ago. As they leant out, looking westward, she said: "About my idea. Couldn't you and I camp out in this house for the night?"

"I don't think we could well do that," said Margaret.

"Here are beds, tables, towels——"

"I know; but the house isn't supposed to be slept in, and Henry's suggestion was——"

"I require no suggestions. I shall not alter anything in my plans. But it would give me so much pleasure to have one night here with you. It will be something to look back on. Oh, Meg lovey, do let's!"

"But, Helen, my pet," said Margaret, "we can't without getting Henry's leave. Of course, he would give it, but you said yourself that you couldn't visit at Ducie Street now, and this is equally intimate."

"Ducie Street is his house. This is ours. Our furniture, our sort of people coming to the door. Do let us camp out, just one night, and Tom shall feed us on eggs and milk. Why not? It's a moon."[5]

Margaret hesitated. "I feel Charles wouldn't like it," she said at last. "Even our furniture annoyed him, and I was going to clear it out when Aunt Juley's illness prevented me. I sympathize with Charles. He feels it's his mother's house. He loves it in rather an untaking[6] way. Henry I could answer for—not Charles."

"I know he won't like it," said Helen. "But I am going to pass out of their lives. What difference will it make in the long run if they say, 'And she even spent the night at Howards End'?"

"How do you know you'll pass out of their lives? We have thought that twice before."

"Because my plans——"

"—which you change in a moment."

"Then because my life is great and theirs are little," said Helen, taking fire. "I know of things they can't know of, and so do you. We *know* that there's poetry. We *know* that there's death. They can only take them on hearsay. We know this is our house, because it feels ours. Oh, they may take the title-deeds and the doorkeys, but for this one night we are at home."

"It would be lovely to have you once more alone," said Margaret. "It may be a chance in a thousand."

"Yes, and we could talk." She dropped her voice. "It won't be a very glorious story. But under that wych-elm—honestly, I see little happiness ahead. Cannot I have this one night with you?"

"I needn't say how much it would mean to me."

"Then let us."

"It is no good hesitating. Shall I drive down to Hilton now and get leave?"

"Oh, we don't want leave."

But Margaret was a loyal wife. In spite of imagination and poetry—

5. A moonlit night.
6. Unattractive, unreceptive.

perhaps on account of them—she could sympathize with the technical attitude that Henry would adopt. If possible, she would be technical, too. A night's lodging—and they demanded no more—need not involve the discussion of general principles.

"Charles may say no," grumbled Helen.

"We shan't consult him."

"Go if you like; I should have stopped without leave."

It was the touch of selfishness, which was not enough to mar Helen's character, and even added to its beauty. She would have stopped without leave, and escaped to Germany the next morning. Margaret kissed her.

"Expect me back before dark. I am looking forward to it so much. It is like you to have thought of such a beautiful thing."

"Not a thing, only an ending," said Helen rather sadly; and the sense of tragedy closed in on Margaret again as soon as she left the house.

She was afraid of Miss Avery. It is disquieting to fulfil a prophecy, however superficially. She was glad to see no watching figure as she drove past the farm, but only little Tom, turning somersaults in the straw.

Chapter XXXVIII

The tragedy began quietly enough, and, like many another talk, by the man's deft assertion of his superiority. Henry heard her arguing with the driver, stepped out and settled the fellow, who was inclined to be rude, and then led the way to some chairs on the lawn. Dolly, who had not been "told," ran out with offers of tea. He refused them, and ordered her to wheel baby's perambulator away, as they desired to be alone.

"But the diddums can't listen; he isn't nine months old," she pleaded.

"That's not what I was saying," retorted her father-in-law.

Baby was wheeled out of earshot, and did not hear about the crisis till later years. It was now the turn of Margaret.

"Is it what we feared?" he asked.

"It is."

"Dear girl," he began, "there is a troublesome business ahead of us, and nothing but the most absolute honesty and plain speech will see us through." Margaret bent her head. "I am obliged to question you on subjects we'd both prefer to leave untouched. As you know, I am not one of your Bernard Shaws[1] who consider nothing sacred. To speak as I must will pain me, but there are occasions—— We are husband and wife, not children. I am a man of the world, and you are a most exceptional woman."

All Margaret's senses forsook her. She blushed, and looked past him at the Six Hills, covered with spring herbage. Noting her colour, he grew still more kind.

---

1. George Bernard Shaw (1856–1950), irreverent Irish playwright and social critic.

"I see that you feel as I felt when—— My poor little wife! Oh, be brave! Just one or two questions, and I have done with you. Was your sister wearing a wedding-ring?"

Margaret stammered a "No."

There was an appalling silence.

"Henry, I really came to ask a favour about Howards End."

"One point at a time. I am now obliged to ask for the name of her seducer."

She rose to her feet and held the chair between them. Her colour had ebbed, and she was grey. It did not displease him that she should receive his question thus.

"Take your time," he counselled her. "Remember that this is far worse for me than for you."

She swayed; he feared she was going to faint. Then speech came, and she said slowly: "Seducer? No; I do not know her seducer's name."

"Would she not tell you?"

"I never even asked her who seduced her," said Margaret, dwelling on the hateful word thoughtfully.

"That is singular." Then he changed his mind. "Natural perhaps, dear girl, that you shouldn't ask. But until his name is known, nothing can be done. Sit down. How terrible it is to see you so upset! I knew you weren't fit for it. I wish I hadn't taken you."

Margaret answered, "I like to stand, if you don't mind, for it gives me a pleasant view of the Six Hills."

"As you like."

"Have you anything else to ask me, Henry?"

"Next you must tell me whether you have gathered anything. I have often noticed your insight, dear. I only wish my own was as good. You may have guessed something, even though your sister said nothing. The slightest hint would help us."

"Who is 'we'?"

"I thought it best to ring up Charles."

"That was unnecessary," said Margaret, growing warmer. "This news will give Charles disproportionate pain."

"He has at once gone to call on your brother."

"That too was unnecessary."

"Let me explain, dear, how the matter stands. You don't think that I and my son are other than gentlemen? It is in Helen's interests that we are acting. It is still not too late to save her name."

Then Margaret hit out for the first time. "Are we to make her seducer marry her?" she asked.

"If possible. Yes."

"But, Henry, suppose he turned out to be married already? One has heard of such cases."

"In that case he must pay heavily for his misconduct, and be thrashed within an inch of his life."

So her first blow missed. She was thankful of it. What had tempted her to imperil both of their lives? Henry's obtuseness had saved her as well as himself. Exhausted with anger, she sat down again, blinking at him as he told her as much as he thought fit. At last she said: "May I ask you my question now?"

"Certainly, my dear."

"To-morrow Helen goes to Munich——"

"Well, possibly she is right."

"Henry, let a lady finish. To-morrow she goes; to-night, with your permission, she would like to sleep at Howards End."

It was the crisis of his life. Again she would have recalled the words as soon as they were uttered. She had not led up to them with sufficient care. She longed to warn him that they were far more important than he supposed. She saw him weighing them, as if they were a business proposition.

"Why Howards End?" he said at last. "Would she not be more comfortable, as I suggested, at the hotel?"

Margaret hastened to give him reasons. "It is an odd request, but you know what Helen is and what women in her state are." He frowned, and moved irritably. "She has the idea that one night in your house would give her pleasure and do her good. I think she's right. Being one of those imaginative girls, the presence of all our books and furniture soothes her. This is a fact. It is the end of her girlhood. Her last words to me were, 'A beautiful ending.'"

"She values the old furniture for sentimental reasons, in fact."

"Exactly. You have quite understood. It is her last hope of being with it."

"I don't agree there, my dear! Helen will have her share of the goods wherever she goes—possibly more than her share, for you are so fond of her that you'd give her anything of yours that she fancies, wouldn't you? and I'd raise no objection. I could understand it if it was her old home, because a home, or a house"—he changed the word, designedly; he had thought of a telling point—"because a house in which one has once lived becomes in a sort of way sacred, I don't know why. Associations and so on. Now Helen has no associations with Howards End, though I and Charles and Evie have. I do not see why she wants to stay the night there. She will only catch cold."

"Leave it that you don't see," cried Margaret. "Call it fancy. But realize that fancy is a scientific fact. Helen is fanciful, and wants to."

Then he surprised her—a rare occurrence. He shot an unexpected bolt. "If she wants to sleep one night, she may want to sleep two. We shall never get her out of the house, perhaps."

"Well?" said Margaret, with the precipice in sight. "And suppose we don't get her out of the house? Would it matter? She would do no one any harm."

Again the irritated gesture.

"No, Henry," she panted, receding. "I didn't mean that. We will only trouble Howards End for this one night. I take her to London to-morrow——"

"Do you intend to sleep in a damp house, too?"

"She cannot be left alone."

"That's quite impossible! Madness. You must be here to meet Charles."

"I have already told you that your message to Charles was unnecessary, and I have no desire to meet him."

"Margaret—my Margaret——"

"What has this business to do with Charles? If it concerns me little, it concerns you less, and Charles not at all."

"As the future owner of Howards End," said Mr. Wilcox, arching his fingers, "I should say that it did concern Charles."

"In what way? Will Helen's condition depreciate the property?"

"My dear, you are forgetting yourself."

"I think you yourself recommended plain speaking."

They looked at each other in amazement. The precipice was at their feet now.

"Helen commands my sympathy," said Henry. "As your husband, I shall do all for her that I can, and I have no doubt that she will prove more sinned against than sinning. But I cannot treat her as if nothing has happened. I should be false to my position in society if I did."

She controlled herself for the last time. "No, let us go back to Helen's request," she said. "It is unreasonable, but the request of an unhappy girl. To-morrow she will go to Germany, and trouble society no longer. To-night she asks to sleep in your empty house—a house which you do not care about, and which you have not occupied for over a year. May she? Will you give my sister leave? Will you forgive her—as you hope to be forgiven, and as you have actually been forgiven? Forgive her for one night only. That will be enough."

"As I have actually been forgiven——?"

"Never mind for the moment what I mean by that," said Margaret. "Answer my question."

Perhaps some hint of her meaning did dawn on him. If so, he blotted it out. Straight from his fortress he answered: "I seem rather unaccommodating, but I have some experience of life, and know how one thing leads to another. I am afraid that your sister had better sleep at the hotel. I have my children and the memory of my dear wife to consider. I am sorry, but see that she leaves my house at once."

"You have mentioned Mrs. Wilcox."

"I beg your pardon?"

"A rare occurrence. In reply, may I mention Mrs. Bast?"

"You have not been yourself all day," said Henry, and rose from his seat with face unmoved. Margaret rushed at him and seized both his hands. She was transfigured.

"Not any more of this!" she cried. "You shall see the connection if it kills you, Henry! You have had a mistress—I forgave you. My sister has a lover—you drive her from the house. Do you see the connection? Stupid, hypocritical, cruel—oh, contemptible!—a man who insults his wife when she's alive and cants with her memory when she's dead. A man who ruins a woman for his pleasure, and casts her off to ruin other men. And gives bad financial advice, and then says he is not responsible. These men are you. You can't recognize them, because you cannot connect. I've had enough of your unweeded kindness. I've spoilt you long enough. All your life you have been spoiled. Mrs. Wilcox spoiled you. No one has ever told what you are—muddled, criminally muddled. Men like you use repentance as a blind, so don't repent. Only say to yourself, 'What Helen has done, I've done.'"

"The two cases are different," Henry stammered. His real retort was not quite ready. His brain was still in a whirl, and he wanted a little longer.

"In what way different? You have betrayed Mrs. Wilcox, Helen only herself. You remain in society, Helen can't. You have had only pleasure, she may die. You have the insolence to talk to me of differences, Henry?"

Oh, the uselessness of it! Henry's retort came.

"I perceive you are attempting blackmail. It is scarcely a pretty weapon for a wife to use against her husband. My rule through life has been never to pay the least attention to threats, and I can only repeat what I said before: I do not give you and your sister leave to sleep at Howards End."

Margaret loosed his hands. He went into the house, wiping first one and then the other on his handkerchief. For a little she stood looking at the Six Hills, tombs of warriors, breasts of the spring. Then she passed out into what was now the evening.

Chapter XXXIX

Charles and Tibby met at Ducie Street, where the latter was staying. Their interview was short and absurd. They had nothing in common but the English language, and tried by its help to express what neither of them understood. Charles saw in Helen the family foe. He had singled her out as the most dangerous of the Schlegels, and, angry as he was, looked forward to telling his wife how right he had been. His mind was made up at once: the girl must be got out of the way before she disgraced them farther. If occasion offered she might be married to a villain or, possibly, to a fool. But this was a concession to morality, it formed no part of his main scheme. Honest and hearty was Charles's dislike, and the past spread itself out very clearly before him; hatred is a skilful compositor. As if they were heads in a note-book, he ran through all the incidents of the Schlegels' campaign: the attempt to compromise his brother, his mother's legacy, his father's marriage, the introduction of the furniture, the unpacking of the same. He had not yet heard of the request to sleep at Howards End; that was to be their master-stroke and the opportunity for his. But he already felt that Howards End was the objective, and, though he disliked the house, was determined to defend it.

Tibby, on the other hand, had no opinions. He stood above the conventions: his sister had a right to do what she thought right. It is not difficult to stand above the conventions when we leave no hostages among them; men can always be more unconventional than women, and a bachelor of independent means need encounter no difficulties at all. Unlike Charles, Tibby had money enough; his ancestors had earned it for him, and if he shocked the people in one set of lodgings he had only to move into another. His was the Leisure without sympathy—an attitude as fatal as the strenuous: a little cold culture may be raised on it, but no art. His sisters had seen the family danger, and had never forgotten to discount the gold islets that raised them from the sea. Tibby gave all the praise to himself, and so despised the struggling and the submerged.

Hence the absurdity of the interview; the gulf between them was economic as well as spiritual. But several facts passed: Charles pressed for them with an impertinence that the undergraduate could not withstand. On what date had Helen gone abroad? To whom? (Charles was anxious to fasten the scandal on Germany.) Then, changing his tactics, he said roughly: "I suppose you realize that you are your sister's protector?"

"In what sense?"

"If a man played about with my sister, I'd send a bullet through him, but perhaps you don't mind."

"I mind very much," protested Tibby.

"Who d'ye suspect, then? Speak out, man. One always suspects someone."

"No one. I don't think so." Involuntarily he blushed. He had remembered the scene in his Oxford rooms.

"You are hiding something," said Charles. As interviews go, he got the best of this one. "When you saw her last, did she mention anyone's name? Yes or no!" he thundered, so that Tibby started.

"In my rooms she mentioned some friends, called the Basts——"

"Who are the Basts?"

"People—friends of hers at Evie's wedding."

"I don't remember. But, by great Scott! I do. My aunt told me about some tag-rag. Was she full of them when you saw her? Is there a man?

Did she speak of the man? Or—look here—have you had any dealings with him?"

Tibby was silent. Without intending it, he had betrayed his sister's confidence; he was not enough interested in human life to see where things will lead to. He had a strong regard for honesty, and his word, once given, had always been kept up to now. He was deeply vexed, not only for the harm he had done Helen, but for the flaw he had discovered in his own equipment.

"I see—you are in his confidence. They met at your rooms. Oh, what a family, what a family! God help the poor pater——"

And Tibby found himself alone.

Chapter XL

Leonard—he would figure at length in a newspaper report, but that evening he did not count for much. The foot of the tree was in shadow, since the moon was still hidden behind the house. But above, to right, to left, down the long meadow the moonlight was streaming. Leonard seemed not a man, but a cause.

Perhaps it was Helen's way of falling in love—a curious way to Margaret, whose agony and whose contempt of Henry were yet imprinted with his image. Helen forgot people. They were husks that had enclosed her emotion. She could pity, or sacrifice herself, or have instincts, but had she ever loved in the noblest way, where man and woman, having lost themselves in sex, desire to lose sex itself in comradeship?

Margaret wondered, but said no word of blame. This was Helen's evening. Troubles enough lay ahead of her—the loss of friends and of social advantages, the agony, the supreme agony, of motherhood, which is even yet not a matter of common knowledge. For the present let the moon shine brightly and the breezes of the spring blow gently, dying away from the gale of the day, and let the earth, who brings increase, bring peace. Not even to herself dare she blame Helen. She could not assess her trespass by any moral code; it was everything or nothing. Morality can tell us that murder is worse than stealing, and group most sins in an order all must approve, but it cannot group Helen. The surer its pronouncements on this point, the surer may we be that morality is not speaking. Christ was evasive when they questioned Him. It is those that cannot connect who hasten to cast the first stone.

This was Helen's evening—won at what cost, and not to be marred by the sorrows of others. Of her own tragedy Margaret never uttered a word.

"One isolates," said Helen slowly. "I isolated Mr. Wilcox from the other forces that were pulling Leonard downhill. Consequently, I was full of pity, and almost of revenge. For weeks I had blamed Mr. Wilcox only, and so, when your letters came——"

"I need never have written them," sighed Margaret. "They never shielded Henry. How hopeless it is to tidy away the past, even for others!"

"I did not know that it was your own idea to dismiss the Basts."

"Looking back, that was wrong of me."

"Looking back, darling, I know that it was right. It is right to save the man whom one loves. I am less enthusiastic about justice now. But we both thought you wrote at his dictation. It seemed the last touch of his callousness. Being very much wrought up by this time—and Mrs. Bast was upstairs. I had not seen her, and had talked for a long time to Leonard—I had snubbed him for no reason, and that should have warned me I was in danger. So when the notes came I wanted us to go to you for an explanation. He said that he guessed the explanation—he knew of it, and you mustn't know. I pressed him to tell me. He said no one must know; it was something to do with his wife. Right up to the end we were Mr. Bast and Miss Schlegel. I was going to tell him that he must be frank with me when I saw his eyes, and guessed that Mr. Wilcox had ruined him in two ways, not one. I drew him to me. I made him tell me. I felt very lonely myself. He is not to blame. He would have gone on worshipping me. I want never to see him again, though it sounds appalling. I wanted to give him money and feel finished. Oh, Meg, the little that is known about these things!"

She laid her face against the tree.

"The little, too, that is known about growth! Both times it was loneliness, and the night, and panic afterwards. Did Leonard grow out of Paul?"

Margaret did not speak for a moment. So tired was she that her attention had actually wandered to the teeth—the teeth that had been thrust into the tree's bark to medicate it. From where she sat she could see them gleam. She had been trying to count them. "Leonard is a better growth than madness," she said. "I was afraid that you would react against Paul until you went over the verge."

"I did react until I found poor Leonard. I am steady now. I shan't ever *like* your Henry, dearest Meg, or even speak kindly about him, but all that blinding hate is over. I shall never rave against Wilcoxes any more. I understand how you married him, and you will now be very happy."

Margaret did not reply.

"Yes," repeated Helen, her voice growing more tender, "I do at last understand."

"Except Mrs. Wilcox, dearest, no one understands our little movements."

"Because in death—I agree."

"Not quite. I feel that you and I and Henry are only fragments of that woman's mind. She knows everything. She is everything. She is the house, and the tree that leans over it. People have their own deaths as well as their own lives, and even if there is nothing beyond death, we shall differ in our nothingness. I cannot believe that knowledge such as hers will perish with knowledge such as mine. She knew about realities. She knew when people were in love, though she was not in the room. I don't doubt that she knew when Henry deceived her."

"Good-night, Mrs. Wilcox," called a voice.

"Oh, good-night, Miss Avery."

"Why should Miss Avery work for us?" Helen murmured.

"Why, indeed?"

Miss Avery crossed the lawn and merged into the hedge that divided it from the farm. An old gap, which Mr. Wilcox had filled up, had reappeared, and her track through the dew followed the path that he had turfed over, when he improved the garden and made it possible for games.

"This is not quite our house yet," said Helen. "When Miss Avery called, I felt we are only a couple of tourists."

"We shall be that everywhere, and for ever."

"But affectionate tourists——"

"But tourists who pretend each hotel is their home."

"I can't pretend very long," said Helen. "Sitting under this tree one forgets, but I know that to-morrow I shall see the moon rise out of Germany. Not all your goodness can alter the facts of the case. Unless you will come with me."

Margaret thought for a moment. In the past year she had grown so fond of England that to leave it was a real grief. Yet what detained her? No doubt Henry would pardon her outburst, and go on blustering and muddling into a ripe old age. But what was the good? She had just as soon vanish from his mind.

"Are you serious in asking me, Helen? Should I get on with your Monica?"

"You would not, but I am serious in asking you."

"Still, no more plans now. And no more reminiscences."

They were silent for a little. It was Helen's evening.

The present flowed by them like a stream. The tree rustled. It had made music before they were born, and would continue after their deaths, but its song was of the moment. The moment had passed. The tree rustled again. Their senses were sharpened, and they seemed to apprehend life. Life passed. The tree rustled again.

"Sleep now," said Margaret.

The peace of the country was entering into her. It has no commerce with memory, and little with hope. Least of all is it concerned with the hopes of the next five minutes. It is the peace of the present, which passes understanding. Its murmur came "now," and "now" once more as they trod the gravel, and "now," as the moonlight fell upon their father's sword. They passed upstairs, kissed, and amidst the endless iterations fell asleep. The house had enshadowed the tree at first, but as the moon rose higher the two disentangled, and were clear for a few moments at midnight. Margaret awoke and looked into the garden. How incomprehensible that Leonard Bast should have won her this night of peace! Was he also part of Mrs. Wilcox's mind?

Chapter XLI

Far different was Leonard's development. The months after Oniton, whatever minor troubles they might bring him, were all overshadowed by Remorse. When Helen looked back she could philosophize, or she could look into the future and plan for her child. But the father saw nothing beyond his own sin. Weeks afterwards, in the midst of other occupations, he would suddenly cry out, "Brute—you brute, I couldn't have——" and be rent into two people who held dialogues. Or brown rain would descend, blotting out faces and the sky. Even Jacky noticed the change in him. Most terrible were his sufferings when he awoke from sleep. Sometimes he was happy at first, but grew conscious of a burden hanging to him and weighing down his thoughts when they would move. Or little irons scorched his body. Or a sword stabbed him. He would sit at the edge of his bed, holding his heart and moaning, "Oh what *shall* I do, whatever *shall* I do?" Nothing brought ease. He could put distance between him and the trespass, but it grew in his soul.

Remorse is not among the eternal verities. The Greeks were right to dethrone her. Her action is too capricious, as though the Erinyes[1] selected for punishment only certain men and certain sins. And of all means to regeneration Remorse is surely the most wasteful. It cuts away healthy tissues with the poisoned. It is a knife that probes far deeper than the evil. Leonard was driven straight through its torments and emerged pure, but enfeebled—a better man, who would never lose control of himself again, but also a smaller man, who had less to control. Nor did purity mean peace. The use of the knife can become a habit as hard to shake off as passion itself, and Leonard continued to start with a cry out of dreams.

He built up a situation that was far enough from the truth. It never occurred to him that Helen was to blame. He forgot the intensity of their talk, the charm that had been lent him by sincerity, the magic of Oniton under darkness and of the whispering river. Helen loved the absolute. Leonard had been ruined absolutely, and had appeared to her as a man apart, isolated from the world. A real man, who cared for adventure and beauty, who desired to live decently and pay his way, who could have travelled more gloriously through life than the Juggernaut[2] car that was crushing him. Memories of Evie's wedding had warped her, the starched servants, the yards of uneaten food, the rustle of overdressed women, motor-cars oozing grease on the gravel, rubbish from a pretentious band.

1. The Furies, female divinities of classical mythology who punish crimes.
2. An overwhelming destructive force, from the Hindi *Jagannāth*, the "lord of the world," the title of the god Krishna, whose followers are sometimes said to throw themselves under the heavy cart on which the idol representing the god is hauled during an annual procession.

She had tasted the lees of this on her arrival: in the darkness, after failure, they intoxicated her. She and the victim seemed alone in a world of unreality, and she loved him absolutely, perhaps for half an hour.

In the morning she was gone. The note that she left, tender and hysterical in tone, and intended to be most kind, hurt her lover terribly. It was as if some work of art had been broken by him, some picture in the National Gallery slashed out of its frame. When he recalled her talents and her social position, he felt that the first passer-by had a right to shoot him down. He was afraid of the waitress and the porters at the railway-station. He was afraid at first of his wife, though later he was to regard her with a strange new tenderness, and to think, "There is nothing to choose between us, after all."

The expedition to Shropshire crippled the Basts permanently. Helen in her flight forgot to settle the hotel bill, and took their return tickets away with her; they had to pawn Jacky's bangles to get home, and the smash came a few days afterwards. It is true that Helen offered him five thousand pounds, but such a sum meant nothing to him. He could not see that the girl was desperately righting herself, and trying to save something out of the disaster, if it was only five thousand pounds. But he had to live somehow. He turned to his family, and degraded himself to a professional beggar. There was nothing else for him to do.

"A letter from Leonard," thought Blanche, his sister; "and after all this time." She hid it, so that her husband should not see, and when he had gone to his work read it with some emotion, and sent the prodigal a little money out of her dress allowance.

"A letter from Leonard!" said the other sister, Laura, a few days later. She showed it to her husband. He wrote a cruel, insolent reply, but sent more money than Blanche, so Leonard soon wrote to him again.

And during the winter the system was developed. Leonard realized that they need never starve, because it would be too painful for his relatives. Society is based on the family, and the clever wastrel can exploit this indefinitely. Without a generous thought on either side, pounds and pounds passed. The donors disliked Leonard, and he grew to hate them intensely. When Laura censured his immoral marriage, he thought bitterly, "She minds that! What would she say if she knew the truth?" When Blanche's husband offered him work, he found some pretext for avoiding it. He had wanted work keenly at Oniton, but too much anxiety had shattered him, he was joining the unemployable. When his brother, the lay-reader, did not reply to a letter, he wrote again, saying that he and Jacky would come down to his village on foot. He did not intend this as blackmail. Still, the brother sent a postal order, and it became part of the system. And so passed his winter and his spring.

In the horror there are two bright spots. He never confused the past. He remained alive, and blessed are those who live, if it is only to a sense of sinfulness. The anodyne of muddledom, by which most men blur and blend their mistakes, never passed Leonard's lips—

> "And if I drink oblivion of a day,
> So shorten I the stature of my soul."[3]

It is a hard saying, and a hard man wrote it, but it lies at the root of all character.

And the other bright spot was his tenderness for Jacky. He pitied her with nobility now—not the contemptuous pity of a man who sticks to a woman through thick and thin. He tried to be less irritable. He wondered what her hungry eyes desired—nothing that she could express, or that he or any man could give her. Would she ever receive the justice that is mercy—the justice for by-products that the world is too busy to bestow? She was fond of flowers, generous with money, and not revengeful. If she had borne him a child he might have cared for her. Unmarried, Leonard would never have begged; he would have flickered out and died. But the whole of life is mixed. He had to provide for Jacky, and went down dirty paths that she might have a few feathers and the dishes of food that suited her.

One day he caught sight of Margaret and her brother. He was in St. Paul's. He had entered the cathedral partly to avoid the rain and partly to see a picture that had educated him in former years. But the light was bad, the picture ill placed, and Time and Judgment were inside him now. Death alone still charmed him, with her lap of poppies, on which all men shall sleep. He took one glance, and turned aimlessly away towards a chair. Then down the nave he saw Miss Schlegel and her brother. They stood in the fairway of passengers, and their faces were extremely grave. He was perfectly certain that they were in trouble about their sister.

Once outside—and he fled immediately—he wished that he had spoken to them. What was his life? What were a few angry words, or even imprisonment? He had done wrong—that was the true terror. Whatever they might know, he would tell them everything he knew. He re-entered St. Paul's. But they had moved in his absence, and had gone to lay their difficulties before Mr. Wilcox and Charles.

The sight of Margaret turned remorse into new channels. He desired to confess, and though the desire is proof of a weakened nature, which is about to lose the essence of human intercourse, it did not take an ignoble form. He did not suppose that confession would bring him happiness. It was rather that he yearned to get clear of the tangle. So does the suicide yearn. The impulses are akin, and the crime of suicide lies rather in its disregard for the feelings of those whom we leave behind. Con-

---

3. From George Meredith's book of poems *Modern Love* (1862), a bitter chronicle of the dissolution of his marriage. Leonard is praised for not drowning his sorrows in drink.

fession need harm no one—it can satisfy that test—and though it was un-English, and ignored by our Anglican cathedral, Leonard had a right to decide upon it.

Moreover, he trusted Margaret. He wanted her hardness now. That cold, intellectual nature of hers would be just, if unkind. He would do whatever she told him, even if he had to see Helen. That was the supreme punishment she would exact. And perhaps she would tell him how Helen was. That was the supreme reward.

He knew nothing about Margaret, not even whether she was married to Mr. Wilcox, and tracking her out took several days. That evening he toiled through the wet to Wickham Place, where the new flats were now appearing. Was he also the cause of their move? Were they expelled from society on his account? Thence to a public library, but could find no satisfactory Schlegel in the directory. On the morrow he searched again. He hung about outside Mr. Wilcox's office at lunch time, and, as the clerks came out said: "Excuse me, sir, but is your boss married?" Most of them stared, some said, "What's that to you?" but one, who had not yet acquired reticence, told him what he wished. Leonard could not learn the private address. That necessitated more trouble with directories and tubes. Ducie Street was not discovered till the Monday, the day that Margaret and her husband went down on their hunting expedition to Howards End.

He called at about four o'clock. The weather had changed, and the sun shone gaily on the ornamental steps—black and white marble in triangles. Leonard lowered his eyes to them after ringing the bell. He felt in curious health: doors seemed to be opening and shutting inside his body, and he had been obliged to sleep sitting up in bed, with his back propped against the wall. When the parlourmaid came he could not see her face; the brown rain had descended suddenly.

"Does Mrs. Wilcox live here?" he asked.

"She's out," was the answer.

"When will she be back?"

"I'll ask," said the parlourmaid.

Margaret had given instructions that no one who mentioned her name should ever be rebuffed. Putting the door on the chain—for Leonard's appearance demanded this—she went through to the smoking-room, which was occupied by Tibby. Tibby was asleep. He had had a good lunch. Charles Wilcox had not yet rung him up for the distracting interview. He said drowsily: "I don't know. Hilton. Howards End. Who is it?"

"I'll ask, sir."

"No, don't bother."

"They have taken the car to Howards End," said the parlourmaid to Leonard.

He thanked her, and asked whereabouts that place was.

"You appear to want to know a good deal," she remarked. But

Margaret had forbidden her to be mysterious. She told him against her better judgment that Howards End was in Hertfordshire.

"Is it a village, please?"

"Village! It's Mr. Wilcox's private house—at least, it's one of them. Mrs. Wilcox keeps her furniture there. Hilton is the village."

"Yes. And when will they be back?"

"Mr. Schlegel doesn't know. We can't know everything, can we?" She shut him out, and went to attend to the telephone, which was ringing furiously.

He loitered away another night of agony. Confession grew more difficult. As soon as possible he went to bed. He watched a patch of moonlight cross the floor of their lodging, and, as sometimes happens when the mind is overtaxed, he fell asleep for the rest of the room, but kept awake for the patch of moonlight. Horrible! Then began one of those disintegrating dialogues. Part of him said: "Why horrible? It's ordinary light from the moon." "But it moves." "So does the moon." "But it is a clenched fist." "Why not?" "But it is going to touch me." "Let it." And, seeming to gather motion, the patch ran up his blanket. Presently a blue snake appeared; then another, parallel to it. "Is there life in the moon?" "Of course." "But I thought it was uninhabited." "Not by Time, Death, Judgment, and the smaller snakes." "Smaller snakes!" said Leonard indignantly and aloud. "What a notion!" By a rending effort of the will he woke the rest of the room up. Jacky, the bed, their food, their clothes on the chair, gradually entered his consciousness, and the horror vanished outwards, like a ring that is spreading through water.

"I say, Jacky, I'm going out for a bit."

She was breathing regularly. The patch of light fell clear of the striped blanket, and began to cover the shawl that lay over her feet. Why had he been afraid? He went to the window, and saw that the moon was descending through a clear sky. He saw her volcanoes, and the bright expanses that a gracious error has named seas. They paled, for the sun, who had lit them up, was coming to light the earth. Sea of Serenity, Sea of Tranquility, Ocean of the Lunar Storms, merged into one lucent drop, itself to slip into the sempiternal dawn. And he had been afraid of the moon!

He dressed among the contending lights, and went through his money. It was running low again, but enough for a return ticket to Hilton. As it clinked Jacky opened her eyes.

"Hullo, Len! What ho, Len!"

"What ho, Jacky! see you again later."

She turned over and slept.

The house was unlocked, their landlord being a salesman at Covent Garden. Leonard passed out and made his way down to the station. The train, though it did not start for an hour, was already drawn up at the end of the platform, and he lay down in it and slept. With the first jolt he was in daylight; they had left the gateways of King's Cross, and were under blue sky. Tunnels followed, and after each the sky grew bluer, and from the embankment at Finsbury Park he had his first sight of the sun. It rolled along behind the eastern smokes—a wheel, whose fellow was the descending moon—and as yet it seemed the servant of the blue sky, not its lord. He dozed again. Over Tewin Water it was day. To the left fell the shadow of the embankment and its arches; to the right Leonard saw up into the Tewin Woods and towards the church, with its wild legend of immortality. Six forest trees—that is a fact—grow out of one of the graves in Tewin churchyard. The grave's occupant—that is the legend—is an atheist, who declared that if God existed, six forest trees would grow out of her grave. These things in Hertfordshire; and farther afield lay the house of a hermit—Mrs. Wilcox had known him—who barred himself up, and wrote prophecies, and gave all he had to the poor. While, powdered in between, were the villas of business men, who saw life more steadily, though with the steadiness of the half-closed eye. Over all the sun was streaming, to all the birds were singing, to all the primroses were yellow, and the speedwell blue, and the country, however they interpreted her, was uttering her cry of "now." She did not free Leonard yet, and the knife plunged deeper into his heart as the train drew up at Hilton. But remorse had become beautiful.

Hilton was asleep, or at the earliest, breakfasting. Leonard noticed the contrast when he stepped out of it into the country. Here men had been up since dawn. Their hours were ruled, not by a London office, but by the movements of the crops and the sun. That they were men of the finest type only the sentimentalist can declare. But they kept to the life of daylight. They are England's hope. Clumsily they carry forward the torch of the sun, until such time as the nation sees fit to take it up. Half clodhopper, half board-school prig, they can still throw back to a nobler stock, and breed yeomen.[4]

At the chalk pit a motor passed him. In it was another type, whom Nature favours—the Imperial. Healthy, ever in motion, it hopes to inherit the earth. It breeds as quickly as the yeoman, and as soundly; strong is the temptation to acclaim it as a super-yeoman, who carries his country's virtue overseas. But the Imperialist is not what he thinks or seems. He is a destroyer. He prepares the way for cosmopolitanism, and though his ambitions may be fulfilled, the earth that he inherits will be grey.

To Leonard, intent on his private sin, there came the conviction of innate goodness elsewhere. It was not the optimism which he had been taught at school. Again and again must the drums tap, and the goblins stalk over the universe before joy can be purged of the superficial. It was

---

4. Clodhopper: clumsy, rustic bumpkin. Prig: fussy, proper conformist. Yeoman: free, independent farmer.

rather paradoxical, and arose from his sorrow. Death destroys a man, but the idea of death saves him—that is the best account of it that has yet been given. Squalor and tragedy can beckon to all that is great in us, and strengthen the wings of love. They can beckon; it is not certain that they will, for they are not love's servants. But they can beckon, and the knowledge of this incredible truth comforted him.

As he approached the house all thought stopped. Contradictory notions stood side by side in his mind. He was terrified but happy, ashamed, but had done no sin. He knew the confession: "Mrs. Wilcox, I have done wrong," but sunrise had robbed its meaning, and he felt rather on a supreme adventure.

He entered a garden, steadied himself against a motor-car that he found in it, found a door open and entered a house. Yes, it would be very easy. From a room to the left he heard voices, Margaret's amongst them. His own name was called aloud, and a man whom he had never seen said, "Oh, is he there? I am not surprised. I now thrash him within an inch of his life."

"Mrs. Wilcox," said Leonard, "I have done wrong."

The man took him by the collar and cried, "Bring me a stick." Women were screaming. A stick, very bright, descended. It hurt him, not where it descended, but in the heart. Books fell over him in a shower. Nothing had sense.

"Get some water," commanded Charles, who had all through kept very calm. "He's shamming. Of course I only used the blade. Here, carry him out into the air."

Thinking that he understood these things, Margaret obeyed him. They laid Leonard, who was dead, on the gravel; Helen poured water over him.

"That's enough," said Charles.

"Yes, murder's enough," said Miss Avery, coming out of the house with the sword.

Chapter XLII

When Charles left Ducie Street he had caught the first train home, but had no inkling of the newest development until late at night. Then his father, who had dined alone, sent for him, and in very grave tones inquired for Margaret.

"I don't know where she is, pater," said Charles. "Dolly kept back dinner nearly an hour for her."

"Tell me when she comes in."

Another hour passed. The servants went to bed, and Charles visited his father again, to receive further instructions. Mrs. Wilcox had still not returned.

"I'll sit up for her as late as you like, but she can hardly be coming. Isn't she stopping with her sister at the hotel?"

"Perhaps," said Mr. Wilcox thoughtfully—"perhaps."

"Can I do anything for you, sir?"

"Not to-night, my boy."

Mr. Wilcox liked being called sir. He raised his eyes and gave his son more open a look of tenderness than he usually ventured. He saw Charles as little boy and strong man in one. Though his wife had proved unstable his children were left to him.

After midnight he tapped on Charles's door. "I can't sleep," he said. "I had better have a talk with you and get it over."

He complained of the heat. Charles took him out into the garden, and they paced up and down in their dressing-gowns. Charles became very quiet as the story unrolled; he had known all along that Margaret was as bad as her sister.

"She will feel differently in the morning," said Mr. Wilcox, who had of course said nothing about Mrs. Bast. "But I cannot let this kind of thing continue without comment. I am morally certain that she is with her sister at Howards End. The house is mine—and, Charles, it will be yours—and when I say that no one is to live there, I mean that no one is to live there. I won't have it." He looked angrily at the moon. "To my mind this question is connected with something far greater, the rights of property itself."

"Undoubtedly," said Charles.

Mr. Wilcox linked his arm in his son's, but somehow liked him less as he told him more. "I don't want you to conclude that my wife and I had anything of the nature of a quarrel. She was only overwrought, as who would not be? I shall do what I can for Helen, but on the understanding that they clear out of the house at once. Do you see? That is a sine qua non."[1]

"Then at eight to-morrow I may go up in the car?"

"Eight or earlier. Say that you are acting as my representative, and, of course, use no violence, Charles."

On the morrow, as Charles returned, leaving Leonard dead upon the gravel, it did not seem to him that he had used violence. Death was due to heart disease. His stepmother herself had said so, and even Miss Avery had acknowledged that he only used the flat of the sword. On his way through the village he informed the police, who thanked him, and said there must be an inquest. He found his father in the garden shading his eyes from the sun.

"It has been pretty horrible," said Charles gravely. "They were there, and they had the man up there with them too."

"What—what man?"

"I told you last night. His name was Bast."

"My God! is it possible?" said Mr. Wilcox. "In your mother's house! Charles, in your mother's house!"

1. A necessary condition, literally "without which not." (Latin)

"I know, pater. That was what I felt. As a matter of fact, there is no need to trouble about the man. He was in the last stages of heart disease, and just before I could show him what I thought of him he went off. The police are seeing about it at this moment."

Mr. Wilcox listened attentively.

"I got up there—oh, it couldn't have been more than half-past seven. The Avery woman was lighting a fire for them. They were still upstairs. I waited in the drawing-room. We were all moderately civil and collected, though I had my suspicions. I gave them your message, and Mrs. Wilcox said, 'Oh yes, I see; yes,' in that way of hers."

"Nothing else?"

"I promised to tell you, 'with her love,' that she was going to Germany with her sister this evening. That was all we had time for."

Mr. Wilcox seemed relieved.

"Because by then I suppose the man got tired of hiding, for suddenly Mrs. Wilcox screamed out his name. I recognized it, and I went for him in the hall. Was I right, pater? I thought things were going a little too far."

"Right, my dear boy? I don't know. But you would have been no son of mine if you hadn't. Then did he just—just—crumple up as you said?" He shrank from the simple word.

"He caught hold of the bookcase, which came down over him. So I merely put the sword down and carried him into the garden. We all thought he was shamming. However, he's dead right enough. Awful business!"

"Sword?" cried his father, with anxiety in his voice. "What sword? Whose sword?"

"A sword of theirs."

"What were you doing with it?"

"Well, didn't you see, pater, I had to snatch up the first thing handy. I hadn't a riding-whip or stick. I caught him once or twice over the shoulders with the flat of their old German sword."

"Then what?"

"He pulled over the bookcase, as I said, and fell," said Charles, with a sigh. It was no fun doing errands for his father, who was never quite satisfied.

"But the real cause was heart disease? Of that you're sure?"

"That or a fit. However, we shall hear more than enough at the inquest on such unsavoury topics."

They went into breakfast. Charles had a racking headache, consequent on motoring before food. He was also anxious about the future, reflecting that the police must detain Helen and Margaret for the inquest and ferret the whole thing out. He saw himself obliged to leave Hilton. One could not afford to live near the scene of a scandal—it was not fair on one's wife. His comfort was that the pater's eyes were opened at last. There would be a horrible smash up, and probably a separation from Margaret; then they would all start again, more as they had been in his mother's time.

"I think I'll go round to the police-station," said his father when breakfast was over.

"What for?" cried Dolly, who had still not been "told."

"Very well, sir. Which car will you have?"

"I think I'll walk."

"It's a good half-mile," said Charles, stepping into the garden. "The sun's very hot for April. Shan't I take you up, and then, perhaps, a little spin round by Tewin?"

"You go on as if I didn't know my own mind," said Mr. Wilcox fretfully. Charles hardened his mouth. "You young fellows' one idea is to get into a motor. I tell you, I want to walk: I'm very fond of walking."

"Oh, all right; I'm about the house if you want me for anything. I thought of not going up to the office to-day, if that is your wish."

"It is, indeed, my boy," said Mr. Wilcox, and laid a hand on his sleeve.

Charles did not like it; he was uneasy about his father, who did not seem himself this morning. There was a petulant touch about him—more like a woman. Could it be that he was growing old? The Wilcoxes were not lacking in affection; they had it royally, but they did not know how to use it. It was the talent in the napkin, and, for a warm-hearted man, Charles had conveyed very little joy. As he watched his father shuffling up the road, he had a vague regret—a wish that something had been different somewhere—a wish (though he did not express it thus) that he had been taught to say "I" in his youth. He meant to make up for Margaret's defection, but knew that his father had been very happy with her until yesterday. How had she done it? By some dishonest trick, no doubt—but how?

Mr. Wilcox reappeared at eleven, looking very tired. There was to be an inquest on Leonard's body to-morrow, and the police required his son to attend.

"I expected that," said Charles. "I shall naturally be the most important witness there."

Chapter XLIII

Out of the turmoil and horror that had begun with Aunt Juley's illness and was not even to end with Leonard's death, it seemed impossible to Margaret that healthy life should re-emerge. Events succeeded in a logical, yet senseless, train. People lost their humanity, and took values as arbitrary as those in a pack of playing-cards. It was natural that Henry should do this and cause Helen to do that, and then think her wrong for doing it; natural that she herself should think him wrong; natural that Leonard should want to know how Helen was, and come, and Charles be angry with him for coming—natural, but unreal. In this jangle of

causes and effects what had become of their true selves? Here Leonard
lay dead in the garden, from natural causes; yet life was a deep, deep
river, death a blue sky, life was a house, death a wisp of hay, a flower, a
tower, life and death were anything and everything, except this ordered
insanity, where the king takes the queen, and the ace the king. Ah, no;
there was beauty and adventure behind, such as the man at her feet had
yearned for; there was hope this side of the grave; there were truer relationships beyond the limits that fetter us now. As a prisoner looks up and
sees stars beckoning, so she, from the turmoil and horror of those days,
caught glimpses of the diviner wheels.

And Helen, dumb with fright, but trying to keep calm for the child's
sake, and Miss Avery, calm, but murmuring tenderly, "No one ever told
the lad he'll have a child"—they also reminded her that horror is not the
end. To what ultimate harmony we tend she did not know, but there
seemed great chance that a child would be born into the world, to take
the great chances of beauty and adventure that the world offers. She
moved through the sunlit garden, gathering narcissi, crimson-eyed and
white. There was nothing else to be done; the time for telegrams and
anger was over, and it seemed wisest that the hands of Leonard should
be folded on his breast and be filled with flowers. Here was the father;
leave it at that. Let Squalor be turned into Tragedy, whose eyes are the
stars, and whose hands hold the sunset and the dawn.

And even the influx of officials, even the return of the doctor, vulgar
and acute, could not shake her belief in the eternity of beauty. Science
explained people, but could not understand them. After long centuries
among the bones and muscles it might be advancing to knowledge of the
nerves, but this would never give understanding. One could open the
heart to Mr. Mansbridge and his sort without discovering its secrets to
them, for they wanted everything down in black and white, and black
and white was exactly what they were left with.

They questioned her closely about Charles. She never suspected why.
Death had come, and the doctor agreed that it was due to heart disease.
They asked to see her father's sword. She explained that Charles's anger
was natural, but mistaken. Miserable questions about Leonard followed,
all of which she answered unfalteringly. Then back to Charles again.
"No doubt Mr. Wilcox may have induced death," she said; "but if it
wasn't one thing it would have been another, as you yourselves know."
At last they thanked her, and took the sword and the body down to
Hilton. She began to pick up the books from the floor.

Helen had gone to the farm. It was the best place for her, since she
had to wait for the inquest. Though, as if things were not hard enough,
Madge and her husband had raised trouble; they did not see why they
should receive the offscourings[1] of Howards End. And, of course, they

1. Dirt, refuse, debris.

were right. The whole world was going to be right, and amply avenge any brave talk against the conventions. "Nothing matters," the Schlegels had said in the past, "except one's self-respect and that of one's friends." When the time came, other things mattered terribly. However, Madge had yielded, and Helen was assured of peace for one day and night, and to-morrow she would return to Germany.

As for herself, she determined to go too. No message came from Henry; perhaps he expected her to apologize. Now that she had time to think over her own tragedy, she was unrepentant. She neither forgave him for his behaviour nor wished to forgive him. Her speech to him seemed perfect. She would not have altered a word. It had to be uttered once in a life, to adjust the lopsidedness of the world. It was spoken not only to her husband, but to thousands of men like him—a protest against the inner darkness in high places that comes with a commercial age. Though he would build up his life without hers, she could not apologize. He had refused to connect, on the clearest issue that can be laid before a man, and their love must take the consequences.

No, there was nothing more to be done. They had tried not to go over the precipice, but perhaps the fall was inevitable. And it comforted her to think that the future was certainly inevitable: cause and effect would go jangling forward to some goal doubtless, but to none that she could imagine. At such moments the soul retires within, to float upon the bosom of a deeper stream, and has communion with the dead, and sees the world's glory not diminished, but different in kind to what she has supposed. She alters her focus until trivial things are blurred. Margaret had been tending this way all the winter. Leonard's death brought her to the goal. Alas! that Henry should fade away as reality emerged, and only her love for him should remain clear, stamped with his image like the cameos we rescue out of dreams.

With unfaltering eye she traced his future. He would soon present a healthy mind to the world again, and what did he or the world care if he was rotten at the core? He would grow into a rich, jolly old man, at times a little sentimental about women, but emptying his glass with any-one. Tenacious of power, he would keep Charles and the rest dependent, and retire from business reluctantly and at an advanced age. He would settle down—though she could not realize this. In her eyes Henry was always moving and causing others to move, until the ends of the earth met. But in time he must get too tired to move, and settle down. What next? The inevitable word. The release of the soul to its appropriate Heaven.

Would they meet in it? Margaret believed in immortality for herself. An eternal future had always seemed natural to her. And Henry believed in it for himself. Yet, would they meet again? Are there not rather endless levels beyond the grave, as the theory that he had censured teaches?[2] And his level, whether higher or lower, could it possibly be the same as hers?

Thus gravely meditating, she was summoned by him. He sent up Crane in the motor. Other servants passed like water, but the chauffeur remained, though impertinent and disloyal. Margaret disliked Crane, and he knew it.

"Is it the keys that Mr. Wilcox wants?" she asked.

"He didn't say, madam."

"You haven't any note for me?"

"He didn't say, madam."

After a moment's thought she locked up Howards End. It was pitiable to see in it the stirrings of warmth that would be quenched for ever. She raked out the fire that was blazing in the kitchen, and spread the coals in the gravelled yard. She closed the windows and drew the curtains. Henry would probably sell the place now.

She was determined not to spare him, for nothing new had happened as far as they were concerned. Her mood might never have altered from yesterday evening. He was standing a little outside Charles's gate, and motioned the car to stop. When his wife got out he said hoarsely: "I prefer to discuss things with you outside."

"It will be more appropriate in the road, I am afraid," said Margaret. "Did you get my message?"

"What about?"

"I am going to Germany with my sister. I must tell you now that I shall make it my permanent home. Our talk last night was more important than you have realized. I am unable to forgive you and am leaving you."

"I am extremely tired," said Henry, in injured tones. "I have been walking about all the morning, and wish to sit down."

"Certainly, if you will consent to sit on the grass."

The Great North Road should have been bordered all its length with glebe.[3] Henry's kind had filched most of it. She moved to the scrap opposite, wherein were the Six Hills. They sat down on the farther side, so that they could not be seen by Charles or Dolly.

"Here are your keys," said Margaret. She tossed them towards him. They fell on the sunlit slope of grass, and he did not pick them up.

"I have something to tell you," he said gently.

She knew this superficial gentleness, this confession of hastiness, that was only intended to enhance her admiration of the male.

"I don't want to hear it," she replied. "My sister is going to be ill. My life is going to be with her now. We must manage to build up something, she and I and her child."

"Where are you going?"

<hr/>

2. Theosophy, a mystical philosophy, which, in some versions, posits the transmigration of souls through different levels of spiritual perfection toward the goal of union with God.
3. Cultivated land owned by the clergy.

"Munich. We start after the inquest, if she is not too ill."

"After the inquest?"

"Yes."

"Have you realized what the verdict at the inquest will be?"

"Yes, heart disease."

"No, my dear; manslaughter."

Margaret drove her fingers through the grass. The hill beneath her moved as if it was alive.

"Manslaughter," repeated Mr. Wilcox. "Charles may go to prison. I dare not tell him. I don't know what to do—what to do. I'm broken—I'm ended."

No sudden warmth arose in her. She did not see that to break him was her only hope. She did not enfold the sufferer in her arms. But all through that day and the next a new life began to move. The verdict was brought in. Charles was committed for trial. It was against all reason that he should be punished, but the law, being made in his image, sentenced him to three years' imprisonment. Then Henry's fortress gave way. He could bear no one but his wife, he shambled up to Margaret afterwards and asked her to do what she could with him. She did what seemed easiest—she took him down to recruit at Howards End.

Chapter XLIV

Tom's father was cutting the big meadow. He passed again and again amid whirring blades and sweet odours of grass, encompassing with narrowing circles the sacred centre of the field. Tom was negotiating with Helen.

"I haven't any idea," she replied. "Do you suppose baby may, Meg?"

Margaret put down her work and regarded them absently. "What was that?" she asked.

"Tom wants to know whether baby is old enough to play with hay?"

"I haven't the least notion," answered Margaret, and took up her work again.

"Now, Tom, baby is not to stand; he is not to lie on his face; he is not to lie so that his head wags; he is not to be teased or tickled; and he is not to be cut into two or more pieces by the cutter. Will you be as careful as all that?"

Tom held out his arms.

"That child is a wonderful nursemaid," remarked Margaret.

"He is fond of baby. That's why he does it!" was Helen's answer. "They're going to be lifelong friends."

"Starting at the ages of six and one?"

"Of course. It will be a great thing for Tom."

"It may be a greater thing for baby."

Fourteen months had passed, but Margaret still stopped at Howards

End. No better plan had occurred to her. The meadow was being recut,
the great red poppies were reopening in the garden. July would follow
with the little red poppies among the wheat, August with the cutting of
the wheat. These little events would become part of her year after year.
Every summer she would fear lest the well should give out, every winter
lest the pipes should freeze; every westerly gale might blow the wych-
elm down and bring the end of all things, and so she could not read or
talk during a westerly gale. The air was tranquil now. She and her sister
were sitting on the remains of Evie's rockery, where the lawn merged
into the field.

"What a time they all are!" said Helen. "What can they be doing
inside?" Margaret, who was growing less talkative, made no answer. The
noise of the cutter came intermittently, like the breaking of waves. Close
by them a man was preparing to scythe out one of the dell-holes.

"I wish Henry was out to enjoy this," said Helen. "This lovely weather and to be shut up in the house! It's very hard."

"It has to be," said Margaret. "The hay-fever is his chief objection
against living here, but he thinks it worth while."

"Meg, is or isn't he ill? I can't make out."

"Not ill. Eternally tired. He has worked very hard all his life, and noticed nothing. Those are the people who collapse when they do notice
a thing."

"I suppose he worries dreadfully about his part of the tangle."

"Dreadfully. That is why I wish Dolly had not come, too, to-day. Still,
he wanted them all to come. It has to be."

"Why does he want them?"

Margaret did not answer.

"Meg, may I tell you something? I like Henry."

"You'd be odd if you didn't," said Margaret.

"I usen't to."

"Usen't!" She lowered her eyes a moment to the black abyss of
the past. They had crossed it, always excepting Leonard and Charles.
They were building up a new life, obscure, yet gilded with tranquillity.
Leonard was dead; Charles had two years more in prison. One usen't
always to see clearly before that time. It was different now.

"I like Henry because he does worry."

"And he likes you because you don't."

Helen sighed. She seemed humiliated, and buried her face in her
hands. After a time she said: "About love," a transition less abrupt than
it appeared.

Margaret never stopped working.

"I mean a woman's love for a man. I supposed I should hang my life
on to that once, and was driven up and down and about as if something
was worrying through me. But everything is peaceful now; I seem cured.
That Herr Förstmeister, whom Frieda keeps writing about, must be a

noble character, but he doesn't see that I shall never marry him or any-one. It isn't shame or mistrust of myself. I simply couldn't. I'm ended. I used to be so dreamy about a man's love as a girl, and think that for good or evil love must be the great thing. But it hasn't been; it has been itself a dream. Do you agree?"

"I do not agree. I do not."

"I ought to remember Leonard as my lover," said Helen, stepping down into the field. "I tempted him, and killed him, and it is surely the least I can do. I would like to throw out all my heart to Leonard on such an afternoon as this. But I cannot. It is no good pretending. I am forget-ting him." Her eyes filled with tears. "How nothing seems to match — how, my darling, my precious——" She broke off. "Tommy!"

"Yes, please?"

"Baby's not to try and stand. — There's something wanting in me. I see you loving Henry, and understanding him better daily, and I know that death wouldn't part you in the least. But I—— Is it some awful appalling, criminal defect?"

Margaret silenced her. She said: "It is only that people are far more different than is pretended. All over the world men and women are wor-rying because they cannot develop as they are supposed to develop. Here and there they have the matter out, and it comforts them. Don't fret yourself, Helen. Develop what you have; love your child. I do not love children. I am thankful to have none. I can play with their beauty and charm, but that is all — nothing real, not one scrap of what there ought to be. And others — others go farther still, and move outside humanity altogether. A place, as well as a person, may catch the glow. Don't you see that all this leads to comfort in the end? It is part of the battle against sameness. Differences — eternal differences, planted by God in a single family, so that there may always be colour; sorrow per-haps, but colour in the daily grey. Then I can't have you worrying about Leonard. Don't drag in the personal when it will not come. Forget him."

"Yes, yes, but what has Leonard got out of life?"

"Perhaps an adventure."

"Is that enough?"

"Not for us. But for him."

Helen took up a bunch of grass. She looked at the sorrel, and the red and white and yellow clover, and the quaker grass, and the daisies, and the bents that composed it. She raised it to her face.

"Is it sweetening yet?" asked Margaret.

"No, only withered."

"It will sweeten to-morrow."

Helen smiled. "Oh, Meg, you are a person," she said. "Think of the racket and torture this time last year. But now I couldn't stop unhappy if I tried. What a change — and all through you!"

"Oh, we merely settled down. You and Henry learnt to understand one another and to forgive, all through the autumn and the winter."

"Yes, but who settled us down?"

Margaret did not reply. The scything had begun, and she took off her pince-nez to watch it.

"You!" cried Helen. "You did it all, sweetest, though you're too stupid to see. Living here was your plan—I wanted you; he wanted you; and everyone said it was impossible, but you knew. Just think of our lives without you, Meg—I and baby with Monica, revolting by theory, he handed about from Dolly to Evie. But you picked up the pieces, and made us a home. Can't it strike you—even for a moment—that your life has been heroic? Can't you remember the two months after Charles's arrest, when you began to act, and did all?"

"You were both ill at the time," said Margaret. "I did the obvious things. I had two invalids to nurse. Here was a house, ready furnished and empty. It was obvious. I didn't know myself it would turn into a permanent home. No doubt I have done a little towards straightening the tangle, but things that I can't phrase have helped me."

"I hope it will be permanent," said Helen, drifting away to other thoughts.

"I think so. There are moments when I feel Howards End peculiarly our own."

"All the same, London's creeping."

She pointed over the meadow—over eight or nine meadows, but at the end of them was a red rust.

"You see that in Surrey and even Hampshire now," she continued. "I can see it from the Purbeck Downs. And London is only part of something else, I'm afraid. Life's going to be melted down, all over the world."

Margaret knew that her sister spoke truly. Howards End, Oniton, the Purbeck Downs, the Oderberge, were all survivals, and the melting-pot was being prepared for them. Logically, they had no right to be alive. One's hope was in the weakness of logic. Were they possibly the earth beating time?

"Because a thing is going strong now, it need not go strong for ever," she said. "This craze for motion has only set in during the last hundred years. It may be followed by a civilization that won't be a movement, because it will rest on the earth. All the signs are against it now, but I can't help hoping, and very early in the morning in the garden I feel that our house is the future as well as the past."

They turned and looked at it. Their own memories coloured it now, for Helen's child had been born in the central room of the nine. Then Margaret said, "Oh, take care—!" for something moved behind the window of the hall, and the door opened.

"The conclave's breaking at last. I'll go."

It was Paul.

Helen retreated with the children far into the field. Friendly voices greeted her. Margaret rose, to encounter a man with a heavy black moustache.

"My father has asked for you," he said with hostility.

She took her work and followed him.

"We have been talking business," he continued, "but I dare say you knew all about it beforehand."

"Yes, I did."

Clumsy of movement—for he had spent all his life in the saddle— Paul drove his foot against the paint of the front door. Mrs. Wilcox gave a little cry of annoyance. She did not like anything scratched; she stopped in the hall to take Dolly's boa and gloves out of a vase.

Her husband was lying in a great leather chair in the dining-room, and by his side, holding his hand rather ostentatiously, was Evie. Dolly, dressed in purple, sat near the window. The room was a little dark and airless; they were obliged to keep it like this until the carting of the hay. Margaret joined the family without speaking; the five of them had met already at tea, and she knew quite well what was going to be said. Averse to wasting her time, she went on sewing. The clock struck six.

"Is this going to suit everyone?" said Henry in a weary voice. He used the old phrases, but their effect was unexpected and shadowy. "Because I don't want you all coming here later on and complaining that I have been unfair."

"It's apparently got to suit us," said Paul.

"I beg your pardon, my boy. You have only to speak, and I will leave the house to you instead."

Paul frowned ill-temperedly, and began scratching at his arm. "As I've given up the outdoor life that suited me, and I have come home to look after the business, it's not good my settling down here," he said at last. "It's not really the country, and it's not the town."

"Very well. Does my arrangement suit you, Evie?"

"Of course, father."

"And you, Dolly?"

Dolly raised her faded little face, which sorrow could wither but not steady. "Perfectly splendidly," she said. "I thought Charles wanted it for the boys, but last time I saw him he said no, because we cannot possibly live in this part of England again. Charles says we ought to change our name, but I cannot think what to, for Wilcox just suits Charles and me, and I can't think of any other name."

There was a general silence. Dolly looked nervously round, fearing that she had been inappropriate. Paul continued to scratch his arm.

"Then I leave Howards End to my wife absolutely," said Henry. "And let everyone understand that; and after I am dead let there be no jealousy and no surprise."

Margaret did not answer. There was something uncanny in her triumph. She, who had never expected to conquer anyone, had charged straight through these Wilcoxes and broken up their lives.

"In consequence, I leave my wife no money," said Henry. "That is her own wish. All that she would have had will be divided among you. I am also giving you a great deal in my lifetime, so that you may be independent of me. That is her wish, too. She also is giving away a great deal of money. She intends to diminish her income by half during the next ten years; she intends when she dies to leave the house to her—to her nephew, down in the field. Is all that clear? Does everyone understand?"

Paul rose to his feet. He was accustomed to natives, and a very little shook him out of the Englishman. Feeling manly and cynical, he said: "Down in the field? Oh, come! I think we might have had the whole establishment, piccaninnies included."

Mrs. Cahill whispered: "Don't, Paul. You promised you'd take care." Feeling a woman of the world, she rose and prepared to take her leave.

Her father kissed her. "Good-bye, old girl," he said; "don't you worry about me."

"Good-bye, dad."

Then it was Dolly's turn. Anxious to contribute, she laughed nervously, and said: "Good-bye, Mr. Wilcox. It does seem curious that Mrs. Wilcox should have left Margaret Howards End, and yet she get it, after all."

From Evie came a sharply-drawn breath. "Good-bye," she said to Margaret, and kissed her.

And again and again fell the word, like the ebb of a dying sea.

"Good-bye."

"Good-bye, Dolly."

"So long, father."

"Good-bye, my boy; always take care of yourself."

"Good-bye, Mrs. Wilcox."

"Good-bye."

Margaret saw their visitors to the gate. Then she returned to her husband and laid her head in his hands. He was pitiably tired. But Dolly's remark had interested her. At last she said: "Could you tell me, Henry, what was that about Mrs. Wilcox having left me Howards End?"

Tranquilly he replied: "Yes, she did. But that is a very old story. When she was ill and you were so kind to her she wanted to make you some return and, not being herself at the time, scribbled 'Howards End' on a piece of paper. I went into it thoroughly, and, as it was clearly fanciful, I set it aside, little knowing what my Margaret would be to me in the future."

Margaret was silent. Something shook her life in its inmost recesses, and she shivered.

"I didn't do wrong, did I?" he asked, bending down.

"You didn't, darling. Nothing has been done wrong."

CHAPTER XLIV

From the garden came laughter. "Here they are at last!" exc
Henry, disengaging himself with a smile. Helen rushed into the gloom,
holding Tom by one hand and carrying her baby on the other. There
were shouts of infectious joy.

"The field's cut!" Helen cried excitedly—"the big meadow! We've
seen to the very end, and it'll be such a crop of hay as never!"

Weybridge, 1908–1910.

Textual Appendix

TEXTUAL VARIANTS

Forster was, by his own admission, a careless proofreader. His handwriting could also be extremely difficult to decipher. As a result, establishing the authoritative text of *Howards End* is no easy task. Notorious errors and obvious misprints have haunted the work over its publishing history. The striking phrase "goblin footfall" was absurdly rendered as "goblin football" through at least three printings. The important epigraph "Only connect . . ." disappeared from British editions of the novel for twenty-seven years. Almost as a harbinger of the instabilities to come, the first American edition of the novel, published by Putnam's in 1911, introduced chapter titles and made many changes in Forster's grammar without his authorization. He managed to get these eliminated in subsequent American editions, but other questions remain about whether the many versions of this often-reprinted novel correspond to the author's wishes. At least five different companies have published *Howards End*, and more than sixty impressions and editions have appeared. Only the 1910 English first edition published by Edward Arnold can claim to have enjoyed the author's close supervision, but even that edition is occasionally flawed.

This Norton Critical Edition of *Howards End* follows the 1910 version with the exception of thirty-seven emendations, which are recorded in the first list of textual variants below. I have introduced changes only when errors in sense or grammar clearly called for correction. This principle is much more conservative than the editorial practices followed in assembling the 1973 Abinger edition, which is widely regarded as the standard text. All Forsterians are much indebted to Oliver Stallybrass, the Abinger editor. His labors, for example, have made the manuscript version of *Howards End* widely available in a readily comprehensible format (see "Selections from the Manuscripts" pp. 250–65). In his edition of *Howards End*, however, Stallybrass often took it upon himself to amend the text according to inferences about Forster's intentions, and a number of his revisions are at best questionable.

Almost all of the changes I have made to the English first edition are straightforward, noncontroversial corrections of errors that were either introduced by a typist or typesetter in the process of production or that escaped the eye of the author and the original editor. For example, the context makes clear that "Mrs." should be "Mr." when Leonard Bast is referred to on p. 84, or that the cigar-smoke is blowing "leeward" rather than "windward" on p. 155, or that only "minutes" rather than "months" had transpired in the conversation on p. 133. Other changes correct egregious and obvious errors of grammar and diction ("matter of fact" instead of "matter fact" on p. 116, for example, or "shrank" instead of "shrunk" on p. 232).

Stallybrass used as his copy text the 1969 Edward Arnold version of the 1947 so-called Pocket Edition, neither of which the author saw through the press. Even more importantly, Stallybrass was considerably more liberal than I have been in using the manuscript or differences between various editions to speculate about improvements that would construct an ideal text. The evidence for Forster's involvement in editions later than that of 1910 is often at most inferential, and the manuscripts are not always a reliable guide to this author's final intentions. Forster made many revisions to the manuscript in the typescript and the proofs (see "Selections from the Manuscripts" for examples). The typescript and the proofs have not survived, and it is consequently often impossible to know with any certainty whether a change in the published version is a typist's or typesetter's error or a revision for which Forster himself is responsible. My policy has consequently been to leave the 1910 edition unaltered unless the evidence for a change is clear and compelling.

The second list of textual variants shows forty-four of the most important changes to the text made in the Abinger edition that I have rejected because they seem unnecessary or speculative. For example, in a number of instances I prefer the word choice in the 1910 edition where Stallybrass has gone back to the wording of the manuscript. Although a case for a typist misreading could be made in these instances, one could also find grounds for thinking "handed" better than "bandied" (p. 90), "circling" an improvement over "circuiting" (p. 122), "bent" just as good as "leant" (p. 63), or "height" a correction of "highest" (p. 134). When reasonable doubt exists, I have let the first edition wording stand. There are, of course, some close calls. Stallybrass argues persuasively that on pp. 49:17, 28 Helen should say "genterman" instead of "gentleman" each time, consistent with one other instance in the printed 1910 text and as indicated in all three cases by the manuscript. I am less sure, however, that on p. 148 "entered" should be seen, as he argues, as a misreading of the manuscript's "ventured into" and not as a desirable simplification of diction introduced by Forster. Similarly, Stallybrass seems overly speculative in changing "she" to "Helen" on p. 139 on the grounds that this alteration, first made in the 1947 Pocket Edition, is so significant that the editor, a friend of Forster's, would not have made it without permission. On this reasoning, many more of the 1947 edition's changes in wording would have to be followed as well, but again this would be based on inference and speculation. (For Stallybrass's explanations of his editorial choices, see "Appendix B: Variants in Editions" in *The Manuscripts of* Howards End, ed. Oliver Stallybrass [London: Edward Arnold, 1973] 356–70.)

There are two instances, however, where Stallybrass uses the manuscript effectively to correct infelicities in the text (awkward or incomprehensible sentences on pp. 136 and 224 where changes somewhat confusingly indicated in the manuscript seem to have been ignored or misunderstood by the typesetter), and I have followed his lead in both cases. In another instance, however, even though Stallybrass persuasively argues that Forster is probably responsible for introducing a new sentence into the 1924 edition (a description of Mrs. Munt on pp. 11–12), I prefer the 1910 version. The change, Stallybrass suggests, was intended to remove a dated reference to railway practices, which had changed since the original publication, but that is to my mind a good reason to retain the first version, since this detail is one of many in the text that roots it in its historical time and place. This choice is consistent with my desire to give readers a version of the novel based as closely as possible on the text at the time of its first appearance.

That has also been my reason for not following Stallybrass in modernizing Forster's punctuation and spelling. The Abinger edition often deletes commas and other punctuation or sometimes introduces commas to clarify sentence structure. It also turns uppercase into lowercase letters, changes semicolons to commas, adds italics for emphasis, turns dashes into commas or commas into colons. I have not indicated all of these changes, but I have left things as they were in the first edition.

Page:line	1910 Edward Arnold	NCE
14:18	north	south
26:35	in major	in a major
46:38	wan't	want
49:17	gentleman	genterman
49:28	gentleman	genterman
50:15	excuse	accuse
84:24	football	footfall
84:32	Mrs.	Mr.
84:33	Tibby	Even Tibby
91:28	to books	to be books
94:1	an universal	a universal
99:33	Charles'	Charleses

102:34	And	As
103:31	arose	rose
109:41	Wilson	Wilcox
116:23	matter fact	matter of fact
121:19	lies	lie
133:25	months	minutes
136:3	steamer gave a further touch of insipidity, drawn up against the pier and hooting wildly for excursionists.	steamer, drawn up against the pier and hooting wildly for excursionists, gave a further touch of insipidity.
139:17	Charles'	Charleses'
155:30	windward	leeward
158:14	walks	walls
158:37	come	came
162:16	begun	began
163:17	gave	give
168:14	Pierpoint	Pierpont
168:23	Pierpoint	Pierpont
174:14	laid	lain
196:33	that	the
199:19	the	this
200:2	with grimy	with the grimy
208:36	of window	of the window
210:36	comfortable	confortable
215:24	them	her
224:39	gravel rubbish on	gravel, rubbish from
231:23	lined	linked
232:21	shrunk	shrank

Page:line	**Abinger Edition**	**1910 Arnold/NCE**
7:13–14	air marvellous	views marvellous
7:27	mother—abroad	mother abroad
10:16	those	most

12:2–5	Mrs Munt secured a comfortable seat, facing the engine, but not too near it	Mrs. Munt, though she took a second-class ticket, was put by the guard into a first (only two seconds on the train, one smoking and the other babies— one cannot be expected to travel with babies)
25:29	We	one
26:12–13	wunderschöning and prachtvolleying	"wunderschöning" and "pracht" volleying
43:25	exclaimed	explained
63:9	leant	bent
69:31	men	man
84:8	would	could
85:34	would	could
90:30	bandied	handed
92:25	a say that	a saying that
109:2	send it toppling	send toppling
110:1–2	failed her	failed her anew
112:25	couldn't	wouldn't
121:22	vanquished	vanished
122:25	circuiting	circling
124:22	down	downs
132:43	side path	side-paths
134:18	those	these
134:37	highest	height
137:42–43	the fellow	this fellow
139:40	Helen continued	she continued
146:41	wouldn't	couldn't
148:17	simile	similes
148:22	relationships	relationship
148:23	ventured into	entered
151:22	packed in	packed
152:8	deeper	deep
160:17	advise	desire

164:28	ashamed at	ashamed of
170:40	so wonderful	is wonderful
171:9–10	real things	real thing
172:33	Nature's	Nature
174:11	would	could
182:40	on her brain	in her brain
186:1	county	country
202:34	distances	distance
219:15	told you	told
227:5	could	would
232:16	and went	and I went
235:15	her	hers
241:28	and have	and I have

SELECTIONS FROM THE MANUSCRIPTS[†]

The original manuscripts of *Howards End* are preserved with Forster's papers at King's College, Cambridge. The manuscripts consist of 520 sheets, for the most part written on one side only. They are bound in four large volumes, with manuscript pages mounted on larger leaves (with holes cut into them, when necessary, so that the reverse side is visible). Twelve sheets contain draft material or are working notes (the latter are reprinted on pp. 275–76 in "The Author and the Novel"). The rest are consecutive pages that comprise a complete longhand draft of the novel. This draft is heavily revised, with numerous deletions and insertions on every page. The manuscript also differs considerably from the first published text. The differences between the manuscript and the published novel suggest that Forster must have made extensive changes to the typescript that he submitted to his publisher or to the proofs returned from the printer for the author's review before publication — or, most likely, to both. But these have not survived.

The selections from the manuscripts reprinted here show a small number of the many changes Forster made during the composition of *Howards End*. Some of these revisions make his phrasing more resonant. For example, Leonard Bast's "half-baked mind" was originally "half educated" (p. 39); the memorable phrase "telegrams and anger" replaced the unremarkable "interviews and diplomacy" (p. 234), and the striking

† The excerpts in this section are taken from *The Manuscripts of* Howards End, ed. Oliver Stallybrass (London: Edward Arnold, 1973). Reprinted by permission of King's College, Cambridge, and The Society of Authors as the literary representatives of the E. M. Forster Estate.

contrast between "the farmyard and the garbage that nourishes it" started out inauspiciously as "the animals and dead" or "inorganic matter"
(p. 172). Other changes seek greater effect through condensation. On
p. 31, for instance, Leonard's embarrassed desire "to pronounce foreign
names correctly" was first "to pronounce names rightly, and to remember who wrote what." The compact "To keep perfection perfect" on
p. 169 had started as "To lift his eyes where there was greatness, and to
keep it great." On p. 239, "the battle against sameness" was originally
wordier and less precise: "the battle against cosmopolitanism and the
universal gray." Some of the most notable passages in the novel were the
result of revision. For example, in Leonard's conversation with the
Schlegel sisters about his night-long walk in the woods, his original
answer to the question "Was it wonderful?" was not the striking letdown
"No" but the more diffuse "Bits of it only" (p. 87). Forster also made
other important changes in details. Leonard's much-discussed umbrella
was originally a walking stick (p. 27). With Leonard, Jacky, and Ruth
Wilcox, Forster experimented with different names, and he also tried
variations on the ages of the Schlegel sisters (see pp. 35, 37, 50, 12). At
the very end of the novel, Forster at first had Henry and Margaret kiss,
then thought better of it, but then added the kiss again, and then finally
left it out.

These changes are fascinating because they seem to offer a glimpse of
Forster's actual intentions by observing his choices as he wrote. There is
a degree of truth to this impression, which is why manuscript revisions
are worth studying, but it may also be misleading. In each case the significance of the revision must still be interpreted and may be open to dispute. For example: Does the discovery that Forster considered closing
the novel with a kiss suggest that he felt more harmony between Henry
and Margaret than do those critics who believe that she does not "connect" with her husband but destroys him? Or does Forster's deletion of
the kiss show that he felt it would misrepresent the estrangement
between them at the end? Or was his decision based on other grounds
altogether, perhaps distaste for the romantic cliché of a concluding kiss?
Revisions of the kind chronicled here are useful critical instruments
because they can clarify what the writer's choices were, but the meaning
of those decisions remains for the interpreter to ponder—and that, one
hopes, will enrich appreciation of the novel.

The challenge of representing manuscript revisions is to design a format that is both economical and readily comprehensible. The selections
reprinted here are taken from Oliver Stallybrass's edition of *The
Manuscripts of* Howards End, (London: Edward Arnold, 1973), and the
symbols he uses to indicate Forster's revisions are adopted as well. The
only exception is the addition of italics to show where further changes
were made at a later stage, a point that Stallybrass's edition leaves
unclear but that I have settled by comparing his edition to the manu-

scripts. Generally speaking, in each case the material to the left of the arrow was substituted by Forster for the material to the right. The words on the left indicate the final form of the text as printed in the 1910 English first edition, on which this Norton Critical Edition of the novel is based, and they are keyed by page and line number to this edition. Unless a passage contains italics, all of the changes that led to it were made in the manuscript. An italicized word or phrase indicates that the published text differs from the corrected manuscript, and the portion in italics is the product of further revisions that must have been made in typescript or proof. An italicized passage to the left of the arrows was added (or otherwise changed as the symbols indicate); italics to the right indicate words deleted in typescript or proof from the final version of the manuscript. Here is a brief explanation of the symbols:

. . . ← . . .	words left of arrow replaced those on right
\. . ./	words between slashes inserted in manuscript
‹. . .›	words within angled brackets deleted
{. . .}	words within braces inserted, then deleted
[. . .]	editor's comments, not Forster's revisions
Italics	changes made in typescript or proof

These symbols are doubled when there are insertions within insertions (thus: \\. . .\. . ./. . .//) or deletions within deletions (thus: ‹‹. . .‹. . .› . . .››).

5:2   *One may as well begin . . . before breakfast.* [5:34][1] ←

                                                              Wednesday.
Dearest Meg
    It is not the least what we expected. The house is quite small. It is just three rooms in a row, of which the middle one is practically a hall. Of course there are kitchens etc. behind, and bedrooms and so on above, but there seem to be only these three rooms when one thinks of the place quickly. Isn't it funny! I nearly cried "Oh you don't ever live here!" as the motor turned in, but fortunately ‹I› saw Mrs Wilcox in the porch. I am not sure that Mr Wilcox would have liked it. He met me. They were dreadfully disappointed about you, and so, dearest Meglet, am I, as you can well believe. I do really think that you might have come. Surely Tibby isn't as bad as he makes out. No doubt hay fever is painful, but it does seem a little much that four people should be kept in London to listen to him sneeze, and I cannot believe that simply

---

1. The epigraph "Only connect" is not in the manuscript (MS). The first two letters, which open the novel, were completely rewritten in typescript or proof and are essentially new. The MS starts immediately with Helen's letter, with no introductory comment from the narrator, and is dated "Wednesday." The date was changed to "Tuesday" and the place "Howards End" added at a later stage.

walking through Covent Garden could have started it. However, it's no good arguing with you. Tell Tibby that Mr Charles Wilcox, the accountant son, has hay fever too, but *he* just ‹walks› \goes/ to his room when he feels bad, and bothers no one. I do think Tibby might have made an effort.

As ‹you are not coming› \I shall not see you till Saturday/, I will write you a long letter. Why *did* we assume that the house would be large and wiggly? I suppose it comes of meeting people in hotels—Mrs Wilcox trailing in those beautiful dresses down long corridors, Mr Wilcox over-tipping waiters etc. Besides it is old—I should say once a farm. One very big tree overhangs it, and the side towards the road is covered with a vine. The side away from the road—i.e. the tree side—looks down a meadow. There is a ‹tennis [court?] in front› croquet court \in front/, on which we have already played several sets—Mrs Wilcox nearly as bad as I am, the two men very good ‹and a great deal too polite. The son is›\. Charles the eldest son is here—fair and/ very good looking. Then there is a daughter of about sixteen—Evie—, and also ‹another› \the second/ son, Paul, who is ‹just now away› \away till Thursday/. How we pack in as it is, is a marvel.

I am writing this in my bedroom before breakfast. ‹Very very early› Early at night we squeeze up in this lovely house. The whole family's here now. It's just like a rabbit warren. Evie is a dear. They want me to stop over Sunday, and I have said I will. Marvellous weather, and the air marvellous—views westward to the high ground over Luton. Thank you for your letter.

                                        Your affectionate Helen.

‹How's Tibby?›

                                                        Sunday
Dearest, dearest Meg: I do not know what you will say: Paul Wilcox loves me and I love him—the younger son who only came here Thursday.

                                                    [no signature]

7:23 Margaret glanced at her sister's note and pushed it over the breakfast-table to her aunt. There was a moment's hush, and then the floodgates opened. ← The dining room at Wickham Place was small and drab, and close to the level of the street. Its lower window panes were of rough grey glass to prevent the passers by from observing the Miss Schlegels as they ate their meals. Its upper window panes occasionally revealed the figures of draymen or of hansom-cab men. The ‹wall-›paper was plain, the furniture inexpensive, the ‹books in the shelves› \book shelves/ ‹were› sombre and chiefly concerned with Political Economy. Only one thing in the ‹apartment› \room/ would have struck the casual observer—a majolica plate, sunk in the wall up to its very rim, and gleaming in the darkness like a jewel.

Here, on the Monday morning, Margaret sat at breakfast with ‹her aunt,› Mrs ‹Yool› \Munt∧, her aunt/. Helen's note had arrived. Mrs ‹Yool› \Munt/ was discussing it volubly. Margaret\,/ ‹was› equally voluble, ‹but› \was/ a little moist about the eyes.

11:7   There was a train *from King's Cross* at eleven. ← Then Mrs ‹Yool› \Munt/ arose. You would have thought she had rehearsed the expedition for years, so competent was she. She even knew the kind of clothes one ought to wear—sombre but not too sombre. Her remark "I think {you would rather it was} a hat, not a bonnet" opens a ‹long› vista of subtleties. A bonnet implies decision. For one thing it cannot be taken off. It is suitable for weddings, ultimatums, and funerals. Whereas a hat, however monumental, denotes ‹an› \the/ open mind, and sympathy with youth. Though inclined to the bonnet, Mrs ‹Yool› \Munt/ had also to consider the wishes of ‹Margaret› \her niece/. She must not be too ‹decided, too› monitory. \She must choose the hat./ And the hat that she ‹selected› \assumed/, though black on the whole, gleamed irridescently in its more secret parts, as if to [*the passage breaks off here, and it continues on the reverse side of a page some 252 pages later, on a sheet whose front side contains material from Chapter 22.*] reassure the Wilcoxes and to hint that the paths of Helen and of Paul might yet be bright with flowers.

Meanwhile Margaret was writing to her sister.

There was a train at eleven.

12:14   when Helen was *five* and Margaret herself but *thirteen* ← ‹when› Helen was ‹ten› {eight} \seven/, and ‹when she herself was only› \Margaret herself but/ fourteen

12:17   *But* her brother-in-law, who was peculiar and a German ← Her brother-in-law, an indescribable person

14:21   studied *Helen's lover a little more. He seemed a gentleman, but had so rattled her round that her powers of observation were numbed. She glanced at him* stealthily. To ← studied ‹Helen's fiancé› {the young man} \Paul Wilcox/ more closely. Her first impression was favourable. He was a ‹handsome› manly ‹young› \young/ fellow, and, to

14:25   *He was dark, clean-shaven, and seemed accustomed to command* ← His clothes were perfect, his voice gentle, \his manners self possessed,/ his complexion healthy but not plebeian. Decidedly things might have been worse

20:26   an electrical discharge. *Yet we rate the impulse too highly. We do not admit that by collisions of this trivial sort the doors of heaven may be shaken open.* To Helen ‹Schlegel›, at all events, *her* life was to bring nothing more intense than the *embrace of this boy who played no part in it.* ← an electrical discharge‹, that Helen›. Yet ‹in England we sneer somewhat too readily› \we indulge the instinct too far/; we do not admit that ‹‹these chan[ce] collisions ‹occasionally› \may/ shake open the doors of heaven›› \by collisions of this sort ‹often› the very doors of heaven may be shaken open/. To Helen Schlegel at all events, life ‹brought no moment greater› \was to bring nothing more intense/ than the ‹‹touch of young Wilcox's lips \on her own/. He himself faded or remained as an absurd memory; the touch of his lips endured, and in all the variable years that followed, she never met ‹the› \their/ like again. She, like her sister, was clear headed, and remembered the ‹incident› \collision/; Paul, like most of us, clouded it over, sneered ‹and forgot› at it, and so forgot›› \gentle brush of ‹his moustache› young Wilcox's moustache upon her cheek/.

22:35   *perhaps* they shine out in it like stars. ← surely they shine out like stars. ‹Their comments› \They/ throw light into our ordered darkness, \their impact generates beauty,/ they are wonderful and therefore they see wonders where other men see four per cent. ‹I promise that they shall› \They may/ suffer \for it/ in the end. But until that happens, pardon them ‹for being› \if at times they are/ economically unsound.

27:31   that lady has, quite inadvertently, taken my umbrella ← the lady has, inadvertently, taken my walking stick

28:38   you despise English music ← you want to go

28:38   *And English art. And English literature, except Shakespeare, and he's a German. Very well, Frieda,* you may go ← And you may go

30:2   "When . . ." ← His voice quivered, and she knew that there was a real person underneath. "When . . ."

31:22   to pronounce foreign names correctly ← to pronounce names rightly, ‹and› to remember who wrote what

35:15   \goblin footfall, as a/

35:17   ill-fed boy ← ill-fed ‹white faced› \suspicious/ boy

35:21   We are not concerned with the very poor ← It is a long way from Wickham Place to the flats behind Vauxhall Station, and the road is full of social ups and downs. No great abyss of poverty is crossed, but the variations of income are sufficiently remarkable, and as much as the imaginations of most of us can realise. With the very poor this story is not concerned

35:22   This story deals ‹only› with gentlefolk ← We are only concerned with gentlefolks

35:23   they are gentlefolk ← they are as good as gentlefolks. Otherwise they would go under

35:25   The boy, Leonard Bast, ← ‹James› {Edward} \Leonard/ Cunningham

35:25   \of gentility/

35:30   as courteous as the average rich man, nor as intelligent, nor as healthy, nor as lovable ← so courteous, nor so intelligent, nor ‹so› \as/ handsome, nor so healthy

35:32   because he was poor, and because he was modern they were always craving better food ← and simply because he was so poor

35:35   his rank and his income ← his social and his financial position

35:36   the angel of Democracy ← Democracy

35:37   leathern wings ← her drab coloured wings

35:38   equal ← equal, gentlemen ← equal

35:38   umbrellas ← *black coats and* umbrellas

36:1   gentility ← equality

36:1   nothing counts, and the statements of Democracy are inaudible ← the voice of Democracy is inaudible

36:4   \Obscurely wounded in his pride, he tried to wound them in return./

36:7   increased ← increased: he often ‹did› felt superior when he was quite alone

36:25   He ← It is no good giving in. With true British pluck he

37:13   cried "Hullo!" with the pseudo-geniality of the Cockney. There
← cried with pseudo-geniality "Hullo!" The electric light was on in the
sitting-room, but there

37:15   \, though the electric light had been left burning/

37:16   A look ← A *slight* look

37:16   flung himself into the armchair ← sat down to rest in a gaily
decorated armchair

37:18   The sitting-room contained ← The room *measured about eight
feet by twelve, and* contained

37:18   a piano, ← a piano, a what-n[ot,]

37:20   the window ← the window, through which the feet of Mr Bast
could ‹now› be seen when it was day

37:21   Cupids ← photographs, tiny vases, and half penny toys

37:23   Goodman ← Goodman, *heavily framed in ‹oak› walnut*

37:23   It was ‹not an› *an amorous and not*/ unpleasant little hole . . .
relinquished too easily [*line 27*] ← Everything was new, with the exception of some of the photographs, and some of the books

37:31   Jacky ← Tootsy ← Nessie [*and similarly in line 32*]

37:33   often photographed with their mouths open ← always photographed showing their teeth

37:33   dazzling whiteness ← dazzling whiteness and enormous size

39:2   half-baked ← half educated

39:17   simplest to say that she was not respectable. Her appearance was
awesome ← quickest to say that she looked a ‹perfect› sight

50:41   Ruth Wilcox ← Yours sincerely [*new line:*] ‹Christabel› \[*inde-
cipherable name*]/ Wilcox

55:27   ". . .what I should have liked to say about them myself." ←
". . . the way I should have liked to put them myself. [*Larger part of page
torn off, now forming the reverse side of MS p. 173:*] Do come and see me

again, Miss Schlegel.—No, I will come and see you. I shall be quite well
after this one day's rest."

    "You wouldn't come to lunch ‹the day after tomorrow› \next
Thursday/?"

    "Thank you; I should enjoy it very much."

    Then Margaret ‹left› put on her disgraceful shawl, and returned to
Wickham Place, well pleased with her visit, and not a little interested.
The tutor was waiting for her. Though clerical and pedantic, he was not
a fool, and offered his own explanation of Tibby's "headaches". He was
also handsome, and as they bent over some papers together she felt
attracted by him. The emotion was easily concealed and quickly forgotten, and the ‹name of this tutor need not be kept in remembrance, or
even remembered› \reader need not keep this tutor in remembrance, or
even be told his name/. He, like Paul, is a storm signal, not the storm.

59:16 For one thing, I'm not ‹feeling› particularly well just today. For
another, you ← You

62:43 *"I want you to see it. You have never seen it. I want to hear what
you say about it, for you do put things so wonderfully."*

63:3 Margaret glanced ← "Now? Let me see," said Margaret, gaining
time. She glanced

63:3 tired face ← face

63:10 *Margaret had been snubbed* ← Margaret bit her lip. She had
been snubbed, and for a moment she ‹welled with anger› felt offended

63:16 *In her turn Margaret became annoyed.*

66:42 *He* suffered acutely. Pain ← ‹He was alone, he had hardly slept,
and bowing his head over his hands he murmured "Oh my God, my
God, I cannot bear it."› *His simple* ‹*affectionate*› *nature* suffered acutely.
The pain

67:23 She lay under the earth now ← And now this life had ended

67:38 the lips, *ambiguous*, were curtained by a moustache. But there
was no external hint ← the lips were veiled by a brown moustache.
There was no trace of grey, and none of age upon his healthy skin; ‹the›
\this/ death had been his first great trouble. His hair, however, had
retreated greatly. But there was no hint

68:1   a bastion that protected his head ← a *sunburnt* bastion that protected the contents of his head

68:3   for fifty years ← for fifty *four* years, and now that ‹sorrow› \a hard
knock/ had come at last, he was equal to that too, and bore it as ‹a steady
man› \an Englishman/ should, ‹unaffectedly,› steadily

70:23   started ← started. He thought beauty in scenery, literature, and
art, bosh too: the only ‹place› \article/ in which he did demand it was a
woman, though he was duly reticent on this point, for it bordered too
closely on passion and the personal. Crane knew his business too, and
he had patience with men who knew their business

75:30   to voyage for a little past the emotions ← ‹for› to voyage for a little past the unseen

75:31   having first *stopped* one another's ears with wool ← having \first/
stopt one another's ears with wool. ← ‹‹ ‹They escaped› By this manoeuvre they escaped death and returned to their property ‹and wives›. ››
‹They returned› They heard ‹nothing, they› \no song, and/ returned
\safely/ to their property in Ithaca: ‹in after years they thought› \they
became old and affirmed/ that there had been ‹nothing› \no song/ to
hear: having taught the younger generation they ‹died› passed into
silence

78:32   "I hope Charles took the hint."
"Yes—that is to say, her husband wrote later on, and thanked me . . ."
← "What did you choose?" said Helen avidly.
"‹Only some› \Some/ novel—I would have chosen more carefully if I
had understood. She meant me to have something that would remind me
of her. Afterwards her husband wrote ‹to me, thanking› and thanked me.

78:34   *and actually gave me her silver vinaigrette. Don't you think that
is extraordinarily generous? It has made me like him very much.* He hopes
← and he hopes

78:37   *I like Mr Wilcox.*

84:22   her thoughts were poisoned ← ‹her thoughts were poisoned:›
she had held her face over one of the cracks in our civilisation

84:24   a goblin footfall, telling of a life where love and hatred had both
decayed ← telling of a life where ‹the human relationships› \love and
hatred/ ‹had› \\‹had› {have} \had/ both// decayed, and where men ‹were›
\are/ incapable of [*illegible word*] tragedy, like a goblin footfall

86:16   "Oh, don't *let us* ‹*let's*› mind," said Margaret, distressed again by
odours from the abyss ← "Come along" said Margaret to her brother,
distressed at the course of events

86:19   "I was somewhere else to what you think, so there!" [*Related to
this remark appears to be the first surviving sentence of the reverse side of
MS p. 227. * * * The fragment provides this much shorter version of the
next two pages:* ". . .] I'm not that sort any more.["]
     Ridiculous creature! skimped humanity. But he had found language
‹at last› \for a moment/, he had spoken straight, and he knew it himself,
and turned and faced them.
     "Saturday night I slept out in a wood. I have always wanted to. But it's
too early in the year and so I contracted this cold. I walked right away
from the office—I could stand it no longer. I took the train to Surbiton
and then just walked. I don't know what came over me—I walked. I felt
like R. L. Stevenson. I went mad ‹—I walked› for the love of the Earth.
I walked."
     "And was it wonderful?" said Helen, leaning forward.
     With unforgettable sincerity he replied "Bits ‹of it only›." And that lit-
tle phrase cancelled all that was ignoble or ‹precious› \artificial/ in his
words, cancelled tiresome R. L. Stevenson and the "love of the Earth"—
even cancelled the cold that he had contracted. In the presence of these
\two/ women he had arrived and he spoke with a flow, an exultation that
he had not known for years.

95:23   "Now that we have to leave Wickham Place, I ‹sometimes› \begin
to/ think it's that. For Mrs Wilcox it was certainly Howards End." ← "For
me no place" said Margaret gravely. "I mind leaving our house dreadfully, but I think and hope that people will always be more important to
me. Whereas for Mrs Wilcox it was certainly Howards End."

104:22   tried to walk by the Pole Star ← slept in the woods near Esher

104:24   the sunrise ← the sunrise and the bank that runs through the
pines

104:25   Laughter ← ‹"Horray!" said› \"You've stopped him" whis-
pered/ Mr Wilcox. "Pile it on!"

105:1   "Can I help you now?" said Mr Wilcox, turning to Margaret.
"*May I have one quiet word with him in the hall?*" ← "You managed that
splendidly" said Mr Wilcox, turning to Margaret.

114:3   in two years, and were really beginning to know each other ←

in two years‹. Though limited in his outlook›, and were really beginning
to converse. That they would ever understand each other was unlikely

114:5   He came, and partook of body-building dishes with humility ←
‹To her it seemed a very thrilling meal: he ate body-building dishes with
enthusiasm, and she did not know that he had eaten a steak at his club
before starting.› \‹In spite of› Busy as he was, he accepted and partook of
body-building dishes with humility. To her it seemed a very thrilling
meal. (She did not know that he had had a steak at his club beforehand.)/ They agreed that it was fun sampling other folk's restaurants, and
their talk was, if anything, more disconnected than it had been at
Simpsons‹‹, ‹darting› \ranging/ from house hunting to the Celtic
Fringe›› in the Strand.

126:29   I don't intend him\, or any ‹woman› man or any woman,/ to be
all my life—good heavens, no! There are heaps of things in me that he
doesn't, and shall never, understand. ← Then I must go through his
virtues. Manliness. Frankness. Tolerance. Cleanness of mind and body.
Very great kindness. Common sense.

134:37   human love will be seen at its height. Live in fragments no
longer. Only connect, and ← love \at its highest/ will be standing on the
summit of the rainbow \arch/. ‹Onl[y]› ‹Do not live in compartments›
Live in compartments no longer‹, and›. Only connect‹. And if (she
would continue)›, and

135:1   *By quiet indications* the bridge would be built ← If she led him
to be more demonstrative \to her/ in public, that \somewhat ludicrous
alteration/ would be enough. The bridge would be built

135:3   But she failed ← But on the morrow, when he did come, she
saw that she had ‹taken› undertaken a tremendous task

135:4   however much she reminded herself of it: his obtuseness. He
simply did not notice *things, and there was no more to be said.* He never
noticed ← however much she reminded herself of it, and however ‹long›
\intimately/ she knew him: ‹‹he ‹never noticed› \did not notice/ things.››
\\\his obtuseness in private relations. \\He simply did not notice what
‹she› \one/ was doing.// For example /// he never noticed

140:37   This conversation made Margaret easier. Their inner life was
so safe that ← This conversation cheered Margaret greatly. \Though she
could not understand her sister, she was assured against estrangement./
The sisters' inner life was, to use Helen's expression, as safe as houses,
and [*a related passage continues on a separate sheet*] ‹knew and never

were to know any slackening of affection.› It was therefore possible to bargain over externals in a way that would have shocked Aunt Juley or the ‹Debating Club at Chelsea› \Chelsea Debating Club/; in a way that would have been impossible for natures like Tibby or Charles. There are moments when the inner life "pays", when the years of self examination, ‹though› conducted for no ulterior end, are useful suddenly. Such moments are still rare‹, at all events› in the West; ‹we, who are determined not to deny the body, must wait for a more distant if nobler reward than those who have taken the short cut of asceticism› that they ‹do› come \at all/ presages a more glorious ‹pow[er?]› future, with fairer relationships than we dream of now. ‹‹The East, we are told, has them frequently, but the East has taken the ascetic shortcut; those who are determined not to deny the body must wait for a more distant if ‹nobler› \more exquisite/ reward.››

169:15 By now he had no illusions about his wife, and this was only one new stain ← it was *one name the more*, one new stain

169:17 To keep perfection perfect ← To lift his eyes where there was greatness, and to keep it great

172:33 Strip human intercourse of the proprieties, and is it reduced to this? ← Man in the smoking room—woman in the drawing room—to meet for a moment in the bedroom. Strip civilisation of its cant [?], and is it reduced to this?

172:37 wider is the gulf between us and the farmyard than between the farmyard and the garbage that nourishes it ← wider the gulf ‹that severs us from the› between us and the animals, than ‹that which› between the animals and ‹dead› \inorganic/ matter

172:40 Men did produce one jewel ← They did produce this

174:10 some explanation was due. ← some explanation was due. \He must connect./ She deserved to be told when he had met Mrs Bast and under what circumstances.
  "If I were conventional" she reflected, "or if I were unconventional, it would be so easy. Those people have each their formula. But I have to wait for the circumstances. What Henry has done is either the greatest of all sins, or else it is no sin at all, and only \the/ circumstances ‹will› \can/ tell me which."

178:40 [*This passage, heavily reworked and revised, occurs on the reverse side of MS p. 395; a clean copy of the final version appears in proper sequence on MS p. 349.*] It is not their names that ‹will› recur in the parish register. It is not their ghosts that sigh among the alders at evening. {Theirs is the kingdom of the future.} They have ‹motored› \swept/ into the valley and \swept/ out of it, leaving a little dust and a little money behind ← Theirs is the kingdom of the future \with its aeroplanes and Marconigrams/—the future of the next five minutes‹—for though they praise patriotism they cannot take root in the earth›. They have swept into the valley and swept out of it, leaving a little dust and a little money behind ‹‹ ‹, and it›\. It is not their ghosts that sigh among the alders at evening/››.

191:32   Here had lived an elder race, to which we look back with disquietude ← The townsman is apt to make his home tasty and bright inside. An elder ‹generation› \race/ had lived here, to which we, with our ‹pied à terres› \week end cottages/ and \our/ bungalows, must look back with astonishment

207:43   but she waited through all, for *there was* no hurry ← *much difficulty and delay*, but she waited through all of it, for ‹the house› \Howards End/ was ‹not in a› \in no/ hurry

214:29   We know this is our house, because it feels ours ← We know that the inner life—oh after endless reservations if you like—but the inner life is the greater really. This is our house. We know it. It \feels as if it/ has been left us by the last person who loved it, and our right to be here is absolute

219:5   You shall see the connection if *it kills* you, *Henry!* You have had ← Connect! You shall connect if I kill you. I have spoiled you in hopes—but you grow worse. You ‹have› had

219:13   I've had enough of your unweeded kindness. I've spoilt you long enough. All your life you have been spoilt ← *If ‹ever› you want my love again, try for clearness of vision.* I've had enough of kindness—unweeded kindness. As I say, all your life you have been spoilt

222:17   I drew him to me. I made him tell me. I felt very lonely myself. *He is not to blame* ← ‹That was the end› \I made him tell me/. I drew him to me. ‹Still I thought "this is \only/ pity".› \I thought it was still only pity./ ‹‹Then ‹suddenly› ›› *I hated not Mr Wilcox but his wife, and kissed him.* ‹Presently› \Afterwards/ *he took me in his arms . . . But he is not to blame*

223:41   their father's sword ← their books

223:45   Margaret awoke and looked into the garden. How incomprehensible that Leonard Bast should have won her this night of peace! ←

Helen awoke and looked into the garden with a shudder of fear. ‹She feared bearing a child.› It was incomprehensible that Leonard, whom she could not find ‹was› should be governing their lives.

226:19   in St Paul's ← in Saint Paul's. It was a terrible ‹and dramatic› moment, far reaching in its consequences

226:22   inside him now ← inside him, rending his heart

226:23   Death alone still charmed him, with her lap of poppies, on which all men shall sleep ← Death alone, with her poppies, still charmed him—Death, contending with ‹Mammon› \Money/ for the soul of man, and her lap on which all the generations of men shall sleep

229:24   since dawn. Their hours were ruled, not by a London office ← for hours. Their lives were ruled not by the hour

229:25   That they were men of the finest type only the sentimentalist can declare. But they kept to the life of daylight. They ← They kept to the life of day light that the whole of England led until the last century ‹and that is now becoming an exception›. That they were men of the finest type, only the sentimentalist will declare; \for/ when they produced any one fine he went to the towns, and ‹produced› \became/ in the third generation Leonard. Still, they

229:28   Half clodhopper, half board-school prig ← Half brutalised, half suburbanized

234:19   *telegrams and anger* ← interviews ‹and diplomacy›

235:28   out of dreams ← out of dreams. She should never love another man‹; constancy was›\, constancy being/ her nature. And she might have loved a better man. But this elderly blundering boy had captured her. His approval had flattered her—‹(had it been thus with Mrs Wilcox?)—› and in a fatal moment she had seen to the depths of his heart and approved of ‹what she found there› \him/. She ought not to have approved. She ought to have known that in those ramifying paths she might herself be ‹entangled› \lost/, that insight is not enough so long as we ‹‹breathe ‹in› this hurtling outer air›› \\are part of this outer ‹life› \world/ too//. ‹Jacky had arisen.› She had expected such an apparition \as Jacky/, ‹but› \yet when it arose/ with difficulty could she lay it. Then Helen and Leonard had arisen—not as Helen and Leonard, people whom she understood, but as more apparitions in Henry's soul, and she had not been able to lay them. She had presumed beyond her powers, and perhaps beyond human powers. At all events she had failed

237:12   No sudden warmth ← ‹‹Margaret comforted him. It was ‹so›
impossible, she said, that any judge would convict. The coroner's jury,
stupid and sensational, might bring it in as manslaughter, but Charles
would surely be acquitted on his trial.›› No sudden warmth

237:12   see that to break ‹and end› him was ‹their only› \\her ‹best›
\only/ // hope ← see in a flash that this final blow would bring them salvation

237:15   Charles ← Charles, *stuttering and purple,*

237:15   *It was against all reason that he should be punished, but the
law, being made in his image,* sentenced *him* to three years' imprisonment. *Then Henry's fortress gave way. He could bear no one but his wife,
he* shambled up to Margaret afterwards ← ‹At the trial› \\‹There he› \He/
was sentenced to three years imprisonment, and// Henry fainted‹. Love
for his son \had/ pierced him to the middle of the brain›\, pierced to the
middle of the brain by love for his son/. He shambled up to Margaret
after the conviction

239:27   It is *part of* the battle against sameness ← ‹The race› It is the
battle against cosmopolitanism and the universal grey

239:31   \Don't drag in the personal when it will not come./

239:33   what has ‹such a man› \Leonard/ got out of life ← what has he
got—

239:36   Not for us. But for him. ← Isn't it everything?

242:45   Nothing has been done wrong ← We are nothing—nothing
but parts of some one else's mind ← You could not know. No one knew
← Nothing was ready

243:1   From the garden came laughter ← ‹They kissed› *They kissed/*.
From the garden came sounds of laughter, and the creak of the perambulator's wheels. The whirr of the cutter had stopped

BACKGROUNDS AND CONTEXTS

The Author and the Novel

E. M. FORSTER
Journal Entries[†]

These excerpts are taken from the unpublished diaries that Forster kept during the years he was working on *Howards End*. He began *The Notebook Journal* in 1903 and broke it off in 1909, when he started *The Locked Journal*, which he continued sporadically until 1969. Both documents are preserved at the King's College Library in Cambridge, but only a photocopy of *The Locked Journal* may be viewed. Some apparently hurtful entries have been masked by the archivist, and all entries after 1949 are as yet embargoed.

From *The Notebook Journal*

1907

Aug. 15 We like the like and love the unlike.

Dec. 31 Shall scarcely write another 'Longest Journey',[1] for it vexed people and I can with sincerity please them. Am anxious not to widen a gulf that must always remain wide; there is no doubt that I do not resemble other people, and even they notice it. Have been strongly attracted * * * to acquiesce in social conventions, economic trend, efficiency, etc., and see that others may do right to acquiesce and that I may do wrong to laugh at them, and that great art was never a conscious rebel. A rebel, surely.

1908

Jan. 27th Last Monday a man—named Farman—flew a ¾ mile circuit in 1½ minutes. It's coming quickly, and if I live to be old I shall see the sky as pestilential as the roads. It really *is* a new civilisation. I have been born at the end of the age of peace and can't expect to feel anything but despair. Science, instead of freeing man—the Greeks nearly freed him

---

† Copyright © 1998 The Provost and Scholars of King's College, Cambridge. Reprinted by permission of King's College, Cambridge, and The Society of Authors as the literary representatives of the E. M. Forster Estate.
1. Forster's second novel (1907), and one of his favorites, about the unhappiness in marriage of a character who finds greater fulfillment in his male friendships.

by right feeling—is enslaving him to machines. Nationality will go, but
the brotherhood of man will not come. No doubt the men of the past
were mistaken in thinking 'dulce et decorum est pro patria more'[2] but
the war of the future will make no pretence of beauty or of being the
conflict of ideas. God what a prospect! The little houses that I am used
to will be swept away, the fields will stink of petrol, and the air ships will
shatter the stars. Man may get a new and perhaps a greater soul for the
new conditions. But such a soul as mine will be crushed out.

Suppose that the thing at the back of things agrees with me and
intends the vanishing quickness to return. (i) there must be a miracle.
We must realise that the Kingdom of God is within us. Our sort do this
fitfully, but we use and increase the machine all the same, and no one
will listen to our little sermons. Passion is necessary—only Wells' comet
is enough.[3] For (ii) the alternative is that the machine should destroy
life, stop itself, and life begin again—perhaps no trees, perhaps not even
water.

March 5th   Have been thinking of the Resurrection of the Body and
what it meant to those who first imagined it—before the Church con-
ventionalized it. Also about the licensing bill, and of the severity of society towards our natural physiological impulses, & of its laxity towards our
acquired desires—e.g. for alcohol. "The brewers are the greatest ratepay-
ers in the country, and to touch them is a crime[.]" So a brute in the
train yesterday. He made me realise what bill a conservative govt. might
introduce: and that the nonconformists, though a force for evil in private
life (self righteousness) are a force for good in public.

May 31st   Uncle Ph. here for day.[4] Squalid stories of flat-life. Husband,
taking up ornament, "You value this, don't you?", and then smashes it.
Wife jumps out of window, breaking both her ancles [sic]. No one can
know any one, nor run the tennis court without quarrelling and forming
a committee.

June 16th   I opened Walt Whitman for a quotation, & he started speaking to me. That the unseen is justified by the seen: which in its turn
becomes unseen and is justified by the other.—He is not a book but an
acquaintance, and if I may believe him, he is more. Others whose work
attract[s] me remain memories, more or less vivid: he as something
objective, convincing me that he knows me personally. That the spiritual view might be robust—!

I am a man, one person, and I have not within me the implement that
will state the problem of life and death impersonally. To me it runs like

---

2. "'T'is a sweet and seemly thing to die for one's country" (Latin).
3. In H. G. Wells's novel *In the Days of the Comet* (1906), a comet passes close to the earth and
   transforms humanity by its effect on the atmosphere.
4. Philip M. Whichelo (1864–98), a brother of Forster's mother.

this: "Is W. correct in saying that he now sees me? And shall I ever see him?" The veil is thinnest just there.

No more fighting, please, between the soul & the body, until they have beaten their common enemy, the machine.

June 26th Idea for another novel shaping, and may do well to write it down.[5] In a prelude Helen [substituted for "the sister"] goes to stop with the Wilcoxes, gets engaged to the son & breaks it off immediately, for her instinct sees the spiritual cleavage between the families. Mrs. Wilcox dies, and some 2 years later Margaret gets engaged to the widower, a man impeccable publicly. They are accosted by a prostitute. M., because she understands and is great, marries him. The wrong thing to do. He, because he is little, cannot bear to be understood, & goes to the bad. He is frank, kind, and attractive. But he dreads ideas.

Aug. 9th Written some of the new novel, Howards End. A deal too cultured, and from hand to mouth. * * *

This afternoon saw Gerry's friends at the loch—a Mr. Baker & a Miss Brown who does fashion plates and said 'When you write your novels, do you use a synonym book, or have you got beyond that?'

1909

Feb. 10th Dined with the Scotts. He, who runs a mining paper, was depressing about America and the future generally. * * * 'Here and there you find individuals with private means and they do very well and the world leaves them alone, for it is doing very well.' He was prone to think 'real life' meant knowledge of finance; but he made me see how wide an abyss opens under our upper class merriment & culture. 'Money is power, and nothing else is, as far as I can see.' He spoke as if America may any minute sweep the pleasing erections of our civilisation away.

April 17th A little French girl, on being invited to have a bath, replies that she has no bathing costume with her. 'But you can lock the door, dear.' 'Mais non, Madame, c'est impossible: j'aurais des mauvaises idées.'[6] In convent schools pupils are taught to fear their own bodies. What horrors unsuspected! In one they are given 'masks for modesty' during bathing.

From *The Locked Journal*

Oct. 16 Would be content if the unseen power was an eternal memory.

---

5. The facing page contains a note, apparently in Forster's hand: "Mention of Howards End," with an arrow pointing to this passage.
6. "But no, Madame. It's impossible. I would have naughty thoughts" (French).

Nov. 29th   Was going to reflect sadly on life, but what's the use of my abuse? A wrong view of S[hakespere]'s sonnets in a book Marsh[7] lent me and an attempted blackmail in this morning's paper are the main cause. How barbaric the world! If a tiny fraction of its energy would go to the understanding of man, we would have the millenium. This bullying stupidity.

Dec. 27th   Two Harrow boys who got up at S.O.[8] to go rabbiting were discovered, and, fearing punishment, started to walk to Cheltenham, where lived the grandmother of one of them. They slept rough, and were so done up that a fire that they lit burned them as they slept. At Cheltenham, the grandmother accepted her own hero, but turned away the other, who was suffering from incipient pneumonia. His friend had no money to give him, but rigged him out with a bicycle, to ride back to Harrow. He got as far as Reading, where he collapsed, and was sent on by the people at the inn to his mother in London, who sent him on the same night to Harrow, where he was caned.—These boys were not popular with their schoolmates, and were sent away from the school.

Dec. 31st   Will review the year, eat an orange, read, and go to bed. * * *
Writing very bad. Two stories published, but do not think I wrote much of either this year. Am only conscious of one drive of inspiration, at Salisbury, where I wrote for several days at a play about S. Bridget.[9] Thought my novel very bad, but though it is pumped it's not quite as bad as I thought, for the characters are conceived sincerely. Will it ever be done? A fortnight ago I should have said not, but am hopeful now. The play may also pan out.—But take it all round, I've lost inspiration, and not adequately replaced it by solidity. Words are more in the foreground than they were: even these I seem to be writing for an audience.

1910

Feb. 14   Yesterday I called on the man two doors off and he said 'In your novels which takes you longest—the writing or the thinking?'

Feb. 19th   Am grinding out my novel into a contrast between money & death—the latter is truly an ally of the personal against the mechanical.

Feb. 22nd   Physical attraction—Universal Brotherhood. Any connection? No.

---

7. Edward Marsh (1872–1953), an influential figure in London literary circles who aided Forster's career and lent him books, including *The Man Shakespeare* by Frank Harris. In a letter to Marsh (18 November 1909), Forster angrily chastised Harris for "smugly absolv[ing] Shakespeare from the 'imputations' of the sonnets" (quoted in P. N. Furbank, *E. M. Forster: A Life*, vol. 1 [London: Secker and Warburg, 1977], 177).
8. Special order (i.e., by special arrangement).
9. Forster's papers at King's College include the manuscript of an unfinished play about St. Bridget of Sweden, a noblewoman and mother of eight children who founded a holy order after her husband's death.

March 19   Falling in love puts daily life out of gear, and makes us irritable, deceitful, and irrational in our judgments. No wonder that a happy marriage renders people remote. Love—and affection too—must be opposed to reason if they are genuine. One 'sees' the faults of the beloved, but cannot register them, and resents their mention by others. Let my own vexations teach me sympathy. I know now *what* Mr. Franks & Elaine, Mr. Lloyd and Miss Marsh[1] see in each other; and *why* I cannot see it myself. A noble adventure—yet distracting in those who are concerned in it and absurd to those who are not.

July 21st   However gross my desires, I find that I shall never satisfy them for the fear of annoying others. I am glad to come across this much good in me. It serves instead of purity.

July 28th   I have nearly done my novel and mean to devote August to athletics and personal appearance. * * *
    Note—on the management of cigarettes. The gentleman makes his part of him. The lower classes practise a sort of intermittent copulation with it, holding it far away meanwhile, where it often goes out. Their opening puffs are violent and ugly. But a pipe they can manage against anyone.

Aug. 6th   'As punctual as a nonconformist.' I stopped a night with the Haslucks,[2] but my pleasure was a little marred by their precision and intolerance. Though amusing, kind, and extremely clever, they had a bestial prejudice against anything spiritual. It is a hideous religion.

Sept. 19th   The last 4 or 5 days have been so unhappy that I cannot keep an outward cheerfulness. * * * I can hardly detail my chief trouble. Mother is evidently deeply shocked by Howards End. The shocking part is also inartistic, and so I cannot comfort myself by a superior standpoint. I do not know how I shall live through the next months. There are Maimie & Aunt Laura too.[3] Yet I have never written anything less erotic.

Sept. 29th   The almost ceaseless worries of the last month have left me more interested in life. I feel older & more competent.

Oct. 9   It is possible to love 2 people, but not on succeeding days. That I have been attractive excites me most.

Oct. 25th   To work out:—The sexual bias in literary criticism, and perhaps literature. Look for such a bias in its ideal & carnal form. Not in

---

1. According to Wilfred Stone, Forster was friends with Mabel Marsh, a delicate, semi-invalid teacher who married a Mr. Lloyd shortly before she died at age forty-three (personal correspondence; also see Stone's interview with Forster in *Twentieth Century Literature* 43 [Spring 1997]: 63–64). The other couple is unidentifiable.
2. Frederick William Hasluck (1878–1920), noted archaeologist and a friend of Forster's from King's College.
3. Maimie Aylward was an intimate, lifelong friend of Forster's mother; Laura Forster was his paternal aunt.

274 E. M. FORSTER

experience which refines. What sort of person would the critic prefer to sleep with, in fact.

Nov. 13th Lust, whether strong or weak, is akin to Romance. The human being of our dreamings is impossible. Lust idealises. Love is passion for an actual person, & the purer the closer it keeps to the fact. Both are good. Lust too can be pure, & dream of unity of souls instead of bodies. But in action it is disillusion & vanity, for souls like bodies can never merge.

Dec. 8th Prayer. Not to imagine people are noticing me, especially when I am with one whom I love. How often I have met Masood the last two months, how little I have enjoyed it.[4] I long to be out of London with him, but that is self indulgence. Let me not be distracted by the world. It is so difficult—I am not vain of my overpraised book, but I wish I was obscure again. Soon I shall be. Let me reenter it with sweetness. If I come an unholy smash let me never forget that one man and possibly two have loved me. In old age I shall look back envious to this year which gave me so much, but it is the material for happiness rather than happiness. I knew I shouldn't and I don't enjoy fame. Never forget nature and to look at her freshly. Don't advance *one step more* into literary society than I have. Let the paper on The Feminine Note in Literature, which I must finish for the Friday Club now, be my last thing of this sort. Henceforward more work & meditation, more concentration on those whom I love.

Dec. 19th Desire for a book.[5] To deal with country life & possibly Paris. Plenty of young men & children in it, & adventure. If possible pity & thought. But no love making—at least of the orthodox kind, & perhaps not even of the unorthodox. It would be tempting to make an intelligent man feel toward an intelligent man of lower class what I feel, but I see the situation too clearly to use it as in Mon Frére Yves, where its author is either deceiving the public or himself. My motive should be democratic affection, and I am not sure whether that has any strength. Am sketching a family—father a Tory candidate, a barrister, moderate, sensible, & generally kind. Lets his children go wrong but expects them to enter their class without difficulty later. Elderly son—Nevil—at Oxford; second Jocelyn, the hero: two girls, 11 & 13, and perhaps another boy. A stepmother, quiet & beautiful, who accentuates the father's faults. And an old bootboy now at the Swindon works, & his two brothers, one a choir boy in the cathedral.

1911

May 14th It struck me a few days ago how lucky I am—health, money, friends. Most of my troubles come from within or because the ill luck of others worries me. Good luck has done me good hitherto but the future is doubtful. My faults are idleness, and inability to admit that I am

4. Syed Ross Masood (1889–1937), whose intense, passionate (but unconsummated) friendship prompted Forster's interest in India.
5. This book was never written.

wrong, unless I love the accuser very much. I might be envious, but the inevitable decline of my literary reputation will test that.

June 16th   Having sat for an hour in vain trying to write a play, will analyse causes of my sterility. 1. Inattention to health—curable. 2. Weariness of the subject that I both can and may treat—the love of men for women & vice versa. Passion & money are the two main springs of action (not of existence) and I can only write of the first, & and of that imperfectly. Growing interest in religion does not help me. 3. Depressing and enervating surroundings. My life's work, if I have any, is to live with a person who thinks nothing worth while.[6]

E. M. FORSTER

Working Notes[†]

One page of the manuscripts contains the following working notes:

ch 10. Mrs. Wilcox, hearing that her husband is returning goes with Margaret to the doctor & insists on her returning to the flat. There she breaks down

She dies & leaves Howards End to M. ‹Who ref› Opinions of the Wilcox family. M. refuses the legacy, and the intimacy between her & Mr W. begins.

Jacky not rude to Helen at the call.
Scene between Dolly & Charles.

Find out: a profession for Mr. W. symptoms of cancer—form of legacy.

Forster made the following notes to himself on another page of the manuscripts:[1]

Mrs Wilcox; her illness & death.
Rapprochement of M. & Mr W.
Return of L. to Wickham Place
M. & Mr W. ‹engaged› \married/. Ructions in the W family—Helen's disapproval. Break up of W. Pl.
The ? of L's separation.

---

6. Forster lived with his mother Alice Clara ("Lily") Forster until her death in 1945. Shortly thereafter he wrote a memorandum, listed in his papers at the King's College library as "Mother,"
   which begins: "Must clear up my relations with my mother, which though never hostile or tragic, did not go so well after my grandmother's death, or even perhaps after Cambridge. I recall
   so few radiant moments."
† From *The Manuscripts of* Howards End, ed. Oliver Stallybrass (London: Edward Arnold, 1977)
   355.
1. See p. 252 above for an explanation of the typographical symbols in the manuscripts.

Mr Wilcox induced to help—\Kind. Sees for Leonard./ meets Jackie & is confronted with idea [?]

M's life at Howard's End.—her child; Mr W. offended that it does not nail her down.

L. & Helen.

"She must be rescued."

Then I think that Charles ‹goes› is sent by his father to horse whip Leonard, and is killed by him, and L flings himself out of the window.

Or it may be that Helen & Leonard die.

Or perhaps Leonard lives.

E. M. FORSTER

Selected Letters[†]

To Goldsworthy Lowes Dickinson[1]

Harnham, Monument Green, Weybridge
12 May 1907

Dear Dickinson,

I do wish you would write again. You know, I meant Stephen, Ansell, and Rickie [from *Longest Journey*] to be likeable, but hardly anyone likes them. On other points, I expect I should agree with your criticisms.

I must say something, not to you but to "you," about sentimentality. All I write is, to me, sentimental. A book which doesn't leave people either happier or better than it found them, which doesn't add some permanent treasure to its world, isn't worth doing. (A book *about* good and happy people may be still better, but hasn't attracted me yet so much.) This is my 'theory,' and I maintain it's sentimental—at all events it isn't Flaubert's. How can he fag himself to write 'Un coeur simple,'—a life of this outline?

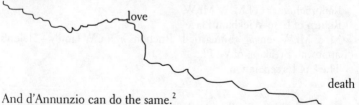

And d'Annunzio can do the same.[2]

† Reprinted by permission of King's College, Cambridge, and The Society of Authors as the literary representatives of the E. M. Forster Estate.

1. Dickinson (1862–1932), a historian and Hellenist, was one of Forster's most influential teachers at King's College and a lifelong friend. The two letters to Dickinson printed in this section are preserved with Forster's papers at King's College.

2. Flaubert's short story "A Simple Heart" (1877); Gabriele D'Annunzio (1863–1938), Italian poet and novelist.

As to seeing life as I write it—certainly I don't do that. The traps are far fewer: perhaps negligeable [sic]. But I can imagine myself liking those three men, if they were alive. The women, certainly, are no go.

Yours ever
E. M. Forster

To Edward Arnold[3]

West Hackhurst, Abinger Hammer, Dorking
13 January 1909

Dear Mr. Arnold,

Thank you so much for your kind letter of congratulation. I am glad to hear that the book is selling[4] and hope that the Spectator review will have a good effect.

I shall be most happy to talk over my next book with you when it is ready, but I am not sure when that will be. I am a little doubtful whether I should be finished in time for publication in the autumn. I have got some short stories which seem to me not bad, and which I have been often asked to republish in book form: would you be inclined to consider these in the meanwhile?[5]

Believe me,
Yours sincerely,
E. M. Forster

Perhaps when you write next, you would very kindly tell me the approximate sales of A Room with a View.

Harnham, Monument Green, Weybridge
12 February 1909

Dear Mr. Arnold,

Thank you for your letter and kind invitation. I am afraid that I cannot have the pleasure of accepting it, as I am very busy just now with lectures and could not come up. It is very good of you to ask me.

I had hoped that the book would have gone a little better, as I had heard it more spoken of than were the other two; but I dare say that only means that more people are reading the same copy at Mudie's,[6] and that considering the times we are doing as well as can be expected. As regards the short stories, I know how uncertain the market for them is, but am anxious

3. Edward Augustus Arnold (1857–1942), publisher of Howards End and other of Forster's works. The manuscripts of Forster's letters to Arnold are preserved in the company archives.
4. Arnold published A Room with a View in October 1908 and supplemented the first printing of 2,000 copies with a second printing of 500 in January 1909.
5. This volume of short stories, The Celestial Omnibus, was eventually published by Sidgwick and Jackson in 1911.
6. A subscription lending library.

to get them published if I can, as they seem to me not bad, nor likely to decrease my reputation among those who may read them. Perhaps the best plan would be for me to collect them together and send them up to you to read before we discuss the matter further. I will do this if I may.

Again thanking you for your kind invitation to lunch.

I remain
Yours sincerely
E. M. Forster

Weybridge
23 March 1909

Dear Mr. Arnold,

I have put together the collection of short stories of which I spoke to you, and am sending them off shortly for your inspection. I should be glad to publish them if possible, though of course we should both anticipate a smaller circulation for them than for a novel. * * *

The novel that I am writing goes forward, but as far as I can tell, it will be rather long, and not ready for publication in the autumn.[7]

Believe me, with kind regards, yours sincerely,
E. M. Forster

Tyn-y-Gamdda, Harlech
19 April 1909

Dear Mr. Arnold,

Thank you for your letter, and for the careful consideration that you and Mr. Mumm have given to my stories. I am sorry that you do not feel inclined to consider publication, though I am compelled to agree that they are in a literary form that is not at present popular. It was not so much with the intention of filling a gap between the longer books that I have collected them together as in the belief that they contained certain merits that the longer books did not. But authors are particularly bad judges of their own productions!

When you return them to my home address, would you very kindly direct "not to be forwarded" to be put on the parcel.

Yours sincerely,
E. M. Forster

Harnham, Monument Green, Weybridge
22 March 1910

Dear Mr. Arnold,

Thank you for your letter. As you would like to see a rough draft, I am sending you 30 chapters instead of 3, but fear you will make little out of

7. The novel Forster refers to is *Howards End*.

them. They contain repetitions and even omissions, and both my hand-writing and method of work may irritate the reader.

I further send a synopsis, with marginal references. This should be helpful.

Would you kindly direct that the packet be acknowledged on arrival, as the loss of it would of course be serious for me. I should further be grateful for its return, registered, when you have read as much as you can manage of the contents.

> Believe me, with kind regards,
> Yours truly
> E. M. Forster

> Harnham, Monument Green, Weybridge
> 6 April 1910

Dear Mr. Arnold,

Thank you for your letter. I need hardly say how glad I am that you think well of the book. I shall be very happy to accept the terms you offer—namely, those of the last agreement with £130 on account of Royalties instead of £100. I am writing in a great hurry, so cannot discuss your criticisms, in both of which I feel great force, & of which I hope to profit. I wanted chiefly to say:—If the book was published in the autumn season, what is the latest date that the MS should be in your hands in its final form? I should be greatly obliged if you could send me an answer by return, as I start for Italy Friday morning, and want to make arrangements accordingly.

Believe me, with many thanks for your letter, and with kind regards,

> Yours sincerely,
> E. M. Forster

> Harnham, Monument Green, Weybridge
> 9 August 1910

Mr. Edward Arnold, Publisher
Dear Sir,

I have thought over shortening the M.S., and am very sorry, but fear it would be impossible. I might have done something earlier, when I submitted the bulk of the M.S. to Mr. Arnold, and indicated the scale on which it would be completed, but he did not make any comment then. I am very sorry that its length should be excessive—though, as I said, I have had a good many complaints that my previous novels were too short.

> Yours faithfully,
> E. M. Forster

> Harnham, Monument Green, Weybridge
> 14 September 1910

Dear Mr. Arnold,

Thank you for your letter. I am afraid that I agree with you about Helen. I was much struck by your original criticism, & tried to do what I could, but the episode had worked itself into the plot inextricably. I hope however that the public may find the book convincing on other counts.

Thank you for sending the proofs to America. I have not much hope myself that it will attract a transatlantic publisher where A Room with a View has failed; still the unexpected may happen.

> Hoping that you have had a pleasant holiday,
> I remain,
> Yours sincerely,
> E.M. Forster

To Edward Garnett[8]

> Harnham, Monument Green, Weybridge
> 10 November 1910

Dear Garnett,

It is awfully good of you to ask me down, and I should enjoy it, but there is such a tangle of relatives and visitors ahead that I fear I can't get away. Are you usually or ever in town on Wednesdays? I am, and would call for you for a talk. Do you dislike the Savile? If not, would you come to lunch there.

I am interested to see what you will write about Howards End, and even more interested to hear what you say privately. Plenty is wrong with the book, but I have not yet located the evil to my satisfaction, though I fancy it suffers from paralysis in its hind quarters. Is that what you mean?

> Yours sincerely,
> E. M. Forster

> Harnham, Monument Green, Weybridge
> 12 November 1910

Dear Garnett

With the possible exception of the Times, which avowedly omitted bad points, your criticism is the only one that strikes me as just.[9] I only hope I may profit by it in the future, and a writer can't say more. Though whether I can profit is another matter. It is devilish difficult to criticise society & also create human beings. Unless one has a big mind, one aim or the other fails before the book is finished. I must pray for a big mind, but it is uphill work—!

> Yours very sincerely
> E. M. Forster.

Do you remember some short stories of mine? I have at last entrapped a publisher into taking them. I am very glad, for I think them better than

---

8. Edward Garnett (1868–1937) was a prolific critic and publisher's reader. This letter and the next are in the collection of the Harry Ransom Humanities Research Center at the University of Texas.

9. See "Contemporary Responses," pp. 381–84, for Garnett's review "Villadom" and for the review in the Times Literary Supplement. The collection of stories Forster mentions is The Celestial Omnibus (1911). From Selected Letters of E. M. Forster, ed. Mary Lago and P. N. Furbank, vol. 1 (Cambridge, MA: Harvard UP, 1983) 117.

my long books—the only point of criticism on which I have ever disagreed with you!

To Goldsworthy Lowes Dickinson

Harnham, Monument Green, Weybridge
21 November 1910

Dear Dickinson,
* * * I don't like popularity. It seems so mad. There isn't any reason
why it should be this book and not another, or another of mine. I go
about saying I like the money, because one is simply bound to be
pleased about something on such an occasion. But I don't even like that
very much. * * * No, it *is* all insanity.

Yours ever,
E. M. Forster

To Arthur Christopher Benson[1]

West Hackhurst, Abinger Hammer, Dorking
13 December 1910

Dear Mr Benson
Thank you for your letter, and for the extract from Mrs Benson's letter; I need not say how flattered I felt by them and how much they interested me. Their tone, though, was much too *respectful*; while reading
them, I felt as if I had made some serious contribution to thought or literature, but I know that I have not. Thus, I agreed with you that the book
is poetical rather than philosophical. This sounds arrogant, but one's
confused little mind is visited by impulses of beauty, whereas systematic
thought can only come to the mind that is both strong and orderly.
However, it is great fun writing, and I am sure I do not want to run
myself down! The house certainly would not appeal so strongly to the
idealists; I had not thought of that. Indeed, though the supernatural element in the book is not supposed to be 'compulsory', I'm afraid that only
those readers who 'take' it, will get through with any ease.
    Again thanking you for your encouragement, and for all the trouble
you have taken in writing to me.

I remain
Yours sincerely
E. M. Forster

1. Eldest son of the archbishop of Canterbury, Benson was a master at Eton and later became
Master of Magdalene College at Cambridge University. See "Contemporary Responses,"
pp. 387–88, for Benson's letter. From *Selected Letters of E. M. Forster*, ed. Mary Lago and
P. N. Furbank, vol. 1 (Cambridge, MA: Harvard UP, 1983) 119.

It would be a great pleasure to come & see you when I am in Cambridge next.

To Edward Arnold

Harnham, Monument Green, Weybridge
23 February 1911

Dear Mr. Arnold,

Thank you for your letter, and enclosures. I shall be most happy to accept Mssrs. Rütter's offer of £20 [for rights to translate *Howards End* into German], but when replying would you very kindly notify that it is on condition that they translate verbatim, without additions or omissions. One has to be careful on this point, for Messrs. Putnam actually inserted chapter headings in the American edition without my permission or knowledge. Mr. Huntington, however, was as annoyed as I was, and thanks to our joint protest, they are to be removed in the second impression. * * *

Yours sincerely,
E. M. Forster

To E. J. Dent[2]

Harnham, Monument Green, Weybridge
7 May 1911

Dear Dent,

* * * Howards End should have appeared as Das rote Haus [The Red House] by now—their title, and I agreed as it wasn't bad though your 'connectings' [*Verbindungen*] were more expressive. But I haven't heard of its publication, nor received any money. * * *

Yours ever
E. M. Forster

To Edward Arnold

Idlerocks, Stone, Staff[ord]s[hire]
3 June 1911

Dear Mr. Arnold,

Thank you for your letter, & for all the kindness and foresight you have shown in this affair. No doubt the verbatim translation may have been a difficulty, but they are clearly no longer keen on the book, & are determined to raise some objection or other. I return their letter.

Believe me, with many thanks,
Yours sincerely,
E. M. Forster

2. Edward Joseph Dent (1876–1957), fellow of King's College and professor of music.

A printer, who is in my Latin Class in the Working Men's College, desires a post with a publisher—apparently as adviser against the iniquities of printers! I have in my possession a letter from him, detailing his qualifications, and if it was likely to be of the slightest interest to you, would send it. But I do not expect that it would be, and please do not trouble to answer this, unless it is. He is an intelligent attractive chap, and I promised to do anything I could for him, so I am soothing my conscience.

To Florence Barger[3]

11 Rue Abbasides, Alex[andria]
8 November 1916

Dear Florence

* * *

This will be a poor letter—I am out of bed from a cold and can't think consecutively—have got through it wonderfully quick thanks to the extreme comfort of this house—hot baths and 3 Arab servants to wait upon me. I only collapsed yesterday—quite the fashionable thing to do during a first visit. My host, a theosophist and a solicitor, is a nice chap. He will persist that I too am "on the path," in fact ~~many~~ several who have read my books here persist in importing creeds into them—rather in the spirit of the Helleno-Christian city, if you come to think of it. e.g. the doctrine of the Incarnation has been found in Howards End. There is plenty of interest and of tolerance in the mixed communities out here but nothing remotely resembling what Cambridge knew as thought. Ingenious muddlements take its place, and the religiously minded are in their element consequently.

* * *

E. M. FORSTER

Recollection of Rooksnest[†]

* * *

* * * It certainly was a lovable little house,[1] and still is, though it now stands just outside a twentieth-century hub and almost within sound of

---

3. Wife of George Barger, who was a student with Forster at Cambridge and who later became professor of chemistry at Edinburgh University. Florence Barger was one of Forster's few close women friends. From *Selected Letters*, vol. 1, 244–45.

† Excerpt from Marianne Thornton: *A Domestic Biography*, copyright © 1956 by E. M. Forster and renewed 1984 by Donald Ambrose Parry, reprinted by permission of Harcourt Brace & Company and The Provost and Scholars of King's College, Cambridge 1997.

1. Rooksnest was Forster's boyhood home in Hertfordshire. It once belonged to a family named Howard.

a twentieth-century hum. The garden, the overhanging wych elm, the sloping meadow, the great view to the west, the cliff of fir trees to the north, the adjacent farm through the high tangled hedge of wild roses were all utilised by me in *Howards End*, and the interior is in the novel too. The actual inmates were my mother, myself, two maids, two or more cats, an occasional dog; outside were a pony and trap with a garden boy to look after them. From the time I entered the house at the age of four and nearly fell from its top to its bottom through a hole ascribed to the mice, I took it to my heart and hoped, as Marianne[2] had of Battersea Rise, that I should live and die there. We were out of it in ten years. The impressions received there remained and still glow—not always distinguishably, always inextinguishably—and have given me a slant upon society and history. It is a middle-class slant, atavistic, derived from the Thorntons, and it has been corrected by contact with friends who have never had a home in the Thornton sense, and do not want one.

Aunt Monie had urged my mother to take the house (provided it was on gravel), so she had no grounds for complaint, and it had seemed to her quite proper that a beautiful young widow should bury herself in the wilds for the sake of a supposedly delicate son. All the same, there was this nagging desire to see us—me particularly. Her thirst for youth had become cannibalistic. My mother's letters fall into three classes—those in which she undertook to go to Clapham, those in which she excused herself from going, and those in which she fed the old lady with amusing bits of news about the Important One, in the hope of keeping her quiet. She was rather cynical—she held that it was as Morgan's mother that she mattered, and she could be proudly silent on the subject of Whichelo affairs.[3] She was not very cynical—she was fond of naughty tiresome Monie, and grateful to her, and liked pleasing her.

*   *   *

2. Marianne Thornton, or "Aunt Monie," was Forster's solicitous (perhaps overly so) great-aunt on his father's side, who left him a legacy of £8,000, which paid for his education and enabled him to travel and write. Battersea Rise was the name of the Thornton family home in Clapham.
3. "Morgan" was Forster's middle name and nickname. His mother's family, less prosperous than the Thornton's, was named Whichelo.

E. M. FORSTER

Map of Rooksnest[†]

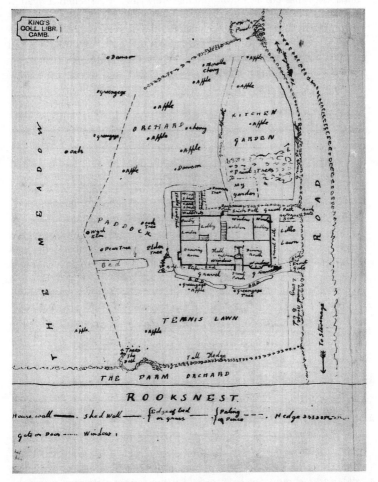

† This pen-and-ink sketch of the house and the garden at Rooksnest can be found in the school notebook in which Forster wrote the recollection of his childhood home reprinted below (286–90). The notebook is preserved with Forster's papers in the library of King's College, Cambridge. The map is located on the reverse side of the second page of the notebook, and the memoir begins on the facing page. Copyright © 1998 The Provost and Scholars of King's College, Cambridge. Reproduced by permission of King's College, Cambridge, and The Society of Authors as the literary representatives of the E. M. Forster Estate.

E. M. FORSTER

Boyhood Recollection of Rooksnest[†]

I have, or think I have, a clear impression of my arrival at Rooksnest. I certainly remember coming in the train and asking the names of the stations as we passed, and pronouncing Welwyn as it is spelled instead of calling it "Wellin" in the approved fashion. I think I remember too coming in the fly and seeing the church and the farm as we passed and also seeing Rooksnest itself but I do not remember entering the house and my next impression is playing with bricks on the drawing-room floor, my next having neuralgia when the doctor called, and my next playing a musical box to the charwoman while she cleaned out the nursery cupboard. I was about four when we arrived which was in March 1883. We came for three years but soon after we arrived mother said we could never stop so long. However we stopped till September 1893 and then only went because we had to.

I suppose I had better begin by a description of the house. It was about one mile from Stevenage walking and one and a half driving and was on a particular bad piece of road which led from Stevenage to Weston, a small village about three miles further on and naturally had very little traffic. Stevenage is on the G.N.R. [Great Northern Railway] and is the highest point on the line between London and York and Rooksnest is a good deal higher than Stevenage so we had a very fine view to the west and north-west over Hertfordshire and part of Cambridgeshire. People who were accustomed to call Herts an ugly county were astonished at this view and the surroundings of the house were altogether very pretty, first and foremost the fine view, and to the north a peep of the park with its little woods of firs and oaks. We could not see beyond the road as there was a high hedge and there were no windows looking out that way. The house faced south-west but it professed to face south. I have made a sketch plan of it and the garden opposite from memory the chief fault of which is that the house is too big for the garden and the back garden should be larger than it is.

I don't know what to speak about first but will perhaps tell about the house. The name Rooksnest was not an ordinary name of a house but the name of a hamlet consisting of us and the farm below. Mother when she came heard that the house was to be called "Chisfield Villa" and nearly had a fit. It was very old. Some said 200 years and some 500, and I should not be surprised if the former statement was right.

† From the Abinger Edition of *Howards End*, ed. Oliver Stallybrass (London: Edward Arnold, 1973) 341–48. This recollection was written by Forster when he was fifteen and away at school. It is his earliest surviving text. Reprinted by permission of King's College, Cambridge, and The Society of Authors as the literary representatives of the E. M. Forster Estate.

It was oblong in shape and built of red brick that had long lost its crudeness of colour. The front was covered with two rose trees and part of a vine. The east side was covered by the same vine. When we came there was only one rose tree and the vine but they grew immensely and with the other rose tree covered two sides of the house. The vine was always a source of debate. Should it be grown this year for grapes or foliage? Sometimes we had the grapes and made wine which people liked very much when they were thirsty but this made the house so bare, for there were no windows on the east side, that we generally had the leafage. The other two sides had no creepers but the roof of the back side was very odd. Two large gables first containing the little spare room and landing windows, then below the back porch and then till the end of the house the roof stretched down from the very top to within six feet of the ground. I was very fond of throwing balls up this roof trying to send them into the front garden but when I broke two windows this was discouraged. The west side of the house was rather bare and only relieved by the larder window and the store-cupboard window above it.

Inside the house was peculiar. You entered through the porch into a tiny ante-room and then into the hall, the pride of the house. It was the kitchen when the house was a farm and sad to say once had an open fireplace with a great chimney but before we came the landlord, Colonel Wilkinson, closed it up, put a wretched little grate instead and made the chimney corner into the cupboard I have marked. Five doors opened out of the hall, the dining-room, the drawing-room, the door to the lobby leading to the kitchen, the door leading to the porch and the door to the staircase which was thus quite shut in and could not be found by new people who wondered how ever we got up. Though the big fireplace was blocked up the big chimney still remained and once the sweep brought a little boy who went up it to mother's great alarm, but came down safe. There were signs of a trapdoor in the ceiling. At the end of the chimney cupboard was a little door which mother once got open and found an old basin which we still have. The ceiling had a beam across as had most of the rooms.

The dining-room and drawing-room were nice rooms but had nothing peculiar about them. On going through the lobby door you came to a door on the left which opened onto a flight of stairs leading to the cellar, which was under the drawing-room. Then from the lobby opened three doors to the pantry, larder, and kitchen. The pantry was a little room but the larder was big and had a yellow brick floor and nice large shelves on which the eatables were put. It was always very cool. In one corner were large red vessels one of which held the bread and the others, at first, our drinking-water. The kitchen was rather warm and paved with squares of red and blue stone. From it opened a cupboard under the stairs. It had a porch with two doors which were useful when parleying with a tramp. All the windows at the back had bars whether they were upstairs or down and all in the front had shutters so we were pretty safe from tramps or burglars.

Upstairs there was the landing which had a window over the back porch and in front three large rooms, the big spare room, the nursery, and mother's room over the dining-room, hall and drawing-room respectively. Mother's was large and cold but she liked it. The nursery was delightful. It had a large cupboard shaped in an L in which my toys were and had also the large wardrobe which took up one side of the room. The big spare room was nice but I did not often go in. Then opposite was the little spare room over the scullery, a later addition which was very nice in winter because of the kitchen chimney. In the passage between it and the big spare room was a trapdoor to the rafters where was a cistern which was filled every day, till we had a regular water supply from the scullery pump. Here was a little window which commanded a view of the back garden. The only other room on this landing was the store-cupboard by mother's bedroom over the larder. Hence always came a mingled odour of apples, mice and jam.

Above were three attics, a bedroom on each side and a boxroom in the middle. This was a curious part of the house, for at the entrance of each room was a beam of wood perhaps 18 inches high by 12 wide on the top of which the door swung. New maids were always much aggrieved at having to stride to bed over these logs. In the attic over the spare room was an L-shaped passage leading nowhere round the chimney-stack. When I arrived I am told I ran to the top of the house and then down this passage. The mice had eaten away all the rafters and I nearly came down quicker than I had come up.

So much for the house. Now for the neighbours. The only houses near us were the farm about 200 yards nearer the village and the lodge of Chisfield about as far the other way. When we arrived the lodge was inhabited by the gamekeeper Mr Plum his wife and two children. Mrs P. paved the way to an acquaintance by leaving some sticks at the back door for us to light the fire the morning we arrived. The little boy she called 'Sizzle", but we called him Baby Plum or Baby Plumbun. From what I remember of him he must have been a truly hateful child. He generally wanted what he had not got. This propensity brought to light delinquencies of the maids who had evidently let the Plum family have the run of our house while we were away. Baby Plum one day kept on saying something we could not understand. At last it resolved itself into:—"I warnt ter see Maaster Morgin's[1] little gla-a-ass b-a-a-alls" ending in a wail. These were marbles which we had never shown him so he must have poked in our drawers to find them. The other child was called Annie. How often have I heard Mrs Plum say in loud tones

---

1. Forster's full name was Edward Morgan; he was generally called "Morgan."

"Sizzle you naughty boy how dare you hit 'littlannie' I'll smack you that I will." While Mrs Plum talked she always pinched pieces out of a box hedge by the lodge. Whether this hurt it I know not but when they left it was cut down.

* * *

* * * Dirty as the farm was I liked it very much. There was a large farm yard, the side of the house forming one side and barns and stables the other three. It was full of mud and manure in the midst of which wallowed enormous pigs. I was very frightened of them though I did not mind cows and horses, and used to steal across in great fear and trembling. Once however across there were great mysterious barns, some full of grain in which I ran about and got my boots and clothes full of, others full of straw, though not often as it was mostly in stacks, and others with curious farm instruments in. Among these was an old winnowing machine that used to be used before the time of threshing engines, and also machines for cutting oilcake and hay. They had large wheels which turned the knives inside, and Frankie used to spread himself out on them like Ixion[2] and whirl round while I stood by wishing I dare do it too. The barns were always full of "dim religious light" but sometimes the great doors were flung open and the whole place lighted up. I was never tired of poking about in the barns for eggs of which I used to find several. The farm had a very nice front garden always bright with flowers but we always went in the back way. * * *

* * *

The map I have drawn of the garden gives a better idea of it than anything else. It was mostly grass but as we had a pony we did not mind. It was level on the whole but in the front garden was a dell known as the "dellole" which was a pond when we came but mother had it drained and filled up, a thing I have always regretted when I saw how pretty the Clarkes' pond looked with bulrushes and flags. There was just such another hole at the other end of the garden but it was full of water. The most interesting thing in the garden was the wych-elm tree. It was of great height and had a very thick stem, but the curious part in it was this. About four feet from the ground were three or four fangs stuck deep into the rugged bark. As far as I can make out these were votive offerings of people who had their toothache cured by chewing pieces of the bark, but whether they were their own teeth I don't know and certainly it does not seem likely that they should sacrifice one sound tooth as the price of having one aching one cured.

All one side of the garden stretched the meadow. It was our meadow

2. Frankie was the grandson of the Forsters' neighbors at the farm; Ixion—a king punished by Zeus by being tied to an eternally revolving wheel.

but we let it to Mr Franklin on the condition that no obnoxious animals should be allowed to be there. By "obnoxious" I suppose we meant animals that would not [sic] hurt the garden if they got in, but the result was we had every animal but a horse. The boundary line between the two was a fence of four wires which we had not to spoil the view, but by the "dellole" it was for some reason very weak and tottery and always had to be supplemented by faggots. The garden was always overrun with animals. There were always hens and guinea-fowls. Those we were used to, but also there was always a sample of whatever animal happened to be in the meadow. If it was large it crashed through by the dell, if small it crawled under the bottom wire of the fence. To the former class belonged cows, calves and sheep, to the latter pigs, lambs, hens, ducks and guinea-fowls. Add to these the occasional animals that strayed in from the road and the keeper's puppies that played in the back garden and you have a good idea what its appearance was. Once a donkey got in, and Mr Stewart suggested that we should tie horns on and have it as a stag. We were very fond of the meadow. It had three fine greengage trees, which we were allowed to have, and a large oak on which was hung a swing. It was of very odd shape, something like this: — [diagram] and was all downhill. It had hedges full of clematis, primroses, bluebells, dog-roses, may, bryony and nuts, with many trees which were nearly all in the hedges. In it was a little dell which communicated with our pond in the back garden to prevent it getting too full. From it were most lovely views of the surrounding country. It was generally used for hay in the summer.

The next thing that occurs to me are the disadvantages. If anyone else had written about Rooksnest they would have begun with them, for our friends were never tired of telling us them. In the first place we lived for six years without water. We were to have had a well but Colonel Wilkinson got out of it by saying that waterworks would soon be made in the valley and that he would then pay to have water pumped up to our house. At length the waterworks were made, but lo! Colonel Wilkinson said we had got on all right for six years and could go on for longer! "Getting on all right" meant that we entirely depended on the rainwater we caught from the roof and on two pails a day of well water from the farm for which we paid a fabulous price. He was at last persuaded to fulfil his promise and the waterworks people built a wonderful erection, a cross between a Noah's ark and a sardine-box perched up on four water-pipes of great height. This in some odd manner supplied us with water, but also spoiled the views for miles round being of an aggressive sea-green hue. When we had our water we had not done, for in the winter it froze. Well I remember one Christmas morning when we woke up to find ourselves waterless. Fortunately we had had hot-bottles, and the kettle had been left on the fire, and with this the Christmas dinner was cooked.

*   *   *

E. M. FORSTER

Interview[†]

INTERVIEWERS: To begin with, may we ask you again, why did you never finish "Arctic Summer"?[1]

FORSTER: I have really answered this question in the foreword I wrote for the reading.[2] The crucial passage was this:

". . .whether these problems are solved or not, there remains a still graver one. What is going to happen? I had got my antithesis all right, the antithesis between the civilized man, who hopes for an Arctic Summer in which there is time to get things done, and the heroic man. But I had not settled what is going to happen, and that is why the novel remains a fragment. The novelist should, I think, always settle when he starts what is going to happen, what his major event is to be. He may alter this event as he approaches it, indeed he probably will, indeed he probably had better, or the novel becomes tied up and tight. But the sense of a solid mass ahead, a mountain round or over or through which (*he interposed*, "in this case it would be *through*") the story must somehow go, is most valuable and, for the novels I've tried to write, essential."

* * *

INTERVIEWERS: You spoke of antitheses in your novels. Do you regard these as essential to any novel you might write?

FORSTER: Let me think. . . . There was one in *Howards End*. Perhaps a rather subtler one in *The Longest Journey*.

INTERVIEWERS: Would you agree that all your novels not only deal with some dilemma but are intended to be both true and useful in regard to it—so that if you felt a certain dilemma was too extreme, its incompatibles too impossible to reconcile, you wouldn't write about it?

FORSTER: True and lovable would be my antithesis. I don't think useful comes into it. I'm not sure that I would be put off simply because a dilemma that I wanted to treat was insoluble; at least, I don't think I should be.

INTERVIEWERS: While we are on the subject of the planning of novels, has a novel ever taken an unexpected direction?

† From *Writers at Work, First Series* by Malcolm Cowley, editor (pp. 26–30, 32–34). Copyright © 1957, 1958 by The Paris Review, renewed © 1985 by Malcolm Cowley, © 1986 by The Paris Review. Used by permission of Viking Penguin, a division of Penguin Books USA, Inc. The interviewers were Forster's biographer P. N. Furbank and F. J. H. Haskell, a friend and professor of art history at Oxford. The interview took place in Forster's rooms at King's College, Cambridge, on 20 June 1952.
1. An unfinished novel that Forster began in 1911, soon after the publication of *Howards End*, but abandoned two years later. He was not to publish another novel until *A Passage to India* (1924).
2. A reading of *Arctic Summer* he gave in 1951.

E. M. FORSTER

FORSTER: Of course, that wonderful thing, a character running away with you—which happens to everyone—that's happened to me, I'm afraid.

INTERVIEWERS: Can you describe any technical problem that especially bothered you in one of the published novels?

FORSTER: I had trouble with the junction of Rickie and Stephen. [The hero of *The Longest Journey* and his half-brother.] How to make them intimate, I mean. I fumbled about a good deal. It is all right once they are together. . . . I didn't know how to get Helen to Howards End. That part is all contrived. There are too many letters. And again, it is all right once she is there. But ends always give me trouble.

INTERVIEWERS: Why is that?

FORSTER: It is partly what I was talking about a moment ago. Characters run away with you, and so won't fit on to what is coming.

* * *

INTERVIEWERS: To leave technical questions for a moment, have you ever described any type of situation of which you have had no personal knowledge?

FORSTER: The home-life of Leonard and Jacky in *Howards End* is one case. I knew nothing about that. I believe I brought it off.

* * *

INTERVIEWERS: I have also never felt comfortable about Leonard Bast's seduction of Helen in *Howards End*. It is such a sudden affair. It seems as though we are not told enough about it for it to be convincing. One might say that it came off allegorically but not realistically.

FORSTER: I think you may be right. I did it like that out of a wish to have surprises. It has to be a surprise for Margaret, and this was best done by making it a surprise for the reader too. Too much may have been sacrificed to this.

INTERVIEWERS: A more general question. Would you admit to there being any symbolism in your novels? Lionel Trilling rather seems to imply that there is, in his book on you—symbolism, that is, as distinct from allegory or parable. "Mrs. Moore," he says, "will act with a bad temper to Adela, but her actions will somehow have a good echo; and her children will be her further echo. . . ."

FORSTER: No, I didn't think of that. But mightn't there be some of it elsewhere? Can you try me with some more examples?

INTERVIEWERS: The tree at Howards End? [A wych-elm, frequently referred to in the novel.]

FORSTER: Yes, that was symbolical; it was the genius of the house.

INTERVIEWERS: What was the significance of Mrs. Wilcox's influence on the other characters after her death?

FORSTER: I was interested in the imaginative effect of someone alive, but in a different way from other characters—living in other lives.

*   *   *

INTERVIEWERS: Do all your characters have real life models?

FORSTER: In no book have I got down more than the people I like, the person I think I am, and the people who irritate me. This puts me among the large body of authors who are not really novelists, and have to get on as best they can with these three categories. We have not the power of observing the variety of life and describing it dispassionately. There are a few who have done this. Tolstoi was one, wasn't he?

INTERVIEWERS: Can you say anything about the process of turning a real person into a fictional one?

FORSTER: A useful trick is to look back upon such a person with half-closed eyes, fully describing certain characteristics. I am left with about two-thirds of a human being and can get to work. A likeness isn't aimed at and couldn't be obtained, because a man's only himself amidst the particular circumstances of his life and not amid other circumstances. So that * * * to ask one and one-half Miss Dickinsons how Helen should comport herself with an illegitimate baby would have ruined the atmosphere and the book. When all goes well, the original material soon disappears, and a character who belongs to the book and nowhere else emerges.

*   *   *

INTERVIEWERS: What degree of reality do your characters have for you after you have finished writing about them?

FORSTER: Very variable. There are some I like thinking about. Rickie and Stephen, and Margaret Schlegel—they are characters whose fortunes I have been interested to follow. It doesn't matter if they died in the novel or not.

*   *   *

INTERVIEWERS: How far aware are you of your own technical clevernesses in general?

FORSTER: We keep coming back to that. People will not realize how little conscious one is of these things; how one flounders about. They want us to be so much better informed than we are. If critics could only have a course on writers' *not* thinking things out—a course of lectures . . . (*He smiled.*)

INTERVIEWERS: You have said elsewhere that the authors you have learned most from were Jane Austen and Proust. What did you learn from Jane Austen technically?

FORSTER: I learned the possibilities of domestic humor. I was more ambitious than she was, of course; I tried to hitch it on to other things.

INTERVIEWERS: And from Proust?

FORSTER: I learned ways of looking at character from him. The modern subconscious way. He gave me as much of the modern way as I could take. I couldn't read Freud or Jung myself; it had to be filtered to me.

INTERVIEWERS: Did any other novelists influence you technically? What about Meredith?

FORSTER: I admired him—*The Egoist* and the better constructed bits of the other novels; but then that's not the same as his influencing me. I don't know if he did that. He did things I couldn't do. What I admired was the sense of one thing opening into another. You go into a room with him, and then that opens into another room, and that into a further one.

*   *   *

E. M. FORSTER

From His *Commonplace Book*[†]

Howards End my best novel and approaching a good novel. Very elaborate and all pervading plot that is seldom tiresome or forced, range of characters, social sense, wit, wisdom, colour. Have only just discovered why I don't care for it: not a single character in it for whom I care. In *Where Angels* Gino, in *L. J.* Stephen, in *R. with V.* Lucy, in *P. to I.* Aziz . . .and Maurice and Alec. . . . and Lionel and Cocoa. . . . Perhaps the house in *H.E.*, for which I once did care, took the place of people and now that I no longer care for it their barrenness has become evident. I feel pride in the achievement, but cannot love it, and occasionally the swish of the skirts and the non-sexual embraces irritate. Perhaps too I am more hedonistic than I was, and resent not being caused pleasure personally.   —May 1958

E. M. FORSTER

People[‡]

Having discussed the story—that simple and fundamental aspect of the novel—we can turn to a more interesting topic: the actors. We need not ask what happened next, but to whom did it happen; the novelist will be appealing to our intelligence and imagination, not merely to our curiosity. A new emphasis enters his voice: emphasis upon value.

*   *   *

[†] From E. M. Forster, *Commonplace Book*, ed. Philip Gardner (Stanford: Stanford UP, 1985) 203–4. Reprinted by permission of King's College, Cambridge, and The Society of Authors as the literary representatives of the E. M. Forster Estate.

[‡] Excerpts from *Aspects of the Novel* by E. M. Forster, copyright 1927 by Harcourt Brace & Company and renewed 1954 by E. M. Forster, reprinted by permission of the publisher and The Provost and Scholars of King's College, Cambridge 1997.

Since the novelist is himself a human being, there is an affinity between him and his subject matter which is absent in many other forms of art. The historian is also linked, though, as we shall see, less intimately. The painter and sculptor need not be linked: that is to say they need not represent human beings unless they wish, no more need the poet, while the musician cannot represent them even if he wishes, without the help of a programme. The novelist, unlike many of his colleagues, makes up a number of word-masses roughly describing himself (roughly: niceties shall come later), gives them names and sex, assigns them plausible gestures, and causes them to speak by the use of inverted commas, and perhaps to behave consistently. These word-masses are his characters. They do not come thus coldly to his mind, they may be created in delirious excitement, still, their nature is conditioned by what he guesses about other people, and about himself, and is further modified by the other aspects of his work. This last point—the relation of characters to the other aspects of the novel—will form the subject of a future enquiry. At present we are occupied with their relation to actual life. What is the difference between people in a novel and people like the novelist or like you, or like me, or Queen Victoria?

There is bound to be a difference. If a character in a novel is exactly like Queen Victoria—not rather like but exactly like—then it actually is Queen Victoria, and the novel, or all of it that the character touches, becomes a memoir. A memoir is history, it is based on evidence. A novel is based on evidence + or − x, the unknown quantity being the temperament of the novelist, and the unknown quantity always modifies the effect of the evidence, and sometimes transforms it entirely.

The historian deals with actions, and with the characters of men only so far as he can deduce them from their actions. He is quite as much concerned with character as the novelist, but he can only know of its existence when it shows on the surface. If Queen Victoria had not said, "We are not amused," her neighbours at table would not have known she was not amused, and her ennui could never have been announced to the public. She might have frowned, so that they would have deduced her state from that—looks and gestures are also historical evidence. But if she remained impassive—what would any one know? The hidden life is, by definition, hidden. The hidden life that appears in external signs is hidden no longer, has entered the realm of action. And it is the function of the novelist to reveal the hidden life at its source: to tell us more about Queen Victoria than could be known, and thus to produce a character who is not the Queen Victoria of history.

* * *

This is perhaps a roundabout way of saying what every British schoolboy knew, that the historian records whereas the novelist must create. Still, it is a profitable roundabout, for it brings out the fundamental difference between people in daily life and people in books. In daily life we never understand each other, neither complete clairvoyance nor complete confessional exists. We know each other approximately, by external signs, and these serve well enough as a basis for society and even for intimacy. But people in a novel can be understood completely by the reader, if the novelist wishes; their inner as well as their outer life can be exposed. And this is why they often seem more definite than characters in history, or even our own friends; we have been told all about them that can be told; even if they are imperfect or unreal they do not contain any secrets, whereas our friends do and must, mutual secrecy being one of the conditions of life upon this globe.

*   *   *

Love. You all know how enormously love bulks in novels, and will probably agree with me that it has done them harm and made them monotonous. Why has this particular experience, especially in its sex form, been transplanted in such generous quantities? If you think of a novel in the vague you think of a love interest—of a man and woman who want to be united and perhaps succeed. If you think of your own life in the vague, or of a group of lives, you are left with a very different and a more complex impression.

There would seem to be two reasons why love, even in good sincere novels, is unduly prominent.

Firstly, when the novelist ceases to design his characters and begins to create them—"love" in any or all of its aspects becomes important in his mind, and without intending to do so he makes his characters unduly sensitive to it—unduly in the sense that they would not trouble so much in life. The constant sensitiveness of characters for each other—even in writers called robust like Fielding—is remarkable, and has no parallel in life, except among people who have plenty of leisure. Passion, intensity at moments—yes, but not this constant awareness, this endless readjusting, this ceaseless hunger. I believe that these are the reflections of the novelist's own state of mind while he composes, and that the predominance of love in novels is partly because of this.

A second reason; which logically comes into another part of our enquiry, but it shall be noted here. Love, like death, is congenial to a novelist because it ends a book conveniently. He can make it a permanency, and his readers easily acquiesce, because one of the illusions attached to love is that it will be permanent. Not has been—will be. All history, all our experience, teaches us that no human relationship is constant, it is as unstable as the living beings who compose it, and they must balance like jugglers if it is to remain; if it is constant it is no longer a human relationship but a social habit, the emphasis in it has passed from love to marriage. All this we know, yet we cannot bear to apply our bitter knowledge to the future; the future is to be so different; the perfect person is to come along, or the person we know already is to become perfect. There are to be no changes, no necessity for alertness. We are to be happy or even perhaps miserable for ever and ever. Any strong emotion brings with it the illusion of permanence, and the novelists have seized upon this. They usually end their books with marriage, and we do not object because we lend them our dreams.

Here we must conclude our comparison of those two allied species, Homo Sapiens and Homo Fictus. Homo Fictus is more elusive than his cousin. He is created in the minds of hundreds of different novelists, who have conflicting methods of gestation, so one must not generalize. Still, one can say a little about him. He is generally born off, he is capable of dying on, he wants little food or sleep, he is tirelessly occupied with human relationships. And—most important—we can know more about him than we can know about any of our fellow creatures, because his creator and narrator are one. Were we equipped for hyperbole we might exclaim at this point: "If God could tell the story of the Universe, the Universe would become fictitious."

For this is the principle involved.

*   *   *

* * * And now we can get a definition as to when a character in a book is real: it is real when the novelist knows everything about it. He may not choose to tell us all he knows—many of the facts, even of the kind we call obvious, may be hidden. But he will give us the feeling that though the character has not been explained, it is explicable, and we get from this a reality of a kind we can never get in daily life.

For human intercourse, as soon as we look at it for its own sake and not as a social adjunct, is seen to be haunted by a spectre. We cannot understand each other, except in a rough and ready way; we cannot reveal ourselves, even when we want to; what we call intimacy is only a makeshift; perfect knowledge is an illusion. But in the novel we can know people perfectly, and, apart from the general pleasure of reading, we can find here a compensation for their dimness in life. In this direction fiction is truer than history, because it goes beyond the evidence, and each of us knows from his own experience that there is something beyond the evidence, and even if the novelist has not got it correctly, well—he has tried. He can post his people in as babies, he can cause them to go on without sleep or food, he can make them be in love, love and nothing but love, provided he seems to know everything about them, provided they are his creations. That is why Moll Flanders cannot be here, that is one of the reasons why Amelia and Emma cannot be here.[1] They are people whose secret lives are visible or might be visible: we are people whose secret lives are invisible.

1. The title characters in novels by Daniel Defoe (1722), Henry Fielding (1751), and Jane Austen (1816).

And that is why novels, even when they are about wicked people, can solace us; they suggest a more comprehensible and thus a more manageable human race, they give us the illusion of perspicacity and of power.

* * *

The novelist, we are beginning to see, has a very mixed lot of ingredients to handle. There is the story, with its time-sequence of "and then . . . and then . . ."; there are ninepins about whom he might tell the story, and tell a rattling good one, but no, he prefers to tell his story about human beings; he takes over the life by values as well as the life in time. The characters arrive when evoked, but full of the spirit of mutiny. For they have these numerous parallels with people like ourselves, they try to live their own lives and are consequently often engaged in treason against the main scheme of the book. They "run away," they "get out of hand": they are creations inside a creation, and often inharmonious towards it; if they are given complete freedom they kick the book to pieces, and if they are kept too sternly in check, they revenge themselves by dying, and destroy it by intestinal decay.

* * *

No, the novelist has difficulties enough, and today we shall examine two of his devices for solving them—instinctive devices, for his methods when working are seldom the same as the methods we use when examining his work. The first device is the use of different kinds of characters. The second is connected with the point of view.

I. We may divide characters into flat and round.

Flat characters were called "humours" in the seventeenth century, and are sometimes called types, and sometimes caricatures. In their purest form, they are constructed round a single idea or quality: when there is more than one factor in them, we get the beginning of the curve towards the round. The really flat character can be expressed in one sentence such as "I never will desert Mr. Micawber."[2] There is Mrs. Micawber—she says she won't desert Mr. Micawber, she doesn't, and there she is. Or: "I must conceal, even by subterfuges, the poverty of my master's house." There is Caleb Balderstone in *The Bride of Lammermoor*.[3] He does not use the actual phrase, but it completely describes him; he has no existence outside it, no pleasures, none of the private lusts and aches that must complicate the most consistent of servitors. Whatever he does, wherever he goes, whatever lies he tells or plates he breaks, it is to conceal the poverty of his master's house. It is not his idée fixe, because there is nothing in him into which the idea can be fixed. He is the idea, and such life as he possesses radiates from its edges

2. The repeated refrain of Micawber's wife in Charles Dickens' novel *David Copperfield* (1850).
3. The comical butler in Sir Walter Scott's 1819 novel.

and from the scintillations it strikes when other elements in the novel impinge. Or take Proust. There are numerous flat characters in Proust, such as the Princess of Parma, or Legrandin.[4] Each can be expressed in a single sentence, the Princess's sentence being, "I must be particularly careful to be kind." She does nothing except to be particularly careful, and those of the other characters who are more complex than herself easily see through the kindness, since it is only a by-product of the carefulness.

One great advantage of flat characters is that they are easily recognized whenever they come in — recognized by the reader's emotional eye, not by the visual eye, which merely notes the recurrence of a proper name. In Russian novels, where they so seldom occur, they would be a decided help. It is a convenience for an author when he can strike with his full force at once, and flat characters are very useful to him, since they never need reintroducing, never run away, have not to be watched for development, and provide their own atmosphere — little luminous disks of a pre-arranged size, pushed hither and thither like counters across the void or between the stars; most satisfactory.

A second advantage is that they are easily remembered by the reader afterwards. They remain in his mind as unalterable for the reason that they were not changed by circumstances; they moved through circumstances, which gives them in retrospect a comforting quality, and preserves them when the book that produced them may decay. The Countess in *Evan Harrington* furnishes a good little example here. Let us compare our memories of her with our memories of Becky Sharp.[5] We do not remember what the Countess did or what she passed through. What is clear is her figure and the formula that surrounds it, namely, "Proud as we are of dear papa, we must conceal his memory." All her rich humour proceeds from this. She is a flat character. Becky is round. She, too, is on the make, but she cannot be summed up in a single phrase, and we remember her in connection with the great scenes through which she passed and as modified by those scenes — that is to say, we do not remember her so easily because she waxes and wanes and has facets like a human being. All of us, even the sophisticated, yearn for permanence, and to the unsophisticated permanence is the chief excuse for a work of art. We all want books to endure, to be refuges, and their inhabitants to be always the same, and flat characters tend to justify themselves on this account.

✻ ✻ ✻

✻ ✻ ✻ A novel that is at all complex often requires flat people as well as round, and the outcome of their collisions parallels life. ✻ ✻ ✻ The

---

4. A courteous member of the aristocracy and a snobbish social climber who are recurring minor characters in Proust's multivolume novel *Remembrance of Things Past* (1913–27).
5. The countess is a socially ambitious adventuress in George Meredith's novel of 1860. Becky Sharp is similarly tireless in her efforts to rise above her station in William Makepeace Thackeray's *Vanity Fair* (1848).

case of Dickens is significant. Dickens' people are nearly all flat (Pip and David Copperfield attempt roundness, but so diffidently that they seem more like bubbles than solids).[6] Nearly every one can be summed up in a sentence, and yet there is this wonderful feeling of human depth. Probably the immense vitality of Dickens causes his characters to vibrate a little, so that they borrow his life and appear to lead one of their own. It is a conjuring trick; at any moment we may look at Mr. Pickwick edgeways and find him no thicker than a gramophone record. But we never get the sideway view. Mr. Pickwick is far too adroit and well trained. He always has the air of weighing something, and when he is put into the cupboard of the young ladies' school he seems as heavy as Falstaff in the buck-basket at Windsor.[7] Part of the genius of Dickens is that he does use types and caricatures, people whom we recognize the instant they re-enter, and yet achieves effects that are not mechanical and a vision of humanity that is not shallow. Those who dislike Dickens have an excellent case. He ought to be bad. He is actually one of our big writers, and his immense success with types suggests that there may be more in flatness than the severer critics admit.

* * *

For we must admit that flat people are not in themselves as big achievements as round ones, and also that they are best when they are comic. A serious or tragic flat character is apt to be a bore. Each time he enters crying "Revenge!" or "My heart bleeds for humanity!" or whatever his formula is, our hearts sink. One of the romances of a popular contemporary writer is constructed round a Sussex farmer who says, "I'll plough up that bit of gorse." There is the farmer, there is the gorse; he says he'll plough it up, he does plough it up, but it is not like saying "I'll never desert Mr. Micawber," because we are so bored by his consistency that we do not care whether he succeeds with the gorse or fails. If his formula was analysed and connected up with the rest of the human outfit, we should not be bored any longer, the formula would cease to be the man and become an obsession in the man; that is to say he would have turned from a flat farmer into a round one. It is only round people who are fit to perform tragically for any length of time and can move us to any feelings except humour and appropriateness.

* * *

* * * The test of a round character is whether it is capable of surprising in a convincing way. If it never surprises, it is flat. If it does not con-

---

6. Pip is the narrator and main character in *Great Expectations* (1861), David Copperfield the main character of the 1850 novel by the same name.
7. The rotund hero of *Pickwick Papers* (1837) must consent to be locked in a closet before he is allowed to speak to the excessively proper mistress of Westgate House, a boarding school. In Shakespeare's comedy *The Merry Wives of Windsor* (1602), the corpulent Sir John Falstaff implausibly hides in a basket of dirty laundry to escape a jealous husband and is carried off by an unspecified number of servants (3.3).

vince, it is a flat pretending to be round. It has the incalculability of life about it—life within the pages of a book. And by using it sometimes alone, more often in combination with the other kind, the novelist achieves his task of acclimatization and harmonizes the human race with the other aspects of his work.

II. Now for the second device: the point of view from which the story may be told.

To some critics this is the fundamental device of novel-writing. "The whole intricate question of method, in the craft of fiction," says Mr. Percy Lubbock, "I take to be governed by the question of the *point of view*—the question of the relation in which the narrator stands to the story." And his book *The Craft of Fiction* examines various points of view with genius and insight.[8] The novelist, he says, can either describe the characters from outside, as an impartial or partial onlooker; or he can assume omniscience and describe them from within; or he can place himself in the position of one of them and affect to be in the dark as to the motives of the rest; or there are certain intermediate attitudes.

Those who follow him will lay a sure foundation for the æsthetics of fiction—a foundation which I cannot for a moment promise. This is a ramshackly survey and for me the "whole intricate question of method" resolves itself not into formulæ but into the power of the writer to bounce the reader into accepting what he says—a power which Mr. Lubbock admits and admires, but locates at the edge of the problem instead of at the centre. I should put it plumb in the centre. Look how Dickens bounces us in *Bleak House*. Chapter I of *Bleak House* is omniscient. Dickens takes us into the Court of Chancery and rapidly explains all the people there. In Chapter II he is partially omniscient. We still use his eyes, but for some unexplained reason they begin to grow weak: he can explain Sir Leicester Dedlock to us, part of Lady Dedlock but not all, and nothing of Mr. Tulkinghorn. In Chapter III he is even more reprehensible: he goes straight across into the dramatic method and inhabits a young lady, Esther Summerson. "I have a great deal of difficulty in beginning to write my portion of these pages, for I know I am not clever," pipes up Esther, and continues in this strain with consistency and competence, so long as she is allowed to hold the pen. At any moment the author of her being may snatch it from her, and run about taking notes himself, leaving her seated goodness knows where, and employed we do not care how. Logically, *Bleak House* is all to pieces, but Dickens bounces us, so that we do not mind the shiftings of the view point.

Critics are more apt to object than readers. Zealous for the novel's eminence, they are a little too apt to look out for problems that shall be peculiar to it, and differentiate it from the drama; they feel it ought to have its

8. In *The Craft of Fiction* (1921), Lubbock tries to demonstrate systematically the claim made by the novelist Henry James that the art of the novel is best realized when the action is portrayed through the consciousness of a central character (his or her "point of view").

own technical troubles before it can be accepted as an independent art; and since the problem of a point of view certainly is peculiar to the novel they have rather overstressed it. I do not myself think it is so important as a proper mixture of characters—a problem which the dramatist is up against also. And the novelist must bounce us; that is imperative.

*   *   *

* * * Indeed this power to expand and contract perception (of which the shifting view point is a symptom), this right to intermittent knowledge:—I find it one of the great advantages of the novel-form, and it has a parallel in our perception of life. We are stupider at some times than others; we can enter into people's minds occasionally but not always, because our own minds get tired; and this intermittence lends in the long run variety and colour to the experiences we receive. A quantity of novelists, English novelists especially, have behaved like this to the people in their books: played fast and loose with them, and I cannot see why they should be censured.

They must be censured if we catch them at it at the time. That is quite true, and out of it arises another question: may the writer take the reader into his confidence about his characters? Answer has already been indicated: better not. It is dangerous, it generally leads to a drop in the temperature, to intellectual and emotional laxity, and worse still to facetiousness, and to a friendly invitation to see how the figures hook up behind. "Doesn't A look nice—she always was my favourite." "Let's think of why B does that—perhaps there's more in him than meets the eye—yes, see—he has a heart of gold—having given you this peep at it I'll pop it back—I don't think he's noticed." "And C—he always was the mystery man." Intimacy is gained but at the expense of illusion and nobility. It is like standing a man a drink so that he may not criticize your opinions. With all respect to Fielding and Thackeray it is devastating, it is bar-parlour chattiness, and nothing has been more harmful to the novels of the past. To take your reader into your confidence about the universe is a different thing. It is not dangerous for a novelist to draw back from his characters, as Hardy and Conrad do, and to generalize about the conditions under which he thinks life is carried on.[9] It is confidences about the individual people that do harm, and beckon the reader away from the people to an examination of the novelist's mind. Not much is ever found in it at such a moment, for it is never in the creative state: the mere process of saying, "Come along, let's have a chat," has cooled it down.

*   *   *

9. In Henry Fielding's novel *Tom Jones* (1749) and in Thackeray's *Vanity Fair*, the narrator often offers editorial commentary on the characters. The narrators in Thomas Hardy's and Joseph Conrad's novels frequently make philosophical observations about human existence, nature, and morality.

E. M. FORSTER

Not Listening to Music[†]

Listening to music is such a muddle that one scarcely knows how to start describing it. The first point to get clear in my own case is that during the greater part of every performance I do not attend. The nice sounds make me think of something else. I wool-gather most of the time, and am surprised that others don't. Professional critics can listen to a piece as consistently and as steadily as if they were reading a chapter in a novel. This seems to me an amazing feat, and probably they only achieve it through intellectual training; that is to say, they find in the music the equivalent of a plot; they are following the ground bass or expecting the theme to re-enter in the dominant, and so on, and this keeps them on the rails. But I fly off every minute: after a bar or two I think how musical I am, or of something smart I might have said in conversation; or I wonder what the composer—dead a couple of centuries—can be feeling as the flames on the altar still flicker up; or how soon an H.E.[1] bomb would extinguish them. Not to mention more obvious distractions: the tilt of the soprano's chin or chins; the antics of the conductor, that impassioned beetle, especially when it is night time and he waves his shards;[2] the affectation of the pianist when he takes a top note with difficulty, as if he too were a soprano; the backs of the chairs; the bumps on the ceiling; the extreme physical ugliness of the audience. A classical audience is surely the plainest collection of people anywhere assembled for any common purpose; contributing my quota, I have the right to point this out. Compare us with a gang of navvies or with an office staff, and you will be appalled. This, too, distracts me.

What do I hear during the intervals when I do attend? Two sorts of music. They melt into each other all the time, and are not easy to christen, but I will call one of them "music that reminds me of something," and the other "music itself." I used to be very fond of music that reminded me of something, and especially fond of Wagner.[3] With Wagner I always knew where I was; he never let the fancy roam; he ordained that one phrase should recall the ring, another the sword, another the blameless fool and so on; he was as precise in his indications as an oriental dancer. Since he is a great poet, that did not matter, but I accepted his leitmotiv system much too reverently and forced

† "Not Listening to Music" from *Two Cheers for Democracy*, copyright 1939 and renewed 1967 by E. M. Forster, reprinted by permission of Harcourt Brace & Company and The Provost and Scholars of King's College, Cambridge 1997.
1. High explosive.
2. Hardened protective wing covers.
3. 3. Richard Wagner (1813–83), German composer of powerfully emotional, theatrical operas based on German mythology. He pioneered the use of the leitmotiv, a brief passage of music connected to a character or incident and repeated to call it to mind.

it on to other composers whom it did not suit, such as Beethoven and Franck. I thought that music must be the better for having a meaning. I think so still, but am less clear as to what "a meaning" is. In those days it was either a non-musical object, such as a sword or a blameless fool, or a non-musical emotion, such as fear, lust, or resignation. When music reminded me of something which was not music, I supposed it was getting me somewhere. "How like Monet!" I thought when listening to Debussy, and "How like Debussy!" when looking at Monet.[4] I translated sounds into colours, saw the piccolo as apple-green, and the trumpets as scarlet. The arts were to be enriched by taking in one another's washing.

I still listen to some music this way. For instance, the slow start of Beethoven's Seventh Symphony invokes a grey-green tapestry of hunting scenes, and the slow movement of his Fourth Piano Concerto (the dialogue between piano and orchestra) reminds me of the dialogue between Orpheus and the Furies in Gluck. The climax of the first movement of the Appassionata (the "più allegro") seems to me sexual, although I can detect no sex in the Kreutzer, nor have I come across anyone who could, except Tolstoy.[5] That disappointing work, Brahms' Violin Concerto, promises me clear skies at the opening, and only when the violin has squealed up in the air for page after page is the promise falsified. Wolf's "Ganymed" does give me sky—stratosphere beyond stratosphere. In these cases and in many others music reminds me of something non-musical, and I fancy that to do so is part of its job. Only a purist would condemn all visual parallels, all emotional labellings, all programmes.

Yet there is a danger. Music that reminds does open the door to that imp of the concert hall, inattention. To think of a grey-green tapestry is not very different from thinking of the backs of the chairs. We gather a superior wool from it, still we do wool-gather, and the sounds slip by blurred. The sounds! It is for them that we come, and the closer we can get up against them the better. So I do prefer "music itself" and listen to it and for it as far as possible. In this connection, I will try to analyse a mishap that has recently overtaken the Coriolanus Overture. I used to listen to the Coriolanus for "itself," conscious when it passed of something important and agitating, but not defining further. Now I learn that Wagner, endorsed by Sir Donald Tovey, has provided it with a Programme: the opening bars indicate the hero's decision to destroy the Volscii, then a sweet tune for female influence, then the dotted-quaver-restlessness of indecision. This seems indisputable, and there is no doubt

4. Claude Monet (1840–1926), French impressionist painter; Claude Debussy (1862–1918), French composer and advocate of musical impressionism.
5. Christoph Gluck (1714–87), German composer of the opera *Orfeo ed Eurydice* (1762) about the Greek mythological figure Orpheus, who descends to Hades in a failed attempt to rescue his wife, Eurydice. *The Kreutzer Sonata* (1891), a short novel in which Leo Tolstoy (1828–1910), attributes powers of sensual dissolution to Beethoven's piece of music.

that this was, or was almost, Beethoven's intention.[6] All the same, I have lost my Coriolanus. Its largeness and freedom have gone. The exquisite sounds have been hardened like a road that has been tarred for traffic. One has to go somewhere down them, and to pass through the same domestic crisis to the same military impasse, each time the overture is played.

Music is so very queer that an amateur is bound to get muddled when writing about it. It seems to be more "real" than anything, and to survive when the rest of civilisation decays. In these days I am always thinking of it with relief. It can never be ruined or nationalised. So that the music which is untrammelled and untainted by reference is obviously the best sort of music to listen to; we get nearer the centre of reality. Yet though it is untainted, it is never abstract; it is not like mathematics, even when it uses them. The Goldberg Variations, the last Beethoven Sonata, the Franck Quartet, the Schumann Piano Quintet and the Fourth Symphonies of Tchaikovsky and of Brahms certainly have a message. Though what on earth is it? I shall get tied up trying to say. There's an insistence in music—expressed largely through rhythm; there's a sense that it is trying to push across at us something which is neither an esthetic pattern nor a sermon. That's what I listen for specially.

So music that is itself seems on the whole better than music that reminds. And now to end with an important point: my own performances upon the piano. These grow worse yearly, but never will I give them up. For one thing, they compel me to attend—no wool-gathering or thinking myself clever here—and they drain off all non-musical matter. For another thing, they teach me a little about construction. I see what becomes of a phrase, how it is transformed or returned, sometimes bottom upward, and get some notion of the relation of keys. Playing Beethoven, as I generally do, I grow familiar with his tricks, his impatience, his sudden softnesses, his dropping of a tragic theme one semitone, his love, when tragic, for the key of C minor, and his aversion to the key of B major. This gives me a physical approach to Beethoven which cannot be gained through the slough of "appreciation." Even when people play as badly as I do, they should continue: it will help them to listen.

6. Wagner wrote an appreciative analysis of Beethoven's overture in which he described Coriolanus as the archetypal figure of untamable force and uncompromising honesty. The Volscii were a warlike people of ancient Italy whom the Romans subdued. Sir Donald Tovey (1875–1940) was a pianist, critic, scholar, and professor of music at the University of Edinburgh.

The Author on Politics

E. M. FORSTER
From Notes on the English Character[†]

First Note. I had better let the cat out of the bag at once and record my opinion that the character of the English is essentially middle-class. There is a sound historical reason for this, for, since the end of the eighteenth century, the middle classes have been the dominant force in our community. They gained wealth by the Industrial Revolution, political power by the Reform Bill of 1832; they are connected with the rise and organization of the British Empire; they are responsible for the literature of the nineteenth century. Solidity, caution, integrity, efficiency. Lack of imagination, hypocrisy. These qualities characterize the middle classes in every country, but in England they are national characteristics also, because only in England have the middle classes been in power for one hundred and fifty years. Napoleon, in his rude way, called us "a nation of shopkeepers." We prefer to call ourselves "a great commercial nation"—it sounds more dignified—but the two phrases amount to the same. Of course there are other classes: there is an aristocracy, there are the poor. But it is on the middle classes that the eye of the critic rests—just as it rests on the poor in Russia and on the aristocracy in Japan. Russia is symbolized by the peasant or by the factory worker; Japan by the samurai; the national figure of England is Mr. Bull with his top hat, his comfortable clothes, his substantial stomach, and his substantial balance at the bank. Saint George may caper on banners and in the speeches of politicians, but it is John Bull who delivers the goods. And even Saint George—if Gibbon is correct—wore a top hat once; he was an army contractor and supplied indifferent bacon.[1] It all amounts to the same in the end.

Second Note. Just as the heart of England is the middle classes, so the heart of the middle classes is the public-school system.[2] This extraordi-

---

† Excerpt from *Abinger Harvest*, copyright © 1936 and renewed 1964 by E. M. Forster, reprinted by permission of Harcourt Brace & Company and The Provost and Scholars of King's College, Cambridge 1997. This essay was originally published in 1926.

1. John Bull, a symbol of the typical Englishman, invented by John Arbuthnot in his allegorical *History of John Bull* (1712). Saint George, the dragon slayer, is the patron saint of England. Edward Gibbon (1737–94) wrote *The History of the Decline and Fall of the Roman Empire* (1776–88).
2. English public schools are elite private institutions, analogous to American preparatory schools.

nary institution is local. It does not even exist all over the British Isles. It is unknown in Ireland, almost unknown in Scotland (countries excluded from my survey), and though it may inspire other great institutions — Aligarh, for example, and some of the schools in the United States — it remains unique, because it was created by the Anglo-Saxon middle classes, and can flourish only where they flourish. How perfectly it expresses their character — far better, for instance, than does the university, into which social and spiritual complexities have already entered. With its boarding-houses, its compulsory games, its system of prefects and fagging, its insistence on good form and on *esprit de corps*, it produces a type whose weight is out of all proportion to its numbers.

On leaving his school, the boy either sets to work at once — goes into the army or into business, or emigrates — or else proceeds to the university, and after three or four years there enters some other profession — becomes a barrister, doctor, civil servant, schoolmaster, or journalist. (If through some mishap he does not become a manual worker or an artist.) In all these careers his education, or the absence of it, influences him. Its memories influence him also. Many men look back on their school days as the happiest of their lives. They remember with regret that golden time when life, though hard, was not yet complex; when they all worked together and played together and thought together, so far as they thought at all; when they were taught that school is the world in miniature, and believed that no one can love his country who does not love his school. And they prolong that time as best they can by joining their Old Boys' society; indeed, some of them remain Old Boys and nothing else for the rest of their lives. They attribute all good to the school. They worship it. They quote the remark that "the battle of Waterloo was won on the playing-fields of Eton." It is nothing to them that the remark is inapplicable historically and was never made by the Duke of Wellington, and that the Duke of Wellington was an Irishman. They go on quoting it because it expresses their sentiments; they feel that if the Duke of Wellington didn't make it he ought to have, and if he wasn't an Englishman he ought to have been. And they go forth into a world that is not entirely composed of public-school men or even of Anglo-Saxons, but of men who are as various as the sands of the sea; into a world of whose richness and subtlety they have no conception. They go forth into it with well-developed bodies, fairly developed minds, and undeveloped hearts. And it is this undeveloped heart that is largely responsible for the difficulties of Englishmen abroad. An undeveloped heart — not a cold one. The difference is important, and on it my next note will be based.

For it is not that the Englishman can't feel — it is that he is afraid to feel. He has been taught at his public school that feeling is bad form. He must not express great joy or sorrow, or even open his mouth too wide when he talks—his pipe might fall out if he did. He must bottle up his emotions, or let them out only on a very special occasion.

Once upon a time (this is an anecdote) I went for a week's holiday on the Continent with an Indian friend. We both enjoyed ourselves and were sorry when the week was over, but on parting our behaviour was absolutely different. He was plunged in despair. He felt that because the holiday was over all happiness was over until the world ended. He could not express his sorrow too much. But in me the Englishman came out strong. I reflected that we should meet again in a month or two, and could write in the interval if we had anything to say; and under these circumstances I could not see what there was to make a fuss about. It wasn't as if we were parting forever or dying. "Buck up," I said, "do buck up." He refused to buck up, and I left him plunged in gloom.

The conclusion of the anecdote is even more instructive. For when we met the next month our conversation threw a good deal of light on the English character. I began by scolding my friend. I told him that he had been wrong to feel and display so much emotion upon so slight an occasion; that it was inappropriate. The word "inappropriate" roused him to fury. "What?" he cried. "Do you measure out your emotions as if they were potatoes?" I did not like the simile of the potatoes, but after a moment's reflection I said, "Yes, I do; and what's more, I think I ought to. A small occasion demands a little emotion, just as a large occasion demands a great one. I would like my emotions to be appropriate. This may be measuring them like potatoes, but it is better than slopping them about like water from a pail, which is what you did." He did not like the simile of the pail. "If those are your opinions, they part us forever," he cried, and left the room. Returning immediately, he added: "No—but your whole attitude toward emotion is wrong. Emotion has nothing to do with appropriateness. It matters only that it shall be sincere. I happened to feel deeply. I showed it. It doesn't matter whether I ought to have felt deeply or not."

This remark impressed me very much. Yet I could not agree with it, and said that I valued emotion as much as he did, but used it differently; if I poured it out on small occasions I was afraid of having none left for the great ones, and of being bankrupt at the crises of life. Note the word "bankrupt." I spoke as a member of a prudent middle-class nation, always anxious to meet my liabilities. But my friend spoke as an Oriental, and the Oriental has behind him a tradition, not of middle-class prudence, but of kingly munificence and splendour. He feels his resources are endless, just as John Bull feels his are finite. As regards material resources, the Oriental is clearly unwise. Money isn't endless. If we spend or give away all the money we have, we haven't any more, and must take the consequences, which are frequently unpleasant. But, as regards the resources of the spirit, he may be right. The emotions may be endless. The more we express them, the more we may have to express.

> True love in this differs from gold and clay,
> That to divide is not to take away,

says Shelley.[3] Shelley, at all events, believes that the wealth of the spirit is endless; that we may express it copiously, passionately, and always; and that we can never feel sorrow or joy too acutely.

* * *

There is one more consideration—a most important one. If the English nature is cold, how is it that it has produced a great literature and a literature that is particularly great in poetry? Judged by its prose, English literature would not stand in the first rank. It is its poetry that raises it to the level of Greek, Persian, or French. And yet the English are supposed to be so unpoetical. How is this? The nation that produced the Elizabethan drama and the Lake Poets cannot be a cold, unpoetical nation. We can't get fire out of ice. Since literature always rests upon national character, there must be in the English nature hidden springs of fire to produce the fire we see. The warm sympathy, the romance, the imagination, that we look for in Englishmen whom we meet, and too often vainly look for, must exist in the nation as a whole, or we could not have this outburst of national song. An undeveloped heart—not a cold one.

The trouble is that the English nature is not at all easy to understand. It has a great air of simplicity, it advertises itself as simple, but the more we consider it, the greater the problems we shall encounter. People talk of the mysterious East, but the West also is mysterious. It has depths that do not reveal themselves at the first gaze. We know what the sea looks like from a distance: it is of one colour, and level, and obviously cannot contain such creatures as fish. But if we look into the sea over the edge of a boat, we see a dozen colours, and depth below depth, and fish swimming in them. That sea is the English character—apparently imperturbable and even. The depths and the colours are the English romanticism and the English sensitiveness—we do not expect to find such things, but they exist. And—to continue my metaphor—the fish are the English emotions, which are always trying to get up to the surface, but don't quite know how. For the most part we see them moving far below, distorted and obscure. Now and then they succeed and we exclaim, "Why, the Englishman has emotions! He actually can feel!" And occasionally we see that beautiful creature the flying fish, which rises out of the water altogether into the air and the sunlight. English literature is a flying fish. It is a sample of the life that goes on day after day beneath the

---

3. From "Epipsychidion" (1821), ll. 160–61, by the English Romantic poet Percy Bysshe Shelley (1792–1822).

surface; it is a proof that beauty and emotion exist in the salt, inhospitable sea.

*		*		*

The main point of these notes is that the English character is incomplete. No national character is complete. We have to look for some qualities in one part of the world and others in another. But the English character is incomplete in a way that is particularly annoying to the foreign observer. It has a bad surface—self-complacent, unsympathetic, and reserved. There is plenty of emotion further down, but it never gets used. There is plenty of brain power, but it is more often used to confirm prejudices than to dispel them. With such an equipment the Englishman cannot be popular. Only I would repeat: there is little vice in him and no real coldness. It is the machinery that is wrong.

I hope and believe myself that in the next twenty years we shall see a great change, and that the national character will alter into something that is less unique but more lovable. The supremacy of the middle classes is probably ending. What new element the working classes will introduce one cannot say, but at all events they will not have been educated at public schools. And whether these notes praise or blame the English character—that is only incidental. They are the notes of a student who is trying to get at the truth and would value the assistance of others. I believe myself that the truth is great and that it shall prevail. I have no faith in official caution and reticence. The cats are all out of their bags, and diplomacy cannot recall them. The nations *must* understand one another, and quickly; and without the interposition of their governments, for the shrinkage of the globe is throwing them into one another's arms. To that understanding these notes are a feeble contribution—notes on the English character as it has struck a novelist.

E. M. FORSTER

What I Believe[†]

I do not believe in Belief. But this is an age of faith, and there are so many militant creeds that, in self-defence, one has to formulate a creed of one's own. Tolerance, good temper and sympathy are no longer enough in a world which is rent by religious and racial persecution, in a world where ignorance rules, and science, who ought to have ruled, plays the subservient pimp. Tolerance, good temper and sympathy— they are what matter really, and if the human race is not to collapse they

† "What I Believe" from *Two Cheers for Democracy*, copyright 1939 and renewed 1967 by E. M. Forster, reprinted by permission of Harcourt Brace & Company and The Provost and Scholars of King's College, Cambridge 1997. This essay was originally published in 1938.

must come to the front before long. But for the moment they are not enough, their action is no stronger than a flower, battered beneath a military jack-boot. They want stiffening, even if the process coarsens them. Faith, to my mind, is a stiffening process, a sort of mental starch, which ought to be applied as sparingly as possible. I dislike the stuff. I do not believe in it, for its own sake, at all. Herein I probably differ from most people, who believe in Belief, and are only sorry they cannot swallow even more than they do. My law-givers are Erasmus and Montaigne, not Moses and St. Paul. My temple stands not upon Mount Moriah but in that Elysian Field where even the immoral are admitted.[1] My motto is: "Lord, I disbelieve—help thou my unbelief."

I have, however, to live in an Age of Faith—the sort of epoch I used to hear praised when I was a boy. It is extremely unpleasant really. It is bloody in every sense of the word. And I have to keep my end up in it. Where do I start?

With personal relationships. Here is something comparatively solid in a world full of violence and cruelty. Not absolutely solid, for Psychology has split and shattered the idea of a "Person," and has shown that there is something incalculable in each of us, which may at any moment rise to the surface and destroy our normal balance. We don't know what we are like. We can't know what other people are like. How, then, can we put any trust in personal relationships, or cling to them in the gathering political storm? In theory we cannot. But in practice we can and do. Though A is not unchangeably A or B unchangeably B, there can still be love and loyalty between the two. For the purpose of living one has to assume that the personality is solid, and the "self" is an entity, and to ignore all contrary evidence. And since to ignore evidence is one of the characteristics of faith, I certainly can proclaim that I believe in personal relationships.

Starting from them, I get a little order into the contemporary chaos. One must be fond of people and trust them if one is not to make a mess of life, and it is therefore essential that they should not let one down. They often do. The moral of which is that I must, myself, be as reliable as possible, and this I try to be. But reliability is not a matter of contract—that is the main difference between the world of personal relationships and the world of business relationships. It is a matter for the heart, which signs no documents. In other words, reliability is impossible unless there is a natural warmth. Most men possess this warmth, though they often have bad luck and get chilled. Most of them, even when they are politicians, *want* to keep faith. And one can, at all events, show one's own little light here, one's own poor little trembling flame,

1. Erasmus (1466?–1536), Dutch scholar and humanist. Montaigne (1533–92), French essayist. See "Tolerance," pp. 318–21, for Forster's explanation of their virtue as opponents of ideological rigidity and absolutism. Mount Moriah: the place Abraham went to sacrifice Isaac (Genesis 22.2). Elysian fields: Greek mythological paradise for heroes favored by the gods.

with the knowledge that it is not the only light that is shining in the darkness, and not the only one which the darkness does not comprehend. Personal relations are despised today. They are regarded as bourgeois luxuries, as products of a time of fair weather which is now past, and we are urged to get rid of them, and to dedicate ourselves to some movement or cause instead. I hate the idea of causes, and if I had to choose between betraying my country and betraying my friend, I hope I should have the guts to betray my country. Such a choice may scandalise the modern reader, and he may stretch out his patriotic hand to the telephone at once and ring up the police. It would not have shocked Dante, though. Dante places Brutus and Cassius in the lowest circle of Hell because they had chosen to betray their friend Julius Caesar rather than their country Rome.[2] Probably one will not be asked to make such an agonising choice. Still, there lies at the back of every creed something terrible and hard for which the worshipper may one day be required to suffer, and there is even a terror and a hardness in this creed of personal relationships, urbane and mild though it sounds. Love and loyalty to an individual can run counter to the claims of the State. When they do—down with the State, say I, which means that the State would down me.

This brings me along to Democracy, "even Love, the Beloved Republic, which feeds upon Freedom and lives." Democracy is not a Beloved Republic really, and never will be. But it is less hateful than other contemporary forms of government, and to that extent it deserves our support. It does start from the assumption that the individual is important, and that all types are needed to make a civilisation. It does not divide its citizens into the bossers and the bossed—as an efficiency-regime tends to do. The people I admire most are those who are sensitive and want to create something or discover something, and do not see life in terms of power, and such people get more of a chance under a democracy than elsewhere. They found religions, great or small, or they produce literature and art, or they do disinterested scientific research, or they may be what is called "ordinary people," who are creative in their private lives, bring up their children decently, for instance, or help their neighbours. All these people need to express themselves; they cannot do so unless society allows them liberty to do so, and the society which allows them most liberty is a democracy.

Democracy has another merit. It allows criticism, and if there is not public criticism there are bound to be hushed-up scandals. That is why I believe in the Press, despite all its lies and vulgarity, and why I believe in Parliament. Parliament is often sneered at because it is a Talking Shop. I

2. Dante (1265–1321), author of *The Divine Comedy* (c. 1308–21). In "Inferno," the poet tours consecutively deeper circles of Hell. Brutus and Cassius were among the main conspirators who assassinated the Roman emperor Julius Caesar in 44 B.C.

believe in it *because* it is a talking shop. I believe in the Private Member[3] who makes himself a nuisance. He gets snubbed and is told that he is cranky or ill-informed, but he does expose abuses which would otherwise never have been mentioned, and very often an abuse gets put right just by being mentioned. Occasionally, too, a well-meaning public official starts losing his head in the cause of efficiency, and thinks himself God Almighty. Such officials are particularly frequent in the Home Office.[4] Well, there will be questions about them in Parliament sooner or later, and then they will have to mind their steps. Whether Parliament is either a representative body or an efficient one is questionable, but I value it because it criticises and talks, and because its chatter gets widely reported.

So Two Cheers for Democracy: one because it admits variety and two because it permits criticism. Two cheers are quite enough: there is no occasion to give three. Only Love the Beloved Republic deserves that.

What about Force, though? While we are trying to be sensitive and advanced and affectionate and tolerant, an unpleasant question pops up: does not all society rest upon force? If a government cannot count upon the police and the army, how can it hope to rule? And if an individual gets knocked on the head or sent to a labour camp, of what significance are his opinions?

This dilemma does not worry me as much as it does some. I realise that all society rests upon force. But all the great creative actions, all the decent human relations, occur during the intervals when force has not managed to come to the front. These intervals are what matter. I want them to be as frequent and as lengthy as possible, and I call them "civil-isation." Some people idealise force and pull it into the foreground and worship it, instead of keeping it in the background as long as possible. I think they make a mistake, and I think that their opposites, the mystics, err even more when they declare that force does not exist. I believe that it exists, and that one of our jobs is to prevent it from getting out of its box. It gets out sooner or later, and then it destroys us and all the lovely things which we have made. But it is not out all the time, for the fortunate reason that the strong are so stupid. Consider their conduct for a moment in the Niebelung's Ring.[5] The giants there have the guns, or in other words the gold; but they do nothing with it, they do not realise that they are all-powerful, with the result that the catastrophe is delayed and the castle of Walhalla, insecure but glorious, fronts the storms. Fafnir, coiled round his hoard, grumbles and grunts; we can hear him under Europe today; the leaves of the wood already tremble, and the Bird calls its warnings uselessly. Fafnir will destroy us, but by a blessed dispensa-

3. A member of the House of Commons who does not hold a post in the prime minister's cabi-net.
4. The department of government responsible for law and order.
5. Richard Wagner's series of four operas, *The Ring of the Nibelungen* (1853–74), is based on German and Scandinavian sagas about the battles of the gods.

tion he is stupid and slow, and creation goes on just outside the poiso-
nous blast of his breath. The Nietzschean would hurry the monster up,
the mystic would say he did not exist, but Wotan, wiser than either, has-
tens to create warriors before doom declares itself. The Valkyries are
symbols not only of courage but of intelligence; they represent the
human spirit snatching its opportunity while the going is good, and one
of them even finds time to love. Brünnhilde's last song hymns the recurrence of love, and since it is the privilege of art to exaggerate, she goes
even further, and proclaims the love which is eternally triumphant and
feeds upon freedom, and lives.

So that is what I feel about force and violence. It is, alas! the ultimate
reality on this earth, but it does not always get to the front. Some people
call its absences "decadence"; I call them "civilisation" and find in such
interludes the chief justification for the human experiment. I look the
other way until fate strikes me. Whether this is due to courage or to cowardice in my own case I cannot be sure. But I know that if men had not
looked the other way in the past, nothing of any value would survive.
The people I respect most behave as if they were immortal and as if society was eternal. Both assumptions are false: both of them must be accepted as true if we are to go on eating and working and loving, and are to
keep open a few breathing holes for the human spirit. No millennium
seems likely to descend upon humanity; no better and stronger League
of Nations will be instituted; no form of Christianity and no alternative
to Christianity will bring peace to the world or integrity to the individual; no "change of heart" will occur. And yet we need not despair,
indeed, we cannot despair; the evidence of history shows us that men
have always insisted on behaving creatively under the shadow of the
sword; that they have done their artistic and scientific and domestic stuff
for the sake of doing it, and that we had better follow their example
under the shadow of the aeroplanes. Others, with more vision or
courage than myself, see the salvation of humanity ahead, and will dismiss my conception of civilisation as paltry, a sort of tip-and-run game.
Certainly it is presumptuous to say that we *cannot* improve, and that
Man, who has only been in power for a few thousand years, will never
learn to make use of his power. All I mean is that, if people continue to
kill one another as they do, the world cannot get better than it is, and
that since there are more people than formerly, and their means for
destroying one another superior, the world may well get worse. What is
good in people—and consequently in the world—is their insistence on
creation, their belief in friendship and loyalty for their own sakes; and
though Violence remains and is, indeed, the major partner in this muddled establishment, I believe that creativeness remains too, and will
always assume direction when violence sleeps. So, though I am not an
optimist, I cannot agree with Sophocles that it were better never to have
been born. And although, like Horace, I see no evidence that each batch

of births is superior to the last, I leave the field open for the more complacent view.[6] This is such a difficult moment to live in, one cannot help
getting gloomy and also a bit rattled, and perhaps short-sighted.

In search of a refuge, we may perhaps turn to hero-worship. But here
we shall get no help, in my opinion. Hero-worship is a dangerous vice,
and one of the minor merits of a democracy is that it does not encourage it, or produce that unmanageable type of citizen known as the Great
Man. It produces instead different kinds of small men—a much finer
achievement. But people who cannot get interested in the variety of life,
and cannot make up their own minds, get discontented over this, and
they long for a hero to bow down before and to follow blindly. It is significant that a hero is an integral part of the authoritarian stock-in-trade
today. An efficiency-regime cannot be run without a few heroes stuck
about it to carry off the dullness—much as plums have to be put into a bad
pudding to make it palatable. One hero at the top and a smaller one each
side of him is a favourite arrangement, and the timid and the bored are
comforted by the trinity, and, bowing down, feel exalted and strengthened.

No, I distrust Great Men. They produce a desert of uniformity around
them and often a pool of blood too, and I always feel a little man's pleasure when they come a cropper. Every now and then one reads in the
newspapers some such statement as: "The coup d'état appears to have
failed, and Admiral Toma's whereabouts is at present unknown."
Admiral Toma had probably every qualification for being a Great
Man—an iron will, personal magnetism, dash, flair, sexlessness—but
fate was against him, so he retires to unknown whereabouts instead of
parading history with his peers. He fails with a completeness which no
artist and no lover can experience, because with them the process of creation is itself an achievement, whereas with him the only possible
achievement is success.

I believe in aristocracy, though—if that is the right word, and if a
democrat may use it. Not an aristocracy of power, based upon rank and
influence, but an aristocracy of the sensitive, the considerate and the
plucky. Its members are to be found in all nations and classes, and all
through the ages, and there is a secret understanding between them
when they meet. They represent the true human tradition, the one permanent victory of our queer race over cruelty and chaos. Thousands
of them perish in obscurity, a few are great names. They are sensitive
for others as well as for themselves, they are considerate without being
fussy, their pluck is not swankiness but the power to endure, and they
can take a joke. I give no examples—it is risky to do that—but the reader may as well consider whether this is the type of person he would
like to meet and to be, and whether (going farther with me) he would

6. Sophocles (c. 496 B.C.–406 B.C.), Greek tragic poet, author of *Oedipus Rex* (c. 429 B.C.).
   Horace (65 B.C.–8 B.C.), Latin poet and critic.

prefer that this type should *not* be an ascetic one. I am against asceticism myself. I am with the old Scotsman who wanted less chastity and more delicacy. I do not feel that my aristocrats are a real aristocracy if they thwart their bodies, since bodies are the instruments through which we register and enjoy the world. Still, I do not insist. This is not a major point. It is clearly possible to be sensitive, considerate and plucky and yet be an ascetic too, if anyone possesses the first three qualities, I will let him in! On they go—an invincible army, yet not a victorious one. The aristocrats, the elect, the chosen, the Best People— all the words that describe them are false, and all attempts to organise them fail. Again and again Authority, seeing their value, has tried to net them and to utilise them as the Egyptian Priesthood or the Christian Church or the Chinese Civil Service or the Group Movement, or some other worthy stunt. But they slip through the net and are gone; when the door is shut, they are no longer in the room; their temple, as one of them remarked, is the Holiness of the Heart's Affection, and their kingdom, though they never possess it, is the wide-open world.

With this type of person knocking about, and constantly crossing one's path if one has eyes to see or hands to feel, the experiment of earthly life cannot be dismissed as a failure. But it may well be hailed as a tragedy, the tragedy being that no device has been found by which these private decencies can be transmitted to public affairs. As soon as people have power they go crooked and sometimes dotty as well, because the possession of power lifts them into a region where normal honesty never pays. For instance, the man who is selling newspapers outside the Houses of Parliament can safely leave his papers to go for a drink and his cap beside them: anyone who takes a paper is sure to drop a copper into the cap. But the men who are inside the Houses of Parliament—they cannot trust one another like that, still less can the Government they compose trust other governments. No caps upon the pavement here, but suspicion, treachery and armaments. The more highly public life is organised the lower does its morality sink; the nations of today behave to each other worse than they ever did in the past, they cheat, rob, bully and bluff, make war without notice, and kill as many women and children as possible; whereas primitive tribes were at all events restrained by taboos. It is a humiliating outlook—though the greater the darkness, the brighter shine the little lights, reassuring one another, signalling: "Well, at all events, I'm still here. I don't like it very much, but how are you?" Unquenchable lights of my aristocracy! Signals of the invincible army! "Come along—anyway, let's have a good time while we can." I think they signal that too.

The Saviour of the future—if ever he comes—will not preach a new Gospel. He will merely utilise my aristocracy, he will make effective the good will and the good temper which are already existing. In other words, he will introduce a new technique. In economics, we are told that if there was a new technique of distribution, there need be no poverty, and people would not starve in one place while crops were being ploughed under in another. A similar change is needed in the sphere of morals and politics. The desire for it is by no means new; it was expressed, for example, in theological terms by Jacopone da Todi[7] over six hundred years ago. "Ordina questo amore, O tu che m'ami," he said; "O thou who lovest me—set this love in order." His prayer was not granted, and I do not myself believe that it ever will be, but here, and not through a change of heart, is our probable route. Not by becoming better, but by ordering and distributing his native goodness, will Man shut up Force into its box, and so gain time to explore the universe and to set his mark upon it worthily. At present he only explores it at odd moments, when Force is looking the other way, and his divine creativeness appears as a trivial by-product, to be scrapped as soon as the drums beat and the bombers hum.

Such a change, claim the orthodox, can only be made by Christianity, and will be made by it in God's good time: man always has failed and always will fail to organise his own goodness, and it is presumptuous of him to try. This claim—solemn as it is—leaves me cold. I cannot believe that Christianity will ever cope with the present world-wide mess, and I think that such influence as it retains in modern society is due to the money behind it, rather than to its spiritual appeal. It was a spiritual force once, but the indwelling spirit will have to be restated if it is to calm the waters again, and probably restated in a non-Christian form. Naturally a lot of people, and people who are not only good but able and intelligent, will disagree here; they will vehemently deny that Christianity has failed, or they will argue that its failure proceeds from the wickedness of men, and really proves its ultimate success. They have Faith, with a large F. My faith has a very small one, and I only intrude it because these are strenuous and serious days, and one likes to say what one thinks while speech is comparatively free: it may not be free much longer.

The above are the reflections of an individualist and a liberal who has found liberalism crumbling beneath him and at first felt ashamed. Then, looking around, he decided there was no special reason for shame, since other people, whatever they felt, were equally insecure. And as for individualism—there seems no way of getting off this, even if one wanted to. The dictator-hero can grind down his citizens till they are all alike, but he cannot melt them into a single man. That is beyond his power. He can order them to merge, he can incite them to mass-antics, but they are obliged to be born separately, and to die separately, and, owing to these unavoidable termini, will always be running off the total-

7. Italian religious poet, hermit, and mystic (1230?–1306).

itarian rails. The memory of birth and the expectation of death always lurk within the human being, making him separate from his fellows and consequently capable of intercourse with them. Naked I came into the world, naked I shall go out of it! And a very good thing too, for it reminds me that I am naked under my shirt, whatever its colour.

E. M. FORSTER

Tolerance†

Everybody is talking about reconstruction. Our enemies have their schemes for a new order in Europe, maintained by their secret police, and we on our side talk of rebuilding London or England, or western civilisation, and we make plans how this is to be done. Which is all very well, but when I hear such talk, and see the architects sharpening their pencils and the contractors getting out their estimates, and the statesmen marking out their spheres of influence, and everyone getting down to the job, a very famous text occurs to me: "Except the Lord build the house, they labour in vain who build it."[1] Beneath the poetic imagery of these words lies a hard scientific truth, namely, unless you have a sound attitude of mind, a right psychology, you cannot construct or reconstruct anything that will endure. The text is true, not only for religious people, but for workers whatever their outlook, and it is significant that one of our historians, Dr. Arnold Toynbee, should have chosen it to preface his great study of the growth and decay of civilisations.[2] Surely the only sound foundation for a civilisation is a sound state of mind. Architects, contractors, international commissioners, marketing boards, broadcasting corporations will never, by themselves, build a new world. They must be inspired by the proper spirit, and there must be the proper spirit in the people for whom they are working. For instance, we shall never have a beautiful new London until people refuse to live in ugly houses. At present, they don't mind; they demand comfort, but are indifferent to civic beauty; indeed they have no taste. I live myself in a hideous block of flats, but I can't say it worries me, and until we are worried, all schemes for reconstructing London beautifully must automatically fail.

What though is the proper spirit? We agree that the basic problem is psychological, that the Lord must build if the work is to stand, that there must be a sound state of mind before diplomacy or economics or trade-

---

† "Tolerance" from *Two Cheers for Democracy*, copyright 1951 by E. M. Forster and renewed 1979 by Donald Parry, reprinted by permission of Harcourt Brace & Company and The Provost and Scholars of King's College, Cambridge 1997. This essay was originally published in 1941.
1. Psalms 127.1.
2. Arnold Toynbee (1889–1975), author of the comprehensive, twelve-volume investigation of the world's civilizations, *A Study of History* (1934–61).

conferences can function. But what state of mind is sound? Here we may differ. Most people, when asked what spiritual quality is needed to rebuild civilisation, will reply "Love." Men must love one another, they say; nations must do likewise, and then the series of cataclysms which is threatening to destroy us will be checked.

Respectfully but firmly, I disagree. Love is a great force in private life; it is indeed the greatest of all things: but love in public affairs does not work. It has been tried again and again: by the Christian civilisations of the Middle Ages, and also by the French Revolution, a secular movement which reasserted the Brotherhood of Man. And it has always failed. The idea that nations should love one another, or that business concerns or marketing boards should love one another, or that a man in Portugal should love a man in Peru of whom he has never heard—it is absurd, unreal, dangerous. It leads us into perilous and vague sentimentalism. "Love is what is needed," we chant, and then sit back and the world goes on as before. The fact is we can only love what we know personally. And we cannot know much. In public affairs, in the rebuilding of civilisation, something much less dramatic and emotional is needed, namely, tolerance. Tolerance is a very dull virtue. It is boring. Unlike love, it has always had a bad press. It is negative. It merely means putting up with people, being able to stand things. No one has ever written an ode to tolerance, or raised a statue to her. Yet this is the quality which will be most needed after the war. This is the sound state of mind which we are looking for. This is the only force which will enable different races and classes and interests to settle down together to the work of reconstruction.

The world is very full of people—appallingly full; it has never been so full before, and they are all tumbling over each other. Most of these people one doesn't know and some of them one doesn't like; doesn't like the colour of their skins, say, or the shapes of their noses, or the way they blow them or don't blow them, or the way they talk, or their smell, or their clothes, or their fondness for jazz or their dislike of jazz, and so on. Well, what is one to do? There are two solutions. One of them is the Nazi solution. If you don't like people, kill them, banish them, segregate them, and then strut up and down proclaiming that you are the salt of the earth. The other way is much less thrilling, but it is on the whole the way of the democracies, and I prefer it. If you don't like people, put up with them as well as you can. Don't try to love them: you can't, you'll only strain yourself. But try to tolerate them. On the basis of that tolerance a civilised future may be built. Certainly I can see no other foundation for the post-war world.

For what it will most need is the negative virtues: not being huffy, touchy, irritable, revengeful. I have lost all faith in positive militant ideals; they can so seldom be carried out without thousands of human beings getting maimed or imprisoned. Phrases like "I will purge this

nation," "I will clean up this city," terrify and disgust me. They might not
have mattered when the world was emptier: they are horrifying now,
when one nation is mixed up with another, when one city cannot be
organically separated from its neighbours. And, another point: reconstruction is unlikely to be rapid. I do not believe that we are psychologically fit for it, plan the architects never so wisely. In the long run, yes,
perhaps: the history of our race justifies that hope. But civilisation has
its mysterious regressions, and it seems to me that we are fated now to
be in one of them, and must recognise this and behave accordingly.
Tolerance, I believe, will be imperative after the establishment of peace.
It's always useful to take a concrete instance: and I have been asking
myself how I should behave if, after peace was signed, I met Germans
who had been fighting against us. I shouldn't try to love them: I shouldn't
feel inclined. They have broken a window in my little ugly flat for one
thing.[3] But I shall try to tolerate them, because it is common sense,
because in the post-war world we shall have to live with Germans. We
can't exterminate them, any more than they have succeeded in extermi-
nating the Jews. We shall have to put up with them, not for any lofty reason, but because it is the next thing that will have to be done.

I don't then regard tolerance as a great eternally established divine
principle, though I might perhaps quote "In My Father's House are
many mansions" in support of such a view.[4] It is just a makeshift, suitable for an overcrowded and overheated planet. It carries on when love
gives out, and love generally gives out as soon as we move away from our
home and our friends, and stand among strangers in a queue for potatoes. Tolerance is wanted in the queue; otherwise we think, "Why will
people be so slow?"; it is wanted in the tube, or "Why will people be so
fat?"; it is wanted at the telephone, or "Why are they so deaf?" or con-
versely, "Why do they mumble?" It is wanted in the street, in the office,
at the factory, and it is wanted above all between classes, races, and
nations. It's dull. And yet it entails imagination. For you have all the
time to be putting yourself in someone else's place. Which is a desirable
spiritual exercise.

This ceaseless effort to put up with other people seems tame, almost
ignoble, so that it sometimes repels generous natures, and I don't recall
many great men who have recommended tolerance. St. Paul certainly
did not. Nor did Dante. However, a few names occur. Going back over
two thousand years, and to India, there is the great Buddhist Emperor
Asoka, who set up inscriptions recording not his own exploits but the
need for mercy and mutual understanding and peace.[5] Going back about
four hundred years, to Holland, there is the Dutch scholar Erasmus,

3. Because of the German bombing of London.
4. John 14.2.
5. After unifying India through bloody wars of conquest, the Emperor Aśoka (d. 232? B.C.)
   renounced violence and made Buddhism the state religion.

who stood apart from the religious fanaticism of the Reformation and was abused by both parties in consequence. In the same century there was the Frenchman Montaigne, subtle, intelligent, witty, who lived in his quiet country house and wrote essays which still delight and confirm the civilised. And England: there was John Locke, the philosopher; there was Sydney Smith, the Liberal and liberalising divine; there was Lowes Dickinson, writer of A *Modern Symposium*, which might be called the Bible of Tolerance. And Germany—yes, Germany: there was Goethe.[6] All these men testify to the creed which I have been trying to express: a negative creed, but necessary for the salvation of this crowded jostling modern world.

Two more remarks. First it is very easy to see fanaticism in other people, but difficult to spot in oneself. Take the evil of racial prejudice. We can easily detect it in the Nazis; their conduct has been infamous ever since they rose to power. But we ourselves—are we guiltless? We are far less guilty than they are. Yet is there no racial prejudice in the British Empire? Is there no colour question? I ask you to consider that, those of you to whom tolerance is more than a pious word. My other remark is to forestall a criticism. Tolerance is not the same as weakness. Putting up with people does not mean giving in to them. This complicates the problem. But the rebuilding of civilisation is bound to be complicated. I only feel certain that unless the Lord builds the house, they will labour in vain who build it. Perhaps, when the house is completed, love will enter it, and the greatest force in our private lives will also rule in public life.

E. M. FORSTER

The Challenge of Our Time[†]

Temperamentally, I am an individualist. Professionally, I am a writer, and my books emphasize the importance of personal relationships and the private life, for I believe in them. What can a man with such an equipment, and with no technical knowledge, say about the Challenge

6. Very generally, these figures all defended freedom and opposed dogmatism: Erasmus (1466?–1536), Dutch humanist and author of *The Praise of Folly* (1509); Montaigne (1533–92), French humanist whose *Essais* (1586–92) are a model of this literary form; John Locke (1632–1704), English philosopher, author of *An Essay Concerning Human Understanding* (1690), and originator of the idea that the state is founded by a social contract among free individuals; Sydney Smith (1771–1845), English clergyman, essayist, and founder of the *Edinburgh Review* (1802); Goldsworthy Lowes Dickinson (1862–1932), English historian, teacher, and friend of Forster's at Cambridge, whose book *A Modern Symposium* (1905) represents an imaginary dialogue among the many points of view across the political spectrum; Johann Wolfgang von Goethe (1749–1832), poet, dramatist, scientist, and author of *Faust* (1808–1832).
† "The Challenge of Our Time" from *Two Cheers for Democracy*, copyright 1939 and renewed 1967 by E. M. Forster, reprinted by permission of Harcourt Brace & Company and The Provost and Scholars of King's College, Cambridge 1997. This essay was originally published in 1946.

of our Time?[1] Like everyone else, I can see that our world is in a terrible mess, and having been to India last winter I know that starvation and frustration can reach proportions unknown to these islands. Wherever I look, I can see, in the striking phrase of Robert Bridges, "the almighty cosmic Will fidgeting in a trap."[2] But who set the trap, and how was it sprung? If I knew, I might be able to unfasten it. I do not know. How can I answer a challenge which I cannot interpret? It is like shouting defiance at a big black cloud. Some of the other speakers share my diffidence here, I think. Professor Bernal does not.[3] He perceives very precisely what the Challenge of our Time is and what is the answer to it. Professor Bernal's perceptions are probably stronger than mine. They are certainly more selective, and many things which interest or upset me do not enter his mind at all—or enter it in the form of cards to be filed for future use.

I belong to the fag-end of Victorian liberalism, and can look back to an age whose challenges were moderate in their tone, and the cloud on whose horizon was no bigger than a man's hand. In many ways it was an admirable age. It practised benevolence and philanthropy, was humane and intellectually curious, upheld free speech, had little colour-prejudice, believed that individuals are and should be different, and entertained a sincere faith in the progress of society. The world was to become better and better, chiefly through the spread of parliamentary institutions. The education I received in those far-off and fantastic days made me soft and I am very glad it did, for I have seen plenty of hardness since, and I know it does not even pay. Think of the end of Mussolini— the hard man, hanging upside-down like a turkey, with his dead mistress swinging beside him.[4] But though the education was humane it was imperfect, inasmuch as we none of us realised our economic position. In came the nice fat dividends, up rose the lofty thoughts, and we did not realise that all the time we were exploiting the poor of our own country and the backward races abroad, and getting bigger profits from our investments than we should. We refused to face this unpalatable truth. I remember being told as a small boy, "Dear, don't talk about money, it's ugly"—a good example of Victorian defence mechanism.

All that has changed in the present century. The dividends have shrunk to decent proportions and have in some cases disappeared. The poor have kicked. The backward races are kicking—and more power to

1. The title of the series of BBC radio talks for which Forster first wrote this essay.
2. Robert Bridges (1844–1930), English poet laureate (1913–30); from his poem "Poor Poll" (1923), which portrays a parrot tethered to its perch as "a very figure and image of man's soul on earth."
3. John Desmond Bernal (1901–71), professor of physics at the University of London (1938–68) known for his left-wing views and a previous speaker in the radio series.
4. Benito Mussolini, the Italian dictator, and his mistress, Carla Petacci, were captured by the Italian underground in April 1945 as the German army retreated. They were court-martialed, shot, and hanged in a public square in Milan.

their boots.[5] Which means that life has become less comfortable for the Victorian liberal, and that our outlook, which seems to me admirable, has lost the basis of golden sovereigns upon which it originally rose, and now hangs over the abyss. I indulge in these reminiscences because they lead to the point I want to make.

If we are to answer the Challenge of our Time successfully, we must manage to combine the new economy and the old morality. The doctrine of *laisser-faire*[6] will not work in the material world. It has led to the black market and the capitalist jungle. We must have planning and ration books and controls, or millions of people will have nowhere to live and nothing to eat. On the other hand, the doctrine of *laisser-faire* is the only one that seems to work in the world of the spirit; if you plan and control men's minds you stunt them, you get the censorship, the secret police, the road to serfdom, the community of slaves. Our economic planners sometimes laugh at us when we are afraid of totalitarian tyranny resulting from their efforts—or rather they sneer at us, for there is some deep connection between planning and sneering which psychologists should explore. But the danger they brush aside is a real one. They assure us that the new economy will evolve an appropriate morality, and that when all people are properly fed and housed, they will have an outlook which will be right, because they are the people. I cannot swallow that. I have no mystic faith in the people. I have in the individual. He seems to me a divine achievement and I mistrust any view which belittles him. If anyone calls you a wretched little individual—and I've been called that—don't you take it lying down. You are important because everyone else is an individual too—including the person who criticises you. In asserting your personality you are playing for your side.

That then is the slogan with which I would answer, or partially answer, the Challenge of our Time. We want the New Economy with the Old Morality. We want planning for the body and not for the spirit. But the difficulty is this: where does the body stop and the spirit start? In the Middle Ages a hard and fast line was drawn between them, and according to the mediaeval theory of the Holy Roman Empire men rendered their bodies to Caesar and their souls to God. But the theory did not work. The Emperor, who represented Caesar, collided in practice with the Pope, who represented Christ. And we find ourselves in a similar dilemma today. Suppose you are planning the world-distribution of food. You can't do that without planning world population. You can't do that without regulating the number of births and interfering with family life. You must supervise parenthood. You are meddling with the realms of the spirit, of personal relationship, although you may not have intended to do so. And you are brought back again to that inescapable arbiter,

5. In 1947, a year after this essay was written, India was granted independence from British rule following a long period of protest and struggle.
6. Noninterference.

your own temperament. When there is a collision of principles would you favour the individual at the expense of the community as I would? Or would you prefer economic justice for all at the expense of personal freedom?

In a time of upheaval like the present, this collision of principles, this split in one's loyalties, is always occurring. It has just occurred in my own life. I was brought up as a boy in one of the home counties,[7] in a district which I still think the loveliest in England. There is nothing special about it—it is agricultural land, and could not be described in terms of beauty spots. It must always have looked much the same. I have kept in touch with it, going back to it as to an abiding city and still visiting the house which was once my home, for it is occupied by friends. A farm is through the hedge, and when the farmer there was eight years old and I was nine, we used to jump up and down on his grandfather's straw ricks and spoil them. Today he is a grandfather himself, so that I have the sense of five generations continuing in one place. Life went on there as usual until this spring. Then someone who was applying for a permit to lay a water pipe was casually informed that it would not be granted since the whole area had been commandeered. Commandeered for what? Had not the war ended? Appropriate officials of the Ministry of Town and Country Planning now arrived from London and announced that a satellite town for 60,000 people is to be built. The people now living and working there are doomed; it is death in life for them and they move in a nightmare. The best agricultural land has been taken, they assert; the poor land down by the railway has been left; compensation is inadequate. Anyhow, the satellite town has finished them off as completely as it will obliterate the ancient and delicate scenery. Meteorite town would be a better name. It has fallen out of a blue sky.

"Well," says the voice of planning and progress, "why this sentimentality? People must have houses." They must, and I think of working-class friends in north London who have to bring up four children in two rooms, and many are even worse off than that. But I cannot equate the problem. It is a collision of loyalties. I cannot free myself from the conviction that something irreplaceable has been destroyed, and that a little piece of England has died as surely as if a bomb had hit it. I wonder what compensation there is in the world of the spirit, for the destruction of the life here, the life of tradition.

These are personal reminiscences and I am really supposed to be speaking from the standpoint of the creative artist. But you will gather what a writer, who also cares for men and women and for the countryside, must be feeling in the world today. Uncomfortable, of course. Sometimes miserable and indignant. But convinced that a planned change must take place if the world is not to disintegrate, and hopeful

7. The counties closest to London, including Hertfordshire, where Forster's childhood home Rooksnest, the model of Howards End, is located.

that in the new economy there may be a sphere both for human relationships, and for the despised activity known as art. What ought the writer, the artist, to do when faced by the Challenge of our Time? Briefly, he ought to express what he wants and not what he is told to express by the planning authorities. He ought to impose a discipline on himself rather than accept one from outside. And that discipline may be esthetic, rather than social or moral; he may wish to practise art for art's sake. That phrase has been foolishly used and often raises a giggle. But it is a profound phrase. It indicates that art is a self-contained harmony. Art is valuable not because it is educational (though it may be), not because it is recreative (though it may be), not because everyone enjoys it (for everybody does not), not even because it has to do with beauty. It is valuable because it has to do with order, and creates little worlds of its own, possessing internal harmony, in the bosom of this disordered planet. It is needed at once and now. It is needed before it is appreciated and independent of appreciation. The idea that it should not be permitted until it receives communal acclaim and unless it is for all, is perfectly absurd. It is the activity which brought man out of original darkness and differentiates him from the beasts, and we must continue to practise and respect it through the darkness of today.

I am speaking like an intellectual, but the intellectual, to my mind, is more in touch with humanity than is the confident scientist, who patronises the past, over-simplifies the present, and envisages a future where his leadership will be accepted. Owing to the political needs of the moment, the scientist occupies an abnormal position, which he tends to forget. He is subsidised by the terrified governments who need his aid, pampered and sheltered as long as he is obedient, and prosecuted under Official Secrets Acts when he has been naughty.[8] All this separates him from ordinary men and women and makes him unfit to enter into their feelings. It is high time he came out of his ivory laboratory. We want him to plan for our bodies. We do not want him to plan for our minds, and we cannot accept, so far, his assurance that he will not.

8. A British law that allows the government to censor or withhold classified information.

Interpretations of Forster's
Liberalism

LIONEL TRILLING
[The Liberal Imagination and *Howards End*]†

E. M. Forster is for me the only living novelist who can be read again and again and who, after each reading, gives me what few writers can give us after our first days of novel-reading, the sensation of having learned something. I have wanted for a long time to write about him and it gives me a special satisfaction to write about him now, for a consideration of Forster's work is, I think, useful in time of war.

* * *

Forster is not only comic, he is often playful. He is sometimes irritating in his refusal to be great. Greatness in literature, even in comedy, seems to have some affinity with greatness in government and war, suggesting power, a certain sternness, a touch of the imperial and imperious. But Forster, who in certain moods might say with Swift, "I have hated all nations, professions and communities, and all my love is for individuals," fears power and suspects formality as the sign of power.[1] "Distrust every enterprise that requires new clothes" is the motto one of his characters inscribes over his wardrobe. It is a maxim of only limited wisdom; new thoughts sometimes need new clothes and the seriousness of Forster's intellectual enterprise is too often reduced by the unbuttoned manner he affects. The quaint, the facetious and the chatty sink his literary criticism below its proper level; they diminish the stature of his short fiction and they even touch, though they never actually harm, the five novels; the true comic note sometimes drops to mere chaff and we now and then wish that the style were less comfortable and more arrogant.

But while these lapses have to be reckoned with, they do not negate the validity of the manner of which they are the deficiency or excess. Forster's manner is the agent of a moral intention which can only be car-

---

† From Lionel Trilling, *E. M. Forster* (New York: New Directions, 1943) 9–10, 12–19, 22–24. Copyright © 1943 by New Directions Publishing Corp. Reprinted by permission of New Directions Publishing Corp.
1. From a letter by the satirist Jonathan Swift (1667–1745) to the poet Alexander Pope (1688–1744) in which Swift explains his skeptical views about human nature (29 September 1725). [*Editor*]

ried out by the mind *ondoyant et divers*[2] of which Montaigne spoke. What Forster wants to know about the human heart must be caught by surprise, by what he calls the "relaxed will," and if not everything can be caught in this way, what is so caught cannot be caught in any other way. Rigor will not do, and Forster uses the novel as a form amenable to the most arbitrary manipulation. He teases his medium and plays with his genre. He scorns the fetish of "adequate motivation," delights in surprise and melodrama and has a kind of addiction to sudden death. Guiding his stories according to his serious whim—like the anonymous lady, he has a whim of iron—Forster takes full and conscious responsibility for his novels, refusing to share in the increasingly dull assumption of the contemporary novelist, that the writer has nothing to do with the story he tells and that, *mirabile dictu*,[3] through no intention of his own, the story has chosen to tell itself through him. Like Fielding, he shapes his prose for comment and explanation, and like Fielding he is not above an explanatory footnote. He summarizes what he is going to show, introduces new themes when and as it suits him to do so, is not awed by the sacred doctrine of "point of view" and, understanding that verisimilitude, which more than one critic has defended from his indifference, can guarantee neither pleasure nor truth, he uses exaggeration and improbability. * * *

* * *

* * * Forster's plots are always sharp and definite, for he expresses difference by means of struggle, and struggle by means of open conflict so intense as to flare into melodrama and even into physical violence. Across each of his novels runs a barricade; the opposed forces on each side are Good and Evil in the forms of Life and Death, Light and Darkness, Fertility and Sterility, Courage and Respectability, Intelligence and Stupidity—all the great absolutes that are so dull when discussed in themselves. The comic manner, however, will not tolerate absolutes. It stands on the barricade and casts doubt on both sides. The fierce plots move forward to grand simplicities but the comic manner confuses the issues, forcing upon us the difficulties and complications of the moral fact. The plot suggests eternal division, the manner reconciliation; the plot speaks of clear certainties, the manner resolutely insists that nothing can be quite so simple. "Wash ye, make yourselves clean," says the plot, and the manner murmurs, "If you can find the soap."

Now, to the simple mind the mention of complication looks like a kind of malice, and to the mind under great stress the suggestion of something "behind" the apparent fact looks like a call to quietism, like mere shilly-shallying. And this is the judgment, I think, that a great many readers of the most enlightened sort are likely to pass on Forster. For he stands in a

2. Flexible and diverse (French). [*Editor*]
3. Strange to say, miraculously (Latin). [*Editor*]

peculiar relation to what, for want of a better word, we may call the liberal tradition, that loose body of middle class opinion which includes such ideas as progress, collectivism and humanitarianism.

To this tradition Forster has long been committed—all his novels are politically and morally tendentious and always in the liberal direction. Yet he is deeply at odds with the liberal mind, and while liberal readers can go a long way with Forster, they can seldom go all the way. They can understand him when he attacks the manners and morals of the British middle class, when he speaks out for spontaneity of feeling, for the virtues of sexual fulfillment, for the values of intelligence; they go along with him when he speaks against the class system, satirizes soldiers and officials, questions the British Empire and attacks business ethics and the public schools. But sooner or later they begin to make reservations and draw back. They suspect Forster is not quite playing their game; they feel that he is challenging *them* as well as what they dislike. And they are right. For all his long commitment to the doctrines of liberalism, Forster is at war with the liberal imagination.

Surely if liberalism has a single desperate weakness, it is an inadequacy of imagination: liberalism is always being surprised. There is always the liberal work to do over again because disillusionment and fatigue follow hard upon surprise, and reaction is always ready for that moment of liberal disillusionment and fatigue—reaction never hopes, despairs or suffers amazement. Liberalism likes to suggest its affinity with science, pragmatism and the method of hypothesis, but in actual conduct it requires "ideals" and absolutes; it prefers to make its alliances only when it thinks it catches the scent of Utopia in parties and governments, the odor of sanctity in men; and if neither is actually present, liberalism makes sure to supply it. When liberalism must act with some degree of anomaly—and much necessary action is anomalous—it insists that it is acting on perfect theory and is astonished when anomaly then appears.

The liberal mind is sure that the order of human affairs owes it a simple logic: good is good and bad is bad. It can understand, for it invented and named, the moods of optimism and pessimism, but the mood that is the response to good-and-evil it has not named and cannot understand. Before the idea of good-and-evil its imagination fails; it cannot accept this improbable paradox. This is ironic, for one of the charter-documents of liberalism urges the liberal mind to cultivate imagination enough to accept just this improbability.

> Good and evil we know in the field of this world grow up together almost inseparably; and the knowledge of good is so involved and interwoven with the knowledge of evil, and in so many cunning resemblances hardly to be discerned, that those confused seeds which were imposed upon Psyche as an incessant labor to cull out, and sort asunder, were not more intermixed. It was from out the

rind of one apple tasted, that the knowledge of good and evil, as two twins cleaving together, leaped forth into the world. And perhaps this is that doom which Adam fell into of knowing good and evil, that is to say of knowing good by evil.[4]

And the irony is doubled when we think how well the great conservative minds have understood what Milton meant. Dr. Johnson and Burke and, in a lesser way at a later time, Fitzjames Stephen, understood the mystery of the twins; and Matthew Arnold has always been thought the less a liberal for his understanding of them.[5] But we of the liberal connection have always liked to play the old intellectual game of antagonistic principles. It is an attractive game because it gives us the sensation of thinking, and its first rule is that if one of two opposed principles is wrong, the other is necessarily right. Forster will not play this game; or, rather, he plays it only to mock it.

*   *   *

Forster's insistence on the double turn, on the something else that lies behind, is sometimes taken for "tolerance," but although it often suggests forgiveness (a different thing), it almost as often makes the severest judgments. And even when it suggests forgiveness it does not spring so much from gentleness of heart as from respect for two facts co-existing, from the moral realism that understands the one apple tasted. Forster can despise Gerald of *The Longest Journey* because Gerald is a prig and a bully, but he can invest Gerald's death with a kind of primitive dignity, telling us of the maid-servants who weep, "They had not liked Gerald, but he was a man, they were women, he had died." And after Gerald's death he can give Agnes Pembroke her moment of tragic nobility, only to pursue her implacably for her genteel brutality.

*   *   *

Perhaps it is because he has nothing of the taste for the unconditioned—Nietzsche[6] calls it the worst of all tastes, the taste that is always being fooled by the world—that Forster has been able to deal so well with the idea of class. The liberal mind has in our time spoken much of this idea but has failed to believe in it. The modern liberal believes in categories and wage-scales and calls these class. Forster knows better, and in *Howards End* shows the conflicting truths of the idea—that on the one hand class is character, soul and destiny, and that on the other hand class is not finally determining. He knows that class may be truly

4. From John Milton (1608–74), *Aeropagitica* (1644), a classic argument against censorship and for freedom of the press. Venus forced Psyche to sort a huge pile of seeds as punishment for her love for Cupid. [*Editor*]

5. Samuel Johnson (1709–84), Edmund Burke (1729–97), and James Fitzjames Stephen (1829–94) were conservative moral and political thinkers. Matthew Arnold (1822–88), the Victorian cultural critic, was the subject of Trilling's first book (1939). [*Editor*]

6. Friedrich Nietzsche (1844–1900), German philosopher who argued that truth is not absolute but varies with perspective. [*Editor*]

represented only by struggle and contradiction, not by description, and preferably by moral struggle in the heart of a single person. When D. H. Lawrence wrote to Forster that he had made "a nearly deadly mistake glorifying those *business* people in *Howards End*. Business is no good," he was indulging his own taste for the unconditioned.[7] It led him to read Forster inaccurately and it led him to make that significant shift from "business people" to "business." But Forster, who is too worldly to suppose that we can judge people without reference to their class, is also too worldly to suppose that we can judge class-conditioned action until we make a hypothetical deduction of the subject's essential humanity. It is exactly because Forster can judge the "business people" as he does, and because he can judge the lower classes so without sentimentality, that he can deal firmly and intelligently with his own class, and if there is muddle in *Howards End*—and the nearly allegorical reconciliation is rather forced—then, in speaking of class, clear ideas are perhaps a sign of ignorance, muddle the sign of true knowledge; surely *Howards End* stands with *Our Mutual Friend* and *The Princess Casamassima* as one of the great comments on the class struggle.[8]

* * *

The great thing Forster has been able to learn from his attachment to tradition and from his sense of the past is his belief in the present. He has learned not to be what most of us are—eschatological.[9] Most of us, consciously or unconsciously, are discontented with the nature rather than with the use of the human faculty; deep in our assumption lies the hope and the belief that humanity will end its career by developing virtues which will be admirable exactly because we cannot now conceive them. The past has been a weary failure, the present cannot matter, for it is but a step forward to the final judgment; we look to the future when the best of the works of man will seem but the futile and slightly disgusting twitchings of primeval creatures: thus, in the name of a superior and contemptuous posterity, we express our self-hatred—and our desire for power.

This is a moral and historical error into which Forster never falls; his whole work, indeed, is an implied protest against it. The very relaxation of his style, its colloquial unpretentiousness, is a mark of his acceptance of the human fact as we know it now. He is content with the human possibility and content with its limitations. The way of human action of course does not satisfy him, but he does not believe there are any new virtues to be discovered; not by becoming better, he says, but by ordering and distributing his native goodness can man live as befits him.

This, it seems to me, might well be called worldliness, this acceptance of

---

7. See Lawrence's letter to Forster of 20 September 1922 in "Contemporary Responses," p. 391. [*Editor*]
8. Novels by Charles Dickens (1865) and Henry James (1886). [*Editor*]
9. Concerned with last things, the end. [*Editor*]

man in the world without the sentimentality of cynicism and without the sentimentality of rationalism. Forster is that remarkably rare being, a naturalist whose naturalism is positive and passionate, not negative, passive and apologetic for man's nature. He accepts the many things the liberal imagination likes to put out of sight. He can accept, for example, not only the reality but the power of death—"Death destroys a man, but the idea of death saves him," he says, and the fine scene in *The Longest Journey* in which Rickie forces Agnes to "mind" the death of Gerald is a criticism not only of the British fear of emotion but also of liberalism's incompetence before tragedy. To Forster, as to Blake,[1] naturalism suggests not the invalidity or the irrelevance of human emotions but, rather, their validity and strength: "Far more mysterious than the call of sex to sex is the tenderness that we throw into that call; far wider is the gulf between us and the farmyard than between the farmyard and the garbage that nourishes it."

He is so worldly, indeed, that he believes that ideas are for his service and not for his worship. In 1939 when war was certain and the talk ran so high and loose about Democracy that it was hard to know what was being talked about, Forster remarked with the easy simplicity of a man in his own house, "So two cheers for Democracy; one because it admits variety and two because it permits criticism. Two cheers are quite enough: there is no occasion to give three. Only Love the Beloved Republic deserves that." He is so worldly that he has always felt that his nation belonged to him. He has always known that we cannot love anything bigger until we first love what Burke called "the little platoon" and so it has been easy for him to speak of his love for his country with whose faults he has never ceased to quarrel; and now he has no void to fill up with that acrid nationalism that literary men too often feel called upon to express in a time of crisis. He is one of the thinking people who were never led by thought to suppose they could be more than human and who, in bad times, will not become less.

*   *   *

FREDERICK CREWS

[Forster and the Liberal Tradition][†]

The relevance of Forster's political views to his novels is far from obvious. Of the novels, only *Howards End* and *A Passage to India* have to do with politics, and these are anything but partisan tracts. The theme of

1. William Blake (1757–1827), English Romantic poet. [*Editor*]
† From Frederick Crews, *E. M. Forster: The Perils of Humanism* (Princeton: Princeton UP, 1962) 19–36. Copyright 1962 by Princeton University Press. Renewed 1990. Reprinted by permission of Princeton University Press. Some of the author's footnotes have been silently omitted.

Howards End is the need not for reform but for broad compromises between men and women, innovation and tradition, intellect and action, the upper classes and the lower. *A Passage to India* moves still farther beyond a simple creed or platform. It suggests that we are doomed by our nature to ignorance of God and isolation from one another—that not prayer nor politics nor social intercourse will save us from this fate. Such a Homeric perspective dwarfs the gestures of anti-imperialism that Forster does occasionally make in the novel. Personal political sentiments cannot seem very urgent in a book about the vanity of human wishes.

In a refined sense, however, it is possible to see considerable political meaning in Forster's novels. Their very lack of overt partisanship is consistent with his version of liberalism, which we can identify as a narrow but by no means private current within the wider liberal tradition. Forster's nonfiction leaves no doubt as to the centrality of political beliefs in his moral framework, and the novels reflect his deepest and most generalized thoughts on the subject. Indeed, the very existence of his novels has political interest if we consider them as a part of cultural history. Trained in the moral absolutes of a Liberal Party which lost both its power and its integrity while they were undergraduates, many of the Cambridge "intellectual aristocrats" of Forster's generation found in art the satisfaction their fathers had found in public life. It is not surprising to learn that Forster's novels are conceived in terms of moral generalizations whose ultimate source is the political philosophy of liberalism.

Forster's unwillingness to be a party man has been evident throughout his career, even in his occasional sallies into political journalism. These have been provoked rather by indignation at abuses of power than by sympathy with the powerful. A typical piece from the postwar era is his poem, "A Voter's Dilemma," which explains in acid couplets that Liberals and Conservatives alike are more concerned with munitions profiteering than with peace and justice. * * * From time to time Forster has lent his services to the British government, but always in the character of a moralist. His Labour Research Department pamphlet, "The Government of Egypt" (1920), for example, is a biting review of colonial policy, written out of an instinctive sympathy for the underdog. When in 1939 he served on the Lord Chancellor's committee to review the Law of Defamatory Libel, he was acting upon his lifelong hatred of censorship. Even his anti-Nazi essays and radio broadcasts during the Second World War bear the stamp of his unwillingness to indulge in political simplifications. While denouncing abuses of liberty in Germany he repeatedly turns back to England and cautions against the same abuses: "Not the beam in Dr. Goebbels' eye, but the mote in our own eye. Can we take it out? Is there as much freedom of expression and publication in this country as there might be?"[1]

---

1. E. M. Forster, *Two Cheers for Democracy* (New York: Harcourt, Brace and Company, 1951) 55. Subsequent references will be given parenthetically and will refer to this text as *Cheers*. [*Editor*]

Though they come late in his career, Forster's pronouncements on the twentieth century's various orthodoxies can give us a more specific idea of his political reasoning. Fascism he finds utterly unthinkable: "Fascism does evil that evil may come."[2] Because of his distaste for "the chaos and carnage of international finance" (*Cheers* 7), he has praised the Communists for their effort to find something better. Communism, however, is too bloody in its methods of reform * * *, and Stalinist Russia is a very imperfect Utopia. Forster is even suspicious of the mildest of collectivist movements, English Fabianism, on the grounds that it is latently autocratic. "Our danger from Fascism," he wrote in 1935, "—unless a war starts when anything may happen—is negligible. We're menaced by something much more insidious—by what I might call 'Fabio-Fascism,' by the dictator-spirit working quietly away behind the façade of constitutional forms, passing a little law (like the Sedition Act) here, endorsing a departmental tyranny there, emphasizing the national need of secrecy elsewhere, and whispering and cooing the so-called 'news' every evening over the wireless, until opposition is tamed and gulled" (*Abinger* 65f.). While he has high praise for Beatrice and Sidney Webb and for Edward Carpenter (*Cheers* 212–18), Forster refuses to commit himself to socialism or to become sentimental over the plight of the working class.[3]

Behind all these judgments lies an uncompromising individualism. Governments are good or bad, for Forster, strictly according to their tolerance of variety and criticism; this is the basis for his grudging "two cheers" for British constitutional democracy. As for the positive achievements that a state might reach under one system or another, Forster counts them as nothing against the dangers that go along with governmental strength. If he is vaguely leftist in his sympathies, he is opposed in principle to the concentration of power that leftist programs require. He can agree, for instance, that housing must be found for London workers, but he cannot approve of commandeering a "satellite town" for them in the uprooted countryside of his own home country: ". . . I cannot equate the problem. It is a collision of loyalties. I cannot free myself from the conviction that something irreplaceable has been destroyed, and that a little piece of England has died as surely as if a bomb had hit it" (*Cheers* 59). Forster's respect for the countryside, the last fortress of individualism in a world of urban sameness, overrides his concern for the material benefit of the majority.

Ultimately we may say that it is Forster's disbelief in the discrete reality of the state that checks his socialism. He sees the nation, not as an

2. E. M. Forster, *Abinger Harvest* (New York: Harcourt, Brace and Company, 1936) 64. Subsequent references will be given parenthetically and will refer to this text as *Abinger*. [*Editor*]
3. The Webbs and Carpenter were prominent members of the Fabian Society, a British socialist group that gave rise to the present-day Labor Party. [*Editor*]

---

entity in itself with international interests to be protected, but simply as a sum total of individual citizens. To "make sacrifices for the state" is thus to trick oneself with words. Occasionally Forster has tried to define a ground where national programs are possible—"We want planning for the body and not for the spirit" (*Cheers* 57)—but in reality he can observe no such distinction. As a nominalist and a moralist he is forever afraid of the arbitrariness, the impersonality, and the blindness of group-power. "The more highly public life is organised," he writes, "the lower does its morality sink" (*Cheers* 74).

In this light it is hardly surprising that Forster has looked with increasing horror and despair upon the twentieth century's tendency to spawn dictatorships and superstates. In his best-known essay, "What I Believe," after explaining that he disbelieves in belief, gives only two cheers for democracy, and is solaced in the modern world only by friendship and art, he concludes: "The above are the reflections of an individualist and a liberal who has found liberalism crumbling beneath him and at first felt ashamed. Then, looking around, he decided there was no special reason for shame, since other people, whatever they felt, were equally insecure. And as for individualism—there seems no way of getting off this, even if one wanted to. The dictator-hero can grind down his citizens till they are all alike, but he cannot melt them into a single man. That is beyond his power. He can order them to merge, he can incite them to mass-antics, but they are obliged to be born separately, and to die separately, and, owing to these unavoidable termini, will always be running off the totalitarian rails. The memory of birth and the expectation of death always lurk within the human being, making him separate from his fellows and consequently capable of intercourse with them. Naked I came into the world, naked I shall go out of it! And a very good thing too, for it reminds me that I am naked under my shirt, whatever its colour" (*Cheers* 76).[4]

Here is rear-guard action of the least hopeful sort. Forster has conceded the political field to the dictator-hero; liberalism will not survive, and individualism can be nearly exterminated in the name of federal authority. "The memory of birth and the expectation of death" will hardly prove adequate consolation when Big Brother has finished his work of molding the ideal citizen, and Forster is understandably reluctant to play an active role in a world heading this way. "We who seek the truth," as he rather dramatically wrote in 1923, "are only concerned with politics when they deflect us from it" (*Abinger* 269).[5]

---

4. One is reminded here of Freud's answer to the charge that he was neither a Fascist nor a Communist, neither black nor red. "No," he replied, "one should be flesh coloured." Quoted by Ernest Jones, *The Life and Work of Sigmund Freud*, Vol. III (New York, 1957), p. 343. Freud, incidentally, took his politics directly from John Stuart Mill.

5. A fuller statement appears in a letter, dated January 13, 1958, to the present writer: "I have never belonged to any political party, and have only become interested in public affairs when the community appeared to be oppressing the individual, or when one community appeared to be oppressing another." (Quoted with Mr. Forster's permission.)

The liberalism evident here would seem to be far removed from the politics of the Liberal Party or of any party, but this is not wholly true. Forster himself recognizes his debt to the tradition of nineteenth-century liberalism, and in one important passage he explains where he agrees and disagrees with his forebears: "I belong to the fag-end of Victorian liberalism, and can look back to an age whose challenges were moderate in their tone, and the cloud on whose horizon was no bigger than a man's hand. In many ways it was an admirable age. It practised benevolence and philanthropy, was humane and intellectually curious, upheld free speech, had little colour-prejudice, believed that individuals are and should be different, and entertained a sincere faith in the progress of society. The world was to become better and better, chiefly through the spread of parliamentary institutions. The education I received in those far-off and fantastic days made me soft and I am very glad it did, for I have seen plenty of hardness since, and I know it does not even pay. . . . But though the education was humane it was imperfect, inasmuch as we none of us realised our economic position. In came the nice fat dividends, up rose the lofty thoughts, and we did not realise that all the time we were exploiting the poor of our own country and the backward races abroad, and getting bigger profits from our investments than we should. We refused to face this unpalatable truth" (*Cheers* 56).

The notion of Victorian liberalism projected here accords well with Lionel Trilling's account of the liberal tradition as "that loose body of middle class opinion which includes such ideas as progress, collectivism and humanitarianism."[6] To be historically scrupulous, however, one would have to point out that Trilling's definition is incomplete and even confused. Collectivism and humanitarianism were once recognized as very antitheses of liberal doctrine. Forster's paragraph refers not to liberalism as a movement but to the practice of a minority of liberals, the descendants of Clapham, whose "benevolence and philanthropy" derived rather from their religion than from their politics. Forster is aligning himself only with those liberals who have rejected *laissez faire* economics while preserving and reinterpreting the liberal ideal of individualism.

Forster's offshoot of liberalism had developed chiefly from John Stuart Mill's critique of Jeremy Bentham. Through most of the nineteenth century the word "liberalism" was considered synonymous with Utilitarianism or philosophic radicalism, the economic theory of Adam Smith, Malthus, Ricardo, Bentham, and James Mill. At midcentury, when the younger Mill was supplanting his father and Bentham as the leading radical theorist, Utilitarianism was little more than the articulation of middle-class capitalist interests. Its calculus of value according to "the greatest happiness of the greatest number" was in practice a ratio-

6. See the selection by Trilling in this Norton Critical Edition, 328. [*Editor*]

nale for free trade, economic expansionism, and democratic government. Utilitarians favored individualism, but only in the business sense
of the word; they recognized no intrinsic rights of individuals for protection against the majority will. It was only because the Utilitarians
happened to concur with Rights-of-Man liberals in opposing the landed
aristocracy and supporting middle-class suffrage that radical economists
found themselves led, in Halévy's words, "to confound economic liberalism with moral liberalism."[7]

This confusion of liberalisms, which widely persisted until Forster's
day and of which the Bloomsbury group was sharply aware, was the central issue in Mill's quarrel with his father's generation of radicals.
Though he always considered himself a loyal Benthamite, Mill set out,
as he later explained, "to show that there was a Radical philosophy, better and more complete than Bentham's, while recognizing and incorpo-
rating all of Bentham's which is permanently valuable."[8] He felt that
Bentham had oversimplified human nature in assuming all pleasures
and pains to be qualitatively equal; because of man's involvement with
moral and religious sanctions, Mill argued, happiness cannot be gauged
by statistics of production and consumption. In politics, too, Mill tempered Bentham's faith in democracy. While previous Utilitarians had
felt that the government should swiftly enact the majority's wishes into
law, Mill saw the long-range value of constitutional restraints. The
Utilitarian principle, once freed from a purely economic definition of
welfare, demanded that dissenters be protected. Society could not afford
to stamp out the vital minority whose unpopular views might later turn
out to be indispensable.

Mill's reasoning is founded on a nominalism very similar to Forster's.
His concern is not with defining the sacrifices we owe to the state, but
with establishing "a limit to the legitimate interference of collective
opinion with individual independence."[9] Again, a love of diversity is crucial in both writers. The power of the majority, for Mill, is valuable only
so far as it is "tempered by respect for the personality of the individual,
and deference to superiority of cultivated intelligence."[1] Forster, living
in a later age, is concerned about the likelihood that this respect for
individuality will be overridden by Benthamite planners. Such men, he
says, "assure us that the new economy will evolve an appropriate morality, and that when all people are properly fed and housed, they will have
an outlook which will be right, because they are the people. I cannot
swallow that. I have no mystic faith in the people. I have in the individ-

7. Elie Halévy, *The Growth of Philosophic Radicalism*, tr. Mary Morris (London, 1934), p. 117.
8. John Stuart Mill, *Autobiography* (New York, 1948), p. 150.
9. John Stuart Mill, "On Liberty," *Utilitarianism, Liberty, and Representative Government* (London, 1931), p. 68.
1. *Mill on Bentham and Coleridge*, ed. F. R. Leavis (London, 1950), p. 88. See also the epigraph to "On Liberty," which proclaims "the absolute and essential importance of human develop-ment in its richest diversity."

ual. He seems to me a divine achievement and I mistrust any view which belittles him" (*Cheers* 57).

If Forster's preference for *laissez faire* in the world of the spirit goes back to Mill, so too does his rejection of *laissez faire* in the economic world * * * . Though he always supported free trade, Mill eventually turned the Utilitarian principle against the prejudices of its founders. By the end of his career he was openly considering the possibility that socialism may be the expression of man's highest political goals.[2] The ultimate social problem, he and his wife decided, was "how to unite the greatest individual liberty of action, with a common ownership in the raw material of the globe, and an equal participation of all in the benefits of combined labour."[3]

This coincidence of liberal individualism with what Englishmen called "progressivism" and Americans "radicalism" has enabled Mill to be a kind of patron saint for two widely different groups. Progressives such as Henry Fawcett, the Webbs, Shaw, and Wells could look to Mill as a theorist of the most sweeping reform of society. These men were opposed to *laissez faire*, but their own politics belong in the Benthamite tradition of serving the greatest-happiness principle at the expense of existing institutions. It is the Benthamite side of Mill that has nourished English socialism. Mill's defense of private liberty, on the other hand, points toward the nonpolitical liberalism that we see in Forster. The liberalism of Walter Bagehot and T. H. Green, and more pertinently of Matthew Arnold and Samuel Butler, seems to belong to this tradition. Such a liberalism does not concern itself with adaptation to new economic and social conditions but with the protection of a fixed ideal of individual freedom. It fears the rule of the mob as well as the rule of the few, and tends finally to disengage itself from party loyalty.

These two divergent branches of liberalism existed side by side within the Liberal Party. Gladstone, the quintessential Liberal,[4] illustrated in his own person the contradictory sources of the party's strength. A High-Church Tory at heart, a friend of private fortunes, and a believer in "the rule of the best," he nevertheless became the spokesman for popular democracy, free trade, Catholic emancipation, reform of the Civil Service, and Irish Home Rule, all but the last of which were congenial to the spirit of Benthamism. Gladstone was anything but "progressive" in his moral outlook. His ambition was to render the morality of private life totally applicable to politics—in other words, to Christianize national policy. He supported repeal of the Corn Laws, for example, not as an economic reform but to satisfy a point of justice, and his campaign to

2. See Michael St. John Packe, *The Life of John Stuart Mill* (London, 1954), pp. 310–314.
3. *Autobiography*, p. 162.
4. William Gladstone (1809–98), leader of the Liberal Party and prime minister four times between 1868 and 1894. [*Editor*]

alleviate poverty rose from a belief that greater material welfare would help to improve the nation's ethics. The distance between this kind of reasoning and the Utilitarian calculus is of course immense, but Gladstone's popularity, together with the concurrence of his policies with Benthamite programs, held the Liberal Party together until the 1890's.

The inconsistency and weakness of the Liberal Party in that decade undoubtedly helped to confirm E. M. Forster in his abstention from partisanship. The Liberals had always been composed of a rather uneasy coalition of Whigs, Radicals, and Peelites, who were united more by their opposition to Disraeli than by any common ground of philosophy.[5] With Disraeli's death in 1881, the debacle of Khartoum in 1885, and the public identification of Gladstone with Home Rule and Parnellism after that year, the party began to disintegrate rapidly.[6] Gladstone's second Home Rule defeat and retirement in 1894 left the party without a widely respected leader. And in the period 1899–1902, when most of the future Bloomsbury writers were undergraduates at Cambridge, the Liberals were further weakened by the divisive issue of the South African War.[7] Almost all the remaining Imperialists in the Liberal Party had gone over to the Conservatives by 1902. Leslie Stephen described what had become, in 1903, an impossible tangle of party lines: "The Radical takes credit for having transferred political power to the democracy, though the democracy sets at defiance the old Radical's hatred of Government interference and of all Socialistic legislation. The Tory boasts that the prejudice against State interference has vanished, though the rulers of the State have now to interfere as the servants and not as the masters of the democracy. Both sides have modified their creeds in the course of their flirtation with Socialism, till it is difficult to assign the true principle of either, or trace the affiliation of ideas."[8]

Where were liberals of the more idealistic stamp expected to turn? Exasperation with the Liberal Party had reached a point where disengagement and reassessment of principles were imperative. This was the case, for example, with the founders of the *Independent Review*, a journal whose principles we must now examine, for E. M. Forster "thought the new age had begun" when he read the first number, and himself became a contributor to later numbers.[9] It is the *Independent Review*

---

5. Whigs, Radicals, and Peelites: opposition political factions that contributed to the formation of the Liberal Party in the early nineteenth century; Benjamin Disraeli (1804–81): leader of the Conservative Party and prime minister in 1868 and 1874–80. [*Editor*]

6. Khartoum: Egyptian city where British imperial forces suffered a humiliating defeat; Home Rule: the cause of independence for Ireland, led by Charles Stewart Parnell (1846–91). [*Editor*]

7. From 1899 to 1902 the British fought the Dutch settlers of South Africa, known as the "Boers," in an especially brutal war, which caused considerable dissent and opposition in England. [*Editor*]

8. *Some Early Impressions* (London, 1924), pp. 81f.

9. E. M. Forster, *Goldsworthy Lowes Dickinson* (London, 1934), p. 116.

that suggests most clearly the connection between liberal politics and Forster's art.

One of this journal's founders was G. Lowes Dickinson, Forster's teacher and friend at Cambridge, whose biography Forster wrote in 1934. There Forster gives us a vivid idea of what the *Independent* promised for disenchanted young liberals of the day: "The first number appeared in October, 1903. Edward Jenks was the editor; Dickinson, F. W. Hirst, C. F. G. Masterman, G. M. Trevelyan and Wedd were the members of the editorial council; Roger Fry designed the cover. The main aim of the review was political. It was founded to combat the aggressive Imperialism and the protection campaign of Joe Chamberlain; and to advocate sanity in foreign affairs and a constructive policy at home. It was not so much a Liberal review as an appeal to Liberalism from the Left to be its better self—one of those appeals which have continued until the extinction of the Liberal party. Dickinson thus defends the opening number of his review against the free-lancing of Ashbee (Letter of November 11th, 1903): 'If Liberals as you say are not "constructive" that perhaps is due to the fact that they believe in Liberty which means that they think all legislation can do is to give the utmost scope to individuals to develop the best in them. That I confess is my own point of view. But I believe that to do that will mean gradual revolution of all the fundamentals of society, law of property, law of contract, law of marriage. Yet all that revolution would be abortive unless people have ideals for which they individually care and which are of the spirit and not mere megalomania. . . .'"

Forster continues: ". . .'The Independent Review' did not make much difference to the councils of the nation, but it struck a note which was new at that time, and had a great influence on a number of individuals—young people for the most part. We were being offered something which we wanted. Those who were Liberals felt that the heavy, stocky, body of their party was about to grow wings and leave the ground. Those who were not Liberals were equally filled with hope: they saw avenues opening into literature, philosophy, human relationships, and the road of the future passing through not insurmountable dangers to a possible Utopia. Can you imagine decency touched with poetry? It was thus that the 'Independent' appeared to us—a light rather than a fire, but a light that penetrated the emotions" (*Dickinson*, pp. 115f).

Here, certainly, the tradition of Mill is unmistakable; Dickinson's statement that "all legislation can do is to give the utmost scope to individuals to develop the best in them" seems to come directly from *On Liberty*. Forster's perception of "avenues opening into literature, philosophy, human relationships" also reflects the liberal belief that a man's political principles should be a consistent extension of his entire moral life. It is noteworthy, too, that Dickinson's remarks align him with the late, "Utopian" Mill rather than with the young defender of *laissez faire*.

He has reached Mill's idea that collectivist legislation is positively necessary to prevent society from exercising a tyranny of fortune and opinion over the individual.

Although Forster's contributions to the *Independent* were not political, the fact that he eagerly submitted short stories and "cultural" essays reflects his admiration for the editors' point of view. We need not assume that he was well versed in the complex problems of trade and Empire that were debated in the review by such experts as Jenks, Masterman, and Trevelyan. It is more likely that his Cambridge years had predisposed him to a general sympathy with the liberalism of Arnold and the later Mill. If he was not exercised by all the collectivist reforms demanded by the *Independent*, he must certainly have approved of its repeated emphasis on freedom of discussion, equality of opportunity, and the importance of the individual man.

* * *

WILFRED STONE

E. M. Forster's Subversive Individualism[†]

I

It is appropriate on this centenary of Forster's birth to take a look at some aspects of his social philosophy—his liberalism, his well-known creed of 'personal relations', his lifelong contention with the vexed problem of *power*. It is appropriate because Forster made his mark not just as a novelist, but also as a humanist; not just as an artist, but as a moral influence; not just as the author of *A Passage to India*, but also as the author of 'What I Believe'. It is appropriate as well because Forster's social attitudes are deeply personal, and now that P. N. Furbank's biography is out, and Forster is out of the closet in other ways, the materials are available for a reassessment. His position as a novelist is, I believe, forever secure, whereas his position as a humanist, as the liberal moral philosopher, is, I think, more problematical. But his influence in this role has been immense, and this centenary year will doubtless be the occasion for many people to reevaluate the impact of Forster's influence upon them.

Let me begin with that striking statement Forster made in his post-war broadcast talk 'The Challenge of Our Time' (1946):

† From *E. M. Forster: Centenary Revaluations*, ed. Judith Scherer Herz and Robert K. Martin (Toronto: University of Toronto Press, 1982), 15–29. Reprinted with the permission of the editors and Wilfred H. Stone.

> I belong to the fag-end of Victorian liberalism, and can look back
> to an age whose challenges were moderate in their tone, and the
> cloud on whose horizon was no bigger than a man's hand. In many
> ways it was an admirable age. It practised benevolence and philan-
> thropy, was humane and intellectually curious, upheld free speech,
> and had little colour-prejudice, believed that individuals are and
> should be different, and entertained a sincere faith in the progress
> of society. The world was to become better and better, chiefly
> through the spread of parliamentary institutions. The education I
> received in those far-off and fantastic days made me soft and I am
> very glad it did, for I have seen plenty of hardness since, and I know
> it does not even pay. Think of the end of Mussolini—the hard man,
> hanging upside-down like a turkey, with his dead mistress swinging
> beside him.[1]

I distinctly remember my shocked reaction when I first read that statement—shortly after I had spent four years in an unwanted military uni-
form. How, I wanted to cry out, did Forster suppose that that hard man
Mussolini got his comeuppance, except at the hands of other hard men,
or men who had been trained to be hard? Did he suppose that some
abstract force of history, operating automatically and inevitably, took
care of these threats to civilization without human intervention? What
kind of bloodless dream of history was this? And by what right did Forster
the non-combatant stand on the sidelines of conflict and assure us that
the hard ones always lost, just a few years after they had come so desperately close to winning? To citizens of the twentieth century who have
known trenches and breadlines and concentration camps for their inheritance, Forster's defence of 'softness' can seem at best unrealistic and at
worst infuriating. Yet the idea of softness is at the heart of Forster's liberal philosophy; it is literally soft at the centre.

So our question is: How valuable is a creed so centred? Is it a responsible code or is it a cop-out—a denial of complexity and a turning away
from history? How seriously can we take Forster's personal witness for
softness in a world increasingly dominated by the hard impersonality of
gigantic armaments, gigantic corporations, gigantic machines, gigantic
populations, gigantic cities? In engaging with that question, I shall consult Forster's fiction and biography as different aspects of one record—as
I believe in essentials they are. And I shall approach the question via
Forster's personal experience, for it is that personal experience more
than any theoretical belief that is written into 'What I Believe' and those
other credal pronouncements of Forster's sixth decade. To ask what
meaning that creed has for our day, we must first ask what meaning it
had for Forster himself.

---

1. "The Challenge of Our Time," *Two Cheers for Democracy*, ed. Oliver Stallybrass (London:
Edward Arnold, 1972), p. 54. [See above in this Norton Critical Edition, 322. *Editor*]

II

As a child, Forster was brought up in virtual protective custody. Fatherless, surrounded by a doting mother and aunts, Forster ('the important one') was the centre of a charmed circle of love from which he never entirely escaped. That charmed circle was both a womb and a prison, a place of safety and of suffocation, and I believe that Forster's life can be largely described as a struggle between his desire to escape that confinement (to hold his own with hardness) and the temptation to return to that womb (to give in to softness). P. N. Furbank points out that Forster even as an adult had the sense of being one specially selected — 'one who, having been specially and royally favoured as a child, had magical feelings about his own life',[2] a sense of being set apart for something like divine favour. I think this magical sense was operating when Forster looked at the dead Mussolini and saw that hardness did not pay: he was looking out at a hard world and seeing, with relief, that his special Providence was at work, that the protectors were doing their job of making things safe for the favoured child. But living within this charmed circle was not all comfort, and Rickie in *The Longest Journey* is eloquent testimony that protective custody could be as much a prison as a paradise:

> The boy grew up in great loneliness. He worshipped his mother, and she was fond of him. But she was dignified and reticent, and pathos, like tattle, was disgusting to her. She was afraid of intimacy, in case it led to confidence and tears, and so all her life she held her son at a little distance. Her kindness and unselfishness knew no limits, but if he tried to be dramatic and thank her, she told him not to be a little goose. And so the only person he came to know at all was himself.[3]

To break out of that feminine confine, Forster could expect help from no-one but himself, and there is real anger at the father who, psychologically, abandoned him. When I was gathering photographs for *The Cave and the Mountain*, Forster gladly gave me pictures of the mother but would not give me one of the father; I felt he simply did not want the father represented in his life story. It is clear, I think, that Forster as a young man fought a kind of losing battle for his own manhood and that his homosexuality is a direct result of his early smothering—a kind of victory in that it was a defiance of the guardians, a kind of defeat in that it was a denial of fatherhood. But Forster did fantasize breaking out: I think those scenes of physical violence in his fiction (like Gino and Philip in *Angels*) and those outbursts of hardboiled petulance in his

---

2. P. N. Furbank, *E. M. Forster: A Life* (New York: Harcourt Brace Jovanovich, 1977), II, p. 131. [Subsequent references will be given parenthetically in the text. *Editor*]

3. E. M. Forster, *The Longest Journey*, World's Classics, No. 578 (London: Oxford University Press, 1960), pp. 27–8. [Subsequent references will be given parenthetically. *Editor*]

essays ('the strong are so stupid') are ways he asserted his masculinity. And that story 'The Machine Stops' is nothing but a fantasy of violent escape from the mother's realm. D. H. Lawrence identified Forster's central crisis, I believe, when in 1915 he wrote to Bertrand Russell (when Forster was 36): 'Will all the poetry in the world satisfy the manhood of Forster, when Forster knows that his implicit manhood is to be satisfied by nothing but immediate physical action?'[4] To become a man, Forster had to fight clear, to use his muscles, to test his courage, to endure pain, to act as a sexual being. Forster knew this, but he also knew the temptation of a powerful tug in the reverse direction, towards softness, pacifism, non-involvement, and what he called 'decadence'—all values that, throughout his life, he accorded deep respect.

The Longest Journey dramatizes this struggle. The essential plot of the book shows Forster killing off a soft, weak, half-wanted self, Rickie, in favour of a hard, strong, longed-for self, Stephen. Stephen the half-brother is the continuator, the stud who breeds the child that continues the family line through the beloved mother. But Rickie, Forster's direct representative in the novel, suffers deterioration and death, and through him the hated father's line is allowed to die out. Thus Forster gets revenge—on the father, and on certain qualities he loathed in himself. That Rickie and Stephen represent two sides of Forster seems to me evident: on the one side is weakness, ugliness, dependency; on the other a craving for strength (even brutality), beauty and heroism. Even relatively late in life Forster looks in his own mirror and sees these two personae contending. Here is part of his New Year's 'summing-up' for 1925:

> Jan. 2 Famous, wealthy, miserable, physically ugly—red nose enormous, round patch in middle of scalp which I forget less than I did and which is brown when I don't wash my head and pink when I do. Face in the distance . . . is toad-like and pallid . . . My stoop must be appalling yet I don't think much of it . . . and am surprised I don't repel more generally: I can still get to know any one I want and have that illusion that I am charming and beautiful. (Furbank, vol. 2, 134)

Stephen is less Rickie's anti-self than he is a wished-for alter ego, another self that could defend and protect the central self. It is significant that in all of Forster's fiction where weak Prufrock-like men appear they save themselves (when they don't simply run away) through the acquisition of protectors. There are two great exceptions—the short stories 'Dr. Woolacott' (1927) and 'The Other Boat' (1957)—but in most of the fiction protection comes from outside, in the form of guardians, class privileges, wealth, 'civilization', or tough guys like Stephen who happen to

4. Letter dated 12 February, 1915. See Harry T. Moore, ed., *Collected Letters of D. H. Lawrence* (New York: Viking, 1962), p. 318. [See below in this Norton Critical Edition, p. 389. Editor]

be on the right side. Meanwhile, outside of fiction, in real life, Forster was deeply drawn to strong men who could be enticed into friendship or love. Perhaps the ideal in this direction was T. E. Lawrence, that close friend who combined heroism and sensitivity,[5] and whom Forster sought in vain as a lover. But there were other hard ones, notably the police officer Bob Buckingham, with whom Forster had more success, to say nothing of the 'reformed and unreformed burglars' and others with whom Forster had affairs (Furbank, vol. 2, 185). Whatever these affairs mean, they do represent the kind of physical engagement D. H. Lawrence called for—an effort to move out of his *cordon sanitaire* and engage with a hard world.

But the hard ones, as Forster experiences them, usually come as enemies, not as friends, and to confront them in the flesh was a terror of his young life. Stephen's opposite in *The Longest Journey* is Gerald the bully, who persecutes rather than protects the weak. This is how Rickie remembers him, years after his school days:

> The horror disappeared, for, thank God, he was now a man, whom civilization protects. But he and Gerald had met, as it were, behind the scenes, before our decorous drama opens, and there the elder boy had done things to him—absurd things, not worth chronicling separately. An apple-pie bed is nothing; pinches, kicks, boxed ears, twisted arms, pulled hair, ghosts at night, inky books, befouled photographs, amount to very little by themselves. But let them be united and continuous, and you have a hell that no grown-up devil can devise. Between Rickie and Gerald there lay a shadow that darkens life more often than we suppose. The bully and his victim never quite forget their first relations. (*Longest Journey*, 43)

The one who has been bullied desires revenge, and Forster openly used the pen as a weapon to avenge himself on those who had hurt him. 'In no book', he said, 'have I got down more than the people I like, the person I think I am, and the people who irritate me'.[6] And in his 1920 essay 'The Consolations of History', Forster expresses frank delight in paying off old scores against the military—a form of organized hardness that, along with bureaucracy generally, he wholeheartedly loathed:

> It is pleasant to be transferred from an office where one is afraid of a sergeant-major into an office where one can intimidate generals, and perhaps this is why History is so attractive to the more timid amongst us. We can recover self-confidence by snubbing the dead.[7]

5. P. N. Furbank points out that T. E. Lawrence's *Seven Pillars of Wisdom* 'supported him in a cherished belief that sensitiveness and introspection could exist side by side with vigour, active heroism and largeness of vision'. Furbank, II, pp. 119–20.
6. E. M. Forster, 'The Art of Fiction', *The Paris Review*, I (1953), 37. See Forster, "Interview," in this Norton Critical Edition, 293.
7. E. M. Forster, 'The Consolations of History', *Abinger Harvest* (London: Edward Arnold, 1961), p. 191.

Yet we should not conclude that Forster disapproved of hardness or even brutality. He just wanted it to be on his side, operating as his vicar. Howard Sholton in 'The Purple Envelope' (1905), for example, 'loved to take life, as all those do who are really in touch with nature'.[8] And in another passage from *The Longest Journey* we are told that Rickie believes 'something can be said' for cruelty and brutality:

> Athletes, he believed, were simple, straightforward people, cruel and brutal, if you like, but never petty. They knocked you down and hurt you, and then went on their way rejoicing. For this, Rickie thought, there is something to be said: he had escaped the sin of despising the physically strong—a sin against which the physically weak must guard. (*Longest Journey* 42)

The school scenes in *The Longest Journey* reflect the spirit if not the letter of Forster's actual experiences at school. Furbank tells us of Forster's profound unhappiness at the various schools he attended from the age of 11. At 'The Grange', for example, where he spent the summer of 1892, Forster learned what it was to be bullied, and his letters home from this place are desperate pleas to be rescued: 'O what is going to happen? . . . I feel utterly wretched, I would like to come away. Every one is against me . . .' Furbank comments:

> There was nothing for it but to withdraw him from the school, and he returned to 'Rooksnest' in floods of tears. His beloved Maimie was there, and between them the two women soon comforted him; but he could tell from his mother's manner that she was ashamed of him as a cry-baby. It had been impressed on him when he went to 'The Grange' that it was a school for the sons of gentlemen, and all through his troubles there the refrain ran through his mind: 'If they were not the sons of gentlemen they would not be so unkind'. (Furbank, vol. 1, 40)

At Tonbridge, where he spent the next eight years and where the 'sons of gentlemen' came a notch lower on the social ladder, he was not so cruelly bullied but was miserable, bored and, as Furbank says, keenly wounded by 'the general atmosphere of unkindness' (Furbank, vol. 1, 42). 'School was the unhappiest time of my life',[9] he wrote later. He came away from the experience with a life-long 'horror of gangs', and his device for recovering his balance after being bullied was, as Furbank reports, 'mentally resolving the gang back into individuals' (Furbank, vol. 1, 43). He was a day student at Tonbridge, so the mother's protection was still extended, one result of which was that he was permitted to ride a bicycle instead of engaging in games—an unprecedented relax-

---

8. E. M. Forster, *The Life to Come and Other Stories*, ed. Oliver Stallybrass, Abinger edn. (London: Edward Arnold, 1972), p. 36.
9. E. M. Forster, 'Breaking Up', *The Spectator*, LXI (July 1923), 110.

ation of the rules. Tonbridge failed utterly to harden Forster; he simply would not rise to the bait. To the degree that the Kiplingesque school anthem expressed the spirit of the place, to that degree Forster despised it, and one of the finer touches in *The Longest Journey* is the small boy who refused to sing the anthem on the grounds that 'it hurt his throat'. Two couplets that Forster exposed to special ridicule were these:

> Here shall Tonbridge flourish, here shall manhood be,
> Serving God and country, ruling land and sea . . .
> Choose we for life's battle harp or sword or pen;
> Perish every laggard, let us all be men. (quoted in Furbank, vol. 1, 41, 42)

The religiosity, the patriotism, the muscularity of those verses all rubbed Forster the wrong way. They were tainted by the bullying that went with them, and Forster's notion of 'manhood' differed fundamentally from the school ideal. To the school's hardness he opposed—with considerable pluckiness—his own softness, and over the years made a creed of it. But his rejection of those school ideals confirmed him forever as an outsider, a pariah, to the main ranks of his own class.

After Tonbridge came Cambridge which, of course, was everything Tonbridge was not. Here too was a muscular 'best set', but it did not dominate, and here Forster the pariah felt welcomed and warmed—particularly after he became accepted as a member of the Apostles. This was the Cambridge of Lord Acton who was saying that 'All power corrupts and absolute power corrupts absolutely', and here were friends who cultivated a pose of irreverence towards the very values extolled in the Tonbridge anthem. The following lines published in *Basileona*, an undergraduate magazine, caught the new mood perfectly:

> I fail to see the reason why
> Brittania should rule the waves,
> Nor can I safely prophesy
> That Britons never shall be slaves;
> It always gives me quite a pain
> Ever to *think* about the main.
>
> Elusive prospects of renown
> Do not excite me in the least,
> A Lion fighting for a Crown
> Is hardly an attractive beast.
> If you are anxious to be shot
> For Queen and Country, I am not.[1]

---

1. *Basileona*, 1900. The verses were found in a *Scrapbook* of Forster's which he let me examine in the autumn of 1957.

Cambridge was once again a kind of charmed circle for Forster, an *alma mater* offering a new kind of protective custody; but it was within those protected bounds that Forster's liberalism, an existential experience, found its first deep reinforcement.

Time permitting, we could trace Forster's contention with the issue of crude power through all his novels, particularly in *Howards End* and *A Passage to India*. Suffice it to say that the issue of softness vs. hardness, sensitivity vs. brutality, is central and that Forster—to his credit—does his best as author to guard against the sin of the physically weak—that of 'despising the physically strong'. He has Margaret marry the redblood Henry and insists on honouring the Wilcox energy and grit: 'If Wilcoxes hadn't worked and died in England for thousands of years, you and I couldn't sit here without having our throats cut'.[2] And Aziz tries to be friends with the English, his imperial oppressors, until the pressures of politics force them apart. In both novels the forces of alienation prove stronger than those of connection, for the reason that the hard ones— those grown-up public school boys—behave too badly. One speech by Ronny Heaslop tells it all:

> I am out here to work, mind, to hold this wretched country by force. I'm not a missionary or a Labour Member or a vague senti- mental sympathetic literary man. I'm just a servant of the Government . . . We're not pleasant in India and we don't intend to be pleasant. We've something more important to do.[3]

Forster is, of course, characterizing himself in that 'vague sentimental sympathetic literary man', and at least one distinguished Indian critic has testified that if Forster's ideal of a 'democratic Empire' had been tried in India—a society based on equal rights and privileges for Indians and Englishmen alike—the British Empire could have been an endur- ing institution.[4] But the imperialist, as Forster tells us in *Howards End*, is a 'destroyer'—and in retrospect, when Forster's ideas for governing India are compared with those that were actually tried, Forster begins to look like a practical politician! But we must return to biography.

The event that perhaps tested Forster's liberal humanism most acute- ly and painfully was the First World War. All Bloomsbury felt, says Furbank, that 'it was not *their* war' (vol. 2, 1), and Forster aligned him- self with this attitude. The war filled him with nothing less than 'panic and emptiness', and his first response was to find refuge in friends, exer- cising the old pattern of dissolving the 'gang' into individuals. 'He was doubly disturbed', Furbank tells us, '—by the war itself, and by the inad- equacy of his own response to it' (vol. 2, 1). That response *was* inade-

2. See 126 in this Norton Critical Edition. [*Editor*]
3. E. M. Forster, *A Passage to India*, ed. Oliver Stallybrass, Abinger edn. (London: Edward Arnold, 1978), p. 44.
4. G. D. Das, *E. M. Forster's India* (London: Macmillan, 1977), p. 25.

quate. Essentially he just ran away—to the safety of a cushy job with the Red Cross in Alexandria—and when in 1916 he was threatened with conscription (technically, the duty to 'attest'), he simply went to pieces. Here is Furbank's account:

> He was now in a serious dilemma. He was determined not to attest, yet could not easily explain his reasons—for he knew that, in a strict sense, he was not a conscientious objector. For a few days he was badly thrown by the contretemps, and—as once or twice later in life in times of stress—he developed a kind of falling sickness and had bouts of hurling himself against the furniture. (Furbank, vol. 2, 26)

He finally managed to stay out of the army through some wire-pulling with high-ranking friends—a conspicuous instance of using his social rank as a 'protector'. 'I am quite shameless over this wirepulling', Forster wrote to his mother in 1916; 'If I can't keep out of the army by fair means then hey for foul! Let alone that there conscience. I know I should be no good, and haven't the least desire to pacify the parrots who cry "All must go"' (Furbank, vol. 2, 27). One cannot, of course, fail to share Forster's horror of the war and his desire to escape it, but neither can one refrain from asking the obvious, embarrassing question: What about those hundreds of thousands who had no high-ranking friends and no wires to pull? This is but one of the many times in his life that Forster invoked special privilege in order to save himself—and is but an extended pattern of that tearful escape home from school.

During these war years in Alexandria Forster experienced an intense retreat inward. There was, of course, a movement outward as well—to an interest in the history and politics of Egypt that led to *Alexandria: A History and A Guide* (1922), *Pharos and Pharillon* (1923), and his long essay 'The Government of Egypt' for the Labour Research Department (1920). It was this period, as Lionel Trilling has said, that gave Forster 'a firm position on the Imperial question'.[5] But I think these outgoing efforts were, in part at least, a kind of moral compensation for having so narcissistically sought sanctuary during the war years.[6] Part of that inward retreat expressed itself as an embrace of 'decadence'. After having read Huysmans' *A Rebours* and Eliot's *Prufrock* in 1917, he wrote: 'Oh, the relief of a world which lived for its sensations and ignored the will . . . Was it decadent? Yes, and thank God'.[7] And speaking specifical-

5. Lionel Trilling, *E. M. Forster* (Norfolk, Conn.: New Directions, 1943), p. 138.
6. In 1917 Forster wrote to G. Lowes Dickinson: 'I have never had the energy or intelligence to understand contemporary civilisation, have never done more than loaf through it and jump out of its way when it seemed likely to hurt me' (Furbank, II, p. 26). In 1939, in 'What I Believe', Forster wrote, 'I look the other way until fate strikes me. Whether this is due to courage or to cowardice in my own case I cannot be sure' (TCD [*Two Cheers for Democracy*], p. 68). These are not simple avoiding reactions, but part of a struggle in Forster, a life-long struggle, between courage and cowardice.
7. E. M. Forster, 'T. S. Eliot', *Abinger Harvest*, p. 106.

ly of Prufrock he wrote: 'Here was a protest, and a feeble one, and the more congenial for being feeble. For what, in that world of gigantic horror, was tolerable except the slighter gestures of dissent?' (*Abinger*, 107). Eliot would have been surprised, I think, to know that anyone read *Prufrock* as a 'protest'. Forster's reasons are interesting:

> He who measured himself against the war, who drew himself to his full height, as it were, and said to Armadillo-Armageddon 'Avaunt!' collapsed at once into a pinch of dust. But he who could turn aside to complain of ladies and drawing-rooms preserved a tiny drop of our self-respect, he carried on the human heritage. (*Abinger*, 107)

This is salvation via nostalgia. What Forster is saying is that he felt safe in such rooms with such ladies—perhaps even saved—and there is little question that his embrace of 'decadence' as a value in this period is a kind of fantasy return to the womb. He loved Eliot's poems because they 'were innocent of public-spiritedness: they sang of private disgust and diffidence, and of people who seemed genuine because they were unattractive or weak' (*Abinger*, 106). Can there be any doubt that this is Forster looking into his own mirror? He is building a defence for the 'unattractive or weak', for softness, and I think that it is during these years that Forster crystallized that defence into something like a principle— and into a political position that touched more than the Imperial question. He was confronted with the clear choice of either being ashamed of himself or being proud of himself, and he elected to be proud of himself. Unless the world is made safe for the soft individual it cannot, for Forster, be a tolerable world: he wanted a literal translation of the hope that the meek should inherit the earth. Decadence? Forster refuses to hear it as a bad word. Years later, in 1939, when these conflicts had been reduced to a creed, Forster declared that decadence is what some people call those intervals in history when 'force and violence' do not 'get to the front'. Forster calls those absences 'civilization' and finds in such interludes 'the chief justification for the human experiment'.[8]

But Forster did not arrive at such views easily. His letters to friends out of Alexandria are full of trouble and sadness, and he by no means managed to 'let alone that there conscience'. Alexandria was a time of sexual awakening for Forster and he was excited by the streams of soldiers pouring into the Montazah Convalescent Hospital where he worked; but he was conscious as well that they came from a hell he had no part of. 'It makes me very happy yet very sad', he writes to Lowes Dickinson in July 1916; 'they come from the unspeakable all these young gods, and in a fortnight at the latest they will return to it . . .' But what comes next? Does Forster consider joining them? Partaking of their suffering like a brother? On the contrary, he clings to his privileged position, and his

---

8. Forster, 'What I Believe', *TCD*, p. 68.

conscience erodes into a daydream of what might be: 'Why not a world like this?' (referring to the comforts the soldiers knew at the hospital). Why not a world 'that should not torture itself by organized and artificial horrors?' (Furbank, vol. 2, 34). This is no way to 'face facts', and friends who were not pacifists (as Dickinson was) criticized Forster for his evasions; but during this period that dream of a world without violence became, in some strange way, confused in Forster's mind with moral action. He looked out on the 'real' world as if from a kind of hibernation, a drugged quarantine; and though he sensed that there was something 'unreal' about his position, he clung to it. Thus he writes to Bertrand Russell in 1917:

> Here I have been for nearly two years. Harmless and unharmed. Here in Egyptian hospitals. I live in their wards, questioning survivors. It has been a comfortable life. How unreal I shan't know till I compare it with the lives others have been leading in the period. I don't write, but feel I think and think I feel. Sometimes I make notes on human nature under war conditions . . . I love people and want to understand them and help them more than I did, but this is oddly accompanied by a growth of contempt. Be like them? God, no.[9]

There is class snobbery here and maybe something worse, but this passage gives us a glimpse at the workings of Forster's 'conscience'. Love warring with contempt measures the degree of Forster's self-contempt—and the guilt (evaded rather than suppressed) arising from his position of special privilege. But such exclusiveness is inseparable from Forster's liberal humanism, for the softness it defends is his own softness, and in that defence Forster again and again implicitly declares himself to be a special case and deserving of special treatment. In spite of having 'magical feelings about his own life' and feeling in some way exempted from the common human fate, he at the same time felt that his situation was somehow 'unreal'. But Forster is never openly apologetic over a position that some people saw as plain cowardice; and Alexandria, I believe, was the testing place where he gained the confidence to accept himself as he was, and to be his own kind of liberal.

During the war, Forster felt that history was sweeping him away, that he could not get anywhere by the exercise of will, that in all the big things he was helpless. Like Cavafy (and perhaps with Cavafy's help), he reduced history to personal relations, to relations—in his case—based on homosexual love.[1] And he elevated 'decadence' to something like an ideal.

But the germ of an opposing attitude was alive in him. And after the war, as if to make up for his wartime retreat, he came out of his cocoon

---

9. Quoted in Jane Lagoudis Pinchin, *Alexandria Still: Forster, Durrell and Cavafy* (Princeton: Princeton University Press, 1977), p. 99.
1. Constantine Cavafy (1863–1933), Greek poet whom Forster knew in Alexandria, author of some notable homosexual erotic poetry. [*Editor*]

and engaged in a wide variety of political actions. Throughout the 'twenties he was an active critic of England's imperialistic crimes in India and Egypt; as first president of the National Council for Civil Liberties, he did what he could to defend free speech on the BBC and elsewhere; he led a wide-ranging assault with his pen on bureaucracy, in the military and in government offices (hitting a high point with that fine satire, 'Our Deputation'); he was active in fighting literary censorship and the prudery behind it, defending Radclyffe Hall's *Well of Loneliness* (1928) and, much later, Lawrence's *Lady Chatterley's Lover* (1960); he was active in the PEN Club and in 1928 became the first president of the 'Young PEN', a club for young and unknown writers; he continually spoke out against homosexual and racial prejudice. As another war loomed, Forster became somewhat disillusioned with activism, and on the eve of the Munich crisis he was asked by Goronwy Rees, assistant editor of the *Spectator*, 'Why have you given up politics?' He replied, 'Because I want just a *little* result' (Furbank, vol. 2, 222).

To be sure, Forster was an activist only in liberal causes, which is to say only causes for which words are weapons. But he had emerged from hiding and become a fighter with words, and he no longer acquiesced in the belief that history operated by its own forces and could not be affected by the will. If Forster became less organizationally engaged in the late 'thirties and early 'forties, he assuredly did not become less articulate. In these years Forster uttered a flood of speeches, broadcasts and essays defining his liberal humanist position—the greatest of which is 'What I Believe' in 1939. In them all, Forster stood his ground in defence of softness, but it was a position toughly held and not weakly acted out. Julian Bell, before he was killed in the Spanish Civil War in 1937, had challenged Forster's pacifism as an archaic posture in a world threatened by Hitlers and Mussolinis. But in reply Forster refused to 'chuck gentleness' and went on to say, 'If one has been gentle, semi-idealistic, and semi-cynical, kind, tolerant, demure, and generally speaking a liberal for nearly sixty years, it is wiser to stick to one's outfit' (Furbank, vol. 2, 224). And it was about this time that Christopher Isherwood in *Lions and Shadows* (1938) had talked about the need for the 'Truly Weak Man' to submit himself to what he called the 'Test'. Forster would have none of this, and wrote to Isherwood in February 1938:

> *Bother the Test*—am so certain I shall fail mine that I can't think about it. Now and then I get toward facing facts, but get too tired to keep on at it. I only hope I shan't let any one down badly: *that* thought does present itself rather alarmingly. (Furbank, vol. 2, 223)

If this is still somewhat self-indulgent, it is at least honest; Forster is sure of who he is and unabashed about acting the part.

During the second war, Forster's stance became one of 'keeping calm and cheerful'. He did not succumb to despair—though he had a tragic sense that the old order had forever 'vanished from the earth'[2] and he turned out, during the war years, a steady stream of propaganda broadcasts, one of them beginning memorably with the words, 'This pamphlet is propaganda'![3] But throughout the war he concerned himself less with winning battles than with reminding his countrymen and women that it was 'civilisation' they were fighting for, not victory. What would be gained if in defeating the Nazis we allowed our culture to become 'governmental' like theirs? All would be lost. And his PEN speech in the autumn of 1941—to a hall full of anti-Hitler writers and refugees, all highly committed—began, 'I believe in art for art's sake'.[4]

III

But all these utterances can be glossed by reference to the one classic statement of 1939, 'What I Believe'. It is all there. Forster in his level speaking voice and colloquial vocabulary, without pomposity or prophetic intonation, made a statement that has become a classic in the modern liberal/humanist tradition. Since most readers probably know this essay almost by heart, I shall dip into it only briefly. He comes out as the defender of weakness ('the strong are so stupid'); of a saving élite ('an aristocracy of the sensitive, the considerate and the plucky'); of free speech ('I believe in [Parliament] *because* it is a Talking Shop'); of something like deconstruction ('The more highly public life is organized, the lower does its morality sink'); and, of course, of personal relations, the key to the whole creed:

> . . . there is even a terror and a hardness in this creed of personal relationships, urbane and mild though it sounds. Love and loyalty to an individual can run counter to the claims of the State. When they do—down with the State, say I, which means that the State would down me.
>
> (*TCD*, 68, 70, 67, 71, 66)

These are tough statements. If this author is not much good with his fists or the sword, he has learned to be very good with words. And if this is a creed born of weakness and dependency, it no longer sounds like a cry from the beleaguered schoolboy. Forster lived in a free country and would not be jailed—not yet—for sounding treasonous. Nevertheless, these are radical things to say on the eve of a war and it took courage to say them. No one could accuse Forster of playing it safe or of currying favour with the powerful.

*   *   *

2. E. M. Forster, 'They Hold Their Tongues', *TCD*. p. 29.
3. E. M. Forster, *Nordic Twilight* (London: Macmillan, 1940), p. 3.
4. E. M. Forster, 'The New Disorder', *Horizon*, IV (1941), 379.

MICHAEL LEVENSON

Liberalism and Symbolism in *Howards End*[†]

Liberalism and symbolism, both unwieldy terms, become more unwieldy when brought together. They seem to belong to such different orders of description and such different strains of modernity that it provokes a small mental shudder to recall that John Stuart Mill and Charles Baudelaire were near contemporaries. Although no one would mistake E. M. Forster for either Mill or Baudelaire, liberalism and symbolism are prominent in his ancestry, and *Howards End* (1910), which occupies a place in both lineages, marks a striking point of connection between political hopes and literary tropes. The only thing more vivid than Forster's perception of social constraint was his perception of imaginative escape. Looking at the world from the standpoint of historical necessity and the standpoint of visionary possibility, he saw depth in modern experience but also incongruity, because he saw with one liberal and one symbolist eye. It is necessary to correct for the parallax. In following the competition but also the cooperation of these perspectives, this chapter * * * asks what happens to the experience of the self when its own modes of understanding come into conflict and when it is unsure whether it has sustained a symbolic victory or a political defeat.

In the work of Forster it is possible to glimpse what the development of the novel might have been if at the turn of our century it had endured an evolutionary, rather than a revolutionary, change. Forster belongs neither with the stout Edwardians, Wells, Bennett and Galsworthy, nor with the lean modernists, Joyce, Woolf, Ford and Lewis. He shared with the latter the sense of an irrevocable historical transformation that necessarily alters the methods of art, but he could never muster the conviction for a programmatic assault on traditional forms. For this reason he continues to occupy an ambiguous position in the history of modern fiction. His own formal experiments, which are by no means negligible, often appear as involuntary expressions of his own sense of loss, and much of their inspiration, as I hope to show, lies in the attempt to revive a dying tradition.

I

"Oh, to acquire culture!" thinks Leonard Bast, "Oh, to pronounce foreign names correctly."[1] He is walking alongside Margaret Schlegel, who has just pronounced Wagner's name (correctly, one must assume) and

† From Michael Levenson, *Modernism and the Fate of Individuality: Character and Novelistic Form from Conrad to Woolf* (Cambridge: Cambridge UP, 1990) 78–93. Reprinted with the permission of Cambridge University Press.
1. E. M. Forster, *Howards End*, 31. [Page references are to this Norton Critical Edition. *Editor*]

who has promised to recover Bast's umbrella, thoughtlessly taken by her sister during a concert at Queen's Hall. Bast stammers, falls silent, takes his umbrella, refuses an invitation to tea, bolts home, reads Ruskin. Then, reminded of the disparity between the flat of an insurance clerk and the stones of Venice, he lays Ruskin aside with this unhappy thought: "Oh, it was no good, this continual aspiration. Some are born cultured; the rest had better go in for whatever comes easy. To see life steadily and to see it whole was not for the likes of him" (42).

Arnold's formulation was a touchstone for Forster who came back to it repeatedly in *Howards End*—its progressive restatements marking the development of the novel's argument. On this first occasion it broaches the problem of modern character, which for Forster (certainly not uniquely) is a problem of lost unity, lost because of related historical pressures: urbanism, imperialism, cosmopolitanism, bureaucracy, the estrangement of social classes. But there is another implication in Arnold's phrase that has particular bearing on Forsterian characterization: the attention to a form of response (seeing) rather than a form of action.

The initial and decisive characterization of Margaret Schlegel identifies her leading quality as "a profound vivacity, a continual and sincere response to all that she encountered in her path through life" (10). Forster thus endows her not with a desire but with a *disposition*; he is concerned less with her will to act than with her "sincere response" to what she encounters. Of the boorish Charles Wilcox we are told that "Want was to him the only cause of action" (71). Forster mentions such an opinion only as a way of dismissing it; he himself is primarily interested in neither wants, nor causes, nor indeed actions in their conventional sense. *Howards End*, like so much of Forster's work, suggests that the incidents which determine the broad course of life, both the intimate movements of the soul and the rude spasms of history, exceed the reach of individual will. One is accountable neither for one's desires nor one's epoch. Both exist as ungovernable forces that change particular lives but resist the workings of human agency, and therefore Forster declines to describe them with precision. He prefers to maintain strict attention upon the subject that interests him most; the region of individual experience that lies between the insurgence of the feelings and the oppressions of history. Part of the reason that Forster has come to seem outdated is that the space between history and the emotions has progressively narrowed in our time, but in *Howards End* there is still room to maneuver. Nevertheless, in the face of such powerful antagonists, what is to be done?

One cannot change one's desires; one cannot alter the movement of history. But it is possible to change the form and style of one's response, and here we come to a telling aspect of the novel's method of characterization: its tendency to describe individuals in terms that refer equally to the English literary tradition. Tibby derives from the Wildean nineties; Leonard Bast connects his aspirations to Ruskin, Meredith and Stevenson; the Schlegel sisters (as others have noted) descend from *Sense and Sensibility*; Miss Avery is a late incarnation of a Gothic housekeeper; and the narrator alternately assumes the tones of Thackeray and Trollope. Through a kind of historical ventriloquism Forster displays the novelistic tradition he has inherited. This is more than an exercise in stylistic virtuosity; it serves to underscore an arresting fact, the intimate connection between fictional character and literary mode. Indeed character in *Howards End* is essentially a mode of aesthetic response, where this is understood not as the casual striking of a pose but as the deepest form of one's engagement with experience. That human responses vary so greatly poses perhaps the chief difficulty of the novel: the heterogeneity of modes, the diversity of styles, tones and manners.

Forster, who acknowledged his great debt to Jane Austen, is commonly linked to Austen and James as a novelist of manners. One might better say that he is a novelist of bad manners, who attends less to the shared norms and values which govern a community than to the moral awkwardness that results when incompatible norms and incommensurable values collide. Thus, Helen's "high-handed manner" (130) competes with the "breezy Wilcox manner" (131); Evie develops a "manner more downright" (110) while Tibby remains "affected in manner" (179); and Margaret finds Leonard's class "near enough her own for its manners to vex her" (29). Forster assumes nothing so stable as a coherent system of human conduct; indeed in his most serious purpose, he dramatizes the search for a moral manner, which becomes one with the search for an imaginative mode.

Beethoven's Fifth Symphony provides a comic and anodyne example. It excites a great variety of reactions—Mrs. Munt's surreptitious foot-tapping, Helen's reverie of heroes and goblins, Tibby's attention to counterpoint—but the variety is unthreatening because it overlays a fundamental point of agreement, namely that the "Fifth Symphony is the most sublime noise that has ever penetrated into the ear of man. All sorts and conditions are satisfied by it" (25). Beethoven, however, is valuable just insofar as he is an exception. Precisely the problem which the novel poses is the difficulty of such agreement and the incongruity of diverse sorts and sundry conditions. When Mrs. Wilcox fails to "blend" with the Schlegel set, when Leonard describes his squalid flat in the style of Ruskin, when Tibby and Charles attempt to converse having "nothing in common but the English language" (219), the painful dissonance establishes an urgent requirement, the need for an appropriate mode with which to confront the facts of contemporary experience. The Arnoldian conception of seeing life steadily and whole represents an ideal mode for the engaged personality but an ideal which seems to have become obsolete. Arnold's phrase, as we will see, has still wider implications, but then so too does the issue of modality.

The agonies of Leonard Bast reflect both the disgregation of the self and the disgregation of its community—the failure of both to advance in the direction which Arnold had so confidently forecast.

> Culture looks beyond machinery, culture hates hatred; culture has one great passion, the passion for sweetness and light. It has one even greater!—the passion for making them *prevail*. It is not satisfied till we *all* come to a perfect man; it knows that the sweetness and light of the few must be imperfect until the raw and unkindled masses of humanity are touched with sweetness and light.[2]

Against such a view, *Howards End* places Bast, whose hopes are kindled only at the cost of great pain, and who, when he burns, gives off no sweetness and little light. Bast will come to mistrust the healing power of culture, as will Margaret Schlegel who thinks of him and arrives at this post-Arnoldian conclusion:

> Culture had worked in her own case, but during the last few weeks she had doubted whether it humanized the majority, so wide and so widening is the gulf that stretches between the natural and the philosophic man, so many the good chaps who are wrecked in trying to cross it. (85)

Instead of Arnold's widening isthmus Forster sees a widening gulf. Moreover, the problem does not end here; it goes beyond the "unkindled masses" to infect the privileged few. Halfway through the novel, just before Henry Wilcox proposes marriage to Margaret Schlegel, the two discuss the burdens of house-hunting. Wilcox insists that she is not as unpractical as she pretends, and Arnold's celebrated dictum makes a second appearance.

> Margaret laughed. But she was—quite as unpractical. She could not concentrate on details. Parliament, the Thames, the irresponsive chauffeur, would flash into the field of house-hunting, and all demand some comment or response. It is impossible to see modern life steadily and see it whole, and she had chosen to see it whole. Mr. Wilcox saw steadily. (117)

The disjunction, steadily or whole, sets out the novel's problem, or to put it better, the disjunction is itself the problem. The novel asks: How can disjunction be overcome? How can Arnold's formulation be rescued and a moral unity restored? The answer, as readers of the novel well remember, is to connect: "Only connect! That was the whole of her sermon. Only connect the prose and the passion, and both will be exalted, and human love will be seen at its highest. Live in fragments no longer. Only

---

2. Matthew Arnold, *Culture and Anarchy*, in *The Complete Prose Works of Matthew Arnold*, vol. 5, ed. R. H. Super (1869; Ann Arbor MI: University of Michigan Press, 1965), p. 112.

connect, and the beast and the monk, robbed of the isolation that is life to each, will die" (134).

At this point we should recall the view of *Howards End* that has dominated the criticism since it was proposed over forty years ago. In an interpretation which first appeared in his book *E. M. Forster* (1943) Lionel Trilling offered a thoroughgoing symbolic reading according to which *Howards End* was to be seen as "a novel about England's fate," "a story of the class war."[3] Under the assumptions of this account the Schlegels exemplify the predicament of the intellectual situated between the victims and beneficiaries of modern capitalism. Their role is to reach downwards towards a depressed clerical class (as represented by Leonard Bast) and upwards towards a thriving business class (as represented by the Wilcoxes). When Helen bears a child fathered by Leonard and when Margaret marries Henry, the Schlegels symbolically fulfill their historical mission, and at the end of the novel, when Henry, Margaret, Helen and Helen's son settle at Howards End ("the symbol for England"), the reconciliation among classes has been achieved. According to Trilling the novel asks the question, "Who shall inherit England?" and it provides its answer in the final image of the child playing in the hay—"a symbol of the classless society."[4]

Trilling, it is evident, offers not merely an interpretation of the novel but an embrace of certain possibilities within it. Placing himself in a line of descent from both Arnold and Forster, he suggests in effect an Arnoldian recovery from Forsterian scepticism. In so doing, he implicitly proposes a solution to a problem that dominated the opening of this study. Both James and Conrad, as we have seen, struggled to find some accommodation between the necessary entanglements of culture and the specific perceptions, reasons and values of the entangled individual. *Heart of Darkness* and *The Ambassadors*, one might say, extend the dominion of culture by showing the extent to which it informs the intimacies of private life, and they preserve a region of individual autonomy only by contracting it severely. Both works create an image of the colossus that is social life and the buzzing gnat that is private moral experience; and both works leave a chasm between the agitation of the central character and the torpor of the community which surrounds him.

Within the terms of Trilling's interpretation *Howards End* successfully overcomes this division of experience. The symbolic equations between characters and classes—and most notably, the allegorical cast of the conclusion—traverse the distance between individual and social life. Through the resources of symbolism the private gesture is at the same time a public gesture. Activities as personal as love and marriage

3. Lionel Trilling, *E. M. Forster* (1943; New York: New Directions, 1964), p. 118.
4. *Ibid.*, pp. 118, 135. Cyrus Hoy also presents a useful reading of *Howards End* "in terms of conflicting principles whose reconciliation serves to define the novel's meaning." "Forster's Metaphysical Novel," *PMLA*, 125 (March 1960) p. 126.

become signs of amorousness among economic groups. The gnat *represents* the colossus; with that one stroke the problem of disproportion is solved. The question is whether it can be solved so easily. There can be no doubt that the symbolic associations which Trilling identifies pertain to the reading of the novel, but the difficulty comes in trying to decide exactly how they pertain. To address that issue is to widen our concerns; it is to acknowledge the problem of the novel's narrator; it is to consider the formal consequences of Forsterian characterization; and it is to ask how symbolic experience bears on the experience of politics.

II

Forster's narrator in *Howards End* retains the formal prerogatives of his Victorian antecedents: the freedom to rove through space and time, the detachment from the affairs he chronicles, the access to the minds of his characters, and the privilege of unqualified ethical assessment. Dolly, we are told, "was a rubbishy little creature, and she knew it" (68). Here is a definitive judgment in the tradition of the Victorian literary moralists, but here also are signs of diminished power. The trenchant dismissal loses some of its force through these colloquialisms—"rubbishy," and "she knew it"—which give it more the tone of a personal crotchet than an Olympian edict. Later, faced with the weighty question of whether Margaret should have been informed of Ruth Wilcox's bequest, the narrator responds with a mild "I think not" (73). Surely someone who knows that Dolly is a rubbishy little creature might be expected to have a stronger opinion on such a momentous question. But Forster gives us a narrator who constructs the fictional universe with all the resources of a narrating divinity, only to halt suddenly, and to gape at what he has made with the incomprehension of any other mortal.

Consistently in *Howards End* the represented world seems to recede from the one who ought to know it best. Consider, for instance, the initial description of Jacky, the woman who shares Leonard's shabby life on "the extreme verge of gentility."

> A woman entered, of whom it is simplest to say that she was not respectable. Her appearance was awesome. She seemed all strings and bell-pulls—ribbons, chains, bead necklaces that clinked and caught—and a boa of azure feathers hung round her neck, with the ends uneven. Her throat was bare, wound with a double row of pearls, her arms were bare to the elbows, and might again be detected at the shoulder, through cheap lace. Her hat, which was flowery, resembled those punnets covered with flannel, which we sowed with mustard and cress in our childhood, and which germinated here yes, and there no. She wore it on the back of her head. As for her hair, or rather hairs, they are too complicated to describe, but one system went down her back, lying in a thick pad there,

> while another, created for a lighter destiny, rippled around her fore-
> head. The face—the face does not signify. (39)

It indicates no disrespect for Forster to say that Jacky disappears within
the description. The passage offers too much information and too little;
like Jacky herself it depends on effects; it reveals no attachment to detail
for its own sake. The ribbons, chains and necklaces represent merely a
gloss on the vague epithets "awesome" and "not respectable," as though
the accumulation of aphoristic insights might finally amount to a coherent image. Moreover, the narrator keeps withdrawing from the descrip-
tive act, back to the mustard and cress of childhood and, more significantly, back to an intense consciousness of the verbal process itself. We
are told what is "simplest to say," what is "too complicated to describe,"
what "does not signify." This mannerism appears persistently; a circumstance is invoked and then held to exceed the reach of language. Having
mentioned the "poetry" of Helen's rash kiss, the narrator can only shrug:
"who can describe that?" (20) Repeatedly, the novel tells us what we will
not be told—"Young Wilcox was pouring in petrol, starting his engine,
and performing other actions with which this story has no concern"
(14–15)—with the result that there seems a vast penumbral field that
exists just beyond the compass of representation. This raises a vexing
formal problem to which we must return, but the opening paragraph of
chapter six reveals that it is more than a formal concern.

> We are not concerned with the very poor. They are unthinkable,
> and only to be approached by the statistician or the poet. This story
> deals with gentlefolk, or with those who are obliged to pretend that
> they are gentlefolk. (35)

Forster mutes the point with irony, but beneath the irony sounds an issue
of consequence: the narrowing of fictional domain. What can the novel
now include? What has passed beyond its bounds? Indeed *Howards End*
does not concern itself with the very poor, nor for that matter with the
very rich, who, one must suppose, are just as unthinkable. Thinkable are
the middle class or, more precisely, a few representative individuals of
that class. *Howards End* makes no attempt to survey social diversity, and
for a novel that broods so heavily over urban life, its London is strikingly depopulated.[5] Forster does not aspire to the capaciousness of the great
Victorians; he does not seek to convey the mass and density of modern
existence; his is a novel, not of three classes, but of three households. In
itself, this restriction is not noteworthy or even unusual, but in Forster it
becomes pointed because he retains such a sharp feeling for what he
excludes, because the question of domain becomes a crux in the novel,
and because it is linked so importantly to the question of Forster's liberalism.

5. Trilling, *E. M. Forster*, p. 118.

Forster frequently remarked upon the obsolescence of the liberal ideal, but he always expressed that opinion from the standpoint of an obsolescent liberal. He placed himself not beyond the tradition of Victorian liberalism but at its deliquescence, once describing himself as "an individualist and a liberal who has found liberalism crumbling beneath him."[6] It is an odd remark. Presumably, he means to suggest that English individualism remained intact while its liberalism declined. But it is a surprising political perception that can distinguish liberalism so sharply from individualism, and it is worth asking what exactly Forster meant.

In 1911, a year after the appearance of *Howards End*, L. T. Hobhouse published a small book called *Liberalism* which tersely summarized the state of contemporary liberal theory and which has for us the additional, and more immediate, virtue of establishing terms in which to approach *Howards End*. Hobhouse, who betrays none of Forster's waning confidence, sees the progress of liberalism as "a steady stream toward social amelioration and democratic government," a long course within which he distinguishes two major phases. The first, "older liberalism" worked to endow the individual with civil, economic and political freedom. It challenged "authoritarian government in church and state," and so constituted "a movement of liberation, a clearance of obstructions, an opening of channels for the flow of free spontaneous vital activity." The "old" liberalism was thus an essentially negative activity, devoted to the removal of constraints, sure in the belief that once individuals were allowed to develop freely, an "ethical harmony" would ensue.[7]

According to Hobhouse, Bentham initiated a second phase in which the highest value attached not to the individual but to the community and its collective will. The utilitarian calculus ensured that individual rights did not remain the sole political consideration; it required an adjustment of claims in conformity to the greatest happiness principle; and it looked to the state to harmonize competing interests. This commitment has led to the positive aspect of the liberal movement: the regulation of behavior, the intervention in markets, the exercise of legal restraints and "social control"—an emphasis which threatens "the complete subordination of individual to social claims."[8] As Hobhouse acknowledges, the collectivist impulse has led some to see a rending contradiction in liberal thought: a radical individualism on one side and a state paternalism on the other.

For Hobhouse, however, no such contradiction obtains. It is merely a

---

6. E. M. Forster, "What I Believe," *Two Cheers for Democracy*, Abinger Edition, vol. 11 (1951; London: Edward Arnold, 1972), p. 72. See Frederick C. Crews for an exposition of the background to Forster's liberalism, *E. M. Forster: The Perils of Humanism* (Princeton NJ: Princeton University Press, 1962), pp. 7–36. [For "What I Believe" and an excerpt from Crews, see above, pp. 310–18, 331–40. *Editor*]

7. L. T. Hobhouse, *Liberalism* (New York: Henry Holt, n.d.), pp. 224, 134, 54, 47, 129.

8. *Ibid.*, pp. 100, 67.

bogey of those who fail to recognize that an individual right "cannot
conflict with the common good, nor could any right exist apart from the
common good." He denies any "intrinsic and inevitable conflict
between liberty and compulsion," and instead brings together the two
emphases which modern liberalism inherits, an individualism and a collectivism. He regards these as mutually dependent commitments: "a fulfillment or full development of personality is practically possible not for
one man only but for all members of a community," and the highest aim
is not personal liberty but "liberty for an entire community."[9] Hobhouse
himself did not expect any immediate realization of this "harmonic conception," but he held to a belief in steady progress, a slow course of
mutual adjustment in which the self and the state would move gradually towards equilibrium. Such a view gives expression to the best hopes of
modern liberalism: a commitment to social reform and an unremitting
respect for personal liberty.

The liberalism that Forster sees crumbling around him is clearly that
"new liberalism" which Hobhouse outlines, with its plans for continued
legislative reform on a large scale. And when Forster holds on to his individualism, he places himself in effect at an earlier stage of liberal ideology when the emphasis had fallen upon the removal of constraints
rather than the regulation of behavior. Unlike Hobhouse, Forster retains
no confidence in an emerging balance between these two concerns, personal freedom and public obligation, and faced with these alternatives,
he unhesitatingly chooses private before public, friend before country,
much as Margaret Schlegel makes this choice:

> Others had attacked the fabric of society—property, interest, etc;
> she only fixed her eyes on a few human beings, to see how, under
> present conditions, they could be made happier. Doing good to
> humanity was useless: the many-coloured efforts thereto spreading
> over the vast area like films and resulting in a universal gray. To do
> good to one, or, as in this case, to a few, was the utmost she dare
> hope for. (93–94)

Later Margaret recalls her sister to this Schlegel creed of moral immediacy, refusing to be bound by abstract principles of justice: "Nor am I
concerned with duty. I'm concerned with the characters of various people whom we know, and how, things being as they are, things may be
made a little better" (163).

This sentiment reflects the novel's much-discussed commitment to
"personal relations," which are what Forster clings to when his liberalism crumbles. But it also bears upon some of its recurrent thematic pre-
occupations, for instance the lively debate over space and size, an issue
which like so many others divides Schlegels from Wilcoxes. When

9. *Ibid.*, pp. 127, 147, 128.

Margaret Schlegel first sees Howards End, she overcomes the "phantom of bigness," remembering "that ten square miles are not ten times as wonderful as one square mile, that a thousand square miles are not practically the same as heaven" (145). Only a few pages later Henry Wilcox, soon to be her husband, insists that "the days for small farms are over": "Take it as a rule that nothing pays on a small scale" (147). Scale is of fundamental concern to Forster, who often saw the problem of modernity as a loss of proportion that could only be recovered through a new respect for *genius loci*.[1] Consistently he teaches the virtues of the small scale, the intimacy that is jeopardized in an age of imperialism. While Henry ceaselessly extends his empire of African rubber holding, Margaret willingly surrenders her "cosmopolitanism" for a house that is "old and little."

A variation on this motif occurs in another issue that follows Wilcox/Schlegel lines, the dispute over the logical categories of experience: types and individuals. After the Schlegels have taken an interest in Leonard Bast, Henry Wilcox tries to intervene: "Miss Schlegel, excuse me, but I know the type," to which Margaret rejoins, "he isn't a type" (107). When Miss Avery frightens Margaret and irritates Henry, the latter erupts: "Uneducated classes are so stupid," and Margaret responds by asking, "Is Miss Avery uneducated classes?" (146). In the last phase of the novel, after the revelation of Helen's pregnancy, Margaret loyally reflects that "Not even to herself dare she blame Helen. . . Morality can tell us that murder is worse than stealing, and group most sins in an order all must approve, but it cannot group Helen" (221). The narrator concurs, observing that "Preachers or scientists may generalize, but we know that no generality is possible about those whom we love" (196). The singular instance thus eludes the coarse generalization; the defense of the small space becomes one with defense of the concrete particular; and the farmer joins hands with the nominalist.[2]

At this point it is possible to recognize the congruence between the various features of the novel that have recently been at issue: the weakness of the narrator and the narrowing of fictional domain, the dismissal of large-scale liberal reform in favor of individual relations, the defense of the small space against the imperial cosmopolis, and the commitment to the concrete instance that resists generalization. In all these respects the novel dramatizes a movement from large things to small, in which the surrender of the broad view makes possible a discovery of value in the rich particular. It should be evident that this emphasis poses insuperable difficulties for a view of the novel as a simple parable of class struggle and national reconciliation, as an allegory of the fate of England. On the contrary, categories such as class and nation frequently

1. Spirit of the place (Latin). [*Editor*]
2. Someone who believes that general or abstract terms do not represent actually existing things. [*Editor*]

appear as the chief villains of the piece. Persistently and passionately, Forster distinguishes between the individual and the class, between "a few human beings" and the "universal gray" of humanity.

And yet no one can dispute that *Howards End* retains grand symbolic aspirations. A novel which finds the very poor unthinkable thinks nonetheless about the state of modern England. A novel which narrows its domain still symbolizes the largest questions that face a culture. How can we square the celebration of the individual with the concern for such high generalities? How does the narrow domain of the plot comport with the broadening symbolic reach? How, that is, can a novel which willfully limits its range dramatize a vision of the social whole? And what do these two commitments imply about character and mode?

Such questions can best be met by a turn to the novel's third reference to Arnold's maxim. Shortly after her wedding, Margaret travels alone to Howards End. As she walks towards the house, she wanders through the Hertfordshire countryside and experiences a sudden and decisive recognition:

> In these English farms, if anywhere, one might see life steadily and see it whole, group in one vision its transitoriness and its eternal youth, connect—connect without bitterness until all men are brothers. (191)

This third instance serves as a rejoinder to the previous two. It is possible, after all, to see life steadily and whole, possible to unify, possible to connect. Still, before we surrender to a warm sense of imaginative triumph, we must raise another question. For what kind of whole is this, that ignores the city, that neglects modern life, that retreats to the farms which, however lovely, are surely not the whole of England? John Martin raises this difficulty in his bluff dismissal of Trilling's reading of the novel: "Lionel Trilling declares that it concerns England's fate, but it does not, for it leaves too much of England out of account."[3] And yet Margaret's vision at Howards End suggests a way both to answer Martin's charge and to amend the symbolic interpretation, because paradoxically it is insofar as Margaret leaves much of England out of account that she learns to address its fate. Only when she narrows her view from the cosmopolis to the little house does she achieve a wide social vision. Only by retreating to the part does she see the steady whole. She thus discloses the novel's presiding symbolic figure, synecdoche.[4]

The novel, one might say, is a long preparation for synecdoche. It withdraws from a broad canvas; it reduces its scale; its battles are all waged among individuals. But in retreating to the partial view, it asks those parts to stand for wholes. Helen assails Margaret's decision to

3. John Sayre Martin, *E. M. Forster* (Cambridge: Cambridge University Press, 1976), p. 109.
4. The rhetorical figure in which a part represents a whole, as when "the crown" stands for the monarchy. [*Editor*]

marry Henry, and Margaret, defending her choice, moves from one man to many: "If Wilcoxes hadn't worked and died in England for thousands of years, you and I couldn't sit here without having our throats cut" (126). Later, Margaret turns to defend Helen and does so in these terms: "The pack was turning on Helen, to deny her human rights, and it seemed to Margaret that all Schlegels were threatened with her" (205). Henry Wilcox signifies all Wilcoxes, Helen Schlegel all Schlegels, and when Margaret must challenge her husband, his son and their doctor, a "new feeling came over her: she was fighting for women against men" (206). This persistent imaginative gesture must be distinguished from that habit of mind which the novel repudiates, the tendency to ignore the individual in favor of the type, or, in the terms of Trilling's reading, to identify a character and a class. Synecdoche, on the contrary, embeds the whole within the part and only achieves its broad amplitude by respecting the concrete instance and by detaching the self from its class.

The history of liberalism is itself a history of negotiations between part and whole, and the "ethical harmony" toward which Hobhouse aims is put in just such terms. His "ideal society" is "a whole which lives and flourishes by the harmonious growth of its parts, each of which in developing on its own lines and in accordance with its own nature tends on the whole to further the development of others."[5] But for Hobhouse, it must be stressed, this relationship between part and whole is real not figural. Individual and community are materially, socially, politically, bound together, making society "a living whole." "National and personal freedom are growths of the same root," writes Hobhouse, "and their historic connection rests on no accident, but on ultimate identity of idea." If in the modern age the "individual voter" feels powerless, then the pressing need is to establish "organizations" which will "link the individual to the whole."[6]

As Margaret approaches Howards End she has a fleeting political insight of her own: "Left to itself . . .this county would vote Liberal" (191). Just here the novel reveals both its lingering attachment to a political ideal and its refusal of a political program. As opposed to Hobhouse's constructive program, Forster's aim is not to secure the bonds that tie the few to the many but to cut those bonds, leaving the county to itself, in the conviction that one can best aspire to the whole by retreating to a part. It is not that Forster abandons hope of social unity: he hopes indeed to "connect without bitterness until all men are brothers" (191), but he sees this as possible only through a *withdrawal* from the large social realm. He asks the part not to stand with, but to stand for, the whole.

Kermode has identified several areas of contact between Forster and the Symbolist tradition, but one point which he does not mention and

---

5. Hobhouse, *Liberalism*, p. 136.
6. *Ibid.*, pp. 133, 232–3.

which deserves particular emphasis here is Forster's keen feeling for *correspondance*: that connectedness between things that things themselves have established, an order which we can only disclose, never impose.[7] Without abandoning political value, Forster seeks to mortify the political will, in the hope that *correspondances* will then reveal themselves to the intelligent eye. He can abandon a large fictional domain; can prefer local roots to cosmopolitan rootlessness; can refuse the general category in favor of the singular instance; and can still address "England's fate," because for him, unlike Hobhouse, the effort to "link the individual to the whole" is a matter not of social organization but of imaginary figuration. Forster avails himself of a visionary possibility absent in James and Conrad, but while we should acknowledge that his technical audacity points beyond the realist norms of early modern fiction, we must also recognize that in *Howards End* the post-realist method is in service of a pre-modern past. Synecdoche allows him to retrieve what he has lost. It gives him a way to retain symbolic connection. It is the trope of a waning liberalism.

* * *

DANIEL BORN

Private Gardens, Public Swamps: *Howards End* and the Revaluation of Liberal Guilt[†]

> "I know that personal relations are the real life, for ever and ever."
> —Helen Schlegel

> "We merely want a small house with large rooms, and plenty of them."
> —Margaret Schlegel[1]

"Reality" and "realty" derive from the same root word, so it is not too surprising that the Schlegel sisters' premium on personal relationships, the "real life" named by Helen, reveals itself to be equally preoccupied with

7. "He declares for the autonomy of the work; for co-essence of form and meaning; for art as 'organic and free from dead matter'; for music as a criterion of formal purity; for the work's essential anonymity. Like all art, he thinks the novel must fuse differentiation into unity, in order to provide meaning we can experience; art is 'the one orderly product that our race has produced,' the only unity and therefore the only meaning. This is Symbolist." Frank Kermode, "The One Orderly Product (E. M. Forster)," in *Puzzles and Epiphanies: Essays and Reviews 1958–1961* (London: Routledge & Kegan Paul, 1962), p. 80.
† From *Novel: A Forum on Fiction* 25 no. 2 (1992): 141–59. Copyright *Novel* Corp. (c) 1992. Reprinted with permission.
1. E. M. Forster, *Howards End*, 126, 111. [Page references are to this Norton Critical Edition. *Editor*]

the business of real estate. Of what, after all, does the "real life" consist? Friendships or property?

The question is never put quite that baldly, and Forster endows it with equally serious, equally comic proportions. But such a query goes to the heart of what has been variously called the liberal "dilemma," "paradox," or, as pejoratively denoted by Marxist critics, "the liberal confusion."[2] Through Margaret and Helen, Forster succeeded in delineating the most comprehensive picture of liberal guilt in this century. As an Edwardian, however, Forster was by no means alone in this obsessive desire to reconcile liberalism's commitment to the life of the spirit, if you will, with the competing tugs of power and property. Forster's contemporaries—journalists such as Masterman and Hobson, and novelists such as Gissing and Conrad—share with him the view that social, collective guilt coalesces around two prime issues: imperial power abroad and growing urban poverty at home. George Gissing's fiction repeatedly examines the plight of the domestic underclass and its effects on intellectuals, while Conrad contemplates most thoroughly the effects of imperialism through the mind of his primary thinker, Marlow. Yet of the Edwardians, it was chiefly Forster who perceived how intimately bound up these two concerns actually were. And it was Forster who wove that sense of interdependence into the fabric of a single literary masterpiece.

The plight of this world's Leonard Basts is connected with the activities of the Henry Wilcoxes: the Schlegels cannot help but see that. Even more importantly, Forster noticed how the privileged vantage point of the liberal intellectual, while it enabled her to see "things whole," still compromised and complicated her disinterestedness: for is the privileged vantage point not dependent on and allied with the very power that liberals mistrust? And corollary to this, is that same power not in part responsible for a socially abhorrent and all too visible poverty? The Schlegel sisters are painfully aware of this condition—at least at the novel's outset.

The unresolved tension of *Howards End* has been stated on many occasions—and, one should note, stated rather gleefully—by critics on both left and right. How can liberal intellectuals reconcile the private activities of aesthetic contemplation, friendships, spiritual formation, with a broader concern for the public and social interest? That is the defining problem for Lionel Trilling's understanding of the "liberal imagination," and, in discussing *Howards End*, he illuminates that question's vital historical importance:

> The 18th century witnessed such a notable breaking up of religious orthodoxies and such a transference of the religious feelings to secular life that it is surely the true seed-time of the intellectual as we

2. D. S. Savage, *The Withered Branch: Six Studies in the Modern Novel* (London: Eyre & Spottiswoode, 1950), p. 46.

now know him. One observes in the social circles of the first generation of English romantic poets the sense of morality, the large
feelings and the intellectual energy that had once been given to
religion.

This moral and pious aspect of the intellectual's tradition is
important. Intellectuals as a class do not live by ideas alone but also
by ideals. That is, they must desire the good not only for themselves
but for all, and we might say that one of the truly new things in
human life in the last two centuries is the politics of conscious
altruism.[3]

Thus liberal intellectuals, if perceived within this historical tradition,
are defined as individuals who seek to integrate their private and public
selves. To a degree, this is exactly what the tension between the pursuit
of the "real life" and of realty is about in *Howards End*. As numerous
critics have noted, the novel is preoccupied with houses, interiors, and
real estate;[4] discussion of values in *Howards End* is never rarefied or
pursued apart from a material context of physical living space. It is as
if Stein's central query in *Lord Jim*, "How to live?" were converted to
that of "Where to live?" and Forster succeeds in treating the question
with utter seriousness, without banality. Real estate permeates the
novel: personal relations never proceed within a material vacuum.
Seen this way, a preoccupation with surfaces, houses, and the substance of material living hardly means *lack* of moral penetration—the
famous charge Virginia Woolf brought against the Edwardian writers;
instead, that preoccupation, at least in Forster's hands, becomes a *strat-
egy* of moral penetration.

Forster, of course, consciously allied himself with a passing intellectual and literary generation. "I belong," he said, in one of his famous
quips, "to the fag-end of Victorian liberalism."[5] By calling himself a
dinosaur, Forster perhaps thought he could escape the charge of being
one. But from our present vantage-point it seems he wrote himself off
prematurely. For why should such an "old-fashioned" narrative—one

3. Lionel Trilling, *E. M. Forster* (Norfolk: New Directions, 1943), p. 123.
4. Wilfred Stone, in *The Cave and the Mountain: A Study of E. M. Forster* (Stanford: Stanford
   UP, 1962), remarks that "houses have the symbolic role in this novel that rooms had in the last"
   (237). [For an excerpt from Stone, see below pp. 396–408. *Editor*.] This is true, but we must
   add that Forster is also concerned with houses in all their literalness and with how those houses, those spaces, impinge on the inner life of values. Especially useful to this examination of
   the connection between living space and inner values are Malcolm Bradbury, "Howards End,"
   in *Forster: A Collection of Critical Essays* (Englewood Cliffs: Prentice, 1966), p. 134 and Paul
   B. Armstrong, "E. M. Forster's *Howards End*: The Existential Crisis of the Liberal
   Imagination," *Mosaic* 8 (1974): 187. Crucial architectural reading that further explains the
   Edwardian attitude toward the country house includes Clive Aslet's *The Last Country Houses*
   (New Haven: Yale UP, 1982), Mark Girouard's *The Victorian Country House* (New Haven: Yale
   UP, 1979), and especially Hermann Muthesius's *The English House*, ed. Dennis Sharp, trans.
   Janet Seligman (1904–05; Oxford Professional Books, 1987).
5. Forster, "The Challenge of Our Time," *Two Cheers for Democracy*, (New York: Harcourt,
   1951). p. 56. [See "Challenge" above, pp. 321–25. *Editor*.]

seeking, in Forster's words, the channel whereby "private decencies can be transmitted to public affairs"[6]—still maintain its grip on us?

Quite simply, the novel vitally engages present debates about the future of liberalism itself. My approach to the book emphasizes the specific texture of Edwardian liberalism, but ends with reflections on how the novel addresses our situation. Particularly interesting is the way this novel serves as a gloss on the contemporary framing of pragmatic liberalism by philosopher Richard Rorty. Rorty, himself much preoccupied with this question of private and public value, ascribes to imaginative narrative and the activity of reading it the highest rewards possible; yet *Howards End* can itself be read as a criticism of Rorty's influential brand of neoliberal thought.

What is especially ironic is that Rorty, who holds Trilling in the highest regard, should disavow the very endeavor that shapes Trilling's understanding of the liberal intellectual: the attempt to fuse private and public virtue. Rorty argues in *Contingency, irony, and solidarity* that "self-creation" and social justice are incommensurate activities. He speaks about the impossibility of ever uniting

> self-creation and justice, private perfection and human solidarity, in a single vision.
>
> There is no way in which philosophy, or any other theoretical discipline, will ever let us do that. The closest we will come to joining these two quests is to see the aim of a just and free society as letting its citizens be as privatistic, 'irrationalist,' and aestheticist as they please so long as they do it on their own time—causing no harm to others and using no resources needed by those less advantaged. There are practical measures to be taken to accomplish this practical goal. But there is no way to bring self-creation together with justice at the level of theory. The vocabulary of self-creation is necessarily private, unshared, unsuited to argument. The vocabulary of justice is necessarily public and shared, a medium for argumentative exchange.
>
> If we could bring ourselves to accept the fact that no theory about the nature of Man or Society or Rationality, or anything else, is going to synthesize Nietzsche with Marx or Heidegger with Habermas, we could begin to think of the relation between writers on autonomy and writers on justice as being like the relation between two kinds of tools—as little in need of synthesis as are paintbrushes and crowbars.[7]

If Rorty is right, then what are we to make of the frequently agonized posture of the Schlegel sisters in *Howards End*, or the central tension of Forster's authorial voice? If Rorty is right, then that agonizing is merely

6. "What I Believe," *Two Cheers for Democracy*, p. 74. [See "What I Believe" above, pp. 310–18. *Editor*.]
7. Richard Rorty, *Contingency, irony, and solidarity* (New York: Cambridge UP, 1989), p. xiv.

wasted energy. Yet, the activity of reading Rorty through the lens of *Howards End* may prove as informative a task as reading *Howards End* through the lens of Rorty. Especially in his portrayal of Margaret Schlegel, Forster seems to anticipate some of the more privatistic conclusions to which Rorty's theory leads. Margaret, like Rorty, eventually abandons the attempt to articulate a unifying vision for her private and public discourse. And the resulting limitations of her character, I want to argue, have premonitory value in anticipating similar limitations in Rorty's argument.

*   *   *

* * * Sometimes a text can be grasped anew only if ossified assumptions about it are swept away. In this respect, Trilling's analysis of the novel, still preeminent, needs revision on one crucial point. Most distorting is his insistence that the novel's characters all belong to the middle class. This denial of class differences obscures far more than it illuminates, yet few readers have bothered to question it. The flaccid term, "middle class," made here to encompass at one stroke the poverty-line Basts, the independently wealthy Schlegels, and the rapidly rising Wilcoxes, might be an indisputable label as defined by Trilling: everyone who is neither destitute nor blueblood royalty. Yet the more we consider the term, the less meaningful it becomes.

There seems to be one reason alone for Trilling's use of the tag: that "the class struggle," as he puts it, "is not between the classes but within a single class" (Trilling 118). Does the finicky distinction matter? It might—but only if one is attempting to combat some narrow strain of Marxist dogma.

There are good reasons to clear away this misleading nomenclature. First, as already suggested, it is descriptively inadequate. When we ponder the enormous differences in cultural outlook, living space, and habits of the Basts, the Schlegels, and the Wilcoxes, the blanket term "middle class" is rendered empty. Second, Trilling's definition, including as it does people of independently wealthy means, alters beyond recognizable form the term "middle class." Imprecise as the term may be, it has always had associations with working for your living, as opposed to living off interest. Finally, and most importantly, one hardly needs claim a Marxist pedigree to suggest that Trilling's framing of social relations in this way takes the edge off the actual struggle depicted in the book. There is a struggle—Leonard's—demanding recognition. There is economic oppression; there are possessors and dispossessed. Although Trilling recognizes the pain underlying the humor—"The situation is sad but comic" (Trilling 125)—his distinctively reassuring, American propensity to see everybody as middle class projects the novel more as livingroom situation comedy than as economic war. As a rhetorical tag, the term smooths out disjunctions and erases difference. It declaws the cat, makes Forster too benign.

The claws reappear rather sharply when we give even the most curso-
ry nod in the direction of history. For the Edwardians, the spread of the
middle-class label was not what it is today. (Of course, for the British, it
has never been so.) Far more prevalent was a perception of plutocracy
on one hand and a growing abyss on the other. Consciousness of the latter pervades *Howards End* and raises several questions: how does Forster
use that term, what is its specific meaning for the Edwardian audience,
and, finally, what is Leonard and Jackie Bast's relationship to it?

The existence and characteristics of the "abyss" were impressed on
the Edwardian reading public most repeatedly by the Liberal journalist
C. F. G. Masterman. In *From the Abyss: Of Its Inhabitants by One of
Them* (1902), Masterman conceived the abyss as a general class marker
and associated it with slum-dwellers' alleged physical characteristics as
well as their living space. Today, perhaps, we too easily lose sight of this
initial sociological significance, when understanding of the word
"abyss," at least since the modernists, more likely conjures generalized
notions of spiritual angst, akin to Helen's experience of the "goblins" in
Beethoven's Fifth and conveyed by the Forsterian voice as "Panic and
emptiness! Panic and emptiness" (26)! The rich, too, experience the
abyss, but as Masterman and Forster remind us, theirs is of a different
kind.

Masterman had first detailed the features of the abyss in *The Heart of
the Empire: Discussions of problems of modern city life in England. With
an essay on imperialism* (1901). There he delineated the composite for
Forster's Leonard Bast, calling him "the New Town type,"[8] someone

> physically, mentally, and spiritually different from the type charac-
> teristic of Englishmen during the past two hundred years. The
> physical change is the result of the city up-bringing in twice-
> breathed air in the crowded quarters of the labouring classes. This
> as a substitute for the spacious places of the old, silent life of
> England; close to the ground, vibrating to the lengthy, unhurried
> processes of Nature. The result is the production of a characteristic
> *physical* type of town dweller: stunted, narrow-chested, easily wea-
> ried; yet voluble, excitable, with little ballast, stamina, or
> endurance. . . . Upon these city generations there has operated the
> now widely spread influence of thirty years of elementary school
> teaching. The result is a mental change; each individual has been
> endowed with the power of reading, and a certain dim and cloudy
> capacity for comprehending what he reads.[9]

The empirical relationship between "stunted" physique and "crowded
quarters" is the controlling hypothesis in Masterman's argument. A year

8. C. F. G. Masterman, *The Heart of the Empire* (T. Fisher Unwin, 1901; Brighton: Harvester
Press, 1973), p. 7.
9. *Heart of the Empire*, p. 8.

later, in *From the Abyss*, Masterman describes that tight space more distinctly:

> The three-roomed tenement forms the staple abode of our people, the characteristic 'home' of the dwellers in the Abyss. In some cases a three-storied house cut into layers; in others tenements in a swarming human hive of 'artisans' buildings;' in the vast bulk four-roomed cottages, of which one is let off to a lodger. The number in these must run to millions; here is being reared the coming race. Civilization has commenced, though in rudimentary form. The oleographs on the wall, the framed burial-cards of defunct relatives, the cheap white curtains pathetically testify to unconquered human aspiration.[1]

Jack London's *The People of the Abyss* (1903), a muckraking, firsthand narrative of the author's experience living in the East End, asserted Masterman's claims even more forcefully. After a lengthy and statistic-ridden account of the cubic feet required to sustain a single human life, London concludes:

> It is incontrovertible that the children grow up into rotten adults, without virility or stamina, a weak-kneed, narrow-chested, listless breed, that crumples up and goes down in the brute struggle for life with the invading hordes from the country. . . .
>
> So one is forced to conclude that the Abyss is literally a huge man-killing machine, and when I pass along the little out-of-the-way streets with the full-bellied artisans at the doors, I am aware of a greater sorrow for them than for the 450,000 lost and hopeless wretches dying at the bottom of the pit. They, at least, are dying, that is the point; while these have yet to go through the slow and preliminary pangs extending through two and even three generations.[2]

Together, Masterman's and London's accounts of the poor city-dweller form the prototype in practically every detail for Forster's own Leonard Bast:

> One guessed him as the third generation, grandson to the shepherd or ploughboy whom civilization had sucked into the town; as one of the thousands who have lost the life of the body and failed to reach the life of the spirit. Hints of robustness survived in him, more than a hint of primitive good looks, and Margaret, noting the spine that might have been straight, and the chest that might have broadened, wondered whether it paid to give up the glory of the animal for a tail coat and a couple of ideas. Culture had worked in her own case, but during the last few weeks she had doubted

---

1. Masterman, *From the Abyss* (1902; New York: Garland, 1980), p. 31.
2. Jack London, *The People of the Abyss* (1903; New York: MSS Information Corp., 1970), p. 47.

whether it humanized the vast majority, so wide and so widening is the gulf that stretches between the natural and the philosophic man, so many the good chaps who are wrecked in trying to cross it. She knew this type very well—the vague aspirations, the mental dishonesty, the familiarity with the outsides of books. She knew the very tones in which he would address her. (84–85)

Now for his depiction of the Porphyrion Insurance clerk, Forster has been much castigated. Commentators have called Bast "one of the most interesting and least convincing characters in the book,"[3] "an inspired guess at an unknown class,"[4] and "Forster's one outstanding failure."[5] Peter Widdowson, who accuses Forster of both condescension and ignorance about people like Bast,[6] is especially incensed by Forster's famous disavowal at the beginning of Chapter 6:

We are not concerned with the very poor. They are unthinkable, and only to be approached by the statistician or the poet. This story deals with gentlefolk, or with those who are obliged to pretend that they are gentlefolk. (35)

Without worrying too much whether Bast has been brought into line with strict standards of literary realism (however those standards may be defined), we can see how carefully Forster relies on contemporary understandings of the abyss to draw his portrait of Bast. Even to the detail of Leonard's death from a weak heart, which we perhaps see too symbolically, Forster's depiction confirms common Edwardian notions about the physical deterioration of the city-dwelling poor. Overlaid on this pattern, there is also much that is reminiscent of Gissing, especially Gissing's proletarian intellectuals who, barely scraping by, manage despite exhaustion to read a little literature in their shortened evenings. Like Gilbert Grail in *Thyrza*, or even Hardy's Jude, Bast has achieved tragic consciousness of his condition. And he is arguably more realistic than many suppose. We might think, in parallel terms, of the university adjunct English instructor. Hopes of finishing the dissertation fade, as he or she signs on to teach one more section of freshman writing. Rent must be paid.

Forster, in his careful description of the Basts' apartment, punctuates both Masterman's and Jack London's observations about the dwellings of the urban poor. The interior of the flat, three rooms railroad-style, seems lifted straight out of *From the Abyss* and is fully visualized, down to the kitschy details of "a draped mantelshelf bristling with Cupids"

3. Stone, *The Cave and the Mountain*, p. 247.
4. John Colmer, *E. M. Forster: The Personal Voice* (1975; London: Routledge & Kegan Paul, 1983), p. 95.
5. H. A. Smith, "Forster's Humanism and the Nineteenth Century," *Forster: A Collection of Critical Essays*, ed. Malcolm Bradbury (Englewood Cliffs: Prentice, 1966), p. 111 footnote.
6. Peter Widdowson, *E. M. Forster's Howards End: Fiction as History* (London: Sussex UP, 1977), pp. 90–92.

(37). It is "what is known to house agents as a semi-basement, and to other men as a cellar" (37). Forster sums it up as "an amorous and not unpleasant little hole when the curtains were drawn, and the lights were turned on, and the gas-stove unlit" (37).

In the phrase "other men," Forster obviously includes himself. To Widdowson's accusation that Forster is calloused, we can point out that he at least reveals the vantage point from which his observations are made. "Realism" is always an illusion, its effect of objectivity achieved by excluding overt reference to the subjective vantage point and biases of the observer. Therefore, Forster's willingness to reveal his own position vis-à-vis Leonard Bast displays not ignorance of Bast, but in fact necessary recognition that "realism" about Bast is problematic. Forster is undoubtedly guilty of condescension toward Bast; remarks that men of Leonard's "type" show a "familiarity with the outsides of books" seem especially gratuitous and cruel. Yet when Forster comments on Bast's attempts at self-education, he shows not only Leonard's inadequate grasp of Ruskin, but also, and just as pointedly, social critic Ruskin's inability to understand men like Leonard. Forster's self-criticism seems almost as harsh. In this passage, his identification with Ruskin, verging almost on confession, can be heard:

> Leonard was trying to form his style on Ruskin: he understood him to be the greatest master of English Prose. He read forward steadily, occasionally making a few notes.
> "Let us consider a little each of these characters in succession, and first (for of the shafts enough has been said already), what is very peculiar to this church—its luminousness."
> Was there anything to be learnt from this fine sentence? . . . Could he introduce it, with modifications, when he next wrote a letter to his brother, the lay reader? For example—
> "Let us consider a little each of these characters in succession, and first (for of the absence of ventilation enough has been said already), what is very peculiar to this flat—its obscurity."
> Something told him that the modifications would not do; and that something, had he known it, was the Spirit of English Prose. "My flat is dark as well as stuffy." Those were the words for him.
> And the voice in the gondola rolled on, piping melodiously of Effort and Self-Sacrifice, full of high purpose, full of beauty, full even of sympathy and the love of men, yet somehow eluding all that was actual and insistent in Leonard's life. For it was the voice of one who had never been dirty or hungry, and had not guessed . . . what dirt and hunger are. (38)

More cruelties ensue, when Forster goes on to describe Leonard's "half-baked mind" (39), his pathetic belief that he could "come to Culture suddenly, much as the Revivalist hopes to come to Jesus" (39). Yet Forster's cutting satire goes both ways, especially later on in the dinner party scene (Ch. 15), complete with the reading of a paper, Bloomsbury-style. Forster's criticism savages those who make a pretense of concern about the plight of people like Leonard, all the while deciding how to dispose of family fortunes. That these women imagine themselves having millions to give away makes scant difference; their leisure time to even speculate about such a thing reveals how comfortable they truly are. (Indeed, Margaret and Helen do have enough of a fortune to allow them independent wealth, and Helen attempts to give hers away, in one of the book's most blatant examples of liberal guilt). The scene reminds us, uncomfortably, that the book is about rich and poor, and that for all their talk, the Schlegel sisters are finally allied with the former. A middle-class label such as that proposed by Trilling glosses over the fundamental social problem. Just a year before publication of *Howards End*, Masterman had summarized England's distress this way: "Public penury, private ostentation—that, perhaps, is the heart of the complaint."[7]

* * *

* * * Must the liberal response to Bast be all heart and no head, or all head and no heart, as Forster suggests in this novel? Perhaps Forster only shows us the wrong roads taken. Perhaps a depiction of other, more successful responses is indeed, as Woolf said, better left to legislators than to novelists. Maybe Richard Rorty is right: attempting to integrate private and public value is an abortive enterprise.

Yet a central observation needs to be made about Forster's final resort to the escape-retreat green world of the Howards End estate. Principally, it must be seen as the typical Edwardian gesture to the urban crises of the time: the pastoral escape hatch has exact parallels, for instance, in Gissing and Masterman. The cry is sounded for the rural virtues. The ideal of the ancient English yeoman is invoked as antidote to modernity, imperialism, and all the attendant crises that made liberals nervous. It almost seems as if these writers, longing for the return of Gabriel Oak, go about composing belated versions of *Far from the Madding Crowd*.[8] Forster's glorification of an organic society is embarrassing stuff: "The feudal ownership of land did bring dignity" (109). And this nostalgic tribute strikingly resembles those of Eliot and Yeats, who never apologized for linking their ideas of spiritual and aesthetic wholeness with a conservative, authoritarian political order located in a golden past.[9]

7. *The Condition of England* (London: Methuen, 1909), p. 25.
8. The most comprehensive study of this pastoralism is Raymond Williams's *The Country and the City* (New York: Oxford UP, 1973). Among the many other critics who have remarked on this phenomenon specifically in *Howards End* are John Batchelor, *The Edwardian Novelists* (London: Duckworth, 1982), pp. 9, 10, 227; Jamie Camplin, *The Rise of the Plutocrats*, p. 151; C. B. Cox, *The Free Spirit*, pp. 90, 91, 171, 172; Samuel Hynes, *The Edwardian Turn of Mind* (Princeton: Princeton UP, 1968), p. 68; Wilfred Stone, *The Cave and the Mountain*, p. 266; and Peter Widdowson, *E. M. Forster's Howards End: Fiction as History*, pp. 89, 90.
9. As C. B. Cox notes, the misguidedness of this brand of "liberalism" is also evident in the Leavisite version of idealized country living (*The Free Spirit*, p. 90.)

What, then, remains at all of Forster's liberal imagination? Commenting on Masterman, from whom Forster seems to derive much of this rosy-hued country gestalt, Samuel Hynes observes:

> The most striking thing about this Liberal's description of the condition of England is its close resemblance to the Tory version. Masterman's account of the loss of national altruism would have pleased Baden-Powell, and his description of suburban idleness and vacuity could have come from any pamphlet of the National Service League. . . . His predictions of increasing lawlessness, his fears of government by violence, and his mood of irresolution and discouragement are all echoed in Tory writings of the time. And so is the note of nostalgia that he struck again and again—nostalgia for a simpler and better past, when life was decent because men were decent, and men were decent because they were in touch with the English earth. This note one expects from Conservatives, but in a Liberal it suggests a facing in the wrong direction. Masterman could write movingly about the things that moved him, and his deep sympathies for the poor sometimes made him sound like a radical reformer; but his emotions were not directed toward action; they were, apparently, sufficient in themselves. If he wrote feelingly about the urban poor, he wrote in the same mood about the decline of the rural peasantry, and in each case the burden of his argument was not reform but decent feelings.[1]

The last phrase is especially telling in the case of Margaret Schlegel. When she towers in righteous fury over Wilcox for his sexual double standard, her intent is that he gain self-awareness, self-consciousness (perhaps to see, as the Forsterian-Schlegelian voice puts it later in Chapter 43, "the inner darkness in high places that comes with a commercial age" [235]); but she hardly proposes any concrete means of reparation to the disenfranchised Basts, whose lives have been sexually and financially destroyed by Henry. On the same note, Jackie Bast's absolute disappearance after Leonard's death is suggestive. She does not come around to spoil the idyll in the hay field; while the child of her husband's and Helen's union seems to trail clouds of glory, the odors of the abyss clinging to her are not allowed to taint this meadow. While the feudal past is glorified, and the unified culture signified by Helen's son deferred to the future, the ignominies of the present hour are avoided. Margaret fully intends to block the chance of any more of that unpleasantness. As she tells Helen,

> ". . .Then I can't have you worrying about Leonard. Don't drag in the personal when it will not come. Forget him."
> "Yes, yes, but what has Leonard got out of life?"
> "Perhaps an adventure."
> "Is that enough?"
> "Not for us. But for him." (239)

1. Hynes, "Undecided Prophets," *The Edwardian Turn of Mind*, p. 68.

Is Forster aware of the frequent chill he puts into Margaret's voice? I think so. In spite of all his identification with her, Forster depicts her in such a way that our disquiet is bound to increase upon every re-reading of the novel. How, we ask, can her rhetoric of connection be reconciled with such coldness?

I would suggest that true connection, to borrow Margaret's term, means at the very least a willingness to ponder, and not forget, the discontinuities between one's private garden and the public swamp, or as the Edwardians named it, the abyss. The connection can be painful, the process of reconciling private pleasures and the public good difficult. Both Schlegel sisters seem perfectly aware of that tension at the outset of this novel, when a man named Leonard Bast walks into their life. And this tension results in guilt, the painful awareness of the gap, in Trilling's words, between one's "ideas" and one's "ideals." The guilt necessarily forces an examination of personal circumstances, as well as the need for some kind of personal gesture or response to the discontinuity.

The dangers of hasty response become all too clear in Helen's behavior, and conservative critics of liberalism are fond of pointing to the often-destructive actions generated by liberal pity.[2] For Margaret, though, a movement beyond liberal guilt seems to be the goal early on, and she accomplishes it by removing herself from the place where class disjunction is most obvious: the city. The quality of this detachment finds uncanny expression in Rorty: "My 'poeticized' culture is one which has given up the attempt to unite one's private ways of dealing with one's finitude and one's sense of obligation to other human beings."[3] Elsewhere Rorty, like Margaret, acknowledges the financial order upon which the life of the mind and culture rests: "We should be more willing than we are to celebrate bourgeois capitalist society as the best polity actualized so far, while regretting that it is irrelevant to most of the problems of most of the population of the planet."[4] Rorty's argument severs all connection between the private pleasures made possible by bourgeois capitalism—including the luxury to contemplate it within the academy, as Rorty does—and the pub-

2. Thomas A. Spragens, Jr., *The Irony of Liberal Reason* (Chicago: U of Chicago Press, 1981), p. 190.
3. Rorty, *Contingency, irony, and solidarity*, p. 68.
4. Rorty, "Method, Social Science, Social Hope," *Consequences of Pragmatism: Essays: 1972–1980* (Minneapolis: U of Minnesota Press, 1982), p. 210. This observation, by way of a footnote, follows the more explicit defensiveness of Rorty against a socialist perspective: "there seems no particular reason why, after dumping Marx, we have to keep on repeating all the nasty things about bourgeois liberalism which he taught us to say. There is no inferential connection between the transcendental subject—of 'man' as something having a nature which society can repress or understand—and the disappearance of human solidarity. Bourgeois liberalism seems to me the best example of this solidarity we have yet achieved, and Deweyan pragmatism the best articulation of it" (207). Rorty does not explain why the imperative for "human solidarity" should be any more convincing than an argument for common "human nature." Nor does he provide any clue as to how bourgeois liberalism translates into solidarity. He simply asserts this to be the case. Maybe Frank Lentricchia's criticism of Rorty is most apt: "Is there culture that is not covert politics?" (*Criticism and Social Change* [Chicago: U of Chicago Press, 1983], p. 14). Rorty's cultural liberalism skirts questions of political commitment, which might give its "solidarity" some content.

lic crises engendered by it. Yet Rorty does not want to admit that the sources of one's private pleasures are quite possibly the sources of others' pain. Rorty's choice of the word "irrelevant" in the above passage may be most liable to question, as Jeffrey Stout suggests:

> If the concession tagged onto the end of this sentence were intended only to say that bourgeois capitalist society is unlikely to solve most of the problems of most of the population of the planet, Rorty is certainly right. But it is hard to see how bourgeois capitalist society could be deemed irrelevant to most of those problems, at least as a source of dramatically important unintended consequences, many of them bad enough to make celebration seem the wrong tack to take. With no more than asides like this to go on, we are left with what seems a dangerously myopic moral vision, apparently blind to relations of interdependence and dominance within the economic world-system from which we derive our wealth, a vision compatible with gross insensitivity to that system's sorrows, injustices, and corrupting influences.[5]

Rorty's position, like Margaret's, is finally meant to relieve us of the burden of guilt—the guilt engendered by seeing systemic connections. And given the supposedly irreconcilable nature of private pleasures and public crises, it should not take us long to realize which distinct order of being, in Rorty's schema, is more likely to be slighted. For once liberalism abandons its traditional concern to integrate private and public modes of discourse, once liberalism becomes exclusively privatistic, it becomes an intellectual game of diminished energy, and then finally altogether unnecessary. Rorty wants to affirm both private ironists and public humanists as ongoing, necessary, albeit separate forms of life. But given the pattern of his thinking, it is almost inevitable that the private ironists—the Tibby Schlegels, perhaps?—will prevail.

That Forster interrupts his final scene with awareness of the encroaching London mass suggests he is not entirely happy with this one-sided vision of serene, private, poeticized culture. The conclusion of the book, which remains stubbornly unsettling, indicates crucial truths about Forster's conception of the liberal imagination: that it cannot relax if it is to remain functional; that any attempt to waft away the odors of the abyss is not only intellectually dishonest but also damaging to one's liberal ideals; and that the spirit of Bast competes with Mrs. Wilcox for the privilege of hovering over the final scene in the meadow. The suggestion in this novel—a suggestion more timely than ever given the giddy and unreflective currents of liberal triumphalism that swirl about—is a simple one. For Forster, the liberal imagination retains its vitality only so long as we are able to revalue, and not dispense with, liberal guilt.

5. Jeffrey Stout, *Ethics After Babel: The Languages of Morals and Their Discontents* (Boston: Beacon, 1988), pp. 229–230.

CRITICISM

CRITICISM

Contemporary Responses

UNSIGNED REVIEW

From the *Times Literary Supplement*†

[*". . . A very remarkable and original book . . ."*]

Mr. E. M. Forster has now done what critical admirers of his foregoing novels have confidently looked for—he has written a book in which his highly original talent has found full and ripe expression. Neither of its three clever, imperfect, slightly baffling predecessors was quite at unity with itself. In each case there was an uncertainty of attack and a want of harmony in the method which prevented an exceptionally fine sense of character from making its proper effect. All this is put right in *Howard's End* [*sic*].[1] * * * Here Mr. Forster has finally got his method under control, and has seized his idea in a grasp that completely encircles it; so that the peculiar freshness and individuality of his gift can now be properly seen and understood. It is in the first place securely founded, this gift, upon a power of generalization which holds the lightly-handled plot compactly together. This is an important point, because for a writer with such a quick eye for detail and such an incisive pen for fine side-strokes there is always the easy resource of constructing a novel out of clever character-sketches and snapshots, arbitrarily thrown together. But Mr. Forster works from the centre outwards, and reaches the graces and humours of the surface of his story with a mind quite clear as to the structure beneath. His generalization starts from the everlasting opposition of the two types which between them hold civilized life together, the people who are not interested in "personal relations" but who alone make the world practically habitable for the other type, the people who are not interested in the thing done but only in the human beings who do it. The Wilcox family stand for the first, English, honest, unimaginative, exasperating, and the Schlegel family for the second, of mixed blood and restless brains and hampering imaginations, certainly not less exasperating, the Wilcoxes being those who deal in realities without understanding them, the

† *Times Literary Supplement* (27 October 1910).
1. This typographical error, also found in the title of the review, haunted Forster's novel throughout its reception.

Schlegels those who understand realities without dealing in them. The Schlegels, indeed, must do all the understanding, and the question is whether they can understand enough for both and so effect an alliance with the Wilcoxes, instead of standing aside and making fun of them. Margaret Schlegel makes the attempt and dares a compromise: "More and more," she says, "do I refuse to draw my income and sneer at those who guarantee it." Helen, her sister, is *intransigeante*, and faces the disaster to which her consistency brings her. Mr. Forster seizes the very essence of the contrast, and again and again pierces his material, with the sharpest of needles, at the exact psychological point. It is another question whether the actual incidents of the story, apart from the perfect justice of the psychology, are well invented and disposed; and here we could make some criticisms. But we are dealing with a very remarkable and original book, and we will not linger over faults which do not touch its central virtue. Nor need more be said of the character-drawing than that it has all the light shrewdness we have seen before in this writer's work, with the added clarity of practice. What gives Mr. Forster's writing its quite unique flavour is something more than this. It is the odd charming vein of poetry which slips delicately in and out of his story, showing itself for a moment in the description of a place or a person, and vanishing the instant it has said enough to suggest something rare and romantic and intangible about the person or the place. It is a refinement which belongs to realism, not romance, for it is simply due justice done to an element in life too momentary and swift for most realism, so called, to overtake. But where quick-fingered lightness and deftness are demanded there Mr. Forster never fails; and he has caught in this book a sensitive reflection of life on which he is very heartily to be congratulated.

R. A. SCOTT-JAMES

From the *Daily News*†

["... A connected novel ..."]

'Only connect . . .' is Mr. Forster's motto. It is because he has taken this motto not only for his book but also for his method of work that he has achieved the most significant novel of the year. Those who seek to express a philosophic view of life in fiction generally strain their characters till they are puppets of their philosophy. Those, on the other hand, who are content to trace individual characters realistically are in danger at all times of losing the scheme and purpose of their work. It

† *Daily News* (7 November 1910).

is because they do not 'connect'; because to write a novel near to nature on the one hand, and true to the larger vision on the other requires tremendous labour of thought making perception and wisdom fruitful; the fitting of the perception of little things with the perception of universal things; consistency, totality, *connection*. Mr. Forster has written a *connected* novel.

Mr. Forster's method is a sort of bridge between that of Mr. Conrad and that of Mr. Galsworthy. The former, I am told, starts the making of a story with an incident which impressed itself on his imagination, and round this primary situation the story is hinged; the latter, starting with a generalisation, selects facts which illustrate it. Both methods are legitimate, and the one by Mr. Conrad, the other by Mr. Galsworthy, have been successfully used. But who could say of *Howard's End* [sic] that the one method or the other had been adopted? The novel rises like a piece of architecture full-grown before us. It is all bricks and timber, but it is mystery, idealism, a far-reaching symbol.

*   *   *

EDWARD GARNETT

Villadom[†]

The habit of orthodox criticism is to be stiff or condescending to a new author when he first appears with an original book, and to increase the measure of praise according to his repeated successes. Mr. E. M. Forster has now given us four novels, and his last, *Howard's End* [sic], will probably receive compound interest on whatever sum of approval was bestowed on *The Longest Journey*. It is as well. *Howard's End*, by its far-sighted criticism of middle-class ideas, is a book that says most effectively those very things that the intelligent minority feel, but rarely arrive at formulating.

*   *   *

The artistic setting of the novel certainly owes much to the spiritual background, which is symbolised by the old-world atmosphere of Howard's End. We require something by which we can measure Mr. Wilcox, busy with his company promoting and his new fortune, made out of oil and rubber, his sound Imperialism, his motoring, his shooting, and his energy in local politics. Mrs. Wilcox and Howard's

† *Nation* 12 November 1910: 282–84. See "The Author and the Novel," p. 280, for the appreciative letter Forster wrote to Garnett the same day this review appeared.

End both have spiritual grace, and the old house reflects the unob-
trusive charm and settled standards which the pushing husband, the
self-assertive son, Charles, and the athletic daughter, Evie, despise.
* * *

                              *   *   *

   In the working out of the fortunes of the two families, now united
by marriage, Mr. Forster shows to great advantage his rare gift of philosophic criticism. His characters are real enough, but their importance
as individuals is less than their significance as contemporary signposts.
It is the ideas behind them, the code of manners and morals, and the
web of forces, material and mental, that are woven before our eyes in
the life of London, that Mr. Forster is deeply concerned with, and from
the standpoint of the interested looker-on we can only admire the dex-
terity with which the disaster that overtakes the Wilcoxes is bound up
with the fate of the insignificant clerk, Leonard Bast, and his disrep-
utable wife, Jacky. * * * The shock of the tragedy of Leonard's death
crumbles down Mr. Wilcox's philistine defences, and the novel ends
with a retrospective chapter, in which a humbled Helen, a calm
Margaret, and a broken-spirited Mr. Wilcox are shown living together
peacefully in the tranquil atmosphere of the old house, Howard's End.
We say that one must admire the ingenuity with which the fabric of
the plot is woven out of the fortuitous yarn of the meetings and the
accidental relations of the three sets of characters; but in closing the
book, we perceive that Mr. Forster has sacrificed the inflexibility of
artistic truth to the exigencies of his philosophical moral. There is too
much ingenious dove-tailing of incidents, too much of accidental hap-
penings, too much twisting and stretching and straining of human
material for *Howard's End* to rank high as a work of art. The individuality of each figure is made obedient to the convenience of the
author's purpose, and, though great pains are taken to make the whole
story and all its parts probable, at critical junctures Helen's action or
Mr. Wilcox's attitude are perceptibly strained to produce a dramatic situation. Not grossly strained, be it remarked, but perceptibly; but it is
just this clever ingenuity that robs the work of artistic inevitability. It
would, however, be doing both the author and our readers poor service to make much of a subsidiary defect in the author's accomplished
method. The novel's original value, which is great, rests primarily on
the acute analysis of the middle-class British code of ideas and standards, typified by the rise and progress of the Wilcoxes. Mr. Forster
understands the outlook of Villadom perhaps better than the fourscore
of writers who speak from the 'vantage ground of its bulwarks. He is
no partisan, but renders justice in a manner that may well bring those
he paints to sue for mercy.

UNSIGNED REVIEW

From the *Westminster Gazette*†

[*"It is in his treatment of the 'personal relations' that he excels."*]

In *Howards End* Mr. E. M. Forster has written a very remarkable book, though he has hardly achieved an altogether satisfactory novel. It is in his treatment of the 'personal relations' that he excels—those factors in human life which stood for 'the real' in the lives of Margaret and Helen Schlegel as against the mere externals of intercourse which in their strange elliptic parlance they sum up in the two symbols 'telegrams and anger.' Symbols mean far more to those two women than the actual facts of life; they are a curious complex pair, living in a world of dreams and ideals, yet with a far-sighted common-sense sometimes materialising, contradictory traits of which we see the germ both in parentage and education. Mr. Forster has handled these two women with an intimacy which is little short of amazing. Perhaps Helen is not always quite convincing, especially at the supreme crisis of her life; but his analysis of the almost more complex Margaret, who can step down from the clouds to make a commonplace marriage with a middle-aged unimaginative gentleman, whom she can love well if not passionately, is quite extraordinary. He gets inside the very soul of the woman, and touches with an equally sure hand the trivial things of every day and the great moments of her development. It is almost with surprise that we realise that the author, who can show such very unusual insight into the rarefied atmosphere of the idealist's inner life, can at the same time appreciate all that goes to the making of the more conventional types. His delineation of the Wilcoxes, who stand for the contradiction of everything which the Schlegels have taught themselves to cherish, is no less admirable than his treatment of the two women and their very individual brother, one of the most lifelike and remarkable portraits in the book. To give an outline of the story would be to give no idea of the value of the book, which is dependent on the 'personal relations' of those involved, in the contrast and balance of character. Mr. Forster has little sense of form; his book has no constructive harmony. But he is something of a seer, something of a mystic, though his mysticism is somewhat intangible, and he can hardly put it into shape. The strange influence of Howards End, realised by the Schlegels rather than by the Wilcoxes, to whom it belonged; the curious personality of Miss Avery, who makes, as it were, a connecting-link between the Schlegels and Howards End, are suggested rather than insisted on. But with Mrs. Wilcox, the real owner of Howards End, who recognised Margaret as her spiritual heir, and who, in leaving her

† *Westminster Gazette* (19 November 1910).

Howards End, felt that she was conveying an atmosphere to one who could appreciate it, Mr. Forster is more definite. 'I feel,' says Margaret to her sister after Mrs. Wilcox's death, 'that you and I and Henry are only fragments of that woman's mind. She knows everything; she is everything. * * *' Mrs. Wilcox thus represents a sort of over-soul. But for this development we had been quite unprepared, and herein lies the real weakness of Mr. Forster's book. He has given us no cause to expect this evolution. He has evidently a strong impression which he wishes to produce, but he fails to produce it because of his treatment of Mrs. Wilcox in the flesh. Spiritualists would doubtless tell us that manifestation on this material plane has but little relation to a higher one. Mr. Forster is working in a particular medium, and he must use that medium to get his effect. He fails with Mrs. Wilcox, perhaps because he takes too much for granted on the part of his reader. And his book suffers in consequence. Nevertheless it remains quite one of the most remarkable novels of the year.

UNSIGNED REVIEW

From the *Athenaeum*[†]

This novel, taken with its three predecessors, assures its author a place amongst the handful of living writers who count. It is the story of a conflict between points of view. The Schlegels are clever, sensitive, refined; they have a feeling for beauty and truth, a sense of justice and of proportion; they stand for what is best in modern civilization: the Wilcoxes are vulgar, blatant, and brutal; such time as they can spare from money-making they devote to motors and bridge and suburban society; they stand for all that is worst. The two families are thrown together. The younger Miss Schlegel, Helen, is uncompromising; one cannot touch pitch without being soiled, she feels; the elder, Margaret, who refuses "to draw my income and sneer at those who guarantee it," marries Mr. Wilcox. Helen and the reader have to watch Margaret's fine edges grow blunt, till at last, by one of those *dei ex machinis*[1] of which Mr. Forster is too fond, the irreconcilables are reconciled, and some of them live happily ever after.

The defects of this novel are that the protagonists are points of view rather than characters; that the two chief events—Margaret's marriage and Helen's seduction—are unconvincing; and that, in our judgment, the moral is wrong. We do not object to didacticism; but we cannot admit that what is bad ought to be loved, or that the finer feelings are not

† *Athenaem* 3 December 1910: 696.
1. The plural of "deus ex machina," literally, "a god from a machine" (Greek). Artificial, implausible devices used to resolve complications in the plot, from the appearance in Greek drama of a god hoisted in on a crane to settle a problem.

too high a price even for enlarged sympathies. The great thing in the book is the sisters' affection for each other; personal relations, except those between lovers, have never, we venture to say, been made more beautiful or more real. But, from beginning to end, it is full of brilliant and delicate strokes, which reveal, with surprising clearness, those subtle states of mind and elusive but significant traits that are apt to escape even the most acute observation.

A. C. BENSON

Letter to E. M. Forster[†]

9 December 1910

You will think me very discourteous or very perverse not to have written to you before about your book. But I wanted my mother to read it and tell me what she thought, because I look upon her as a remarkable instance of a very feminine woman and at the same time a highly intellectual one. She is Henry Sidgwick's sister, and has much of his power. * * * She says 'Might not the drift of H.E. be called Pragmatism? What chiefly seems to me to emerge is that, so to say, situations make their own ethics: that instead of having a fixed code of morals, a better thing is to be led by desire and impulse, and to find in the situations this leads to the true moral of fact. And that this leads to great general misunderstanding of other people and their lives, and to an absence of all "being shocked". To this is to be added "connect, connect", by which I suppose the author means that it finds and also establishes hitherto unthought-of connections in the one life, and with all the others who share in the problem. . . . This is most inadequate, and please let us talk about it. It interested me enormously, and one will never forget it. It certainly hits the want of elasticity in some codes, and accounts for the general mellowing in all good lives; but it also has tremendous dangers?'

I think this criticism which I copy down just as it was written will interest you. My own feeling about the book—which stirred me very much—was much the same; but being partly a determinist and partly a pragmatist I didn't feel the emphasis as my mother does. (I felt it to be poetical rather than philosophical.) My own belief is that people *do* act by desire and impulse, almost invariably, and that moral codes are mere names of psychological genera and species, without any particular inspi-

† From *E. M. Forster: The Critical Heritage*, ed. Philip Gardner (London: Routledge & Kegan Paul, 1973) 152–53. See "The Author and the Novel," pp. 281–82, for Forster's appreciative response to this letter. Benson was an acquaintance of Forster's from King's College, Cambridge. His mother Mary Sidgwick Benson was the sister of Henry Sidgwick, a professor of moral philosophy at Cambridge.

ration or power of restriction. I took the book rather to be a study of the immense strength of sturdy and conventional humanity, just as the sparrow fares best among the birds—and the contrast between Margaret and Helen seemed to me to be another point—the emotional and intellectual nature, with and without moral force.

I felt throughout that the appeal of the *house* was a little strained—I should rather have expected the *conventionalists* to have felt that than the idealists. . . . But I must not go on—the book interested me very greatly, and gave me the beautiful sensation of a sudden *up-lifting* of thought every now and then, like a mountain breaking out of a cloud!

KATHERINE MANSFIELD

Journal Entry[†]

May 1917

Putting my weakest books to the wall last night I came across a copy of *Howard's End* [sic] and had a look into it. But it's not good enough. E. M. Forster never gets any further than warming the teapot. He's a rare fine hand at that. Feel this teapot. Is it not beautifully warm? Yes, but there ain't going to be no tea.

And I can never be perfectly certain whether Helen was got with child by Leonard Bast or by his fatal forgotten umbrella. All things considered, I think it must have been the umbrella.

FRIEDA LAWRENCE

Letter to E. M. Forster[‡]

Greatham, Pulborough, Sussex
Friday [5 February 1915]

Dear Mr Forster,

Thank you for *Howard's end* [sic]—It got hold of me and not being a critical person I thank the Lord for it, and what he gives me. Only per-

[†] From *Journal of Katherine Mansfield*, ed. J. Middleton Murray (London: Constable & Co., 1954) 120–21. Mansfield (1888–1923) was a short story writer, born in New Zealand, who came to London in 1908. In an epigraph to this section of her journal, Mansfield wrote: "In these notes—so help me, Lord, / I shall be open and above board. K.M." (119).

[‡] From *The Letters of D. H. Lawrence*, vol. 2, ed. George J. Zytaruk and James Boulton (Cambridge: Cambridge UP, 1981) 277–78. Reprinted by permission of Laurence Pollinger Limited and the Estate of Frieda Lawrence Ravagli. Forster visited the novelist D. H. Lawrence and his wife Frieda 10–12 February 1915. This tumultuous visit, during which Lawrence lectured Forster about the need to transform his life, prompted the important letter to Bertrand Russell excerpted below (p. 389). For an account of the visit, see P. N. Furbank, *E. M. Forster:*

haps the end—broken Henry's remain Henry's as I know to my cost—It's a beautiful book, but now you must go further—We had violent discussions over your letters, L[awrence] and I—(Three cheers for the 'firm').[1] What ails you modern men is that you put too high a value on [Lawrence interjects: ready-made] 'consciousness' on the revealed things; Because you cannot utter the 'unutterable' you are inclined to say it does not exist—Hope and that sort of thing is *not* your strong point—You are so frightened of being let down, as if one couldn't get up again!—As to the firm you *did* hit a little sore point with me—Poor author's wife, who does her little best and everybody wishes her to Jericho—Poor second fiddle, the surprise at her existence! She goes on playing her little accompaniment so bravely! Tut-Tut, tra la-la! Thank you again for *Howard's end*, it had a bucking-up effect on me!

Yours sincerely   die zweite Flöte[2]—
And come soon—

* * *

D. H. LAWRENCE

Letter to Bertrand Russell[†]

Greatham, Pulborough, Sussex
12 Feb 1915

Dear Mr Russell,

We have had E. M. Forster here for three days. There is more in him than ever comes out. But he is not dead yet. I hope to see him pregnant with his own soul. We were on the edge of a fierce quarrel all the time. He went to bed muttering that he was not sure we—my wife and I—weren't just playing round his knees: he seized a candle and went to bed, neither would he say good night. Which I think is rather nice. He sucks his dummy—you know, those child's comforters—long after his age. But

---

A Life, vol. 2 (London: Secker and Warburg, 1978) 4–14. Late one evening, according to Furbank, Forster "asked Lawrence if there were anything, anything at all, in his books that he could praise, and Lawrence, surprisingly, said yes, the character of Leonard Bast in Howards End" (vol. 2, 10).

1. Saying he refused to "have dealings with a firm," Forster had earlier expressed his dislike of joint letters from the Lawrences (Furbank 2:7). [*Editor*]
2. The second flute (German).
† From *Letters of D. H. Lawrence*, vol. 2, ed. George J. Zytaruk and James Boulton (Cambridge: Cambridge UP, 1981) 282–85. Reprinted by permission of Laurence Pollinger Limited and the Estate of Frieda Lawrence Ravagli. Bertrand Russell (1872–1970) was a British philosopher and social reformer who taught at Trinity College, Cambridge, from 1910–16. [*Editor*]

there is something very real in him, if he will not cause it to die. He is *much* more than his dummy-sucking, clever little habits allow him to be.

* * *

Forster is not poor, but he is bound hand and foot bodily. Why? *Because he does not believe that any beauty or any divine utterance is any good any more.* Why? Because the world is suffering from bonds, and birds of foul desire which gnaw its liver.[1] Forster knows, as every thinking man now knows, that all his thinking and his passion for humanity amounts to no more than trying to soothe with poetry a man raging with pain which can be cured. Cure the pain, don't give the poetry. Will all the poetry in the world satisfy the manhood of Forster, when Forster knows that his implicit manhood is to be satisfied by nothing but immediate physical action. He tries to dodge himself—the sight is pitiful.

But why can't he act? Why can't he take a woman and fight clear to his own basic, primal being? Because he knows that self-realisation is not his ultimate desire. His ultimate desire is for the continued action which has been called the social passion—the love for humanity—the desire to work for humanity. That is every man's ultimate desire and need. Now you see the vicious circle. Shall I go to my Prometheus and tell him beautiful tales of the free, whilst the vulture gnaws his liver? I am ashamed. I turn my face aside from my Prometheus, ashamed of my vain, irrelevant, impudent words. I cannot help Prometheus. And this knowledge rots the core of activity.

If I cannot help Prometheus—and I am also Prometheus—how shall I be able to take a woman? For I go to a woman to know myself, and to know her. And I want to know myself, that I may know how to act for humanity. But if I am aware that I cannot act for humanity—? Then I dare not go to a woman.

* * *

* * * The ordinary Englishman of the educated class goes to a woman now to masterbate [*sic*] himself. Because he is not going for discovery or new connection or progression, but only to repeat upon himself a known reaction.

When this condition arrives, there is always Sodomy. The man goes to the man to repeat this reaction upon himself. It is a nearer form of masterbation. But still it has some *object*—there are still two bodies instead of one. A man of strong soul has too much honour for the other body—man or woman—to use it as a means of masterbation. So he remains neutral, inactive. That is Forster.[2]

* * *

---

1. Zeus punished Prometheus, a powerful Greek god, for defiance by chaining him to a rock while a vulture continually picked at his liver. [*Editor*]
2. According to Furbank, Forster felt Lawrence was obtuse about his own homosexuality as well as Forster's (see vol. 2, 12). [*Editor*]

THE NOVELS OF E. M. FORSTER

D. H. LAWRENCE

Letter to E. M. Forster[†]

Taos. New Mexico. U.S.A.
20 Sept. 1922

Dear E. M.

We got here last week from San Francisco—from Sydney—Found your letter. Yes I think of you—of your saying to me, on top of the downs in Sussex—'How do you know I'm not dead?'—Well, you can't be dead, since here's your script. But I think you *did* make a nearly deadly mistake glorifying those *business* people in *Howards End*. Business is no good.

* * *

VIRGINIA WOOLF

The Novels of E. M. Forster[‡]

There are many reasons which should prevent one from criticizing the work of contemporaries. Besides the obvious uneasiness—the fear of hurting feelings—there is too the difficulty of being just. Coming out one by one, their books seem like parts of a design which is slowly uncovered. Our appreciation may be intense, but our curiosity is even greater. Does the new fragment add anything to what went before? Does it carry out our theory of the author's talent, or must we alter our forecast? Such questions ruffle what should be the smooth surface of our criticism and make it full of argument and interrogation. With a novelist like Mr. Forster this is specially true, for he is in any case an author about whom there is considerable disagreement. There is something baffling and evasive in the very nature of his gifts. So, remembering that we are at best only building up a theory which may be knocked down in

† From *The Letters of D. H. Lawrence*, vol. 4, ed. Warren Roberts et al. (Cambridge: Cambridge UP, 1987) 301. Reprinted by permission of Laurence Pollinger Limited and the Estate of Frieda Lawrence Ravagli. Two years later, writing to a friend to recommend *A Passage to India*, Lawrence wrote about Forster: "I think he is about the best of my contemporaries in England" (*The Letters of D. H. Lawrence*, vol. 5, ed. James T. Boulton and Lindeth Vasey [Cambridge: Cambridge UP, 1989] 91).

‡ From Virginia Woolf, *The Death of the Moth and Other Essays* (New York: Harcourt, Brace, and World, 1967), 342–50. Copyright 1942 by Harcourt Brace & Company and renewed 1970 by Marjorie T. Parsons, Executrix. Reprinted by permission of the publisher. Originally published 1927. The novelist Virginia Woolf (1882–1941) and her husband, the publisher and writer Leonard Woolf (1880–1969), are often linked with Forster as members of the so-called Bloomsbury Group, an informal association of artists and intellectuals named after the quarter of London where the Woolfs lived.

a year or two by Mr. Forster himself, let us take Mr. Forster's novels in the order in which they were written, and tentatively and cautiously try to make them yield us an answer.

The order in which they were written is indeed of some importance, for at the outset we see that Mr. Forster is extremely susceptible to the influence of time. He sees his people much at the mercy of those conditions which change with the years. He is acutely conscious of the bicycle and of the motor-car; of the public school and of the university; of the suburb and of the city. The social historian will find his books full of illuminating information. In 1905 Lilia learned to bicycle, coasted down the High Street on Sunday evening, and fell off at the turn by the church. For this she was given a talking to by her brother-in-law which she remembered to her dying day. It is on Tuesday that the housemaid cleans out the drawing-room at Sawston. Old maids blow into their gloves when they take them off. Mr. Forster is a novelist, that is to say, who sees his people in close contact with their surroundings. And therefore the colour and constitution of the year 1905 affect him far more than any year in the calendar could affect the romantic Meredith or the poetic Hardy. But we discover as we turn the page that observation is not an end in itself; it is rather the goad, the gadfly driving Mr. Forster to provide a refuge from this misery, an escape from this meanness.

*　*　*

*　*　* Let us look for a moment at the nature of the problem he sets himself. It is the soul that matters; and the soul, as we have seen, is caged in a solid villa of red brick somewhere ·in the suburbs of London. It seems, then, that if his books are to succeed in their mission his reality must at certain points become irradiated; his brick must be lit up; we must see the whole building saturated with light. We have at once to believe in the complete reality of the suburb and in the complete reality of the soul. In this combination of realism and mysticism his closest affinity is, perhaps, with Ibsen.[1] Ibsen has the same realistic power. A room is to him a room, a writing table a writing table, and a waste-paper basket a waste-paper basket. At the same time, the paraphernalia of reality have at certain moments to become the veil through which we see infinity. When Ibsen achieves this, as he certainly does, it is not by performing some miraculous conjuring trick at the critical moment. He achieves it by putting us into the right mood from the very start and by giving us the right materials for his purpose. He gives us the effect of ordinary life, as Mr. Forster does, but he gives it us by choosing a very few facts and those of a highly relevant kind. Thus when the moment of illumination comes we accept it implicitly. We are neither roused nor

1. Henrik Ibsen (1828–1906), Norwegian playwright, author of bleak, realistic works including *A Doll's House* (1879), *The Wild Duck* ((1884), *Hedda Gabler* (1890), and *The Master Builder* (1892). [*Editor*]

puzzled; we do not have to ask ourselves, What does this mean? We feel simply that the thing we are looking at is lit up, and its depths revealed. It has not ceased to be itself by becoming something else.

Something of the same problem lies before Mr. Forster—how to connect the actual thing with the meaning of the thing and to carry the reader's mind across the chasm which divides the two without spilling a single drop of its belief. At certain moments on the Arno, in Hertfordshire, in Surrey, beauty leaps from the scabbard, the fire of truth flames through the crusted earth; we must see the red-brick villa in the suburbs of London lit up. But it is in these great scenes which are the justification of the huge elaboration of the realistic novel that we are most aware of failure. For it is here that Mr. Forster makes the change from realism to symbolism; here that the object which has been so uncompromisingly solid becomes, or should become, luminously transparent. He fails, one is tempted to think, chiefly because that admirable gift of his for observation has served him too well. He has recorded too much and too literally. He has given us an almost photographic picture on one side of the page; on the other he asks us to see the same view transformed and radiant with eternal fires. The bookcase which falls upon Leonard Bast in *Howards End* should perhaps come down upon him with all the dead weight of smoke-dried culture; the Marabar caves should appear to us not real caves but, it may be, the soul of India. Miss Quested should be transformed from an English girl on a picnic to arrogant Europe straying into the heart of the East and getting lost there.[2] We qualify these statements, for indeed we are not quite sure whether we have guessed aright. Instead of getting that sense of instant certainty which we get in *The Wild Duck* or in *The Master Builder*, we are puzzled, worried. What does this mean? we ask ourselves. What ought we to understand by this? And the hesitation is fatal. For we doubt both things—the real and the symbolical: Mrs. Moore, the nice old lady, and Mrs. Moore, the sibyl. The conjunction of these two different realities seems to cast doubt upon them both. Hence it is that there is so often an ambiguity at the heart of Mr. Forster's novels. We feel that something has failed us at the critical moment; and instead of seeing, as we do in *The Master Builder*, one single whole we see two separate parts.

* * *

* * * None of the books before *Howards End* and *A Passage to India* altogether drew upon the full range of Mr. Forster's powers. With his queer and in some ways contradictory assortment of gifts, he needed, it seemed, some subject which would stimulate his highly sensitive and active intelligence, but would not demand the extremes of romance or passion; a subject which gave him material for criticism, and invited

2. The Marabar Caves is a place in, Miss Quested and (below) Mrs. Moore characters in, Forster's *A Passage to India* (1924). [*Editor*]

investigation; a subject which asked to be built up of an enormous number of slight yet precise observations, capable of being tested by an
extremely honest yet sympathetic mind; yet, with all this, a subject
which when finally constructed would show up against the torrents of
the sunset and the eternities of night with a symbolical significance. In
Howards End the lower middle, the middle, the upper middle classes of
English society are so built up into a complete fabric. It is an attempt on
a larger scale than hitherto, and, if it fails, the size of the attempt is largely
responsible. Indeed, as we think back over the many pages of this elaborate and highly skilful book, with its immense technical accomplish-
ment, and also its penetration, its wisdom, and its beauty, we may
wonder in what mood of the moment we can have been prompted to
call it a failure. By all the rules, still more by the keen interest with which
we have read it from start to finish, we should have said success. The reason is suggested perhaps by the manner of one's praise. Elaboration, skill,
wisdom, penetration, beauty—they are all there, but they lack fusion;
they lack cohesion; the book as a whole lacks force. Schlegels, Wilcoxes,
and Basts, with all that they stand for of class and environment, emerge
with extraordinary verisimilitude, but the whole effect is less satisfying
than that of the much slighter but beautifully harmonious *Where Angels
Fear to Tread*. Again we have the sense that there is some perversity in
Mr. Forster's endowment so that his gifts in their variety and number
tend to trip each other up. If he were less scrupulous, less just, less sen-
sitively aware of the different aspects of every case, he could, we feel,
come down with greater force on one precise point. As it is, the strength
of his blow is dissipated. He is like a light sleeper who is always being
woken by something in the room. The poet is twitched away by the
satirist; the comedian is tapped on the shoulder by the moralist; he never
loses himself or forgets himself for long in sheer delight in the beauty or
the interest of things as they are. For this reason the lyrical passages in
his books, often of great beauty in themselves, fail of their due effect in
the context. Instead of flowering naturally—as in Proust, for instance—
from an overflow of interest and beauty in the object itself, we feel that
they have been called into existence by some irritation, are the effort of
a mind outraged by ugliness to supplement it with a beauty which,
because it originates in protest, has something a little febrile about it.

Yet in *Howards End* there are, one feels, in solution all the qualities
that are needed to make a masterpiece. The characters are extremely
real to us. The ordering of the story is masterly. That indefinable but
highly important thing, the atmosphere of the book, is alight with intelligence; not a speck of humbug, not an atom of falsity is allowed to settle. And again, but on a larger battlefield, the struggle goes forward
which takes place in all Mr. Forster's novels—the struggle between the
things that matter and the things that do not matter, between reality and
sham, between the truth and the lie. Again the comedy is exquisite and

the observation faultless. But again, just as we are yielding ourselves to the pleasures of the imagination, a little jerk rouses us. We are tapped on the shoulder. We are to notice this, to take heed of that. Margaret or Helen, we are made to understand, is not speaking simply as herself; her words have another and a larger intention. So, exerting ourselves to find out the meaning, we step from the enchanted world of imagination, where our faculties work freely, to the twilight world of theory, where only our intellect functions dutifully. Such moments of disillusionment have the habit of coming when Mr. Forster is most in earnest, at the crisis of the book, where the sword falls or the bookcase drops. They bring, as we have noted already, a curious insubstantiality into the 'great scenes' and the important figures. But they absent themselves entirely from the comedy. They make us wish, foolishly enough, to dispose Mr. Forster's gifts differently and to restrict him to write comedy only. For directly he ceases to feel responsible for his characters' behaviour, and forgets that he should solve the problem of the universe, he is the most diverting of novelists. The admirable Tibby and the exquisite Mrs. Munt in *Howards End*, though thrown in largely to amuse us, bring a breath of fresh air in with them. They inspire us with the intoxicating belief that they are free to wander as far from their creator as they choose. Margaret, Helen, Leonard Bast, are closely tethered and vigilantly overlooked lest they may take matters into their own hands and upset the theory. But Tibby and Mrs. Munt go where they like, say what they like, do what they like. The lesser characters and the unimportant scenes in Mr. Forster's novels thus often remain more vivid than those with which, apparently, most pain has been taken. But it would be unjust to part from this big, serious, and highly interesting book without recognizing that it is an important if unsatisfactory piece of work which may well be the prelude to something as large but less anxious.

*   *   *

Essays in Criticism

WILFRED STONE
Howards End: Red-Bloods and Mollycoddles[†]

> Life without Industry is sin, and Industry without Art, brutality.
>
> —Ruskin

> Culture without character is . . . something frivolous, vain, and weak; but character without culture is . . . something raw, blind, and dangerous.
>
> —Matthew Arnold

With *Howards End* Forster broadened his subject from a private to a public world, confronting for the first time not just personal or domestic antagonists, but representatives of England's social, political, and economic power. The motto of Margaret Schlegel, who can be said to speak for Forster, is "Only connect," and the book is a test of the ability of Bloomsbury liberalism to survive a marriage with the great world. Can personal relations and public relations join in creative harmony? This crucial problem has worried Forster from the beginning. Unless liberalism can show a more edifying view of reality than the Christian warfare between the flesh and the spirit, the world and the soul, unless it can effect some healing of the ancient dualisms, then it has small hope, or reason, for survival—nor should we lament its passing. Margaret's plea is a distant echo of the "Only believe" of St. Mark:[1]

> Only connect! That was the whole of her sermon. Only connect the prose and the passion, and both will be exalted, and human love will be seen at its height. Live in fragments no longer. Only connect, and the beast and the monk, robbed of the isolation that is life to either, will die.[2]

[†] Reprinted from Wilfred Stone, *The Cave and the Mountain: A Study of E. M. Forster* (Stanford: Stanford UP, 1966), 235–37, 243, 246–49, 255–63, 265–66 with the permission of the publishers, Stanford University Press. (c) 1966 by the Board of Trustees of the Leland Stanford Junior University. Some of the author's notes have been silently omitted.
1. Mark 5.36.
2. *Howards End*, p. 134. [Page references are to this Norton Critical Edition. *Editor*]

* * *

* * * This great theme, this joining of power and sensibility, the heroic and the civilized, male and female, springs directly from a personal
worry; and whatever universality the theme has is due in part at least to
the representative nature of Forster's personal experience. We evoke that
problem immediately if we remember Dickinson's dichotomy between
the Red-bloods and the Mollycoddles.[3] The Red-bloods had their origi-
nals in the wellborn bullies and roughs of the "best set," those cricket-
playing conformists of the public school (and university) who were destined to rule Britain and her Empire; the Mollycoddles were those, like
Dickinson and Forster, almost as wellborn, who hated and envied the
strong ones and consoled themselves with dreams that one day the meek
and the sensitive would inherit the earth. The issue of crude power pervades everything Forster writes: how can one handle the authorities, the
bosses, the parents? This book confronts that issue and broadens its
scope. But it is interesting to note that here for the first time Forster
relinquishes the hero-role entirely to women. The two Schlegel sisters,
and especially Margaret, are his personal representatives, and they take
on the male adversaries, the Wilcox Red-bloods, with feminine
weapons. The attempt to compete as a man, abandoned with *The
Longest Journey*, is not resumed; instead the author pours his contempt
into that lost identity, lets it live briefly as Henry Wilcox, and takes shelter in female bodies that men do not normally strike.

So it might be said that Forster is hiding out in this book—in the very
book that seems in some ways to move most bravely into the public
arena. His doing so would be in keeping with his well-known "shy crab-
like sideways movement"[4], that oblique and feminine way of meeting
opposition, and would suggest that Forster may be facing the great world
more out of duty than inclination. Such possibilities make one question
whether Forster will be able to give the problem of connection, especially connection between men and women, a fair trial. Lionel Trilling
calls *Howards End* Forster's masterpiece because it "develops to their full
the themes and attitudes of the early books and . . . justifies these attitudes by connecting them with a more mature sense of responsibility."[5]
But is the book more responsible than the earlier ones? Does it represent
a summit or a crisis of achievement? These are critical questions.
Connection, not division, is the theme, and Forster's fictional trans-
vestism does not increase our confidence that he will be an impartial
mediator between Red-bloods and Mollycoddles, or indeed that he will

3. Goldsworthy Lowes Dickinson (1862–1932), Forster's teacher at Cambridge, makes this distinction in *Appearances, Being Notes on Travel* (1914). [*Editor*]
4. Forster, *Aspects of the Novel* (London 1927) 158. [For an excerpt from *Aspects*, see above, pp.
294–302. *Editor*]
5. Lionel Trilling, *E. M. Forster* (Norfolk 1943) 114–15. [For an excerpt from Trilling, see above,
pp. 326–31. *Editor*]

even try to be. But in spite of these misgivings—and because of them—this book commands an unusual degree of interest and respect.

* * *

* * * The two sisters are quite different. Trilling suggests that the names Margaret and Helen may derive from the heroines of the two parts of *Faust*, "one the heroine of the practical life, the other of the ideal life." Forster has denied any borrowing, but the association, though it fits the theme of the book better than it does the characters of the girls, is suggestive. One of the book's narrative rhythms is their drawing apart and their final coming together.

Helen is ardent, impulsive, idealistic, and easily disillusioned. * * * If Helen is guilty of the radicalism of extremes, Margaret, Forster's chief ethical representative, is presented as an example of "proportion." Her truth, we learn, is * * * a synthesis, an organic whole which is greater than the sum of its parts. To achieve this Moorean (or Arnoldian) state is the whole point of connecting, and Helen is finally reconciled to Margaret's marriage because she sees the action as a heroic attempt to "keep proportion" in spite of the goblins and their terrible universal message.

But the connections Helen makes are worth study, partly because it is her energy that gives the book much of its momentum. She is the first, we remember, to meet the Wilcoxes at Howards End, and these new connections briefly fascinate her.

The Wilcox children—Charles, Evie, and Paul—are all less pleasant versions of their father. Devotees of the outer life of "telegrams and anger" (rather than "sweetness and light"), they are known and know themselves in terms of stinking cars, cricket averages, and the financial pages of the *Times*. But Helen is at first swept off her feet; she even enjoys being bullied by Henry Wilcox into believing that all her fancy ideas about equality, votes for women, socialism, art and literature, are nonsense. "When Mr. Wilcox said that one sound man of business did more good to the world than a dozen of your social reformers, she had swallowed the curious assertion without a gasp, and had leant back luxuriously among the cushions of his motor-car" (19). These enchantments quickly became hateful, but one Wilcox stands apart from the tribe and is exempted from Helen's general condemnation. Ruth, the mother, the unassertive presiding spirit of Howards End, is almost a myth-like figure, and seems to float rather than walk through the book. She inhabits the house of realism like some ghostly deity. It is Helen who first meets and admires her:

> She seemed to belong not to the young people and their motor, but to the house, and to the tree that overshadowed it. One knew that she worshipped the past, and that the instinctive wisdom the past can alone bestow had descended upon her—that wisdom to which we give the clumsy name of aristocracy. High born she might not

be. But assuredly she cared about her ancestors, and let them help her. (18)

But Helen's most vital relationship is with Leonard Bast, one of the most interesting and least convincing characters in the book. Leonard, who bears some resemblance to Butler's Ernest Pontifex,[6] is a poor insurance clerk who lives "at the extreme edge of gentility" with Jacky, a lower-class woman whom Forster treats with unqualified—and even cruel—contempt. Leonard has staked his salvation on his ability to acquire "culture." To this end he goes to Queen's Hall concerts, looks at pictures, and reads Ruskin, Meredith, and George Borrow—believing that one day he will "push his head out of the grey waters and see the universe." Having no conception of "a heritage that may expand gradually," Leonard hopes "to come to Culture suddenly, much as the Revivalist hopes to come to Jesus" (39), a vulgar error for which his author does not let him off lightly. No easy atonement is available to those not born in the ranks of the elect.

Leonard is a fictional test of Arnold's belief that Culture, if it is to be realized at all, has its best chance among the Philistines. "The era of aristocracies is over," wrote Arnold; "nations must now stand or fall by the intelligence of their middle class and their people." For all its grievous faults, the middle class is the broad base of the nation, its source of power, and England's hope lies in the possibility that this class can be transformed, "liberalised by an ampler culture, admitted to a wider sphere of thought, living by larger ideas, with its provincialism dissipated, its intolerance cured, its pettinesses purged away."[7] Here if anywhere, thought Arnold, can be recruited the "saving remnant," that community of the best who can rise above the interests of class and sect to the true equality: they can become the representatives of humanity and "the heavenly Gods."[8] Can Leonard qualify? Can the "pursuit of perfection" and "sweetness and light" operate as strongly in him as mere class interest? That is his test, and Forster is brutally clear about limiting the scope of this novel to that class which has, on Arnold's terms, some fair hope of achieving culture. That Forster is consciously testing Arnold's belief is evident from this rather shocking statement: "We are not concerned with the very poor. They are unthinkable, and only to be approached by the statistician or the poet. This story deals with gentlefolk, or with those who are obliged to pretend that they are gentlefolk." (35)

Only those who have some chance of inheriting "England" are of interest, and once Forster has let Leonard into his novel, he seems

6. The inept and unhappy hero of Samuel Butler's satirical novel *The Way of All Flesh* (1903). [*Editor*]
7. "A French Eton; or Middle Class Education and the State," *Matthew Arnold, Poetry and Prose,* ed. Bryson, p. 342. Preceding quotation from Lionel Trilling, *Matthew Arnold* (New York, 1949), p. 229.
8. "Equality," *The Portable Matthew Arnold,* ed. Trilling, p. 581.

pressed to decide whether he should let him stay, just as the Schlegels debate whether they should invite Leonard to Wickham Place. Is he good enough? Can he be made good enough? The name Bast is itself a satiric tag,[9] and Forster several times burlesques his character, as in the following internal monologue: "Oh, to acquire culture! Oh, to pronounce foreign names correctly! Oh, to be well informed!" (31).

This is cheap playing to the Bloomsbury galleries. Nevertheless, it is Leonard's connection with Helen and with Schlegel sensibilities that gives this book its social conscience. Just as he stands on the edge of the social "abyss," so he affords the Schlegels a glimpse into it—increasing both their "panic and emptiness" and their guilt over class and money.
✻ ✻ ✻

✻   ✻   ✻

We have seen that this morality play begins, as morality plays must, with certain prejudices in favor of the angels. But what about Margaret's "connection"? Less prudish and absolute than Helen, in her exogamic[1] marriage to Henry Wilcox she makes a definite effort to join the prose and the passion. She knew Henry's faults and took the connubial risk with her eyes open. She says to Helen:

> "There is the widest gulf between my love-making and yours. Yours was romance; mine will be prose. I'm not running it down—a very good kind of prose, but well considered, well thought out. . . . I know all Mr. Wilcox's faults: He's afraid of emotion. He cares too much about success, too little about the past. His sympathy lacks poetry, and so isn't sympathy really. I'd even say"—she looked at the shining lagoons—"that, spiritually, he's not as honest as I am. Doesn't that satisfy you?" (126)

It is an astonishing statement to come from one who will soon be a bride. Is her honesty about Henry matched by an equal honesty in examining her own motives? The evidence is interesting.

First we must admit that the case against Henry is a strong one. He treats people as things; he turns Howards End (i.e., England) into a warehouse; he is a prude and defensively conventional. He is mad with rage over Helen's affair with Leonard, yet he cannot see that his own adultery with Jacky is morally the same. When the Jacky affair comes to light, Margaret, to save him from panic, has to help him "rebuild his fortress and hide his soul from the world" (176). He can never admit to being wrong, whereas the Schlegels did not mind being wrong: "To them nothing was fatal but evil." Margaret's frankness even allows her to

9. Besides the obvious connections with bastard, the name also could evoke St. Sebastian, who, full of the arrows of outrageous fortune, still manages to live on and not despair. The connection of Leonard with "odours from the abyss" also brings to mind that the Roman saint, after his martyrdom by stoning, was thrown into a sewer.
1. Outside of one's tribe or social unit. [*Editor*]

hope that someday, "in the millennium," her husband's "type" will be expendable. But for the present, the Wilcox virtues of "neatness, obedience, and decision" (though they kill imagination) remain necessary for the race's survival, and deserve homage "from those who think themselves superior, and who possibly are" (117).

These thoughts about her husband-to-be bring out the missionary in her. She thinks of her love as a means of setting "his soul in order" (158), of making him a "better man," of helping him "to the building of the rainbow bridge that should connect the prose in us with the passion" (134). "How wide the gulf between Henry as he was and Henry as Helen thought he ought to be! And she herself [Margaret]—hovering as usual between the two, now accepting men as they are, now yearning with her sister for Truth. Love and Truth—their warfare seems eternal" (165).

How easily Margaret turns from talking about Henry to talking about "men"—as though Henry were not an individual but a symbol! And this, in large part, is what her problem in connection comes to. Seeing that her influence over him depends on what she calls "the methods of the harem," she increasingly feels association with him to be a humiliation, an aspect of the eternal contention between male and female. When, for example, Henry owns up to his affair with Jacky, Margaret knows that he is "not so much confessing his soul as pointing out the gulf between the male soul and the female" (175). Again and again we hear echoes of the melioristic notion advanced by Carpenter[2] and Dickinson of the emergence of a "third sex," a new synthesis that will transcend sex, as the notion of the classless society would transcend class: "Are the sexes really races, each with its own code of morality, and their mutual love a mere device of Nature to keep things going? Strip human intercourse of the proprieties, and is it reduced to this?"

> Her judgment told her no. She knew that out of Nature's device we have built a magic that will win us immortality. Far more mysterious than the call of sex to sex is the tenderness that we throw into that call. . . . We are evolving, in ways that Science cannot measure, to ends that Theology dares not contemplate. (172)

Is it possible for Margaret to love anyone who does not also hear this millennial call—to this "truth" which is greater than love? Implicit in her whole relationship with Henry is the nagging question of whether she should make do with "men" in the relativistic present, or anticipate the classless and sexless society, now, in her own sensual being.

Her decision—or better, her drift—is strongly influenced by the first Mrs. Wilcox. From the first, Margaret is touched and chastened by this uncontentious spirit. At a time when Margaret is "zig-zagging with her

2. Edward Carpenter (1844–1929), champion of love, sex, and the body, who defended homosexuality and argued that love between men of different classes would break down social barriers. [*Editor*]

friends over Thought and Art" in the New English Art Club, Ruth Wilcox declares: "We never discuss anything at Howards End." "Clever talk alarmed her, and withered her delicate imaginings; it was the social counterpart of a motor-car, all jerks, and she was a wisp of hay, a flower" (58, 56). This wisp of hay nevertheless can sting like a nettle, as Margaret discovers when she is snubbed for refusing Ruth's first invitation to visit Howards End—for failing to recognize the importance of Howards End and the favor that was being shown her. (Ruth is the only character with greater spiritual authority than Margaret, and she is merciless on lapses of intuition.) She acts as an influence rather than a mover, thinking it "wiser to leave action and discussion to men," but when called upon to "separate those human beings who will hurt each other the most," she moves with uncompromising dispatch. But there is no hurry in her character: "She took her time, or perhaps let time take her" (60). Without any obvious messianic equipment, she moves on the earth as an incarnation of spiritual absolutes, an embodiment of "England's" best self. Even Henry Wilcox recognized her "unvarying virtue," the "wonderful innocence that was hers by the gift of God" (67), and the tenderness of his grief when she dies is perhaps his highest recommendation. But their union raises some vexing questions: What could possibly have led her to marry him—the same motives that moved Margaret? Then why does her spiritual power not have a greater effect on her brood of Wilcox barbarians? Does this mean that Margaret, in her missionary attempts with Henry, is defeated before she starts—that prose and passion cannot mix? If Ruth had so little influence on Henry, what can Margaret do? These questions demonstrate, in part, the near impossibility of bringing the worlds of myth and of realism together in the same book. But the difficulty, one feels, is not just technical; the more one reads this novel, the more one is disturbed by its ethical evasiveness.

Howards End is Ruth's temple. To the Schlegels, as to Rickie,[3] houses are "alive," whereas the Wilcoxes treat houses as things to buy, sell, lease, and improve. "We know this is our house," says Helen about Howards End, "because it feels ours" (214). Though the Wilcoxes hold the "title-deeds" and the "door keys," these evidences of ownership do not impress the Schlegels. The clash between realism and romance is marked. When Margaret marries, in a sense she marries both Henry and Ruth—the one in the flesh, the other in the spirit. The first union gives her legal title to the house, but the second gives her spiritual title, and there is no doubt which one Forster respects more. Mrs. Wilcox alone had "possessed" Howards End, for she had loved it, had sensed its inner and continuing life. The ancient wych-elm, where pigs' teeth had been buried by the country people in the belief that the bark would then cure

---

3. Rickie Elliot, the sensitive, literary, and congenitally lame hero of Forster's novel *The Longest Journey* (1907).

the toothache, is to her no mere curiosity, but a precious and true inheritance, the soul of the past impinging on the present. So when Mrs. Wilcox on her deathbed pencils a hasty note (which she fails to sign) leaving Howards End to Margaret, it is a spiritual rather than a material bequest (though the Schlegels ultimately get the material house as well). The Wilcoxes, of course, see in Ruth's act only illegality and "treachery":

> To them Howards End was a house: they could not know that to her it had been a spirit, for which she sought a spiritual heir. And— pushing one step farther in these mists—may not they have decided even better than they supposed? Is it credible that the possessions of the spirit can be bequeathed at all? Has the soul offspring? (73)

The joining of a house to a spirit, of treasure upon earth to treasure in heaven, is part of Margaret's problem in connection; and Forster, like the Claphamites,[4] deals with spiritual questions in the language of the court and the marketplace. But in exploring these "mists," Forster brushes against the more broadly symbolic issue of homelessness itself. The loss of the "mythical home, the mythical source," writes Nietzsche, is a cause of the "stupendous historical exigency of the unsatisfied modern culture,"[5] and Forster is first among contemporary writers to exploit the symbolic reality of a house that is a home, one of those simple universals evoking the critical need of modern man to "find his way back to a world in which he is no longer a stranger."[6]

As the novel proceeds, Margaret becomes more and more identified with Mrs. Wilcox, eventually assuming not only her married name but much of her nature. Ruth represents the achievement of "proportion," an ideal which has always ranked highest with Margaret. Margaret tells Helen,

> "To be humble and kind, to go straight ahead, to love people rather than pity them, to remember the submerged—well, one can't do all these things at once, worse luck, because they're so contradictory. It's then that proportion comes in—to live by proportion. Don't *begin* with proportion. Only prigs do that. Let proportion come in as a last resource, when the better things have failed." (55)

In fact many of the "better things" do seem to have failed for Ruth Wilcox: she no longer enjoys art, literature, conversation, sex, family life, or even personal relations. Proportion amounts to Arnoldian "disinter-

---

4. A group of Evangelical reformers of which Forster's grandfather Henry Thornton was a prominent member and who were active in such political causes as abolition of the slave trade. [*Editor*]
5. *The Birth of Tragedy from the Spirit of Music*, in *Modern Continental Literary Criticism*, ed. O. B. Hardison, Jr. (New York, 1962), p. 238.
6. C. J. Jung, *The Archetypes and the Collective Unconscious*, trans. R. F. C. Hull (New York, 1959), p. 110.

estedness," a kind of middle ground between partisanship and indifference, a rising above competition, and Margaret drifts toward it. Like
Ruth, she becomes less and less "enthusiastic about justice," saying to
Helen at Oniton: "There is to be none of this absurd screaming about
justice. I have no use for justice" (163). Nor, at last, does she care any
more about "duty," art or literature, political or social problems. "She
had outgrown stimulants," writes Forster, "and was passing from words to
things" (187), moving toward that strange spiritual autism which also is
to overcome Mrs. Moore in *A Passage to India*.

As part of this process, she turns against the city and toward the country, as Ruth had done. Earlier, Margaret had been surprised to hear Ruth
say "there was nothing to get up for in London" (52), but as her eyes
open to the architecture and the language of "hurry" she too comes to
despise cosmopolitanism. "This craze for motion," she says, "has only set
in during the last hundred years. It may be followed by a civilization that
won't be a movement, because it will rest on the earth" (240). Earlier in
the novel, Forster had written: "Month by month the roads smelt more
strongly of petrol, and were more difficult to cross, and human beings
heard each other speak with greater difficulty, breathed less of the air,
and saw less of the sky. Nature withdrew: the leaves were falling by midsummer; the sun shone through dirt with an admired obscurity." (79)
The psychic withdrawal of Ruth and Margaret is but an aping of
Nature's defeat, and a recognition that the city is a form of death. As
Lewis Mumford writes: "The metropolis is rank with forms of *negative
vitality*. Nature and human nature, violated in this environment, come
back in destructive forms. . . . In this mangled state the impulse to live
departs from apparently healthy personalities. The impulse to die sup-
plants it."[7] It is through Ruth, not through marriage, that Margaret finds
relief from "flux." It is through Ruth, not through Henry, that she finds
a home amidst the "civilization of luggage." Yet the "proportion" both
the women achieve or seek is hardly anything more than a form of the
negative vitality Mumford speaks of, an opting out of active life. Though
Margaret's moves from Wickham Place to Oniton to Howards End are
all away from metropolitan deathliness, away from the secular city to the
holy country, she is nonetheless tainted by this negativism, and led further into it by Ruth. Margaret is no Christian "in the accepted sense"
and does not "believe that God had ever worked among us as a young
artisan." But Ruth Wilcox is evidence to her that God works in other
ways, the living affirmation that "it is private life that holds out the mirror to infinity" (61). The child of an unbelieving though churchgoing
age, Margaret finds in Ruth everything she can retain as religion.
"Though it is impossible to tell," writes J. Hillis Miller, "whether man
has excluded God by building his great cities, or whether the cities have

---

7. Lewis Mumford, *The Culture of Cities* (New York, 1938), pp. 271, 291–92. Italics in original.

been built because God has disappeared, in any case the two go togeth-er." And Forster—with Margaret concurring—would agree with him that "life in the city is the way in which many men have experienced most directly what it means to live without God in the world":[8]

> Certainly London fascinates. One visualizes it as a tract of quiver-ing grey, intelligent without purpose, and excitable without love; as a spirit that has altered before it can be chronicled; as a heart that certainly beats, but with no pulsation of humanity. . . . Nature, with all her cruelty, comes nearer to us than do these crowds of men. . . . London is religion's opportunity—not the decorous religion of the-ologians, but anthropomorphic, crude. Yes, the continuous flow would be tolerable if a man of our own sort—not anyone pompous or tearful—were caring for us up in the sky. (79–80)

Margaret's following of St. Ruth is a direct consequence of her repudia-tion of London. But we feel it as a negative discipleship, an escape to a kind of pleasant despair; for the city remains and needs some good force to "connect" with it.

What, finally, can we say of Margaret's connection with Henry? Does she love him and give the marriage a fair trial, or does she only go through the motions? Her early feelings for him describe an ascending order of impatience: he had cheated on Ruth, he sells Oniton without consulting his wife, he is underhanded about the irregular will (this is discovered later), and he even refuses to let the pregnant Helen spend a night in Howards End. While he forgets his own immorality, he is con-ventionally outraged at Helen's, causing Margaret to deliver a speech that marks her final emotional deliverance from him. Though the word "love" is used after this, one feels it is only the return to a verbal habit.

> "Not any more of this!" she cried. "You shall see the connection if it kills you, Henry! You have had a mistress—I forgave you. My sis-ter has a lover—you drive her from the house. Do you see the con-nection? Stupid, hypocritical, cruel—oh, contemptible!—a man who insults his wife when she's alive and cants with her memory when she's dead. A man who ruins a woman for his pleasure, and casts her off to ruin other men. And gives bad financial advice, and then says he is not responsible. These men are you. You can't rec-ognize them because you cannot connect. I've had enough of your unweeded kindness. I've spoilt you long enough. . . . No one has ever told what you are—muddled, criminally muddled. Men like you use repentance as a blind, so don't repent. Only say to yourself, 'What Helen has done, I've done.'" (219)

---

8. "The Theme of the Disappearance of God in Victorian Poetry," *Victorian Studies*, VI (1963), 209.

Later, remembering her words, "her speech to him seemed perfect." "She neither forgave him for his behaviour nor wished to forgive him." "It had to be uttered," she claims, "to adjust the lopsidedness of the world"; and—significantly—"It was spoken not only to her husband, but to thousands of men like him—a protest against the inner darkness in high places that comes with a commercial age. . . . He had refused to connect, on the clearest issue that can be laid before a man, and their love must take the consequences" (235).

But has she adjusted the world's lopsidedness, or has she made it more lopsided? To address herself not just to Henry but to "men," to those imaginary "thousands," is evidence enough that she has, unconsciously perhaps, rehearsed this speech before. It is evidence, too, that her relation to him is not simply "personal," but abstract; he is in fact a figure in her personal allegory even as he is in her author's. In one of her ponderings Margaret reflects: "It is pleasant to analyse feelings while they are still only feelings, and unembodied in the social fabric" (125). Yes, and it is equally pleasant to discuss love this way, before it is invested in a man. The purity of detachment strongly appeals to her, and it is impossible not to feel the profound relief, and even pleasure, in her casting-out speech to Henry. But to divide fact from feeling and love from flesh in this way is the essence of sentimentality; and Margaret's "love" is not exempt from the cruelty that so often accompanies the sentimental attitude. Before Henry, we are told, she had often loved, "but only so far as the facts of sex demanded: mere yearnings for the masculine, to be dismissed for what they were worth, with a smile" (120). But why with a smile? Could her yearnings for the feminine, her loyalties to Helen and to Ruth, be dismissed so lightly? Something is indeed lopsided here. Henry's commitment to Margaret has of course its shortcomings—he could be "a little ashamed of loving a wife" (134), and he is as ascetically furtive about sex as he is about money—but Margaret is essentially virginal from the start. Her real design is to save Henry, not to marry him; and their actual relations are a power struggle. * * *

* * * The book ends with the two girls and their misbegotten heir in complete and undisputed possession of Howards End, in its real as well as its spiritual estate—and with all the human creatures they connected with either maimed, imprisoned, or dead. Once again things had gone on until there were no more men. Henry is still physically present, and we are told that Margaret still loves him, but he is broken, a man no longer. Margaret had said that she would make him see the connection if it "killed" him, and she very nearly has had her wish. After Charles goes to prison convicted of manslaughter for his part in Leonard's death, Henry's "fortress" gives way, and he simply turns himself over to Margaret "to do what she could with him." Margaret dismisses him dryly: "He has worked very hard all his life, and noticed nothing. Those are the people who collapse when they do notice a thing" (238). If there

is love in that remark, it is not recognizable in any ordinary sense. Margaret's may be one of the unfairest marriages in modern fiction.

*　　*　　*

The Schlegel experiments in connection mean a little expansion outward of their femininity, a little relaxing of their frigidity and fear, and then a closing again into a tight circle of safety and inviolability. They make of Howards End a place of sterile quarantine for the best self of England, but there is no indication that these defenders will ever again do battle with the enemy. The symbolic hope, of course, is Helen's son. He is continuance. But we have no reason to suppose that Helen and Margaret will be better child-rearers than Ruth Wilcox. The burden of the book's conclusion is that Forster does not really want connection at all, but only the rewards of connection; he does not want sex, but only the heir. He wants, in short, ends without means. As Margaret says: "Alas! that Henry should fade away as reality emerged, and only her love for him should remain clear, stamped with his image like the cameos we rescue out of dreams" (235). This is the love of love, not the love of people, and while it may be sound Moorean ethics, it is a disastrous program for practical humanism.[9] "She, who had never expected to conquer anyone, had charged straight through these Wilcoxes and broken up their lives" (242). The girls are "finished" almost before they begin, yet Forster calls their retreat a "victory":

> And all the time their salvation was lying round them—the past sanctifying the present; the present, with wild heart-throb, declaring that there would after all be a future, with laughter and the voices of children. Helen, still smiling, came up to her sister. She said, "It is always Meg." They looked into each other's eyes. The inner life had paid. (212)

The sisters' victory, to be sure, is not complete—it will take two thousand years of development to attain it fully—but they have won the battle.

We end with sensitivity quarantined from impulse, and an attendant promise of decadence and brutality. It is too bad, for this is a fascinating and ambitious book, and few readers will easily believe that this is what Forster really wants his fable to say. The malignancy inherent in a spiritual-esthetic withdrawal is a subject Forster knows well, and has warned about in his essays.[1] But in fictionalizing the problem, he has presented a moral failure as a triumph—and, in the name of much that is beautiful and fine, has become the partisan of much that is sick and corrupt. The forces of value do not "connect," but pursue each other in a lonely

---

9. G. E. Moore defined "the pleasures of human intercourse and the enjoyment of beautiful objects" as ideal goods, "worth having purely for their own sakes" (in his *Principia Ethica* [1903]). [*Editor*]
1. See "Virginia Woolf," *Two Cheers for Democracy* (London, 1951).

and circular futility. And the circle is especially vicious because Forster seems to see only its "proportion" and not its "emptiness."

*   *   *

BARBARA ROSECRANCE

[The Ambivalent Narrator of *Howards End*]†

The conscious intent of *Howards End* is to resolve conflict and affirm possibility. Yet throughout the novel Forster undercuts his attempts at an optimistic synthesis by repeatedly projecting chaos. The real source of problems in *Howards End* is neither imbalance between "inner" and "outer" values nor contradiction between the aims of conciliation and victory, but rather a deeper tension that these difficulties mirror, between Forster's efforts to "prove" his humanistic values and to sustain Western society through reversion to rural virtues, and a countercurrent of disbelief, a deepening pessimism expressed through images and motifs that evoke, in a new and menacing world, a vision of cosmic disorder and loss of meaning. The rhetoric affirms connection, but the undercurrent describes collapse. This tension invades all aspects of the novel. It explains the disjunctions in theme and character; it pervades and determines Forster's narrative voice.

*   *   *

The contradictory impulses of *Howards End* infuse Forster's narrative voice and have important implications for its quality and function. The voice contains the schism that the action also reflects, for throughout the novel the narrator strains to bring his disparate materials into congruence and the competing formulations of his own voice into compatibility. In an accelerating tension between the impassioned rhetoric of the authorial voice and the ambivalence it attempts to suppress lies the explanation of the peculiar narrator of *Howards End*. Ultimately the increasing pressure of the negative vision undercuts the voice that contains it and alters its very nature.

It seems appropriate that *Howards End*, the novel that seeks most directly to locate ultimate value within the context of human relationships, should reveal an intensely personal narrative voice. The narrator's techniques of omniscience and engagement are familiar, but his voice goes further in self-dramatization, in manipulation of the reader, in the frequency and length of intervention than in any other Forster novel. The tendency of the narrator to step out of the action to formulate its

† From Barbara Rosecrance, *Forster's Narrative Vision* (Ithaca, NY: Cornell UP, 1982) 111, 131–42. Copyright (c) 1982 by Cornell University Press. Used by permission of the publisher.

larger significance also reaches its height in *Howards End*. No other Forster narrator establishes so personal a hegemony. His use of Margaret is instrumental to his scope, for he enters her generalizing imagination so often that Margaret functions as an extension of his voice. The narrator's omniscience, his relationship with the reader, and his self-dramatization distinguish him from Margaret. Uniquely in this novel, Forster's narrator indicates his gender, as, speculating on the difference between male and female friendships, he notes that "when men like us, it is for our better qualities. . . . but unworthiness stimulates woman."[1] His language defines a variety of roles. As celebrant of England's glory he is a visionary bard, his literary diction means to a precarious decorum. He emphasizes his manipulations and the centrality of his function more than he does the story itself, intervening, for example, to excoriate Wilcox's repudiation of Mrs. Wilcox's will: "the discussion moved toward its close. To follow it is unnecessary. It is rather a moment when the commentator should step forward. Ought the Wilcoxes to have offered their home to Margaret?" (73). The long essay that follows displays the narrator's judicial wisdom. But he can also present himself as a fellow-citizen, permitting the reader a rare glimpse of domestic intimacy as he extrapolates from Henry Wilcox's failure to mention the mews behind Ducie Street when he hopes to sublet his flat: "So does my grocer stigmatize me when I complain of the quality of his sultanas, and he answers in one breath that they are the best sultanas, and how can I expect the best sultanas at that price?" (131).

Through diction and tone, the narrator seeks control of his structure and reader. With deceptive self-effacement he casts himself as the mind behind the action: "one may as well begin with Helen's letters to her sister" (5). As the narrator continues, his grammatical emphases imply reader agreement — "Certainly Margaret was impulsive. She did swing rapidly from one decision to another" (11). He moves toward fuller control of the reader through frequent mediations between reader and characters, in which he often furthers intimacy by direct address. Thus, defending Leonard Bast's reticence about the adventure of his all-night walk, Forster admonishes the reader: "You may laugh at him, you who have slept nights out on the veldt, with your rifle pat beside you and all the atmosphere of adventure pat. And you may also laugh who think adventures silly. But do not be surprised if Leonard is shy whenever he meets you, and if the Schlegels rather than Jacky hear about the dawn"(91). This passage is singular in the degree to which it defines reader as well as character and commenting voice; its hostility to the imagined reader is perhaps Forster's coy attempt to produce sympathy appropriate to his character. But the passage is also noteworthy for its erosion of the boundary between experience and fiction. The rhetorical

---

1. *Howards End*, p. 174. [Page references are to this Norton Critical Edition. *Editor*]

nature of Forster's narrative technique is not new, but the frequency in
Howards End of conflations like this is unique in his fiction.

As he intrudes into a comic scene between Margaret's Aunt Juley and
Charles Wilcox, the narrator interrupts his narrative to suggest its irrelevance: "Young Wilcox was pouring in petrol, starting his engine, and
performing other actions with which this story has no concern" (14–15).
The narrator's qualification, itself an aside, renders the action he
excludes parenthetical also. Yet, in a comic anticipation of *A Passage to
India*, his very exclusion includes. For his distinction implies the existence of his characters in a realm of reality that is not the story, a world
in which the reader may be presumed to function also. More directly,
the narrator identifies Margaret with "others who have lived long in a
great capitol," a classification that implies her shared reality with potential readers. Like these city-dwellers, Margaret has "strong feelings"
about railway stations, emotions that become the narrator's truth: "They
are our gates to the glorious and the unknown" (11). From Margaret the
narrator moves to the implied reader who coexists with her in the world
outside his fiction, with the judgment that "he is a chilly Londoner who
does not endow his stations with some personality, and extend to them,
however shyly, the emotions of fear and love" (11). The use of direct
address intensifies the reader's participation in the narrator's rhetoric.
Hoping that Margaret's connection of King's Cross Station with infinity
"will not set the reader against her," he intrudes further to insist on
Margaret's insight: "If you think this is ridiculous, remember that it is not
Margaret who is telling you about it; and let me hasten to add that they
were in plenty of time for the train" (11–12). The assumption of potential conversation between Margaret and the reader merges the double
fiction of character and narrator with the reader's world of experience,
for it is the narrator who, ostensibly in the character's behalf, confronts
the reader. The commentary has become not only a direct conversation
but an argument, in which the narrator disarms potential opposition,
assumes responsibility for his characters' perceptions, and buttresses his
case with apparent considerations of common sense. These techniques
are significant because they reveal the intensity of Forster's need in this
novel to persuade, and suggest the degree of his extremity.

For despite the narrator's brilliance, his persuasion must ultimately be
regarded as unsuccessful. He does not achieve a harmonious integration
of ideology and dramatic representation, of content and form. His reflections are often disconnected from the action, so that the novel appears
to present an uneven alternation between essay and scene, comment
and action. To a degree found in no other Forster novel, the narrator's
diction is abstract, metaphorical, hyperbolical; the anxiety and inflation
of his tone suggest the desperation of his attempt to harmonize and persuade. The prominence, the intimate tone, the rhetorical techniques of
this narrator are evoked by the impossibility of his task. Equal intensity

seems to attend each exhortation. Nowhere does he acknowledge incompatibility among contending values. It is as if Forster is trying to bridge the gap between desire and disillusion by the insistence of his presence, to cover his inconsistencies of attitude and the unlikeliness of character and action by the sheer weight of his rhetoric as narrator. Consequently he is eloquent and hysterical, strained, elaborate, evasive, intimate, familiar, powerful, and unconvincing as he attempts to impose on the world of the novel a coherence that action and voice alike belie.

The narrator's rhetoric thus embodies its own limitations, which appear in all the novel's contexts. The portrayal of Mrs. Wilcox, for example, is an attempt to establish the mythic significance of an unsubstantial character. First seen by Helen, Mrs. Wilcox wears a long dress, she "trails," she picks up a piece of hay, she smells flowers, she is tired, she is "steadily unselfish." The corroborating narrator assures that Mrs. Wilcox is "just as Helen's letter had described her, trailing noiselessly over the lawn, and there was actually a wisp of hay in her hands" (18). But in the absence of dramatic context, Forster asserts a larger significance: "One knew that she worshipped the past, and that the instinctive wisdom the past can alone bestow had descended upon her—that wisdom to which we give the clumsy name of aristocracy" (18). Mrs. Wilcox, described throughout as shadowy, is too shadowy to bear this weight. To the degree that her behavior is recorded, she is rather a caricature of the traditional wife and mother, naive, submissive, and insular. The preciosity of Margaret's guests at a luncheon she gives for Mrs. Wilcox is balanced by the parochiality of the lady herself. Margaret's brief experience of Mrs. Wilcox doesn't warrant her belief that she and her family "are only fragments of Mrs. Wilcox's mind," and that Mrs. Wilcox "[knew] everything" (222). Nor does the characterization support the narrator's direct claim that Mrs. Wilcox is "nearer the line that divides daily life from a life that may be of greater importance" (58). Assertion seeks unsuccessfully to bridge the gap between intention and presentation.

Forster's relation to Leonard Bast is at best uneasy, a mixture of compassion and condescension. The significance of Leonard Bast is in his origin, in his pivotal position as cause célèbre for the liberal intellectuals and victim of the capitalists, and in his sentimental apotheosis into England's future. An uncertainty of narrative tone pursues Leonard throughout. Initially Forster demythifies him: "he was inferior to most rich people, there is not a doubt of it. He was not as courteous as the average rich man, nor as intelligent, nor as healthy, nor as lovable" (35). Leonard has a half-baked mind; his conversation is querulous and banal; he is "one of the thousands who have lost the life of the body and failed to reach the life of the spirit" (84). Margaret's assessment contains no hint of irony, although it catches her in violation of her own individualistic credo: "She knew this type very well—the vague aspirations, the mental dishonesty, the familiarity with the outsides of books" (85). Leonard's capacity for spontaneity and his questing spirit redress the balance, but even in this Forster undercuts his praise: "Within his cramped little mind dwelt something that was greater than Jeffries' books—the spirit that led Jeffries to write them" (88). When ultimately Forster transfigures Leonard, his invocation does not create heroic significance: "Let Squalor be turned into Tragedy, whose eyes are the stars, and whose hands hold the sunset and the dawn" (234).

In comparable interventions the narrative voice asserts dimensions that the action cannot substantiate, as when Forster tries unsuccessfully to cover Margaret's crisis with sister and husband by a rhetoric of benediction: "For the present let the moon shine brightly and the breezes of the spring blow gently, dying away from the gale of the day, and let the earth, who brings increase, bring peace" (221). The inflation and unease of these assertions is compounded in many of the essaylike passages that stud the novel. Forster's evocation of a rainbow bridge is replete with questionable images:

> . . . she might yet be able to help him to the building of the rainbow bridge that should connect the prose in us with passion. Without it we are meaningless fragments, half monks, half beasts, unconnected arches that have never joined into a man. With it love is born, and alights on the highest curve, glowing against the gray, sober against the fire. Happy the man who sees from either aspect the glory of these outspread wings. The roads of his soul lie clear, and he and his friends shall find easy going. (134)

How is the reader to interpret the implied parallel between prose and passion and monk and beast, the location and meaning of fire, the literal and metaphorical discrepancy of gray, the location and condition of the man "who sees from either aspect" and to incorporate into all this the sudden appearance of roads in the man's soul? One has only to contrast this jumble with the powerful and coherent imagery of arch and echo of *A Passage to India*. Groping in *Howards End* for the way to embody his thought, Forster too often substitutes preachiness for the integrated imagery of a coherent position.

The narrator presides over the survival theme, and most of the passages that celebrate England emanate from his voice. Elegiac and passionate, sentimental and unabashed, they transcend the focus on personality even as they represent a desperate attempt to retain the civilization for which it was a primary value.

> Branksea Island lost its immense foreshores and became a sombre episode of trees. Frome was forced inwards toward Dorchester, Stour against Wimborne, Avon towards Salisbury, and over the immense displacement the sun presided, leading it to triumph ere he sank to rest. England was alive, throbbing through all her estu-

aries, crying for joy through the mouths of all her gulls, and the north wind, with contrary motion, blew stronger against her rising seas. What did it mean? For what end are her fair complexities, her changes of soil, her sinuous coast? Does she belong to those who have moulded her and made her feared by other lands, or to those who had added nothing to her power, but have somehow seen her, seen the whole island at once, lying as a jewel in a silver sea, sailing as a ship of souls, with all the brave world's fleet accompanying her towards eternity? (127)

F. R. Leavis cites this passage to note that Forster "lapses into such exaltations quite easily," and he criticizes the vagueness that Forster's use of "somehow" creates in the last sentence.[2] But do we not react more to the inflated diction of "leading it to triumph ere he sank to rest," to the frenetic personifications of "England was alive," "throbbing," and "crying"? Besides the hyperbole, of which one can find in *Howards End* surpassing examples, the passage is noteworthy for revealing Forster's ambivalence of preoccupation and uncertainty of mode. The rhetorical question about England's fate leads not to concern with "the brave world's fleet" but to an expression of conflict between power and the creative imagination. In this it reflects the disjunction between the goals of reconciliation and victory seen in the action and implies the ascendancy of those who see life whole, who have "seen the whole island at once." These, of course, are the Schlegels, and, as the only voice capable of the rhetorical question, the narrator himself. Thus while appearing to transcend the concern with personality, Forster displays the superiority of the mind whose insight includes but discounts "those who have moulded her and made her feared by other lands." Yet Leavis's uneasiness with "somehow" ought to have extended to the literary echoes and second-hand images, which suggest limitation or, as I. A. Richards put it, a "forcing" of the creative imagination.[3] Again to contrast the ungrounded abstraction of this language with the concrete diction and integrated imagery of *A Passage to India* is to envision the distance Forster still has to travel.

The inner tensions that these "forcings" imply may also be seen in direct expressions of ambivalence within the narrative voice. Noteworthy here is the degree to which Forster's apprehension contains something other than concern for the civilization he loves, for underlying the exhortation to human relations is a striking sense of recoil from humanity.

Their house was in Wickham Place, and fairly quiet, for a lofty promontory of buildings separated it from the main thoroughfare.

2. F. R. Leavis, "E. M. Forster," *The Common Pursuit* (London: Chatto & Windus, 1952), reprinted in *Forster*, ed. Malcolm Bradbury (Englewood Cliffs, N.J.: Prentice-Hall, Inc., 1966), p. 42.
3. I. A. Richards, "A Passage to Forster: Reflections on a Novelist," *The Forum*, 78 (December 1927), 914–920, reprinted in *Forster*, ed. Bradbury, p. 19.

One had the sense of a backwater, or rather of an estuary, whose waters flowed in from the invisible sea, and ebbed into a profound silence while the waves without were still beating. Though the promontory consisted of flats—expensive, with cavernous entrance halls, full of concierges and palms—it fulfilled its purpose, and gained for the older houses opposite a certain measure of peace. These, too, would be swept away in time, and another promontory would rise upon their site, as humanity piled itself higher and higher on the precious soil of London. (8)

The narrative voice discriminates between house and city and, more significantly, between human life and nature. Noise, vulgarity, meaningless aggregation cover simultaneously the flats of a burgeoning city and the ephemeral but continuous flow of humanity they enclose.

This ambivalence may also be seen in Forster's treatment of characters. It is curious that this most personal narrator should display so little real sympathy for the characters of whom he claims such profound knowledge. But the intimacy of his rhetoric obscures the indifference or hostility that underlies his professions of concern. To the gap between Forster's theory and his practice with Henry Wilcox and his condescension to Leonard Bast we must add the overt repugnance he feels for Jacky Bast: "A woman entered, of whom it is simplest to say that she was not respectable. . . . Yes, Jacky was past her prime, whatever that prime may have been" (39). Even the Schlegels, though in a more disguised manner, receive a share of this ambivalence. Helen is passionate and truthful, the only character to act on the doctrine of personal responsibility that Margaret and the narrator espouse. But Forster's disapproval of Helen's excesses and his fear of her enticements undercut his support of her perceptions. On Margaret the narrator renders little judgment, but whether from unconscious intention or inability to separate himself from her characteristics, Forster has produced a character whose stridency evokes a certain recoil. And the narrator's impulse to protect himself from the vulgar crowd and the less comfortable realities of existence is mirrored in Margaret, to whom the appearance of Leonard Bast's wife, "Mrs. Lanoline," causes an anxiety that is not solely concern for the Basts: "She feared, fantastically, that her own little flock might be moving into turmoil and squalor, into nearer contact with such episodes as these" (84).

Thus, even as Forster describes with some compassion the consequences for Leonard Bast of his entrapment in class (Mrs. Lanoline is such a consequence), he draws back from contact with the imperfectly washed. Concerned though he is with social equity and social cost, Forster shrinks from humanity in the aggregate. His ideology may be seen partly as an expression of this ambivalence: the individual is nearer to the "unseen" than any organization, humanity as a concept is associated with isms and programs. The consequences of this position engender what has been described as Forster's critique of liberalism. But although he dramatizes the impotence of the liberal intelligentsia to solve the problems of modern society, there is little evidence of Forster's separation from liberal values.

Portrayed as inhabitants of a feminine culture and divorced from power, the intelligentsia are dilettantes. While Forster yearns for masculinity, he can conceive it only as Henry Wilcox, whom he repudiates, or as Leonard Bast, who is so disadvantaged he doesn't signify. With apprehensions about the feminization of culture, expressed in his criticism of Margaret's effeminate brother Tibby and in the sisters' awareness of the need for balance, he nevertheless places his moral weight behind the Schlegels. To women as a group he is less generous. Margaret and Helen's all-female discussion club presents something of a parallel to the Apostolic session of *The Longest Journey*. But the women discuss social questions whereas the men engaged in metaphysical speculation, a Forsterian estimate of their relative capacities, as the narrator's misogynistic comment that "the female mind, though cruelly practical in daily life, cannot bear to hear ideals belittled in conversation" (93) suggests. One should note, however, that both discussion groups are equally ineffectual.

Although Forster treats Leonard Bast more as representative of a class than as an individual, he does not conclude that social or economic action to improve the situation of Leonard Basts is desirable. On the contrary, the members of the debating society avoid the issue by bequeathing their fictional millionaire's legacy within their own class. Margaret wishes to help only the individual, but the very values of integrity and honor that comprise the "inner" ideal nullify this possibility in the novel itself. For when Helen undertakes to realize Margaret's ideal of personal philanthropy, the near-starving Leonard Bast declines her offer. His refusal, "very civil and quiet in tone" (183), aligns him with the gentlemanly standards of Forster's own class. One could wish that Forster had shown here the hardheaded sophistry of his contemporary Shaw, whose Mr. Doolittle is concerned only about his translation to gentility.[4] At any rate, Leonard's "higher" instincts doom him even more effectively than the indifferent machinations of capitalism. Nice guys finish last, as the contrast of his honorable behavior to Jacky with Henry's sexual opportunism also demonstrates. But although Forster dramatizes these ironies, he clings to the old formulations of honor. For him, the only alleviation of the modern condition lies in escape from the encroaching mass and its urban hive.

Forster's authorial voice itself expresses the conflicts that character and action embody. More than in any other novel Forster directs, exhorts, emphasizes, and seeks to harmonize, as the realities he presents become increasingly intractable to his hopes. Attempting for the last

4. See Bernard Shaw, *Pygmalion* (New York: The Modern Library, 1953), p. 288.

time to demonstrate a hopeful synthesis, straining to bring recalcitrant materials into conformity with his ideology, Forster's voice projects an anguish that moves us but does not solve the novel's problems. The narrator's intense rhetoric is a last, desperate exercise of personality, a final attempt to celebrate the creed of individuality through the colorful tonalities of a highly personal voice.

But *Howards End* demonstrates the limits of the personal, and Forster's movement away from the values of individual fulfillment and personal relations engenders the eventual effacement and withdrawal of his narrator. A valedictory persona, the narrator spends himself in a last violent effort to sustain, through his intense relationship with the reader and through characters in whom he no longer believes, his commitment to individual effort and personality. As the action converges upon Howards End, the narrator begins to withdraw. This is not a dramatic movement, but as his presence diminishes, the narrative voice abandons its exhortations and its intimate tone: in the final pages it appears only to validate Margaret's ominous apprehension of the end of rural civilization and to underline briefly the last revelations of plot, as Margaret discovers that Mrs. Wilcox had bequeathed her Howards End long ago. With this withdrawal the novel approaches the mode, the insights, and the austere voice of *A Passage to India*.

* * *

PERRY MEISEL

Howards End: Private Worlds and Public Languages[†]

If we begin to inspect the novel's language in any detail at all, * * * we find that Forster's vaunted (and only apparent) thematic intent—his myth of the modern—is simultaneously undermined as programmatically as it is set up by a rhetorical contamination or slippage of the oppositions that put it in place. Central among the novel's dualities is the classic modernist antagonism between self and society, private and public, and one that leads Forster to recommend the Moorish ideal of "'personal relations'" as a means of building that "rainbow bridge" between self and community that turns out to be unnecessary because the two are already conjoined.[1] Even Terry Eagleton remains captive to the belief in a straightforward "Forsterian affirmation of the 'personal,'" as though there

---

† From Perry Meisel, *The Myth of the Modern: A Study in British Literature and Criticism after 1850* (New Haven: Yale UP, 1987) pp. 173–82. Reprinted by permission of Yale University Press.
1. *Howards End*, pp. 126, 134. [Page references are to this Norton Critical Edition. *Editor*]

is no real irony in Forster's art.[2] "Personal relations" is, however, an oxy-
moron, since, as Pater and Joyce—and even Eliot—have shown, self and
world are mutually constitutive in the semiotic play of culture that produces subjects and objects alike in a series of gestures that privileges neither side of what is a productive rhetorical opposition rather than one
expressive of a condition in the world. A thorough focus on Forster's
vocabulary will show just how the oppositions that organize his manifest
myth of the modern also turn into one another so as to wreak semantic
havoc with the categories the novel's manifest thematic has erected.

If Bloomsbury is indeed programmatic in its use of the unseen poetic
arrangements of ordinary language, the real object of a text such as
Howards End is to join linguistically those colloquial terms that are customarily articulated as oppositions. Thus the novel's oppositions turn out
to link, paradigmatically, human and fiduciary relations—private and
public, spiritual and material, "personal" and "relations"—in a common
set of signifiers, throwing the relationship between denotation and con-
notation into chaos as one of the numerous side-effects that render
privacy a function of its dependence on the publicity to which it is normally counterposed. Most pervasive as well as most focused are the
similarities rather than differences between psychic and real economy
and their mutual interdependence in the tropology that identifies the
vocabulary of business or the Wilcoxes with the vocabulary of private
emotion or the Schlegels. Private virtue itself, for example, is thereby
always grafted, linguistically at least, to the same terms by which we cal-
culate the world of material value to which it is customarily opposed
("worth . . . ," 120, 185, 187, 208), making it no wonder that an idiom
such as "'tender hearts'" (123) suddenly reveals an economic aspect to
the figure that cautions the degree of epistemological integrity we like to
assign to our private worlds. Thus a surprising parade of tropological
identifications: one can be "'worthy'" (50) or "'unworthy'" (175) as a person; "tender" (175) emotionally; repose "trust" (29) in another person
(shades, too, of *The Confidence Man*);[3] or take an "interest" (76) in
someone else. Even more exactly, Helen's stocks, like her emotions, are
characteristically "reinvested" (183), while the contrastingly stable Mrs.
Munt possesses stock in her more appropriate style of "safe investments"
in "Home Rails" (12). One can, moreover, "cancel . . ." one's "mistrust"
(29) in a person by means of the same idiom by which one cancels a
check. Thus, too, a "'girl with no interests'" (43) is, like the otherwise
comfortable Helen, tropologically at least, nevertheless akin to a girl
with no money at all—Jacky, for example, with whom Helen in fact
changes places when she becomes Bast's lover. Likewise, "'the will to be
interested'" (43) directly implicates the vocabulary of the personal in

2. Terry Eagleton, *Walter Benjamin* (London: Verso, 1981), 138.
3. Novel by Herman Melville (1819–91). [*Editor*]

that of the public. "'The very soul of the world is economic'" (46), admits Mr. Wilcox, not only for the materialist reasons that escape him even in the first instance, but also because of the semiotic spillage that thwarts his like investment in the absolute difference between what is one's own and what is another's.

The vocabularies of the marketplace and stock exchange, in short, programmatically collide with the vocabulary of personal relations. Even throwaway colloquialisms denoting (connoting?) one's private mood such as "on Helen's account" (53) or to give an "account" (64, 78) of something coincide figurally with the public language of commerce and exchange. Such common or idiomatic usage almost endlessly infects the difference between private and public throughout the novel, whether we "'make a great deal of it'" (56), "evoke our interests" (59) or "withdraw" them (59). Thus an emotional "check . . ." (71, 80) has fiduciary connotations, much, amazingly enough, as does Mrs. Wilcox's extraordinary "tenderness" (67) and what is "tender . . ." (131, 139, 226, 231) in others throughout the novel. The property of Howards End has "tenderness" chief among its manifest atmospheric qualities (148), legal tender as it is of the value of the property as real estate. Indeed, one goes on "trusting" one's "husband" (69) or shows "mistrust . . ." (59) for someone in implicitly economic figures meant to describe the private alone, even when it comes to one's "life interest" (74). Though life is, says Forster, "unmanageable" (79), his descriptions of it are, by contrast, scrupulously managed by a language that joins the "alien associations" of the public discourses of management, finance, and exchange with those we (also) use to describe what is most private to us.

Hence the sudden resonance of apparently innocent idioms such as "'on no account'" (89, 177), "on her account" (118), "on his account" (227); the wish to "'tender . . . apologies'" (85); the economic murmur of phrases describing personal relations such as "'managed him'" (105), "trading on" (107), "deposited" (108), "cost" (115), even the matter-of-fact "owing to" (114). People try in short "to balance their lives" (109) through the management of psychic investments etymologically laced with economic ones such as those that make up Henry's bank balance. Thus Margaret's annoying recollection of "the stock criticism about Helen" (197) raises still another series of economic murmurs in an otherwise purely personal idiomatic signification. Even to be "rent into two people" (224) by psychological shock carries the quite alien associations that intimate the settled or unsettled state of one's psyche as a form of tenancy. Late in the novel, Helen's "'interests'" (216) slip between fiduciary and psychological meanings almost overtly, the family "'goods'" (217), like Moore's,[4] both blessed and tainted by the oscillation of philo-

---

4. G. E. Moore (1873–1958), professor of philosophy at Cambridge who emphasized the value of personal relationships and beautiful things. [*Editor*]

sophical and material meanings in the same signifier. And once Forster describes the condemned Leonard as one who does not "count for much" (221), his fate is sealed tropologically and representationally in the same figure.

Hardly random events in the novel, *Howards End*'s linkage of the public and private in an exemplary set of shared or common expressions not only projects a Keynesian[5] vision of the interdependencies that represent society as a matrix of relations rather than as a set of autonomous atoms, but also serves as a continual reminder of our nonimmediate relation to the world altogether, whether private or public, a world in which we are always belated because "'some medium of exchange'" (113) — some social mediation — is always required for anything to signify at all. Neither self nor world is in itself either independent or immediate; as a set of representations in the first instance, life is a secondary rather than a direct phenomenon from the start it can never be said properly to have (had). Foreshadowing Woolf's rather more overt vision of a world without a given self, Forster must conclude by implication that nothing exists autonomously, and that autonomy itself — the very token of the will to modernity whose typology and nature as a notion the novel elaborates — is a defensive reaction to its own impossibility within the semiotic grid of a culture to which we come belatedly and as a function of the bewildering overdeterminations of its signs and history. The novel's characters may try to act out the will to modernity in their various quests for the self-erasing ideal of "personal relations" that stands for a directness supposedly lost after an implied Eliotic "dissociation" divides modernity from tradition. As Forster's language shows, however, such acting out fails to work through the paradox of liberation that forever forbids the possibility of immediacy or of any kind of transcendent autonomy at all.

If the self-contamination of Forster's metaphors begins to emerge in the novel's habitual identification of psychic and real economy at the level of language — of "goods" and "goods," "worth" and "worth" — such an identity is even more trenchant and etymologically exacting in the movement of another of the novel's chief tropological systems, that of property. As we have seen in Pater's deconstruction of Arnold's selfsame ideals of originality and cleanliness, "property" is a figure etymologically bound to a series of what are, for Forster as well, epistemologically identical structures of desire: for property as such (as in Mrs. Wilcox's "property" [54] or in simple "possessions" [73]); for propriety in manners and sensibility (refinement and serenity); for the properness or integrity of a work of art; and for that self-possession or stability of ego that we equate with mental health. We should recall that *propre* also means what is clean or unspoiled, the graphic and/or tactile representation of

---

5. John Maynard Keynes (1883–1946), economist and member of the Bloomsbury circle of intellectuals with Forster and Virginia Woolf. [*Editor*]

the wishful desire for originality or autonomy central to the will to modernity in art and experience alike. Forster's use of the tropology of "property" is both exact in the novel's enduring deconstruction of its myth of the modern, and exacting in the strategic play of the figure throughout the text. Even one example suggests that behaving "'properly'" (9) and avoiding "impropriety" (13) will result in "self-possession" (14)—the possession of oneself is metaphorically akin to the solidity or ground of epistemological certainty and of plain real estate as well.

The figure's strategic vicissitudes organize the novel's language in a striking way. One wants one's "muddles" or dirt "tidied up" (52), for example, so as to let "self-possession," the propriety of one's own being, take on its apparently proper privacy (hence Bast's role as a grossly thematic reminder that the state of one's psyche and of one's economy are disastrously intertwined). Similarly, a "sloppy" soul (77) and the physically "untidy" (90) are figurations that epistemologically join what would otherwise be put asunder. Any "truth" is, as the Arnold to whom Forster sometimes alludes would have it, one of "clearness of vision" (131), freed from the haze or uncleanliness of outside influence. Thus Margaret's Arnoldean desire that Leonard "'wash out his brain and go to the real thing'" (106). We are in fact all in a "'mist'" (171), and therefore want our "vision cleared" (171)—we want to make a "clean breast" (177) of things. Even the apparently universal and nonliterary ideal of love is figured in the register of property and cleanliness, too: "She loved him," says Forster of Margaret's feeling for Henry, "with too clear a vision to fear his cloudiness" (158). The metaphorical chain is maintained when, for example, Jacky Bast's affair is described as "one new stain on the face of a love that had never been pure" (169). Of course, in a precise instance of Forster's wit, the last figuration again returns us, not to the will to modernity undiagnosed, but to the structure of modernism that produces its emergence. The origin or home—Jacky—to which Leonard wishes to return is, like Molly, already admittedly stained, the figure contaminating the origin as a precondition of the desire for it, its warmth a function of its distance.

With the categories and structure of modernism Forster's subject, then, *Howards End*, otherwise a proto-wastelander picture of London as full of "'rubbish'" (114, 117), "'slime'" (125), and "'heaps'" (126), is neither mimetic transcription nor a rehearsal of Eliot's anxiety about tradition as it will be projected in the ruinous landscape of *The Waste Land*. Instead, Forster's myth of the modern, with all its detailed characteristics, is, like Hardy's, an enormously prescient anticipation and prior critique of the ideology of a High Modernism yet to be misread. To say, then, that "the mind is overtaxed" (228) by the novel is to describe the effect of Forster's apparently flat prose as well as to cite still another example of its surprising spillage that scrambles the oppositions necessary to maintain a myth of the modern without being obvious about it.

The privacy of the "mind" is troped as the form of a public system, "tax-ation." The sanctity of privacy itself—that "paradise within thee happier far" still sustaining English Romantic tradition as late as 1910—can, must be signified, alas, only in relation to that which it is not, the pub-lic, the traditional, the outside. Because property is, ironically, privacy, it is public enough for Forster to dub the age itself the "Age of Property" (149). Like "personal relations," "Age of Property" is, however, also an implicit contradiction, implying as it does a shared or communal belief in the kind of privacy such a public articulation forbids.

If, moreover, what is private is available only as a function of what is public, the belated status of modern experience and of the modern imagination are once again redoubled, too. Like literary language, the lineaments of being itself are already used, handed down—woven and rewoven, to recall Joyce. This is why Forster grows reflexive as a direct function of his realism rather than as a reaction against it. If the world itself is already taken to be a world of signs or representations from the start, it not only puts all its denizens in the belated role that the modern writer has toward tradition; it also makes the practice of writing about such a world an inherently reflexive procedure, since narrative repre-sentation must thereby be a representation of a world already under-stood to be a set of representations. As taxonomist and diagnostician of the ideology of modernism, then, Forster finds the lifelike objects of his fiction to be already fictions or representations in their own terms. As with his own burlesque pathetic fallacies, Forster will sometimes even provide us with clues as to just how equivalent life and letters (another version of the supposedly opposed public and private) can get to be, sometimes by affirmation, sometimes by negation. Helen, for example, writes to Margaret very early in the novel that though (as Meg has said) "'life is sometimes life and sometimes only a drama,'" "'it really does not seem life'" at all "'but a play'" (6). Tibby's sense of family life as scripted ("a scene behind footlights" [199]) is also in line with the novel's habit-ual systems of usage by which Forster's reflexive realism represents the real by representing the representations that compose it in the first place. Like his own mock-heroic allusions (e.g., 75), the terms by which everyone lives derive from quite discernible mythologies rather than from a natural expressiveness on Forster's own part. London is a "vast theatre" (94); Mrs. Munt "rehearse[s]" (12) for actual events, expecting her niece to "imitate" (12) her in turn; even Leonard's oaths are "learnt from older men" (38), a rather overt sign that the vocabulary of candor and earthiness, too, is belated because derivative or learned. Margaret's desire to have Ruth Wilcox as a friend is likewise figured in an overtly textual metaphor ("Desiring to book Mrs. Wilcox as a friend, she pressed on the ceremony, pencil, as it were, in hand" [59]), while the mourners surrounding Mrs. Wilcox's "grave" (another recurrent term that con-notes writing and links it with death) are described as virtual letters in another writerly metaphor: they "moved between the graves, like drops of ink" (65). The life Forster represents in all its forms is, in other words, represented in the first instance as a system of texts or codes already in place when any new or original subject arrives on the scene.

Woolf and, more especially, Strachey[6] will go on to show us, with even greater precision and far clearer intent, the world itself as a set of texts or representations like the textual representations that represent them. Even the various pastoral landscapes upon which *Howards End* dwells so fondly—and tries to separate from the "theatre" of the "Satanic" (63) city—are figured by Forster as "system after system" (121) in their own right, much as Charles and Dolly's newest child is, however humorously, "a third edition" (134). And while such vocabulary may be taken to suggest the dehumanization of life under technology, the measured repetition of Forster's strategic figurations should remind us instead that his focus is not on a world as such, but on the "reverberations" (19), as he puts it himself, of the dominant codes or discursive polarities by means of which the discourses of ideology produce rather than merely respond to the real.

What, however, is the point of the elaborate romance machinery at book's end? Does it mean to repress the contamination of its modernist categories in the hidden service of the kinds of ideals it otherwise puts in question? But while the book's modernist wishes may be summed up in Helen's rather Moorish remark that "'One is certain of nothing but the truth of one's own emotions'" (123), we know that "one's own" is hardly certain as a category. Ironically, the aesthetic pleasure of the book's ending is its most enduring source of pain. The ending of *Howards End* is an overcompensatory romance whose desire to soothe despite the horrors involved is sociologically pathetic and, epistemologically, symptomatic of something else. Its attempted (or merely staged) dialectical resolution—the kind of structure made readily apparent in the tripartite shape of the later *Passage to India* (1924)—may or may not be but another programmed moment in a novel that is otherwise really a metatext that represents and interrogates the systematic self-representations of life itself rather than our chaotic experience of them. Not only must we ask why Bast dies, but also why it is Charles who kills him. In fact, Charles kills Bast as the function of a double Oedipal displacement. After all, Charles's father has not once but thrice slept with women Charles himself desires—his real mother (naturally), but also Jacky and Margaret, the latter he once fancies flirting with him early on in the story. Thus Bast, who has a sexual connection to Charles's father through his wife

---

6. Lytton Strachey (1880–1932), prominent member of the Bloomsbury group, author of *Eminent Victorians* (1918). His younger brother James Strachey (1887–1967) was Freud's translator. [*Editor*]

Jacky's affair with him, provides Charles with a reason for investing him with a son's displaced fury. Bast thereby becomes his ironic surrogate father as the husband of the Jacky with whom his father has slept. As a subjective structure, it also has the effect of psychologizing away class differences in favor of personal ones, even though, as we shall see in a moment, Forster's psychoanalysis is political as well as poetical. Symbolically, Bast represents the father that Charles cannot in law kill, though he can—and almost does—ruin him by his attack upon the poorer man. More than that, however, Bast as displaced symbolic father substitutes not just for Mr. Wilcox himself, but, in the process, also suggests, by virtue of his own mobile symbolism, that even the real father is not an immediate origin either. The real father is real because he is a symbol, and a symbol of authority because he is a real father. The father actually represents, not himself, but the law that he serves by symbolizing or substituting for it in the eyes of the futurity that will organize itself retrospectively around his legacy. Even the ambiguity in the possible historical play of the Wilcoxes' Christian names, Charles and Henry (both kings of England, it is up to the reader to fashion a relation in accord with a given interpretation), encourages ambiguities as to whom it is that gains the ultimate, if sad, privilege, and encourages in turn the startling psychoanalytic ambiguities that Forster's Oedipal structure is designed to provoke. The father is himself the symbol or surrogate for something else even more primary than his own supposedly seminal authority. The original original—the father—is belated in relation to himself, ironically prior to himself as father since he can only stand for his purported natural authority by virtue of his symbolism. Even Freud himself (in James Strachey's translation) is momentarily explicit about it. Writing of the Wolf Man, Freud says, "He resisted God in order to be able to cling to his father; and in doing this he was really upholding the old father against the new." "The totem, I maintained, was the first father-surrogate, and the god was a later one, in which the father had regained his human shape."[7]

What is repressed in the killing of Bast, then, is not just an expression of Charles's personal Oedipal rage, but the constitutive protest of subjectivity against its formation through categories that make its autonomy impossible. Thus Forster's machinery at novel's end performs double duty, framing Bast's murder in apparently suavely psychoanalytic terms so as to keep us away from the deeper problem to be repressed, not just in the static sociology of English life, but also in the epistemology of psychoanalytic reasoning (another instance of Forster's early scrutiny rather than expression of modernist ideologies): the failure of the notion of the Oedipus complex itself as a route to original truth. Hence Forster allows

7. Sigmund Freud, "The History of an Infantile Neurosis" (1918), from *The Standard Edition of the Complete Psychological Works of Sigmund Freud*, vol. 17, ed. James Strachey (London: Hogarth, 1953–74) 66, 114.

us to see just what Arnold has tried to hide more than anyone else: that origins, fathers central among their (ironic) figurations, are themselves but symbols or substitutes for something else absent but supposedly more primary, more original than the father even in the immediacy of his flesh.

Also a caution as to the ease or certainty with which we use the notion of authority at large, the novel's surprising psychoanalytic implications are at the same time at the hinge of the poetics of reflexive realism as a project in its own right. The original father's only symbolic power suggests that, in its narratological counterpart, the immediate—the thing represented—is also already a sign for something else at the very moment that it is what it is. A sign is what it is because it is, by the definition that allows it to signify in the first place, something different from itself to begin with. Hence, too, in both reflexive realism and in the transference that structures the analytic session (at least in the younger Strachey's formulation), the real is only symbolic, while only the symbolic is real. If Forster's text is reflexive because of its realism—because the world it refers to is already a tissue of signs—Forster's implicit notion of symbolism here suggests in turn that the real is precisely the symbolically authoritative.

Forster's reflexive realism in *Howards End*, then, is, like the later work of Woolf and Strachey (and of Conrad and Hardy before them, along with Ford), implicitly but efficiently pedagogical as well. Taking as his subject the systems by which we exist and the by-products or effects of them that make up our lives, Forster produces an allegory of reading in *Howards End* that asks its reader to decide—or not to—a mode of response within the wide spectrum of possibilities the book's complex operations may detonate reader to reader. If Joyce focuses on the minute *paroles* of life, forcing the reader to deduce from them the *langues* or codes that contextualize and so give each the meaning the reader requires them to have, Forster instead appeals directly, if invisibly, to the *langues* or ideological paradigms themselves in a cultural metafiction that sets the model for Bloomsbury prose to come. So organized are the components of the ideology of modernism in Forster's text that we can in the final instance only classify *Howards End* as a novel of classification that in turn asks us to classify it. Much, for example, as one may ask fruitlessly who one really is once the vagaries of "property" are exposed, so, too, may one read the book's famous "wych-elm" (the preeminent sign of fixity and established grace in the novel's myth of the modern) as the rather more transient sign to be found in reading it interrogatively— as a Joycean pun that asks instead, through an inversion of its normative meaning, the reflexive question "which elm?" that both frees the text from its denotative referents while simultaneously reaffirming their coherence by virtue of such educative transgression. The novel thereby demonstrates the ever-shifting possibilities produced by the play of both fixed codes and floating signifiers, enjoying just the kind of pleasure *The Waste Land* in particular cannot.

Like Helen's desire that Margaret "'Burn'" (6, 7) her letters at the novel's start, or like the Wilcoxes' decision to "tear the note up" (73) with which Mrs. Wilcox has bequeathed Howards End to Margaret, the novel itself functions—like the psychoanalytic transference—as a double operation that asks us both to absorb and destroy its variously incompatible messages at one and the same time. It wishes to leave "no traces behind" (76), even if its language continues to broadcast both its myth of the modern and the contamination of the dichotomies that sustain it. Such simultaneous absorption and cancellation—a structure also figurally identical with Freud's representation of the unconscious in the "Note upon the 'Mystic Writing-Pad'" (1925)—is a strong and decisive response to the problematic of modernist belatedness. Like psychoanalysis, it secures the wishful primacies its representations of them habitually undercut.

KENNETH GRAHAM

[The Indirect Style of *Howards End*]†

At the very end of *Howards End*, as the book swells a little fulsomely towards reconciliation, the redeeming of Henry Wilcox through Margaret's love, and the symbolic gathering-in of the hay harvest, a single sentence cuts abruptly across this mood of sober fruition. The other Wilcoxes, snarling in defeat, have been summoned from their various suburban villas to hear Mr Wilcox's decision to leave Howards End to Margaret, and from the witless Dolly drops a careless reference to the long-concealed fact that Mrs Wilcox's dying wish will thereby be fulfilled after all. Then we have this:

> From Evie came a sharply drawn breath. 'Good-bye', she said to Margaret, and kissed her.
> And again and again fell the word, like the ebb of a dying sea.
> 'Good-bye.'
> 'Good-bye, Dolly.'
> 'So long, father.'
> 'Good-bye, my boy; always take care of yourself.'
> 'Good-bye, Mrs Wilcox.'
> 'Good-bye.'[1]

† From Kenneth Graham, *Indirections of the Novel: James, Conrad, and Forster* (Cambridge: Cambridge UP, 1988) 156–79. Reprinted with the permission of Cambridge University Press. Some notes have been silently omitted.
1. *Howards End*, 242. [Page references are to this Norton Critical Edition. *Editor*]

The deployment of these sentences is very characteristic. Evie kissing Margaret (keeping up false appearances to the end) focuses our attention on Margaret and makes us associate the next and crucial sentence with Margaret's own consciousness: 'And again and again fell the word, like the ebb of a dying sea.' The allusion is extreme, not quite explicable, and certainly very chilling: the first half of the sentence made resonant with its Biblical echo, and the whole made to stand out not only by being printed on its own but by its quite unprosaic rhythms (five anapaests and an iamb). The following chorus of 'Good-byes' to which it refers (like the same hollow chorus at the end of Section 2 of 'The Waste Land') is a part of triviality and reality—but quite drained of any consolation by that interpolated falling, ebbing, and dying. And when Margaret then gently asks her husband about the incident in the past, he is as always—and despite his 'redemption'—quite unperturbed by any possibility of having been dishonest:

> Margaret was silent. Something shook her life in its inmost recesses, and she shivered.
> 'I didn't do wrong, did I?' he asked, bending down.
> 'You didn't, darling. Nothing has been done wrong.' (242)

If Margaret's inward shudder is not to be taken as a frisson of that dying sea, an ebbing of her new security at this reminder of unassuageable betrayals, and is no more than a shiver of fearful pleasure at seeing how Mrs Wilcox's wishes have come right in the end, then her 'Nothing has been done wrong' is an egregious self-betrayal and self-delusion. And on the other hand if her 'Nothing has been done wrong' is a tragically conscious gesture of ironic pacification towards the Wilcox crassness, then her shudder is indeed an echo of that momentary cosmic sense of disaster and chaos. Either way—like Maggie Verver burying *her* knowledge of marital treachery in a self-conscious embrace[2]—it is a deathly note to strike amid the celebration of new life, Helen's baby, and the joy of harvest. It seems not quite to be controlled—though the sense of artistic control, in language, tone, and commentary, is one of the most active constituents of our total response to this novel. It is, in fact, a classic and powerful instance of Forster's 'double turn' (as identified by Trilling): one of these moments where a totally different register suddenly declares itself within the bland or witty cadences of his prose, jolts our attention to a quite different line of thought or feeling, and casts a new light of suggestiveness on everything that has gone before, hinting at contradictory combinations or ramifying echoes in the text that has been already unfolded. As a device, the double turn presents sudden new possibilities of meaning; makes us look back differently at comparable 'surprises' in style, scene, or phrase; and keeps

2. In *The Golden Bowl* (1904) by Henry James. [*Editor*]

us conscious of how this narrative, in its textures and nuances, is to be apprehended as perpetually *at work*.

'At play' is an equally accurate phrase, since the manipulation of tones, from the waggish to the stiffly solemn, makes Forster's writing a notable instance of the ways in which fiction is a game—and a participative game at that. The stance of the manipulator * * * is a complicated one, and is itself part of the game. For one thing, by drawing attention to itself it manages to give the impression not just of the events and characters being subject to a confidently omniscient commentator but, on the contrary, of their retaining some vital freedom of movement away from that manipulation and evaluation. The novel's very first sentence is of this kind, drawing attention to the conscious act of presentation yet at once preparing the way for what seems to exist in a dimension beyond the presenting: 'One may as well begin with Helen's letters to her sister.' The narrator shrugs nonchalantly and a little ruefully, contemplating the daunting otherness and multiplicity of the 'events' his narration must try to set in motion—and the letters that are now allowed to begin the narrative emphasize this sense of space and opening-up by their own youthful sprightliness of style, and their own description of surprises, false expectations, and vulnerability to a world where values and feelings might be stood on their head at any moment. The narrator's 'One may as well', just like James's 'As I have had the honour of intimating', in *The Europeans*, is a gesture that creates a little leeway between him and these apparently uncontrollable and interesting events. And across that leeway, within that narrated field, characters and scenes can take on a certain independence, and can eventually be seen to cast their own shadow, while the narrator's shadow falls at a slightly different angle— the true Forster angle.

Even when the narrating stance is less self-deprecatory than this, and more assertive, the effect is not necessarily restrictive. For example, in chapter 2 we have this paragraph:

> Margaret was silent. If her aunt could not see why she must go down, she was not going to tell her. She was not going to say: 'I love my dear sister; I must be near her at this crisis of her life'. The affections are more reticent than the passions, and their expression more subtle. If she herself should ever fall in love with a man, she, like Helen, would proclaim it from the house-tops, but as she only loved a sister she used the voiceless language of sympathy. (9)

The effect here is interesting, and intensely Forsterian. Having taken us behind Margaret's silence and told us how it might have articulated itself in speech (*le style indirect libre*),[3] the narrator then suddenly expands into a general aphorism. But the generality does not really limit or final-

---

3. Free indirect discourse (French). A technical term for a narrated monologue that renders a character's thought or speech. [*Editor*]

ly judge the situation. Rather, it seems to detach itself momentarily, in a brooding, self-communing way, from the immediate 'scene' of Margaret's hypothesized inner self, partly by the different angle of self-confidence and abruptness. Beneath the universalized comment—or rather, on each side of it, in terms of the paragraph—her fictional life continues, touched upon by the remark, but only guaranteed and countenanced by it rather than finally 'placed' or subsumed into it.

It is the variation of mode and outlook—as here, between the dramatized intimacy of word and feeling on one hand and a sudden sententiousness on the other—that helps to create the freedom within Forsterian narration that I have called 'play'. Of course the narrator quite frequently asserts something more directly dogmatic: an endorsement of the Schlegel faith, for example, or an uncompromising gibe that seems to leave the Wilcoxes pinned like butterflies to the wall. But such partisanship is in continual interplay with other things and styles, some of them quite irrelevant to the mode of commentary, some of them contradictory of what the commentary has said. Along with the strong sense of masterful control in plot and in general analytic intelligence, there is unsteadiness of an enlivening kind that challenges the reader's attention at every moment. Nuances of tone keep suggesting alternative vistas. The prose sometimes lumbers portentously in one direction, then suddenly darts in another with an almost Wildean glee. Or a sentence progresses towards a shaped conclusion, then in the last words unexpectedly opens itself up, wittily, vivaciously, even ungraspably—like the effect of the word 'possibly' in this: 'Some day—in the millennium—there may be no need for [Henry Wilcox's] type. At present, homage is due to it from those who think themselves superior, and who possibly are' (117). Direct dramatization or solemn authorial adjuration, even occasional flatness of description and dialogue, are all interspersed with jocosity and occasionally falsetto laughter. A sudden lyricism swells up, only to be cut short by a neat irony, a cool disclaimer. The naturalistic and the highly stylized are in perpetual interplay, so that the reader is in a state of surprise and restlessness—a state of aesthetic response that then finds its conceptual equivalent within Forster's view of the world. For example, we find ourselves almost simultaneously noting the narration's realistic grasp of how social types behave—how Charles Wilcox bullies a railway porter, or drives his car in a certain arrogant way—and responding imaginatively and consciously to the more 'de-naturalizing' features of the telling, even tiny stylizations like an occasional arch inversion—'Most complacently did Mrs Munt . . .'—or the comic reductiveness of 'the form of Mrs Munt, trying to explain things, sprang agreeably up and down among the red cushions' (12, 15). The narration is liberated by such textual display, gives itself freedom to ramify and to experiment—and, in the end, to embrace more of the area of human experience that concerns it. For its continual modulations, as well as giving pleasure by their own energy and colour, also move in the direction of suggested meaning, no matter how tentative that meaning. And at one level of our reading them these modulations are recognized as repeating, with novelty and clarity, certain modulations that the book wishes to suggest are in real life: in *its* textures of gaiety, surprise, and dismay. As one small example, in the chapter where the Schlegels hear Beethoven we have this modulation:

> Helen said to her aunt: 'Now comes the wonderful movement: first of all the goblins, and then a trio of elephants dancing'; and Tibby implored the company generally to look out for the transitional passage on the drum.
> 'On the what, dear?'
> 'On the *drum*, Aunt Juley.'
> 'No; look out for the part where you think you have done with the goblins and they come back,' breathed Helen, as the music started with a goblin walking quietly over the universe, from end to end. Others followed him. They were not aggressive creatures; it was that that made them so terrible to Helen. They merely observed in passing that there was no such thing as splendour or heroism in the world. (26)

The opening voices are comically, 'realistically' disconnected: Helen apparently affected and whimsical in her image of the trio of elephants; Tibby no less affected, even pretentious; Mrs Munt floundering. Then suddenly Forster's absolute seriousness rises up, with the goblins and the universe, in mid-sentence. Mid-sentence is so often the perfect place for Forster's particular view of the tragic, as for Conrad's casual linkage, 'like evil or truth': a devastating observation, in passing, that no values exist. At the beginning normality seems ready to jog on, in its usual syntax— only a little ridiculous. Then a goblin, which began as a girl's whimsy, suddenly becomes real, and with the unforeseeableness of an accident the paragraph as it flows uncovers an abyss of 'panic and emptiness'. This is the way it happens, the manner suggests to us. Visions of emptiness can come like a modulation in a sentence: a sudden horrifying fall, like the ebb of a dying sea, before language, like Beethoven's energy, returns us to terra firma and the Queen's Hall.

Sometimes, such is the unease that lurks below the groomed surfaces of this book, there is an opposite modulation: say, from the scathingly sardonic to the passionately ideal and romantic. These 'positive' outbursts are more difficult to accept than their acerbic opposites: the lyricism is a little frenetic and highly coloured. But they can be seen as part of a larger rhythm, as a rhetorical compensation through which the necessary components of desire and dream can enter into the book's dialectic of feeling, and can serve not only to counterbalance but to define and explain the opposing sense of loss or detestation. For example, chapter

21 is a brief and pungently satirical vignette of the junior Wilcoxes breeding, complaining, and being arrogant. It ends: 'a perambulator edition is squeaking; a third edition is expected shortly. Nature is turning out Wilcoxes in this peaceful abode, so that they may inherit the earth' (134). Then in quite stark contrast, as if to offset such virulence, the next chapter opens in almost dithyrambic mode:

> Margaret greeted her lord with peculiar tenderness on the morrow. Mature as he was, she might yet be able to help him to the building of the rainbow bridge that should connect the prose in us with the passion. Without it we are meaningless fragments, half monks, half beasts, unconnected arches that have never joined into a man. With it love is born, and alights on the highest curve, glowing against the gray, sober against the fire. Happy the man who sees from either aspect the glory of those outspread wings. The roads of his soul lie clear, and he and his friends shall find easy going. (134)

These are extreme words for a transcendental goal glimpsed in a dream, made extreme by fear of the opposite, the vision of the world's panic and emptiness. And our unease and half-embarrassment at some of the cadences and epithets — 'the rainbow bridge', 'love is born, and alights on the highest curve', 'Happy is the man', 'the roads of his soul' — testify to the instability of the dream. It is energized by desire, but the suspicion of hysteria is functional, since it dramatizes for us the hopelessness that also lies somewhere within such desire, and it therefore belongs totally to the basic stresses of the narration. And typically (and savingly), the very next paragraph sinks to a wry irony that half-mocks the lyrical excesses of the previous sentence: 'It was hard going in the roads of Mr Wilcox's soul.'

There is a well-known test case in any consideration of the rhetoric, particularly the extreme rhetoric, of *Howards End*: that is the celebrative description of England as viewed from the Isle of Purbeck, at the beginning and end of chapter 19 (and therefore at the exact spatial centre of the novel). Even a critic like John Beer, who has defended it against the strictures of Leavis — Leavis considered it Wilcox-like in its immaturity — has had to concede some embarrassment at Forster's flourishes.[4] But the final flourish cannot properly be considered on its own, only in the full context of the reader's response: that is, the reader's involvement in the intricate movement of the whole chapter and in the surrounding currents of preparation and aftermath. As a test case, therefore, it will call for some detailed consideration.

In the previous chapter, where Mr Wilcox proposes to Margaret in his house in Ducie Street, we have encountered the illogicality and the disturbing impersonality of love. The love between Margaret and Henry

---

4. *The Achievement of E. M. Forster*, 1962, pp. 187–9. Leavis's criticism is in *The Common Pursuit*, 1952, pp. 271–2.

causes the reader problems later in the book, but at the beginning its sheer unlikelihood becomes part of its verisimilitude, so much in the book up to this point, at every level of plot, scene, conversation, and even syntax, having reconciled us to the advent of the unexpected. Even the casual 'mid-sentence' quality of their love—'Just as this thought entered Margaret's brain, Mr Wilcox did ask her to be his wife ...' (119)—is a part of that narrative rhythm we noted in the 'Beethoven' passage, a rhythm that expresses the inadvertency of experience, great or small, and, having already offhandedly ushered in death in the case of Mrs Wilcox ('The funeral was over'), now does the same for love. Not only is the love illogical, unexpected in its syntax, it is also—which may be the same thing—impersonal: a 'central radiance' which 'had nothing to do with humanity, and most resembled the all-pervading happiness of fine weather' (119). There is a strong degree of naturalism in all this, too, of course, and Forster's other level of operation, that of psychological perceptiveness and a knowledge of manners (as revealed, for example, in the decor of a smoking-room, and a woman's response to a masculine room), bolsters and qualifies the invocation of love as a mystery. But the proposal scene nevertheless ends in a ghost, lightly introduced: 'Mrs. Wilcox strayed in and out, ever a welcome ghost; surveying the scene, thought Margaret, without one hint of bitterness' (120). And we are left feeling that love's contingency and impersonality—out of which zone strays a benign ghost—are so beyond our sense of proportion and control that despite benignity there must be a mystery in such a presence.

Out of this complex experience, then—and out of such intimacy of encounter with both the everyday and the unseen—comes the suddenly panoramic and oratorical consideration of landscape that opens chapter 19:

> If one wanted to show a foreigner England, perhaps the wisest course would be to take him to the final section of the Purbeck Hills, and stand him on their summit, a few miles to the east of Corfe. Then system after system of our island would roll together under his feet. Beneath him is the valley of the Frome, and all the wild lands that come tossing down from Dorchester, black and gold, to mirror their gorse in the expanses of Poole. The valley of the Stour is beyond, unaccountable stream, dirty at Blandford, pure at Wimborne—the Stour, sliding out of fat fields, to marry the Avon beneath the tower of Christchurch. The valley of the Avon—invisible, but far to the north the trained eye may see Clearbury Ring that guards it, and the imagination may leap beyond that onto Salisbury Plain itself, and beyond the Plain to all the glorious downs of Central England. Nor is suburbia absent. Bournemouth's ignoble coast cowers to the right, heralding the pine trees that mean, for all their beauty, red houses, and the Stock Exchange, and extend to the gates of London itself. So tremendous is the City's

trail! But the cliffs of Freshwater it shall never touch, and the island
will guard the Island's purity till the end of time. Seen from the
west, the Wight is beautiful beyond all laws of beauty. It is as if a
fragment of England floated forward to greet the foreigner—chalk
of our chalk, turf of our turf, epitome of what will follow. And
behind the fragment lie Southampton, hostess to the nations, and
Portsmouth, a latent fire, and all around it, with double and treble
collision of tides, swirls the sea. How many villages appear in this
view! How many castles! How many churches, vanquished or triumphant! How many ships, railways and roads! What incredible
variety of men working beneath that lucent sky to what final end!
The reason fails, like a wave on the Swanage beach; the imagination swells, spreads and deepens, until it becomes geographic and
encircles England. (120–21)

This is far more than a romantic flourish or an indulgence; far more,
even, than the compensatory outburst it resembles in *The Nigger of the
'Narcissus'*, on England as 'ship mother of fleets and nations'.[5] It is a further
attempt * * * to confront and to mediate the impersonal, even the infinite. The narration, with a theatrical panache, is trying to grasp the
ungraspable, to know, through landscape, the elemental presence more
quietly encountered in Ducie Street by Margaret, and uttered in a different mode by Beethoven's music in the Queen's Hall. The strangeness
of love, strange beyond proportion and, despite her hopes, beyond
Margaret's capacity to 'connect' fully with the mundane, is being
brought by Margaret through this very landscape towards the watchers:
towards the waiting, mundane complexity of her family relationships in
the shape of Helen, Mrs Munt, and her cousin Frieda, taking in the
view. The landscape is a challenge and an entanglement—and, at
beginning and end, frames a chapter which is itself dominated by shocks
of encounter and revelation. The vision is of an England so extensive, so
rich, so ever-receding and beyond proportion, that 'the reason fails', and
only the imagination can deal with it by becoming more than personal:
that is, 'geographic' (as Maisie's newly visionary knowledge, on the sands
at Boulogne, swelled poetically from 'Most' to 'All', and from self to 'sky'
and 'air').[6] Like the vision which the whole novel seeks to 'encircle' by
the imagination and to re-create, this landscape both baffles the mind
and is accessible to it. It has its definite names and colours, its human
history, its graspable forms—'system after system', the stages of the Stour,
the implied vistas, beyond seeing, of the Midlands and of London, the
Isle of Wight as an 'epitome' of the larger island, Southampton as an
entry, the tides as measurably 'double and treble'. Then measurement
and formal gradations threaten to break down in the half-ironic, half-

---

5. A novella (1897) by Joseph Conrad. [*Editor*]
6. In *What Maisie Knew* (1897) by Henry James. [*Editor*]

hysterical apostrophes at the end, 'How many! . . . How many! . . . How many!' And in the unresolved images in the last sentence—the reason ebbing like a wave, the imagination flowing like an all-encompassing tide, together with the acute sense of anxiety and impossibility, and the straining, oceanic desire to transcend and embrace—we recognize, here, halfway through the novel, one of its most important and persistent symbols (wave, sea, tide, river) bearing its most characteristic burden of irreconcilable feelings.

Whatever is exalted in that first paragraph is at once deflated, and whatever is unsteady in it is elaborated, by the comedy of Frieda and Mrs Munt clashing over the merits of English and German landscapes: a typical Forsterian transposition from the grand to the self-mockingly petty, within which, nevertheless, certain social and even political realities declare themselves. And this alternating movement is confirmed by the way the focus of narration changes throughout the first half of the chapter from the close-at-hand, the personal and domestic chatter of those waiting on Nine Barrow Down, to the panoramic, as we take a bird's eye view of Margaret's train chugging from Wareham to Swanage, and then of the pony-cart bringing her, and her revelation, closer and closer. The emotional exchanges that follow between the two sisters are dramatically and intimately direct, on a distinctly new register, without any of the earlier shiftings of tone:

> 'Look here, sit down.'
> 'All right; I'll sit down if you'll sit down.'
> 'There. (One kiss.) Now, what ever, what ever is the matter?'
> 'I do mean what I said. Don't; it wouldn't do.' (125)

But in a subtle involvement the landscape still enters parenthetically and frequently, no longer embraceable or an enhancement to the imagination but now—exactly what the opening paean half-feared in its conclusion—irremediably other, shapeless, cold, and indifferent in its elemental impersonality. Despite mid-sentence appeals to it, the landscape only reinforces the darkness, the weight of incommunication and powerlessness that settles on Margaret and Helen. It is the goblin footfall, the ebbing wave, the falling word, with a vengeance: '[Helen] broke right away and wandered distractedly upwards, stretching her hands towards the view and crying' (125). Margaret follows her 'through the wind that gathers at sundown on the northern slopes of hills', and 'suddenly stupidity seized her, and the immense landscape was blurred.' She finds no aid to understanding: 'With her arm around Helen, and her eyes shifting over the view, as if this county or that could reveal the secret of her own heart . . .' (125). Helen 'in her turn, looked outwards'; and Margaret, admitting her knowledge of the spiritual dishonesty of the man she is about to marry, looks down 'at the shining lagoons'; and when she tries to argue for the merits of the Wilcox practicality she adduces the view of England as evidence of those merits: 'She waved her hand at the landscape, which confirmed anything' (126). The effect is to reinforce the sense of division, contrary to that all-unifying vision of the first paragraph, as we hear the subdued, tense voices of two intimates, despairing, pleading, failing one another, high on the crest of a chalk down above an ungraspable and annulling vista.

Then the frame of the chapter closes by returning overtly to the landscape, testing it anew, as it were, for what it can yield and where it resists. We read the peroration with our awareness attuned to what has gone before, and thereby sensitized to the inner turnings that qualify the superficial impression it gives of a performance now in the major key, putting the goblins to flight with a noise of trumpets. It begins with an enigmatic statement and ends in a rhetorical series of questions tinged — like the apostrophes that closed the chapter's opening description — with the possibility of mockery:

> There was a long silence, during which the tide returned into Poole Harbour. 'One would lose something', murmured Helen, apparently to herself. The water crept over the mud-flats towards the gorse and the blackened heather. Branksea Island lost its immense foreshores, and became a sombre episode of trees. Frome was forced inward towards Dorchester, Stour against Wimborne, Avon towards Salisbury, and over the immense displacement the sun presided, leading it to triumph ere he sank to rest. England was alive, throbbing through all her estuaries, crying for joy through the mouths of all her gulls, and the north wind, with contrary motion, blew stronger against her rising seas. What did it mean? For what end are her fair complexities, her changes of soil, her sinuous coast? Does she belong to those who have moulded her and made her feared by other lands, or to those who have added nothing to her power, but have somehow seen her, seen the whole island at once, lying as a jewel in a silver sea, with all the brave world's fleet accompanying her towards eternity? (127)

At first, Helen's 'One would lose something' is a little unclear. Can she be making a concession, in the pause that follows her argument with Margaret about the Wilcoxes? Does she mean, 'I agree, without the Wilcox values one would lose something'? Or even more limitingly, is Helen partly retracting her angry claim, of a moment before, that 'It makes no difference thinking things out'? Only after pausing — delaying the progress of the paragraph, and emulating the slow return of the tide — does the reader consider that Helen seems to be simply reiterating her position against the Wilcoxes, and above all against Margaret marrying into them: in so doing, a Schlegel would, and will, lose much. Our doubt about the remark is functional. It gives it an added salience, as though the ambiguity had cleared some space around it. The space has created unease, and into the unease creeps the incoming tide. An 'immense displacement' is moving a little ominously, even abstractly in its generality, towards 'the blackened heather', forcing the rivers back on themselves and creating 'a sombre episode'. This is an encounter with a presiding power—inhuman and inexplicable. The sudden change to 'England was alive, throbbing through all her estuaries, crying for joy' is in startling contrariety: a celebration of energy, after the fear of it. The change is imaged further in the reference to the wind, 'with contrary motion', blowing *against* the encroaching sea. The paragraph, true to the overall narrative mode of which it is a part, leaves the two opposite motions deadlocked— or rather, unresolved and unstilled. It is appropriate that a direct questioning should be thrown up from such a situation. 'What did it mean?' sends us straight back into the welter of hints and opposites. If we cannot understand those elemental opposites of land and sea, river and tide, how can we hope to impose a pattern of coherence on such human opposites as Wilcox and Schlegel: practical power displacing sensitivity, sensitivity poeticizing and losing the real world? For that is the minor irony that is now drowned out by the major bravura of the closing cadences. The rhetorical excess and the very literary allusiveness, just touched by cliché—'A jewel in a silver sea', 'all the world's brave fleet'—more than hints at the incipient dangers of the Schlegel sensibility, which have been touched on often enough in the novel before now. And Forster also tries to distance himself from the purple of the prose by attributing the lyricism to others, to 'those who have added nothing to her power'. The climax is clearly not mock-heroic; and the mingling of tones is perhaps not assured, not quite stable, with the urge to endorse the romantic celebration being almost audibly in conflict with the need to be sceptical. But this instability is not the same as confusion: it expresses clearly, and in other terms, a dilemma that is central to the novel, and gains coherence from the role it plays in that surrounding drama.[7]

*   *   *

* * * Any close reading of the novel must qualify beyond tenability the idea that this is a liberal-humanist essay, rather than an intricate (and no doubt imperfect) drama in which—again, as with James—many of the features of liberal humanism are set in train, amid much that negates them, or passes them by. It is the pressure among these different currents, the air of challenge and change, the perplexing and at times perplexed movement from a meditative expounding down to an awkward twining of desires and fears, that makes the book what it is. The commentary some-

---

7. An example of the more typical criticism that the instabilities of this passage *are* simply confusion and self-contradiction and not a complicated dialectic is K. W. Gransden's comment: 'the over-writing, the over-ripeness here ... is too like that of a travel advertisement. And the swelling optimism of such words as "but the cliffs of Freshwater it will never touch" is belied by numerous other passages in the book which say the opposite and in which the author's critical and prophetic sense proves a surer judge than his "poetic" one' (*E. M. Forster*, 1962, pp. 58–9).

times recommends change, vulnerability, openness to the flow of experience; but what is narrated (and sometimes the commentary, too) shows a
horror of the deathliness that such flux also contains—hence the doubleness that everywhere attaches to the dominating images of sea, river, and
tide. Beneath the line of witty, moral analysis that suggests a faith in the
prospect of change there is a depth of fear, a touch of panic that is not only
Wilcox panic but panic in something of that etymological sense used
more explicitly elsewhere by Forster, an extreme and contagious terror
caused by the influence of Pan:[8] in the case of this book, the influence of
a half-perceived but unapprehendable absolute, far less absurdist than the
reductive absolute of Razumov or of *The Shadow-Line*, purposeless but
still full of varied signs, sometimes enigmatically confirming the shapes of
civility and intercourse, at other times sweeping them away implacably.[9]
The force of it comes in surprises, passions, deaths, cruel snobberies,
adventitious births, broken photograph frames. It is felt in the book's ubiq-
uitous rumours of war, its overheard political conversations, slight family
altercations, a Schlegel German sword, hung up for peace, that inadvertently kills the weakest of Englishmen; Germany and England, person
and person, moving towards Armageddon. Even Mrs Wilcox is both truth-
bearer and shadow: she values continuity, 'the inner light', instinctual wisdom; but is always dying, inarticulate, even boring; ghostly in characterization even when shown as alive. The unseen world she so insubstantial-
ly emanates from, and which is recognized by Margaret, is one that can
enrich and take on human or humanistic shape: a house, say, or a dream
of harvest. But it is a world equally that devastates; and its emanations—
like the memory or the ghost of Mrs Wilcox—can be simply frightening,
doors into the darkness, as well as encouragements to the initiate like
Margaret. Moments of cosmic fear float through the book, though never
quite overwhelming the resistances of wit, hopefulness, idealism,
patience, and artistic form. Yet one of the profoundest and most challenging of these moments comes in the very centre—the representative
centre—of a great resistant form.

> [Margaret] went for a few moments into St. Paul's, whose dome
> stands out of the welter so bravely, as if preaching the gospel of
> form. But, within, St. Paul's is as its surroundings—echoes and
> whispers, inaudible songs, invisible mosaics, wet footmarks crossing
> and recrossing the floor. *Si monumentum requiris, circumspice*: it
> points us back to London. (200)

The misapplication—or reapplication—of the famous epitaph to Wren
is brilliant. Where 'circumspice' properly invites the beholder to glory in

---

8. On 'Pan' and 'panic' in Forster, see, e.g., Alan Wilde, 'The Naturalization of Eden', in *E. M.
Forster: a Human Exploration*, ed. Das and Beer, pp. 196–207.
9. Razumov is a character in Joseph Conrad's novel *Under Western Eyes* (1911), and Conrad is
also the author of the novella *The Shadow-Line* (1917). [*Editor*]

the ordered structure of the great church all around him, here it breaks through that form to point at the surrounding and interpenetrating chaos of London which is, for the moment, more ultimate than art or rationality. And London, from which Helen has so appallingly disappeared, is the sea, the encroaching unseen, at its most inhuman:

> The mask fell off the city, and she saw it for what it really is—a caricature of infinity . . . Helen seemed one with grimy trees and the traffic and the slowly flowing slabs of mud. She had accomplished a hideous act of renunciation and returned to the One. (199–200)

But Margaret's faith goes on with dynamism and energy, opposing such visions of absolute contingency, seeking humane 'connection' even where the adventitious or taunting connections of narrative, like a cleverly annulling echo, seem to deny its possibility. To the very end, in its context of harvest and a new birth, her view rejects the full implications of the Wilcox lie to others, her husband's lies to himself, the deathliness of every falling and repetitive word, and the death—as for Conrad's Marlow—that exists in every act or phrase of dishonesty, including her own final act of connivance:

> And again and again fell the word, like the ebb of a dying sea . . .
> . . . Margaret was silent. Something shook her life in its inmost recesses, and she shivered.
> 'I didn't do wrong, did I?' he asked, bending down.
> 'You didn't, darling. Nothing has been done wrong.'
> . . . 'The field's cut!' Helen cried excitedly—'The big meadow! We've seen to the very end, and it'll be such a crop of hay as never!' (242–43)

For a book so often criticized as essayistic and contrived, it ends with surprising—if disguised—tentativeness, far more tentativeness than, say, *The Bostonians*,[1] that other notable diagnosis of a national culture in stress and internecine division, sexual, regional, moral, and psychological. Its options are still open, its opposed feelings brought to a point not of closure but of perfected and communicative strain, and all kept at a pitch of drama. Everything that is expressed and hinted at in such an ending makes it less a conclusion than a just-suspended rhythm of these two things: consummation and loss, a harvest and a falling.[2]

---

1. A novel (1886) by Henry James. [*Editor*]
2. Very many critics have found the conclusion less rhetorically complex and less satisfying than I suggest. Wilfred Stone, for example, is led by his sense of dissatisfaction into a strangely insensitive dismissal: '[The Schlegels] make of Howards End a place of sterile quarantine for the best self of England, but there is no indication that these defenders will ever again do battle with the enemy . . .The burden of the book's conclusion is that Forster does not really want connection at all, but only the rewards of connection; he does not want sex, but only the heir. He wants, in short, ends without means' (*The Cave and the Mountain: a Study of E. M. Forster*, Stanford, 1966, pp. 265–6). [For an excerpt from Stone, see above, pp. 396–408. *Editor*]

ELIZABETH LANGLAND

Gesturing toward an Open Space: Gender, Form, and Language in E. M. Forster's *Howards End*[†]

E. M. Forster is a difficult writer to approach because he appears simple. His work presents none of the stylistic resistance and technical virtuosity characteristic of his notable contemporaries like Joyce and Woolf. Further, he seems to have recourse to a nineteenth-century liberal humanism in resolving his novels, an emphasis that sets at naught the complexities of literary modernism.[1] So, at best, Forster claims a precarious stake in the twentieth-century canon. But Forster accomplished something difficult and important in his novel *Howards End* that a gendered politics of reading can uncover. In his personal embattlement with gender and his embattlement with patriarchal culture, Forster exposes the constructed nature of gender and his own ambivalent relationship to traits coded "masculine" and "feminine" in his culture.

This gendered politics of reading begins with an acknowledgment of Forster's homosexuality and outspoken misogyny, a textual politics that is tied to a sexual politics. There is substantial evidence that Forster was deeply troubled and preoccupied by his own gender identity during this period. He had spent his childhood largely in the female company and sheltering presence of his mother and aunt, who no doubt gave him his "knowledge" of women and female friendship. At the same time, he was uncertain of his own sexual orientation and uncertain of even the basic facts of male/female reproduction, which Forster claimed he never fully grasped until his thirties. The conviction of his homosexuality came

---

[†] From *Out of Bounds: Male Writers and Gender(ed) Criticism*, ed. Laura Claridge and Elizabeth Langland (Amherst: U of Massachusetts P, 1990) 252–67. Copyright (c) 1990 by The University of Massachusetts Press. Reprinted by permission. Some notes have been silently omitted.

1. After the early, enthusiastic appreciation of Forster's work set in motion by Lionel Trilling, *E. M. Forster* (New York: New Directions, 1943), and Trilling's identification of *Howards End* as "undoubtedly Forster's masterpiece," because it develops into their full the themes and attitudes of the early books and connects them "with a more mature sense of responsibility" (114–15), other critics have not been content to rest with the thematic coherence of his work and have disagreed with Trilling's assessment. They have located Forster's reliance on nineteenth-century modes as a source of the novel's weakness. See, for example, Frederick Crews, who feels that Margaret's "'connection' with the Wilcoxes is merely diagrammatic" and that Forster's "plot must finally retreat to an unconvincingly 'moral' ending" (*E. M. Forster: The Perils of Humanism* [Princeton, NJ: Princeton University Press, 1962], 122). See also Wilfred Stone, who claims that "The forces of value do not 'connect,' but pursue each other in a lonely and circular futility. And the circle is especially vicious because Forster seems to see only its 'proportion' and not its 'emptiness'" (*The Cave and the Mountain: A Study of E. M. Forster* [Stanford, CA: Stanford University Press, 1966], 266).

I hope my own analysis identifies a new way to see the narrative strengths and challenges of Forster's novel, to perceive those techniques and questions that align him with other literary modernists. At the same time, my goal in this essay is to give another perspective from which to assess the novel's difficulties, which have been too readily grouped under the rubric of Forster's return to a nineteenth-century liberal humanism. [For excerpts from Crews and Stone, see above, pp. 331–40, 396–408. *Editor.*]

shortly after publication of *Howards End* when George Merrill, the
working-class homosexual lover of Forster's friend Edward Carpenter,
"touched Forster's backside 'gently and just above the buttocks.'" Forster
continued: "The sensation was unusual and I still remember it. . . . It
seemed to go straight through the small of my back into my ideas, without involving my thoughts."[2] That touch conceived *Maurice*, Forster's
novel about homosexual love published only posthumously.

It wasn't until 1916 that Forster found "total sexual fulfillment—or, as
he put it, 'parted with respectability'"[3]—and not until 1917 that he finally fell in love: with an Egyptian tram conductor, Mohammed-el-Adl.
After that fulfillment, Forster wrote to Florence Barger: "It isn't happiness. . . . it's rather—offensive phrase—that I first feel a grown up man."[4]
The offensiveness lies in the implication that a man becomes grown up
through sexual mastery.

Thus, in 1910, while composing *Howards End*, Forster was in a great
deal of confusion, which we can understand more fully if we consider
the Victorian notion of homosexuality: *anima mulieris in corpore virile
inclusa* or "a woman's soul trapped in a man's body."[5] Ironically, that
confusion and dissatisfaction precipitated a misogynistic homosexuality,
which I suggest we see in light of Forster's fear of the feminine in himself.[6] This understanding also gives us some insight into the process by
which the confusions that produced this misogyny in Forster also fueled
a desire for something other than the classical opposition between male
and female, masculine and feminine, and so initiated his embattled relationship with patriarchy. In *Howards End* we see this relationship played
out through the narrator, the leading female characters, certain thematic oppositions, and the connections between all of these and the dramatic structure of the novel.

At a first glance, Forster appears to offer neither a radical literary practice nor a liberal sexual practice in this story of a younger woman's conventional marriage to an older and successful businessman, who looks
upon women as "recreation." But textual evidence suggests that this conventional image is an anamorphosis[7] reflecting Forster's attempt to manage a site of conflict in himself. A close analysis of the textual maneuvers

2. Francis King, *E. M. Forster and His World* (New York: Scribner, 1978), 57.
3. Ibid., 64.
4. P. N. Furbank, *E. M. Forster: A Life*, 2 vols. (New York and London: Harcourt Brace
Jovanovich, 1977, 1978), 2:40.
5. D. A. Miller, *The Novel and the Police* (Berkeley and Los Angeles: University of California
Press, 1988), 154–55.
6. Eve Kosofsky Sedgwick, *Between Men: English Literature and Male Homosocial Desire* (New
York: Columbia University Press, 1985), 20, has made an important connection here between
misogyny and fear of the feminine. She argues that "homophobia directed by men against men
is misogynistic, and perhaps transhistorically so. (By 'misogynistic' I mean not only that it is
oppressive of the so-called feminine in men, but that it is oppressive of women)." Sedgwick also
notes that, although antihomophobia and feminism are not the same forces, the bonds between
them are "profound and intuitable."
7. A distortion. [*Editor*]

in *Howards End* discloses a radical sexual politics that has been obscured by psychobiographical approaches and by assumptions about Forster's literary allegiance to the nineteenth century. We may begin to excavate the layers of the text through its narrative stance, which is ambiguous, uneasy, and defensive. The following passage from the middle of the novel first brought me to examine *Howards End* because of the ways it makes problematic the omniscient narrator's voice:

> Pity was at the bottom of her [Margaret's] actions all through this crisis. Pity, if one may generalize, is at the bottom of woman. When men like us, it is for our better qualities and however tender their liking, we dare not be unworthy of it, or they will quietly let us go. But unworthiness stimulates woman. It brings out her deeper nature, for good or for evil.[8]

The problem emerges from the "us," which initially appears to refer back to "woman," used to essentialize all women, with whom the narrator seems to identify.[9] A closer reading suggests that "us" simply refers to all people, that is, "when men like people. . . ." The temporary confusion arises here because, previously, the events have been focalized through the female protagonist, Margaret Schlegel, and "us," the first-person-plural pronoun, invokes the feminine perspective.[1]

The "us" feels problematic, too, because the narrator's previous narrative intrusions have been characterized by an uneasy authority that hovers between irony and sympathy, creating an overall impression of indefiniteness. The narrator opens deferentially: "One may as well begin with Helen's letter to her sister" (5). Shortly thereafter we are told: "To Margaret—I hope that it will not set the reader against her— the station of King's Cross had always suggested Infinity" (11). The special pleading is intrusive here and later: "That was 'how it happened,' or, rather, how Helen described it to her sister, using words even more unsympathetic than my own" (20). Comments on the underprivileged seem to attempt sarcasm but end up sounding defensive: "We are not concerned with the very poor. They are unthinkable" (35); or, "take my word for it, that [poor woman's] smile was simply stunning, and it is only you and I who will be fastidious, and complain that true joy begins in the eyes" (37). Later addresses to the reader fail to achieve either authority on the one hand or familiarity on the other: "It is rather a moment when the commentator should step forward. Ought the Wilcoxes have offered their home to Margaret? I think not" (73); and, "Margaret had expected the disturbance. . . . Good-humour

---

8. *Howards End*, p. 174. [Page references are to this Norton Critical Edition. *Editor*]
9. One critic who has observed that the narrator is female is Kinley Roby, "Irony and Narrative Voice in *Howards End*," *Journal of Narrative Technique* 2 (May 1972).
1. There is some evidence from contemporary reviews that Forster's narrator and the narrative point of view were problematic. Indeed, some reviewers were persuaded that E. M. Forster must be a woman who had adopted a male pseudonym.

was the dominant note of her relations with Mr. Wilcox, or, as I must now call him, Henry" (128).

Forster is more assured when he avoids omniscient comment and focuses on Margaret Schlegel, from whose perspective we see the events of the novel. It is not merely that we share the point of view of a woman here (although that is important to Forster's ends) but also that we tend to take her perspective as representative of the female point of view in general. As the novel develops, Forster complicates this identification of Margaret with the "female" or the "feminine," but initially it undergirds the binary oppositions informing the novel. The novel is built upon a dialectical opposition between male and female, under which several others are subsumed. The most significant oppositions for this analysis are those of class—rich and poor; those of philosophy—logic and vision; and those of language—word and intuition. Under the male side of the equation fall wealth, logic, and the word; under the female, poverty, vision, and intuition. These oppositions are worked out on the level of theme and plot.

On the level of theme, that resolution is fairly straightforward, although we should note that those terms subsumed under the aspect of male and female perpetuate a hierarchical tradition that relegates women to an inferior status. We may want to applaud Forster for attempting to redress the balance by privileging the feminine, but we are still caught in a net of stereotypes that perpetuate hierarchy and binary opposition, ideas that inscribe male perspectives in the world, as we shall see in a moment.

Although I have relegated wealth to the male side of the equation and poverty to the female, in fact, the female protagonists of the novel, Margaret and Helen Schlegel, are well-to-do women. Their sympathy with the poor, however, initiates Forster's interrogation of class distinctions. The Schlegels are distinguished from the Wilcoxes, the masculine protagonists, by their recognition of the privilege that money confers. Margaret asserts that the rich "stand upon money as upon islands" in the sea of life (46). As a result of this perception, she and Helen are able to look beneath the social surface of a poor individual like Leonard Bast to the "real man, who cared for adventure and beauty" (224).

Yet, even as the novel attempts to redress the imbalance between rich and poor, it cannot transcend certain class attitudes which are implicit in Forster's uneven characterization of the workingman and explicit in Margaret's discovery that Jackie Bast has formerly been Henry Wilcox's mistress. She writes to Helen that "The Basts are not at all the type we should trouble about" (173), and Helen, who is ready enough to sympathize with Leonard Bast, condemns Jackie as "ready enough to meet" Henry Wilcox and laments that such women "end in two ways: either they sink till the lunatic asylums and the workhouses are full of them . . . or else they entrap a boy into marriage before it is too late" (181). That

Jackie is a victim of patriarchy is understood imperfectly, although Margaret strenuously criticizes Henry's double standard. Helen's disclaimer, "I can't blame her," sounds unconvincing as the novel seeks to deconstruct sexist and class values on the level of theme, which it then reconstructs on the level of plot when Helen has a sexual relationship with Leonard—a woman's classic offering of her body in sympathy—and then arrogantly seeks to compensate him with cash, admitting that "I want never to see him again, though it sounds appalling. I wanted to give him money and feel finished" (222). Both of these episodes play out basic patriarchal expectations about relationships between men and women, between the rich and the poor. The pattern we see here, where plot reconstructs what the theme interrogates to deconstruct, will be replicated in working out Forster's other binary oppositions.

Thematically, vision is privileged over logic, intuition over word. Of course, logic and the word are related: They are in this novel the logos, the word of the fathers. Forster is committed to an ideology that seeks to defy the phallic mode and, from the novel's opening, logic and the word are made to appear irrational. Charles Wilcox's blustering question to his brother, Paul, about his engagement to Helen Schlegel—"Yes or no, man; plain question, plain answer. Did or didn't Miss Schlegel"—is corrected by his mother's response: "Charles, dear Charles, one doesn't ask plain questions. There aren't such things" (18). When Henry Wilcox confronts Margaret over Helen's seemingly irrational behavior at the end of the novel, he echoes his son: "Answer my question. Plain question, plain answer" (202). Henry's plan to trap Helen like some hunted animal and Margaret's resistance provoke her recognition that the plan "is impossible, because—. . . it's not the particular language that Helen and I talk" and his counterclaim that "No education can teach a woman logic" (202). Margaret's later rejoinder—"leave it that you don't see. . . . Call it fancy. But realize that fancy is a scientific fact"—refuses Henry's reductive dichotomies. Margaret is given the final word in the novel as she reflects that, "Logically, they had no right to be there. One's hope was in the weakness of logic" (240), and she is vindicated in the conclusion as the Wilcox clan gather to hear the word of the father—"And again and again fell the word, like the ebb of a dying sea"—which belatedly, yet inevitably, affirms the intuitive vision of the mother in seeing that Margaret is the "spiritual heir" she seeks for Howards End.

And yet Margaret's "final word" is problematic because definitive answers belong to the male-inscribed discourse the novel seeks to deconstruct. We might want to argue that the apparent difficulty is only a matter of semantics. But, in fact, my introduction of a teleology of final word here anticipates the deeper problems we discover on the level of plot.

Forster's central opposition between man and woman would seem, initially, to be played out between Henry Wilcox and Margaret Schlegel. It begins on the level of houses. Margaret recognizes that "ours is a female house. . . . It must be feminine and all we can do is to see that it isn't effeminate. Just as another house that I can mention, but I won't, sounded irrevocably masculine, and all its inmates can do is to see that it isn't brutal" (34). This summary prepares us for the dialectic to follow, but Forster's feminist vision removes Margaret as a single term within the traditional dialectic, replaces her with Helen, and reinterprets Margaret as the principle that will complicate the hierarchical oppositions and provide a new kind of connection. That new connection is not the old androgyny, a merging or blurring of terms and traits;[2] it is a condition that preserves difference.

Whereas Henry Wilcox remains inscribed in a male mode of discourse, set within masculine imagery of dominance and conquest, Forster's descriptions of Margaret transcend the traditionally feminine and reinscribe her within a rhetoric of reconciliation and connection. Through Margaret Schlegel, the traditional terms of masculinity and femininity are scrutinized and subjected to the demands of higher integration. Margaret's point of view, then, is ultimately not representative of a view we might code as essentially female or feminine. Forster is sensitive both to essentialist conceptions of the female and to the social coding of the feminine. He subverts both in his characterization of Margaret Schlegel, who can calmly state, for example, "I do not love children. I am thankful to have none" (239), thus debunking ideas of a natural, maternal female.

And Margaret remains constantly alert to social expectations of feminine behavior, decoding those expectations. She turns the notion of "reading the feminine" into a lever against the men who are dependent on and limited by its convenient categories. When Henry proposes, Margaret has anticipated his action, but "she made herself give a little start. She must show surprise if he expected it" (119). Later, when a man hits a cat with his automobile and Margaret jumps out of the car, we learn that "Charles was absolutely honest. He described what he believed to have happened. . . . Miss Schlegel had lost her nerve, as any woman might." But the narrator reveals that "His father accepted this explanation, and neither knew that Margaret had artfully prepared the way for it. It fitted in too well with their view of feminine nature" (154). Later, in response to a question, Margaret "knew . . . but said that she did not know" (158) because "comment is unfeminine" (172).

Throughout the novel, Margaret resists being controlled by this

---

2. The subject of androgyny has become a vexed one in contemporary feminist discourse. In early stages of the feminist movement, the argument for equal treatment of women and men seemed to depend on detecting similarities: the masculine in the feminine and the feminine in the masculine. Then androgyny seemed the ideal. Subsequently, women have wanted to argue for the authority of the female perspective and values, and androgyny as a concept has become less attractive. It is interesting, in this light, that Forster doesn't advocate the merging of traits androgyny implies but instead insists on preserving distinctions. He is, in that regard, closer to the spirit of a contemporary discourse that speaks of escaping hierarchies.

dichotomous thinking and instead manipulates the terms with the goal of dismantling and transcending them. From the beginning, she is suspicious of hierarchies, as we discover in her mediation of the English and German claims to superiority. She announces, "To me one of two things is very clear; either God does not know his own mind about England and Germany, or else these do not know the mind of God" (24). The narrator pronounces her, ironically, "a hateful girl," acknowledging that "at thirteen she had grasped a dilemma that most people travel through life without perceiving" (24). That dilemma focuses on the logic of binary thinking. Margaret resists such dichotomous thought and chastises Helen's binary oppositions as "medieval," telling her "our business is not to contrast the two, but to reconcile them" (77). Not surprisingly, it is Margaret who is capable of concluding that "people are far more different than is pretended. All over the world men and women are worrying because they cannot develop as they are supposed to develop" (239).

In his reconceptualization of Margaret, Forster generates a new integrative principle that is associated with a woman but not ideologically coded as feminine. Part of his success here depends, as I have suggested, on using Helen to reevaluate the traditionally feminine by associating her with emotion and the inner life.

Helen Schlegel, in contrast to Margaret, is emotional, impulsive, impatient of logic, impatient of all restraint on her generous impulses. She scoffs at moderation and is incapable of balance; she is first seduced by the Wilcox men and then violently rejects them. She extols the "inner life" and, unlike Margaret, refuses to acknowledge the value of Wilcox energy, which has created a civilized world in which her sensibilities and the inner life can have free play. When Margaret must protect a pregnant and unmarried Helen from the interference of Wilcox men, Margaret herself codes the struggle as a sexual one: "A new feeling came over her; she was fighting for women against men. She did not care about rights, but if men came into Howards End, it should be over her body" (206). Although Margaret prefers not to be locked into a struggle between opposed faces, under duress she will privilege what Helen represents. Forster has anticipated this moment earlier in the novel when Margaret and Helen disagree over the older sister's impending marriage to Henry Wilcox. Their "inner life was so safe," we are told, "that they could bargain over externals. . . . There are moments when the inner life actually 'pays,' when years of self-scrutiny, conducted for no ulterior motive, are suddenly of practical use" (140). The narrator adds that "Such moments are still rare in the West; that they can come at all promises a fairer future." Forster codes the inner life within another set of oppositions—Eastern mysticism versus Western pragmatism—but he reverses the usual hierarchy to privilege the East and the inner life.

In contrast to Helen, Henry is associated with an imagery of war, battle, and self-defense. When Margaret discovers that Jackie Bast was

Henry's mistress, the narrator claims that, "Expelled from his old fortress, Mr. Wilcox was building a new one" (175). Margaret is forced to play "the girl, until he could rebuild his fortress and hide his soul from the world" (176). Henry believes that "Man is for war, woman for the recreation of the warrior, but he does not dislike it if she makes a show of fight. She cannot win in a real battle, having no muscles, only nerves" (185). At the end of the novel, in the crisis over Helen, Henry speaks "straight from his fortress," and Margaret at first fails to recognize that "to break him was her only hope." It is only when "Henry's fortress [gives] way" that Margaret can initiate the process that leads to the integration, the connection, she enacts in the novel's conclusion by bringing Henry and Helen together at Howards End.

It is significant in *Howards End* that the most moving scene occurs between two women, Helen and Margaret. When the sisters meet at Howards End and Margaret discovers Helen is pregnant, she asserts, "It all turns on affection now" (207). Although at first they feel themselves in antagonism, unconsciously they move toward communion:

> The triviality faded from their faces, though it left something behind—the knowledge that they never could be parted because their love was rooted in common things. Explanations and appeals had failed; they had tried for a common meeting-ground, and had only made each other unhappy. And all the time their salvation was lying round them—the past sanctifying the present; the present, with wild heart-throb, declaring that there would after all be a future, with laughter and the voices of children. Helen, still smiling, came up to her sister. She said: "It is always Meg." They looked into each other's eyes. The inner life had paid. [212]

In stark contrast stands Charles Wilcox's relationship with his father:

> The Wilcoxes were not lacking in affection; they had it royally, but they did not know how to use it. It was the talent in the napkin, and, for a warm-hearted man, Charles had conveyed very little joy. As he watched his father shuffling up the road, he had a vague regret—a wish that something had been different somewhere—a wish (though he did not express it thus) that he had been taught to say "I" in his youth. He meant to make up for Margaret's defection, but knew that his father had been very happy with her until yesterday. How had she done it? By some dishonest trick, no doubt—but how? [233]

The traditionally feminine mode is clearly affirmed in these final contrasting scenes that sanction the inner life and "voiceless sympathy."

In privileging the inner life, as we have seen, Forster reverses the usual hierarchy in the oppositions of inner/outer, female/male, East/West, intuition/logic. This affirmation is a part of Forster's achievement. More significant, he takes a further step and sets up through Margaret a double reading in which the poles indecidably include each other and the *différance*[3] of this irreducible difference. It is a process made familiar to us by Derrida.[4] We are forced to think or imagine the "inconceivable," what we have seen as mutually exclusive; we are forced to form conceptions of that for which we have no concepts. The novel's epigraph — "Only connect" — stands at the heart of this difficult process through which Margaret hopes to enable Henry's salvation: "Only connect! That was the whole of her sermon. Only connect the prose and the passion, and both will be exalted, and human love will be seen at its height. Live in fragments no longer" (134). At Howards End, Margaret senses this connection of comrades between the house and the wych elm tree: "It was a comrade, bending over the house, strength and adventure in its roots, but in its utmost fingers tenderness. . . . It was a comrade. House and tree transcended any similes of sex" (148). Significantly, Forster has chosen representative terms — a house and a tree — that resist hierarchical placement and the classical oppositional structure of patriarchal thinking. Margaret reflects that, "to compare either to man, to woman, always dwarfed the vision. Yet they kept within limits of the human. . . . As she stood in the one, gazing at the other, truer relationship had gleamed" (148). Margaret also argues for connection — this discovery of mutual inclusivity — in her conception of proportion: "truth, being alive, was not halfway between anything. It was only to be found by continuous excursions into either realm, and though proportion is the final secret, to espouse it at the outset is to insure sterility" (140). Finally, in the novel's conclusion, Margaret looks toward an "ultimate harmony" (234).

To summarize, the connection that Margaret seeks is obviously not born out of an attempt to merge or to blur or reverse oppositions. She fights the "daily grey" of life, the blending of black and white. Rather, she seeks to dismantle the hierarchical privileging of one term over another. She expresses it as a celebration of "Differences — eternal differences, planted by God in a single family, so that there may always be colour; sorrow perhaps, but colour in the daily grey" (239).

Ironically, however, although the resolution thematically insists on connections and although the patriarch Wilcox is unmanned, the plot appears to encode the patriarchal structures that the novel seeks to escape. I began this essay with the narrator's ambiguous sexual identification. I then quoted a paragraph which is followed by one that reads,

3. Jacques Derrida's term for the process whereby signs both defer and differ from what they signify, thus making meaning elusive and unstable. [*Editor*]

4. Although I find *différance* a fruitful concept for allowing us to see Forster's achievement in a new light — for allowing us to perceive a radical dimension to his art obscured by previous insistence that he belongs to a nineteenth-century tradition of liberal humanism — I am not doing a Derridean deconstruction on this text. Indeed, the conclusion I postulate — Margaret's ultimate spiritual insight outside language — Derrida would probably see as a metaphysics. I am, however, inevitably led to see the parallels between Forster's conception of connection and Derrida's notion of *différance*, both of which are crucial to the problem of sexual difference.

> Here was the core of the question. Henry must be forgiven, and made better by love; nothing else mattered. . . . To her everything was in proportion now. . . . Margaret fell asleep, tethered by affection, and lulled by the murmurs of the river that descended all the night from Wales. She felt herself at one with her future home, colouring it and coloured by it, and awoke to see, for the second time, Oniton Castle conquering the morning mists. [174]

We notice the imagery of proportion, of connection, of mutuality monopolizing the paragraph which, nonetheless, concludes with an image of domination, "Oniton Castle conquering the morning mists." It is possible Forster is being ironic because Oniton is not to be Margaret's home and she is, perhaps, mistaken in so valuing it. Yet, if this is irony, it is irony of a very subtle sort.

I suggest instead that the pattern is not ironic; rather, it anticipates the resolution of the novel where the value of connection, represented by the presence of Henry and Helen at Howards End, is enacted in the plot by Margaret's conquest of Henry. Henry, in masculine style, has earlier told Margaret, "fix your price, and then don't budge," and she has responded, "But I do budge" (113). Nonetheless, on the issue of connection, she, like her masculine counterparts, won't budge: "He had refused to connect, on the clearest issue that can be laid before a man, and their love must take the consequences" (235). And in the novel's closing paragraphs, Margaret reflects, "There was something uncanny in her triumph. She, who had never expected to conquer anyone, had charged straight through these Wilcoxes and broken up their lives" (241–42). Margaret has triumphed, conquered, and broken up their lives. This conclusion to a novel about connection is ironic although not, I would suggest, deliberately so.

The irony arises because Forster inscribes the value of connection within the patriarchal dialectic of conquest and defeat, domination and submission, and within a narrative form that demands a resolution instead of "continuous excursions into either realm" (140). Although the themes of the novel indicate a desire to deconstruct the patriarchal ideology, ultimately, it seems, Forster is forced to reconstruct that ideology in the structure of the novel, in Margaret's "victory" over Henry. Plot has demanded a hierarchical ordering of terms for a resolution to conflict even though the novel's themes have argued for replacement of conquest with connection. Forster's often trenchant interrogation of patriarchal language and perspectives appears to give way before the resistless temptation to expropriate the authority available to him in patriarchy. What he *wants* to assert, of course, is the value of the feminine perspective as a first step to dismantling hierarchy, but in the *act* of assertion, he affirms the value of the masculine mode, remaining dependent on patriarchy's hierarchical structures for authority, resolution, and conclusion. Ultimately, Forster recuperates an authority that would thematically seem to be repudiated.

Reaching this point in my argument—where the need to conclude a paper definitively is as imperative as the requirement to resolve a novel—I nonetheless stepped back from my own recuperation of authority, stepped from form to language. Perhaps Forster's critique of patriarchal modes and binary thinking was more trenchant and thoroughgoing than I first perceived. Forster had certainly appropriated the language of conquest, but he had also recontextualized it and, in the process, forestalled expropriation by that masculine terminology. A deep suspicion of conquest in its most notable manifestations—imperialism and war—lies at the very heart of *Howards End*. The narrator simply asserts, contrasting the yeoman who is "England's hope" to the Imperialist who "hopes to inherit the earth," that "the Imperialist is not what he thinks or seems. He is a destroyer. He prepares the way for cosmopolitanism, and though his ambitions may be fulfilled, the earth that he inherits will be grey" (229). Strong biblical cadences underline this apocalyptic vision of a world shaped in a masculine mode.

Perhaps, then, Forster is having his joke when Margaret characterizes her success as a conquest. "She, who had never expected to conquer anyone, had charged straight through these Wilcoxes and broken up their lives" (242). In fact, she has not "charged through"; she has simply done what "seemed easiest" (237). "No better plan had occurred to her" (238). She confesses, "I did the obvious things" (240). "Conquer," in this context, is not an act of self-assertion and dominance but is redefined as nonassertion, an opening up of space, a refusal to accept the exclusivity of opposition between Henry and Helen. "Everyone said [living together at Howards End] was impossible" (240), but Margaret defies this patriarchal logic.

The futility of binary thinking appears in the lives of both Henry and Helen, both of whom declare they are "ended." Henry confesses, "I don't know what to do—what to do. I'm broken—I'm ended" (237). As if in echo, Helen rejoins, "I'm ended. I used to be so dreamy about a man's love as a girl, and think that, for good or evil, love must be the great thing. But it hasn't been" (239). The man of action and the woman of emotion reach the bankruptcy implicit in their exclusive positions. Margaret's conquest or victory, then, is not the patriarchal one demanding suppression of an other but one that emerges as the traditional oppositions destroy themselves and clear a space for difference.

Forster has anticipated this conclusion, as we have seen earlier, in identifying a warfare mentality with Henry Wilcox. But we may now discover a further step Forster has taken. While Henry Wilcox persistently refers to casualties such as Leonard Bast as "part of the battle of life" (137) as if such casualties were in the "nature" of things, Margaret decodes his metaphor: "We upper classes have ruined him, and I suppose you'll tell me it's part of the battle of life" (161). Margaret herself is a master of words, as we see in her first encounter with Leonard Bast when her speeches "flutter away from him like birds" (31). But Margaret's strength lies in recognizing the way ideologies are encoded in language and in acknowledging the social privilege behind her "speech." She early argues, "all our thoughts are the thoughts of six-hundred-pounders, and all our speeches" (46), underlining both the intensity and the futility of Leonard Bast's desire "to form his style on Ruskin" (38). Ruskin's style cannot "speak" Leonard Bast's life.

When Margaret rejects Henry's language and metaphor of life as a battle, she rejects his patriarchal ideology and introduces new terms into the novel. She reflects that "Life is indeed dangerous, but not in the way morality would have us believe. It is indeed unmanageable, but the essence of it is not a battle. It is unmanageable because it is a romance, and its essence is romantic beauty" (79). This passage informs the entire novel and encourages us to reread the metaphors of conquest conclud-ing the novel within a romance topos[5] put into play by the figure of Ruth Wilcox, Henry's first wife.

Margaret's own sense of victory is severely qualified when she learns that Ruth Wilcox had "willed" Howards End to her, had designated her as its "spiritual heir," many years earlier: "Something shook [Margaret's] life in its inmost recesses, and she shivered" (242). Ruth Wilcox is intro-duced into the novel as one who always "knew," although no one "told her a word" (21). Ruth Wilcox is represented as beyond language deployed as power, beyond the words that cripple communication among the other characters, implicated as they are in ideology. Margaret ultimately asserts to Helen: "I feel that you and I and Henry are only fragments of that woman's mind. She knows everything. She is every-thing. She is the house, and the tree that leans over it" (222).

Miss Avery, who after Mrs. Wilcox's death becomes her representa-tive, prophesies to Margaret: "You think you won't come back to live here [at Howards End], but you will" (194), and Margaret, who has dis-counted her words, is disturbed to find them fulfilled when she and Helen sleep in the house: "It is disquieting to fulfill a prophecy, howev-er superficially" (215). She will, of course, fulfill it much more deeply, making Howards End her permanent home, as, increasingly, Margaret herself recognizes the "power of the house. It kills what is dreadful and makes what is beautiful live" (213).

As Margaret moves toward insight and vision, she, too, moves away from language. The narrator comments, for example, that Margaret's "mind trembled toward a conclusion which only the unwise will put into words" (147). And later we learn that Margaret "had outgrown stim-ulants, and was passing from words to things," an inevitable process "if the mind itself is to become a creative power" (187). Finally, Margaret admits to Helen, who calls her life "heroic," "No doubt I have done a lit-

5. The conventions of romance. [*Editor*]

tle towards straightening the tangle, but things that I can't phrase have helped me" (240).

At best, because of its ideological character, language can take characters to the brink of understanding as it does when Margaret exposes Henry's hypocrisy in committing adultery himself and refusing to forgive it in Helen. Margaret confronts Henry: "I think you yourself recommended plain speaking." And the narrator reveals that "they looked at each other in amazement. The precipice was at their feet now" (218). Language takes them to the abyss, but it cannot reconstruct their lives on a new basis because they cannot form conceptions of that for which there is no concept. Margaret simply relies on "the power of the house."

As we reconsider Forster's resolution in light of Mrs. Wilcox and the spiritual heir she seeks for Howards End, we notice that the novel moves toward resolution, but it is a resolution that existed from the beginning as a "part of Mrs. Wilcox's mind" (224). In that respect, the plot subverts its own commitment to hierarchy and sequence, to prior and subsequent events. In addition, the power that has "defeated" Henry Wilcox, the patriarch, is diffused over the universe. At the end of the novel, Henry Wilcox lies suffering with hay fever, confined to the house, recalling Miss Avery's words with their echoes of battle imagery: "There's not one Wilcox that can stand up against a field in June" (195). The patriarch is "shut up in the house," and his wife pronounces, "It has to be. . . . The hay-fever is his chief objection to living here, but he thinks it worth while" (238).

As previously noted, the novel's last words belong to Helen, who rushes into the house with her child and the neighbor boy accompanied by "shouts of infectious joy": "We've seen to the very end," she cries, "and it'll be such a crop of hay as never" (243). To see "to the very end," in this scene and in the novel as a whole, is to discover the beginning of possibility: "such a crop of hay as never." The last phrase is appropriate, too, concluding with a "never" that has already been subverted. In its closure, the novel gestures toward an open space, like a field in June, that "not one Wilcox . . . can stand up against." It is a "closure" that echoes Hélène Cixous on *écriture féminine*. Though Cixous is speaking of women writers, she describes what I am arguing that Forster has achieved:

> [Writers] must invent the impregnable language that will wreck partitions, classes, and rhetorics, regulations and codes, they must submerge, cut through, get beyond the ultimate reserve-discourse, including the one that laughs at the very idea of pronouncing the word "silence," the one that, aiming for the impossible, stops short before the word "impossible" and writes it as "the end."[6]

6. Hélène Cixous, "The Laugh of the Medusa," in *New French Feminisms: An Anthology*, ed. Elaine Marks and Isabelle de Courtivron (New York: Schocken, 1981), 256.

This reading seems more true to the narrative and linguistic proce-
dures of Forster's *Howards End*. But it raises further questions. Can
Forster thus evade the connection between discourse and power by pos-
tulating an unspoken knowledge? Indeed, the pressure of resolution may
seem inevitably to produce an evasion as Forster gestures toward an
alternative to binary thinking, a "conclusion that only the unwise will
put into words." It is, at best, an uneasy truce. And this final inaccessible
metaphysics may leave us frustrated by our own continuing embattlement with language, power, and patriarchy.

FREDRIC JAMESON

[Modernism, Imperialism, and *Howards End*]†

The hypothesis to be explored here is both more formalistic and more
sweeping than the affirmation that imperialism as such produced its specific literature and left palpable traces on the *content* of other metropolitan[1] literary works of the period. I want in fact to suggest that the
structure of imperialism also makes its mark on the inner forms and
structures of that new mutation in literary and artistic language to which
the term modernism is loosely applied. This last has of course multiple
social determinants: any general theory of the modern—assuming one
to be possible in the first place—would also wish to register the informing presence of a range of other historically novel phenomena: modernization and technology; commodity reification; monetary abstraction
and its effects on the sign system; the social dialectic of reading publics;
the emergence of mass culture; the embodiment of new forms of the
psychic subject on the physical sensorium. Nor is the relative weight and
importance of the emergence of a whole new global and imperial system in this constellation of "factors" at all clear, even in a speculative
way. The present essay is limited to the isolation of this determinant
alone, the presence of a new force, which cannot be reduced to any of
those aforementioned.

* * *

* * * Colonialism means that a significant structural segment of the
economic system as a whole is now located elsewhere, beyond the
metropolis, outside of the daily life and existential experience of the

† From Fredric Jameson, "Modernism and Imperialism" in *Nationalism, Colonialism, and
Literature*, A Field Day Company Book (Minneapolis: U of Minnesota P, 1990) 43, 50–59.
Reprinted by permission of the University of Minnesota Press.
1. In what follows, the word "metropolis" will designate the imperial nation-state as such, "metropolitan" then applying to its internal national realities and daily life (which are of course not
exclusively urban, although organized around some central urban "metropolis" in the narrower sense).

home country, in colonies over the water whose own life experience and life world—very different from that of the imperial power—remain unknown and unimaginable for the subjects of the imperial power, whatever social class they may belong to. Such spatial disjunction has as its immediate consequence the inability to grasp the way the system functions as a whole. Unlike the classical stage of national or market capitalism, then, pieces of the puzzle are missing; it can never be fully reconstructed; no enlargement of personal experience (in the knowledge of other social classes, for example), no intensity of self-examination (in the form of whatever social guilt), no scientific deductions on the basis of the internal evidence of First World data, can ever be enough to include this radical otherness of colonial life, colonial suffering, and exploitation, let alone the structural connections between that and this, between absent space and daily life in the metropolis. To put it in other words, this last—daily life and existential experience in the metropolis— which is necessarily the very content of the national literature itself, can now no longer be grasped immanently; it no longer has its meaning, its deeper reason for being, within itself. As artistic content it will now henceforth always have something missing about it, but in the sense of a privation that can never be restored or made whole simply by adding back in the missing component: its lack is rather comparable to another dimension, an outside like the other face of a mirror, which it constitutively lacks, and which can never be made up or made good. This new and historically original problem in what is itself a new kind of content now constitutes the situation and the problem and the dilemma, the formal contradiction, that modernism seeks to solve; or better still, it is only that new kind of art which reflexively perceives this problem and lives this formal dilemma that can be called modernism in the first place.

Now of course one's simplest first thought, faced with this problem of a global space that like the fourth dimension somehow constitutively escapes you, is no doubt to make a map: nor is *Ulysses* by any means the first, let alone the only, literary work of the imperialist period that stakes its bet on the properties of maps. The very title of Conrad's *Heart of Darkness*, whatever other resonances it comes to have, is literally determined by the reference to cartography. But cartography is not the solution, but rather the problem, at least in its ideal epistemological form as social cognitive mapping on the global scale. The map, if there is to be one, must somehow emerge from the demands and constraints of the spatial perceptions of the individual; and since Britain is generally thought of as the quintessential imperialist power, it may be useful to begin with a sample of English spatial experience:

> The train sped northward, under innumerable tunnels. It was only an hour's journey, but Mrs. Munt had to raise and lower the win-

dow again and again. She passed through the South Welwyn
Tunnel, of tragic fame. She traversed the immense viaduct, whose
arches span untroubled meadows and the dreamy flow of Tewin
Water. She skirted the parks of politicians. At times the Great North
Road accompanied her, more suggestive of infinity than any railway awakening, after a nap of a hundred years, to such life as is conferred by the stench of motor-cars, and to such culture as is implied
by the advertisements of antibilious pills. To history, to tragedy, to
the past, to the future, Mrs. Munt remained equally indifferent;
hers but to concentrate on the end of her journey, and to rescue
poor Helen from this dreadful mess.[2]

This episode, from the opening pages of *Howards End*, is characteristic
of Forster's duplicities, and offers an amiable simplicity filled with traps
and false leads. Pockets of philosophical complexity are hidden away
beneath its surface, and they include reflections on nature and industri-
alization, on authentic and inauthentic existential time (Mrs. Munt's
version of Heideggerian *Sorge*),[3] and a firm but tactful consciousness of
English class realities. The novel will then undertake to spell these out
and to make sure that what the reader has been encouraged to overlook
here becomes at length an unavoidable message, in terms of which we
may then leaf back and gloss the present text in some detail. But it will
remain a gloss on what is essentially a spatial representation and a spatial perception: the philosophical thoughts (which in any case involve
space, as we shall see) will finally have been dependent on space, and
inexpressible without it. This is of course a cinematographic kind of
space, with its Einsteinian observer on a train moving through a landscape whose observation it alters at the very moment that it makes it possible. But what is most significant is not some possible influence of
nascent cinema on Forster or on the modernist novel in general, but
rather the confluence of the two distinct formal developments, of movie
technology on the one hand, and of a certain type of modernist or pro-
tomodernist language on the other, both of which seem to offer some
space, some third term, between the subject and the object alike.
Cinematographic perception is in that sense neither subjective nor psychological: there is nothing private or personal about it (and it was for
that reason that * * * characterizations of the modern as some inward
turn were misleading). But it is not objective either in any conventional
sense of realism or empiricism: nothing is indeed quite so perverse or
aberrant for the truly postmodern person as the polemic expression
"photographic realism"—as though photography, today so mysterious
and contradictory an experience, had anything reassuringly trustworthy
or reliable about it, for us a most unlikely guarantor of verisimilitude!

2. *Howards End*, p. 13. [Page references are to this Norton Critical Edition. *Editor*]
3. According to the German existential philosopher Martin Heidegger in *Being and Time* (1927),
the care (*Sorge*) we exercise toward people and things defines our being. [*Editor*]

This is why, although the category of *style* remains a fundamental one of the various modernisms, emerging with them and disappearing again when the psychic subject is notoriously eclipsed in the postmodern moment, it seems urgent to disjoin it from conventional notions of psychology and subjectivity: whence the therapeutic usefulness of the cinematographic parallel, where an apparatus takes the place of human psychology and perception. But this can most effectively be achieved by recoordinating the concept of style with some new account of the experience of space, both together now marking the emergence of the modern as such, and the place from which a whole bewilderingly varied set of modernisms begins to flourish.

Forster, at best a closet modernist, may seem an unlikely enough illustration of this process; but it was its tendential emergence that interested us, and not the full-blown thing itself. Meanwhile, if it is argued that England, the very heartland of imperialism, is also that national terrain which seems to have been the least propitious for the development of any indigenous modernism,[4] then that is surely also relevant for our present topic.

Yet at least one moment in the present passage seems to hold all the possibilities of some properly modernist language, past and future, instinct within itself, from Baudelaire to Eliot: a figure which speeds by like Mrs. Munt's surroundings, only its false modesty drawing attention to itself (as always in Forster). It is "the Great North Road . . . suggestive of infinity." One sees what is meant, of course, and the reader dutifully recomposes some inner film around the visual properties of the highway, its great sweep and curve away from the train tracks; its empty endlessness, on which a few (multiple) vehicles reinforce the investment of the observer by a single massive conveyance; its desolation, finally, denuded and thereby closer to the Idea than the unavoidable contamination of the railway interior by a modernizing and commercial history. This is at least what the figure gives us to see; but, particularly when you come to know that Forster continues to use the word "infinity" as though it really means something, the meaning itself grows less and less evident. Or perhaps it might be better to characterize this moment of a properly modernist *style* as one in which an appearance of meaning is pressed into the service of the notation of a physical perception. In fact, the reading problem turns on the objective uncertainty as to the structure of this figure: it is undecidable whether the Great North Road is the tenor or the vehicle;[5] whether the roadway is intended, as in analogous moments in Baudelaire, to concretize the nebulous metaphysical concept, "infin-

4. It is, I take it, the position of Terry Eagleton's stimulating *Exiles and Emigrés* (New York: Schocken, 1970) that all the most important modern writers of what we think of as the *English* canon are in fact social marginals of various kinds, when not outright foreigners. * * *
5. The "tenor" and the "vehicle" are the literal and figurative parts of a metaphorical expression. In the phrase "man is a wolf," for example, "man" is the tenor and "wolf" is the vehicle. [*Editor*]

ity," and by a momentary transfer of its visual properties to make that vague but lofty word a more vivid linguistic player in the textual game; or whether, on the other hand, it is rather the metaphysical prestige of the more noble Idea that is supposed to resonate back on the banal high-way, lending it *numen*[6] and thereby transforming it into the merest promise of expressivity without having to affirm it as some official "symbol" of the conventionally mendacious kind. Modernism is itself this very hesitation; it emerges in this spatial gap within Forster's figure; it is at one with the contradiction between the contingency of physical objects and the demand for an impossible meaning, here marked by dead philosophical abstraction. The solution to this contradiction, which we call "style," is then the substitution of a spatial or perceptual "meaning" (whatever that now is) for the other kind (whatever that was, or might be in the future).

But Forster's figure also turns out to have a more conventional "meaning," as the rest of his novel instructs us: it will be perfectly proper to unravel it, provided we do not lose sight of its initial spatial and percep-tual ground, and of the work of some new modernist language on our bodies and our sensorium that is its precondition. He goes on, indeed, to develop his ethos of place, as "the basis of all earthly beauty" (147), which he elaborates into something like a twofold salvation system, the twin paths of intimate human relations and of an immediate landscape: "We want to show him," says Margaret about the wretched Leonard Bast, "how he may get upsides with life. As I said, either friends, or the coun-try, some . . . either some very dear person or some very dear place seems necessary to relieve life's daily grey, and to show that it is grey. If possi-ble, one should have both" (106). The place is of course the country house itself, the Howards End of the title; and the "dear person" the late Mrs. Wilcox, who begins to merge with her dwelling to the point of becoming almost literally a "*genius loci*."[7] Yet the representational dilemma remains, as in our earlier figure: Mrs. Wilcox as a character draws her possibilities from that concrete place that is Howards End, while this last draws its evocative power from the spirit of Mrs. Wilcox. The transformation of chance encounters ("only connect") into a utopi-an social community presided over by a woman who is its providential spirit in a virtually literal sense;[8] and the recovery of a utopian landscape orchestrated by the well-nigh Shakespearean glorification of an ideal (and an antipatriotic) England in chapter XIX—the combination, indeed, the identification of these two visionary constructions is Forster's political as well as his aesthetic agenda in his novel.

---

6. Spiritual power. [*Editor*]
7. Spirit of the place (Latin). [*Editor*]
8. Formally, the position of Mrs. Wilcox in this novel demands comparison with that of Mrs. Ramsay in Virginia Woolf's *To the Lighthouse*, an analysis of which forms a part of the larger version of the present essay.

Yet as he himself makes clear, it is not evident that the operation can be historically realized and completed (even though the novel itself gets written). For he will go on to suggest that the tendential conditions of modern civilization—"modernization" now, rather than aesthetic "modernism"!—are in the process of closing off one of these two avenues of personal and spiritual "salvation" (if that is not too lofty a word for it). Landscape is in the process of being obliterated, leaving only the more fragile and ephemeral safety net of the interpersonal behind it:

> London was but a foretaste of this nomadic civilization, which is altering human nature so profoundly, and throws upon personal relations a stress greater than they have ever borne before. Under cosmopolitanism, if it comes, we shall receive no help from the earth. Trees and meadows and mountains will only be a spectacle, and the binding force that they once exercized on character must be entrusted to Love alone. (186)

But what we must now add, and what now returns us to our starting point, is that London is very precisely that "infinity" of which we caught a glimpse on the Great North Road, or at least a "caricature" of it (Forster's word, 199). But now suddenly a whole set of terms falls into place and begins to coincide: cosmopolitanism, London, the nomadic, the stench of motorcars, antibilious pills, all begin to coalesce as a single historical tendency, and they are unexpectedly at one with "infinity" itself, which equally unexpectedly becomes the bad opposite of place, of Howards End, of the salvation through the here and the now (and incidentally of the regeneration of some older England that never existed, the utopian England of chapter XIX). But this is not simple romantic antiurban or antimodern nostalgia; it is not at all the conservative revulsion before the faceless industrial masses of the Waste Land, the modern urban world. And that for a final decisive reason, a final identification in this linked chain of phenomena: for infinity in this sense, this new grey placelessness, as well as what prepares it, also bears another familiar name. It is in Forster *imperialism*, or Empire, to give it its period designation. It is Empire which stretches the roads out to infinity, beyond the bounds and borders of the national state, Empire which leaves London behind it as a new kind of spatial agglomeration or disease, and whose commercialism now throws up those practical and public beings, like Mr. Wilcox, around whose repression of the personal Forster's message will also play, taking on new forms we have no time to examine here:

> In the motorcar was another type whom Nature favors—the Imperial. Healthy, ever in motion, it hopes to inherit the earth. It breeds as quickly as the yeoman, and as soundly; strong is the temptation to acclaim it as a superyeoman, who carries his country's virtue overseas. But the Imperialist is not what he thinks or seems. He is a destroyer. He prepares the way for cosmopolitanism, and

though his ambitions may be fulfilled, the earth that he inherits
will be grey. (229)

With this identification—the coincidence of "infinity" with "imperialism"—we come full circle, and a component of the imperialist situation
appears in human form, or in the representational language of a narrative character. Yet the representation is incomplete, and thereby epistemologically distorted and misleading: for we are only able to see that
face, the "Imperial type," turn inward, toward the internal metropolitan
reality. The other pole of the relationship, what defines him fundamentally and essentially in his "imperial" function—the persons of the
colonized—remains structurally occluded, and cannot but so remain,
necessarily, as a result of the limits of the system, and the way in which
internal national or metropolitan daily life is absolutely sundered from
this other world henceforth in thrall to it.[9] But since representation, and
cognitive mapping as such, is governed by an "intention towards totality,"[1] those limits must also be drawn back into the system, which marks
them by an image, the image of the Great North Road as infinity: a new
spatial language, therefore—modernist "style"—now becomes the marker and the substitute (the "tenant-lieu," or place-holding, in Lacanian
language) of the unrepresentable totality. With this a new kind of value
emerges (and it is this which is generally loosely and misleadingly
referred to as modernist aestheticism): for if "infinity" (and "imperialism") is bad or negative in Forster, its perception, as a bodily and poetic
process, is no longer that, but rather a positive achievement and an
enlargement of our sensorium: so that the beauty of the new figure
seems oddly unrelated to the social and historical judgment which is its
content.

What I have tried to suggest about this "event" on the border or limit
of representation might also have been shown for the representation of
inner or metropolitan space itself, for the national daily life which must
remain its primary raw material. Because in the imperial world system
this last is now radically incomplete, it must by compensation be formed
into a self-subsisting totality: something Forster uniquely attempts to
achieve by way of his providential ideology, which transforms chance
contacts, coincidence, the contingent and random encounters between
isolated subjects, into a utopian glimpse of achieved community. This

9. Africa is set in place by the mediation of Paul Wilcox, who works in Uganda for his father's
   Imperial and West African Rubber Company (see 141). About *A Passage to India*, what needs
   to be said here is (a) that Forster's luck lay in the fact that one of the many Indian languages is
   the one called Indian English, which he was able to learn like a foreign language; and (b) that
   the novel is restricted to British and Muslim characters (Islam being, as Lévi-Strauss instructs
   us in *Tristes Tropiques*, the last and most advanced of the great *Western* monotheisms), the
   Hindus specifically designated as that Other are inaccessible to Western representation.
1. Georg Lukács, *History and Class Consciousness* (Cambridge, Mass.: MIT Press, 1971), 174
   (where the German "*Intention*" is translated "*aspiration*").

glimpse is both moral and aesthetic all at once, for it is the achievement of something like an aesthetic pattern of relationships that confirms it as a social reality, however ephemeral; and the coincidence of the social (grasped in moral terms) and the aesthetic is then what allows other related works (such as those of Virginia Woolf) to refocus it by way of operations which look more aestheticizing than Forster's. Here also the internal social totality will remain incomplete; but the internal social classes are nonetheless explicitly designated by their absence (thus, Leonard is carefully characterized as nonproletarian, as standing "at the extreme edge of gentility. He was not in the abyss but he could see it, and at times people whom he knew had dropped in, and counted no more") (35). This internal subsumption is sharply to be distinguished from the exclusion of an external or colonized people (whose absence is not even designated): the distinction would correspond roughly to that which obtains in Freud between repression (neurosis) and foreclusion (psychosis).

＊　＊　＊

Reviews of the Merchant-Ivory Film

VINCENT CANBY
[A Triumphant Adaptation]†

It's time for legislation decreeing that no one be allowed to make a screen adaptation of a novel of any quality whatsoever if Ismail Merchant, James Ivory and Ruth Prawer Jhabvala are available, and if they elect to do the job. Trespassers should be prosecuted, possibly condemned, sentenced to watch "Adam Bede" on "Masterpiece Theater" for five to seven years.

In case you've been living inside a pinball machine for the last several decades, Mr. Merchant, the producer; Mr. Ivory, the director, and Mrs. Jhabvala, the writer, are the team responsible for, among other films, the screen adaptations of Henry James's "Bostonians," E. M. Forster's "Room With a View" and Evan S. Connell's "Mr. and Mrs. Bridge."

They triumph again with their entertaining, richly textured film translation of Forster's fourth novel, "Howards End" * * *.

Like the novel, which was published in 1910, the film is elegant, funny and romantic. Though intensely serious in its concerns, it is as escapist as a month in an English countryside so idyllic that it probably doesn't exist.

Forster is not passé, but time has played tricks on his work. The shapeliness of his prose and his plotting still satisfies. The wit remains piercing and seemingly painless. "All men are equal," he writes in "Howards End," "all men, that is to say, who possess umbrellas."

Yet our world is now so different from Forster's that we follow the drawing-room war in "Howards End," seen in the confrontation of the two high-minded Schlegel sisters with the members of the rich, acquisitive Wilcox family, as if it were a fantastic spectacle, a time out of time.

"Howards End," set at the end of the Edwardian era, doesn't even dimly perceive World War I, to say nothing of World War II, the Holocaust, the Bomb and the possibility of the planet's extinction. The

† *New York Times* 13 March 1992, sec. C1:3. Reprinted by permission.

stakes being fought over in this film are high, but no one is killed, with the exception of poor Leonard Bast, and he scarcely counts (this is a Forster irony), since he is of the lower orders.

It's easy for us to shake our heads with Forster over the inequities built into England's class system, although that same system provides the stability of the structure in which such drawing-room wars can be fought. Forster was a social critic capable of savagery, but for today's film audiences, "Howards End" is so much fun that it becomes a guilty pleasure. Thank heaven for inequities.

Although Leonard Bast (Sam West), a rather dull bank clerk who aspires to culture, is the unwitting instrument for the story's optimistic resolution, he is at the center of the film only when he is invited to call by the brainy Margaret Schlegel (Emma Thompson) and her younger, prettier, more headstrong sister, Helen (Helena Bonham Carter).

The Schlegel sisters are well-bred, well-read, music-loving people for whom the life of the mind is as natural as fine food and drink. Their serene London existence is forever destroyed by the richer, cruder, altogether (it seems at first) more dynamic Wilcoxes, whom they have met (before the film starts) while on a holiday abroad.

Sticking to the novel with unhurried fidelity, Mrs. Jhabvala's screenplay traces Helen's brief, doomed infatuation with the younger Wilcox son, Paul (Joseph Bennett). There follows the friendship of Margaret with the otherworldly Ruth Wilcox (Vanessa Redgrave), mother of Paul and two other children and wife to Henry (Anthony Hopkins). After Ruth's death, Margaret marries Henry, whom Helen sees to be a barbarian, if a very rich one.

The war that ensues has as its main issue Henry Wilcox's high-handed treatment of the dopey Leonard Bast and Leonard's good-natured, tarty wife, Jacky (Nicola Duffett), who, it turns out, had once been Henry's mistress.

Standing first as décor, then as a concept, is Howards End, the Wilcox family's comfortable old country house, which Forster saw as a symbol of England. It is Forster's conceit that the house must fall if the Schlegels, the Wilcoxes and the Basts cannot somehow be reconciled within Howards End. The grace with which this is accomplished is just one of the delights of this film, which is nothing if not symmetrical.

Though full of plot, "Howards End" is a comedy of character, expertly realized in performances that match any on the screen now or in the recent past.

Ms. Thompson, who was a charming asset to "Henry V" and "Dead Again," both directed by her husband, Kenneth Branagh, comes into her own as the wise, patient Margaret Schlegel. Hers is the film's guiding performance. Ms. Thompson even manages to be beautiful while convincingly acting the role of a woman who is not supposed to be beautiful, being all teeth and solemn expressions.

The film is also a breakthrough for Ms. Bonham Carter. No more the pouty ingénue, she here gives a full-length portrait of a pretty young woman who, disappointed by life, gathers a sort of mad force as she ages and proudly assumes the role of one of society's outcasts.

Mr. Hopkins is splendid and easy as the Edwardian era's equivalent to a corporate raider, outwardly tough and willful but, at heart, almost fatally fragile. Miss Redgrave is not on the screen long, but hers is also a strong performance as a woman not quite in touch with the quotidian world. She looks grandly haggard, as she is supposed to, while her niece, Jemma Redgrave (daughter of Corin Redgrave), is very comic as her spoiled Wilcox daughter. Prunella Scales bustles through the movie as the Schlegel sisters' managerial aunt.

That Mr. Ivory and Mrs. Jhabvala work well together is not exactly news. What continues to astonish is Mrs. Jhabvala's magical way of putting herself in the service of another writer's work, preserving as she distills. The film unfolds chronologically. No narrator is used. Yet the Forster voice is heard in virtually every scene, chatting, being discreetly sarcastic, sometimes sounding worried and, at other times, laughing with pleasure.

Like all Merchant-Ivory productions, "Howards End" looks terrific, the colors mostly muted, the light dim. Occasionally the physical opulence does become excessive, as with the wisteria, which may be all nature's doing. Yet there is so much wisteria clinging to the roof and walls of Howards End that the place would seem in danger of collapse, no matter how the characters pair off to save England.

That's an extremely minor reservation. "Howards End" need apologize only for its bracing high spirits and the consistency of its intelligence. A great pleasure.

JOHN SIMON

Demolition Jobs[†]

Adaptations have always been one of the great problems of the cinema. Can a novel, a story, a play be successfully adapted to the screen? Of course, when the movies were young and called photoplays, many of them were just that: photographed plays or novels, and horrible. But the cinema became more technically advanced and sophisticated, hiring better writers to adapt other people's or their own fiction and drama, and the results were an improvement. Not much better most of the time, but enough to enable people to say, "No, I haven't read the book, but I saw

† *National Review* 13 April 1992: 55–57. (c) 1992 by *National Review*, Inc., 150 East 35th Street, New York, NY 10016. Reprinted by permission.

the movie." And it took smart people, behind or in front of the screen, a long time to realize that, in the case of great books and plays, seeing the movie meant nothing.

Many years ago, I posited something that a fellow critic dubbed Simon's Law (which, to be sure, applies rather more to stage adaptations): If it is worth doing, it can't be done; if it can be done, it wasn't worth doing. The reason a great play or fiction cannot be properly adapted to the screen is that form is content. Can you imagine any great sonnet that could have done as well as a sestina or villanelle? Even less conceivable than transposition from one poetic form to another is transferral into another genre, prose. Similarly, what was envisioned and embodied as a novel or novella cannot be recast as a play or movie. Not if it is a true work of art, that is. A lesser novel might make a good movie — might even improve as one.

But the lure of turning a classic novel into a film is enormous. To the hack director it means riches and prestige: all those non-readers who have heard so much about *Moby-Dick* and *The Brothers Karamazov* will simply have to see the picture, and bring you cash and cachet. For the good but deluded director the challenge is equally great: "They said you cannot make a movie out of *Faust* or *Middlemarch*; well, I'll show them!" And they end up, with few exceptions, with a noble flop, artistic and commercial.

Some very good directors have been thus seduced, and a couple even beat the odds. So, along with the rare exceptions, we get all those mangled masterpieces and near-masterpieces, which also bleed. Indeed, there are those deplorable bunglers who make a point of rushing in where angels fear to tread, and who have made, by their very dishonesty or deludedness, careers out of vulgarizations. * * *

                              *   *   *

Merchant and Ivory should have been ivory merchants, a field in which fakery thrives. Not to worry, though: they have made a phenomenal career out of peddling plastic as cinematic art, as their latest, *Howards End*, triumphantly confirms. Let us recall that M & I, with their devoted screenwriter Ruth Prawer Jhabvala, have already laid waste Henry James's *The Europeans* and *The Bostonians*, and have similarly attacked two by E. M. Forster, *A Room with a View* and *Maurice* (not to mention a foray into Jane Austen). Though they successfully demolished *Room*, *Maurice*, Forster's sentimentalized fictionalization of his own homosexuality, had a tone congenial to the filmmakers, who, in this instance, were also helped by the master cameraman Pierre Lhomme.

When they are not razing masterworks but addressing Indian matters, M & I do better. Merchant, after all, is Indian, as is the husband of Mrs. Jhabvala, who has lived in India and written about it. But with *Howards End*, the Merchant-Ivory-Jhabvala team is firmly back in Masterpiece Theatre, which is where their talent for subversion leaps to the fore.

I approached this film with benevolence, because I happened to like the trio's last venture, *Mr. and Mrs. Bridge,* based on two novels by Evan S. Connell, although even there the ending was a bathetic failure of nerve. With *Howards End,* however, it is business as usual, start to finish. When Forster's novel appeared in 1910, the *Saturday Review* (to quote P. N. Furbank's *E. M. Forster: A Life*) wrote that "to express his genius in using everyday speech to betray 'cunning shadowings' of personality, the term 'Forsterian' was now a necessity." Forster's Bloomsbury colleague, Virginia Woolf, writes more critically: "We are to notice this, take heed of that. Margaret or Helen, we are made to understand, is not speaking simply as herself; her words have another and a larger intention." So, Mrs. Woolf argues, we are repeatedly forced into "the twilight world of theory."

In the movie, we are also shoved into another world, though not one of subtle shadowings or larger, symbolic intention. No, it is a smaller, indeed diminutive, world of farce, of rather mechanistic, caricatural exaggeration. If I do not go into the plot, consider this my attempt to get you to read the novel, marvelous even if flawed, and to find out for yourselves just how far short, for all its superficial faithfulness, the movie falls.

The reductive technique can be demonstrated with the treatment of the famous passage near the beginning, where two of the principal characters are deeply affected by the Beethoven Fifth they hear at a concert. Forster's description both of the music and of its effect on the listeners is a justly famous purple patch in modern literature—perhaps even in music criticism. Granted this is hard, even impossible, to translate to the screen, surely better could have been found than having Simon Callow, in an uncredited cameo performance as a music-appreciation lecturer, whose mother plays illustrative passages on the piano, act smug and condescending to his audience. The scene does incorporate passages from Forster's text, but it reduces them to comic rubble.

There are fine British actors in the film, doing their level best to stem the leveling into farce; I feel especially for Anthony Hopkins and Emma Thompson. One thing, though, works: wonderful English landscapes and houses, flashily but still invitingly shot by Tony Pierce-Roberts, the M & I house photographer.

TERRENCE RAFFERTY

Yes, But[†]

James Ivory's movie version of the 1910 E. M. Forster novel "Howards End" is a handsome and intelligent piece of work: a faithful, well-paced, and carefully crafted dramatization of a very good story. Of Forster's six novels, "Howards End" is the most nearly perfect, the one whose characters and events come closest to being adequate representations of the large spiritual themes that drive his fiction. In "Aspects of the Novel" he expressed, in his characteristically modest and companionable manner, his ambivalence about the value of narrative: "Yes—oh, dear, yes—the novel tells a story. . . . That is the highest factor common to all novels, and I wish that it was not so, that it could be something different—melody, or perception of the truth, not this low atavistic form." If Forster had written for the movies, that resigned assent to the primacy of storytelling might have had a bitterer, more exasperated tone—"oh, dear, yes" with an edge of frustration—because conventional movies charge through their narratives more swiftly and more relentlessly than conventional novels do, and allow even less latitude for reflection.

Without that latitude, Forster isn't Forster. All his stories seem haunted, in varying degrees, by the suspicion of their own insufficiency. In each novel, a third-person narrator maintains a running commentary on the motivations of the characters and the meanings of the events, in an attempt to supply an extra dimension to the story materials of the traditional English novel. Nothing in a Forster novel ever quite speaks for itself; the narrator's voice constantly prods us to see beyond the story, to see through it, to transcend it. Forster's subject is always the middle-class English society of his time—a society that is, in his terms, spiritually inarticulate—and his stories are designed to bring his level-headed bourgeois characters to some awareness of the mystery and the awe and the beauty that their everyday life doesn't provide. Forster's novels, for all the witty exactness of their dialogue and descriptions, are romances that are aware of, and a little embarrassed by, their artificiality. Not one of his novels is completely persuasive, yet there's something moving and brave about all of them. To respond to Forster fully, you have to be able to understand the gap between his artistic achievement and his human aspiration: he wants desperately to imagine the possibility of a consciousness that would lift the English above the petty particularities of their daily lives—so desperately that he's willing to undermine his greatest gift as a novelist, which is for realistic, precise observation.

It's odd, then, that Forster's work has attracted so much attention from moviemakers in the past few years. Movies can't reproduce the intimate, searching tone of the novels' narrators. All that survives the transition from the page to the screen is, yes, story; and when Forster's stories are isolated from the voice that comments on them and acknowledges their inadequacy they can seem terribly contrived. Charles Sturridge's recent "Where Angels Fear to Tread," which is based on Forster's first novel, is a textbook example of bad literary adaptation. It marches us through the book's events with a grim literal-mindedness that makes the story seem foolish—naïve, old-fashioned, clumsily symbolic.

Ivory and his screenwriter, Ruth Prawer Jhabvala, are far more skillful and sensitive, but their approach isn't really so different: they stick to the story and try to get what they can out of it. They're fortunate here, because in "Howards End" Forster's ideas appear to flow more naturally, more inevitably, from the story than in his other books. The heroine, Margaret Schlegel (played by Emma Thompson), is a thirtyish Englishwoman of German ancestry who lives with her sister, Helen (Helena Bonham Carter), and her brother, Tibby (Adrian Ross Magenty), in a pleasantly unostentatious London town house. The Schlegels move in intellectual circles and consider themselves enlightened; their Germanness, in Forster's scheme, confers on them a somewhat un-English taste for art and philosophy, and a tendency toward idealism. Margaret is the best and the most complex of them, and in all Forster's work there is no character who more clearly embodies the seemingly contradictory values that he's always trying to reconcile. She's kind and sympathetic and down-to-earth, in the self-effacing English manner, but she's also (like her creator) a striver. Even when she's engaged in the most highminded chat, she doesn't seem quite satisfied with herself. It's as if she sensed that the shared beliefs, fine as they might be, of her family and friends were somehow too abstract and too easily articulated to be of much use to her. The plot brings Margaret and her siblings in contact with a very different sort of family, the Wilcoxes, who appear to represent English values at their most infuriatingly solid and complacent. Henry Wilcox (Anthony Hopkins) is a pragmatic, no-nonsense businessman, and his wife, Ruth (Vanessa Redgrave), looks like his exact feminine counterpart—a traditional middle-class wife and mother, content to live for her husband and her children and her property. Within this limited scope, though, Ruth Wilcox is far less unimaginative than she seems. She and Margaret strike up a brief, unlikely friendship, and Margaret discovers an unanticipated beauty in the older woman's attachment to her small patch of the world—especially to Howards End, the modest country house where Ruth was born.

Mrs. Wilcox, who dies early in the story, is a remarkable creation. She's English to her fingertips, and unshakably conservative in her beliefs, and yet she inhabits her narrow world so profoundly, and with such enormous feeling, that she transforms it. If there is—as Forster obviously hopes there is—a thoroughly English kind of spirituality, Ruth Wilcox is its incarnation. The character is a novelist's leap of faith, and it's so extravagantly conceived that it should be unplayable; perhaps it would be unplayable by anyone but Vanessa Redgrave, whose relationship to her art is as mysterious and as miraculously complete as Mrs. Wilcox's relationship to Howards End. Redgrave is at her most radiant in this role: she makes Ruth Wilcox seem both the most deeply rooted and the most ethereal woman imaginable, and even after she's gone her words and gestures linger like remembered lines of poetry. Since the story depends on the strange affinity between Ruth and Margaret, on the older woman's recognition of the younger as her spiritual heir, the actress who plays Margaret has to be up to the nearly impossible standard of Redgrave's genius. Emma Thompson is a worthy heir. She never seems to be copying Redgrave's style, but we can feel that she has been inspired by it. She finds her own way: the performance is thrilling and original. Her previous work has been marked chiefly by a wicked adeptness at caricature, but here her acting is unmannered, daringly straightforward. Thompson is required to carry the movie, and she does, with an unusually graceful combination of wit and feeling.

These luminous performances go a long way toward putting Forster's ambitious ideas across on the screen. (Hopkins, in a less complex role, is awfully good, too.) The elusive, magical resources that Redgrave and Thompson seem to be drawing on for their portrayals feel, in some peculiar way, like proof of the inexpressible virtue that Forster wanted to find in the English character. The story holds us for the full two hours and twenty minutes that the movie takes to tell it, and we leave the theatre with a satisfied feeling. Still, it's difficult not to feel—as Margaret Schlegel does after a long intellectual discussion—that something important is missing. You sense it in the lack of sympathy shown to some of the minor characters, like Jacky Bast (Nicola Duffett), the lower-class wife of a clerk whom Helen has taken on as a protégé, and Charles Wilcox (James Wilby), Henry's stiff-necked elder son. These characters, who are essential to the story but peripheral to Forster's real concerns, have no vitality on the screen; there's no commentator to reduce their cartoonishness, to disguise their purely functional status. They stick out as unwelcome survivors of the "low atavistic form" that Forster worked so hard to transcend.

The movie's most serious flaw is probably an irresolvable one. At one point in the novel, Margaret launches into a spirited defense of German art, responding to the "tasteful contempt" of the English for the romantic sensibility that most stirs her: "'Oh, Böcklin,' they say; 'he strains after beauty, he peoples Nature with gods too consciously.' Of course Böcklin strains, because he wants something—beauty and all the other intangible gifts that are floating about the world. So his landscapes don't come off, and Leader's do." (This speech is not in the movie.) Ivory's "Howards End" is the work of a canny storyteller. It comes off superbly, in Margaret's sense. Perhaps it's perverse to complain about something that has been done so well, but those of us who love Forster might miss the sense of strain, the awkward human beauty of his artistic failure.

ANNE BILLSON

Our Kind of People[†]

I'm like everyone else. I take film reviews—including my own—with a
pinch of salt. But seldom have I been struck by such a chorus of praise
as that which greeted the release of *Howards End*. "Genuine triumph."
"Seamless adaptation." "Masterful film." "A great movie."

Even *Time Out*, to which one might once have looked for the dis-
senting view, chimed in. "Action-packed saga . . .performances are
impeccable." Golly, I thought, perhaps director James Ivory and producer Ismail Merchant and screenwriter Ruth Prawer Jhabvala *have*
pulled out the Big One. I haven't ever been a Merchant-Ivory fan, but I
liked *The Deceivers*, and rather enjoyed *A Room with a View*. So I shuf-
fled along to see with my own eyes this paradigm of the film-maker's art.

Whatever else one might say, this is a film that has found its target
audience. They laughed each time one of the actors delivered a particularly arch line of dialogue. They swooned with pleasure at the sight of
a bluebell wood. They chirruped with delight each time a steam train
chuffed into frame.

Now, I'm all for pretty pictures and nice frocks, but there's a limit. The
limit is reached when these things start being hailed as a great movie.
After 20 minutes, I realised I was trapped in a sub-standard slice of
British heritage.

The actors may have been illustrious, but just because they had an
exceptionally large amount of dialogue—and were allowed to deliver it
uninterrupted by any sort of tiresome editing or camerawork—didn't
mean they were giving the performances of their lives. Anthony
Hopkins, Emma Thompson, Vanessa Redgrave and Helena Bonham-
Carter have all been better.

Cinema should be more than what the *Daily Telegraph* called "connecting prose and passion with pictures". And on all levels but the picturesque, this film fails to connect. Whenever the film-makers are faced
with adapting a conversation too long for even them to transplant whole-
sale, they reduce it to a series of edited highlights punctuated by fades to
black—virtually an admission that they lack the cinematic wherewithal
to cope. And I found it impossible to understand why the lively blue-
stocking Margaret Schlegel (Thompson) should decide to marry the
stuffy widower Henry Wilcox (Hopkins). One minute she's playing hostess to feminists, the next she's sunk in the little woman role.

This jars, not because the match is inconceivable, but because there
is nothing in the performances or the filming to suggest that she has
grown particularly fond of Wilcox, or that she's desperate not to become

† *New Statesman and Society* 29 May 1992: 32–33. Reprinted by permission of the publisher.

an old maid, or that she had always wanted a big ballroom, and here is a man who can provide her with one. This is where cinema should have an advantage over the printed word. It would take only a glance, a touch, or a lingering camera movement for one to be convinced of such a *volte-face*. But Ivory saves all his lingering for the vintage motors and the bluebell woods.

As for social comment, the film treats its lower middle-class characters with as much condescension and contempt as do the snotty Wilcoxes and the do-gooding Schlegels. Leonard Bast and his wife are presented as *different*, pathetic interlopers, caricatures to be pitied and despised. Once Mrs Bast has served her purpose (getting drunk, shocking the gentry), the film washes its hands of her. *Yeuchh*. Now let's get back to *our kind of people*.

If *Howards End* is supposed to be an indictment of snobbery and greed, it fails, because it revels in the snobbish and greedy way of life: the idyllic country cottages, the grand mansions, the perfect lawns. The qualities of such illustrated English Lit are not cinematic, but are those of the Edwardian theme park. This film should be bought up by the National Trust, though it doesn't need to be preserved. It has already been pickled in the formaldehyde of nostalgia.

It is not a world to which I can relate at any level, nor one of which I want any part. Maybe this is my problem and not the film's; I certainly seem to be out of step with the rest of the human race on this one. Hell, it even won a prize at Cannes.

E. M. Forster: A Chronology

1879	Edward Morgan Forster born January 1, in London, to Edward Morgan Llewellyn Forster and Alice Clara "Lily" Whichelo Forster. Their only child.
1880	Father Edward dies of tuberculosis on October 30; leaves Lily and Morgan an estate worth £6,000 (approximately £260,000 [$416,000] in current value).
1883	Moves with mother to Rooksnest in Stevenage, Hertfordshire, the original of Howards End.
1890–93	Attends Kent House, a preparatory school in Sussex.
1893	Lease on Rooksnest not renewed, moves to Tonbridge and attends Tonbridge School as a dayboy until 1897.
1897–1901	Attends King's College, Cambridge University; studies classical literature, elected in 1901 to the Apostles, an illustrious group of intellectuals.
1901	Queen Victoria dies on January 22.
1901–2	Travels to Italy with mother.
1904	Moves with mother to Harnham, a house on Monument Green in Weybridge, their home until 1924.
1905	First novel, *Where Angels Fear to Tread*, published in October.
1907	*Longest Journey* published in April.
1908	Begins occasional lecturing at University of London and teaches Latin at the Working Men's College, eventually a regular commitment. First mention of *Howards End* in diary on June 26.
1910	*Howards End* published in October to excellent reviews and strong sales. Reprinted four times in November and December.
1912–13	First trip to India.
1914	World War I begins.
1915–19	Works in Alexandria for the Red Cross, questioning the wounded for information about soldiers missing in action.
1921–22	In India as secretary to the Maharaja of Dewas, visits friend Syed Ross Masood in Hyderabed.

1924	A *Passage to India* published in June to critical acclaim, the last novel to appear in his lifetime.
1925	Moves with his mother to West Hackhurst and rents an apartment in London near Leonard and Virginia Woolf and other Bloomsbury friends.
1930	Meets Bob Buckingham, a police constable, with whom he has a life-long relationship that continues after Buckingham marries and has children.
1935	Speaks against fascism at International Writers' Congress in Paris.
1939–45	World War II; delivers regular BBC radio talks on political and literary topics.
1945	Mother dies on March 11 at age ninety.
1946	Elected honorary fellow of King's College, moves to Cambridge.
1970	Suffers stroke in May and dies on June 7 in Coventry home of Bob and May Buckingham.

Selected Bibliography

Forster's Major Works

Novels

Where Angels Fear to Tread (1905)
The Longest Journey (1907)
A Room with a View (1908)
Howards End (1910)
A Passage to India (1924)
Maurice (1971)

Short Stories

The Celestial Omnibus (1911)
The Eternal Moment (1928)
The Collected Tales of E. M. Forster (1947)
The Life to Come (1972)
The New Collected Short Stories (1985)

Essays and Other Writings

Alexandria: A History and a Guide (1922)
Pharos and Pharillon (1923)
Aspects of the Novel (1927)
Goldsworthy Lowes Dickinson (1934)
Abinger Harvest (1936)
Two Cheers for Democracy (1951)
The Hill of Devi and Other Indian Writings (1953)
Marianne Thornton, 1797–1887: A Domestic Biography (1956)
Albergo Empedocle and Other Writings (1971)

Other Materials

Commonplace Book. Ed. Philip Gardner. Stanford: Stanford UP, 1985.
The Manuscripts of Howards End. Ed. Oliver Stallybrass. London: Edward Arnold, 1973.
Selected Letters of E. M. Forster. Ed. Mary Lago and P. N. Furbank. 2 Vols. Cambridge, MA: Harvard UP, 1983–85.

Bibliographies

Kirkpatrick, B. J. A *Bibliography of E. M. Forster.* 2nd ed. Oxford: Clarendon P, 1985.
Summers, Claude J. *E. M. Forster: A Guide to Research.* New York: Garland, 1991.

Biographies

Beauman, Nicola. *Morgan: A Biography of E. M. Forster.* London: Hodder & Stoughton, 1993.
Furbank, P. N. *E. M. Forster: A Life.* 2 Vols. London: Secker and Warburg, 1977–78.
Stape, J. H. *An E. M. Forster Chronology.* London: Macmillan, 1993.

Criticism

• indicates works included or excerpted in this Norton Critical Edition.

Armstrong, Paul B. "E. M. Forster's *Howards End*: The Existential Crisis of the Liberal Imagination." *Mosaic* 8 (Fall 1974): 183–99.
Bedient, Calvin. *Architects of the Self: George Eliot, D. H. Lawrence, and E. M. Forster.* Berkeley: U of California P, 1972.
Bloom, Harold, ed. *E. M. Forster: Modern Critical Interpretations.* New York: Chelsea House, 1987.
• Born, Daniel. "Private Gardens, Public Swamps: Howards End and the Revaluation of Liberal Guilt." *Novel* 25 (1992): 141–59.
Bradbury, Malcolm, ed. *Forster: A Collection of Critical Essays.* Englewood Cliffs, NJ: Prentice-Hall, 1966.
• Crews, Frederick C. *E. M. Forster: The Perils of Humanism.* Princeton: Princeton UP, 1962.
Das, G. K., and John Beer, eds. *E. M. Forster: A Human Exploration. Centenary Essays.* New York: New York UP, 1979.
Delaney, Paul. "'Islands of Money': Rentier Culture in E. M. Forster's *Howards End.*" *English Literature in Transition* 31 (1988): 285–96.
Duckworth, Alistair M. *Howards End: E. M. Forster's House of Fiction.* New York: Twayne, 1992.
Dowling, David. *Bloomsbury Aesthetics and the Novels of Forster and Woolf.* London: Macmillan, 1985.
Eagleton, Terry. "Evelyn Waugh and the Upper-class Novel." *Exiles and Émigrés: Studies in Modern Literature.* New York: Schocken, 1970. 33–70.
Feltes, N. N. "Anyone of Everybody: Net Books and *Howards End.*" *Modes of Production of Victorian Novels.* Chicago: U of Chicago P, 1986. 76–98.
Gardner, Philip. *E. M. Forster: The Critical Heritage.* London: Routledge and Kegan Paul, 1973.
Gibson, Mary Ellis. "Illegitimate Order: Cosmopolitanism and Liberalism in Forster's *Howards End.*" *English Literature in Transition* 28 (1985): 106–23.
Gillen, Francis. "*Howards End* and the Neglected Narrator." *Novel* 3 (1970): 139–52.
• Graham, Kenneth. *Indirections of the Novel: James, Conrad, and Forster.* Cambridge: Cambridge UP, 1988.
Green, Martin. *The English Novel in the Twentieth Century: The Doom of Empire.* London: Routledge, 1984.
• Herz, Judith Scherer, and Robert K. Martin, eds. *E. M. Forster: Centenary Revaluations.* Toronto: U of Toronto P, 1982.
Hewitt, Douglas. "E. M. Forster: The Proclamations of the Liberal Agnostic." *British Fiction of the Early Modern Period.* London: Longman, 1988. 66–82.
Hoy, Pat C. II. "The Narrow, Rich Staircase in Forster's *Howards End.*" *Twentieth Century Literature* 31 (1985): 221–35.
• Jameson, Fredric. "Modernism and Imperialism." *Nationalism, Colonialism, and Literature.* Essays by Terry Eagleton, Fredric Jameson, Edward W. Said. A Field Day Company Book. Minneapolis: U of Minnesota P, 1990. 43–66.
Kazin, Alfred. "*Howards End* Revisited." *Partisan Review* 1 (1992): 29–43.
Lago, Mary, guest ed. "E. M. Forster Issue." *Twentieth Century Literature* 31 (Summer/Fall 1985): 137–341.
• Langland, Elizabeth. "Gesturing toward an Open Space: Gender, Form, and Language in E. M. Forster's *Howards End.*" *Out of Bounds: Male Writers and Gender (ed) Criticism.* Ed. Laura Claridge and Elizabeth Langland. Amherst: U of Massachusetts P, 1990. 252–67.
• Levenson, Michael. *Modernism and the Fate of Individuality: Character and Novelistic Form from Conrad to Woolf.* Cambridge: Cambridge UP, 1990. 78–93.
Martin, John Sayre. *E. M. Forster: The Endless Journey.* Cambridge: Cambridge UP, 1976.

May, Brian. "Neoliberalism in Rorty and Forster." *Twentieth Century Literature* 39 (1993): 185–207.

McDowell, Frederick P. W. *E. M. Forster.* Rev. ed. Boston: Twayne, 1982.

• Meisel, Perry. "The Bloomsbury Novel and the Production of the Real." *The Myth of the Modern: A Study in British Literature and Criticism after 1850.* New Haven: Yale UP, 1987. 159–226.

Page, Norman. *E. M. Forster.* New York: St. Martin's P, 1988.

Rapport, Nigel. *The Prose and the Passion: Anthropology, Literature, and the Writing of E. M. Forster.* New York: St. Martin's P, 1994.

• Rosecrance, Barbara. *Forster's Narrative Vision.* Ithaca, NY: Cornell UP, 1982.

Schwarz, Daniel R. "The Originality of E. M. Forster." *Modern Fiction Studies* 19 (1983): 623–41.

Stewart, Garrett. "Connective: Forster." *Death Sentences: Styles of Dying in British Fiction.* Cambridge, MA: Harvard UP, 1984. 181–213.

• Stone, Wilfred. *The Cave and the Mountain: A Study of E. M. Forster.* Stanford: Stanford UP, 1966.

Summer, Claude J. *E. M. Forster.* New York: Ungar, 1983.

Thickstun, William R. *Visionary Closure in the Modern Novel.* London: Macmillan, 1988.

• Trilling, Lionel. *E. M. Forster.* Norfolk, CT: New Directions, 1943.

Widdowson, Peter. *E. M. Forster's* Howards End: *Fiction as History.* London: Chatto and Windus, 1977.

Weatherhead, Andrea K. "*Howards End*: Beethoven's *Fifth*." *Twentieth Century Literature* 31 (1985): 247–64.

Weissman, Judith. "E. M. Forster: Gasoline and Goddesses." *Half Savage and Hardy and Free: Women and Rural Radicalism in the Nineteenth-Century Novel.* Middletown, CT: Wesleyan UP, 1987. 262–90.

Wilde, Alan. *Art and Order: A Study of E. M. Forster.* New York: New York UP, 1964.

——, ed. *Critical Essays on E. M. Forster.* Boston: G. K. Hall, 1985.

• Woolf, Virginia. "The Novels of E. M. Forster." 1927. *The Death of the Moth and Other Essays.* New York: Harcourt, Brace, 1967. 342–50.